George Augustus Sala

The Seven Sons of Mammon

George Augustus Sala

The Seven Sons of Mammon

ISBN/EAN: 9783741186288

Manufactured in Europe, USA, Canada, Australia, Japa

Cover: Foto ©Andreas Hilbeck / pixelio.de

Manufactured and distributed by brebook publishing software
(www.brebook.com)

George Augustus Sala

The Seven Sons of Mammon

THE

SEVEN SONS OF MAMMON:

A Story.

BY

GEORGE AUGUSTUS SALA,

AUTHOR OF "AFTER BREAKFAST," "DUTCH PICTURES," &c., &c.

NEW EDITION.

LONDON:

TINSLEY BROTHERS, 18, CATHERINE ST., STRAND
1864.

LONDON:
BRADBURY AND EVANS, PRINTERS, WHITEFRIARS.

PREFACE.

A Book without a Preface has, ere now, been likened to a Palace without a façade; but I am afraid that in too many instances the prefatory observations which authors think themselves called upon to make, more closely resemble that cumbrous attic story added, by an after thought, to the Mansion House, and which enabled the architect to spoil an originally excellent edifice. As, however, the postulate of excellence as regards this work may be extremely questionable, I do not think that a brief exordium is calculated to make it much better or much worse. The only tribulation it has caused me, has been in the endeavour to make it serve some useful purpose. For, by this time, I should imagine those who peruse novels must have grown somewhat tired of being called " courteous readers "—of being grinned and simpered at, and tickled, and flattered, and cajoled by a person they never saw, and whom most probably they do not care to see. How do I know that the reader of these lines is " courteous " ? He may be Ursa Major for aught I can tell, and be grumbling and growling fiercely because the tale does not finish to his liking. Why should I endeavour to conciliate some unknown reader, whose favour can do me

no good, and whose displeasure no harm ? If the public
don't approve of the show, they need not patronise it.
There are other ways, thank Goodness, of getting a livelihood, besides dabbling in literature. There are shoes to
mend and stones to crack ; and, bearing this in mind, I can
afford to dispense with the deprecatory or complimentary
preface, and to brand it as useless and absurd.

I have something, however, to say ; and it could not be
said in a better place than this. The title of " The Seven
Sons of Mammon" may be regarded by some persons as a
misnomer, and others may assume that I have failed in
carrying out the plan I originally proposed to myself. I
beg to state, that, in commencing the first chapter, I knew
perfectly well what the last one was to be about; and that I
no more contemplated giving a distinct biography of each
Son of Mammon than of dancing on the tight rope and
cooking an *omelette in medio*. You see that, had each of
the Seven Sons an equal space apportioned to him, this
work had need to be in six volumes instead of one ;
and I am afraid that the modern reading public is not
inclined to tolerate works of the dimensions of the " Grand
Cyrus," or even of " Clarissa Harlowe." Whether there is
to be a sequel to what I have already given—whether any
more of Mammon or his Sons is to be heard at a future
period, must depend on the inclination of the public. If
they cry " Hold—enough !" I shall stay my hand ; if they
are anxious for additional particulars, they shall have them.
C'est à prendre ou à laisser. I have designed my little
Human Comedy on the model of an American *table d'hôte*,
and the guests may drop in as they choose, eat their fill, go
away, or come back again as the humour takes them. How

many incarnations, if you please, had Balzac's Vautrin?
How many times, and in how many novels, does Mr.
Cooper's Natty Bumppo turn up; and who would ever
grow tired of the Marquis of Steyne, were he met with
twenty times in Mr. Thackeray's fictions? You may object
that *my* characters are dull and stupid and uninteresting.
That is, again, a matter of opinion.

With respect to the reception this novel may meet with
from professional critics, I am indifferent. Of course, for
my Publisher's sake, I should wish it to be lauded to the
skies; but so far as I am personally concerned, criticism,
hostile or amicable, is a matter of no moment whatsoever.
Did I earn my bread by writing novels, or did I look to
booksellers for patronage, the praise or the condemnation
of a new work might make or break me;—were I young, or
hopeful, or ambitious, I might be overjoyed or driven to
despair by eulogy or blame. But I have reviewed too many
books in my time, and known too many reviewers, to care
much about such things. I have found that slander has not
diminished my income, and that the lies that have been told
about me have not injured my digestion; and although it is
a very nice thing to be a popular author, and a very terrible
one to be castigated as a dullard and an ignoramus by critics,
I have come to be of the opinion of *Candide* "*qu'il faut
cultiver son jardin,*" and that, so long as a man goes on
cultivating his cabbages in a quiet laborious manner, and
earning his daily bread by the sweat of his brow, and thank-
ing God for it, he need not trouble himself in any great
degree about the applause or censure of the world. Therefore, my intimate enemies, or my inimical friends, if you
feel inclined for the attack, come on. Gentlemen of the

Guard, fire first. I have, myself, a faculty for sound hearty abuse, and if you choose to brawl at me over the hedge, I shall be very happy to look up from my spade-husbandry, and return half a dozen good set terms of invective for every six you may be pleased to favour me with.

GEORGE AUGUSTUS SALA.

UPTON COURT, BUCKS,
  December, 1861.

CONTENTS.

THE SEVEN SONS OF MAMMON.

CHAPTER I.

WHAT CAME OUT OF A COURT IN THE CITY.

"GOLD is a chimera," I heard a man sing in the opera of
"Robert le Diable." *L'or est une chimère.* Gold a chimera! Is
it? Ask Sir Jasper Goldthorpe.

He was the richest man on 'Change. The richest man in the
Bank Parlour. The richest man in the East India Directory.
The richest man at innumerable Boards, whose members sat and
coined money out of green baize. He was the richest man in
that Square full of palaces, near to where stood an ugly monument
that poor rogues used to be suspended from, hard by the Edge-
ware Road. He was the richest man in the county where he had
his estate and his "place," and of which he was High Sheriff.
When he went down for a week to Brighton, his riches awed the
wealthiest stockbrokers and the grandest members of the fast-
decreasing class of nabobs. And Rothschilds and Baring? and
the Amsterdam Hopes? and the Hamburg Heines? Pshaw!
Pshaw! Sir Jasper Goldthorpe was deemed to be richer than all
these, for he was alone on his throne of gold. He had no partners. Mammon would not even let one of his sons come into the
firm. No shares were to be purchased in the house of Goldthorpe
and Co. The Co. was a myth. Sir Jasper was the Co.—himself
and company. He had no fears that the Antwerp house would
warn him against undue speculations; that the Leghorn branch
would remonstrate if he drew too largely on them, or the Frank-

fort firm give cause for remonstrance by drawing too heavily on
him. He stood alone. His agents and correspondents were his
obedient and trembling slaves, and he the most generous but the
most exacting of taskmasters. There was no trifling with Sir
Jasper Goldthorpe. How could one jest with a man who had so
much money? He had had rivals. Now and then some gorged
Hebrew capitalist of Paris or Madrid would strive to shoulder his
way past him with bank-notes and bonds; but Sir Jasper Goldthorpe, with icy English politeness, would drop a couple of heavy
golden ingots on the capitalist's toes, and force him to retreat,
howling and discomfited. Once or twice some lucky speculator
in Australian wool, some enriched digger, some auriferous bubble-
monger of railway shares and mining-schemes, would make a dead
set at Sir Jasper's supremacy,—would strive to outvie him by
taking a bigger house, giving grander parties, purchasing more
acres of park-land, subscribing to more charities and packs of
hounds. Then Sir Jasper would smile his frigid smile, step down
to a little shooting-box, if it were in autumn, or to the sea-side if
in spring; pop away at the pheasants, or stroll about in a jacket
and a slouched hat, as though he were some miserable wretch
of eight hundred pounds a year; and then, coming quietly back
to town, would manage somehow to crush his rivals. He always
crushed them. The Australian wool-speculator would spend
some thousands in a contested election—lose it; or, gaining it, be
unseated for bribery, and be forced to retrench. The digger's
agents would fail, or he drink himself into a cerebral congestion.
The bubble-monger would burst and turn out a common cheat.
Alone, triumphant and immovable, without a wrinkle in his brow
or a crease in his waistcoat, would stand Sir Jasper Goldthorpe.
At last people gave up contending with him, and were content to
agree that he was a wonderful man.

His beginnings had been small enough.' It was rumoured
that his father was but a small tradesman in a country town.
There were found even those bold enough to whisper, " Bankrupt
in 'twenty-five; didn't pay twopence in the pound,"—alluding to
the paternal Goldthorpe. Sir Jasper always spoke of his sire as
" my excellent and worthy father; " and you may be sure that no
word of detraction against his progenitor was ever audible in his

presence, or within a good distance thereof. He had himself first
made an appearance in public with a company which certainly did
not succeed after he left it, but which realised tremendous profits
while he was on the direction. He had gone largely into government contracts, and had been the special object of several commissions of inquiry; but it always turned out that it was
somebody else, and not he, who was to be blamed for shoes that
wouldn't go on, and muskets that wouldn't go off; and commissioners, witnesses, and accountants were all loud in their praises
of Mr. Goldthorpe's—he was Mr. Goldthorpe then—public spirit
and unimpeachable integrity. He had always been a prosperous
man, with that wondrous Midas faculty for turning everything
which he touched into gold; but the termination of a particularly
searching committee, which had been moved for in a series of
vehement speeches by two Radical members, and had very nearly
been the means of ejecting the Government of the day from
office, seemed the turning-point in his greater fortune. How the
man's riches swelled and swelled after his contract rum had been
denounced as a fiery poison, and his contract rice sneered at
as the sweepings of the dock-warehouses! He thenceforward
devoted himself to politics: one of the Radical members was
regularly coughed down for several sessions, and the other, at the
next general election, lost his seat, and, more than suspected of
debt, was compelled to fly to Brussels in Brabant. Mr. Hemp of
the Sheriff's Court makes proclamation of outlawry against him
with admirable regularity. After this, naturally Mr. Goldthorpe
gave up contracts altogether. It was about this time that he
made such immense sums in the shipping line of business. He
had a fleet which sailed to the East Indies, and a fleet which
sailed to the West; and his Australian bullion dealings and
speculations in wool, copper, and tallow were prodigious.
With great meekness and condescension he consented to serve
the office of Sheriff in the metropolis. He might have been
Alderman and Lord Mayor, of course, had he so chosen; but
these latter dignities he declined. He got into Parliament; his
constituents, touched with gratitude and reverence, it is to be
supposed, for the immense wealth he possessed, insisting on
paying his election expenses to the uttermost farthing. When

he was supposed to be worth about a million of money, a committee of merchants and bankers met at the London Tavern, and boldly put down their hundreds and their fifties for a testimonial, which—a *chef-d'œuvre* of the ateliers of Mr. Benson of Cornhill, and forming a pleasing pyramidal composition in burnished and frosted gold, including dolphins, the Three Graces, emblematic figures of Peace and Commerce, a nautilus-shell, an Egyptian pyramid, and an Arab steed—the malicious described it as three race-cups hammered into one—was presented to him at a grand banquet held at the "Albion," Aldersgate Street. He was master of the Mystery of Battleaxe-makers, and gracefully presided over the patronage in the gift of that wealthy company, in the shape of fat livings in the Church and presentations to the Company's schools. He was great at Goldsmiths' Hall; for if he didn't make actual plate and jewellery, he made the raw material, gold, by heaps:—which is far better. Soon after he entered Parliament he was made a Baronet;—'twas the least tribute that could be paid to his transcendent merits and riches. He was received with immense respect in the House of Commons, and his opinions on financial questions, although he scarcely ever spoke, were looked upon as incontrovertible. The Chancellor of the Exchequer was generally thought to be sure of another six months' tenure of office if he could only be seen walking with Sir Jasper Goldthorpe on the river-terrace. He was usually lucky enough to get excused from committees; it was known how rich a man he was, and how much he had to. Had he not been so useful to the Government, there is little doubt that, ere this history opens, he would have been made a Peer.

The year 1847, and the succeeding year of revolution and political turmoils, shook, as you will remember, the commerce of the Continent to its very centre, and some shocks of the universal earthquake were felt even in the sound and stable city of London. Many brave and ancient firms utterly vanished. It was then, so the gossips said, that Sir Jasper Goldthorpe made his famous *coup* of purchasing, at about a third of their value, the diamonds and other regalia of the distressed and fugitive sovereigns of Europe. When confidence was restored, and the reign of legitimacy recommenced diamonds were at a premium again, and Sir Jasper Goldthorpe realised. He had done with all his mercantile speculations now,—had no longer large ventures on the sea, or trains of obsequious shipping and colonial brokers at his heels. He dealt in Money, and money alone. He turned money over, and in the summersault it made itself into more money. He crumpled a piece of paper, and it distilled drops of gold into his coffers. The more bankrupt was a European state, or a South-American republic, the richer became Sir Jasper Goldthorpe. He purchased railways, but he did not carry them out. He farmed mines and revenues, but he neither worked nor collected them. They remained with him but a few days; but every thing of which he took hold was a golden orange, and he managed to squeeze it so long as he held it.

In the year 1849, Sir Jasper Goldthorpe was just fifty years of age. As Christmas came round, he was good enough to remember, on returning thanks for the proposal of his health at a grand feast at Battleaxe-makers' Hall, that he was born on the twenty-seventh of December, Anno Domini seventeen hundred and ninety-nine. He said "Anno Domini;" for though his words were few, they were always sonorous, and had a rich metallic sound. His admirers declared that they were worth their weight in gold. The cheers at the announcement of the date of his nativity were deafening. About Christmas time 1849, then, Sir Jasper Goldthorpe, Bart., M.P., F.R.S. (he had contributed a wonderful paper on the Greek drachma to the transactions of the Royal Society, and was dignified moreover with many more initials than I care to enumerate), was a hale fresh-coloured gentleman, slightly corpulent, and with a very slight stoop in his shoulders, but looking on the whole a model of health and strength. He was not in the least bald,— so rich a man could not afford to lose even a hair,—and his locks, thin as they were, were not even gray, but of a dull flaxen colour. "Tow head" Sir Jasper had been opprobriously nick-named by political opponents at election time. He was quite cleanly shaven and very fresh-coloured. His eyes were blue-gray, and mirrors of placidity—that is, when you could get him to look at you; for Sir Jasper was short-sighted. He read with a double eye-glass, and when he was not reading usually bent his eyes downwards. He was a tall man, and wore a white hat in winter. His hands

were very fat, smooth, and dimpled, his fingers very short and
thick at the tips. Much handling of money had blunted them,
perhaps. A black frock-coat, gray trousers, the invariable buff
waistcoat already mentioned, the double eye-glass, a plain black
necktie, a very high shirt-collar, of the old tape-tied kind, not
buttoned; no rings or trinkets of any kind. Imagine the form I
have described so attired, and you will have a definite notion of
Sir Jasper Goldthorpe. He came down to the Office every
morning with unvarying punctuality (save during the vacations
he methodically allowed himself) at ten o'clock. He always came
down in his carriage—a double-bodied, high-hung, two-hundred-
guinea-pair-of-horses one. He would as soon have thought of
riding in a brougham at the east end as of paying nineteen shillings in the pound. At his villas and palaces he had plenty of
broughams, and phaetons, and curricles, and things; and in the
country he did not disdain to ride on a shaggy little pony, or to
drive a tiny wicker-work carriage, like a clothes-basket upon
wheels; but between Temple Bar and Eastcheap the carriage was
part of his state and the handmaiden to his riches. But, though
he would not ride eastward in a brougham, it was touching to mark
the humility with which this very rich man would hire a common,
lowly, four-wheeled cab for conveyance to public meetings or railway stations. Those who knew how rich he was said he looked
ten times richer, meekly sitting on the shabby cushions of the
four-wheeler, with his bundle of papers—contracts for the new
loan perhaps—or his little locked travelling bag beside him. He
was fond, too, of walking; and, with his umbrella in one hand
and his buckskin gloves (which he never wore) in the other, might
often be seen peacefully strolling towards the Royal Exchange,
the Bank, or the India House, quite unmoved, apparently, by the
rush and turmoil of the Poultry, Cornhill, or Leadenhall Street.
He was never in a hurry; you might see him serenely gazing in
at the windows of the bullion-dealers and jewellers, or blandly
contemplating the fire-proof safes and cash-boxes at Chubb's, as
though time was no object to him; although you knew that hundreds of people were at that moment anxiously waiting to see
him, and hungering for one of his golden smiles. What need
had he to be in a hurry? He knew that he, being so rich, would

be waited for ; and yet Sir Jasper Goldthorpe was proverbial for punctuality, and in most cases, where any matters of business were concerned, contrived to be a little beforehand with those he had transactions with.

Who knows Beryl Court? It lies between Temple Bar and Eastcheap, as aforesaid. Need I be more explicit ? Well, it is not a hundred yards from St. Mary Axe. I daren't say more, for fear of compromising people. The street from which Beryl Court leads is very narrow, and very poor, and very dirty ; and although it is the centre of a hive of wealth and industry, of lordly counting-houses, board-rooms, and wholesale groceries, is given up to the meanest description of commerce. Petty little hucksters' and chandlers' shops nestle under the wing of the merchant princes, iron safes, crammed with gold and notes. One side of the street may, however, for all its dirt and squalor, be secretly wealthy ; for it is almost exclusively occupied by the unwindowed shops of Jew-dealers in oranges, grapes, and almonds, the which spread a very pleasant odour in Beryl Court. It would be pleasanter, perhaps, were it not mingled with the smell of fried fish and strongly-pickled vegetables, retailed in the few little stalls forming the exception to the rule of fruit-selling. The Caucasian proprietors of these establishments are dirty and wretched-looking from Sunday to Friday night ; but on Saturdays they are splendid in brave garments and rich gems. They all had the most intense respect for Sir Jasper Goldthorpe and Sir Jasper Goldthorpe's carriage ; and their little black-eyed chaffering children sometimes penetrated into Beryl Court, and peered admiringly at the Palace of Gold erected there.

For it was a palace ; a marble-fronted house, with wings forming three parts of a square ; the fourth a red brick wall, with a porter's lodge in one corner. The court itself beautifully flagged with gray and white stone in chequers ; and in the centre a pretty fountain, where a little boy with nothing on him spouted water from a conch-shell all day long. The stream seemed to be mur-muring odes in praise of riches. The windows were all plate-glass, the wire-gauze blinds had golden beadings ; over the door was sculptured the Goldthorpe family cognizance,—three martlets on a field *or* ; the bloody hand of its proper blazon ; motto, *Ex sudore, aurum,* the whole emblazoned on a richly-framed marble escutcheon. On the well-polished mahogany door glittered the brass-plate of the firm " Goldthorpe and Co."—a plate burnished much brighter than gold. The architecture of Beryl Court, exteriorly, was entirely Italian Renaissance, and had been commanded by Sir Jasper,—in a letter of four lines to his architect,—just after he achieved his baronetcy. But his decorative fancy was an odd one; for, inside, the house was at least a hundred and fifty years old. Some South-Sea director had lived here in the reign of George I.; and there was a vast staircase painted with the story of the Golden Fleece, and a pagan apotheosis sprawled on the ceiling of almost every room. The staircase, up which you might have driven a coach-and-four, was of polished oak, with richly carved balustrades, and its stairs were laid with an oil-cloth painted in imitation of tiger's skin. All the rooms were panelled, with enriched marble mantelpieces and curiously inlaid floors; but all this work was of the old time of the South-Sea director. No gas was permitted in Beryl Court. The numerous staff of clerks worked in winter time by the light of dumpy wax candles. The balance of the petty cash account exceeded the salary of a county court judge. The heads of departments had Turkey carpets laid in their rooms, rosewood escritoires to write upon, morocco-covered easy-chairs to sit upon. Silent and civil messengers glided in and out on their behests. Lunch was brought to them when they asked. Were those repasts charged in the petty cash, I wonder? Broughams came for many of the superior clerks when office hours were over. Perhaps it was for that reason that Sir Jasper Goldthorpe repudiated, while in the City, the vehicles just spoken of. Everybody employed by the firm, from the heads of departments to the youngest office-boy, was paid so highly that embezzlement was unheard of. A young man's fortune was thought to be made if he could only be got into Goldthorpe's house, although there was not the remotest chance of his ever obtaining a partnership therein; and parents and guardians used to intrigue for years to obtain junior clerkships for their sons and wards, just as they would intrigue for Indian cadetships or commissions in the Guards.

What did all these chiefs of departments, clerks, messengers, aud office-boys do from nine in the morning until five at night? None but those employed by the firm could tell. They wrote, wrote, and wrote : took letters off files and put them on others ; consulted huge vellum-covered volumes, and made entries in other tomes similarly bound, perpetually ; but what they did was a mystery. There was no faint odour about, of samples of rice, indigo, coffee, sugar, opium, as in merchants' and brokers' offices. No sea-captains showed their bronzed faces in the counting-house. No actual cash was ever seen : but nobody had the least doubt that the one great subject of work at Gold-thorpe's was Money. All day long a stream of junior clerks with pocket-books secured by leather-covered chains wound round their waists would drop Bills for Acceptance into the great letter-box by the brass-plate in Beryl Court ; and all day long a counter-stream of Goldthorpian messengers would issue from Beryl Court, and from their leather chain-secured pocket-books drop Bills for Acceptance in other letter-boxes all over the City.

Sir Jasper's room was the plainest in the entire establishment. It was papered a sober drab, and matted ; but it was a very Ear of Dionysius for gutta-percha tubing and ivory mouth-pieces. Nearly one side of the room was taken up by a huge iron safe, which, with its many locks and knobs and handles, looked like a monument to Mammon.

Add to Beryl Court the palace in Onyx Square, with its picture-gallery, its grand ball-room, and its belvedere towering above the neighbouring mansions, sumptuous and superb. Add to these the princely domain of Goldthorpe in Surrey, with its deer-park and its home-park, its Vitruvian palazzo ; its con-servatories, graperies, pineries, kennels, model-dairies, lawns, terraces, mazes, grottoes, and temples :—its stables and coach-houses, its pavilions and lodges. Add to these a fine house at Kemp Town, Brighton, and the little shooting-box I have already glanced at. Surely it needs no more to convince you that Sir Jasper Goldthorpe was a power in the state and a prince in the land.

So gold is a chimera, is it ? Ah, my romantic friends, you little know what a reality gold is. See what it had given this fortunate man. Power and influence, respect, adulation, worship almost. Houses and parks and palaces, carriages and horses and hounds : a red hand in his escutcheon, a handle to his name, a seat in the Parliament of the country, a peerage in prospect;—and Gold, nothing but gold, had done it all.

CHAPTER II.

"And if ever," exclaimed Lady Goldthorpe, puffing with over-exertion,—"if ever I try to get a Christmas-tree into a clarence again, I'm a Dutchman, — that's to say, a Dutchwoman, — that's all."

Lady Goldthorpe was stout in figure and mature in years, and might be excused for puffing. Moreover, although it was a very cold winter's day, Lady Goldthorpe had on a very thick dress of black velvet, beneath which was revealed an underskirt of quilted silk; and a long seal-skin mantle trailed from her broad shoulders, and a crimson silk scarf was tied round her comfortable chin, and purple plush gloves defended her hands, and goloshes covered her feet, and a bonnet of velvet and lace sat closely to her round jovial-looking face; and there were plenty of rugs and shawls and mufflers about her in the carriage where she sat, and a muff of rich fur bolstered her up on one side, and a very fat shaggy Skye terrier on the other. The very gold chain she wore round her neck was heavy enough to make her warm; and as Lady Gold-thorpe's clarence—she had taken out the clarence that day—was cosily lined and padded and cushioned, and had elastic stuffed cushions and a fleecy rug at the bottom, it would not, I think, have been a thing to be wondered at if Lady Goldthorpe had puffed even without excessive exertion.

But there was that Christmas-tree into the bargain. Now you may get almost anything—some people say everything—into a carpet-bag; but I much doubt whether, under any circumstances, a Christmas-tree can be comfortably stowed away in the carriage called a clarence. It isn't within the laws of nature or the fitness of things. A flower-pot is bad enough; a vivarium can with difficulty be conveyed in a hackney-coach; but a Christmas-tree,

never! Not that this adjunct, which we have borrowed from the
German Vaterland to make our Christmas festivals merrier, was
of the largest size. 'Twas but a poor little sapling evergreen, a
supplementary tree, designed to act as satellite to the monarchs
of the forest in Lady Goldthorpe's saloons. Her ladyship always
had half a dozen trees at Christmas. But one had caught fire
from the premature illumination by infantine hands of the waxen
tapers among its branches the night before, and had not only been
consumed to its roots, but had very near burned the belvedered
palace in Onyx Square along with it. The twenty-seventh of
December was the day on which it was Lady Goldthorpe's im-
memorial custom to have all her trees in full bloom. It was
essential to repair at once the loss of the burnt-up *arbuste;* and
so Lady Goldthorpe had ordered the clarence, and driven down to
Fortnum and Mason's to buy an additional tree, ready-hung with
toys, and fit to be lighted up instanter.

The tree was duly purchased—that was a very easy matter;
but the difficulty was to get it into the carriage, for Lady Goldthorpe was an impulsive lady and a determined one; and when
she could have her own way—which she generally had—liked to
have it. She had said she would carry home the tree with her,
and, notwithstanding the apparently insurmountable impediments
to the accomplishment of her design, she insisted upon its being
carried out. First her embroidered, buttoned, and striped foot-
page tried, but lamentably failed in the attempt; and, under the
humiliating threat of having his ears boxed—a menace rendered
still more galling by its being proffered in the presence of a
momentarily increasing circle of street-boys, who looked at the
whole affair with the liveliest interest—he retired to the coach-box
and snivelled; whereupon he was called by the coachman, in a
wheezy undertone, a " young warmint." The domestic who drove
Lady Goldthorpe's clarence was so fat, so warmly clad and
wrapped up, and had so broad and jovial a countenance, that he
might have passed for a poor relation of her ladyship's, whom the
inexorable logic of necessity compelled to hold the reins, but who,
off the box, was a Goldthorpe and a brother.

One of Messrs. Fortnum and Mason's young gentlemen—I
dare not term them young men—having likewise done his best,

and been stigmatised as an idiot for his pains, at which he blushed, smiled, rubbed his hands—as was seemly in the presence of a lady-customer who ran such heavy bills, and, what is more, paid them with unvarying regularity—Lady Goldthorpe took the re-fractory tree (which wasn't more than a foot and a half high) in hand herself. But the tree was as obstinate as her ladyship. It wouldn't stand up, or lie down, or lean against the side of the carriage. It would protrude its branches either from one window or the other. Once it fell a-top of the fat terrier, irritating with its twigs that animal's nose, and causing him to yelp piteously; and at last Lady Goldthorpe's unsuccessful struggles with the mutinous fragment of vegetation gave rise to the exclamation recorded at the commencement of this chapter.

" Drat the tree! " the lady cried out, in increasing exasperation. "There's two drums off, and a banjo, and a flying Cupid, and a sugarstuff parrot. *Now* will you, then, obstinate ? "

She gave a vigorous pull and a wrench at the recalcitrant tree. The last appeal seemed to have touched its obdurate heart, and by dint of more coaxing and a little propping up with the muff and a couple of shawls, it gradually consented to assume an erect and stationary position.

"Home!" cried Lady Goldthorpe to the page, who jumped down as Messrs. Fortnum and Mason's young gentleman tele-graphed to him that peace was restored. The little street-boys gave a cheer,—why they scarcely knew, only, as a reflective young butcher observed, "the old un," meaning her ladyship, looked "such a jolly party; " the young gentleman who had been called an idiot retired into the emporium of Christmas and colonial luxuries to which he was attached, and indulged in comments with his comrades on Lady Goldthorpe's hasty temper, and on the munificent Christmas boxes she always distributed; and away drove the clarence, with its two showy horses, in the direction of Park Lane, the toy-laden branches of the Christmas-tree bobbing round Lady Goldthorpe's jovial face, until she looked like a fat Fair Rosamond in an ambulatory bower.

"Thank goodness for all things!" said the wife of the Prince of Beryl Court. There couldn't be two Lady Goldthorpes, you know, —the scheme of the universe couldn't stand it. "Thank goodness!" her ladyship repeated, when she had recovered her breath, and her usual equanimity of temper, "one of my troubles is over. Not that I've any thanks to give you, Magdalen Hill," she continued, "sitting quiet and cool there like a stuck pig, and me breaking my heart over the thing, and the mother of Seven Children, all boys too."

Yes; Lady Goldthorpe had the number of children she alluded to: and there were Seven Sons to the Mammon of Beryl Court.

"I can't see, mamma," answered a calm quiet voice on the other side of her ladyship, "that seven children have anything to do with your trouble. Was the Christmas-tree an eighth one?"

"Then why didn't you help me, Miss Icicle?"

"I knew I couldn't be of any use. You know how weak and awkward I am. And besides, I thought that you would desist, and allow the people at the shop to do that which they should have done in the first instance :—send the thing home."

"Ah, I dare say," grumbled, but not ill-humouredly, the mother of seven children. "It's always the same:—weak and awkward. You're not weak and awkward when you're playing the harp or the pianoforte like an angel, or painting saints with gold cheese-plates round their heads, and their toes turned in :—poor deluded creeturs. You're not weak and awkward when you're writing letters five pages long, let alone the crossing, to somebody in India, are you?"

A faint blush rose on the pale face, and a fainter smile played on the firm lips of Lady Goldthorpe's companion.

What companion? Muffs don't blush, at least not inanimate ones; and Skye terriers, although they sometimes grin and snarl, seldom smile. Who was Lady Goldthorpe's companion, occupying, indeed, the remaining back seat of the carriage, the dog sitting in conscious majesty between?

Why, Magdalen Hill, to be sure. And who was Magdalen Hill? A very few words will suffice to introduce her to you. She was very tall, and very slender, and had an odd prejudice against wearing crinoline, which, if you will carry your remembrance back, began to show itself in England as a French impor-

tation about ten years ago.* She had very large gray eyes, veiled
with very long lashes, and which had a fixed and stern and not
very pleasant expression. Her lips were, as I have hinted, firmly
cut—"chiselled" is I believe the proper term—and when she
opened them, very bitter words issued occasionally from between
them and her white teeth. Her feet—what do I know about a
lady's feet? and what gross dullards are those, who, looking on
Woman, cast down their eyes to the earth she walks upon,
instead of looking upward to the heaven in her face! Well, her
feet. They were hidden, as a lady's feet should almost ever be;
and she never danced, and he who describes her never met her on
a wet day. She had very long white hands, and I can assure you
that her fingers were not tapering; for, albeit their hue was exquisite, long practice on the pianoforte, on which she was an accomplished performer, had given somewhat of a muscular character
to her digits, and to the nerves and muscles that belonged to
them. Her hair—yes, her hair, how well that is remembered!—
was raven black, was glossy, worn in two plain *bandeaux*. I spoke
of her pale face. It was pale almost to the pallor of Death.
You know the pallor I mean—the first camellia-lke waxiness
of the mortal that has put on immortality, not the dreadful hues
of after days.

Such was Magdalen Hill. She dressed habitually in that which
Chief Justice Hale advised his children to dress in, "sad colour"
—grays and fawns, and lilacs and blacks, relieved by lighter rays.
She wore high-necked dresses always; and for all ornament carried a plain cross of dead gold at her throat. And she seemed
one of those women who look neither happy nor unhappy, despairing nor resigned, quick nor slow, clever nor stupid; but who
are ready and able for anything—to run away with you, or to go
into a convent and wear spiked girdles, and scourge themselves
thrice a day; to be the idol of a Parisian *salon*, or to teach a
Sunday-school full of clod-hopping children; to say spontaneously

---

* Lest the author should be accused of an anachronism, he begs to refer his
readers to a comic publication called the *Man in the Moon*, which may be consulted in the reading-room of the British Museum, and in Volume II. (under the
date of 1847) of which work he will find this paragraph : "All the cab-horses in
Paris are said to have lost their tails in consequence of the demand for crinoline.

"I love you," or to a fervent protestation of love to answer, "Sir, I don't understand you;" to go to the end of the world for an idea, or to go home to their mothers, to bear blows, ill usage, coarse language,—anything but infidelity; or to take offence at the omission of a finger-napkin at dinner, and serve you with a citation in the Divorce Court for cruelty because you have taken them to the Opera in a cab instead of a brougham. Who has not known these fathomless, inscrutable women; looked upon those eyes, whose glance would either beam out a message of happiness to you, or turning towards the executioner send you to the block, and yet do neither; but behave always in conformity with *les parfaites convenances!* Such was Magdalen Hill, with her eyes, and her lips, and her long demure but cruel hands, and her set phrases, and her sarcastic parentheses, and the great mystery of Heart and Soul within her, which would have baffled you, La Bruyère, in all your skill in character, and you, John Wilkes, with all your boast of subduing the untractable fair. And of such there are thousands, who are born to be riddles and paradoxes, and the despair of passionate men.

Magdalen Hill was an orphan. Her father had been a colonial judge, and had died of the yellow fever just at the time when he had laid by enough money to give a dowry to his little daughter, then at boarding-school, a mere child, in England. Magdalen was not a favourite at school. She never played, never got into disgrace, never did anything that her governesses had to forgive her for, and love her more for the atonement of her fault. She was always calm, equable,—not silent, but incomprehensible.

"Upon my word," said, in despair, Miss Mirabelle, the duenna of Selina House, Brixton, "if Miss Hill had not had sixty thousand pounds to her fortune, I do believe that the best thing that could have happened to her would have been to be an articled pupil, and turn out a 'trotting governess;'" by which appellation was meant, I believe, those unhappy females who, collected and resigned, go out daily in rain, or sleet or snow, to give lessons in middle-class families, and are spoken of by the servant who opens the door as "that young pusson who comes at twelve, and will *not* wipe her feet." Poor wearied creature, with an English lady's soul within you, how much mud have you carried away from rich

men's houses, when you should have shaken off the dust of your
feet on the scraper !

But Magdalen Hill had sixty thousand pounds to her fortune.
She was a rich little girl and a rich young woman. Sir Jasper
Goldthorpe had been her guardian. Her holidays had been spent
in his family. After she came of age,—for she was now twenty-
two,—his house became her home. And, as we have seen, she
called good old Lady Goldthorpe her "mamma."

I come back to the blush and the smile—both faint—awakened
by the good-natured taunt that she was neither weak nor awkward
when she wrote those voluminous epistles to "somebody in India."

"You know that he is coming home, mamma," she said, laying
her hand on her companion's arm, and in a voice that would have
been soft and kindly, had there not been, as in an old harpsichord,
a string broken somewhere.

"Yes, my darling Maggie, my own good girl," the wife of the
British baronet responded, "I know it well. He has promised,
he has tried ; he will, I'm sure, if human will can prevail. He
knows that the twenty-seventh of December is his father's birthday. He knows that he is my own dear son, which I bore him in
travail and in sorrow twenty-seven years ago, when we were poor,
Magdalen Hill—when we were poor, when my Goldy wasn't the
great man he is now ; when Goldy walked ten miles over the snow
to fetch a doctor, and the good gentleman said that I bore up
more bravely than mortal woman ever did, and—Heaven bless
him for it—left half a sovereign on the mantlepiece of his own
gentleman's money, and hid the guinea fee my husband had
scraped together sixpence by sixpence, at the very back of the
Bible on the chest of drawers. I know that my son will come
home from the far East Indies. I know he will. He has timed
his time ; and if wind and weather don't stop him, he'll be
here to-night. He was born in '23. He got his cadetship in '40.
and Goldy thought it a good catch; although I'm sure, situated
as he now is, he'd make my youngest boy Emperor of Rooshia.
My son Hugh will be back to-night, and you know what he's
coming for. He's a captain in the army. He's coming back, not
alone to see his father and mother and brothers, but he's coming
home to marry you, Magdalen Hill, which he fell in love with

c

you five years back, when he was home on leave ; and I know, for
all your face that frightens me, that you love him, and that he
loves you; and though I am but a poor woman which was ill
brought up, and wasn't always so, I love my son and daughter
which is to be, and I've had seven children, all boys."

It was a very indecorous thing to do at Grosvenor Gate, Park
Lane ; but it is none the less true that Lady Goldthorpe, the
mother of seven children, all boys, and the wife of the richest man
in the City of London, did, there and then, and within the very
shadow of Grosvenor Gate, and in her own clarence, throw her
arms about the neck of her companion, and vehemently kiss her.
Who let her kiss, and returned the embrace.

"I'm sure," the good lady remarked, affectionately smoothing
the dark bands of Magdalen Hill, which had become slightly dis-
arranged, "that we've all got our troubles, even to the richest of
us. It was years, my dear, before I could receive company without trembling all over, or give an evening party without wishing
that I might sink through the drawing-room carpet. When I
married my Goldy, I hadn't an *h* in my alphabet,"—in making
this confession Lady Goldthorpe very nearly succeeded in putting
an h *to* the alphabet she mentioned,—"and now every thing's
prospered with us. I'm sure that the very potato peelings
seemed to turn to gold in Goldy's hands ; and you're going to
marry Hugh, and I'm the happy mother of seven children."

Yes ; the Goldthorpe quiver was furnished with that number
of arrows. Let us mark off, one by one, the Seven Sons of
Mammon.

First came Hugh Jasper Goldthorpe. His first name from a
godfather, Mr. Hugh Desborough, who during Sir Jasper's early
career had been intimately connected with him in friendship and
in business. Hugh was twenty-six years of age. He was but a
captain in a regiment of native infantry in the service of the East
India Company ; but he had held important staff appointments,
had been resident and political agent at the court of more than
one native prince, and had obtained great renown during the last
campaign against the Sikhs as the commander of that famous
corps of indigenous troopers, the Daglishwallah Irregular Cavalry.

Second came Ernest, born in the year 'twenty four, and consequently that number of years old at the commencement of this history. Ernest had early manifested a serious and studious disposition ; had passed with great distinction through Rugby school ; gained high honours at Cambridge ; took holy orders ; and had been recently inducted into the rectory of Swordsley, worth a good nine hundred per annum, one of the comfortable benefices in the gift of the Battleaxemakers' Company.

The third son, William, who was now twenty-three, had chosen, like his eldest brother, the army for his profession ; but the times being very different with his papa to those in which he had been glad to obtain a humble cadetship for his first-born, a commission in a crack cavalry regiment had been purchased for him, and he was now a lieutenant in the 19th Hussars.

The fourth Son of Mammon, Henry, was at sea. He had entered a line-of-battle ship as naval cadet, and having served his time as midshipman, and passed his examination with much *éclat*, was now a mate, awaiting his lieutenant's commission on board the *Magnanimous*, ninety-one gun ship, at Malta.

George, the fifth son, aged nineteen, was an undergraduate at Oxford, and was destined for the bar; his mother having the firmest persuasion that Sir Jasper Goldthorpe had only to say the word to have her George made Lord-Chancellor the moment after he had donned his wig and gown.

Charles, the sixth son, was scarcely eighteen, but he was already installed in a clerkship in the Foreign Office; and Sir Jasper's great friend, the Earl of Mount Olympus, had promised Charles the very first foreign attachéship—at a nice court where there was plenty of good society and a healthy climate—that should become available.

Alfred, the seventh son, and who at Christmas 1849 was nearly eleven years of age, was a boy at school at Eton, where he had much more pocket-money, and had very nearly as much respect paid to him as though he had been a little Duke. Having a taste for history and a turn for recitation, his career was destined to be "politics," by which Lady Goldthorpe understood that her youngest son was to be made Prime Minister of England so soon as he arrived at years of discretion.

At the grand Christmas party given in Onyx Square on the

twenty-seventh of December, in honour of the double event,—the joyful season and the birthday of Sir Jasper Goldthorpe,—five of the Seven Sons of Mammon were present. The Reverend Ernest Goldthorpe, who was pale and demure, and wore a high black silk waistcoat that met his bow-less white neckcloth, came and talked church decoration and illuminated literature with Magdalen Hill. Lieutenant William, of the 19th Hussars, danced and flirted and supped copiously, and was admired—chiefly for his moustaches and his impertinence—by all the young ladies present, and was positively idolised by the said young ladies' mammas. George, the fifth arrow in the auriferous quiver, was there from Oxford. Charles, the sixth, the most languid of bureaucratic dandies, was there from the Foreign Office. Alfred, the seventh, was there from Eton; and although he declined dancing, on the ground that it was "so precious slow," made ample amends for his inactivity by energetic attacks on the sweet things and the champagne at supper-time.

It was a juvenile party as well as an evening one. Good-natured Lady Goldthorpe loved to have other people's children besides her own around her at Christmas time. A bright band of children overran the gorgeous saloons, and mingled with the throng of grown-up fashionables and celebrities, who were but too glad to pay their court at Onyx House and to its potent master. Many pages would be needed to describe that distinguished company, or even to enumerate their names and dignities. There were peers and peeresses, numerous foreigners of rank and celebrity, immensely rich bald-headed old gentlemen, belonging mostly to Banks and Boards, from the City; marriageable young ladies, marriage-making old ladies, and unmarriageable middle-aged ladies. There were members of parliament, barristers, doctors, wealthy solicitors, proctors from Doctors' Commons, wild slips of college-lads, friends of Willy Goldthorpe, Eton boys, young ladies from boarding-school, and a sprinkling even of artists and literary men; for Sir Jasper Goldthorpe liked to be well with all classes, and by his bounty golden rays were cast into the humblest homes. Amidst this varied, glittering, rejoicing throng, the Great Millionnaire glided about bland, serene, and silent. Nobody found fault with him for his taciturnity. It was sufficient to look upon him, to talk about his wealth in whispers, on staircases, in conservatories, by mantle-pieces, and in retired corners. The talking department of the firm of Goldthorpe and Co. fell entirely to the share of her lady-ship, whose conversation was not very profound, nor, to tell truth, very grammatical, but who gossiped and laughed, and pressed people to dance and eat and drink, until every body was delighted with her. If she had been as mum as her husband, or, talking, had given utterance to the baldest nonsense, the admira-tion expressed for her would yet have been universal. Was she not the wife of the master of Beryl Court?

So all these fine folks enjoyed themselves in junketing and feast-ing till the night was very old, and the small hours began to chime from the buhl clocks. But a certain gloom and anxiety had stolen in among the gaiety and rioting, and sat on the coun-tenances of three persons—Sir Jasper Goldthorpe, his wife, and Magdalen Hill. No Hugh Goldthorpe had made his appearance. Midnight came, and no Hugh. The time when his arrival might have been expected was long past. Had he missed a train from Marseilles? Had he been detained in Paris? Had he fallen ill on the road? His brothers did not know that his coming was so imminently looked for. It was to be a surprise to all—to his relatives as to his friends.

One, two o'clock in the morning, and no Hugh Goldthorpe. The gay company broke up and went home to talk of the delight-ful evening they had spent, the boundless riches of Sir Jasper, the charming eccentricity—had she been poor they would have called it vulgarity—of Lady Goldthorpe. The Sons of Mammon bade their parents good night, and retired to their rooms—all save the subaltern of hussars, whose cabriolet was waiting for him, and who drove down gaily to his club to spend the evening. Three persons were left in the stately crimson drawing-room in Onyx Square: Sir Jasper, evidently perturbed; Lady Goldthorpe, who made no secret of her approaching intention of seeking consolation in a flood of tears; and Magdalen Hill, with her pale face.

CHAPTER III.

CAPTAIN HUGH GOLDTHORPE, M.N.I., ex-commander of the Daglishwallah Irregulars, ex-Resident at the Court of Duffa Khan Sahib, Rajah of Jowlapore, is weary of Indian service. Barely five years have elapsed since he was last in England on sick leave; but he has sought and obtained fresh *congé*. He contemplates a much longer stay in Europe; and, indeed, it is exceedingly problematical whether he will ever return to either of the three Presidencies. He has shaken the branches of the Pagoda tree quite long enough, and longs to enjoy his *siesta* at the foot thereof. Six feet two in his stockings stands Hugh Goldthorpe, strongest and coolest *sabreur* of his corps, skilful in diplomacy, wise in durbar. He is of the stuff of which great soldiers and statesmen are made; but his father is too rich, and his allowances have been too handsome, for him to continue seeking fresh advancement in either career. He has had enough of glory, both in soldiering and negotiation, and is only desirous of rest, and the enjoyment of the wealth that is to be, or is already his, and the wife long since promised to him. His desires are modest, you see. The affianced one—the Beloved One—is a stately lady, and a haughty one, withal; but she has told him that she loves him with her whole heart and soul, and that is enough for Captain Hugh. So the hero of many intricate negotiations with crafty Asiatics, and of fifty hand-to-hand combats with fierce Sikhs and Afghans, tranquilly puffs his cheroot in the expectation of a speedy return to England, home, and beauty. He has engaged a saloon berth in the Peninsula and Oriental Company's ship *Isis*, and, by the last days of December, he gaily augurs that he will be in London. He feels happier than many passengers on board, albeit they may be nearly as rich as he, can feel; for he has been fortunate enough

to bring his liver away with him.   He is broad of chest and sturdy
of limb, with handsome straight-cut features, a mobile yet determined mouth, shaded with a thick Saxon moustache, and a long
silken beard curling down nearly to his waist.   He will have that
latter appendage trimmed within moderate limits when he reaches
the shores of Albion.   He is very brave, and strong, and resolute;
but he is none the less joyous and amiable in private life.   A lion
in the field, a fox in the council, he is a very lamb in the compound ; and scores of blushing virgins of all ages—from innocent,
trusting seventeen to perspicacious thirty-five—who had been
imported to India by *rusée* female relatives, with a view of putting
a stop to their dreary state of celibacy, have ogled Captain Hugh,
and sung songs at him, and embroidered pretty trifles for him,
and laid siege to his heart in a hundred different ways, every one
of which, for all his lamb-like demeanour, have proved totally
unavailing.   Perhaps there was no citadel to besiege, nothing but
embankments and outworks; the heart itself was in England, in
Onyx Square, with Magdalen Hill.   He has been away five years;
but as he paces the deck of the *Isis* he can scarcely persuade himself that so long a period has passed away.   He leans against the
bulwarks of the vessel ploughing her way through the long rolling
waves of the Red Sea.   He puffs at that cheroot again, and gazes
upward at the fleecy clouds, passing gingerly—as though they
feared to take too great a liberty with the Queen of Night—across
the face of the shining moon.   He thinks on his boyhood, on
the happy day when he received his direct appointment in the
Honourable Company's service, on his transition period of "griff-
dom," of his efflorescence as a full-blown subaltern.   The dead
dull heat of the climate falls harmlessly on him now; for he has
sweltered year after year in the tightest of uniforms, and the
heaviest of accoutrements, and again in all the charming *abandon*,
full of wild sartorial reveries, and of his irregular costume, beneath
the hottest-blazing sunshine.   The mere heavy sultry languor of
the Red Sea feels comparatively cool to him ; but he recollects his
sensations when, as a boy, he first reached that "other side" which,
to Anglo-Indians, means all the country that lies eastward beyond
the Egyptian desert, and firmly believed that his young life would
be fairly scorched out of him before he reached his destination.

Freshly came back to him the old doubts and fears, and surmises of what his career in India would end in; whether he would be slain in battle, or rise in civil employments, or in any case vindicate the old *sobriquet* of "Cockey Goldthorpe" bestowed upon him at school. How well he remembered his first sword, new and slender and shining! now he has half a dozen blades with him, all notched and red-rusted from deadly frays. He is coming Home. That one thought has absorbed, for weeks, all the thoughts of his waking hours, and even of his dreams.

Home! He has reached Aden on his way; he has gone down into Egypt, and come to Cairo. At Shepherd's Hotel, where the Overland caravan rests for a night, he declines joining the dinner-party, and devotes his brief period of repose to eagerly devouring the contents of the English newspapers, brought by the outward-bound party of young cadets and yellow civilians who have just arrived. As the mail nears England, Hugh's impatience and home-sickness increase. The three days between Alexandria and Malta are spent almost in a fever. At the Valetta post-office he gets a packet of letters from Home,—letters which breathe love and tender interest in every line,—letters that tell him of the glorious reception that awaits him when he reaches his father's house. He sees no reason why he should not arrive in England on the long-looked-for day,—his father's birthday.

He leaves Malta for Marseilles. The confinement of the vessel becomes almost intolerable to him. He indulges in wild speculations of days when monster viaducts shall cross the Mediterranean, and express trains run without stopping from Marseilles to Malta. He sits in the bows of the *Messageries Impériales* steamer all day long; and when a sudden squall comes on in the Gulf of Lyons, and delays the way of the ship by some three or four hours, Captain Hugh becomes almost frantic with impatience. Why can't squalls be put down by Act of Parliament?

Marseilles has been made, at last. Captain Hugh, during the last portions of the trip, has had his wits sufficiently about him to make friends with the mail-agent, who, he knows, will go straight through to London at express speed, and whom he has persuaded to accept him as a companion.

Up the steep hilly streets of Marseilles dashes the post-waggon.

Cutting in between long tumbrils drawn by long-horned oxen, and driven by Spanish-clad, swarthy, sleepy varlets, dashes and rattles, but never too rapidly for Captain Hugh, the homeward-bound convoy of letters and newspapers. Then he comes on to the French railway, and finds himself in mid-winter, and discovers that the pelisse he has been careful enough to bring with him, lined throughout with fur, is none too warm. Away over the flat dusky plains of the Midi flies the express train with its one carriage attached, shrieking, and sputtering, and roaring, but not too fast for Captain Hugh. He cannot sleep. Wakeful and lynx-eyed, he remains up and anxious; while his companions, the English and French post-couriers, are slumbering in their respective corners. There is no time for set breakfasts or set dinners. Long dusky loaves, with slices of Lyons sausage and fragrant-smelling Brie cheese are thrust into the carriage at certain stations, and then and there devoured by the three travellers. The repast is washed down by great gulps of Médoc, imbibed in the most primitive fashion from the bottle's mouth.

Paris at last, and in time to catch the 7·30 p.m. express from Paris. In the rapidest of cabs, Captain Hugh scurries from the terminus of the Lyons railway to that of the Chemin de Fer du Nord. He makes such haste that he is there twenty-five minutes before the departure of the Calais train. He has parted company by this time with his friends the mail-agents, English and French; and they are quite busy enough over the stowage of their innumerable boxes to dispense with his society. Captain Hugh is admitted by special favour on to the platform, instead of having to wait in the *Salle d'attente*. That is the last favour the English courier shows him. Captain Hugh secures a place for himself in a particularly comfortable-looking carriage, and places on the corner seat his pelisse lined throughout with fur, and his Russia-leather-covered despatch-box. He strolls into the refreshment-room, and has even five minutes for the discussion of his beloved cheroot.

About seven o'clock there has drawn up at the entrance to the terminus a pretty little one-horse brougham, with a coachman in a livery that has something of an English fashion. A lacquey who sits beside him dismounts, and assists a lady, who is the sole occupant of the carriage, to alight. A porter comes up, and, touching his cap, asks politely whether Madame is going by the *train express.* No; Madame has not any such intention. She is merely here to see a friend off. She bids the coachman go away, and away he drives. Then, followed by a little Blenheim spaniel, Madame walks into the great entrance vestibule of the station, where porters are rushing about with trucks full of luggage, and people are crowding to the ticket office, and vendors of cheap periodicals are offering their wares for sale, and idlers are wandering about and staring, and police agents are watching.

Madame is very short and slight in stature, and is richly clad in very wide-spreading skirts. The hems of her garments are marvels of fine linen and needlework. She is exquisitely *gantée.* She has sparkling bracelets on her arms. Her bonnet is a paragon. She wears her veil down ; but it is transparent enough for you to see, beneath, that her face is very pretty, that she has a very fine colour in her cheeks, that her teeth are very white, that her mouth is very smiling, and that she has very fair flowing ringlets.

She looks about her, and stamps her little foot as though in impatience. Anon she espies a diminutive and shabbily-attired man, with curly grey hair, and a peaked nose somewhat purple in hue. In face and gesture he is not unlike a ferret. She beckons to him imperiously ; and the little man comes smirking and bowing up to her, rubbing his hands.

"Is he here, Sims ?" Madame asks in the English language.

"He is, and, O be joyful," answers the little shabby man, with a grin that makes his face look more and more like a ferret, " our agents have not deceived us. The telegraphic message from Marseilles was perfectly correct. He came with the courier in charge of the mails, and I have just seen him in the refreshment room. This has been a day of great grace."

"Do your errand," Madame says, tossing her ringlets, and turning to caress her Blenheim spaniel.

The little shabby man hurries away, and at the door of the *Salle d'attente* he meets a stalwart young Englishman with a fair moustache and a silky beard.

"Captain Hugh Goldthorpe?" the little man says, tentatively rubbing his hands and grinning again.

"That's my name," answers the individual so addressed; "and what might you want with me?"

"There's a lady close by who would just have one moment's conversation with you."

Hugh's thoughts revert to his mother and Magdalen Hill. Could they have come to Paris to meet him?

"A lady! where is she?" he cries out eagerly.

"Yonder," answers the messenger, and points to where the lady who has despatched him stands, her back turned, and caressing her little spaniel.

The loving eyes of Hugh could see at a glance that this was neither Lady Goldthorpe nor Magdalen Hill. Whom could it be? He knew scarcely any one in Paris, and certainly he had no female acquaintances in that capital. He laughed, and looked at his watch.

"It's twenty-two minutes past seven," he says; "I've not much time to talk to a lady. Does she know me, and how long will she keep me?"

"She knows you perfectly well, and she won't detain you an instant," the shabby messenger replies.

With another laugh, thinking there must be some mistake, gallant Captain Hugh advances to a lady, takes off his hat, and, with a low bow, asks in French of what service he can be to her.

"The lady speaks English," remarks the shabby little man, with the most peculiar grin he has yet given.

The lady turns round, raises her veil, and looks Captain Hugh Goldthorpe full in the face. He starts back with something very like a cry of horror.

"Merciful Heavens!" he exclaims, "it is Mrs. Armytage!"

But time and the express-train will wait for no man. The bell rings. The cry of "*Prenez vos places—en voiture*" is heard. The passengers rush through the open doors of the *Salle d'attente* on to the platform. A stalwart young man, with a thick beard and moustache, hurriedly opens the door of a carriage, sees a furred pelisse and a Russia-leather despatch-box lying on one seat, and jumps in.   Doors are slammed, a shrill whistle is audible, and the Calais express starts.

On that selfsame evening of the 27th of December, shortly before midnight," an appalling accident happened to the express train from Paris.   Close to a station called Armentières, between Arras and Hazebrouck, the engine ran off the rails and into a luggage-train going up the line.   Both trains came into dire collision.   The damage was tremendous, the carnage awful.   Seven persons were killed and nearly thirty frightfully injured.

When assistance had been procured, the labourers and police who had hastened to the scene of the catastrophe proceeded to extricate the dead and dying from the shattered ruins of the passenger train.   One carriage was found positively crushed to pieces, and a full hour elapsed before it could be ascertained whether any traveller lay buried beneath its fragments.   At last the task was accomplished, and a doleful spectacle presented itself.   One corpse was found; but it was so awfully disfigured, so crushed and pounded and mashed and battered and gashed, as to have scarcely any human semblance left.   Of the countenance, indeed, there remained positively nothing that could lead to the discovery of its identity.

"*Rien dans les poches;*" nothing in the pockets save French and English money, and his watch, marked "Benson, London, 55,304," the chief of the station remarks, with a melancholy shake of the head, after such dreadful superficial examination as was possible had taken place of the dead thing's garments.   "Stay, what is this beside the *cadavre?*"

The assistants turned their lanterns to the spot pointed out by the inspector.   Close to the side of the corpse, drenched with blood, but quite intact, they found a despatch-box covered with Russia leather, and a pelisse lined throughout with rich sable fur.   The leathern case was locked; but in the side pocket of the pelisse was a morocco pocket-book, which being examined was found to contain a packet of letters, with the English and Maltese postmarks, addressed to Captain Hugh Goldthorpe, H.E.I.C.S.; and a passport five years old, covered with *visas*, in which the principal Secretary of State for Foreign Affairs of her Britannic Majesty requested all authorities, civil and military, to allow free passage, and afford assistance in case of need, to Captain Hugh Gold- thorpe, captain in the service of the Honourable East India Com- pany, travelling abroad.

"*Il n'y a plus de doute*," said the inspector, with a melancholy shrug of the shoulders. "That mass of bloody clay must be the captain. *Pauvre enfant!* And he has a mother, perhaps, *là-bas*, in England."

CHAPTER IV.

THE Rue Grande-des-Petites-Maisons runs at right angles from the Boulevard Pompadour to the Place Dubarry. Are any further particulars needed to tell you that the thoroughfare just named is in the very centre of fashionable Paris? But you may be exigent. Therefore, let it be also hinted that, branching from the Rue Grande-des-Petites-Maisons, runs that well-known arcade full of old curiosity dealers, jewellers, and print-sellers, the Passage Agnes-Sorel. You are scarcely a stone's throw, either, from the Rue Diane-de-Poictiers, which has for termination the Cité La Vallière; and, parallel to the Rue Grande, stretches the great, teeming Faubourg Ste. Frédegonde, the chosen mart of silk-mercers and antique furniture sellers. This being all duly mapped down, you are now recommended to take your Galignani's Guide, and find out the Rue Grande-des-Petites-Maisons if you can.

It is a street of the very newest, and belonging wholly to new France. The old site, once occupied by those quiet, sombre, narrow thoroughfares, the Rue-des-Bons-Epiciers, the Rue Cherche-cinq-francs, and the Carrefour-des-vieilles-parapluies, had been cleared shortly after the revolution of '48, to form the approaches to a certain Golden House of Nero, which had been centuries a-building. The Rue Grande appertains, stucco and soul, to the fresh dynasty. No grim hotels, *entre cour et jardin*, as in the Faubourg St. Germain, tenanted by fossil legitimists, whose hearts are in the highlands of Frohsdorff, and who call the proprietor therefore Henri Cinq, are to be found in the Rue Grande. It is disfigured by no shabby *maisons meublées*, or tenth-rate hotels, smelling all day long of cabbage-soup. It is debased by no mean *crémeries*, greengrocers, or *gargotte* restaurants. No; the street is long and wide, and clean and comely, gas-lit, well-paved, full of new, handsome, dazzling white houses, with green blinds, with plate-glass windows, with veined and varnished doors, or else with entrance-gates in elaborate iron filagree. Its railings are of gilt bronze, and its door-steps of granite. The houses all seem to be striving to effect a compromise between solid English comfort and flimsy French luxury; but they are altogether as unlike the old mansions of Bourbon or Orleanist Paris as a snug little *remise* rolling swiftly up the Avenue Marigny is unlike the lumbering old *coucou* that used to creep to Versailles and St. Cloud. For a new Paris has sprung up over the water; a Lutetia that has knockers to its doors; partakes of lunch — sometimes, it must be admitted, spelt "laounch;" rides in pill-box broughams and Hansom cabs; stares, eye-glass on cheek, out of the casements of clubs, instead of sipping barley-syrup at a marble table outside a café-door; and has recently Gallicised "*blackballer*," as a verb signifying "to exclude;" bets at its Tattersall's; reads its *Bell's Life* and its city article, rigs its market and posts its ponies in the purlieus of the Bourse. Paris *est mort*—the old, the witty, the polite; *vive* Paris the new, the impudent, the brazenfaced, the speculative! But vice and frivolity are undying, and Paris is still as vicious and as frivolous as ever.

In 1849 the Rue Grande-des Petites-Maisons had not attained the imperial splendour it now enjoys. Cæsar was not yet emperor. He scarcely was dictator, and every day of his tenure of power he was badgered, well nigh to the death, by politicians of every degree. In 1849 the Rue Grande smelt of scarcely dried cement and fresh paint. It had not received the impress of imperialism. At the present time, on reference to the *Almanach des vingt-cinq milles Adresses*, I find that it is tenanted by one Grand Referendary, two auditors of the Cour des Comptes, one Austrian Archduchess, one Moldo-Wallachian Kaimakan, and at least a dozen female celebrities of the Parisian minor theatres, whose individual salaries average about thirty shillings a week, and who certainly do not spend less than a hundred thousand francs per annum, each and every one of them. Unless I am very much mistaken, too, the Rue Grande-des-Petites-Maisons contains the charming

little Pompeian house of the Princess Rostolka, with "*Salve*"
on the pavement of the vestibule, and "*Cave canem*" on the wall,
and "*Hic lætantur Lares*" over the porch; and all the rest of it.
Likewise the sumptuous hotel of M. Israel Portesac des Trois
Chapeaux, millionnaire of Marseilles, formerly of the Temple,
dealer in ancient garments, and genealogically of Judea; but
lately, alas! of Mazas, and now, I know not of what *Maison
centrale* of detention and correction.   Finally, I think I discover
in the Rue Grande the gorgeous bachelor quarters of M. Roguet
de la Poguerie, member of the Council of State, journalist of
Napoleonic tendencies, formerly deputy for the department of the
Haute-Dou, and member of the *Académie des jeux floraux* of
Rascaille-sur-le-Nève.   In 1840 there was no Rue Grande to
boast such illustrious occupants.   Plain Israel Portesac bought
and sold old cocked hats, and was not above dealing, occasionally,
in the furry robes of departed rabbits; and simple Jeannot
Roguet was a doctor's boy in his native town of Rascaille, vigorously pounding medicaments in a mortar.   Still in 1849 the new
street was very fashionable, and very wealthy, and very gay.   How
could it be otherwise when its dainty tenements were already the
residence of two Russian princesses, one English nobleman (Lord
Barrymore of Wharton, who had not been to England since the
revolution of '30, bought more pictures in a month than Mr.
Farrer could sell in a year, and whose morals were not quite
secure from the tittle-tattle of the English community in the
neighbouring Faubourg St. Honoré); of the mysterious and
fabulously wealthy Grand Duke of Grimgribberstadt; of Mes-
demoiselles Henriette Coquillard, Nini Cassemajou, Euphrosine
Turlupin, Aspasie Catin, Herminie Languedouce, Jenny Fagotin,
and other dramatic heroines; and, to sum up, of LA DAME AU
PREMIER?

La Dame au Premier, or, to come down to plain Saxon, the
Lady on the First Floor, lived at Number one, Rue Grande-des-
Petites-Maisons, and in a house seemingly large enough to lodge
a regiment of dragoons; but having neither husband nor children
she contented herself with the first floor, and was but a lodger,
condescending to permit a banker to occupy the *rez-de-chaussée,* a
stockbroker to live on the second floor, a *premier sujet* of the

opera to be installed on the third, and any body who liked, and
could afford to pay an enormous rent for somewhat straitened
accommodation, to shelter themselves in the fourth or attic
story. The name of the lady on the first floor was Mrs.
Armytage.

She was a rich English widow, whose husband had died in the
Indies. That the *concierge* knew well. The great Indies, he
called our Oriental Empire. To that functionary she was the
most adorable of her sex. A superb woman, he declared, pursing
in his lips. A queen-like creature. An angel. She showered
five-franc pieces on him. That woman should have the ribbon of
the Legion of Honour, or the *prix Monthyon*, opined the *concierge*.
She did not give anything to the poor: they are always in the
way, *ces gens*, those poor (muttered the *concierge*), but she was
liberal, nay, munificent to him, to the postmen, to her servants, to
her tradespeople. She received the very best society—the very
best of the semi-imperial court of the Elysée Bourbon, the
plutocracy of the Chaussée d'Antin, the most distinguished
illustrations of the world of the Bourse, the Palais, the Green-
room, the Republic of Letters, and the Jockey Club. The
Faubourg St. Germain stood aloof from her; for had not
Madame proclaimed her enthusiastic adhesion to Bonapartism?
Was not her bed-chamber hung with green velvet, powdered with
Napoleonic bees? Did she not wear an eagle in diamonds in her
blonde tresses? The Faubourg St. Germain, in its dynastic
sense, stayed away from the Rue Grande, and the fascinating
first-floor lodger thereof, and was not missed; but many a son
and heir of the Faubourg, many a haughty young vicomte, with
more quarterings in his scutcheon than thousands of francs in his
purse; many a wrinkled old chevalier or parchment-faced *Vidame*,
with the cross of St. Louis at his button-hole, and the memory of
the dear wicked old times when Charles the Tenth was only the
Comte d'Artois, in his heart, stole away from the crumbling
quarter of Divine Right to bask in the smiles of Madame on the
first floor. Her salons were crowded to the vestibule every
evening. The ladies and gentlemen of the English community
before named came from the Faubourg St. Honoré to eat, and
drink, and sing, and dance, and play. The gentlemen were in

D

raptures with the rich Indian widow. The ladies were all but unanimous in abusing her. She was a little too charming to be admired by her own sex. On her part the lady on the first floor frankly accepted all invitations from foreigners of distinction, and contributed to the *délices* of many French, German, and Russian salons; but she resolutely declined visiting, under any circumstances, her own countrymen and countrywomen. " Let them come to *me*," she said, tossing her pretty head ; "I don't want to go to them." The English community had no excuse for cutting Mrs. Armytage, or for sending her to Coventry ; for we English carry a Coventry about with us wherever we go—whether it be to the North Pole or the Andaman Islands. There was no mystery about her. Her conduct as a wife had been irreproachable. Scores of yellow-visaged Anglo-Indians resident in the French capital had known her husband, Major Armytage, of the Queen's army, who died of a fever at Goggerdebad in 1843. People knew that she had a pension ; people surmised from her manner of living that the major had died rich. She had resided alternately in Paris, London, and Brighton during the seven years of her widowhood, keeping open house everywhere, receiving the cream of society, but never returning visits. Why should the English ladies of the Faubourg and the Cité Beaujou be continually girding at her, and yet be glad to rustle their flounces in the grand suite of apartments where Mrs. Armytage reigned supreme ?

The first floor in which she lived might have belonged to a palace of the Arabian Nights. Major Armytage must have shaken the Indian pagoda-tree to some purpose, if all the fine things belonging to his widow had come out of her jointure and the pensionary liberality of the Honourable East India Company. She lived *en princesse*. The suite of rooms on the first floor of the Rue Grande comprised a vestibule (coloured marble, fresco copy of Cephalus and Aurora, statuary, alabaster vases, &c.), a dining-room (inlaid *parquet*, pictures of game by Mytens, boar-hunt by Snyders, fruit after Rubens, insects by Abraham Mignon, silver Venetian frames, Japanese bird-screen, &c.); a grand saloon for receptions (needlework, tapestried furniture, ebony, mother-of-pearl, *consoles, guéridons, cabarets* full of porcelain, ceiling painted by Diaz, carpet of velvet pile *d'Aubusson*, pianoforte by Pleyel, harp by Erard, &c. &c.); a little drawing-room (pink silk and malachite, Turkish scenes by Décamps, aquarelles by Eugène Lamy, statuettes by Pradier, &c.); a delicious boudoir (white and gold, select library in alternate vellum and crimson morocco bindings, stained-glass windows, porcelain door-panels, aquarium, miniature conservatory, aviary, *priedieu* in carved oak, every conceivable variety of arm-chair, ottoman, divan, sofa, tabouret, *dormeuse, causeuse*, and *boudeuse*, and the entire apartment not much bigger than a butler's pantry, &c. &c. &c.). Finally, there was my lady's own chamber, the *chambre-à-coucher*,—remember that we are in Paris, and that there is consequently no impropriety in alluding to a lady's sleeping apartment,—with the famous green velvet hangings, powdered with golden bees, and a bed in carved rosewood and gold standing in an alcove; quilt of eider-down enclosed in apple-green brocade; gauze curtains; a plenitude of mirrors; floor of polished oak, inlaid, with rugs of lion and tiger skins; Beauty's altar in the shape of a toilet-table; infinite trifles from Froment Meurice and Tahans'; tiny arsenal of pistols, damascened sabres, poignards, and fowling-pieces,—an odd fancy for a lady's chamber, but they were perhaps trophies belonging to the defunct major,—and massive Elizabethan wardrobe. The bed-chamber was, according to continental custom, thrown open on reception nights, and, lighted up by scores of wax-tapers, produced sensations of delight in the spectator, which frequently approached frenzy.

It is time to send the upholsterer away, and bid the broker's man close his inkhorn and pocket his inventory. Mrs. Armytage is on her way home even as I write, and it might be dangerous to be detected in enacting the part of Paul Pry in her apartments. There is just time to let you know that the *valetaille*, the inferiors of Mrs. Armytage's household, had their quarters, as beseemed their degree, on the same vast first floor of No. 1, Rue Grande-des-Petites-Maisons. Where the kitchen was situated remained a mystery; but there must have been one on the premises, else how could M. Estragon (formerly of the Chimborazan embassy), the accomplished *chef* of the lady on the first floor, have concocted those delicate little dinners, those exquisite little suppers, for

which he and Mrs. Armytage were alike renowned, and which had
extorted the admiration of the most exacting epicures of Paris—
epicures before whose searching gaze the butler of the Trois
Frères faltered, and the waiters of the Café de Paris trembled.
Mrs. Armytage's wines had a special celebrity of their own. She
had a dry champagne which made fools witty and ugly women
look handsome. She had a sparkling Burgundy which seemed to
sing songs of its own accord as it danced in the glass. She had a
Romanée Conti, after drinking which authors rushed home and
wrote thrilling romances, and M. Israel des Trois Chapeaux added
hundreds of thousands of francs to his fortune by bold speculations
on the *hausse*.

For servants there were M. Estragon, erst of the Chimborazan
embassy, cook and *maître d'hôtel* as aforesaid—of foolish fat scul-
lions, I say nothing ; Mademoiselle Reine, lady's maid, tall,
supple, and discreet ; Monsieur Bénoît, *valet de chambre*, butler
and factotum, grave, solemn, silent, clean shaven, clad in raven
black, and on gala occasions appearing in black shorts and silk
stockings. When the Grand Duke of Grimgribberstadt came—
he was expected on the very night of which I am speaking—M.
Bénoît appeared with a slender silver chain round his neck,
ruffles, and a slim mourning sword by his side. The ladies of the
English community sneered at what they stigmatised as ridiculous
ostentation. Mrs. Armytage laughed—she was always laughing
—and declared that Bénoît had served crowned heads in his time,
and that if she did not allow him to wear his sword and chain
on state occasions he would give her warning. She did not even
resent the satirical inquiry of the young Marquis Boissec de
Puitssec, as to whether her *valet de chambre* was in the employ of
the Pompes Funébres,—and indeed his ceremonial costume did
not ill resemble that of the head undertaker at a French funeral.
This was the same M. de Boissec de Puitssec who was shortly
afterwards slain in a duel in the Bois de Vincennes by M. Hector
de Viellesouche, formerly of the Gardes du Corps, on a quarrel
arising from a bet as to the number of Mrs. Armytage's flaxen
ringlets. Boissec said there were fifteen on one side and fourteen
on the other ; Viellesouche betted that the numbers were equal.
They could not agree about payment ; so they quarrelled and

fought, and he died, and she—the lady on the first floor—laughed louder than ever.

I have omitted to mention one domestic of Mrs. Armytage's following; yet Hercule Moustachu deserves a word. He was the lady's *chasseur*, and wore a green pelisse elaborately embroidered, a gigantic cocked hat and plumes, Hessian boots, and an ivory-handled hunting-knife in his belt. Again the English community of the Faubourg had something to sneer at. "What does she want with that ruffianly creature, six feet high, with whiskers like blacking-brushes, and his absurd masquerade dress?" they kindly asked. Mrs. Armytage shrugged her pretty shoulders and laughed. Moustachu was her *chasseur*, she simply remarked, and wore the ordinary uniform of his station. Go to the hotel of the Chimborazan ambassador, of the Baratarian minister, or of the Ashantee envoy even, and you would find *chasseurs* similarly accoutred. He *was* a droll creature certainly, she admitted, with his cocked hat and his big whiskers; and she laughed till her ringlets shook like the leaves in a summer's breeze. She was but a mite of a woman, and Moustachu was her protection. He sat on the box of her brougham beside the coachman; and when she walked abroad on the boulevard, or in the Bois de Boulogne, he followed her, bearing a great golden-tipped staff of office, colossal, imposing, and severe. In the winter he wore a pelisse of bearskin, which made him look, to say the least, tremendous and appalling. Great men—the very greatest—have their foibles, and Moustachu's weakness was *absinthe*. When excited by that stimulant, he was at first ferocious and the terror of peaceful wineshop-keepers, but would ultimately subside into the tears of happy infancy. The malicious whispered that Moustachu had once been a giant at the fairs; and sarcastic M. de Boissec (only a week before the duel) declared that he recognised the *chasseur* as a former assistant to a travelling quack doctor, and that he had seen him in a scarlet toga and a Roman helmet grinding the organ in the dickey of a phaeton, while Dulcamara, his master, vaunted his pills and potions to the simpletons around.

"What a droll idea!" cried Mrs. Armytage, laughing, when some kind friend—I think it was an English lady of the community—repeated M. de Boissec's words to her.

The English community—the female part of it, at least—had once endeavoured to put down Mrs. Armytage. There was positively nothing against her,—not a speck on the ermine of her fair fame,—not a flaw in her diadem of good repute,—not the tiniest peg whereon to hang scandal; but they tried to put her down notwithstanding. "That serpent must be crushed," said Lady Eaglesborough emphatically; and when Lady Eaglesborough said a thing, important results generally followed. She was the leader of the serious (Anglican) world of Paris, was very nearly as tall as Moustachu, had four daughters almost as tall as herself, whom, rumour said, she caned, and was altogether a woman not to be trifled with. Mrs. Cowpon, the banker's wife (Cowpon, Pécule, Filicoteaux, et Cᵢᵉ., Rue St. Lazare), entered into an offensive and defensive alliance with Lady Eaglesborough; Mrs. St. Leger Levius, about whom scandal had more than once, and with some appearance of reality, been whispered, petitioned to be allowed to join the league; the Honourable Mrs. Dipton, whose husband led her such a sad life; the two Miss M'Caws whose father made that unfortunate mistake about the trust-money : gathered round Lady Eaglesborough. The serpent *must* be crushed, they all agreed. The terms "basilisk," "cockatrice," "crocodile," and "syren," were freely applied to Mrs. Armytage. She was to be cut, repudiated, ostracised, blackballed, sent to that terrible Coventry more dreaded than Norfolk Island ever was. The news of the conspiracy soon reached the widow of the Rue Grande-des-Petites-Maisons, and she laughed for at least twelve consecutive minutes. "*They* crush me!" she repeated, almost with a shriek of merriment. "The insensates! You may tell them," she continued, turning to Mr. Simperleigh, of the British embassy, who was her informant as to the hostile intentions of the Faubourg, "that if I hear any more of this nonsense, Lord Barrymore shall produce all Mrs. St. Leger Levius's letters to him, written while her husband was in Jamaica. The plain reasons why Frank Dipton shot himself shall be put down in writing by my man Sims. I've got the newspaper report of the bankruptcy of that wicked old Dr. M'Caw, who was a schoolmaster at Greenock, and starved his pupils, the wretch, besides spending his ward's trust-money. Young Mistigris, the artist of the Rue de Bohême, sketches capi-

tally in pen and ink, and he shall draw me *such* a caricature of
Lady Eaglesborough caning her grenadier daughters; and as for
Mrs. Cowpon, all Paris shall know how she pretended to go to
Aix-la-Chapelle for her health, went on to Baden-Baden instead,
lost five thousand francs at roulette,—on a Sunday night, Mr.
Simperleigh,—and, not daring to face her red-headed husband, had
to borrow money of Captain Lovelace to pay her hotel-bill and
come home. They crush me, indeed! Unless ample apologies
are made to me, I'll tear off all their false fronts and have half
their young men in Clichy in a fortnight."

Mrs. Armytage did not insist upon the apology, but the conspiracy melted at once into thin air. Lady Eaglesborough called
on her to beg a subscription for the Destitute Couriers and
Footmen out-of-place Relief Fund, and publicly declared that she,
Mrs. Armytage, was a person of superior attainments and great
energy of character. Mrs. St. Leger Levius went to spend six
months at Bagnères de Bigorres; and when next old Lord Barrymore of Wharton dined *en petit comité* with the lady of the first
floor, they both laughed till the *vermeil* and porcelain on the
damask clinked again. His Lordship liked to dine in the Rue
Grande-des-Petites-Maisons. He was to have dined there on the
27th of December, 1849, but, having a prior engagement with the
Grand Duke of Grimgribberstadt, sent an apology, and promised
to look in during the evening. For Lord Barrymore of Wharton
belonged to the old school, and liked to dine as well as sup.

The half-past seven *train express* had started a good hour ere
Mrs. Armytage left the vicinity of the Northern Railway terminus. "My man Sims"—the diminutive personage of ferret-
like appearance—had quitted her, and Mrs. Armytage was alone.
She had not even Moustachu the *chasseur* to protect her; but she
was a woman of great mental resources, and feared nothing. She
hailed a little *voiture bourgeoise* and bade the driver proceed to the
Boulevard Pompadour; and just as the multitude of clocks scattered all over her apartments were tinkling out the hour of nine,
Mrs. Armytage was in her *cabinet de toilette*, arraying herself for
a festal evening. It was a *fête* every night with Mrs. Armytage.
Her sands of life were diamond dust, and Time gave her his
arm with dainty politeness, and conducted her along a path all

strewn with flowers.   How old was she?   You might have asked
yourself the question a hundred times looking at her as she sat
on one of the luxurious couches in her boudoir waiting for her
guests, and have reaped only bewilderment and perplexity from
your inquiries.   As a rule, you are aware, it is difficult to tell the
ages of blondes.   Their complexion keeps; wrinkles and crows'
feet are slow to appear, and their furrows cast no deep shadows;
their hair rarely becomes grey.   Fair women of fifty may often
pass for their own daughters, unless indeed they become fat,
when the secret is at once disclosed.   Fat is fatal to either sex,
and under any circumstances.   Mrs. Armytage had no tendency
to *embonpoint*.   She was the rather *svelte*, slim, tiny, slender.
You saw none of her bones, but you did not see too much of her
flesh.   Her shoulders were much whiter than the whitest opera
cloak she could wear.   Her eyes were very large and very blue,
and they laughed at you to the full as much as her mouth did.
As to the laugh itself, it was almost incessant, but it was neither
a simper nor a snigger.   You know the blondes who laugh in that
manner, and who are, for the most part, utter and hopeless simpletons.   Mrs. Armytage's laugh was by no means a hollow one—
nothing like that dreadful cavernous "he-hee" of the actress on
the stage—the laugh which is twin-sister to the stereotyped grin
of the ballet-dancer.   It was not a jocund laugh; it was not a
"bitter" laugh (*risus sardonicus*); and the merriment in which
this lady indulged was by no means contagious.   Very few people
felt inclined to laugh with, or at, or after the laughing lady of the
Rue Grande-des-Petites-Maisons.   "She is a mermaid whose mother
was a laughing hyena," said Lord Barrymore of Wharton of the
lady, with whom he was so fond of dining.

All this brings us no nearer the solution of the problem as to
Mrs. Armytage's age.   She was not the kind of person to let you
into the secret herself.   There were ladies and gentlemen in plenty
who came to her saloons, and who had known her, some for ten and
some for fifteen years; but they were no closer to certainty than
her most recent acquaintances.   She had always looked young.
She always had that fresh bloom on her cheeks, the bloom
which didn't look like rouge, and which I don't believe was rouge.
There were no *fossettes* in her neck, no creases beneath her eyes,

not a touch of the Enemy's finger round the muscles of her mouth. There she sat on the couch in the boudoir, radiant in sea-green silk and pink bows and point-lace, and blazing with diamonds and rubies, and shaking her blonde ringlets as she played with and laughed at her little Blenheim spaniel.

She had dined alone, and in this same boudoir. M. Estragon had taken the same pains with her solitary repast as though it had been a banquet for fifteen. Moustachu the *chasseur* brought the dishes to the door, but he was not suffered to pass the magic portal. M. Bénoît, in full dress, himself, served the lady on the first floor. She tasted a little *purée*, a morsel of *turbot à la crème*, a tiny corner of *vol-au-vent*, a delicate slice of *chevreuil en poivrade;* but she ate up the whole of a fat little bird in a very nimble and cat-like manner, and crunched its succulent bones with great apparent gusto. Wines were presented to her in due course, the still and sparkling, the vintages of Bordeaux and of the Côte d'Or. She barely put her lips to the glittering crystal, but she drank a little glass of Curaçoa after her thimblefull of black coffee served up in a tiny cup of eggshell porcelain—real Sèvres, you may rest assured.

So she sat and played with the lap-dog, laughing at his gambols, and, anon, took down a daintily-bound novel—it was one of the admired works of M. Pigault-le-Brun, I am afraid, although on the back the volume was lettered *Œuvres de Racine.* She sat and laughed, and read and waited, but not long. Ere ten o'clock the *salons* were full of company. It was the most refined of Liberty Halls, and the guests wandered about pretty much as they pleased; only they were expected to take their departure at midnight. Special invitations were issued to the favoured few who partook of Mrs. Armytage's famous suppers.

I look back years, and stroll in spirit across the years through the dazzling chambers. I see the groups at the card-tables, piles of napoleons by them, silently but eagerly playing *écarté* or *baccara. Lansquenet* was never heard of in this particular house of the Rue Grande. Respectable English fogies played whist sometimes for five-franc points. The starched married ladies of the English community generally kept together, and whispered disparagement of the hostess. "That horrid gambling" they

were chiefly severe against. Young English lads were warned by
prudent mammas against *baccara*, and, stealing into the contiguous
saloon, began immediately to play at the pleasing game denounced;
young English ladies were warned, by the same anxious parents,
not to enter into flirtations with those "dangerous Frenchmen;"
but the peril of the Gallic element was overrated, so far at least
as the daughters of Albion were concerned. Plenty of French
dandies came from the Jockey Club, the Faubourg St. Germain,
and the Café de Paris; but, as the knowledge of the English
language possessed by the majority of their number was infinitesimal, their active flirtation with *les blanches meess* did not extend
beyond ogling the fair ones, and twirling their moustaches at them
in a fascinating and engaging manner.

I look back across the years, and see the boudoir whose threshold only the *élite* of the company dared, by a tacit kind of un-
derstanding, to pass. It is there the lady on the first floor by
preference remains. She glides in and about all her rooms and all
her company, and performs all the duties of hospitality with irreproachable ease and grace; but her home is in the boudoir, and
there chiefly she sits enthroned. On one divan you may see the
rigid form and coal-black beard of the Grand Duke of Grimgribberstadt. He was reigning Grand Duke once; but political com-
plications, culminating, to tell truth, in the summary burning of
his palace about his ears, caused his separation from an ungrateful
people, and the enforced abdication of a remarkably prickly crown.
His Effulgency—such is his Teutonic title—is very wealthy and
very peculiar. It is said that his cheeks are painted, and that his
beard is dyed. It is reported that he keeps the whole of his fortune in ready money between the mattress and the palliasse of his
bed; and that around his couch is a terrible assortment of spring-
guns, and twenty-bladed poniards that dart forth at the slightest
touch like the instruments of a cupper. It is rumoured also that
he will trust no servant of his to prepare his meals—having a
dread of poison—and that his daily repasts are sent to him hot
and hot each day from a different *restaurant*. Certain it is that
the Grand Duke of Grimgribberstadt is a mysterious-looking
personage, and that his eye is an evil one. He has a cluster of
diamond rings on every finger. The buttons of his waistcoat are

brilliants of the purest water. His studs in rose diamonds are prodigious. He is the only man in Europe who possesses an orange tawny diamond, with, wonder of wonders, the Grand Ducal arms of Grimgribberstadt engraved thereupon. He sits rigid and superb, and blazing. His conversation is limited to one topic, the Italian Opera, and, it must be further admitted to one opera, *The Barber of Seville*. "*Est-ce qu'on se fatigue jamais du Barbier?*"—"Do we ever grow tired of the Barber?"—asks his Effulgency, and poses you. Then he is silent for half an hour. "*Mais l'air de la Calomnie!*" he interposes clinchingly, when something is said about evil speaking. Another half-hour of silence elapses. Suddenly he rises, murmurs, "*Buona sera*," recalling the famous concerted piece in his beloved opera, and, dislocating for one instant one of his cervical vertebræ, by which it is understood that his Effulgency bows, he sails away, and is conducted by M. Bénoît, bearing waxen tapers, to his carriage— that heavy vehicle with the panels and shutters said to be of iron and shot-proof, and of which the two coal-black horses with the silvered harness have been pawing the flags impatiently these two hours.

About eleven, a little brougham drives up to the door of Number One. A tall footman jumps off the box, darts upstairs, pulls the crimson silk cord at Mrs. Armytage's door, says to the *chasseur*, "*Madame la Baronne*," darts down-stairs again, flings open the brougham door, cries "*On attend Madame*" to the inmate, and hustles or carries, or pushes,—he seems to do it so rapidly, —rather than conducts, a little ball of rich sable fur, surmounted by a little sky-blue hood, up to the apartments of *La Dame au Premier*. Mademoiselle Reine is in waiting, and unwinds the little cocoon of sable and sky-blue. With lightning rapidity you see Mrs. Armytage in her boudoir, curtseying to a dumpy little woman in black velvet and amethysts, with a towering plume on her little head. She looks like Humpty Dumpty who has fallen off the wall and has been half submerged in an ink-bottle. The company crowd about the silken hangings of the boudoir portal, and listen with rapt attention while, in a deep contralto voice, the little dumpy woman declaims something; it may be the grand tirade from *Mary Stuart*, the *Hélas!* scene in *Les Horaces*, the

"*Es ist nicht lange*" speech from *William Tell*, the *Timbaliers* of
Victor Hugo, or the "*Pour nous conserver purs*" passage from
Lamartine's *Jocelyn*. She declaims, perorates; there is a burst of
applause; Mrs. Armytage curtseys again; fifty people say what
they do not in the least mean; the dumpy little woman hurries
away again, is robed by Mademoiselle Reine, caught up again by
her footman, popped into her carriage, and rattled away to the
far end of the Rue de Lille, where she will favour the guests of
La Princesse de Chinon-Croisy with a similar burst of elocution.
Mrs. Armytage's guests burst out laughing, and whisper,
"*La Baronne* is madder than ever." This is the Baronne de
Biffinbach. Her spouse, M. de Biffinbach, formerly Hof Kam-
merer to the Landgrave of Sachspflugen-Hamstein, is an entomologist, and passes the best part of his existence in the society
of spiders, alive and dead. The Baronne has a rage for elocution. She will probably declaim at five or six houses this evening.
Last year her *lune* was for fresco-painting, and she insisted on
being suspended in a basket to the ceiling of her dining-room
while she executed Cupids and Muses thereupon. Some wet
plaster got into the Baroness's eye one day, and she abandoned
Art for Eloquence. She has had manias for animal magnetism,
for ascetic devotion, for *lansquenet*, for St. Simonianism, and
for tricks of legerdemain; but she has always been a very charitable, kind-hearted woman, and every body likes her.

That grand old man, so grave, so dignified, so venerable in his
flowing white locks, with such an exquisite hand, such a symmetrical
foot—*le beau vieillard*—is M. Laplace de Fontenelle the Acade-
mician? Not in the least. Yonder mean-looking little old man,
dabbing his forehead with a blue cotton pocket-handkerchief, is the
illustrious writer and *savant* you mean. Well, it must be my
Lord Barrymore. You are wrong again. His lordship is the jovial,
red-faced gentleman with the white teeth and the black whiskers
who is bending over Mrs. Armytage, and slyly chuckling over some
story she is telling him. The grand and dignified patriarch is no
less than old Monsieur Fourbel—Papa Fourbel—Nini Fourbel,
the wags of the small satirical journals call him. He has been a
chemist and druggist, and has made a fortune out of lollipops to
cure catarrh. He has been a stockbroker, and made another

fortune out of the *hausse* and the *baisse*. He has been manager of the Opera, and made fortune number three out of the throat of Duprez and the ankles of innumerable *coryphées*. He has been proprietor of the Republico-Monarchico-Orleanico-Bonapartist journal the *Girouette*. He started the Carpentras and Brives-la-Gaillarde Railway, and realised early. He sold, at premium, all his shares in the Docks Elagabale, the *Société anonyme des Marchands de Marrons chauds*, the *Compagnie d'Assurances contre la Migraine*, and other notable speculations. Had he resided in England, Sir Jasper Goldthorpe would have been proud of his acquaintance. This lucky old man might have rivalled the great Hebrew M. Portesac des Trois Chapeaux in wealth, but for his insatiable devotion to eating and drinking. The magnificence of his dinners is only equalled by that of his breakfasts. In oysters alone he spends a princely revenue. He is the one *gourmet* who has ortolans on his table all the year round. "To others the fame of Crœsus, of Ouvrard, or Paris-Duvernay," he says, proudly : "I am the emulator of Lucullus ; I am the successor of Cambacérès. I would settle fifty thousand francs a year on the widow of the man who would consent to be thrown into a fish-pond to feed my carp ; and were Vattel alive he should be cook to Casserole Fourbel."

Back across the years, back till I can see the journalists, the dandies, the political adventurers, the foreign counts, the financiers, the stock-jobbers, the painters and poets of a perturbed period of transition and suspense. Things had not fallen into their places in 1849, and every one wondered at the position in which he found himself. Back! I hear a voice, sonorous, solemn, touching, wild almost in its searching tones, through the doorway of the chamber where the grand piano is. Ah! I know who this is. The Princess Okolska is singing. "Princess, you must sing," Mrs. Armytage has said laughing ; "Society entreats this favour from you." The Princess rises and goes to the piano. She is a gaunt, bony woman, in an ill-fitting dress of tartan poplin, and a head-dress made of gold coins of Oriental look. She has big black eyes, and blue-black hair. Her husband, it is whispered, helped to strangle a certain emperor, and she herself is reported to be the daughter of a Circassian slave. She sings some strange

ballad in an unknown tongue. The song, at first monotonous and
faint, rises first to plaintive dolence, then to a passionate wail,
then to a sort of cry of rage and despair. "That woman has
been devoured by passions," says a journalist to a painter. At the
end of the song, the Princess Okolska faints away. She always
faints on these occasions. She is restored to consciousness, and
caressed and complimented, and has a glass of hot sugar and
orange-flower water brought her, in which, I am afraid, there
is something stronger than either of the ingredients above-
named.

This was the twenty-seventh of December, 1849. Seldom had
so brilliant a gathering been seen in the Rue Grande-des-Petites-
Maisons. There were richer guests, perhaps, at that very moment
at a certain family party in Onyx Square, Tyburnia, London—a
party where a father and a mother, and a tall girl with a pale face,
were waiting; but for rank, and talent, and wit, Mrs. Armytage's
visitors had undoubtedly the superiority. And while the lights
shone brightly, and the music streamed in either brave house on
either side of the Channel, the Calais express was ploughing
through the night towards the shores of the cold and complain-
ing sea.

The majority of the company left, as was the custom, at midnight. After that came supper, of the richest and rarest, to the
chosen ones who remained. Songs were sung, arrowy jests flew
about, political intrigues were dissected, wicked anecdotes were
told. There was deep drinking; there was deep play; and Mrs.
Armytage laughed continually.

At last she was alone. The bed-chamber was being prepared
for her. Mademoiselle Reine awaited her coming. She stood
with her white shoulders and her sea-green robe, and daintily
toasting one little foot at the embers that glowed on the polished
hearth. Tiny tongues of flame came out of the logs, as if to lick
her garment's hem in homage. The mirror on the velvet-hung
mantel reflected something else beside lustres and Sèvres vases
and Buhl clock. It reflected a woman's face and yellow ringlets
and dancing gems. Something else, too. A face haggard and
pallid, eyes vengeful and terrible.

She struck her little hand on the mantel with violence enough to wound it. She looked angrily at her bruised wrist, and twisted it in her other hand. She laughed no more.

"I would kill myself, if I dared," she muttered. "I am as beautiful now as I was four years since; and he has spurned me, spurned me again as he did before. I am richer than ever. There is not a penny belonging to his wretched father but I could call it mine; and he has spurned me. . . . But I will crush him; yes, Hugh Goldthorpe," she continued,—and seeming to address a locket which she took from her bosom,—" I will crush you, body and soul, and the woman who is waiting for you yonder shall see you no more."

She made as though to kiss something inside the locket, which she held open before her. But she closed the bauble with a sudden click, and thrust it into her white breast; and then Mrs. Armytage went to bed.

She was breakfasting at noon the next day—breakfasting in her little purple Morocco slippers and her morning wrapper of China silk, when M. Bénoît announced M. Sims.

M. Sims was as diminutive and as ferret-looking, but he looked more excited than usual.

"Have you heard the news?"

"What news?" the lady asked disdainfully. "That you smell of tobacco, as you do always, and do now? That is no news to me."

"You are cross this morning, ma'am," Mr. Sims remarked, shrugging his shoulders. "I have something here that will put you in a better temper."

With trembling hands he unfolded a copy of that morning's *Girouette*, and read out :—

"Telegraphic despatch from Armentières. *Epouvantable Sinistre* on the Northern Railway. Calais express came into collision with up luggage-train. Thirty-seven persons killed and wounded. Among the sufferers has been recognised by his papers the body of M. le Capitaine Hugh Goldthorpe, officer in the military service of the Honourable Company of the Oriental Indies, and son of Sir Goldthorpe, Baronet, and member of the Chamber of Lords of Great Britain. Further details will be given in our edition of the evening."

Mr. Sims had probably never in his life executed a translation from the French with such rapidity. Nor, I should think, was the recital of an appalling occurrence often received in so strange a manner as it was by Mrs. Armytage. It is a fact that she burst out laughing, and laughed so long and so loudly that the Blenheim spaniel, thinking that he too would be of the party, began to bark in doggish merriment.

" Was there anything ever so fortunate ?" said the lady, at last panting for breath.

"It is a joyful thing," responded Mr. Sims, rubbing his peaked nose.

" There, Sims!" cried Mrs. Armytage, catching up her spaniel and bestowing a kiss upon his snub nose. "You must go to the Préfecture and get my passport *viséd*. I start for England to-night. I hope the train won't have another accident, and kill poor little me. Ha! ha! ha!"

CHAPTER V.

ON A FIELD, OR; A CROSS, SABLE.

THE blackest winter baked the earth to stone; and in the fields
thin spikes of grass just contrived to pierce the hoar crust, naked
and rigid. It was a black frost. The roads, the kennels, the
pavements, the bare trees were dark and glossy. The roofs only
were white with frozen snow, and had been so for weeks.

Strong handed Labour, frozen out of bread-earning, stalked
starving through the town; wretched women whined and cowered,
but hungry men wandered scowling and with folded arms about
the shells of houses they should have been building. It was
winter everywhere, and Misery came abroad, forlorn and piteous.
Thousands were enjoying themselves on the glassy surface of the
park-waters, skating, and sliding, and shouting, and tumbling over
one another for joy; but thousands more looked on from the
banks, silent, savage, and famished. Vast blocks of ice floated
down the river, and, collecting in creeks, ground up against each
other with sharp noises. News came from the country of trains
snowed-up, of whole flocks of sheep lost in drifts, of villages in the
Yorkshire wolds cut off from all communication with towns and
markets; of gullies between them choked with snow, of cattle
frost-bitten, villagers half-starving. The Old Year laid himself
down to die in an adamantine coffin, and the New Year was swad-
dled in icy bands. There was much feasting and merry-making
in rich men's houses; yule-logs were burned, Christmas-trees
shaken; dancing and singing were heard. The cold was not
severely felt in warmly-lined carriages; and in thick-carpeted
drawing-rooms and bed-chambers thickly-curtained, the price of
fuel was not of much account. But in the narrow courts and
dens, and over the London border, and on the skirts of docks and
factory yards, and in the avenues of police courts, before the

E

relieving officer's strong door, and by the Union Workhouse's pitiless walls, Starvation and Destitution cowered in their rags, and moaned their lack of common food, and warmth, and shelter, and made the evil season more hideous to the view.

If you take a million-rich man, and put him naked and without victuals or a roof to cover him, on a rock, and expose him to the nipping frost and the January blast, it will not be long ere he begins to shiver, and anon to howl in agony and despair; and at last he will crouch prone to his jagged bed and die. But in the very centre of London, with his palaces and his vassals around him, it is difficult for the rich man to feel the cold. On that bare rock his millions in gold or crisp paper would not warm him, unless haply he had needles and thread to sew the money-bags together for raiment. When he is in London, however, the money will buy furred robes and Wallsend coals, and sand-bags to exclude the wind, and well-closed chariots to ride in, and Welsh wigs to draw over his head, plush gloves to cover his hands, and hot water bottles to put to his feet. Railway rugs, scalding soups and drinks, shawls and comforters, are all ready for him and purchaseable. The theatres, the churches, the counting-houses, the board-rooms, the marts and exchanges which he frequents, have all their warming apparatus, and become snug and cosy. No; I cannot see how it is possible for the English Dives to shiver,—were even Siberia brought to London, and the North Pole set up in the Strand in lieu of the Maypole which once adorned that thoroughfare. The milliners that serve Dives' wives and daughters may sell as many fans for Christmas balls as for Midsummer picnics; and after Dives' New-year's feasts the ice-creams and the ice-puddings are positively refreshing after the spiced viands and generous wines.

Sir Jasper Goldthorpe was the richest of rich men. The quilt of his bed might have been stuffed with bank-notes instead of eider-down. He could have afforded, had he needed caloric, to have burned one of his own palaces down, and warmed his hands by the conflagration. From his warm bed-room, breakfast-room, and study, his warm carriage took him, swathed in warm wrappers, to the warm sanctum of his warm counting-house. His head clerks wore respirators, and had mulligatawney soup for lunch.

The *Times*' City article was carefully warmed for him ere he perused it. His messengers comforted themselves with alamode beef and hot sausages and fried potatoes before roaring fires; and, when they were despatched on errands, slipped into heated taverns in little City lanes, where they hastily swallowed mugs full of steaming egg-hot and cordialised porter. The only cold that could seemingly touch so rich a man as Sir Jasper Goldthorpe was a cold in the head; and what possets, white-wine wheys, gruels, footbaths, doctors' prescriptions, and hot flannels, were there not in readiness to drive catarrh away from him! Lived there in the whole realm of England one man or boy mad or desperate enough to cast a snow-ball at the millionaire of Beryl Court? I think not. He was above the cold. It was street people only who were cold, just as the little princess asked the painter who came to take her portrait whether it was not true that "only street-people died." So Sir Jasper Goldthorpe, his sons and their thralls and churls, their tributaries and feudatories, let the street-people shiver as beseemed their degree, flinging them cheques and sovereigns sometimes in their haughty unbending way, and went on, warm and glowing, from a prosperous old year to a prosperous new one, when suddenly a Hand of Ice, that thrilled them all to the very bones and marrow, was laid just above the heart of Mammon, and of his wife, and of his children.

It was the Hand of Death, and it touched each with a cold pang, and went onwards, to touch some transiently, but to grasp others without release. Whoever felt its lightest pressure was chilled and benumbed. The icy hand came to Beryl Court and to Onyx Square, and all the gold of Mammondom could not, for that season, bring cheerful warmth again.

The News had come. A brief telegraphic message like a thunderbolt first fell. Then followed the lightning flashes of more messages; then the driving tempest of full details,—and the happiness of a household was scathed and blasted. No doubt, no hope could glimmer in the black night of their woe. The crushed, mangled, unrecognisable corpse had been gathered up at Armentières: the fragments of clothes, mingled with its remnants, were such as a man of Hugh's degree would have worn. There was the conclusive evidence of the furred coat, the writing-

E 2

case, the pocket-book, and the passport. Hugh Jasper Goldthorpe
was surely dead. According to the law of France, the remains
should have been interred within four-and-twenty hours following
the decease; but telegraphic messages stopped the interment.
The dust of so rich a man's son was not to be lightly disposed of.
The prefect of the department was written to; the English
ambassador in Paris condescended to wait upon the Minister of
the Interior and tell him of what golden parentage the young man
came; and orders were issued to permit the transmission of his
body to England.

The Reverend Ernest Goldthorpe remained in Onyx Square to
comfort his bereaved parents. Lieutenant William Goldthorpe
and his brother Edward, the Oxford Undergraduate, had to
undertake a sad pilgrimage to Calais. They were preceded two
days beforehand by Mr. Screwm, foreman to that eminent firm
Messrs. Ravenbury Brothers, of St. James's Street. All the
melancholy arrangements necessary were confided to this well-
known, and, indeed, historical house. They had buried the
Princess Charlotte; and old Mr. Simon Ravenbury, who used
facetiously to say that the elm wasn't grown nor the lead dug from
the mine that would be needed for his shell and coffin, had
married the grand-daughter of the undertaker to whose care had
been intrusted the disposal of the decollated remains of the last
nobleman executed for high treason in England—Lord Lovat.

The ill-omened messengers did their work, and met the two
brothers at Calais. A party of French actors and actresses were
coming over in the mail-steamer, but, though the night was wild
and stormy, they huddled themselves on deck, and dared not enter
the cabin, knowing what lay in the hold beneath. A hearse, all
plumed and garnished, with a mourning coach and four, waited on
the Admiralty Quay at Dover. The family lawyer, Mr. Drossleigh, head of a confidential department in Beryl Court, and Mr.
Plumer Ravenbury himself, junior in the historical firm of St.
James's Street, were also in attendance. Mr. Ravenbury's own
black brougham, with the showy long-tailed black horse—its dam
a Flanders mare that had assisted at the obsequies of William the
Fourth—followed the coach that contained the brothers, the
lawyer, and the confidential Mr. Drossleigh. A slight sojourn

took place for refreshment at the " Lord Warden ; " and it must
be mentioned, as a stroke of genius on the part of Mr. Ravenbury, that the chambermaids who conducted the brothers to their
apartments had black bows in their caps, and that the waiters
who served breakfast were the most mournful looking of their
class, and had strips 'of black crape on their arms. This last,
indeed, may not be so very surprising ; for from the waiter to the
mute there is but half a step, and *vice versâ*.

Mr. Ravenbury, so far as was consistent with his professional
woe, thoroughly enjoyed himself. It was his and his firm's pride
and pleasure to furnish rich men's funerals in the first style of
Black Art. He was a little, bustling, bald-headed man, whose
voice 'scarcely ever rose above a whisper, and every one of whose
plaited shirt-fronts was worth three guineas. The black brougham
and black horse were merely his professionally private equipage ;
and when a very rich "party" was to be conveyed to town, he
took the sable vehicle and its grim steed down by rail. In Hyde
Park, away from business, Mr. Ravenbury, covered with gold
chains, with a white hat and a black band,—it is said that he
continually wore mourning for a defunct earl, regarding whose
funeral he had given too lax reins to his imagination, and whose
executors had refused to pay the bill,—drove a dashing mail
phaeton, with two grays full of fire and action. He gave joyous
dinner parties and balls at St. John's Wood, and at Gunnersbury.
His wife was a handsome lady, with a mezzo-soprano voice and a
mania for Verdi. Her musical *matinées* were delicious ; and the
same embroideress who arabesqued the hems of her underskirts
pinked the shrouds and ruffled the winding-sheets for Ravenbury
Brothers. Plumer Ravenbury betted ; but he had a keen eye for
safe joint-stock speculations. Sir Jasper Goldthorpe did not
disdain to bow to the undertaker when he met him at boards and
public dinners. "Why should not an eminent upholsterer, who
performs the last sad offices for the very highest nobility, go into
Parliament?" asked Ravenbury's friends after dinner at St.
John's Wood. His sparkling hock was superlative! "Why
indeed?" mused Mrs. Plumer Ravenbury, as her jewelled fingers
paused on the keyboard of her Broadwood's grand. "I wish he
would, and cut the bone-grubbing business," savagely cried

Tressel Ravenbury, gentleman cadet at Woolwich; when his comrades taunted him on the paternal vocation, and nicknamed him "Hatchment." "Stuff and nonsense!" wheezed old Mr. Simon Ravenbury; "let him stick to the shop." Plumer's only son was destined for the Artillery. His papa would have preferred the Church—with an eye to a cemetery chaplaincy, the ill-natured surmised; and he had always had a great penchant for classical studies, being supposed to know all the Latin mottoes on his hatchments by heart; but Mrs. Plumer Ravenbury declared there was quite enough black already in the family, and Tressel was sent to Woolwich.

A dense crowd, whispering comments on the fabulous wealth of the Goldthorpe family, followed the mournful train from the hotel to the railway station. A special train had been secured, and Death and Sorrow sped through the icebound Kentish country to London Bridge. The same lugubrious ceremonial took place at the metropolitan terminus. Waggoners and cabmen stared in crowded Cannon Street, and Fleet Street, and Oxford Street, as the embryo funeral swept along. In the western part of Oxford Street, and the Edgware Road, where some of Sir Jasper's tenants dwelt, the shutters of the shops were closed. There was a great silent throng in Onyx Square as the dead man was brought home to his father's house.

Sir Jasper Goldthorpe had seen no one but his wife, his body-servant Argent, and the confidential Mr. Drossleigh, since the news came. He alternated between his bedroom and his study, and his children;—nay, Magdalen Hill even, did not dare approach him. Argent described him to his familiars, the lady's maid, the housekeeper, and the butler, as being less overwhelmed by grief than furious at his loss. The unhappy man's ravings and complaints had been fearful. He, usually so silent, had poured forth, hour after hour, torrents of passionate ejaculations. He disputed the justice of the decree that had taken his son from him. He menaced and defied the ravisher Death. His first-born could not, should not die, he wildly repeated. It was a shame. It ought not to happen. He was the richest man in the City of London. Then he relapsed into a silence that seemed to approach stupefaction. Let us draw a veil over this dismal spectacle. Who

meets Death or bears its visitations in the same manner? Piety
and Faith oft await its coming, shrinking and terrified; while
sceptic cynicism turns its face to the wall, smiling. Nothing is
there so unjust as to estimate man or woman's reality by the way
they die, or undergo the bereavements in which Death is for ever
dealing. Judge not from the dried-up eye; from the common-
place remark at the very grave's brink; from the solicitude for
petty things while yet It is in the house. Judge not from the
floods of tears, from the agonising wailings, from the days and
nights passed crouching on carpets, or on stairs; from the hands
that are wrung, the eyes that stream, the hair that is disheveled.
From earliest time men have set up a conventional standard of
sorrow to be observed at the death of their fellows. But it so
rarely is the nature of humanity to act exactly up to the standard:
there is so much grief that cannot be seen, and so much that is
simulated and over-acted, that it is the rather a commendable convenience than a hypocritical formula to have professional howlers
and mourners—hirelings who will tear their hair, and blacken
their faces, and rend their garments; or their modern substitutes,
who will carry staves in their hands and trays of feathers on their
heads for a given sum. Let them do their office for the sake of
the World and its usages, and we shall have time to grieve, each
in our own fashion.

And as each of these children of Mammon so grieved, at their
great and appalling loss, I leave the father and the mother: their
woe is not for contemplation. If a man were as rich in children
as Numenius, he is not to be comforted for the loss of his first
child, any more than a woman can ever be comforted for the
destruction of her first love. But those to whom Hugh had been
brother felt the loss in more mingled kind. The Reverend Ernest
Goldthorpe was now the Heir. His profession forbade that he
should ever become occupant of the throne of Mammon in Beryl
Court; yet still he might expect to enter one day into the possession of a title and almost boundless wealth. Would he rest
content with a country rectory? Would his golden thousands
prove stepping-stones to a bishopric? The second son of Sir
Jasper Goldthorpe became at once a mark for eager eyes. He
was but twenty-five years of age. He was unmarried. The nine

hundred a year he had from his living could matter but little to
him now. What a prospect lay before! Did he love his dead
brother? Did he regret his loss? The Reverend Ernest made
no sign. He was a pale bloodless man, and ordinarily reserved.
Solemn and severe, he took up his quarters in his father's house,
and obeyed the behests which, almost hourly, were transmitted
to him either in Sir Jasper's hand-writing, or by word of mouth of
the confidential Mr. Drossleigh. There was an immensity of work
to do. Drossleigh took care of the City business, and, had he
even not attedned to affairs in Beryl Court, there is no doubt
that Sir Jasper's money-bags would have turned themselves over
of their own accord, and multiplied themselves spontaneously.
There were perpetual interviews with Mr. Plumer Ravenbury and
his prime minister, Mr. Screwm. There were servants' and family
mourning to be ordered : for the superior womankind of Onyx
Square were quite beyond direction and advice. Mrs. Cashman,
the housekeeper, had *carte blanche*, or rather *carte noire*, for the
habiliments of woe. A select committee of Lady Goldthorpe's
female friends kindly assisted her ; and Cashman, installed in one
of the Goldthorpe carriages, was continually driving backwards and
forwards between Onyx Square and Mr. Jay's in Regent Street.
That urbane and distinguished purveyor of ladies' mourning took
her at once to the Unmitigated Woe Department. Whole bales
of the paraphernalia of inconsolable grief were despatched to
Onyx Square. Mr. Jay's young ladies plied their busy needles :
tried on bonnets, and mantles, and skirts. All the lower rooms
of Mammon's house were littered with funeral trappings, and the
maid-servants dreamt of crape and bombazine.

There were hundreds of letters to be written to the vast circle
of Goldthorpe's friends and clients, bidding them to the funeral,
or merely apprising them of the loss. There were the long and
pompous advertisements to be drawn up for the *Times* and
Morning Post. There was a sad letter to be sent to Malta, that
the young sailor on board the *Magnanimous* should know that
Mammon had one son the less.

It was premature as yet to speak of the tomb or the inscription.
" I suppose Ernest Goldthorpe will write that himself. His Latin
was never very good," opined many a clerical and scholastic

admirer of the Goldthorpian grandeur. "He fought bravely enough at the Sutlej. They can't do less than give him a statue down at Goldthorpe, or at least a couple of busts for town and country," reasoned Tom Praxtiles the sculptor, fondly regarding his unsold Bacchante and his unsuccessful design for a monument to Lord Hill, in his not too frequented studio in Charlotte Street, Fitzroy Square.

"And then there'll be the monument in the cemetery, Praxtiles, my chick," would hint friendly George Gafferer, Praxtiles' boon companion, Boswell, and critic, who had looked in to inform him that there was a neat little paragraph about his last bust (Pessawee Ramjetjee Bobbajee Lal, the rich Parsee of Bombay) in that morning's *Comet*, smoke a quiet pipe, drink a bottle of pale ale, and give him another sitting for his own (complimentary) bust.

"There'll be no stonecutters' work where a Goldthorpe's concerned, my chick," George would continue. The worthy soul was thus naïvely affectionate with every body, and would have called the judge who sentenced him to death "my chick." "No broken columns, or quenched torches there, you may depend. Why, they'll have a mausoleum, Praxtiles, with slabs of Carrara, and verde antique and scagliola columns, with gilt capitals and a bronze railing, and a weeping Victory at top. Write in at once, my dearest chick."

Praxtiles didn't write, but he left his card with kind inquiries, that afternoon, in Onyx Square; and meeting the Lieutenant of Hussars moodily walking through Bayswater, grasped his hand with a depth of sympathy that would have drawn tears from one of Praxtiles' own marble blocks. The sculptor had had the honour of dining more than once at Sir Jasper's, and he never dined with a rich man without at once laying the foundation of a plot for hewing his bust while alive, or his statue when dead.

Lieutenant William was constrained to walk moodily about Bayswater, for he could not sit all day in the darkened house, or in the frigid Jermyn Street Hotel where he slept. He scarcely knew his dead brother; but he was very sorry—the sorrier because his kind father and mother were in such dire grief. He was a good-natured young man, who could not think much. The most he could say about the dreadful catastrophe at Armentières was that it was " a shocking thing," and that " poor Hugh was gone, you know." He did not know how to employ his time. He wrote to his colonel and to one or two friends about the " shocking thing," and the gallant officers of the Nineteenth repeated at mess that it *was* shocking, and that " poor Hugh Goldthorpe had gone to the bad." But they talked much more about his father's money, and indulged in many surmises as to whether the parson would come in for the bulk, or whether Willy Goldthorpe would sell out and turn money-grubber in the City.

The subaltern would have liked to look in at his club in St. James's Square, but he knew that etiquette inhibited his going there. He dared scarcely enter the shop of his cigar-dealer in ordinary. The Reverend Ernest was too busy to talk with him. Miss Hill did not leave her room. He had an odd disdain for his three younger brothers, to whom he could not talk, and who could not talk to him. It was inconvenient to walk about Bayswater all day long; but at last he hit upon a happy expedient and compromise, and retaining a private room at his hotel, did there entertain a select circle of tall, stupid, good-natured fellows, mostly with tawny moustaches, and belonging to the profession of arms, who drank sodawater dashed with cognac, smoked very large and powerful cigars, made occasional bets on current events, and bade him " cheer up, old fellow." Lieutenant William got on very well with these friends until the funeral. It was just the kind of consolation he needed. He was not hard-hearted—only somewhat obtuse, and nearly a stranger to the kinsman he had lost. Who shall say that he was not as sorry as he might reasonably be expected to be ?

The undergraduate and the clerk in the Civil Service had been mere boys when Hugh had paid his visit to England. They were bewildered and shocked by the awful intelligence of his death, but they could scarcely bewail it. They talked incessantly about it to each other, canvassed every item of the tragedy as lads will do ; but how were they to weep, and what were they to weep about ?

As for Alfred Goldthorpe, he was a child. The best thing that could be done for him was done ; and the Honourable Mrs. Cony-

beare, who had a whole tribe of boys home for the holidays, took
temporary charge of him. The little fellow did not understand
much about the bereavement his family had suffered. He had
never seen Hugh. He was chiefly sorry when the lady's maid
told him that Miss Magdalen, of whom he was dotingly fond, was
ill with grief. But the laughter of his playmates—their toys, and
games, and sponge-cakes, and oranges, soon controlled him; nor
could Alfred resist an odd feeling of gratification at the thought
of the fine clothes for which the tailor had measured him, and
which he was to wear, or banish from his young mind the knowledge that the sad misfortune that had happened in his family
would invest him with a strange importance and interest when
he went back to school.

Should these brothers of the dead have shown their sorrow
otherwise ?—and if so, in what manner ?

CHAPTER VI.

"RESURGAM."

In the early days of January 1850, the solemn funeral of Hugh Jasper Goldthorpe took place. The locality chosen was the cemetery at Kensal Green. The Goldthorpe family had been too recently inscribed in the *Libro d'Oro* of provincial aristocracy (Burke's *Landed Gentry*) to claim sepulture in some ivy-grown country church, the pavement of whose chancel was sown thick with monumental brasses and cross-legged figures, couchant, of mediæval Goldthorpes, dead and gone. Hugh could not be laid with his ancestors; and Sir Jasper had ever calmly repudiated the convenient insinuation of heraldic parasites, that it might be possible to find a Goldthorpe well known as a Saxon franklin whose fathers had been here long before the Conqueror's coming, and the registration of whose land and swine had been unaccountably omitted from Domesday-book. The potentate of Beryl Court prided himself on being the Rodolph of Hapsburg—read "Lucksburg"—of his race. There had been some talk of a mausoleum in the park at Goldthorpe; but this idea was abandoned at the earnest instance of the mother of the deceased. Where her son's ashes were laid, she was determined, she said, to lie some day; and it should be, she insisted, in a Christian graveyard, not among the deer in a park. There were those among the Goldthorpe following who expressed themselves of opinion that Westminster Abbey was the most appropriate place for interment. Why had not Captain Hugh been killed at the Sutlej?—his representatives might have demanded a niche in the Abbey for him then, as of right. Sir Jasper knew the Dean. What were Deans good for but to be civil and do what they were asked? In the end, Kensal Green was fixed upon, and the freehold of a huge family grave purchased there. Praxtiles the sculptor knew its super-

ficial area to an inch two days before the funeral. So did Fiddyas
of Eccleston Street, Pimlico ; so did Roubiliac Tompkins of the
Euston Road. Now was the time. Tompkins fondly pictured to
himself the means of getting rid of that long-completed group,
" Pity weeping over Valour," which, in despair at seeing marble
lie idle, he had begun to think of exhibiting at Canterbury Hall,
or selling to the proprietor of a tea-garden.

The day of the funeral was kept as a kind of mournful *fête* in
Onyx Square. The little Miss Sardonixes (Dr. Sardonix, physician to the Court), next door to the house of Mammon, were
excused that morning from attendance at the Hyde Park College
for Young Ladies. They stood at the dining-room windows instead,
and glued their young noses to the panes thereof, until the last of
the brave funeral had disappeared from the Square. Pappadaggi,
the music-master, was bidden to forego his bi-weekly lesson at
Number Twelve. The Miss Bosuns (Admiral Bosun) were eagerly
scanning the funeral from their drawing-room casements. Mrs.
Twizzle from Maida Hill, Miss Ashtaroth, the old maid from the
Harrow Road, who regularly attended the marriages at St.
George's, Hanover Square, and (by special favour of a subsidised
pew-opener) was permitted to weep plenteously in the organ-loft,
with Captain Hawksley, R.N., and one or two evening-party young
men, looked in before noon. There was a nice hot lunch at two.
The Bosuns didn't know the Goldthorpes. The dead man was
no kinsman of theirs. What harm was there in their having a
little singing, and spending a most delightful afternoon ? Old
Chewke, the plethorically wealthy retired timber-merchant, formerly of Riga, went purposely two hours later to the Union Club
that morning. He had declined an invitation to the funeral. He
was a selfish old man, who ate hot veal cutlets in bed, and was
afraid of the weather ; but he watched the start of the procession
narrowly, and to Chipp, his body servant, imparted his opinion
that it was deuced well done, and a credit to Goldthorpe. Chewke
knew Plumer Ravenbury quite well, and nodded familiarly to
that monarch of funeral-furnishing as he saw him hand the chief
mourner into his coach ; then, remembering the solecism in
etiquette he had committed, he retreated to his study, and took
Chipp severely to task for daring to peep at the *cortége* through

the half-opened door. "Think of my health, sir," thundered the
retired timber-merchant. Mr. Chewke did not like draughts in
his house—always excepting hot ones (with spices and sugar)
before going to bed.

Truly, it was the grandest funeral that had ever been seen in
Onyx Square. There was no cheap local papers in those days
(capital institutions are those cheap local papers), else some
Bayswater Chronicle or *Paddington Gazette* would have described
the order of the procession: the hearse and plumes, with the
cypher of the deceased embroidered on the horses' trappings; the
long train of mourning coaches; the longer file of private carriages
—from those of dukes and marquises downwards, all with shutters
closely drawn up, all with coachmen and footmen with long hatbands;—the policemen who cleared the way and closed the procession; the crowds that lined the streets through which it passed.
The chief daily newspapers did indeed each devote a paragraph to
the description of the melancholy spectacle.

Throughout, it was the strangest mixture of the things of this
world and those that belong no more to the world at all. You
could *not* keep wealth and pride and feasting away from the
black, dreary drama of death. Those who were being arrayed for
mourners could not help fingering their scarves and hatbands, and
wondering at the thickness and richness of the silk. There was
cake and wine everywhere; and people could not help taking port
and sherry with one another. The maid servants could not help
looking prettier than usual in their new black and glossy-ribboned
caps. There was a buzzing of murmuring conversation most mundane while the last dread preparations were going on above—and
till murmuring was hushed by the creaking of the stairs and the
coming down of the bearers. Dr. Sardonix was one of the family
physicians. His little daughters wagged their heads affectionately, and pointed their innocent fingers, until reproved by
Zenobia, their mamma, when they saw the Doctor emerge,
pilloried in the highest of white cravats, from Mammon's portals,
and bow gravely to the undertaker's aide-de-camp, who assisted
him into the mourning-coach. Dr. Sardonix knew the man by
sight; and, in good sooth, Beaver, the functionary in question,
had often officiated as toastmaster at the anniversary festivals of

the hospital of which the Doctor was chief physician. In the
dining-room, pending departure, Dr. Sardonix was, as usual,
gravely eloquent. He was shorn of one customary subject of conversation, for he could not dilate on the curative treatment to
which he had subjected the deceased:—"but Nature was too strong
for us—too strong, my dear sir," would the Doctor wind up.
But he was a ready man, and atoned for the loss of his topic by
pleasing anecdotes of railway accidents. Here Bolsover, M.P.—
who always went in for his borough as a red-hot Liberal at every
general election, spoke and voted as a determined Tory till the
last month of the session, then turned Liberal again, and was
triumphantly re-elected after the dissolution—cut in with quota-
tions of celebrated epitaphs, and " Sidney's sister, Pembroke's
mother," " *Martini Luigi implora pace*," and similar mortuary
inscriptions that have become historical, were handed about with
the cake and wine.

It was the same in the carriages during the dreary ride up the
Harrow Road. The lawyers talked of abstruse conveyances, and
notable wills, and picturesque Chancery suits, in which all the
costs were costs in the cause, and none of the suitors got anything:—" Not a rap, sir," whispers Mr. Probate of Bedford Row,"
suiting the action to the word on his silver snuff-box, and treating
himself to a pinch of Macabaw. The legislators talked politics.
The clubmen talked club scandal and girded at the committee ;
the clergymen talked schools, missionary societies, Ecclesiastical
Commission, and the *Times* newspaper;—I don't know how it is,
but the clerical body seem better read in the contents of the
leading journal than the members of any other class in the community ;—and the merchants and money-dealers, of whom there
were very many in the funeral following, talked stocks and shipping, bullion, bills, and bankruptcy, and Mammoniana generally.
The most direct reference to Sir Jasper Goldthorpe was made by
Mr. Deedes (Deedes, Ferret, and Wax, the great bank solicitors),
who opined that, after all, Sir Jasper would be better for his
calamity, for that "they could hardly keep him out of his peerage
now."

At every funeral there is a mourner—in mien, the gravest
among the whole company—who makes jokes. I suppose he

cannot help being jocose. His notorious propensity does not
prevent his being bidden to funerals. The strangest thing about
him is that he is only facetious at funerals, and that at ordinary
dinner-parties he is the dullest dog present. There was such a
joker present at the solemnity now recorded. His name was
Grygger. He primed himself well with old Madeira before
starting. He was funny (behind the largest white pocket-handkerchief) all the way from Onyx Square till the tombstone-
cutters' yards that herald the vicinity of the cemetery began to
loom in sight; and he never forgot to precede each joke with a
chuckle, and end it with a sigh. He was universally popular,
although all his hearers were strongly of opinion that he ought to
be thrown out of the coach-window.

And so, with faces that belie their thoughts, these children of
mrotality follow the poor crushed mortal who has put on immortality. There is a larger crowd at the cemetery gates. The
spectators are packed closely in the street of tombs, up which
the black train passes. The chapel is densely filled; the last
orisons are said; the grave has been reached; the handful of
earth thrown in; the cords are dragged rattling up; the company throng round the frost-covered planks that edge the grave,
and peep over each other's shoulders to read the inscription on
the gilded coffin-plate :

HUGH JASPER GOLDTHORPE,
Captain H.E.I.C.S.
&c. &c. &c.
Died, Twenty-seventh December,
1849,
aged Twenty-seven Years.
" Resurgam."

" What does the last word mean ? " timidly asks of Doctor
Sardonix a little milliner's girl in a skimping plaid shawl, who has
come to the funeral as to a show, and has edged herself in among
the mourners.

Dr. Sardonix looks condescendingly over his pillory of starched
muslin at the inquisitive *modiste*.

"'*Resurgam*,' my young friend," he responds in a dulcet under-tone, "is a Latin word, and signifies '*I shall arise again.*'"

"Thank you, sir," says the little milliner with a curtsey, and runs off to tell Amy, her friend, who is staring at the tomb of the late Mr. Ducrow, of the grand crimson velvet coffin she has seen, with its gilt handles and cherubim heads, and golden plate, and how kindly the nice old gentleman in the white neckcloth answered her.

"*Resurgam.*" One need not look into a grave to read that motto. You may see it painted on the hatchments in every undertaker's shop-window.

It was all over. The sexton who locked the chapel-door just paused as he noticed a fresh line of furrows on the great wooden turntable bier, covered with thousands of dints, in the centre of the edifice. "What a heavy coffin, to be sure!" he said medita-tively. "Might have held three. Ravenbury Brothers have made a good thing of it this time." And so locked all up, and went to smoke his pipe at the little beershop hard by. The undertaker's men crammed the rich pall into the hearse, and hauled the plumes off their several pegs as though they were extinguishing so many corpse-candles. Then they rattled off to town, their legs swinging over the sides of the vehicle, and their jolly noses brightening up with the bracing motion and the thoughts of the bowls of punch they would partake of that night. For Ravenbury Brothers gave an annual supper to those who did "black work" for them, and this festival happened to be concurrent with the grand funeral at Kensal Green Cemetery.

The carriages, of which the shutters had been so closely drawn up, and whose attendants had assumed such mournful adjuncts to their garb, did good service that evening in the conveyance of their distinguished proprietors to balls, and suppers, and panto-mimes. Everybody went about his several business, and was business-like or convivial, sleepy or snappish, preoccupied or simply indifferent, as circumstances or inclination led him. Only Grygger the joker had the blues, slipped off to his lonely chambers in Duke Street, Adelphi, sipped mutton-broth for his dinner, and passed the evening in the perusal of Sir Thomas Browne's "Urn Burial."

F

Mr. Plumer Ravenbury had not conducted the funeral on foot. Members of the firm never did. It was Mr. Screwm who, ebony baton in hand, marshalled the procession, and walked valorously through the frozen mud to Kensal Green. He would not have derogated from his position by accepting a "lift" on the road, for worlds. Inferior undertakers might do it; but, as Mr. Screwm observed to his immediate subordinate, Beaver (by night a check-taker at the Olympic Theatre, Wych Street, Strand,—and much success to you, Messrs. Robson and Emden), "hif Ravenbury Brothers' 'ed man can't afford shoe-leather, and charge chilblains to the 'ouse, the dickens is in it. I'll have the next warm, my dear." The colloquy took place at the Mute's Head, Church Passage, Jermyn Street, the favourite house of call for gentlemen who did black work. Mr. Plumer Ravenbury followed the *cortége* at a decorous distance in his black brougham; but he was on the ground and at the grave, and adjusted the chief mourner's cloak, and placed his Prayer-book for him. He had a civil word to say, too, for the Cemetery Chaplain, a pallid young man with a fishy eye, one of a race of hapless curates who had desperately clutched at the large salary attached to a charnel-house chaplaincy. Do these chaplains ever go raving mad from incessantly repeating the same solemn ritual, I wonder? We who listen to the noble Burial-service of the Church of England, and dwell upon its beautiful language, its austere eloquence, sit with charmed ears and reverent awe to hear the priest; but how is it with the unhappy ecclesiastic who has to read the service perhaps fifty times a day?

Sir Jasper Goldthorpe went straight from the cemetery to the South-Western Railway Station. Argent, his body-servant, waited for him with one of his own close carriages at the gate. The Baronet had borne up wonderfully. Natural emotion, and of the bitterest, he had shown in the chapel, and at the grave of him who had been his hope, his pride, and his joy; but he was soon nearly himself again; and save that there were deep-sunk cavities beneath his eyes, and that his hands and knees trembled (perchance with the cold), you would scarcely have thought that he had suffered this dreadful blow. He bowed to the company on leaving the grave, said a kind word to Mr. Ravenbury who was thrilled

to the soul with gratitude thereby, pressed the hand of each
of his children present, and, leaning on his second son's arm, proceeded to his carriage. Plumer Ravenbury scarcely thought it in
accordance with strict etiquette that the chief mourner's departure
should take place in this abrupt manner; but he consoled himself
with the thought that grief so intense and wealth so prodigious
must be humoured, and, when the carriage had driven away, conducted Ernest Goldthorpe and his four brothers to the mourning
coach (for even little Alfred had been brought thither) with a
dignity worthy of a *chambellan* of Louis Quatorze.

Sir Jasper Goldthorpe found a companion within his carriage.
Magdalen Hill was there. The blinds were down. The girl flung
herself into his arms. They sobbed in concert, till the vehicle
stopped at the entrance to the Terminus an hour afterwards;
scarcely a word had been exchanged; and both were the better
for their undisturbed grief.

Everybody in office at the Railway Station knew whom they
were, and turned their heads away as they alighted, that they
might not be seen to notice the swollen eyes of Sir Jasper and
his companion. Argent had secured a carriage. Officials conducted them to it with silent respect, and policemen stood on the
platform near, quietly warning off inquisitive travellers with a
whisper that Sir Jasper Goldthorpe was there.

An hour's journey brought them to Goldthorpe Station, formerly
Pogthorpe Road, but which had been rechristened in honour of
the contiguity of Goldthorpe Manor, Sir Jasper's marvel of a
place hard by. The mansion was a good two miles' distance from
the station. Another carriage was in waiting; the servants in
deep mourning. The lodge-keeper at Goldthorpe who flung open
the gilded gates was in profound black. The little charity-children
who passed them on the road had crape on their arms. Tears
trickled down the cheeks of the ancient butler and housekeeper,
who received them in the grand entrance-hall; and Plutus, the big
mastiff, whined as he crept towards his master and licked his
hand.

There was a bright and cheerful fire burning in the dining-
room: and when Sir Jasper and Magdalen had removed their
travelling wrappers, the ancient butler, who had been nervously

twitching his fingers and scraping his feet, as though he had some message to deliver about whose reception he was not quite certain, said, bowing deferentially :

" If you please, Sir Jasper, I was to give you this card, and the lady has been waiting more than an hour to see you.

The card was slim and limp, and glazed and scented. There was a crest engraven on it, and a name ; and beneath, these words in pencil :—

" I must see you, instantly, and alone. I learnt that you were coming here, this morning. You cannot refuse me. I saw the last of Hugh."

Sir Jasper Goldthorpe hastily glanced at Magdalen, murmured " Some City business," crumpled the card in his hand, and hurried to the door. He darted across the hall into his study, where, sitting before a fire as bright and as cheerful as that which he had left, was a lady in very deep but very rich black, with a very elaborate black bonnet, and pretty little black kid-gloved hands. The drapery beneath her sombre dress was wonderfully embroidered, and she had just lifted it to toast one of her little feet, daintily arrayed in a shining little black *bottine*, at the fire.

" Alone ? " said the lady in black, inquiringly, when the Baronet entered.

" We are alone."

" Be kind enough to lock that door. Doubly. There's no bolt ? Well, never mind. Thank you."

The lady rose, and put out one little gloved hand to Sir Jasper Goldthorpe, smiling, showing her dazzling white teeth, and shaking her sunny ringlets—of which she had a profusion—as she did so. The Baronet took her hand, shuddering, but let it fall again as though he had come in contact with some noxious reptile.

"And so you have buried your son ? " she continued, quite jauntily. " Poor fellow ! He was with me only five minutes before the train for Calais started."

Sir Jasper Goldthorpe groaned, and hid his face in his hands.

" Only five minutes," the lady in black repeated.

There was no response.

"You see I wear mourning for him. It was due to his memory. It is fit that I should go into the very deepest black for Hugh. I killed him."

The Baronet turned his eyes, wild in amazement, towards the speaker.

"Yes!" the lady in black airily repeated. "I killed him. I'm not a luggage-train, though; I had nothing to do with that horrid accident."

"Do you wish to drive me mad?" moaned the father.

"Not at all. Only to make you remember old times and old promises. Look here, Sir Jasper Goldthorpe," the lady went on, and seating herself coquettishly on one arm of the chair in which her companion crouched rather than sat, "you once threatened to have me transported."

"Woman, there were circumstances—"

"There were Devils, and there is one," interrupted the lady in black, with pretty testiness, and swinging one of the dainty *bottines* to and fro. "You threatened to transport me—poor little Me! And to think that I should have killed your son, the heir to your riches and your baronetcy! Sir Jasper Goldthorpe, I killed him with THESE!"

As she spoke she produced a charming little *bijou* of a pocket-book in morocco and gold. She took out an oblong packet of papers, the topmost one seemingly covered with faded writing, and crossed at right angles by more manuscript.

"*Regardez donc,*" she said; "how pleasant the old writing looks. 'Accepted payable at '—— wherever is the place?"

A minute afterwards she had unlocked the door, and stood in the hall, calling for "somebody, please!"

"Ah! there is Miss Hill," cried Mrs. Armytage cheerfully, as Magdalen's blanched face showed at the dining-room door. "Quite *éplorée* she looks. Oh! here is a servant. If you please," she continued, addressing the butler, "you had better bring some water, or some brandy, or some smelling salts, or something. I don't think Sir Jasper is very well."

CHAPTER VII.

MRS. ARMYTAGE IS AS MUCH AT HOME AS EVER.

MRS. ARMYTAGE did not care to stay for the succour she had requested to be afforded to Sir Jasper Goldthorpe. She had done all that, in her opinion, was due to the claims of humanity. Could she, a lady and a comparative stranger, assist with propriety in the resuscitation of a gentleman—such a very rich one, too—who had fallen down in a fit, caused, no doubt, by excessive grief and by reaction of the nerves after the melancholy ordeal through which he had just passed? Sir Jasper was in his own house, and surrounded by his own attached domestics. The presence of Mrs. Armytage was clearly no longer needed; so she slipped through the throng of frightened servants, who were crying out that their master was dying; brushed past Magdalen Hill, who was hastening towards the study, and who regarded her with a look of haughty aversion mingled with amazement, and tripped down the great marble steps on to the terrace. Mrs. Armytage and Magdalen were old acquaintances. The house-dog Plutus sprang towards her with a growl; but she waved him off with her tiny kid-gloved hand. She was very fond of dogs, and called this one "poor fellow;" but as the animal stood regarding her with uncertain eyes, and uttered a low querulous baying, she sighed to herself, "Will nobody love me,—not even a dog?" The golden and purple peacocks, in their house by the frozen lake, craned forth their necks as Mrs. Armytage approached in her way down a lower terrace into the park that stretched for full a mile before Goldthorpe Manor. It was quite pretty to see her picking her way along the carriage-drive between the tall old trees. She saw the woodman with his billhook pruning the dead branches. The man made a clumsy bow to her fair face and rich clothes. Her golden ringlets seemed to belong, somehow, to Mammon. She smiled graciously, and put a shilling into the man's leathern-covered paw—at least, it looked a paw, swathed in his huge verderer's glove. "A civil fellow," she thought. "What would he do to me if I were a ragged, barefooted girl caught stealing dead wood in Sir Jasper's park? There is a cage in the village, I suppose. Would they send poor little Me to gaol, or put me into the stocks?" And she broke into a bitter little fit of laughter, which rang very strangely through the frosty air of the evening. It was twilight when she reached the lodge-gates. The ancient keeper came out with a lantern to open the portals for her. The light shone upon her sombre dress, upon her white skirts and tinselled hair. It shone, too, upon the heavy gate-posts, upon the gilding and tracery, and the armorial bearings of the rich man displayed above the entrance to his demesne. "A pretty place," murmured Mrs. Armytage, giving the lodge-keeper another shilling. "And it might all belong to poor little Me!"

"You've seen Sir Jasper, my lady, may be?" Huggins the lodge-keeper inquired, in a respectfully sympathetic voice.

"I have just left the house," Mrs. Armytage replied.

"Do he bear up, my lady?" added Huggins, in a tone of affectionate solicitude.

"Wonderfully. He will soon get over it. A little this way with the lantern. Thank you. Good night." And the gates closed with a clang, and Mrs. Armytage was gone.

"A nice-spoken lady as ever was," remarked Mr. Huggins to his wife, as he dropped the shilling through the orifice in a missionary society's box. "She didn't come up, though, with Sir Jasper and Miss Magdalen, surely. Didst thou let the lady in, Moggy?"

"Not I," answered Mrs. Huggins, his wife, addressed as "Moggy." "A'nt I been down to Pogthorpe till a quarter of an hour ago?"

"Then 'twas you, Tib."

"I never saw the lady," protested the young person hight Tib, who was a red-headed girl of fifteen, the lodge-keeper's grand-daughter.

"That's strange," grumbled old Huggins, settling himself down in a rush-bottomed chair to enjoy his customary afternoon's cough,

which as customarily followed the afternoon's pipe, from which he
had been disturbed by Mrs. Armytage's summons to open the gate.
"That's pertickler strange," he continued. "I thought I should
ha' recklected all that gold-coloured hair if I'd seen it afore. My
memory must be getting uncommon bad, sure*ly*." And here, the
customary cough overtaking Mr. Huggins, he substituted a bark
for a wheeze, and so went off to a growl and a rattle, until his tea
was ready.

Meanwhile Mrs. Armytage walked through the black winter
gloaming. She met a rural policeman, and wished him good night
with much sweetness. She was troubled with no fears of poachers
or rustic burglars; although there were some very coarse, ruf-
fianly-looking fellows lounging about the door of the Goldthorpe
Arms, half way between Pogthorpe and the manor. She was a
courageous little woman, and went straight on. There was no
village at Goldthorpe Station, formerly Pogthorpe Road; only a
few stucco villas run up by a speculative builder, who had gone
mad immediately after mortgaging the carcasses of his houses for
thrice their value, and who was now expiating his taste for architecture at Colney Hatch. Two or three forlorn little shops had
been started by traders who hoped to get some custom from the
occupants of the villas; but as half of these edifices were not
finished, and the other half had hitherto found only insolvent and
fraudulent tenants, and one also, as it was, had already the reputation of being haunted, from the fact of a retired pig-jobber of
evil disposition having cloven his wife's skull with a chopper in
the front parlour the preceding Christmas Eve, commercial activity
was not very remarkable at Goldthorpe Station. In fact, but for
its vicinage to the manor of Mammon, the Company might have
shut it up altogether without much detriment to the traffic.
There was an unhappy little beershop, "The Railway Arms;"
but the topers of the neighbourhood preferred either the "Goldthorpe Arms" or the "Jolly Beggars" at Pogthorpe village
proper, which was distant a mile from Sir Jasper's. The great
man had once thought of taking Pogthorpe Road in hand, and
had he deigned to smile upon it, it would doubtless by this time
be as prosperous as Wimbledon or Kingston; but one of the
porters happened to offend him one morning, by omitting to hand

him his *Times* before he entered the train, and thenceforth deso-
lation gathered over the yet uncompleted station of Pogthorpe
Road.

It looked gay and cheerful enough, however, to Mrs. Armytage,
as she terminated her dark walk, and was accosted at the entrance
to the station by the driver of the solitary fly with the knock-
kneed horse attached to Pogthorpe Road, who, as she wished to
proceed to town, wanted, of course, to drive her " any where, any
where out of the world." There was light, there was warmth at
the station—brilliant gas and a roaring fire in the waiting-room.
The clerk was a species of Robinson Crusoe, in a sealskin-cap,
who resided in a small hutch surrounded by skirting boards, and
who, in the intervals of the arrival and departure of trains, amused
himself by cutting out models of Hansom cabs in cardboard.
There were two porters, moody and saturnine men, one of whom
perpetually studied the time-bill, the proclamations against smoking, and the " awful examples " shown in placards announcing the
recent conviction of Keziah Bopps, of Portsea, for travelling without
a return ticket, and the fining of Wilhelmina Lightfoot, of Basing-
stoke, for leaving the train while in motion. As he studied, he
whistled a lugubrious melody that began like "Old Dan Tucker,"
and ended like " The Dead March in Saul." The other porter used
habitually to sit on his truck on the platform, inspecting the interior
of his bell, as though to find out if it were possible to ring it without agitating the clapper ; while the odd boy who ran errands,
attended to the newspaper department, and had to be carefully
watched lest he should get at the electric telegraph, continually
ascertained his own ponderosity by standing on the weighing-
machine, and, when he could do it without observation, pasted
luggage-labels on the knees of his corduroys. It was a very
dreary little station, but hundreds of times its solitude had been
enlivened and its dreariness converted into splendour and gaiety by
the guests who had come down to visit Goldthorpe Manor. The
flyman had conveyed peers of the realm and foreign ambassadors,
when they had missed the Goldthorpe carriages. The gorgeous
vehicles last named—barouches, curricles, broughams, dog-carts,
chars à banc—had gathered by droves at the station door, and
towering, powdered, purple-and-yellow footmen had condescended

to quaff the mildest of mild ales at the little beershop. The dull platform had been swept by the robes of beautiful women; it had been trodden by statesmen, diplomatists, and millionaires; but where is the use of telling you of the had-beens?—it was silent and deserted now, and there was no one who sought warmth at the waiting-room fire save Mrs. Armytage.

She would have to wait a full hour, the odd boy told her, for the eight p.m. up-train. The moody porter paused in his study of the time-bill, hushed his whistling, and stared vacantly at the visitor. The Robinson Crusoe of a clerk, who had just made a slip with his penknife, and severed two of the spokes of a cab wheel from the axle, opened the sliding panel of his hutch, and angrily bade the odd boy, for a "young limb," hold his noise. When Robinson Crusoe was not modelling Hansom cabs, or performing his ticket-dispensing duties, he cultivated hollyhocks on the slope of the embankment. He used to envy his brother, who was an agent for coals about a hundred yards beyond the station. He envied the landlord of the beershop. He envied the guards, engine-drivers, and stokers, who were at least continually going up and down the line. Nature may have fitted him to be a poet, an artist, an orator; stern Fate condemned him to be a station-master. He used to say, like Mariana, that his life was dreary, and that he was a-weary, a-weary. Promotion came not, he said. He did not wish that he was dead, mainly, I think, because he was a full-blooded young fellow, only three-and-twenty years of age, and keenly interested in the eventualities of the next New-market meeting.

As there was an hour to wait, and no refreshment-room and no book-stall at the station, Mrs. Armytage found time hang rather heavy on her hands. She got over about five minutes of the sixty by her favourite employment of toasting her little *bottines* at the fire. Then she read all the advertisements, chromo-lithographed and otherwise, which hung framed and glazed on the walls, and wondered what manner of artists they could be who devoted themselves to the composition of cartoons representing gentlemen's hats, boneless corsets, taps for beer-barrels, iron bedsteads, and isometrical views of ginger-beer manufactories at Bermondsey.

Then, what with her two miles' walk, the cold without, the

warm fire within, the deathlike stillness, relieved only by the
ticking of the waiting-room clock, Mrs. Armytage grew drowsy.
Her little head fell gently back, her hands sank down among her
drapery, she released her hold of a tract which some pious well-
wisher had left on the table, and she sank into a profound sleep.

The tract was solemn, and rather fierce in its solemnity. It
was entitled " Where are you going ?" and on its title-page was
a neat woodcut of a young woman bearing a basket of flowers,
rapidly descending a mountain-path, at whose base was couched a
grisly bear. Mrs. Armytage had glanced at the tract with considerable interest just before she went to sleep. She was a well-
read little woman, and liked literature for its own sake. " Where
are you going ?" she repeated, with a tinkling laugh. " Ah, if
one could but tell ! *Sait on où l'on va ?* Didn't Diderot ask the
question ? Does any one know whither they are going ? " and
so fell into a slumber.

I declare that she slept as peacefully and as prettily as a baby.
Her little lips were just parted, and a brighter glow than ordinary from the fire would momentarily come and tip her teeth with
pellicles of crimson. As she lay back in the chair, her head
reclining, the deep shadows were on her forehead and above her
cheeks. Her fair throat shone radiant above the lace of her
collar ; while, enshrined in the trappings of her bonnet, lay, all
tumbled and flung back, those waves of golden ringlets. Had the
moody porter, or he who pored into the bell, or the Robinson-
Crusoe clerk, entered while she so slept, they would have been
asses had they not kissed her, whatever might have been the
penalty. There was no Aggravated Assaults Act in 1850. She
looked so calm, so tranquil, so happy. No shadow of the clouds
that sometimes pass over the sea of sleep disturbed her closed lids,
with those long lashes trailing gently, like the fringe of some
gorgeous drapery that veils a cabinet of gems. She smiled once
or twice, meekly, gently, coaxingly enough to melt a man whose
heart was triply plated ; the beadwork of her mantle just glanced
in the light as it rose and fell with the beating of her heart ; and
a soft sigh stole from those half-opened lips, as if to reproach the
waiting-room clock for its remorseless ticking, and hush it while
the fair creature slept.

And so she slept for about twenty minutes; when with a quick, sharp, painful scream, she started up, erect, trembling, fluttering like a bird become suddenly aware of the ruthless hawk above him; first flushed, then pale, almost breathless.

"Hands off!" she cried; "you shan't touch me. I'll go quietly. It isn't—Miss Hill," she continued hurriedly,—"am I dreaming?"

Mrs. Armytage had not been dreaming. Hands had been laid upon her, but with no stern grasp. Only Magdalen Hill, draped from head to foot in her mourning raiment, and with the rime of the night-frost upon her, was there, and had awakened her.

The two women—the girl and the widow—had been acquainted for years; had been at the same balls and feasts; but they had never been alone together until this moment. Mrs. Armytage was evidently flurried; but then you must recollect how suddenly she had been aroused from a comfortable sleep. In less than a minute she was herself again,—shook her ringlets and arranged her dress. She stayed the laugh that was rising to her lips; but, as she eyed Magdalen keenly, she laughed internally, in what sleeve of her soul I am not psychological milliner enough to determine. "The little weasel was very nearly being caught asleep," thought Mrs. Armytage.

The girl stood looking at her with sad eyes. Remorseful, wistful, well-nigh imploring—not haughty, not full of aversion now.

"Oh, Mrs. Armytage," she said, in a low pleading tone, "what is this? What have you told Sir Jasper? He is dreadfully ill. I thought he would die. He had but just recovered consciousness when I started, hearing from the lodge-keeper that you had left, in the endeavour to find you. What terrible business could it have been to bring you to our house at such a time?"

"My dear Miss Hill," asked the widow, "before I answer your question, allow me to ask you another. Is Sir Jasper in danger?"

"I scarcely know," replied Magdalen, in a broken voice. "There was not time. I hurried after you. I rushed into a carriage. Fortunately the house-steward bled him, and Dr. Medley has been sent for."

"I am very sorry, then," interposed Mrs. Armytage; "but I don't see that I have anything more to do with the matter. Had the news I conveyed to Sir Jasper Goldthorpe brought about fatal or even dangerous consequences, no one would have regretted it more than I. As it is, he has just had a fit of syncope, and will get on nicely. As I am neither a village apothecary nor a member of the Royal College of Surgeons, I can't be of any use; and as I am going to London by the 8 p.m. train, you will permit me to remain your most humble servant to command."

So saying, and with a sarcastic laugh which seemed irrepressible, she dropped a very low curtsey, and would have passed out. But Magdalen Hill was determined. She put back Mrs. Armytage with a calm sternness before which the Lady on the First Floor, courageous as she was, could not avoid quailing, and in a tone of resolution, placing herself before the door, she said:—

"Pardon me, madam, you cannot, you shall not, leave me thus. We have but to consult each our own instinct to know that we are no great friends. It is not through affection for you that I am here. I come through love for my dear dead Hugh; I come through love for my dearest friends and guardians. What has brought you to sow additional sorrow among us, wretched as we are? It is something that concerns poor Hugh's memory, it is something that concerns Sir Jasper; and I ask because I feel that I have a right to know."

"I will not answer one word," quoth Mrs. Armytage, clenching her little hands.

"I entreat, I implore you, then," Magdalen went on, her sternness failing her, and her voice choked with sobs. "Oh, Mrs. Armytage, you cannot be so cruel! Is there any peril that can be averted from Sir Jasper? Is there anything you know of Hugh's last moments that can inflict pain on his relatives, on me, on any one? Oh, speak, I adjure you!"

Mrs. Armytage took from her pocket a little jewelled *bon-bonnière*, took out a chocolate *praline*, and began daintily nibbling it.

"The train-bell must ring presently," she remarked, "and you will be compelled to let me go. As it is, you have laid yourself

open to an action for assault and false imprisonment. Imagine,
'Armytage v. Hill. Extraordinary case, cross-examination of
witnesses.' Ha! ha!"

"If I interposed somewhat abruptly—" Magdalen broke in,
apologetically.

"There, there," continued the widow, " no harm is done ; you
want to be told something that I won't tell you. You thought to
frighten me with your Tragedy-queen airs, and now you are fit to
cry your eyes out. You are an overgrown school-girl, and I am a
woman of the world—a clever woman, you understand. Go, and
paint your missals, and leave serious things to men and women of
business. What I know, I know ; and it is a matter between Sir
Jasper Goldthorpe and myself. Be a good girl, and get from
before that door. Will you have a *praline?*"

She held out the box of sweetmeats to her rival with a merry,
roguish twinkle in her eyes. She was quite at home again. The
weasel was thoroughly awake. Poor Magdalen felt very much
like a bird in the clutches of a fine silky-furred cat. She was
powerless, and dropped her head, and almost involuntarily moved
away from the door.

"That is better," laughed Mrs. Armytage. "There's nothing
like common sense. Common sense has been worth six thousand
a year to me, a poor little Indian widow, with a twopenny-halfpenny pension. It was sensible in you to stand away from the
door as I bid you ; because, if you had not, and for all that you
are the grand young lady Miss Magdalen Hill, I would have torn
your bonnet off your head and your dress off your back."

What could Magdalen do ? How could she cope with this
affable tigress ? She averted her gaze, and drew herself closely
together, as the widow, in all the pride of her rustling skirts, swept
onwards.

"A word ere we go," she said, in a hot whisper that almost
blistered Magdalen's cheek. "Just now you said, and truly, that
we needed but to consult our instincts to know that we were not
friends. We are not. We are enemies. I am glad that Hugh
was killed ; and had he come home and made you his wife, you
cat, I would have poisoned or shot you before ever you sat at his
table or lay in his bed. Good-by, and bless you!"

These were the last words of Mrs. Armytage, on that occasion
at least, heard at Goldthorpe Station, erst Pogthorpe Road; and
with this farewell and benediction she went out into the night,
and on to the platform.   The moody porters, the clerk who made
the models, the boy who weighed himself, all woke up to temporary life and activity as the bell rang out, and the train rattled
and screeched into the station.   The little platform shook; the
people on it drew back, lest they should be sucked into destruction by the monster's breath, and smashed to paste among its
whirling wheels.   It came out of a deep cutting, and disappeared
in a dark tunnel.   Green and red lights fitfully shone as it dashed
away.   The red smoke made lurid the face of the engine-driver, as
he stood with arms folded, thoughtful, at his post.   From the
carriage windows dozens of visages of men and women peered out
on to the station; many of them seeing it for the first time, and
being seen by those who peopled it for the last time in their lives.
So away sped the up-express, carrying its load of loves and hatreds,
and hopes and fears, and joys and sorrows; bearing mothers,
perchance, as bereaved as she of the House of Mammon was;
sons as fair and brave as he who had been slain at Armentières;
girls as young and haughty and as loving as Magdalen; foreigners
and British men, lisping children and doddering dotards, honest
people and foul rogues, Cornelia going to her children and Laïs
going to a masked ball, millionaires whose ships have come home,
and bankrupts flying from a fiat—hundreds of patches towards
the make-up of that vast motley counterpane we call society; but
not, in all its medley company, one woman, I will wager, prettier
or wickeder than the lady in black, who tripped with such grace
into a first-class *coupé*, and displayed such dainty white drapery to
the admiring eyes of the guard.

The train was gone.   It had its goal; but whither went its
occupants?   "Where are you going?" asked the station-room
tract.   Whither are we all going, and where is the terminus
where the last tickets shall be asked for in a Trumpet tone?

The romancer's privilege can assign a destination to two persons who so parted on this January night.   Foiled and repulsed,
Magdalen Hill wept no more.   The hot fire of the waiting-room,
the hotter farewell whisper of the widow, had dried her tears for

good. "She will tell me nothing," she murmured, "nothing, although I know that she is working fearful evil to me and mine. Heaven grant me strength and patience to watch and pray." The carriage was waiting for her, and, sad and sorrowful, but calm and resigned now, she was borne back to Goldthorpe Manor, where physicians and nurses were bending over an old man very different to the blandly strong man who lorded it in Beryl Court, and who lay now feebly moaning and half unconscious in his great bed of state. A messenger on horseback passed Magdalen, or ever she had cleared the environs of the station. He had been bidden to telegraph to Dr. Sardonix, in London, desiring his immediate attendance. The Doctor was called away from the dinner-table of a rich East Indian Director, who, having quarrelled with most of his friends, and turned his children out of doors, had adopted a liver complaint as his son, and, indeed, his heir,—for he had made his will in favour of a Special Hospital,—and now got on very well with curry, mulligatawny, and Doctor Sardonix in the evening, and tarraxicum, blue-pill, and Dr. Sardonix in the morning. The Doctor used to remonstrate with the Director; but how could you coerce a man who had sat under the pagoda-tree until a golden apple had dropped on his nose, and imbued him with directorial gravity; who had tossed up heads or tails with Sir Mungo Chutnee, in Leadenhall Street, as to whether the Rajah of Cadmore should be maintained in his sovereignty or deposed, whether the Begum of Boocherabad (vehemently sus-pected of having boiled her pet dwarf in Macassar oil, specially imported from Europe for the purpose, and buried a nautch girl under a marble pavement, alive) should be prosecuted or pen-sioned; and who gave away commissions in the Bengal cavalry as though they were soup-tickets? The claret-bell had just rung when one of Sardonix's black-worsted footmen brought him the telegraphic message from his house. He rose in haste, had scarcely time to take his usual after-dinner dose of carbonate of soda in the hall, and was very nearly committing a robbery in a dwelling-house, by cramming one of the Director's damask napkins into his pocket. "I thought so," he said, in a soothing tone, apologising to his host. "Poor dear Sir Jasper! Nerves, my dear sir, nerves. We must be very cautious. We cannot take too much care of ourselves. Such a precious life must be guarded by the minutest precautions." It was Dr. Sardonix's practice, whenever he found it feasible, to pay double-barrelled compliments, or to hit two birds with one flattering bullet. The Director felt grateful for the allusion to his " precious life," and growled out an expression of admiration as the Doctor took his departure. " Sensible man that," he said, half inclined to put the Doctor in his will by the side of the Hospital for Dyspepsia, but for economy's sake resolving to get the Doctor appointed physician extraordinary to the special establishment in question. " Bobus," he continued to the butler, " now he's gone I won't have claret, I'll have port. The 'tawny' twenty-four, you know : Herringpond's port,—the banker fellow who was hanged. Capital port he had."

Dr. Sardonix paid a whole academy of compliments before he reached Goldthorpe Manor. He asked the butler after his gout, and called that delighted servitor " my good friend." I believe that if the footman had consulted him as to the malady which prevented the calves of his legs from fattening, he would have given him the most friendly advice. He complimented the cabman on the swiftness of his pace, and even presented him with an extra sixpence. " We doctors are hard masters to horseflesh," he sympathetically remarked. The black-worsted footman who accompanied his master to the station had not failed to tell the driver how distinguished a practitioner he was carrying ; and the charioteer, could he have mustered up courage, would have begged a prescription for the bronchial affection under which his horse was suffering. The South-Western Railway officials were deeply impressed with a sense of Doctor Sardonix's talents and affability before the special train that he had ordered—no expense was spared when Mammon was sick—could be got ready. The keeper of the book-stall bowed to him, handed him the third edition of the *Express*, damp with the latest news, and respectfully informed him that the sale of his work, " The curative Properties of stuffed Sweetbread in its Action on the human Pancreas," by E. Mollyent Sardonix, M.D., F.R.S., was going on wonderfully. The guard would have allowed him to smoke like Etna had the Doctor felt so disposed, and numerous hats were lifted as his "special" quitted the terminus. Such homage is due to the princes of science. There are some modest and retiring princes who never get it, and don't want it; but Dr. Sardonix had long since determined that the barque in which he navigated the sea of life should be a golden galley and a pleasure-barge. He greased the ways assiduously at launching, and, with a fair start, the craft went on swimmingly. He had no need to puff himself in print; his natural suavity was far more effective than leaded type. "One compliment is worth a hundred advertisements" was a favourite apophthegm with this astute physician. He has long since got his baronetage; and I have no doubt that the next generation will hear Sardonician orations delivered at the Royal College of Physicians by practitioners as polite as he was.

The special train that took the Doctor down to Goldthorpe passed the ordinary up express, and the illustrious medical man was near enough at one moment to a certain first-class *coupé* to have shaken hands with its occupant had he chosen to run the risk of fracturing his arm in so doing. Mrs. Armytage no more dreamed of the Doctor's proximity, nor the Doctor of Mrs. Armytage's, than you or I when we pass in the street our dearest unknown friend or our bitterest unknown enemy—the woman who would marry us to-morrow were we to ask her, or the man who would force a dose of strychnine down our throats for twopence. There are human parallel lines which are continued to infinity, and never meet. Mrs. Armytage arrived at Waterloo, quite unconscious as to whom her transient neighbour had been, and comforting herself with a Bath bun—of which she ate little more than the sugared top and the carraway-seeds—and a bottle of lemonade, entered a cab—I am ashamed to say that it was a Hansom—but she was of *so* frolicsome a disposition!—and was driven to the Victoria Hotel, Euston Square. Properly, her palfry with embroidered housings, or her armoried litter drawn by *dos arrogantes mulas*, like Gil Blas' uncle, the canon's: with her squire and seneschal and page, should have been waiting for her; but I am writing in a prosaic time, and the characters in my drama must have recourse for their more or less momentous movements to such prosaic modes of conveyance as railways and steamboats, cabs and broughams.

She had brought her bower-maiden, Mademoiselle Reine, with her to London. That young lady detested England and the English; and when not required at her mistress's toilet, sat immured in her bedroom, sipping sugar-and-water, and perusing the charming novels of M. Xavier de Montépin. She was an oral *cabinet de lecture*. The Blenheim spaniel was on duty also, and yowled fractiously at the inferior quality of the London chickens, and the shameful adulteration of the London cream. Moustachu, the *chasseur*, was likewise in attendance, officiating, when Mrs. Armytage travelled, as courier; on which occasions he appeared elaborately got up in a braided pandour jacket lined with silver-fox skin, a gold laced cap, and a tawny leathern pouch slung round him, containing an assortment of every European coinage. Moustachu had been fearfully seasick in crossing the Channel. He consoled himself with potent draughts of the brown beer of Albion when he landed; and his mistress very nearly caught him smoking a silver-mounted meerschaum at the corner of Seymour Street as her cab drove by.

Nor, finally, was "my man Sims" wanting to complete the train of the Princess who lived in that sumptuous first-floor in Paris yonder. It was, however, Mr. Sims's invariable practice to keep himself in the background. I question if he had even a passport of his own; or passed among Mrs. Armytage's "suite." While the accommodation afforded to Mademoiselle Reine and the Sieur Moustachu heavily contributed to the expansion of the widow's hotel-bill, the modest Sims took up his quarters at a neighbouring coffee-shop, where he dined off saltpetred bacon and boiled tea-leaves, read papers five days old, played draughts with a contemplative signalman from the station over the way, and was regarded by the landlord as a quiet party from the manufacturing districts, who was seeking for a situation as a clerk in a London house. If I had committed a murder and wished to avoid detection, I would hide in a coffee-shop close to a railway station. Pay as you go, and nobody will take any notice of you, save perhaps to remark to you how strange it is that the detectives haven't captured that sanguinary villain Slaughterford yet.

Mrs. Armytage was very well known and highly respected at the hotel. Faithful to her taste for a first-floor, she always had a

G 2

suite of apartments one story high, and retained a brougham while staying in town. Her little malachite card-basket was on the drawing-table, and when she returned it was full of scented and heraldically emblazoned cards. The announcement, " At the Victoria Hotel, Euston Square:—Mrs. Armytage and suite," met her eyes among the "fashionable arrivals" in the *Post*. Sims had seen to that. Sims was in attendance, having been fetched by Moustachu from the coffee-shop. " *Quoi de nouveau?* " the lady carelessly asked of Mr. Sims in French, for a waiter was present solemnly lighting a galaxy of wax candles. Darkness was the only thing that made Mrs. Armytage nervous.

" *Il fait gros temps dans la chiourme,*" enigmatically replied Mr. Sims. " *Madame attendra que ce butor soit parti.*"

The solemn lamp-lighter spoken of so uncomplimentarily as a "*butor,*" a blockhead, having taken his departure, Mr. Sims, as was his wont when conferring alone with his patroness, lightly turned the key in the door.

" What is it? " Mrs. Armytage asked, speaking very rapidly, and a feverish flush rising to her cheeks.

" Bad as bad can be. The reddest of red lamps. Total, dangerous. Prospect, smash."

" Don't torture me. Go on."

" Saddington and Dedwards."

" Well! "

" Won't renew.—Whittle and Gumtickler."

" Well! "

" Have had the two five hundreds returned from New Orleans. Furious, but don't suspect any thing."

" Any thing else? " Mrs. Armytage's foot was drumming on the carpet, and her fingers were twitching at her dress.

" Something to tickle your fancy, as the valentines say. Ephraim Tigg of Stockwell."

" What of him? "

" Ephraim Tigg of Stockwell," slowly and quietly continued Mr. Sims:—he had been reading the names just quoted from a scrap of paper, taken from a greasy pocket-book, and now carefully closed it, strapped it up, and replaced it in his pocket—" Ephraim Tigg of Stockwell is a Rasper."

"Go on, go on; I shall lose my wits."

"Ephraim Tigg *knows all about it, and won't wait.* He found the counterfoil; you must have been silly to leave *that.*"

A piercing scream was rising to the pretty woman's lips; but she checked herself, biting her lips till the blood came. Then she started up, shaking her yellow hair about her like a Fury, and wringing her hands.

"I am ruined, I am ruined!" she panted out. "Why did I ever go near that horrible old man? I have never lost sight of his white face and red eyelids. He has haunted me for days. The others are nothing. Fool that I was not to get the money from Goldthorpe before I struck him down: to-morrow may be too late. O Sims, Sims, help me; what am I to do?"

I know that what I am going to relate is exceedingly improbable; but it is true, nevertheless, that the brilliant widow of the Rue Grande-des-Petites-Maisons, with starting eyes, with swollen veins, with dishevelled hair, threw herself on her knees before the modest Mr. Sims, who lived at a coffee-shop, who had a face like a ferret, and whose nose was not only peaked but purple at the ends.*

"Mercy, mercy!" she repeated, in scarce articulate accents. It was well that the door was fastened. The solemn torch-bearing waiter would have been scandalised; but an artist would have rejoiced in the disordered folds of her drapery, spread over the carpet; in her attitude of despairing supplication. She was not acting. Her laughing mask was thrown aside; real grief and terror raged beneath. She might, for her wild and scared looks, have been a Helen, remembering that the woes of Troy were due alone to her, that she was growing old, and that Paris had frowned upon her. She might have been a Brinvilliers, with all her wiles

* "It is scarcely possible to quit this horrid subject without observing that the facts which have now been demonstrated were in the highest degree improbable. Who could have believed that two wretches of the ages of fifteen and sixteen years could have continued . . . . . Let us not, then, too hastily conclude on other occasions that what does not appear probable is necessarily false, nor rashly reject every proposition for which we cannot fully account. Let our inquiry be cool, critical, and deliberate; but as evils multiply beyond probability, let our vigilance be not only constant but scrupulous, not resting on slight appearances, but passing on to facts."—EDMUND BURKE *on a celebrated Criminal Case,* A.D. 1767.

detected, and the *lieutenant criminel*, with his exempts, thundering at the door.

"Get up," was the unceremonious response made by Mr. Sims to the impassioned appeal made to him. "For laughing like a Cheshire cat, and going on your knees like Ada the Outcast, I never did see your equal. What's the good of play-acting to me?"

"I'm not acting," groaned Mrs. Armytage. I have said as much for her already.

"Well, get up, at all events," Mr. Sims continued. "For such a plucky one as you generally are, you do break down shamefully sudden sometimes. You'll show the white feather at the C. C. C. some of these days, if you don't take care. Think of your dignity. There's nothing like dignity; and the shorter you are, the more dignified you ought to be. I'm too old for it, and always liked a quiet life; but you're just young enough to dignify yourself into a coronet."

Mrs. Armytage no longer knelt; she sat rather in the midst of the carpet, looking up with a strange expression of mingled fear and curiosity in Mr. Sims's face.

"Is there any hope?" she asked.

"To be sure there is," replied Sims. "Every thing's as right as can be."

She arose radiant, but trembling. She summoned up her laugh, but it died away in a fitful gasp, and she had to place her hand on her labouring heart.

"Why did you frighten me?" she said, in broken tones. "I have been in tortures, in agony."

"To let you know what an excellent friend you can always reckon upon in an emergency, and may reckon on if you only follow his advice. Ephraim Tigg and I have done business for years in all sorts of things, from lottery-tickets to the lead off roofs. He daren't squeak; but he *would* have squeaked but for me. You went to him without my sanction, and you see the scrape you have nearly got yourself into. The money was a mere fleabite, a miserable fifty. But your confounded imprudence has nearly knocked down your palace, just as if it had been made of cards. At your time of life, too, and after all the experience you have had, you really ought to know better, ma'am."

There was nothing openly disrespectful in Mr. Sims's tone, even when he had used his rudest words of expostulation. He spoke calmly and quietly, as though he were despatching a matter of business, such as conferring about a schedule with an insolvent, and a schedule concerning which it was necessary to speak without disguise. And so soon as Mrs. Armytage had reached a sofa, and had sunk down upon its luxurious cushions, the normal state of things between mistress and man seemed of itself to return: Mr. Sims addressing her with his customary deference, and she treating him with her usual familiar disdain. The little Blenheim spaniel on the hearthrug, who had perhaps been dreaming of pullet prepared in the superior Parisian fashion, woke up when his mistress, on her knees, was adjuring Sims. He yelped peevishly; but no notice being taken of his complaints, turned himself round, like a sensible dog, and went to sleep again. This was by no means the first scene in which Mrs. Armytage had figured as an actress, and at which Mouche the Blenheim had assisted. Matters assuming a more cheerful aspect, he leapt up to his mistress's lap, and took her caresses with much complacency.

"And how," demanded Mrs. Armytage gaily, and toying with the dog,—"how did you manage it all, my good faithful Sims? Stay, you are sure there is no one at the door."

"Unless walls have ears," was the answer, "we are unheard. There are some fools who, when they lock a door, put the key in their pocket. Always leave it inside. Nobody can look through the keyhole then."

"You are wondrous wise, Sims, but tiresome. Proceed, my excellent agent."

"I sha'n't take you long. Saddington and Dedwards must have the diamonds; you can't wear them. It's a bad moment for selling, though. We've glutted too many markets already, and another sale might bring on a stoppage of the firm of Armytage and Co. Besides, you have jewels enough already to cover the Queen of Sheba."

"Let the diamonds go! I don't like to part with them: those nice glittering things are so compact, tell such few tales, and sew up so neatly in one's dress. For a rainy day, at the North Pole or at the Tropics, there's no umbrella so good as a diamond."

"It's a pity you can't keep these ; but the figure is heavy. Whittle and Gumtickler could have done nothing but sue. Had Somebody been alive at New Orleans, it might have been a different matter. Fortunately, a champagne supper and the yellow fever—only thirty-six hours—kept your secret for you."

Mrs. Armytage just raised her eyes, and her hand rested for a moment immobile on the silken head of the dog.

"Dead?" she rather looked than spoke as she made the inquiry.

"Dead as mutton," echoed Mr. Sims; "our dear brother departed, and so on. He left a good crop of debts behind him, and a large family."

"Poor Bellasis!" mused the widow. "He was always too fond of champagne, and *would* take the miss at loo." And she went on playing with Mouche.

"Ephraim Tigg," went on Mr. Sims, "was the worst. As I told you, he is a Rasper."

"What is a rasper?" asked the widow, elevating her eyebrows.

"You would be one if you had only a little more decision. He vowed vengeance, and was going to do all sorts of things. But for some little business transactions of old date between us, when my name was Des—" he checked himself—"when it wasn't Sims, Ephraim might have done all he threatened. But I paid him. I burnt the ugly bit of paper, and there's an end of that business. But he knows what he ought not to know, ma'am, and that's a red lamp as big as a pumpkin."

"Is he a man to kill, to gain over, or to tell lies to ? and what should be done to prevent him annoying us ? "

"He is a man," remarked Mr. Sims, with much calmness, "to die. He is a man to have another paralytic stroke. He's had one, and I think the next will be pretty nearly his good-by to stamped paper. He's got just about strength enough to creep into a witness-box, and that's all. He's got a hundred thousand pounds, lives in a kitchen, and feeds on the rats and blackbeetles that swarm in it, I think. I never did see such an old atomy. No ; there's nothing to be feared from him, unless"—he paused in his speech, and spoke very slowly and deliberately—"unless you've been making him any more morning calls, ma'am."

"On my honour, no!" asseverated Mrs. Armytage, turning nervously among her cushions. "I never saw the old brute but once, and never wish to see him again."

"Then you can go to bed and sleep comfortably on your honour. Do you want me any more to-night? I think I shall go to the play."

"*You* go to the play!" repeated his patroness, in some astonishment. "Why, you don't go once in six months. What on earth has put that into your head?"

"Well, I like theatricals," Mr. Sims explained, slowly rubbing his hands together. "They're warm, and bright, and cheap; and you can let the people on the stage talk away without bothering yourself. Then you can look at the people in the boxes; and you're so close-seated in the pit, that you can't well help hearing all that your neighbours have got to say among themselves. Oh, I like the play! I used to be fond of going to chapel; but it's the audience there who are acting, and you can't tell what they are really up to."

"I think I know where you would like to be much better, Sims," his mistress observed, with good-humoured contempt. "What a pity there is no hazard left, no roulette, no rouge-et-noir!"

Mr. Sims shrugged his shoulders, and was silent; but a tiny red spot on either cheek showed that the widow's lance had hit home.

"Well, go to the play, most virtuous Sims," Mrs. Armytage resumed, with a slight yawn. "If you want any thing to drink, they will give it you down-stairs. Please come to me very early in the morning, and send Reine to me."

She waved her hand in gracious dismissal, and Mr. Sims, with a jerk that may have been meant for a bow, turned on his heel, unlocked the door, and departed. He walked gingerly along the richly carpeted corridor of the hotel, stopping ever and anon before some particular door, and studying the number with a look of owl-like wisdom. He also meditated for full three minutes before a vast pyramid of bedroom candles, and meeting a pretty chambermaid bade her good night in a fatherly manner. To the waiter, whose life seemed to be passed in torch-bearing, and who was just lighting up a county magistrate in a private room, he imparted his lady's behests ; and as the bells began to ring for somebody to tell somebody that number eleven's maid was wanted, Mr. Sims stepped into Euston Square.

"A clever woman, but rash, and cannot resist her impulses," he soliloquised,—"her One impulse, at least. That is irresistible, and will be the ruin of her. Who can overcome one's little fancy? I can't. With proper management that woman ought to be a Russian archduchess, at least ; but she'll end badly, I fear, all through impulse."

He was decidedly the most retiring and least ostentatious of mankind, Mr. Sims. He walked all the way from Euston Square, through Covent Garden, to the Strand, and was positively not above supping off a dozen oysters at a stall beneath the pillars of Clement's Inn. Then, after a sober libation of stout, he resumed his walk westward.

"No hazard left!" he thought. "No hazard, eh? not a tiny nook and corner where a gentleman from the Continent can sport a fifty? Well, we'll have a try."

Mr. Sims went to the play, but he passed both the Haymarket and Adelphi theatres without availing himself of the privileges of half-price. Where he went to, what play he saw, and in how many acts, and who were the players, it is no business of mine to inquire.

The lady's-maid came, disrobed her mistress, and went back to long-protracted vigils of sugar-and-water and M. Xavier de Montépin. Mrs. Armytage did not read ; but it was late ere she sought her couch in the adjoining bed-chamber. They brought her a little *carafon* of Maraschino, and she sipped a tiny glassful now and then. She had drawn an easy chair to the fire, and wrapped in her China silk *peignoir* had got to her old trick of toasting her little feet at the fire. There were no *bottines* to toast now, and the little feet, covered with a film of open worked silk, looked ravishing in the morocco slippers.

"It is a hard life," she said to herself. "A convict, or a minister of state, can't be much harder worked. It is all sowing and ploughing, and harrowing, and weeding, and what will the harvest be? Do I shrink? do I falter? am I afraid? No ; but the life is very wearisome. It makes my head ache. It makes my heart ache. I suppose I have a heart as well as other people. I know I feel it more than other people do, and that I shall die some day of palpitation, or aneurism, or something. Heigho! heigho!"

The little dog, snoozling on the hearthrug, lifted up his blinking eyes, as though in surprise at the unwonted sounds. Screams and laughter he was accustomed to—but sighs!

"Down, Mouche," his mistress cried pettishly, as though offended that the animal had heard her. "What was it that the stupid tract said at the railway?" she went on cogitating. "'Where are you going?' Do the good people know where they are going? I should like to be good, but I can't. I used to scream, 'I will be good! I will be good!' as a child, when they punished me; but I never could be good when the smart was over. I suppose it isn't in me. There *must* be some pleasure, though, in being able to sleep without horrid dreams, in being able to walk without looking over one's shoulder every five minutes. Good people pray. Where is the good of my praying? Will the words of a prayer help me? My thoughts used to wander away from the words of the service at church. What am I to do, where am I going, and where am I to go?"

She uttered these words against her wicked will, and aloud. The innermost voice had started up unbidden, and overwhelmed her with the imperious suddenness of its summons. It was not a still small voice—the creeping uneasiness of conscience:—that had been stifled long ago. No; this was a sharp, harsh cry. It seemed as though her name were pronounced close to her,—as if some one said, "Florence Armytage, Florence Armytage, where are you going?"

Among the trinkets and the gold-bedizened scent-bottles of her dressing-case, in the next room, was a little crystal phial, carefully stoppered, and half-full of a dark liquid. She opened it, and, holding it from her, allowed its vapid odour to exhale.

"But a little courage, and it would all be over. Bah! 'tis an idiot's resource to kill oneself. I may win the *grand coup*, and leave this life. But that isn't it. I haven't the courage."

She never lied to herself; she was too clever.

"Why can't I cry?" she exclaimed passionately, looking at herself as in the mirror at Paris. "Why can't I squeeze a few tears out? I never could. That white-faced puss at Goldthorpe can whine and sob. I can't even weep when I think of Hugh. Am I to begin to learn whimpering now?"

She had yet some little business to go through ere she sought her bed. From a secret drawer in her jewel-case she took a common red penny memorandum-book and opened it. The columns were full of figures in English and foreign moneys. These she dwelt long over. Then she turned to another page with writing on it.

"Amiens, St. Lazare, La Bourbe, Nice, Preston, Philadelphia, Kilmainham, Kirkdale, Lewes, Manheim, Milan: a pretty catalogue!" she said, with a bitter smile. "Ah, I have been a great traveller. Where is the journey to end?"

Once more, as though dreading to go to rest, she went from her sleeping to her sitting room, took writing materials, and, sitting down, penned a long letter on foreign post paper. She carefully folded it, gummed the envelope all round, sealed it, and addressed it thus :

> "Dominique Cosson,
>   Frère laïque,
> Aux Pères Maristes des Bonnes-Œuvres,
>   Hoogendracht (près Louvain),
>   Brabant,
>   Belgique."

"Sims must post this the first thing in the morning," she said almost gaily, as she rose from her seat. And then for the second time I leave her to her bed, and to Sleep, which comes alike to the evil and the just, to the criminal in his cell and the anchorite on his pallet, and covers all over with the Death that is in the midst of Life.

CHAPTER VIII

SIXTEEN months had passed, and crazy fanatics who had predicted the end of the world before the year was out—not forgetting to take houses at long leases meanwhile—found for the thousandth time that their reckoning was confusion, and that their prophecies were wind. The old world went on, and men children were born to supply the loss of those who had been taken away; and kings and cadgers alike gave up the ghost; and Death as usual met the wedding guest on the threshold, and with unvarying politeness bade him pass in first, as there would be plenty of time for him.

It was the merry month of May of the year eighteen fifty-one, and London was in a frenzy about the Great Exhibition. The glass-house in Hyde Park has, directly, nothing to do with the conduct of this story; and you will hear little about it from me. But the influence of the fever that raged in London was felt in the remotest portions of the English provinces. A gadding-about mania seized on all ranks and conditions of men. Women went up in droves to London professedly to see the Exhibition—actually to stare at the dresses and bonnets in the shop windows. Ancient hedgers and ditchers who were scarcely yet familiar with the high street of their market town, were put into clean smock-frocks, and paraded by their pastors through the giant metropolis, and the wonderful structure in the park. The very paupers in rural workhouses were dressed in their best, taken to town, permitted to croon forth feeble notes of admiration in nave and transept, and were regaled with unwonted meat and beer. Some such kindly feelings from the rich towards the poor are generally brought forth by great public festivals. He who has all is even anxious to let him who has nothing share—in the infinitesimal

degrees. Exclusive possession palls. If Flag gets a couple of
thousand pounds as prize-money, he flings fourteenth-class half-a-
crown as *his* portion. A man who has a blue diamond, or a
cabinet full of Rafaelles, is frequently most liberal in permitting
the gratuitous inspection of his treasures.

It has been said that the Great Exhibition made itself felt all
over the land. The press and the post-office between them distributed hundreds of thousands of journals teeming with woodcuts,
and glowing with descriptions of the rare contents of Paxton's
Palace. Every rustic Paul who found himself in London wrote
letters to his kinsfolk. The humours of the Great Exhibition and
"Lunnon town" were put into the Lancashire dialect, and
chanted by the descendants of those Troubadours, of whom Tim
Bobbin was the Blondel. Somersetshire, Westmoreland, Yorkshire, Northumbria had ballads in their vernacular about the great
carnival of industry in the capital—ballads which would have
delighted Prince Lucien Solomon Bonaparte. This was the time
when lads ran away from home to seek their fortune, and expect-
ing to find London paved with gold, discovered that pockets might
be so lined, but that the streets themselves were jagged and
muddy ; and so, Bow Bells seeming to chime out more to the
effect that they were fools for their pains, than to bid them turn
again and be Lords Mayor of London, betook themselves to their
homes, and were feasted on the fatted calf, or the cold shoulder,
as the case might be. It was in all respects—you, who remember
it, will agree with me—an exceptional year. Gentlemen fell in
love at first sight, not in three-volume novels, but in actual
reality, with young ladies they met in railway carriages, or at
Osler's Crystal Fountain, and married them out of hand. Freemasons from Mount Atlas fraternised with Freemasons from
Primrose Hill, and the Polish Lodge entertained a Babel of
foreign brethren. The oldest *habitués* of the Park and the Opera
were forced to confess that they saw daily and nightly in Rotten
Row and the Halls amazons and amateurs with whose faces they
were not familiar ; and the learned in social statistics ascertained
for a fact, that from May to September—such was the molli-
fying effect of the season—vast numbers of born and well-
born Englishmen and Englishwomen made no scruple of con-

versing with persons to whom they had never been formally
introduced.

But, as in the midst of a railway loopline, or between its
parallels, or midway between its horns, you shall find some hamlet
—some small country town sometimes—which has no station, no
omnibus nor fly communication, no gas, no police, and no roads
much better than bridle-paths, and which is, to all intents and
purposes of civilisation, five hundred years behind the age; so
down in the county of Kent was there a village whose inhabitants
did not trouble themselves in the slightest degree about the Great
Exhibition—and many of them had but a very hazy and uncertain
knowledge of what an exhibition was—at all.

This place was called Swordsley; and the rector of Swordsley
was the Reverend Ernest Goldthorpe. The village was of some
size, its population numbering nearly nine hundred. It was not
a specially ignorant or uncouth village; it was simply indifferent
to all that went on out of its precincts. If a Swordsley man had
designed the House of Fame in Hyde Park, or the heir of the lord
of the manor of Swordsley—who was a Captain in the Guards—
had been sent to the House of Correction for assaulting a policeman in Rotten Row, the villagers might have taken some interest
in the World's Fair. As it was, none of those in whom they
interested themselves had anything to do with it; so they left the
Great Exhibition to its own devices.

To the inhabitants of this tranquil place the world was bounded
by the limits of Swordsley parish. The ancient cathedral town of
St. Becketsbury was not very far distant,—scarce ten miles, in
fact; but that was a matter concerning the rector and his curate,
and not the laymen of Swordsley. There was a station at Daiseybridge, four miles distant, belonging to the South-Eastern Railway,
and the aristocracy of Swordsley might avail themselves of it; but
the Swordsleians were profoundly indifferent and all but unconscious of the existence of such things as trains and locomotives.
An early village bard had made a satirical song, in days gone by,
against the railway movement generally, deriding it as a new-
fangled invention, and lampooning it as a "Long Tom's Coffin,"—
a hit which told immensely, more for the sound of the phrase than
for its actual signification. When a Swordsley man was pressed

to accede to a branch line from Daiseybridge through Swordsley, and so on to the little seaport of Shrimpington-super-Mare, he ordinarily made answer, " We want none of your Long Tom Collins hereabouts," and was supposed thereafter to have irretrievably demolished his adversary. A sharp lawyer from St. Becketsbury once threatened the intractable villagers with an Act of Parliament which should compel them to have either a railway, or gas or water pipes, or some other filaments of the crinoline of civilisation; but Chuff the saddler, who was the village oracle, and the " Cromwell guiltless of his country's blood" of Swordsley, cried, " Let un try it. I'll Parliament House un. I'll sow their Acts up like so much pig-skin." And it was universally believed (in Swordsley) that any attempt on the part of the Legislature to coerce Swordsley into light, or cleanliness, or activity, would be met by the erection of barricades, and the invocation of the Patron of battles.

There was a society, less convivial than conservative and inquisitorial, held at the " Old Dun Horse " tavern, called " The Leave-us-alone Club," in Swordsley. It was particularly active in suppressing new-fangled inventions. It was stanchly Protectionist, had burnt Peel and Cobden in effigy, and debated the propriety of presenting a silver pitchfork to the once illustrious, but now forgotten, champion of costly corn—Chowler. The St. Becketsbury lawyer, aided by one or two incendiaries among the neighbouring gentry—for at Swordsley, and not for the first time since the Creation, it was the patricians who were strong liberals, and the yeomen and peasantry who were bigoted Tories—had actually got a Bill affecting Swordsley sufficiently into work as to have complied with the standing orders of the House. There was an indignation meeting among the villagers, and a secret sederunt of the " Leave-us-alone Club," who, from their own funds, despatched a deputation, consisting of Chuff the saddler, Muggeridge, mine host of the " Old Dun Horse," and Scrase the corn-chandler, to London, with strict injunctions to spare neither labour, expense, nor physical force—even to the " punching " of the St. Becketsbury lawyer's head—to defeat the abhorred measure. The Bill came to nothing, which was a triumph to Swordsley; but the end of the deputation was curious. The delegates were absent a long time, and wrote more than once for remittances to the Club. Muggeridge informed Mr. Pearkle-borough the grocer (chairman *pro tem.* of the " Leave-us-alones ") that parliament business was terribly dry work. On his return he evinced a remarkable taciturnity, merely deigning to observe occasionally that the deputation had had " awful times of it ;" and the face of Mrs. Muggeridge, his spouse, should properly have been as flat as the countenance of a Kalmuck, for, as she informed Miss Chuff, the saddler's daughter, Muggeridge was in the prac-tice, when spoken to, of biting her nose off from morning till night. There was a dreadful to-do about auditing the account, and the examiners objecting to an item of nine pounds for " sundries," Mr. Muggeridge offered to fight the committee all round (four being a *quorum*) ; and as the host of the " Old Dun Horse " was a notoriously hard hitter, the auditors perpended and passed his account. Two members of the deputation remained for a considerable period unaccounted for, which neces-sitated the sending of fresh envoys to the capital in search of them. Chuff the saddler was discovered at an hotel in Old Palace Yard, reduced by a reckless course of hot suppers and heavy lunches to a state of semi-idiocy. He was rapidly being converted to liberalism by an unscrupulous attorney's clerk who used the coffee-room ; but was rescued by his friends just in time to save his political principles and discharge his bill before it grew too heavy to be paid anyhow.

The catastrophe which overtook the third delegate, Scrase the corn-chandler, was even more tragic. Scrase was a vain old fellow, of a bilio-sanguineous temperament, and was a continual butt for the shafts of Love. The wretched man had the folly to propose marriage to a lady who sang comic duets at an East-end coffee-room with a negro vocalist, who said that he came from Alabama, but who sprang in reality from Agar Town. Love, harmony, and Jamaica rum were his ruin. The great breach-of-promise case of De la Quaverdille (otherwise Siphkins) *versus* Scrase must be fresh in the recollection of my middle-aged readers. Heliogabalus Jones, Q.C., was for the plaintiff. Wumpkins, Q.C., made nothing of the defence. The judge—he was a joking judge, and his father had been a hanging judge—riddled Scrase

II

with witticisms upon his love-letters. The jury gave swingeing
damages. Scrase was hooted by the populace, and pursued to a
cab by those infuriated females with umbrellas, who always seem
ready to enact gratuitously the part of out-door Nemesises to the
courts of justice. Scrase sold his business, paid the damages and
costs, and retired in dudgeon to St. Becketsbury, where he set up
as a stationer, dealt in cheap literature, and became the most
rampant of radicals. His former comrades sorrowed sternly over
the defection of this Erastian. His name was erased from the
club-book,—to add to his crimes, he had left three half-years'
subscription unpaid,—and over his portrait (painted by Spillme-
gelp, author of the restorations in the sign of the " Old Dun
Horse ") was wafered a copy of *Bell's Weekly Messenger*.
Unconsciously, the Leave-us-alones followed the example of the
Venetian counsellors, who hung the black veil over the picture of
Marino Faliero.

It was to wrestle with these somewhat obstinate and prejudiced,
albeit very worthy people, that the Reverend Ernest Goldthorpe
came to Swordsley. The living was a handsome one, certainly :
that was something ; but had Ernest not been an upright and conscientious man, anxious and determined to do his duty in his state
of life, the first month of his residence in Swordsley would have
disgusted him with his preferment, and he would have left the place
to a curate, and only regarded it as a milch-cow. The Reverend
Ernest Goldthorpe took a different view of his obligations. He
would fertilise, he thought, this intellectual desert ; he would clear
away all this tangled jungle of bigotry and prejudice. So, axe in
hand, he walked into the wilderness, and began to lay about him
lustily. He was not unpopular at first. The former rector had
been deaf, paralytic, and all but blind. There had been a curate
who stammered, a curate who couldn't pronounce his H's—the
Swordsley men, although they had a pretty broad dialect of their
own, were vastly critical as to cockneyisms,—and a curate with a
red head—all abominations in the sight of Swordsley. Ernest at
first made himself liked. He preached eloquently ; he visited the
sick sedulously ; he kept port wine in his cellar much more for the
poor and ailing than for himself; and on Sundays, after morning
service, he would give his arm to some fair parishioner, and, arrayed

in his gown and bands, conduct her through the churchyard. The
Swordsley people were pleased at this. " I like to see a parson in
his cassock—it shows he knows his station," was the sage observation made by Mr. Pearkleborough the grocer. As for Ernest's
liberality, the villagers did not care much about his open purse.
They were very well to do. They had scarcely any paupers; and
the infirm were mostly provided for by their relatives, or in the
ancient almshouses of the Battle-axe Makers' Company. Many
bed-ridden octogenarians turned up their noses at the rector's
port wine; and as for the flannel petticoats which his housekeeper
made for them, they preferred their own hooded cloaks, dyed in
grain. The neighbouring farmers, who had been totally ruined at
intervals during the half-century, were generally very wealthy;
and "purse-proud Swordsley" was a by-word to the country-
side.

It was an evil hour for Ernest Goldthorpe, so far as his professional peace of mind was concerned, when he became by his
brother's lamented death heir to the title and the vast treasures of
Mammon. When the season of mourning was drawing to a close,
the gentry of the vicinity made a point of offering him their more
than tacit congratulations. A rector already passing rich, and
who in all human probability would be a baronet and a millionnaire, was not a person to be slighted. The great country families
called assiduously on the incumbent of Swordsley. He was unmarried, and the fact of how eligible a match he was did not escape
the notice of numerous wary mammas. But in proportion as the
consideration in which he was held among those of his own degree
increased, so did it decline and diminish among his immediate
parishioners. They began to sneer at his bounty as ostentation,
to stigmatise his shy and reserved demeanour as pride. The surest
way of making a shy man proud is to tell him of his haughtiness.
By somewhat of the feeling, *si vult decipi, decipiatur*, one feels inclined, in sheer retaliation, to become distant and austere. The
gulf between the rector and his flock widened every day; and it
wanted but one element of discord to make it impassable. The
men and, worse than all, the women of Swordsley began to take
exception to the Reverend Ernest Goldthorpe's doctrine. The
unlucky young man had a taste for mediæval art, and he held

H 2

notions somewhat advanced of the kind advocated in certain famous Tracts for certain troubled Times. If he was not a Puseyite, at least his congregation declared he was one; and he did a good deal towards encouraging the belief. At his own expense he had done much towards restoring the fine old early English church of St. Mary-la-Douce, at Swordsley; but the clearing away of the hideous wainscoting flaming with the golden names of departed churchwardens, and the rubbing off the smearing of whitewash which concealed some fine old fresco paintings,—both parts of the process by which the church had been "beautified" during the Georgian era,—involved him in unseemly broils with his own churchwarden, and caused him to be denounced by the "Leave-us-alone Club" as a pervert, an Escobar, an Ignatius Loyola, who was moved by the horrid intention of once more inflicting Popery, brass money, and wooden shoes on this free and Protestant land. Presuming to decorate the church with evergreens at Easter and Whitsuntide as well as at Christmas time, his harmless horticulture raised a shout about pagan idolatry and popish mummeries. He preached in a surplice, whereupon Pearkleborough the grocer positively wrote, and had printed at St. Becketsbury and circulated at his own expense, an eight-page pamphlet, headed "The Wolf in the Fold." It commenced with "Remember the Smithfield fires," and ended with the quotation from King John about Italian priests tithing and tolling in the English dominions. Ernest had spent much more in Swordsley than he had ever got out of it; but no account was taken of that. Finally, he put the climax to his offences in the eyes of his parishioners by presenting one of the Sunday-school children with a prize in the shape of a church-service, on which was embossed a cross in crimson morocco. It was about this time that the vestry wrote to the bishop about Ernest's proceedings—his "shameful goings on," as they were termed in Swordsley. They likewise memorialised the Battle-axe Makers' Company; and Chuff threatened the rector that "some of these fine mornings he would have him in the privy council." I have not dwelt on the commotion raised when Ernest took eight little boys from frightening birds and picking up stones in the fields, arrayed them in little white nightgowns worn over their clothes, taught them the Gregorian chant, and called them his

choristers. Less need also is there to mention the rumour that
he had set up the tribunal of Penitence in his back parlour,
and that by dint of strong cordials and pecuniary gratifications,
he had induced old Biddy Cubley, the habitually inebriated
washerwoman of the village, to confess her manifold sins and
do penance.

It may thus be imagined, when this state of things is borne in
mind, that the inhabitants of Swordsley had quite enough to do in
the month of May, 1851, without troubling themselves about the
Great Exhibition. The very few comments that were bestowed
upon it generally concurred in the opinion that Exhibitions were
a dangerous encouragement to foreigners, and a consequent upholding of papistry. The *odium theologicum* against Ernest alone
was sufficient to engross all the evil passions of the little community ; their better sympathies were, I trust, reserved for their
relations and friends. What slight surplus of hatred there remained was liberally bestowed, in fee simple, upon Miss Magdalen
Hill, who, desirous of being near her almost kinsman Ernest, had
for the last six months resided at the old mansion-house, known
as "The Casements," not half a mile from Swordsley on the St.
Becketsbury Road. The Casements, which was said to have fifty-
two windows, named each after a popish saint, which had been the
hiding-place of one of the Gunpowder-Plot conspirators, which
had stood a siege (for the king) during the civil wars, and was said
to be triply haunted, through an agreeable series of assassinations
which had occurred there,—this old Elizabethan brick-house, with
stone gables and quaint terraces and complicated carvings, belonged
to Lady Talmash. There was no mistake about Lady Talmash's
theological views. She was of the very highest church, and very,
very old, and very arbitrary, and very active, and one of Ernest
Goldthorpe's most influential supporters. She had known Magdalen from a child, and regarded the young woman with a sincere
affection. My lady was a widow, and wealthy. Before Magdalen
had come to cheer her solitude, she had had no other companions
save a High-Church parrot,—which had been taught to scream
" Canting Roundheads," and " wicked old Pope," with much dis-
tinctness of utterance and acrimony of tone,—a rigid old lady's
maid, and her own temper, which was of a somewhat hot and

intolerant nature. Lady Talmash was only too glad to have Magdalen near her. The girl was rich in her own right, and knew that
she could not be looked upon as a dependent. Above all, she was
near her adopted brother's church and flock, and persuaded herself
that she could find congenial and useful employment for herself
within Ernest's sphere of action.

Magdalen was very pale and thin,—much thinner and paler
since the awful day when the news came from Armentières,—and
her eyes had a strange look; but to most men she seemed eminently beautiful ; and, although the other sex would rarely admit
her good looks, they were generally unanimous in being jealous of
her. What did she want, they asked, in Swordsley ? She had
lost one husband among the Sons of Mammon ; was she seeking a
new one in the heir to the title and the riches ? If Ernest Goldthorpe wanted a wife, and if he disdained to seek a partner among
the ancient county gentry of Kent, he could surely find one
among his fine friends in London. Everybody knew that Magdalen was sensible and good ; but the knowledge of her many
excellent qualities rather embittered the feeling against her than
otherwise. Had she been perfect, she would not have escaped
censure ; but it was a point in favour of her detractors that she
missed perfection by one fatal failing—the weak pinion in the wings
of the fallen angels : Pride. Ernest was merely shy ; Magdalen
was really proud. The settled melancholy which had come upon
her since the death of her affianced husband rendered her even
more frigid and repellent. She had been sarcastic ; she was so no
more, but silent and preoccupied. The girls who came to The
Casements when, as rarely happened, Lady Talmash gave a party,
or who returned the old lady's visits, could find nothing to talk
about with Magdalen Hill. They dared not prattle about fashions
and flounces to her. It was known that she held balls, operas,
and flirtations to be sinful. They could not talk to her about the
Early Fathers, about the Council of Trent, or German art or
Gothic architecture. Not that her hose was in the slightest degree
tinged with blue. She knew much theoretically and practically ;
but with men who could converse with her on letters or on art she
disdained to interchange information or ideas. Even Ernest, who,
enthusiast as he was on High Church and mediæval revivalism,

was not devoid of a certain amount of timidity, was half afraid of
the beautiful sister-in-law that should have been. You see that
one can be afraid of other things besides ghosts or dragons; and
to the strongest mind it might be unpleasant to sit up all night
in a sculpture gallery, with the moonbeams glancing on Pallas
Athene's marble figure. Magdalen seldom went to the rectory;
but she ruled the rector's domain, both there and in the church.
She gave audience at The Casements to stainers of glass windows,
to carvers of rood-screens and bench-ends, to embroiderers of altar-
cloths, to makers of brass sconces and emblazoned candles. To
her was due the episcopal Faculty which permitted the erection in
the chancel of St. Mary-la-Douce, of a magnificent memorial, in
the form of a window, to Captain Hugh Jasper Goldthorpe, deceased. She controlled the discipline of the Reverend Ernest's
own proprietary schools; punished or rewarded the children as
she liked,—much to the discontent of the schoolmaster and
mistress,—and deluged the school library with little mediævalising
tracts about Saxon saints and Cappadocian martyrs. In the Sunday-school the young ladies of the environs, and even the tradesmen's daughters of the village who were teachers there, made a
bold stand against her sway. They rapped the knuckles of the
girls she favoured, they presented surreptitious plum-cake to those
who fell under her displeasure. Miss Chuff, driven to desperation
by her assumption, stoutly demanded one Sunday morning whether
Miss Hill thought herself Empress of Rooshia? Magdalen vouchsafed no response; but Chuff, speedily collapsing into floods of
tears, and adding irrelevant riders to her queries by demanding
whether she was a door-mat for Miss Hill to wipe her feet upon;
whether her connections were not to the full as respectable as
Miss Hill's, although they were not money-grubbers that lived on
the taxes got by grinding poor people's faces; with similar incongruities—she was easily vanquished by the stately silent lady, who
withered people with one glance of her proud eye.

To the poor, Magdalen was a sedulous benefactor and an affectionate friend. But she could not get on even with them. The
bed-ridden old women regarded her bounty with greater distaste
than they did that of the rector. They would not look at her
tracts; they did not care for her cold, measured accents when she

read to them. They wanted something warm and comforting, they said, and they found only coldness and discomfort in Magdalen's ministrations. They hesitated to take the remedies she brought them. They regarded her with vague distrust. Even the curly-headed little children were afraid of the proud, severe lady in mourning who never smiled. She felt, though she was straining every nerve to do her duty as a Christian woman, that there was something that impeded her progress,—something that she could not remove or quell. Where was *she* going ? Truly she was pursuing the narrow, thorny path that should probably lead to reward; but was her mode of travelling the right one ? Should she have trampled on the brambles and the sharp pebbles instead of gently moving them aside ? She asked herself the question sometimes,—asked if she could not conciliate instead of command-ing, invite instead of repelling. Pride stepped in and forbade further research ; and in pride and silence she wrapped herself up, and went on her lonely way. The women, as I have hinted, regarded her with a lively aversion ; the gentlemen admired, but gradually avoided her. She was a little too freezing. Now and then William the dragoon, whose regiment was by this time in garrison at St. Becketsbury, came over to The Casements. He was highly popular, even with Lady Talmash, and he could make his brother laugh ; but so soon as he was gone the temporary gaieties of the Elizabethan mansion were discontinued, and Mag-dalen resumed her icy empire, not only there, but at the rectory and the church. " One doesn't like sitting next to a snowball, you know," the jolly young fox-hunting squires used to say ; so Lady Talmash's severe although hospitable table became as deserted as she liked it to be,—not for economy's sake, but for pride. The two women, the old hermit and the young anchorite, used to sit opposite each other in state, eating scarcely anything. The table was loaded with plate; wine sparkled in the decanters; yet the dinner was more barren than a Barmecide's feast. The butler and his subordinates went through all the forms of a ceremonial dinner; but they knew that it was given for Pride's sake; that Pride sat bodkin between the two ladies, and was the only guest that went away filled from that dreary board.

The Casements was, however, Magdalen's only home. The

dragoon was wild; the clergyman was celibate; none of the other
Sons of Mammon were old enough to offer her a home. The
position she held was anomalous. The link of the dead man was
wanting to bind her to the family who should have been her
brothers. She felt this, and mourned, and said nothing. Sir
Jasper Goldthorpe had happily recovered the shock brought about
by his great grief, and which had culminated in a series of fainting
fits at Goldthorpe Manor on the evening of the funeral. But he
was sadly shaken. His physicians had insisted that he should
temporarily abstain from the cares of business. He went away
to Nice, to Naples, to Malta, with Lady Goldthorpe; came back
in the autumn of 1850; once more made his appearance among
the clerks in Beryl Court; but suffered a relapse on the very
anniversary of his son's death, and went abroad again. He was
now in Belgium, whither he had come from Paris, and was staying
at the residence of some great financial dignitary of the Low
Countries. His affairs in Beryl Court had gone on prosperously
during his absence, and he was richer than ever. But Sir Jasper
was expected back: of course, being so rich a man, he had been
made a commissioner of the Exhibition, foreman of a jury, and all
sorts of things. From ill health he had been unable to attend the
opening ceremonial, but he was now convalescent; and on his
return Magdalen was to join him in Onyx Square: only for a few
days, however, for the girl loathed London and the gilded palace
there, and seemed to prefer her residence in the village where she
was hated. Had she gone away from Swordsley for good, there
would have been probably, with the exception of the rector and
Lady Talmash, but one person who would have regretted her
absence. That person was the Reverend Ruthyn Pendragon,
B.A., the Reverend Ernest Goldthorpe's curate, and who, in his
clumsy fashion, had fallen madly in love with Magdalen Hill.

CHAPTER IX.

A LAY Brother came out of the convent on the hill, and so by the winding road into the valley where lay the village of Hoogendracht. It was an evening in May, and the far landscape was bathed in mellow hues. A fat and fair prospect was that Belgian champaign to look upon. Far as the eye could reach, to east and west the corn-fields ranged and waved, and the warm sun had just begun to sprinkle their green expanse with golden patches—pale gold as yet, and unalloyed by July fierceness. To the south the valley rose again into thick-wooded heights, where the birds held high harmony all day long, and partridges and pheasants might have thanked their stars that Flanders had a code of game-laws as well as England, and that their respite lasted until the latter days of August. Embowered in the woods shone out two or three blocks of white masonry, pierced by many windows, on which the sun gleamed with an arrowy sharpness, and which, I grieve to say, for the sake of the picturesque, were also provided with tall chimneys, from whose tops smoke curled and diapered the woodland distance. These were cloth factories; for Hoogendracht was rich in manufacture of woollens. Right down in the midst of the valley was the straggling village of Hoogendracht proper, with its church of St. Josse-ten-Groode, its fountain, its antique stone cross, and quaint little Town-house, now the quarters of the village mayor. It was girt about by farm premises, rich in kine, in sheep, in pigs, in breweries, in wheelwrights' shops, and in beetroot-crushing mills. Half-way down the winding road which the Lay Brother traversed was the château of St. Hendrik, held for ages by the noble family of Vandercoockenhagen, now represented by Wilhelm, twenty-second baron of that name; and to the north, on the summit of a high hill, the only object, barren,

savage, and gloomy to look upon in the whole cheerful picture,
was the monastery of the Pères Maristes des Bounescœuvres,—the
Marist Fathers of Goodworks,—a religious community of the very
strictest discipline and rule of life, and who were generally considered to be a succursal offshoot of the stern ascetics of La
Trappe.

When you had turned your back to the grey, timeworn abode
of the monks, and looked around to the corn-fields swelling in
lazy undulations; to the umbrageous thickets where the partridges
and pheasants rejoiced and the cloth factories nestled; to the
prosperous village in the middle of the vale, and on whose southern
side the little river Dracht babbled and struggled, all seemed
happy, smiling Peace. Beyond that bare hill not an inch of
ground lay waste. What ponds or rivulets the vale had,—tiny
tributaries to the Dracht,—were either the elected swimming-
baths of ducks and geese, or turned the wheels of mills, or were
rich in roach and dace and trout, sternly tabooed to piscatorial
interlopers by threatening notices. The abundant manure-heaps
in the farm-yards, the turkeys that gobbled over the scandal of
the poultry-yard, the well-stored barns, the sturdy Flemish cocks
that continually crowed forth their shrill pæans of defiance to all
the Gallic cocks beyond Lille and Verviers, the pigs that grunted
a Brabançonne in bassetaille, the sheep that fed, not forty, but four
hundred like one, on the beetroot peelings, the fat lazy horses that
had grown epicures in pasturage, and tired of grazing, rubbed their
noses against palings, or with dull thuds beat now one hoof, and
now the other on the turf to while away the time: all these spoke
of Peace. The cows were too proud to rise and stalk away as a
stranger passed, but looked at him instead with their vast chests
prone to the grass and their haunches bent, with a lazy, landed-
proprietor kind of air, chewing the cud disdainfully as though
they thought, " We are the cows that Cuyp and Karl du Jardin
painted in the sheeny fields and the golden sunset, and that
Verbeckhoeven paints so well now. We are historic cows. Reason
not about us. Regard our horns, our mild eyes, our well-set
bones, our heaving flanks. Regard, and pass."

The château of St. Hendrik had been recently redecorated, for
the Baron Vandercoockenhagen XXII. was rich, and a nobleman

of taste. But the old forms and the old carvings had been well
imitated, and the mansion-house had a respectably mediæval look.
It had need to have been renovated. We are in 1851. Five-
and-thirty years before, the château of St. Hendrik had been
turned inside out. The walls had been riddled by bullets,
the roof blown off by grenades, the rich furniture smashed, the
windows torn from their frames. Of the orchard only a few
blackened ʼstumps of apple-trees remained. The bearded barley
that was threshing in the barn was trampled into a gory mud,
and among the parterres of the flower-garden men had hacked
and hewed each other until the life-blood floated the tall lilies,
and made the red roses pale beside it. Here the warriors of
Napoleon the Great had left their sign, and cast their crimson
shadow. Here, as there, as far beyond, and to every point of the
compass, there had been slaughter and rapine, and burning of
houses, and outraging of women, not alone in the year of the
Waterloo campaign, but for many, many ages—almost since
Christianity began. For Gaul is divided into parts three, and
this was Belgic Gaul, " the cockpit of Europe ; " and men had so
cut each other's throats here and hereabouts, for the last sixteen
hundred years, that Prælium would have been a far more appropriate name for the village in the vale than Hoogendracht.
Scarcely a farmer was there in the place but whose fore-elders
had been burnt out or slain, or pillaged by the Romans or
Frenchmen, Imperialists or Republicans : Spaniards, Englishmen,
Italians, Walloons, Croats, and Pandours had come to this out-of-
the-way place to fight. The husbandman could scarcely trace a
furrow without turning up a splinter of bone ; and in the church
a stately monument to Don Esteban de Lara y Lara, killed in a
skirmish at Hoogendracht A.D. 1580, was neighboured by a
humble mural tablet, setting forth in lean English characters that
Captain Basil Horton, who fell by a hand-grenade in defending
Hoogendracht against the French king's troops A.D. 1707, had
been buried (he belonging to the ancient faith) in the adjoining
graveyard, and that this memorial had been erected by the High
and Mighty Prince John Churchill, Duke of Marlborough, to
whom the deceased was aide-de-camp.

  Flanders, however, has always been remarkable for a sound

flesh and a healthy skin, and the wounds inflicted upon her speedily heal. So soon as the blood has ceased to flow and the anguish is over, the patient begins to smile again; and in a year's time or so, scarcely a cicatrix remains to tell of the hideous gash. The husbandmen of Hoogendracht, when they had escaped the conscription, troubled themselves very little with the thought that their fathers had been forced into the ranks to lose their lives in quarrels that did not concern them. Peterkin's beet-root crop was abundant. What mattered it to Peterkin if his great uncle's acres had been grubbed up, his homestead ruined, and half-a-dozen ruffian soldiers of the Danube or the Douro quartered on him? Jan walked firmly and trippingly. His ancestor's wooden leg did not lie heavy on his soul. He hummed the Brabançonne at his work, and thought King Leopold the very best sovereign in Christendom, St. Gudule, St. Hendrik, and St. Josse-ten-Groode the very pinks and pearls of sanctity, and Geneviève de Brabant the cynosure of noble damsels. He ate his rye-bread, drank his sour beer, clumped about in his sabots, said his prayers, burnt his tallow-candles to the Virgin, and sold his bees-wax to the dealers at Louvain, kept his kermesses, hoarded his money in earthen pots and worsted stockings, and paid his taxes without grumbling. What more could he do to repeat in his Flemish tongue the spirit, if not the words, of the Latin inscription on the old house in Brussels, "From plague, famine, and war, good Lord, deliver us!"

So peace reigned in Hoogendracht, and the corn and flowers grew above the mouldering bones, the shattered blades, the rusty cannon-balls, and the dinted head-pieces; and every man lived under the shield of the law, and in the quiet possession of his own flocks and herds, till it should please some conqueror to come and root up Hoogendracht again, and strip every peasant as bare as a forked radish. Meanwhile the place smiled and gladdened every man's eyes to behold it. It might have gladdened those of the Lay Brother; but as he walked he kept them bent resolutely to the ground. He was a tall and stalwart brother, with a Saxon face, and closely shaven. He had not assumed the tonsure, but his hair—what little, at least, could be seen under his coarse woollen cap—was rigidly cropped to his head. For all raiment he had a long, loose, amply-sleeved, and hooded frock, of some rough woollen stuff, reaching from his neck to his heels, and girt about his waist by a cord, from which hung neither cross nor rosary. Those simple ornaments of monachism were reserved for the fathers of the convent. His unstockinged feet were thrust into wooden shoes, hay being stuffed into the interstices between his flesh and the rough wood. And so in mean and sordid garb, that had a mixture of the monk and of the farm-labourer in it, the Lay Brother stalked silent and with his eyes cast down.

His life was a hard one. He was but *servus servorum*, the slave of the slaves of self-mortification. The intervals between his rude labours, or his menial services, might be filled up in pious meditation; but he was not yet admitted even to the noviciate. He might remain for life a lay brother; and his companions in solitude were stolid and ignorant—Flemish boors, in fact, of a serious turn of mind, who were content to hew wood and draw water for the good fathers, without a chance, or indeed a hope, of ever putting on the cowl. The Lay Brother, however, was on a partial equality, so far as his material life was concerned, with the monks. He was allowed to share their toil and their privations. He rose with them in the middle of the night and at dawn to attend mass, and to hear gloomy chants. He stood with them in the refectory, listened during meal-time to the same austere homilies against the lusts of the flesh, read by the Father Prælector, partook standing of the same Spartan diet of lentil-soup, brown bread, black radish, cheese, and cold water. He, as a lay brother, was allowed to eat meat at Easter; but his comrades, the boors, did not eat it, and he abstained. He worked and vegetated. Were he to die here, he would again be put on an equality with the brethren, and be thrust into a hole in his rope-girt gabardine, unshrouded and uncoffined, with a plain wooden cross above his grave. For this consummation the Lay Brother devoutly prayed. For him, peace was not in the cheerful vale of Hoogendracht, but in the field behind the convent, on the plateau, which served as a cemetery.

There were forty Fathers of Goodworks at the convent. They had been dispossessed at the Revolution, and persecuted with unrelenting severity by the elder Napoleon. Their passive, uncomplaining forbearance under unmerited oppression irritated the Emperor and King much more than overt resistance would have done. "*Sapristi!*" cried his Majesty one day, I will turn every one of these forty shavelings into grenadiers of the Guard. His Imperial Majesty did a great many more quiet little things in the way of despotism—things much more cruel and arbitrary than shooting Palm the bookseller, or sending the brave guerillas of Major Schill, as though they were felons, to the galleys—than even his bitterest enemies in England are aware of. It was thought an act of clemency on his part when he permitted the intractable, albeit inoffensive, Marist Fathers to emigrate to America. After Waterloo a poor and scattered remnant, most of them feeble and ancient men, but who had preserved the traditions of their discipline intact, came back to Belgium. They were soon driven out again by the Dutch dynasty, to whom the Low Countries had been apportioned; but after 1831, the conciliatory government of Leopold permitted them to return, and to enjoy their humble own again.

They wore long-cowled frocks, of form like unto that of the lay brothers, but of coarse white flannel. Their feet were bare and sandalled, their heads, but for the ring of hair at the base of the skull, shaven. They ate little; they worked long hours in the rudest employments of field industry. They taught a school of vagrant children sanctioned by the State, and were the physicians and the relieving officers to the poor. Their farm-lands brought them in rich annual profits, but not one brother had a sou of his own, or even a purse to put it in. The consolation of literary study was even denied them; and in their wretched cells, on their hard pallets, they were expected to meditate on death, and not to read. They observed the rule of silence with a severity even more frightful than ever reigned in a modern penitentiary; and the deadliest sin against conventual discipline, was the utterance of a word not warranted by the actual requirements of labour. No ghastly reminders of "Brother, we must die," were interchanged between them. They plied their spades and broke their clods in mute companionship. The Guest-master only, or *Père Hospitalier*, and the Reverend Superior of the convent, who wore a golden chain above his flannel robe, but lived as poorly and worked as

hard as his brethren—these and the lay brethren who fetched and
carried from the village were permitted to speak on matters of necessity. So, without books to read, without human converse to hear or
smiles to cheer them, without shirts, without shoes, without pocket-
handkerchiefs, or sheets, or pillows,—with no money to spend, no
meat to eat, no kindly words to soothe their last moments, lived
the Marist Fathers of Goodworks—sternly and gloomily, and confident that the road they were treading was the sure one, and
torturing themselves in hopes of a blessed immortality. The
publications of the Tract Society never reached their grim abode.
They would have spurned such heretical pamphlets; and yet I
think more than one of these devoted friars might have asked
himself with advantage the question, " Where are you going ? "

Among these forty men who herded in one common living
sepulchre, there were the usual number of Fathers Hulbert,
Austin, Jerome, Francis, Joseph, Stephen, Philip, Luke, and so
forth. They assumed their new baptism in taking the cowl; but
they did not all belong to one nation, and in the great outside
world they had gone by very many different names. Thus,
Father Hulbert may have been a once famous tenor-singer at the
Grand Opera in Paris, to whom Emperors had sent diamond
snuff-boxes, and who had lain in the alcoves of princesses of the
blood royal. Father Austin had been a chamberlain at the court
of Leopold; Stephen a wealthy iron-master at Liège; Jerome an
officer in the Royal Guard; Joseph a brilliant poet and wit;
Francis a fashionable roué; Luke a ——; but there is no need
to pursue the catalogue further. The world was quite shut out
from the convent of Hoogendracht, and all the pomp, pride, and
ambition of man disappeared beneath the flannel frock and the
hempen girdle.

As the Lay Brother neared the château of St. Hendrik, he
found a handsome barouche and pair standing at the gates. M.
le Baron Vandercoockenhagen XXII. had visitors staying at the
château, and he was about to take an airing with two guests, one
of whom had been an invalid. The horses champed, the postilion,
in the lightest of jackets and the brightest of top-boots, clacked
his whip. Two spruce outriders reined their horses in, a little in
advance. M. le Baron Vandercoockenhagen XXII. was a burly

Belgian magnifico, with quite a conservatory of coloured ribbons at his button-hole. He came forth from the château with a lady and gentleman, whom, with the utmost politeness, he assisted into the barouche. The lady was stout, and had been comely and cheerful, but she looked pale and careworn. The gentleman was tall and broadly built. His hair was light; his age might have been a little over fifty; but he stooped and shook painfully, and could only walk with the assistance of a stick. At length the three were comfortably seated in the barouche; the Baron waved his hand, the postilion gave another clack to his whip, and the rapid wheels rolled down the winding road.

The Lay Brother had stood apart, by a wayside cross. When the party had left, he made to resume his way; but the gate-porter, a fat Fleming, in a gorgeous livery of green and gold, recognised, stopped him, and bade him good even.

The Lay Brother turned his feet towards Hoogendracht, bowed his head and would have passed on; but the gate-porter was not so to be put off.

"Have you heard the news, Brother Dominique?"

"We hear no news. I have heard nothing."

"Our guests leave us to-morrow. They are called to England. And you, whither may you be bound?"

"To the post-office, for the Reverend Superior's letters."

"Ah, the barouche will be there long before you. M. le Baron does not feed his horses with broken bottles; and when they go it is with a will. Do you know whom our guests are, Brother Dominique?"

"I am not permitted to ask. No."

"Well, they are English; no conceited beggarly upstarts of Frenchmen. Oh, no. The invalid gentleman you saw is a great English milord,—Sir Jasper Goldthorpe by name, a member of the British parliament, and richer they say than Rothschild."

"Ah!"

"And the *belle dame*, whom should she be but Miladi Gold-thorpe, his wife."

"Good evening," said the Lay Brother, turning his eyes to the ground and walking on.

"*Sont-ils rustres, ces frères laïques?*" muttered the porter, as

I

he closed the gate. "That Brother Dominique is as surly as a bear. I wonder to what nation that lay brother belongs. He can speak no Flemish, and his French is decidedly not of Paris. Perhaps he is a Walloon."

When the Lay Brother arrived at the post-office in the main street of Hoogendracht, the official handed him a packet of letters for the Reverend Superior. He bowed his head and was going away, when the postmaster called him back.

"Stay," he said, "there is a letter for you, Brother Dominique, with the English postmark, and in a very pretty female hand. *Vous êtes en bonne fortune, mon frère.*"

"It is from my sister," observed Brother Dominique coldly; but as he extended his hand for the letter his fingers trembled, and he clutched rather than took it.

"I don't believe in lay brothers' lay sisters," was the sage remark of the postmaster, as he proceeded to stamp the contents of the outgoing letter-bag.

The Lay Brother pursued his road back towards the convent on the hill until he had passed the château of St. Hendrik by full a hundred yards. Then he drew the letter in a woman's hand from the bosom of his gaberdine, broke the seal, and eagerly tore open the envelope. His pale face was flushed, and his whole frame shook.

"At last," groaned the Lay Brother, and in the English tongue. "At last. A letter in January, and a letter in May, and sixteen months have passed in this prison, and yet no hope."

CHAPTER X.

WHAT is a gentleman? Who is a gentleman? I pause for a reply. Of course there will be at once as many score thousand answers, indignant, sarcastic, explanatory, and argumentative, to my queries as there are readers to this story. But I must repeat them nevertheless. "What is a gentleman? and who, if you please, has a right to be considered one?" Maginn once, discussing the vexed question, quoted an Irish authority, who laid it down that for duelling purposes any one might be considered a gentleman who wore a clean shirt once a week. The present generation is more fastidious, and would not be satisfied with such a standard of gentility. The Byronic idea of a gentleman we are all familiar with : small hands and feet, a high forehead (warranted alabaster), curly hair, and a fine taste for hock and soda-water in the morning; but when we find a being so endowed squabbling with his wife, recommending Mr. Grimaldi, the clown, to take soy with his apple-tart, and composing a scurril poem under the inspiration, not of Rhenish wine, but of diluted Geneva, one begins to doubt somewhat of the correctness of the Byronic theory. It is plain, I am afraid, that manners have little to do with making a gentleman—in the world's sense of the term. The Plantagenets ate their meals with their fingers, slept on straw, and did not use pocket-handkerchiefs; and Charlemagne, not being able to write, was compelled to dip the fore-finger of his glove in ink and smear it over the parchment, when it was necessary that the imperial sign-manual should be affixed to an edict. Imagine "Carolus Magnus **X** his mark"! The best-bred men of modern times have often been of the most plebeian extraction. The French Duke de Noailles-Noailles confessed that the dancing-master Vestris, if his demeanour was to be taken as a criterion,

was the most polished gentleman he ever saw; whereas, *per contra,*
read what St. Simon has to say of the bearish and brutish manners
of the great Dukes and Peers of his time.   Brummell, the pattern
of English patricians, was the son of a petty lodging-house keeper,
and the grandson of a menial servant;—if he ever had a grandfather at all. Again, as to appearance. Take down your Lavater's
Physiognomy, and, placing your hand over the names appended
to the portraits, just strive by guesswork to determine who are
the nobly descended and who the base-born in that long panorama of faces.   Long odds may be laid that when you come to
remove your hand, you will discover that this eagle-nosed, lofty-
browed worthy, who by his countenance should be of the bluest-
blood of Castile, is the son of a cobbler; and that this bull-necked,
snub-nosed, thick-lipped, clod-hopping-looking fellow is a grandee
of a hundred quarterings, or a prince of an imperial house.   Now,
do you think I am about to launch into some hotly democratic
invective against the folly and fallacy of claims of long descent;
that I am about to quote the "grand old gardener and his wife;"
or ask, with Wat Tyler's crew, who was a gentleman when the
gardener delved and his wife span; or chuckle over the ambas-
sador-poet's proposed epitaph :

> " Ladies and gentles, by your leave,
>   Here lies the body of Matthew Prior ;
>   The son of Adam and of Eve :
>   Can Bourbon or Nassau go higher ?"

No : I have not any wish to attempt sarcasm either one way or
the other—either about "tenth transmitters of foolish faces," or
poor varlets whose blood "has crept through scoundrels ever since
the Flood." Blood, quotha ! If I am pricked, will not my veins
yield the life current; and if I choose to wear blue spectacles,
may I not declare it to be the real tap—the genuine *sangre azul?*
Blood, forsooth ! What are your two-penny-halfpenny Howards
and Percys to *my* ancestry,—to yours, my descendant of five hundred cattle-lifters,—to yours, Fitz Bogie designed of Macgilli-
cuddy ; to yours, M. de Sidonia, who carry three trumpets proper
in memory of your ancestor who helped to blow the walls of
Jericho down ? and what are all our boastings of ancient descent
compared with those of the Chuggs of Suffolk, who have held the

plough and cracked the clods for twice five hundred years. Let us all be proud of our progenitors, and think ourselves each and severally the very finest gentlemen that ever stepped; and when a rude person says, "Sir, you are no gentleman," let us answer him, "Sir, you are no judge."

And yet: Who is a gentleman? What is a gentleman? The question is as far from solution as ever. *I* don't know, for one; but if, as we are generally compelled to do, the general verdict of the world is to be fallen back upon, it is very certain, not only that the Reverend Ruthyn Pendragon was no gentleman, but that he was, on the contrary, an exceedingly vulgar person.

There had been curates and curates at Swordsley. The rector, who was deaf, paralytic, and all but blind, had been taken care of for a long period by his relatives, who found the mild and genial climate of Torquay most suited to his infirm state of health. The large revenues of the incumbency had been carefully paid in to the bankers of the Reverend Mr. Marrowfat—that was the name of the invalid rector; and the successive curates had been as punctually paid their small and not increasing stipends. The evil-tongued, who were neither more nor less numerous at Swordsley than elsewhere, averred that the patroness in ordinary to ecclesiastical preferment under the Rector of Swordsley was a certain Mrs. Gryphon, by the mother's side a Marrowfat, by conjugal relation the widow of a broken ship-broker, and who was good enough to officiate as housekeeper, companion, and general *locum tenens* to the infirm clerical gentleman. She did everything for him. She opened his letters and read those which he received; nay, after the Reverend Mr. Marrowfat's death, human malignity went so far as to say—in the great probate case of Marrowfat and Wife *versus* Gryphon—that this indefatigable widow lady made the rector's will for him, and had it all her own way in making it. This, however, is only by the way. I am afraid that she did appoint the curates, and that the advent of the ecclesiastic who stammered, and of the other one who had no H's, must be laid to her charge. Of the red-headed curate, however, Mrs. Gryphon must be held blameless. He of the scarlet locks was a nominee of the Chuckle-buxes, a rival branch of the Marrowfat family, who obtained temporary dominion over the poor old clergyman during an absence of Mrs. Gryphon in London. The widow had a graceless nephew,—a Gryphon, not a Marrowfat,—who, having spent a large legacy, principally in hire of dog-carts, and the purchase of cherry-brandy, shirts of extraordinary pattern, and coloured litho- graphs of eminent dramatic performers, had enlisted in the Hussars, but was speedily bought off from the draff and husks of the depôt at Maidstone by his affectionate aunt. Having unsuc- cessfully tempted fortune as a commercial traveller for an article in general demand (the celebrated steel-edged wooden razors), as a billiard-marker, and as a frequenter of certain dry skittle-alleys, whither gentlemen of agricultural appearance were brought to play, and where, it is said, they were sometimes drugged and robbed, young Ripton Gryphon again enlisted; this time in her Majesty's infantry of the line. He was again bought off; and after enjoying for a short time an appointment in the metropolitan police force, from which he was dismissed for a fault, harmless in itself but highly subversive of discipline, being that of offering to fight his inspector for half-a-crown, this gay youth became an omnibus conductor, a waiter at a tavern where the hours were rather early than late, and an attendant at fictitious auctions, where his business was to bid for gigantic plated cruet-stands, and, with an air of extreme solicitude, to inspect curiously-inlaid writing- desks, handed round for that purpose on a japanned tea-tray. In this place of business he was ordinarily known by the familiar sobriquet of "Rip the Bonnet." If I have mentioned the pecu- liar phases in the career of this sportive young man, it has been merely to mark the strong points of contrast in his character. Ripton Gryphon was exceedingly intelligent. His education had been excellent. He was a good classical scholar, a ready speaker, and he wrote a beautiful hand. These acquirements did not in the least militate against his being, root and branch, a hopeless and incurable scamp. With that odd perversity not uncommon to her sex, Mrs. Gryphon positively adored this lamentable scapegrace; and as he happened to be at the same time tall, curly-haired, straight of limb, bright of eye, and generally good-looking, the widow declared that her Ripton was born to be a gentleman; that he would sow his wild oats; that he should go into the Church, and that a country curacy was the very thing to suit him, pending,

of course, his elevation to the episcopal bench. To all appearance,
it certainly appeared that the soil of Mr. Ripton Gryphon's moral
nature had been exhausted by the cultivation of wild oats, and
that unless it lay fallow for a time it was not likely to produce
anything but an abundant crop of hemp; but with the energy and
audacity characteristic of a lady accustomed to deal only with
weak and timid people, and to work her will upon them, Mrs.
Gryphon set about converting a young fellow who was bidding fair
to graduate at the hulks into a candidate for holy orders. She
found out the easy chaplain to an easy bishop, who had already
ordained a gentleman not quite right in his head for a living near
the Land's End, and another who was not quite right in his morals
for a chaplaincy in the West Indies. Mrs. Gryphon learned to
know, as some of us know, and as all of us ought to know, that
other means exist for wearing a cassock and bands, and tacking
"reverend" to one's name, besides taking a university degree.
The easy chaplain recommended her to a tutor for her Ripton,—
a college man, a ripe scholar, who had taken deacon's orders, who
was as proud as Lucifer and as poor as Job, and whose name was
Ruthyn Pendragon. The graceless nephew was confided to the
care of this instructor, and in a quiet retirement at Clapham,
supported from the widow lady's funds, did, for a certain period,
make some progress in leaving off sack and living cleanly, like a
gentleman. What is a gentleman? It was during the sojourn of
Mrs. Gryphon in London, of course in the interests of her *protégé*,
that the Chucklebux faction achieved a momentary triumph; and
the reverend gentleman who had no H's, having married a lady
who had two thousand pounds, and so resigned his appointment,
brought in the curate with the red head. Mrs. Gryphon returned
to Torquay in a rage, and the shock of her temper was almost too
much for the poor old rector. She was appeased, however, by
abject concessions, and the immediate and ignominious dismissal
or the entire Chucklebux faction (the danger was imminent; for
there was one Chucklebux who was medical, of the homœopathic
persuasion, and who was also a distinguished amateur will-maker)
and she soon resumed her empire over her reverend patient and
relative. So hard did this lady work towards the accomplishment
of her purpose, so various were her resources, so strong was her

will, so feeble were those with whom she had to deal, that I for one should not have been surprised if success had crowned her enterprise, and if Ripton Gryphon had at last crept through the hawse-holes on board the ecclesiastical bark. Stranger things have happened, believe me. I am not writing from imagination or without book. All the widow's plots and schemes were, alas, foiled by Ripton Gryphon taking it into his head to vindicate his natural character. He ran away from Mr. Pendragon, his tutor, and was not heard of any more. Many a similar scapegrace, whose relatives are vainly inquiring after him, or, through the medium of newspaper advertisements, as vainly entreating him to return, is quietly tried under a false name at some provincial assizes,. and quietly transported, without anybody save some chance gaoler being the wiser for it. "That's a baronet, sir," said a convict's warder to me once on Southsea Common, pointing to a peculiarly villanous-looking individual in cross-barred canvas and an oil-skin hat, who was leisurely tickling the turf with his spade,—"that's a baronet, and kep' his 'osses and his 'ounds. But, Lord love you, sir, he ain't at Portsmouth, leastways as his genteel fam'ly think. Must live abroad for his 'elth, sir. He's at Paw, in the Pyrenees, a living in his own chatow, is that baronet." But what became of Ripton Gryphon there was no deponent to say. He went away, and didn't come back. He may have subsided into penal servitude, as has already been hinted. He may have turned up swollen, blue, ghastly, and drowned, in the ooze of some riverain creek, and have passed from a parish dead-house to a parish grave. He may have enlisted again, have died on board a transport, and been flung to the fishes. He may have been murdered. Who knows? Men pass and pass in the great glass of Life like the Kings in Macbeth's vision; and there is no remembrance of those that have gone before, and no knowledge of those that are to come afterwards.

Who, for instance, could have foretold that Ruthyn Pendragon, the tutor of the graceless scion of the Gryphons, would have ever become curate of Swordsley! yet it was his *kismet*, his fate, to occupy that post. By one of those odd coincidences which are perpetually baffling and perplexing us, Pendragon, having passed into priest's orders, was recommended to the new rector of

Swordsley,—poor old Mr. Marrowfat having been gathered to
his fathers,—and obtained employment from the Reverend Ernest
Goldthorpe. It is not fitting to tell how the widow, at once
bereaved of her rector and of her nephew, raged and stormed at
the course which events had taken. It wasn't Ruthyn Pendragon's fault if Ernest Goldthorpe chose to take him. He wanted a
curacy, and Ernest wanted a curate: what was more natural?
Why should Mrs. Gryphon charge him with the blackest ingratitude, and accuse him of being a traitor and an intriguer? He
had not solicited the appointment. It had fallen in his way, and
he had taken it. The widow would have liked to say all kinds of
possible things against the new curate; but there was nothing to
be said against him. He was staunchly recommended by college
magnates. He was eminently learned. His poverty was notorious; but his moral character was without stain. Ernest
Goldthorpe was glad to be able to do a service to so able and
respectable a young man. So the Gryphon was finally discomfited,
—she had got all the rector's money though, and all the Mar-
rowfats and Chucklebuxes, with their lawyers to boot, failed in
dispossessing her thereof,—and the Reverend Ruthyn Pendragon
was curate to the Rector of Swordsley.

Stay,—learning, respectability, character, all granted,—there
might have been one little thing to be alleged against the
Reverend Ruthyn Pendragon. He *was* a very vulgar person.
He had plenty of H's, and used them in the right place, but he
was desperately vulgar. He looked like a vulgar person. He
talked like one. He ate and drank like one. He dressed like
one. There was a vague but uncertain vulgarity in his face, his
smile, his demeanour. His bold, firm, defined handwriting was
vulgar to every cross of a *t*, to every dot of an *i*. When he first
entered the presence of Lady Talmash, that aristocratic church-
woman held up her hands, and whispered to Magdalen, "However
comes that bore by the name of Pendragon?"

By lineage Ruthyn was a gentleman of the most ancient
descent. What were Normans, Saxons, Danes, to his old stock?
He sprang from the genuine Phœnician *souche*, as I suppose all
the Tre, Pols, and Pens of Cornwall do. Ruthyn came from that
famous although somewhat remote province. Unhappily there

were no tin-mines in his family, nor, had Pendragon died, would
there have been twenty thousand or ten under-ground in Cornwall
anxious to know the reason why. He had no money. He was
an orphan, and alone in the world.

An old grandmother at St. Mawes had brought this vulgar person up. She did what she could for him, and her small savings
were laid out for his benefit. Ruthyn's father was a gentleman,
who, about the year 1825, in company with other adventurous Cor-
nishmen, had gone in quest of some silver-mines in Peru, and found
the *vomito nero* instead, of which, at Lima, he straightway died.
The old grandmother did what she could for the orphan, which was
not much. The father had, on the principle of conveying coals to
Newcastle, taken most of the available ready money of the family
with him to the silver-mines of Peru. In after years Ruthyn
Pendragon did not mind confessing that in his boyhood he had
made a voyage in a fishing-smack, with a view to see whether he
would like to be apprenticed to the sea; and that he had served a
short probation behind the shop-counter of a chemist, who likewise sold grocery and haberdashery, at Truro. These early associations may have been instrumental in planting the first seeds of
that vulgarity for which Ruthyn Pendragon was always noted, and
for which he eventually became famous. In process of time a
Cornish gentleman of means, who had known the paternal Pendragon, advised Ruthyn's grandmother to send him to a certain
ancient and well-known grammar-school in the West Country.
He made great progress in his studies here, and was commended
by his master as a very diligent and capable boy, while he was
excepted to by his schoolfellows as being a pitiably vulgar one.
He obtained an exhibition at last, and took that, and his vulgarity, and a huge stock (for a boy) of book-learning, and a vast
fund of natural shrewdness, observation, and humour, with him to
college. Anything else? well, he had a slender wardrobe, and
his grandmother's blessing. His successes at the university were
solid, if not brilliant. It is said of him, that leaving school, and
entering the mail-coach which was to convey him to town, Ruthyn
Pendragon flung his hat into the air, and cried, "Here goes for
Archbishop of Canterbury;" but at the university it was speedily
decided that such a vulgar fellow would never obtain a fellowship,

while doubts were expressed as to whether any gentlemanly
bishop could ever be persuaded to ordain such a lout. He was
not likely to go wrong at the university. His health was of the
rudest, his frame of the strongest; and excesses of dissipation
would have hurt him no more than excess of study; but he was
wise, and chose the latter. He read desperately and continuously.
All that the gay youth of the university could say against him
was that he was vulgar. They could not in their charmingly contemptuous manner call him a "cad." There was no denying
his gentle blood. There was no finding a blot on his scutcheon.
His great-great-grandfather was duly enshrined in Fuller's
Worthies; a great-grand-uncle was mentioned in Anthony à
Wood. The university tradesmen refrained from soliciting his
custom; they knew that he could do them no good, and that they
could do him no harm. Of what use were well-cut coats and
brilliant scarves to one who, winter and summer, wore a plain
black coat, which he acknowledged to have bought second-hand,
and which he himself mended when it required repair; and
beneath that a waistcoat and trousers of coarse grey serge, made
by his old grandmother at St. Mawes? Where he first purchased
his cap and gown was a mystery; the triflers declared that he had
bought them at a London masquerade warehouse, on his way to
college. They were certainly curiosities of faded shabbiness.
His linen was dreadfully coarse, but scrupulously clean. He was
in the habit of biting his nails to the quick, and no scissors were
needed for his large healthy-looking hands. His hair was naturally dark and glossy, and he wanted no Macassar. He looked
like a man who washed with yellow soap. He never had a row
with the bargemen on the river. They respected and feared him,
not alone for his strength, which was palpably prodigious, but for
his homely, kindly manners; for he was not above holding the
poorest and roughest in discourse, and would talk to them by the
half-hour together of common things and their daily avocations.
He was not vulgar to them. Some called him a "true gentleman," but more frequently working-men exclaimed: "We likes
him, for he talks like one of us." Clearly a very vulgar person,
this Ruthyn Pendragon.

There were young gentlemen of his college whose quar-

terly cigar bills came to ten, nay, twenty, pounds.   Viscount
Racquetborough, indeed, owed his tobacconist two hundred and
odd ; but, then, most of that was discount.   Ruthyn rarely smoked,
but he casually mentioned that the use of a short pipe had been
habitual to him before he was twelve years of age ; and when
from time to time some new man who thought him an original
persuaded him to come to his rooms, he indulged in a calumet of
that very strongest cavendish which young undergraduates buy,
like Editions of the Fathers, more for show than use.   Such
strong meat is not fit for babes.   He was by rule a water-
drinker ; but sometimes after rowing he would drink of the
country beer that labourers drank.   Somebody mentioned All-
sopp's bitter ale to him, and he returned for answer, " What
is that ? "   The Dons could not like him ; he was too vulgar, and
yet he was not offensive.   He was innocent of any sins against
collegiate discipline ; but he neither invited nor seemed thankful
for praise.   The Dons were of course absolved from toadying him,
and he seemed to be utterly ignorant of the fact that anything
was to be got from toadying the Dons.   He was a great eater,
although occasionally it was known that he passed the twenty-
four hours without any sustenance more solid than bread and
butter ; yet those who watched him—and he was strange enough
to have many observers—remarked that he could eat voraciously
of cold meat, of suet pudding, and of buttered toast.   He was not
taciturn, for he was always ready to speak when spoken to ; but
he seldom volunteered conversation.   Those who most objected
to his vulgarity could not help admiring his honest discourse, full
of manly and sensible reflection.   He was one in whose presence
young men were somehow ashamed to swear, to talk of loose and
shameful things, or, indeed, to talk nonsense, if they could avoid
it.   The most brilliant conversationalists were on their mettle in
the presence of Ruthyn Pendragon.   And yet he could enjoy
humour, and at a droll story, proper for a decorous man to hear,
would open his large mouth and laugh sonorously.   The only
overt act against the usages of society which he had been known
to commit was this.   He had gone to a man's rooms to return
some books he had borrowed—he was not above borrowing books.
A dozen young fellows were present, and as Ruthyn Pendragon

turned to depart, he saw a pack of cards which had been inadver-
tently left exposed on a table. Without any more ado he seized
the cards, flung them into the fire, put his back before it, folded
his arms, and said, "I am no censor of manners, Proctor, or
Puritan, and you may think that this is no business of mine.
But it is. Cards are the Devil's books. Wherever I find them,
I burn them. Good morning. If anybody thinks he has a right
to complain, I will fight him, here or elsewhere." But nobody
cared to complain, or to fight Ruthyn Pendragon; so he went,
and, indeed, the sound that accompanied his departure much more
resembled a cheer than a murmur of discontent. The story was
told about and gained him much esteem, although men were
careful not to invite this rigid hater of graven images to their
card-parties. It was known that he was not a hypocrite, and
would not lie. Lord Racquetborough expressed himself much
pleased when he heard of the story. "By Jove," he said, "the
Grisly Bear is a trump. I wish I could lend him fifty pounds.
He looks so deuced hard up. I wish my father could put a living
by for him." Viscount Racquetborough's papa was the Earl of
Tenniscourt (family name De la Paume), very noble, but impo-
verished. Viscount Racquetborough was always wishing good
things to everybody, but his lordship's habits were expensive and
his means were limited. He ended by owing the tobacconist
many hundreds of pounds ; and, going through the court, retired
to Baden-Baden until such time as he should be called to the
House of Lords to legislate for vulgar people.

In the second year of Ruthyn's residence the old grandmother
at St. Mawes died. The few pounds that were left of her savings
barely sufficed to bury her, and to pay the expenses of her grandson to Cornwall and back. He had no kindred now, no money,
and no friends. The country gentleman who had advised his
being sent to the grammar-school was dead. He was known at
the university, and might have earned some money by reading
with men ; but he preferred to leave college for a while. He
went away, and found a situation as usher in a school near London.
The master was an ignorant brute, who had been bankrupt in the
linen-drapery line, and who, when his certificate was definitely
refused, had hesitated whether he should turn corn-cutter, low

comedian, or school-master. He had an aptitude for the two former vocations; for the latter his capacity was limited to the possession of a very strong arm and a cruel disposition. Broomback, of Clapham Rise (he is Dr. Broomback now, a German degree), was glad to secure the services of a good classical scholar, and a university man to boot, for forty pounds a year. So Ruthyn Pendragon taught the boys, and Broomback beat them, and his wife took tithe and toll on their clothes and linen ; and thus the division of scholastic labour was complete. The boys used to laugh at the usher's odd, rough ways, as he read Greek Testament to them, with a great hole under the arm of his black coat; but he was kind and just, and I think that before he went away nine out of ten of those children loved the poor usher. By great good luck there was a boy at Broomback's who was the son of a lady of some fortune. It having occurred to Broomback to beat this lad (who was frail and delicate) into a fever, he was removed from Clapham Rise ; and when he got well, he begged so earnestly that his studies might be directed by his dear old usher,—so he called Ruthyn,—that his mamma forthwith engaged the friendless Cornishman as domestic tutor to her darling. In time Pendragon saved enough money to take a small house of his own, and advertise for pupils ; and one of those pupils was the Ripton Gryphon you have heard of. I don't know what Ruthyn Pendragon thought of the preposterous plan of turning a scamp into a clergyman, indulged in by the vain and self-willed housekeeper of the Reverend Mr. Marrowfat ; but he did his duty by the prodigal, even to the extent of having one or two up and down fights with him. In these combats it must be admitted that Rip, although for his youth a somewhat experienced bruiser, invariably got the worst of it. He was the last pupil that Ruthyn Pendragon took. He was rich enough to go back to the university and take his degree. He was ordained on the strength of a miserable cure offered him by the proprietor of a large bone-boiling manufactory in the Essex marshes, who had a chapel on his premises for the benefit of his work-people, and thought it rather a grand thing to entertain a chaplain at his own expense. The young curate—he was now five-and-twenty years of age—did not stay long in Essex. The people were willing enough to receive religious instruction ; but when they were not at work they straggled away to the adjacent beer-shops and got tipsy, and on Sundays they generally had the ague ; and finally the bone-boiler breaking, it was discovered that he had been robbing everybody for the last fifteen years (he was the man who did eighty-seven thousand pounds worth of bills in one morning, assuring the firm who discounted them that every bill " had bones at the bottom of it," but it turned out rather that every bill was fundamentally fraudulent) ; and Ruthyn Pendragon lost his chaplaincy. He was for a while unemployed ; but, on the recommendation of a college-acquaintance, he became known to the Reverend Ernest Goldthorpe, whose views on Church matters, in the latter part of 1849, had not become so strongly pronounced, and who was happy to have a person so fitted by education and principles for the responsible position confided to him, and who, by family descent at least, was undeniably a gentleman.

Such was the curate of Swordsley, who had not been six months in the village before he was idolised by the inhabitants, and who, when Ernest began to lean towards High-Church doctrines, became, by tacit consent, and without the slightest manifestation of open opposition on his part, the leader of the Low-Church party. "Ah, if he was only our rector ! " cried the men of Swordsley. The women, too, were unanimous in his praise,—all save the haughty maiden at The Casements, Miss Magdalen Hill.

This young lady took no pains to disguise her disdain and aversion for the curate. He was from the very first eminently distasteful to her. She shuddered at the contrast between the pale, thoughtful, refined Ernest, with his high white brow, his crisply curled chestnut locks,—he was a delicate copy of his brother Hugh,—his tiny hands and feet, his neat and well-fitting garments, and this brawny, swarthy, hirsute, round-shouldered, bull-necked, large-limbed, Ruthyn Pendragon. The man's head was capacious enough, but his black hair grew thick and tufted down to within a couple of inches of his bushy eyebrows. Had he let Nature have her way, he would have been bearded like a pioneer. His hands were uncouthly shaped, and corrugated with knotty veins. Although he had the arms and the torso of a Hercules, he was short and clumsy in stature, and his legs were slightly bowed. She raged within herself to think that this

ragged, vulgar, truncated colossus, who blew his nose with a
trumpet-sound, who trampled rather than walked over the flowers
of a carpet, who clattered his tea-cup and ate his food ravenously,
who dragged books from shelves, and if he took notice of a lap-dog
only forced open its mouth to look at his teeth, who never wore
gloves,—should be a gentleman of long descent; whereas Ernest,
with all his refinement and his address, and the title that was in
store for him, was but the son of a city money-spinner of mush-
room extraction. Why should this vulgar person, she thought,
be a gentleman? What right had he to a proud name,—he who
looked like some Cornish miner fresh from wielding the pick?
She did not soften in the least when she heard how good and kind
and thoughtful he was to the poor. Had she no goodness, no
kindness, and no thought? Was Ernest destitute of these good
qualities? She bit her lip in anger when she heard that this
rough, awkward man, who could not speak French, who had
plainly said that people should come to church to pray, and not to
look at pictures, and that the best mural decoration for the chancel
was a fresh coat of whitewash; who lodged at Pearkleborough's
the grocer's, and bought his own chop or steak at the butcher's
(who could scarcely bring himself to charge the curate anything
for it)—should be revered and beloved by the parishioners, who
looked on Ernest with a dislike that was little short of hatred.
She heard that this man, who could scarcely handle a knife and
fork, and was not fit to be trusted with a teacup, could bandage
wounds, could bleed a horse, or put leeches on a child's temples;
could dandle babies, could make out petty tradesmen's bills, could
appease lovers' quarrels, and prevent contentious neighbours from
going to law; and that he did all this without currying favour
with the poor (who are as easily and as often toadied as the rich),
but always with a homely, sensible, simple-mindedness. Magdalen
knew that the curate disapproved of the rector's views. She disliked him for that. She disliked him for his popularity. She
disliked him for his very goodness. She did. And yet she was
a virtuous, pious, and—so far as her purse went—a charitable
young woman. How much more reason had she to dislike Ruthyn
Pendragon, when, as he had the ineffable presumption to do, he
told her that he loved her?

CHAPTER XI.

"HE did," Magdalen exclaimed indignantly,—almost passionately for one of her composed manner. "He told me so in this very room."

"And what if he did, Maggy?" was the reply of the person to whom Miss Hill addressed herself. "Did you expect him to tell you so in the church-porch, or in front of the village-inn? If you have curates here, you must expect them to make love to you. It stands to reason."

This conversation took place one May morning in the antique drawing-room of The Casements. Magdalen Hill was sitting at her perpetual hard labour of illuminating select martyrologies on vellum; and her sole companion was a lady of about her own age, who, in certainly an easy if not elegant posture, reclined in a large arm-chair just opposite to Miss Hill's working-table, and contemplated, with that complacent interest which only habitual laziness can give, the delicate and minute pursuit in which the other was engaged.

The lady was young—a year in advance of Magdalen perhaps, and although not beautiful, comely to look upon. She had more than what is termed "a tendency to *embonpoint*," for she was decidedly plump, tottering on the verge of corpulence, so to speak. Now of fat girls there are several varieties. There is your fat baby-girl, a delightful little dumpling of a child, every one of whose dimples is a mine of delight, and every one of the creases in whose rosy limbs inspires you with an irresistible propensity to tickle it. These are the little baby-children that Rubens painted so gloriously. He made their little puffed-out cheeks celestially roseate; he curled their flaxen locks like unto the young tendrils of the vine; he tipped their little heels and elbows with rich carnations; he

K

took away their sex, and made them epicene; and when he had added little wings of green and golden plumage to their shoulders, they were no longer baby-children, but angels, ministering in the apotheoses of kings and emperors, who, I sincerely trust, have reached the destination which the courtly pencil of Peter Paul ascribed to their dead majesties. Then there is your fat school-girl, with long, fair ringlets, profuse as a Louis-Quatorze perruque, with fixed blue eyes that remind you unpleasantly of the Pantheon Bazaar and Madame Montanari's wax-work shop, and with a dull, listless fixity of demeanour that makes one always wish to find out whereabouts the string is, in order to pull it, and cause the eyes to move and the great doll to squeak "pa-pa" and "ma-ma." Yet another variety of the fat school-girl is there in the romp, or "tom-boy," who has cheeks as ruddy and as hard as a Ribstone pippin; who is continually grazing the skin off her arms, and tearing the trimming off the ends of her trousers; who, if she lives in the country, is in the habit of catching young colts, and riding them without saddle or bridle round paddocks; who is always getting into domestic trouble through her transactions with a big black dog fond of the water and of chivying cats; who is always laughing, has a tremendous appetite, and once fought with a Boy and came off victorious. The decline of the old-fashioned system of education, and the rise of seminaries and collegiate institutions, where young ladies attend lectures on the Od force and the Therapeutic Cosmogony of Ancient Art, has made the tom-boy fat girl an exceedingly rare specimen of femininity; but she is still occasionally to be met with—notably in Westmore-land boarding-schools, and in farm-houses of the West. I lament the progressive extinction of the merry fat girl. She usually grew up to be a jolly, comfortable matron, with a tribe of sunny children, all as great romps as she had been. Her pickled wal-nuts were perfection. She was one of those admirable women who always give you something to eat when you call upon them, and if you are neither hungered nor athirst, insist on your carry-ing away a pot of preserves or a slice of bride-cake with you. It was in the golden age, and England was merry England indeed, when those fat matrons who had been fat girls flourished. They used to entertain you at "meat teas"—bounteous repasts, where there were sausages and pressed beef, soused mackerel, and potato-cakes.

The fat young lady need not have been a fat child. Some are of the lean kind in early girlhood, and fall into fatness as others fall into love. The Germans are the most prolific in fat young ladies. Their names are Ermengarde, Hilda, Dorothea. Their eyes are blue, but not doll-like, for they are full of sentiment. They call each other "*Du*," and continuously embroider cigar-cases, tobacco-pouches, nay, carpet-bags even, for officers in the Grand-Duke's army, or students of the university of Katzelstein. They sit and sigh, and carve Ludolf or Heinrich's names on the bark of linden-trees. They write pretty little sonnets to the sky and the birds in fat albums bound in blue watered silk. They make little sketches in coloured crayons, representing Körner going to the wars, the Fahnenwacht keeping his lonely watch, and not daring to name the lady of his love. They wish they were not quite so fat; but they are above drinking vinegar to make themselves thin. Perhaps they eat a little too much. They, too, marry, and have prodigious families; but they don't become jolly. They go through life with a meek smile of placid resignation, eating plentifully, and reading many novels. "Elle a peaucoup zouffert, Matame la Paronne, tans le temps," tawny-moustached Captain Kalbsfleich whispers to you at the *table-d'hôte*. You look at "Matame la Paronne," and see that she has got very well through two courses, and is making a vigorous onslaught on the third,—let us say of stewed trout and maca-roons, hot roast-veal and raspberry-jam, or some equally anomalous German dish,—and find it difficult to persuade yourself that the Baroness has ever suffered from anything more serious than indigestion.

The lady who sat in the great arm-chair opposite Magdalen Hill by no means belonged to the sentimental or to the doll-like category of stout young ladies. Far more probable that ten years before she had belonged to the order of tom-boys; indeed, it may be as well to make a clean breast of it at once, and avow that, at fourteen years of age, there had never been a franker, merrier, or noisier hoyden than the Honourable Lætitia Salusbury. She was an only child; that may have had something to do with it. The lady her mother—a meek woman, who was frightened at mice, and firmly believed in the Apparition of Mrs. Veal, as related by Daniel Defoe—had died during her infancy, which may have had more to do with it. At all events, Letitia grew up through childhood petted, caressed, and humoured in every caprice, and if she was not spoiled herself, she spoiled, at least, innumerable frocks, pinafores, pairs of socks, and garden-hats. To enumerate the panes of glass fractured by this young lady, the lustres, china monsters, rare tea-cups, irrevocably smashed; the dolls she dismembered ; the injuries she did to marqueterie tables and costly carpets ; and the immense benefit she conferred on the bookselling trade by destroying every book that came within her reach, and so increasing the consumption of juvenile literature—would be a task as wearisome as to learn the annual speeches on the Army and Navy Estimates by heart, throwing in the Chancellor of the Exchequer's financial statement by way of epilogue. She condescended to learn very little, but what she did learn she learned very well. She was the bane, terror, and despair of eight successive governesses, native and foreign ; but she took a fancy to the Swordsley curate who stammered, and actually went through the Latin Accidence with him. Her indulgent papa, after vainly explaining to her that it was necessary for a young lady of her high station to attain some proficiency in the Continental languages, in music, and in drawing, despatched her to a Parisian *pensionnat*. After an enforced sojourn of three years, equally irksome to parent and child, Letitia returned to Swordsley a very fair French scholar. Of her drawing, it may be sufficient to say that she had a particular aptitude for sketching horses and dogs ; but as to music, I am afraid that her progress had not extended farther than enabled her to whistle sundry lively airs familiar to the youth of Paris, and to join in the chorus of numerous convivial melodies, of which the wonder was to know where she had picked them up. It is certain, however, that she had publicly diswigged the dancing-master at the establishment of Madame Givry de la Roncière in the Champs Elysées ; that she had organised numerous hot suppers in the dormitory, the preparation of one of which surreptitious banquets had nearly set the school on fire ; and that she had blown up the bust of the sainted

M. de Fénélon, Archbishop of Cambrai, which stood in the
garden, with gunpowder. She was the delight of her school-
fellows; but the diswigged dancing-master called her "*une belle
mégère.*" Madame Givry de la Roncière bore with her eccentricities, for the quarterly bills sent to her papa, and so punctually
settled by his solicitor at St. Becketsbury, were very large, and
made her a valuable pupil; but after the departure of the
Honourable Miss Salusbury, the much-suffering schoolmistress
spoke of her privately, only as "*cette petite diablesse,*" and in
public, warned her flock against the example of "*la conduite
inconcevablement dévergondée d'une demoiselle que la convenance
m'empêche de nommer.*"

The Honourable Letitia had, as a child, always had her own
way; and she was not likely to abandon it on coming to woman's
estate. Her papa was very old, and adored her. She returned
all his love with interest, but that did not hinder her from tyran-
nising over him in a manner quite as good-natured as it was
arbitrary. She had been, at school, and with the exception of her
brief probation under the curate who stammered, a very close
imitation of a dunce; but on her return to England she began
to read with much avidity. The bent of her literary studies was
peculiar. She had a healthy scorn for French romances, and
esteemed them all, from beginning to end, as so much vicious
humbug. The historians, essayists, and moralists, whose bulky
tomes graced the morocco-valanced shelves of her father's library,
she classed, generically, as "old fogies," and she kept fishhooks
in a very splendidly bound copy of Elegant Extracts. Nor did
our English three-volume novels, mainly relating to the cultivation of the affections among the upper classes of society, please
her any more than the little *brochures*, full of paper poison, which
are so plentiful in Paris. "Trash," "rubbish," and "rigmarole"
the Honourable Letitia Salusbury called the staple products of
the circulating library at St. Becketsbury. But, for the enlivening works of Captain Marryat and the other nautical novelists,
and for the *Ingoldsby Legends*, Miss Salusbury took an immense
liking. She had the dreadful heresy to declare all poetry—
except it was "funny"—a bore; but she luxuriated in the
perusal of Nimrod's Sporting Sketches. She yawned over Sir

Walter Scott, and intimated her opinion that Diana Vernon was
a designing minx, who only put on a riding-habit to hook Frank
Osbaldistone; but I much fear that she had heard of a work
written by the late Mr. Pierce Egan, and called *Boxiana*. It
is terrible to tell, but the Honourable Letitia Salusbury was an
assiduous student of *Ruff's Guide to the Turf* and the *Racing
Calendar*. You see that I wish to extenuate nothing of her
faults; but in order that nothing may be set down in malice concerning her, I must, while admitting that she did shoot, fish,
hunt, drive,—tandem occasionally,—and bet, deny in the most
unqualified manner what has been averred by the malevolent,
viz. that the Honourable Letitia Salusbury smoked cigars and
drank brandy-and-water. As to her conversation, you will be
enabled to judge of its tenor; and as to another accusation which
has been brought against her, of swearing, you may be sure that,
if Miss Salusbury did now and then rap out an ugly word, I shall
always, for good manners' sake, suppress it.

I say that she was not beautiful, but was still comely to look
upon. She had great flashing brown eyes and a quantity of
vagrant brown hair, which was ordinarily thrust into a net, or
tumbled off her forehead anyhow. She had a great deal too much
colour—at least, of that colour which is not sold by the per-
fumers, and that won't rub off. Her mouth would have been
handsome had it been a little smaller. Her teeth were very
white, but they were large and square. Her nose wavered
between the mild *retroussé* and the decided snub. But her
whole face beamed with candour, happiness, and good-nature, and
these amply redeemed the irregularity of her features. Her
figure, for all its plumpness, was graceful and supple, and she was
as agile as a squirrel. Nobody could precisely say that Miss
Salusbury was masculine, although she delighted and excelled in
most of the pursuits and the exercises of men. No; she was *not*
masculine, and yet she had, it must be confessed, something of the
Amazon of the Cirque about her, with a more considerable
admixture of a good-looking milkmaid. It is very improper to
say so. No doubt it is unpardonable to unveil a heroine who,
albeit she was a peer's daughter, frequently spoke of money as
"tin," of a carriage as a "trap," of a gentleman as a "fellow."

She could not help it, she said, when remonstrated with by Magdalen. It was her way. There was no harm in it, and she hated humbug. So, as it was her way, there was but one course open, and that was to let her have it.

I have hinted that the papa of this young lady, who knew quite as much about horses, dogs, rats, and badgers as one of her own grooms, was a peer of the realm. You may take down your peerage and look for Chalkstonehengist (Viscount). Jehan de Salusbury did good service at Agincourt. Sir Mulciber Salusbury, of Chalkstonehengist, was summoned as a baron to Henry the Eighth's first parliament. The Salusburys fought on the King's side during the civil wars, and the possessor of the title was made a Viscount at the Restoration. " *Le roy, la foy, la loy,*" was the Salusbury motto. The Lord Chalkstonehengist, regnant, was a very old gentleman, born while the American War was at its hottest. He was the most consistent, but the mildest and most benevolent, of Tories of the old school. He spoke of the Reform Bill as "that grievous error in legislation," and of the Reformers as "gentlemen who hold the pernicious doctrines of Mr. Hunt and Mr. Cobbett." A bitter Tory lord held his proxy, for Lord Chalkstonehengist seldom made his appearance in the senate-house. He wore a blue coat and brass buttons, low-crowned white hat and top-boots. He had not forgotten his scholarship, and the composition of Latin verses sometimes served to while away an odd hour. It was even said that he had been engaged for years in writing a history of the American War, in which the Stamp Act was incontrovertibly defended, and Mr. Washington very hardly dealt by. Until years and infirmities had overtaken him, he had been an enthusiast in the sports of the field; and it was with an irrepressible pleasure, mingled with an odd sensation that the thing wasn't exactly proper, that he heard of the daring deeds of his daughter, in riding 'cross country, leaping gates and clearing ditches. For Miss Salusbury was in all respects a worthy descendant of the old monastic huntress, Dame Juliana Berners; and, from her own practical experience, could have capped the sporting wisdom of the noble lady who wrote

> " Wheresoever ye fare by fryth or by fell
> My dere chylde take heede how Trystram do you tell
> How manie manere bestys of veneric there were,
> Lysten to youre dame, and she shalle you lere :
> Four maner bestys of veneric there are,——
> The fyrst of them the harte, the second is the hare ;
> The boore is one of tho : the wulfe and not one more "

—only, Dame Letitia Salusbury would have taken away the "boore" and the "wulfe," and added the fox.

Father and daughter lived pleasantly and comfortably enough in their old house on the older estate of Chalkstonehengist, about a mile and a quarter from The Casements. Lord Chalkstonehengist was not very rich, but had enough and to spare. His high Tory predilections did not prevent him from being kind, hospitable, and benevolent, to his neighbours, to his tenants, and to the poor. As a landlord he was of the most liberal, and, although he preserved his game in moderation, never refused a farmer a day's shooting. As a magistrate he was of the most merciful. They used to tell a story of one Giles Conybeare, an incorrigible poacher, who was brought before his lordship sitting in petty sessions. It was about the twenty-fifth time that Giles had so fallen into trouble for wilful contravention of the Game Laws. His lordship put on his sternest expression of countenance, which at the worst was but dove-like. "Here again, Giles Conybeare," he thundered, or at least tried to thunder. "Were I your lordship, I should make an example of him," whispered the clerk. "Yes," answered the noble magistrate, "an example, certainly—an example must be made of Giles Conybeare." "For the sake of the public," whispered the clerk. "For the sake of the public," his lordship repeated. The wretched Giles began to blubber. He could not deny that he had been taken red-handed, with one pocket full of hares, and the other full of springes; but he pleaded his grandmother bedridden with the "rheumatiz," his own want of employment, his large family. For Giles was a philoprogenitive poacher, and had no less than eleven children. "It makes his offence worse," murmured the clerk *sotto voce.* "All this only aggravates your offence, prisoner," said his lordship aloud ; and he went on to tell the captive that he ought to be hanged, that he ought to be transported; that he was a disgrace to the village, to the estate, to the country, and so forth. Wurzel, the steward, inclined his head towards the bench, and delivered a pitiable character of Giles from behind his hand. The prisoner could only continue to blubber, to wring his handcuffed hands, and to talk about his bedridden grandmother and his eleven children.

"This must be put a stop to," continued his lordship, glancing with benign severity at the culprit. " I'll—no, I won't. How many children did he say he had? Eleven! Ah, dear me! And his grandmother bedridden, too. And no work. Ah! poor fellow. I—*I'll give him a pig.* Wurzel, give him a pig," quoth Lord Chalkstonehengist, throwing himself back in his arm-chair. You may understand from this that his lordship was not unlikely to be a somewhat indulgent parent.

"And what answer did you return to this lovelorn swain?" said Miss Salusbury, breaking a somewhat irksome silence which had ensued.

" I told him," Magdalen replied, " that I should feel it my duty to acquaint my brother—I mean Ernest—with his conduct, if he presumed to repeat it."

" Well, that wasn't very encouraging; but it's an answer that may cut both ways. Appeals to one's brother may mean anything. Don't you remember the story of the young lady in Australia—I should like to go to Australia—who wrote just this in a book, and left it, quite by accident of course, in the way of a bashful swain, 'If he doesn't propose to-morrow, I'll get my brother to thrash him?' "

" I must beg you, Miss Salusbury—" interrupted Magdalen, looking up from her work—

" I must beg you, my dear Maggy," retorted the daughter of the House of Chalkstonehengist, " to remember that there is nothing, after all, so wonderful in the conduct of Mr. Pendragon. He is a gentleman of good family, and although he is only a curate now, why, bless us, he may be made Archbishop of Canterbury some fine morning."

" He had the miserable vanity to tell me as much. He vaunted his poverty, and said that he would hew steps out of the rock of knowledge, whereby to mount to fame and fortune."

"I think I've heard that before," Miss Salusbury remarked with semi-gravity. "It sounds like poetry. I hope it isn't; for I hate poetry, except when it's jolly; and I should be sorry if Pendragon turned out a humbug. Did you ever hear the 'Ratcatcher's Daughter,' Maggy? I made Willy Goldthorpe sing it to me the last time he came over from St. Becketsbury."

It is scarcely necessary to say that Lord Chalkstonehengist's daughter was an immense favourite with young men, both of sporting tendency and the military profession, who voted Lady Talmash a dragon, and Magdalen Hill a snowball. She was declared to be a stunner, a screamer, an out-and-outer,—all kinds of superlatives of admiration were applied to her. She was perfectly frank and unrestrained with the young men. They would have liked to elect her an honorary member of the cavalry mess at St. Becketsbury. At the cover-side her gray riding-habit, and the red feather in her cap, were as well known as Lord Chalkstonehengist's white pony,—he could not follow the hounds now, but liked to see the meet and chat with his neighbours,—or as Farmer Turmut's big brown horse with the star on his forehead. She tolerated smoking after permission had been asked; but woe betide the luckless wight who lit his cigar without leave being granted, or who by word or deed took a liberty with the Honourable Letitia Salusbury! An unhappy cornet, raw to the service, was once rash enough to chaff her, whereupon the daughter of Chalkstonehengist pulled his ears till they were as crimson as his sash, flung his undress cap out of window, and bade him follow it, or she would make him, she added significantly. You could not take a liberty with her, although she did know the "Ratcatcher's Daughter," and had besides an astounding répertoire of ballads and melodies more popular than refined. The Onzeport hounds met near St. Becketsbury, and Letitia rode regularly to them. There had come down a certain celebrated sportswoman— who but the famous Miss Southbank indeed!—who sometimes hunted other animals besides hares and foxes. She thought it would be capital fun to engage the eccentric daughter of Lord Chalkstonehengist in conversation. Up rode the dashing Southbank, splendid in a scarlet riding-habit, spatter-dashed with patent leather, with the big diamond horseshoe given to her by Lord Racquetborough, just previous to his insolvency, at her throat, and the riding-whip with the emerald handle presented to her by that well-known sporting blade, Charley Pettycash, who kept so many race-horses, theatres, and dancers, who spent so many thousands a year, and who, when he was transported for life for his innumerable forgeries, turned out to have been all along a clerk in a bank with 150*l*. a year salary. Up rode the Southbank, saucy and radiant, on her noted black mare "Shiny Face." I wonder the horse had not a jewelled surcingle. His mistress was always covered with splendour, and jewels, and shame; and every one of her gewgaws had some history of sin or of folly connected with it. The Southbank presumed to "pass the time of day" to Miss Salusbury, and to ask her whether she meant to put the pot on for the Metropolitan? Letitia started back so as nearly to throw her steed on his haunches, and, trembling with passion, made this reply, "You are an abandoned hussy. I know all about you; and if you dare to speak to me again, I'll cut your wicked face in two with my whip." The Southbank was not very remarkable for placidity of temper, but she was somehow cowed as much by Miss Salusbury's manner as by the matter of her answer. She rode away quite crest-fallen, and at the Ouzeport hounds was seen no more. She alluded subsequently to Letitia as an "uppish party," but without bitterness. The Southbank was sensible. Of course the blame of having incited her to address Letitia was laid at the door of Puffin, the wretched cornet, who had had his ears pulled. She vainly denied the charge; but it did not much matter. Some months afterwards that well-remembered and eccentric captain of dragoons, Lord Snowstorm, having rendered Puffin's life a burden to him by cutting up hair-brushes in his bed, filling his boots with coal-tar, charging his cigars with moistened gunpowder, corking his face, and shaving off one of his whiskers, the cornet's mamma indignantly interfered, and caused her darling to sell his commission, and quit the wicked, depraved service, just after Lord Snowstorm had been turned out of it by the Commander-in-Chief.

Letitia and Magdalen were very good friends; but the intimacy was one-sided. William the dragoon was a favourite with the Amazon, and she extended her fondness to Miss Hill; drove over two or three times to see her, invited her to Chalkstonehengist much oftener than Miss Hill chose to come, and persisted in calling her Maggy. But the haughty illuminator never went beyond " Miss Salusbury " in addressing her.

The subject of the curate was anything but an agreeable one; but Letitia, for some capricious reason of her own, continued to press it.

" Well," she went on. " He did repeat his ' conduct,' as you call it, didn't he ? "

" He wrote," Magdalen replied, with cold severity.

" And you—"

" Returned his letter. More than that, I felt it my duty to carry out my threat. I made my brother—I made Ernest acquainted with the affair."

" In other words, you tried to get this poor curate the sack," the unaffected Letitia remarked. " That wasn't very kind-hearted of you, Maggy. And what did the reverend say ? "

" He agreed with me that I was not to be insulted with impunity."

" Insulted ! where's the insult ? "

" Miss Salusbury ! " Magdalen exclaimed in proud surprise, and with a positive blush on her pale face.

" Miss Hill ! " the other rejoined, mimicking her. " Dear Maggy," she continued, "you are a good girl, after all, although you are as proud as a dog with two tails,"—whence the Honourable Miss Salusbury gathered her prolific collection of similes was always a matter of intense surprise. " What great offence has Pendragon committed ? You are both young. He is a clergyman and a gentleman. You are a lady. Surely you can strike a balance between High Church and Low Church. You can't go on for ever moping here, and grizzling about that poor dear Hugh Goldthorpe."

" You forget my position," Magdalen said, in a sad low voice.

" Well, I do perhaps. I forgot that you had a fortune. But what does that matter ? Is Pendragon the first man who has

wanted to marry a rich woman?   Don't you remember the old
lines?

> " 'Cloth of frize, be not too bold
>   If thou art match'd with cloth of gold:
>   Cloth of gold, do not despise
>   If thou art match'd with cloth of frize.'

Besides," she added, " I don't think that Bruin is mercenary after
all."

" No, indeed," quoth Magdalen, half to herself.

" Then why not have him.   Better to be a curate's wife than a
lonely spinster, painting away at those everlasting saints and
martyrs with their heads on one side, and worrying yourself about
High Church and Low Church and Ernest Goldthorpe, who would
be a good fellow enough if he didn't wear swanshot in his shoes,
and live on pickled eggs and boiled soda-water."

Again, and at the mention of the rector's name, Magdalen
blushed.   " I declare," continued Miss Salusbury, " that if Bruin
asked me, I'd marry him myself, and beg papa to get him made
something better than a curate; though for the matter of that, I
think Pendragon would do best in the Life Guards.   I'm getting
tired of the life I lead.   It's very jolly, but it's lonely.   I don't
seem to know where I'm going.   I suppose nobody does.   Sometimes, when I'm reading *Bell's Life*, I seem to fancy that I should
like to be a man.   They have a good many advantages over us,
those men.   Why can't I play at nurr and spell, and walk a
thousand miles in a thousand hours?   Why can't I match my
novice to fight any man in England, bar the ' Mumper'—who is
the Mumper?—at catch-weight for a hundred pounds a side?
Why can't I show toy-dogs?   or patronise the noble sport of
ratting?   or frequent the Bendigo's Head, where *Boxiana* is kept
at the bar, and gloves are always ready for the convenience of
gentlemen?   Why can't I go to the festive board, where harmony
prevails, and the eccentric Joey Jones is in the chair?   Who is
Joey Jones, and why is he eccentric, and called Joey? and is he a
broker's man, that he is always taking the chair?   I should like
to be a man.   No; I should like to be a Bloomer, or Dr. Elizabeth
Johnson, or Madame Ida Pfeiffer, and travel the whole world
over; or Richard Carr, the female sailor.   What a brick Grace

Darling was? I wonder whether Joan of Arc's armour hurt her.
I tried on one of the old helmets in our hall the other day, and
had a frightful headache for hours afterwards. Perhaps the best
thing to do would be to marry somebody."

"I think so too," responded Magdalen, glancing with solemn
pity at this misguided young woman.

"The difficulty is to find somebody. The daughter and heiress
of Lord Chalkstonehengist can't go to the barracks at St. Becketts-
bury, and say, Messieurs of the dragoons, or gentlemen of the
Onzeport hunt, will you marry me? I can't pickle and I can't
preserve. I can't play and I can't sing, but I can leap a five-
barred gate, make the best flies in Kent, and shoot a trout in the
water. Heigho!"

"Truly, the daughter of Lord Chalkstonehengist could not do
this; but might she not find pursuits more in keeping with her
rank in life, and to that which society expects from her?"

"Society is all humbug," cried the Honourable Miss Salusbury,
in something like a passion; "and I've tried all the pursuits in
keeping with my rank in life, and they're all botheration."

"There remains marriage as a resource open to you; and surely,
if the gentleman in whom you take so great an interest—"

"Pickles!" exclaimed the Honourable Miss Salusbury. Her
expletives were positively unprecedented in lack of refinement.
"My honest persuasion is, that if I let Pendragon know that I
liked him, he would calmly tell me that he didn't want to have
anything to say to me. I know the man. Besides, I was but
jesting about him. He is and can be nothing to me. You know
that he is over head and ears in love with you, Maggy; and cold
and angry with him as you seem, I can't help fancying—"

"It is too late," said Magdalen, poising her brush, and resolutely
driving a spike into the bosom of a martyr on the vellum before
her. "Ernest knows all. He was justly shocked and indignant.
He summoned Mr. Pendragon before him. High words passed
between them only yesterday; and I believe that Mr. Pendragon
will shortly leave this part of the country."

"Then, I'm very sorry for it; and the fat's all in the fire,"
Miss Salusbury remarked, and rising in dudgeon. "I shall go
home to lunch; will you come? I've got the trap and the two

piebalds on the lawn. St. Gengulphus the Great can wait a couple of hours for his eyebrows," she concluded, glancing in great disdain at the spiked martyr.

Magdalen sadly shook her head, and declined the offer.

"Then I'm off. Good-bye, Maggy. Why don't you turn nun, or Sister of Charity, or something of that sort? You might be a martyr then yourself, without the trouble of painting whole armies of them on parchment. Bye, bye."

"A nun or a Sister of Charity," repeated Magdalen, when, having coldly returned the good-natured shake of the hand which her easily-pacified friend had proffered her, the door had closed upon the Honourable Miss Salusbury. "A nun or a Sister of Charity! why not, indeed?" And she went on very carefully and deliberately marking in the eyebrows of St. Gengulphus the Great.

"Poor Pendragon!"

Who said "poor Pendragon?" Letitia Salusbury or Magdalen Hill? You see the words are between inverted commas, so the exclamation can't be mine.

The Amazon's "trap," a pretty little phaeton, with two prettier piebald ponies, and a diminutive groom in gray-and-black livery, and perhaps the tiniest buckskins and top-boots ever seen since the visit of General Tom Thumb to this country, awaited their mistress on the lawn before The Casements. Letitia was very anxious before she took the reins, and settled herself on the high cushion of the vehicle, to know if Twitters had had his beer. Twitters was the Lilliputian groom; and he, smacking his lips, made answer that he had had a pint of the right sort, but that it might have been a trifle older. Miss Salusbury delighted in this Twitters. He was so charmingly wicked, she said. He was, indeed, a most precocious imp. He betted; his talk was essentially "horsy;" he was the proprietor of a terrier which could be backed to kill a maximum of rats in a minimum of minutes, and which had been favourably noticed in the sporting journals; and when his mistress was at a loss for a line in the "Ratcatcher's Daughter," she would turn round to Twitters and seek his infallible aid.

Chalkstonehengist was towards St. Becketsbury, and thither the

Amazon drove at a smart trot. Just where another road turns off in the direction of Tiburnhurst is a blackened and jagged stump of timber; and here, according to the legend, once stood the gibbet where, a hundred and fifty years ago, had swung in a grisly apparatus of chains the corpse of an atrocious murderer. By this spot of ill omen there stood a short, broad-shouldered man with his arms folded. He raised his hat, and, with a grim bow, would have turned down the Tiburnhurst road, but for the adjuration of "Hillo there!" by which Miss Salusbury commanded him to stop.

"Why, it's Pendragon," she cried. "Come over to the house and have some lunch. Don't stand staring there, man, like a stuck pig. Get in."

No other young lady in the neighbourhood would have dared to ask a clergyman to enter the phaeton which she was driving; and had any dared to do so the pendulum of scandal would have so incessantly wagged between Swordsley and St. Becketsbury, that one might have thought the perpetual motion had been discovered. But Miss Salusbury frankly owned that she did not care one brass farthing for public opinion, and that she would do what she liked when she liked. There was perhaps some consideration due to what might be said concerning the curate's acceptance of the proposition ; but ladies who do as they like are not much in the habit of considering the interests of other people. At any other time, Ruthyn Pendragon would have felt bound to decline the invitation. As it was, perhaps for sundry good reasons of his own, he chose to accept it now, and took his seat beside Miss Salusbury. As he said never a word, that young lady chose to inform him that he was as "grumpy" as ever. Then she adjured the piebalds to "come up." Then she entered into a short conversation with Twitters relative to a new collar for Betty the near piebald, and the propriety of putting a kicking-strap on Harlequin the off one; —he was vicious when separated from his companion—when she drove him in the tax-cart. For the Honourable Letitia delighted in driving a neat vehicle under duty, on the conspicuous sides of which were painted the style and titles of Lancelot Brian De Crux Salusbury, Viscount Chalkstonehengist, of Chalkstonehengist, Kent.

They reached the house, and had lunch; the Amazon proving

by ocular demonstration that she had a keen appetite for game-pie, and fully understood the flavour of old Madeira. Then she took the curate to her own little boudoir, with the carved oak fittings and the walls hung with antlers, brushes, guns, fishing-rods, eel-spears, whips, spurs, and similar sporting gear.

"We don't allow pipes here," she said quite gravely, and without the slightest touch of irony. "Papa even objected to Mr. Neilgherry's hubble-bubble. You know;—the yellow man who was so long in India, and talks about pig-sticking and tiger-hunting so well, though every other word he says is a crammer, I do believe. You can have a cigar, if you like; but, for my part, I think they make the curtains smell much worse than pipes do. Mrs. Major Kanaster at St. Becketsbury says so too."

Pendragon, who had not spoken ten words since he entered the house, respectfully declined the cigar. He had definitively given up smoking, he said.

"Is there anything else you have given up," asked Letitia, in a dry voice.

"I am going away," he said, for all explanation.

"Then you've had a quarrel"—she was nearly saying a "row" —"with the reverend."

"It is so," he answered, bowing his head sadly.

"Where are you going?"

"To London."

"What to do?" It is melancholy to have to record it, but Letitia was within an ace of asking "what's your game?"

"To work."

"That's right," said the heiress. "I only wish I could work at something. And so you are going. Poor old Pendragon. Poor old fellow. I know all about it. Give us your hand."

She held out her honest palm and left it in the curate's grasp, while he pressed it long and cordially. He looked in her face, and saw nothing in that wild, wilful face but truth and generosity. He would have liked to have kissed her.

"You are a good woman," he murmured, going towards the door. "God bless you."

"Stop," cried Letitia hastily; "London's a long way off, Pen-

L

dragon, and the pigs have left off running ready roasted through the streets. Do you want any money ?"

" I have enough and to spare," the curate made answer, after expressing his gratitude for the offer.

" Well, if you ever do want any money," she resumed, "write to me, under cover to papa. You *will* go ? Well, good bye, Pendragon."

She gave him her hand again, and again he pressed it and departed. She watched him long from her window striding towards the spot where she had met him. When his form had disappeared, she took up a book —it was Strutt's *Sports and Pastimes*,—and tried to read, but the letters danced before her eyes, and she flung the volume down. Then she took up a parchment portfolio and ran through her collection of salmon flies, gorgeous in pheasants' feathers and yellow floss silk and golden wire. And then she threw herself into a chair, and burst into a passionate fit of weeping.

" A good cry always does me good when I've got the blues," she said, drying her eyes. "Poor Pendragon! I wish I was a man, or a dressmaker, or a charwoman, or a fairy, or anything else that would enable me to help him ; but it's no good ; and now I think I'll go and see how Brindle gets on." Brindle was the newest-imported Alderney calf in the byre, and the Honourable Miss Salusbury forthwith proceeded to inspect him.

As for the curate, he walked passed the old gibbet stump and past The Casements, towards whose glancing windows he never looked, and to his lodgings in Swordsley village. His rent was paid. His chattels had already been sent to St. Becketsbury Station, and thence to one farther up the line towards London. He purposed to reach the station by a circuitous route of about eight miles. There was no leave-taking to be got through. He had strictly enjoined his landlady to keep his departure a secret for at least twenty minutes after he was clear of the town ; and the good woman, who loved him, promised to obey. Words of hot displeasure, of furious wrath, had passed between him and Ernest. Each had said things which he would gladly have recalled. It was too late now. The notice he might have demanded had been foregone by mutual consent. The curate was paid the balance of his wages, and was free to go wheresoever he listed.

The station he was bound for was Tiburnhurst; but by a long walk round he could reach it without retracing his steps and passing The Casements again. He had to leave the Church of St. Mary-la-Douce, which lay at the back of the village, to his left. He halted as he wound round the grassy knoll on whose summit the timeworn fabric stood.

"In that grey and crumbling fane," the curate murmured low, as with arms folded he gazed long and earnestly at the church, "I have prayed and I have preached, when my lord the rector would grant me his high permission. There I have married, and buried, and christened. There is no grave in that yard that holds a corpse more dead than I am to that which I once was. And my lord rector and my lady Magdalen have trampled on the wretched curate, have they? Old Church," he finished, raising his right hand almost menacingly, "the struggle is henceforth between you and me."

And so Ruthyn Pendragon turned his face away from the Church of England, and went on his journey, whitherwards he deemed best. And I have heard a wise man say that what is said to be done for Conscience' sake is often done for spite.

CHAPTER XII

It was on a Tuesday in the month of May, 1851; and Mr. Sims, having business to transact in Coger's Inn, Strand, betook himself thither at about ten o'clock on a sunshiny morning. He eyed those who passed him, as was his wont, narrowly; yet he seemed with his bent-down eyes to be occupied in counting the number of iron plates in the pavement that covered the coal-holes. It should be mentioned that Mr. Sims was accustomed to wear a broad-brimmed hat, which was convenient for many reasons, and that his eyes possessed the faculty of looking round corners.

Sixteen months, or thereabouts, had elapsed since we last had the pleasure of meeting Mr. Sims; and he was then going to the play. He was bent on the same errand now, although the theatres do not usually open their doors at ten o'clock in the morning. But the whole of human life was a play to Mr. Sims, and he was always, to use a Gallicism, "assisting" at the representations of the Theatre Royal Humanity. He did not care to be a conspicuous actor on the noisy stage thereof. He was content to be Signor N. N., *non nominato*, as the Opera play-bills call the illustrious incogniti who, in a bar and a half of recitative, announce that the coach is at the door, or that the fatal hour has arrived. Or rather he liked to be prompter, or to have the care of the trap-door department, or to stand patiently at the wing with a pan of blue fire, waiting to light up the last scene with a lurid glare.

Time had not thinned the flowing locks of Mr. Sims. He had none that flowed for the Great Gleaner to operate upon. Nature had provided him with a close-set and spiky black caul of hair much resembling a horsehair cushion. Time had inserted, since January '50, a few thousand spikes of rusty grey among the sable stubble, and on the crown of his head had mown a little circular tonsure quite bald. His nose was a little more peaked, and a trifle more purple in hue, and that was all.

Mr. Sims came from the west, and set his watch by the Horse Guards. The watch very much resembled the model of a potato in silver, and the disc which prudent housewives sometimes slice off that esculent, to allow the steam to escape while boiling, was represented by the dial. It had belonged to a railway engine-driver, and to it was attached a history. At the corner of St. Martin's Lane it is on record that Mr. Sims purchased a penny-worth of apples. There is nothing so very strange in this fact; but it may be just hinted that Mr. Sims entered into a somewhat lengthy conversation with the fruit-seller, who was an Irishwoman of the purest growth, and earned a considerable addition to her weekly income by colouring cutty pipes for gentlemen whose heads were too weak to allow them to swallow about an ounce of nicotine every day. A clean pipe, half a pound of the strongest tobacco, half-a-crown, and a week's fair smoking, given to Biddy McGrath, and she would colour a cutty for you as black as my hat.

"Five times within a fortnight, eh?" said Mr. Sims, as he turned down King William Street. "For watching closely, and never losing a minute, there's nothing like an apple-woman. She never moves, and nobody suspects her. For following, give me an orange-girl." So you see that Mr. Sims did business even as he walked.

In Mid-Strand Mr. Sims held brief parley with a Hansom cabman, which ended in that charioteer giving him a ticket, receiving a shilling, laying his forefinger by the side of his nose, and driving on. Had Mr. Sims designed to take a drive anywhere, and had he suddenly changed his mind? At all events, he reached Coger's Inn on foot, and entering the open doorway of No. 20, mounted briskly to the third floor.

Coger's Inn is not in the Strand, but off it, and is about the dingiest, rottenest old inn of Chancery in the metropolis. It should have been pulled down a century since; but as, let out in tenements, it realises a considerable and tolerably safe annual rental, its proprietors—whoever they may be—have excellent reasons for allowing it to stand. The windows are never cleaned;

the staircases are never swept; the mangy old courtyard is never weeded or rolled. It is a sandy desert in fine weather, and a miry puddle in wet weather. It was a place of legal habitations once, but very few men of the law care to abide in it now. Its tenants are all cloudy and mysterious. They come nobody knows whence, and go nobody knows where. They have slips of foolscap pasted on their doors, saying that they will be " back in five minutes;" return in ten years, paste a fresh slip over the old one, saying that they will be " back in a quarter of an hour," and never return at all. Letters fall through the slits of the door, and moulder away there; cats die of starvation, and the crannies of lonely chambers are fusty with the skeletons of mice. It would be a bold flea that took up his quarters within those pinched precincts, thinking to live on the fat of the land, or of the lodgers, and hoping to drink his pint of blood a day like a gentleman. Coger's Inn was the very place to suit Mr. Sims, and for that reason he had chambers there.

The third-floor back, No. 20, had a huge outer door, which was a mass of knobs and staples, and iron bands and plates, and great cross-beams of oak. You might have murdered a man behind that door, and nobody on the staircase would have been the wiser for it; nor if, by holding the ear to the letter-slit, the screams of the dying man had been heard, could any one without a dozen sledge-hammers, or an engineer's petard, have burst the massive portal open. When Mr. Sims had reached this door, and produced his latch-key, he tapped one of the iron plates approvingly with that instrument, remarking, in a satisfied under-tone, that it (meaning the door) was uncommonly strong, and quiet, and safe. The key looked large enough to have fitted the great door of Newgate, and to it, by a piece of red tape, was attached a tiny little Chubb that might have opened a lady's portfolio or a pocket-ledger. Mr. Sims applied the big key, which made a noise of mingled ferocity and anger as it was turned twice or thrice round in the lock, and so passed into his chambers. It has been omitted to state, that in the midst of the mass of iron and oak forming the door was painted in faded white letters the name of " Filoe and Co." Whether Mr. Sims was Filoe and Co., or Filoe and Co. had once lived there, but had left the place a quarter of a century since, or the day before yesterday, is uncertain and immaterial.

There was an inner door, panelled, smooth, and knockerless, and with the minutest of keyholes, to which Mr. Sims applied his Chubb, and was fairly within his premises. He who was behind the smooth-panelled door might have seen that it was backed by one solid sheet of iron. "An Englishman's house is his castle," soliloquised Mr. Sims; "and, egad, I think Coger's Castle would stand a pretty strong siege."

Mr. Sims's chambers comprised three rooms, each with a single window, through whose infinitely dirty panes could be faintly descried an agreeable perspective of roofs and chimney-pots. For this was the third-floor back, and the background of Coger's Inn was Cadger's Market. The rooms were *en suite;* and as Mr. Sims stood at the first one he heard a great noise of scuffling and stamping, the clatter of some metallic substance, and the sound of a human voice crying,

"Saha! Saha! there! Come on, three, six, twelve of you! Come on, ye wolves! Buffalmacco the Ruthless never yields!"

Mr. Sims did not seem in the least disconcerted by this strange discourse, but entered the room, which was low and dusty, very bare of furniture, but, with what little there was, of a counting-house character; and in the centre of whose carpetless floor stood a tall youth about seventeen, marked with the small-pox, and endowed with a shock head of hair of the hue that may be called a fine sunset, inasmuch that it was flaming red. He was stamping very violently on the deal boards, and brandishing an old broadsword, and occasionally dealing a sounding thwack to an office-desk, adjuring some imaginary enemy, by the name of Spadacapo, to "come on."

"At it again, Buff," Mr. Sims tranquilly remarked. "Where are the letters, and has anybody called?"

"Buffalmacco the Ruthless," or Buff, as by default of any better name I must call him, was almost breathless with excitement and the broadsword exercise. He did not appear at all ashamed in being detected in his strange occupation, but, leaning on the hilt of his weapon, informed his master that there was a heap of letters in the next room, and that nobody had called

except the Gas, who had looked at the meter, and found they had
only burned eighteenpennyworth during the last quarter.

"And quite enough, too, Buff," Mr. Sims cheerfully remarked.
"When gas is given away, we will burn more of it. As I'm
going to be very busy for the next hour, you will oblige me by
suspending your infernal row during that period; after which, I
will see anybody who calls."

Mr. Sims passed through the second room, which was entirely
empty, unless a huge splash of ink in the middle of the floor
could be called furniture. He entered the third room, his own
private *sanctum*, and carefully locked the door, leaving, according
to his already-mentioned principle, the key therein. Buffalmacco the Ruthless, being temporarily prohibited from indulging
in the broadsword exercise, betook himself to his library, which,
in a very greasy, tattered, and coverless condition, stood on a
shelf by the window, and consisted of copies of the exciting dramas
of *The Castle Spectre*, *Jonathan Bradford*, and *The Iron Chest*,
an odd volume of the *Newgate Calendar*, the *Sam-Hall Songster*,
and sundry numbers of a thrilling romance entitled *Murder Castle ;
or, the Heads of the Headless*. Buff had commenced taking in
The Hatchet of Horror ; or, Love and Madness ; but he found
Murder Castle more attractive, and so dropped *The Hatchet*.

"An invaluable boy, that," Mr. Sims said, taking off his plain
black frock, and donning a dressing-gown of grey striped flannel.
"He lives in the realms of fancy and the Victoria Theatre. His
wages enable him to go four times a week to the upper gallery,
and he is happy. He could rob me if he liked very conveniently,
but he is scrupulously honest. So long as he has enough for the
gallery, thousands might pass through his hands without a penny
sticking to his fingers. I know it, for time out of mind I have
laid traps for him. Here's one, for instance." And from a
pyramid of at least two hundred and fifty penny-post letters Sims
turned up one, the seal of which he carefully broke, and, from
several thicknesses of paper in the envelope, took out twenty-four
postage-stamps. Mr. Sims had himself posted this letter to himself on the preceding afternoon; but he had been careful to have
the address written in a strange hand. He usually tried this
little manœuvre about four or five times every week, always

selecting a different handwriting, and had never found one of his letters miscarry.

"Here's another little test," muttered Mr. Sims as he opened another letter, and, peering anxiously into its enclosure, took forth, with the greatest caution, a human hair, which he held up for an instant to the light, and then blew away.

"Letters may be unsealed and resealed," thought Mr. Sims; "but if I tell my correspondent, by word of mouth, to pluck out one of his hairs and pop it into the envelope before he sends it, I don't think it very probable that a letter would be opened without the hair being displaced."

Mr. Sims said, luckily, none of this aloud, else Buffalmacco the Ruthless might by chance have heard the things he should not. Mr. Sims addressed himself to his own inner self, and hugged his secrets in his own secretive bosom. He continued opening letters until long past the hour of which he had spoken had expired, when a discreet tap was heard at the door, accompanied by a more discreet cough.

"What is it, Buff?" he asked, opening the door to the red-headed youth.

"She's here," the fencing clerk, if clerk he was, responded, and pointing with his thumb over his left shoulder.

"Phew!" and Mr. Sims gave utterance to a prolonged whistle. "Dear me, Mrs. Clapperton," he continued, pushing past Buff, and eagerly ushering a handsomely-attired lady into his sanctum, "to what may I ascribe the honour of this unexpected visit?"

He knew very well, did Mr. Sims, that the handsomely-attired lady's name was not Mrs. Clapperton. Perhaps Buffalmacco the Ruthless knew it quite as well; but it was the invariable practice with Mr. Sims never to address a client who called upon him by his or her proper name. It kept things so snug, he was wont to say. The handsomely-attired lady was a client of Mr. Sims, and her name was Mrs. Armytage. She was out of mourning, and looked prettier than ever.

"*Fait-il gros temps dans la chiourme?*" asked Mr. Sims,—what necessity was there for him to speak French?—when he had handed the lady to a chair, had locked the door and left the key inside. "Is it business? or is it on purely sentimental grounds that we are come to see our Sims, all in the morning early? Has the obdurate heart at Hoogendracht relented?"

"It is not that," replied Mrs. Armytage; "the heart you speak of is as hard, and I am as wretched as ever."

She looked more scared and terrified than she had done at the room in the hotel that night.

"Then there is a red lamp out; where is the danger?"

"I want five hundred pounds."

"Five hundred jars of pickled gherkins! Why, to my certain knowledge, ma'am, you had five thousand pounds at your banker's only yesterday."

"I know that, but I want five hundred pounds directly: this instant."

"Draw a cheque, then. Here are pens, ink, and paper."

"It's of no use, he won't take it."

"Who won't take it?"

"Sims, I want five hundred pounds. Let me have them at once, for mercy's sake, or all is over."

"Is it a real smash?" Mr. Sims asked searchingly.

"It is ruin and despair. You know that I never lie to you."

"I don't think you do; but you keep back the truth till the last moment, which is quite as bad; and then the train shunts away on the branch line, that leads to smash, and after that we come to our Sims and eat humble pie."

"Will you give me the money?"

"I haven't got it. I've only a bunch of keys, sevenpence halfpenny, and half an Abernethy biscuit,—my breakfast, ma'am,—in my pocket, and eight pounds fourteen in postage-stamps. There has been a joyful delivery this morning."

"Draw me a cheque, then."

"You know I never draw cheques myself. I have a blank one, however, with somebody else's name to it; but where's the use of it? He won't take a cheque."

"Yes he will, with a line from you."

"Who will?"

"His man is down stairs."

"Whose?"

"Tigg's."

" Ephraim Tigg of Stockwell!" Mr. Sims repeated, with another prolonged whistle; "I thought so. And so you've found out again that he's a Rasper, have you?"

" Will you let me have the money?"

" I must, ma'am," responded Mr. Sims, shrugging his shoulders. "I can't afford to let the concern go to smash, although, if this kind of business continues, I shall be obliged to take my capital out of the firm. Why on earth can't you come and see me before you pay that walking museum of the College of Surgeons a visit, instead of afterwards? Did your Sims ever refuse you the genial loan?"

" I can't help it," said Mrs. Armytage, with a murmur that was half a groan.

" I don't think you can," observed Mr. Sims, scanning her from beneath his eyebrows, as from a huge leathern pocket-book he produced a blank cheque and filled it up. " There, Ephraim will take Filoe and Co.'s signature, particularly if I put this upon it."

He made a minute tick in the corner of the cheque, partly with a pen, partly with his nail, and handed the document to her.

" You have a flying pen, ma'am," he observed calmly, " and the bump of imitation ought to be strongly developed somewhere among those pretty curls; but I think that mark will puzzle even *you*, my lady. I suppose you don't want me any more, till the next time; but take care. It's a long lane that has no turning, and, as sure as my name's Des—— Sims, I mean,—the very next thoroughfare on the wrong-hand side is C. C. C. Street."

She had scarcely heard his concluding remark. She crumpled the cheque in her hand, and walked to the door, and was gone.

" Impulse again," Mr. Sims muttered; " I thought so. Five times within a fortnight. *La chiourme chauffe.* If that woman doesn't put a stopper on her impulse, it will most inevitably end in the cultivation of the science of botany in the pleasant bay of that name. Buff," he continued, " I'm at home to everybody. I think I shall have a harvest this morning."

And Mr. Sims went on opening letters, and taking out postage-stamps.

CHAPTER XIII.

EMBARRASSMENTS OF A RICH YOUNG MAN.

It is but weary work opening letters; but when every other one or so contains from half a dozen to half a crown's worth of postage-stamps, the operation becomes profitable, and the labour may be borne. Mr. Sims got through his work quite cheerfully, and whistled as he went, not certainly for want of thought, but as a little accompaniment to a pleasant task. Now and then he came upon a letter which contained, not postage-stamps, but a coin carefully stuck in a card or secured under a seal,—now a sixpence, now a shilling, and now actually a half-sovereign; and at the discovery of such a treasure Mr. Sims would shake his head: in a very placable manner, however.

"When *will* the public learn common prudence and caution?" asked Mr. Sims, suspending his whistling, and carefully pocketing a golden effigy of her Majesty, which for greater security had been carefully wrapped up in a piece of soft paper crumpled enough as to texture, and oleaginous enough as to surface to warrant the surmise that it had originally served as a confining locket for the tresses of some unknown Pyrrha. "Are the repeated warnings of the Postmaster-General, are the innumerable convictions at the C.C.C., are the pleasing pamphlets of the Ordinary of New-gate—'A double Rap at the Postman's Conscience,' and so forth, —of no avail? It is wicked, it is cruel, to send coin by post. You mus'n't send leeches, and you mus'n't send lucifer-matches, and you mus'n't send sucking-pigs, and you decidedly oughtn't to send money. It places undue temptations in the way of the humble and ill-remunerated postman, and it wears out the letter-boxes. Besides," he continued, slipping three fourpenny-pieces into his waistcoat-pocket, "money may be marked, may be sent for sinister objects, and may lead to unpleasant revelations concerning one's little business transactions before the stipendiary magistrates.   Hum: what have we here ? "

No postage-stamps had to be taken out this time.   A common, cheap, salmon-coloured envelope being opened, disgorged a piece of coarse sugar-paper, in which were rather crammed than folded at least a dozen halves of what seemed to be five and ten pound notes of the Bank of England.   Mr. Sims carefully took account of the numbers of these documents ; then as carefully lighted a little taper, walked to the hearth, set the notes on fire, watched them crackle into flame and smoulder into black powder, embossed here and there with "five " and "ten " in grey gothic, and finally stamped and ground them with his heel into an impalpable smear of dust.

"Plenty more where they come from," he softly remarked, walking back to his letters ; " but those half-notes will never find their brothers and sisters, I fancy, nor call out for gum-water."

Mr. Sims had not the slightest appearance of belonging to the nautical profession, nor of having recently assisted in the capture of an enemy's vessel, and so come into the possession of prize-money ; and yet what he had just done was suggestive of the old stories current at the Common Hard, Portsmouth, of the brave old days when Jack-tars kindled their pipes with bank-notes, or ate them, sandwich fashion, between slices of bread-and-butter. Was he about to fry a gold watch, toss all his loose silver out of window, or paper the ceiling with postage stamps, next ?   Not at all ; he went on opening letters.

They were all addressed to Coger's Inn, but not by any means were all of them superscribed with Mr. Sims's name.   Some were for " Professor Merryscope, Ph. Dr.;" others were for " Aber-nethy Halford Hunter, M.D. ; " others for " Miss de Rosen-burg ; " others for " Nemo," " Aliquis," " Tamen ; " others for nearly every letter in the Greek alphabet, and almost every combination of initials.   Some contained, in addition to postage-stamps, and wrapped in more or less greasy scraps of paper, locks of hair,—brown, grey, black, auburn, chestnut, sandy, and fiery red, coarse and fine, curled and straight.   Professor Merryscope, Ph. Dr., had to deal with these ; and the senders of the stamps and the locks of hair all made urgent requests to be favoured

with certain information, mainly relative to love, marriage, and
the pursuit of riches, which, it appeared, only Professor Merryscope, when duly provided with postage-stamps, could give.
There were people who wrote to Abernethy Halford Hunter,
M.D., eagerly asking to be relieved, by return of post and on
receipt of stamps, from "nervous fluttering," "unaccountable
sensations," "general depression," "dreadful all-overishness," and
kindred ailments for which remedies are not to be found in the
ordinary pharmacopœia. Scores of people corresponded with
Miss de Rosenburg, enclosing scraps of their handwriting,—
villanous scrawls in most cases,—and demanding revelations concerning their personal characters and future prospects in life.
Some were anxious with regard to hair-dyes, cosmetiques, and
"Ninon de l'Enclos' Revivifier," which was warranted (for eighteen
postage-stamps) to make people of sixty look younger than youths
of sixteen. Denizens of Dorsetshire were desirous to know how
they might earn a genteel livelihood by ornamental leather-paint-
ing and decorating Japanese lacquer-ware. Correspondents from
Sunderland presented their compliments to "Nemo," and were
perfectly certain that they were the parties rightly entitled to the
9,089*l*. 13*s*. 4*d*. unclaimed dividends then lying in the name of
Scrookidge in the Bank of England. A confiding party at
Bolton-le-Sands was wistful to learn the nature of the desirable
investment by which (only eight hundred pounds outlay) a permanent income of five hundred per annum could be secured.
Applications for pecuniary loans, accompanied by offers of every
kind of security, from landed estates and dock-warrants, to piano-
fortes and silver spoons, were numerous. But almost every body
who wrote either to Professor Merryscope, Ph. Dr., to Miss de
Rosenburg, to Abernethy Halford Hunter, M.D., to "Nemo," or
"Aliquis," or "Tamen," or "Beta," or "Sigma," to "A.B.C." or
"X.Y.Z." sent postage-stamps or coin of the realm.

"If I could only make my mind up to take post-office orders,"
thought Mr. Sims, "'Nemo' alone would be worth twenty pounds
a week. But I won't. That's an impulse I *can* subdue. Many
a man of business has found his bill of indictment in a P.-O.
order."

He arranged the letters in different piles methodically, tied up

some, filed others. About a dozen or so he burnt. These did not
enclose any stamps. The contents, indeed, were generally brief,
and not complimentary. "Swindler," wrote one defaulter, "if I
didn't live at Berwick-upon-Tweed, I'd hunt you out and kick
you." "Villain," a second one had the ill manners to express
himself, "your plausible humbug won't go down with me;" and
"Scoundrel" was the coarse commencement of a third; the fourth
beginning with the rude apostrophe, "Rascal." One enemy—
even Mr. Sims had enemies—mingled a spice of humour with his
malice. There was something round, flat, and hard in his letter,
which any one might have reasonably conjectured to be either a
sixpence or a half-sovereign. On examination it proved to be a
farthing, and was encircled by this legend, "Ha, ha! you thought
you'd caught me, did you?" Mr. Sims was not at all vexed, nay,
seemed somewhat tickled. He burnt the letter, but pocketed the
farthing with a smile.

"A droll dog, a very droll dog," he said, whistling between
whiles. "After all, it's cash. A pin a day is a groat a year. A
farthing put out at interest will make a man as rich as Crœsus, if
he can only live to the age of Methusaleh. What do I care for
their loud words? Let 'em abuse as much as they like. Let 'em
come here. If even they get into Coger's Castle, they won't get
anything out of Buffalmacco the Ruthless and Filoe and Co."

He walked to the window and tapped his nail against the dirty
pane.

"If one cared to call a charwoman in, and have all this grime
cleaned off," he chuckled, "and if there was anything down there
besides cats and sparrows and chimneys, I might pass my leisure
time in seeing the fools pass. How many hundreds a minute, I
wonder?"

His principal work was over, and he had begun to dally with
the rest. The letters, tied and taped and filed, he swept into a
cupboard and locked up. A special pile which bore either his
own name, Sims, Coger's Inn, or that of the mysterious firm of
Filoe and Co., he reserved on his table. The silver was all in his
pocket. The stamps he had entombed in a drawer. And whenever Mr. Sims opened any thing it was with a key, and he always
locked everything after him. His very trousers and waistcoat

pockets seemed ruled by Chubb and Bramah, so tightly did they close.

" I wonder," mused Sims, frugally lunching off the Abernethy biscuit of which he had spoken to Mrs. Armytage, and perhaps also in compliment to the illustrious surgeon whose name he had borrowed,—" I wonder who the ' married gentleman ' is who advertises for unruly children to tame ? I think I could tame 'em at a guinea a lesson. Dear me, even Mr. Van Amburg might have saved himself a good deal of trouble, if he'd brought a Bengal tiger or two to Coger's Inn. Unruly children! Why, Buff could tame a dozen of 'em before breakfast. Hark! he's at it again."

Long quiescence had proved unbearable to Buffalmacco the Ruthless, and emboldened by the interval that had occurred since he was last summoned, he was stamping on the floor and thwacking the office desk with the broadsword more fiercely than ever.

" 'Ear me,"—to this effect was Buffalmacco the Ruthless's voice heard through the door,—" 'ear me, minions, were yon blue skyey a sea of bl-l-ludd, were hevry blade of grass a bleeding corse in my path, I would not falter; no! Saha! slaves of the vile Oppimo, come on ! " And the slaves of Oppimo the Vile apparently coming on, in theory, Buffalmacco the Ruthless went at them in practice until the crazy room shook again.

Mr. Sims unlocked his door and called out, " Buff."

" Before you go quite mad, my young friend," he remarked firmly but mildly, " you will oblige me by putting that sword away, and doing something towards earning your wages. Fill up twenty-six characters by handwriting, a dozen Ninon de l'Enclos recipes, and fourteen genteel livelihoods directly; do you hear ? You may do a few nervous affections, and futures foretold too, for stock. We're sure to want 'em."

Buffalmacco the Ruthless, who from the fiercest had suddenly become the meekest boy in all Coger's Inn, betook himself to a high stool at the office desk, from the recesses of which he produced sundry packets of note-paper, partially filled up with lithographed characters in imitation of manuscript, and in ink of various hues.

Mr. Sims went back to his room, and read his own letters, and

those destined for Filoe and Co. They were of a very different
character to the previous instalment of his correspondence. There
was no question now of paltry postage stamps, or shillings, or half-
sovereigns. Mr. Sims was up to his eyes in thousands. He read
of mortgages, and post-obits, of deeds and bonds, of bills and pro-
missory notes, of assignments and reversions.

"Lord Racketborough," he mused inwardly. "Is he good for
twopence-halfpenny yet? Poor old Tenniscourt is very nearly
done up. The Southbank has got young Draff Huskisson of the
Blues. Good-bye to the broad acres of Vealsborough. Can Mrs.
Mountain Earsleigh have five thousand on her note of hand? No,
she can't. Will I lend Sir Paul Pindar any more on the Wake-
field estate? No, I won't. Will I give Mr. Fishton Shiftleigh
time, because he's got neuralgia and has lately lost his aunt? No,
I won't. What have I to do with his neuralgia? Hang his
neuralgia! Why didn't his aunt leave him money enough to take
up his bills with? Now then, Buff, what is it?"

Buff had knocked at the door. When his master opened it, he
handed him a card. Mr. Sims looked at it, and said curtly, "Show
him in." He flung his door wide open, sat down before his great
leathern-covered table,—there was not a letter or a vestige of
created paper on it now, all had been spirited away with pantomimic rapidity,—thrust his hands into his pockets, and looked
prepared for anything.

He was quite prepared for his visitor, who turned out to be Sir
Jasper Goldthorpe, neat and spotless as to outward appearance as
ever, but very pale and careworn, and bowed; not at all the man
he was at Christmas Eighteen hundred and forty-nine.

Mr. Sims scanned him narrowly under his lids. "He outran
me bravely he thought, but I have caught him up. Aha! I have
caught him up."

It might have been long illness and long mental suffering, but
Sir Jasper, before whom all men were wont to tremble, seemed
quite meek and humble—almost cowed, to tell the truth, before
the mean little man with the grey head and the purple nose.

"Shall I close the door?" the baronet asked.

"No," returned Mr. Sims shortly, and almost snappishly.

"I had better," Sir Jasper softly urged.

M

"No," repeated the other. "The boy is deaf and blind, save when I tell it."

"DESBOROUGH!" cried Jasper, appealingly.

"Hay!" exclaimed Mr. Sims. "What's that? You've made a mistake. Buff," he continued, rising, and calling to the ruthless clerk, "the gentleman's come to the wrong chambers. There's no Mr. Desborough here. These are Filoe and Co.'s offices."

But Buffalmacco the Ruthless continued filling up the lithographed papers, as though he had been in good sooth as deaf as his master had declared him to be.

"Show the gentleman out," Mr. Sims went on.

But Buffalmacco the Ruthless being blind as well as deaf for the nonce, didn't see the gentleman, and never turned his red head.

"Desborough, Mr. Desborough!" Sir Jasper broke in, catching the little man by his garment. "For Heaven's sake hear me. I conjure you, I entreat you. Here, let me shut the door."

Mr. Sims made a faint show of resistance, but eventually suffered the rich man to do as he asked. He who had always been accustomed to have doors—golden doors, too—opened and shut for him; he who could raise the rate of discount by a nod, and make money tight in the City by crooking his little finger!

Mr. Sims sat down as before in his chair, his hands in his pockets and his lips close set.

"Once more, you will hear me, Des——," the baronet was beginning.

"Don't know the party," broke in Mr. Sims: "he's dead. Dead and gone years ago. There used to be a Mr. Sims here, but he's gone away. He went off to Australia by the Black Ball line of packets last January twelvemonth, and is supposed to have been lost in the bush, and eaten up by Bungaree, King of the Blacks."

"What am I to call you, then? But for mercy's sake, hear me."

"Say Filoe and Co., and I'll listen to you. I'm Filoe, and the boy in the next room's the Co."

"I should know the name well enough," Sir Jasper retorted, with a transient touch of his old haughtiness. "Much stamped paper bearing that endorsement has passed through my hands."

"Curiously," replied Mr. Sims *alias* Filoe, "I've a quantity of it myself accepted by one Captain William Goldthorpe, of whom you may know something, and which I'm going to endorse this afternoon to a friend of mine in the City."

The baronet bit his lips. "I'm no stranger to my son's embarrassments," he said. "Munificent as his allowance has always been, I know that he has exceeded it, and that he has plunged into a vortex of profligate expenditure."

"Do you know that he bets?" Mr. Sims asked calmly.

"I have heard so."

"Do you know that he gambles?"

"I fear that he has become addicted to the unhappy passion of play."

Mr. Sims might have winced a little, but he did not; he only sneered.

"Mere paralysis in the elbow," he said. "There used to be a Mr. Desborough who was afflicted with that complaint, and died. Do you know that the Captain's up to the eyes in all manner of wickedness that costs money, and that next Wednesday is the Derby Day, and that he has backed Orcus,—as if that three-legged brute could ever get round Tattenham corner,—and that he stands to lose twenty thousand?"

Sir Jasper slightly groaned, and hid his face in his handkerchief.

"You were always an old humbug," Mr. Sims remarked contemptuously: it was Belphegor bearding Mammon. "You knew very well that he was deep in Filoe and Co.'s books, only you weren't quite aware of the fact that I was Filoe. Why couldn't you look at the name over the door when you came hunting for dead men, you old stupid?"

It was a peculiarity of Mr. Sims, when he used harsh words, never to make them audible in a harsh voice. As he upbraided Mrs. Armytage, so he upbraided Sir Jasper Goldthorpe; and the tone of his last speech had been quite mellifluous.

"It was not on his account, I called upon you," Sir Jasper answered, with an unquiet look towards his tormentor.

"Of course it wasn't, it was on your own; but, if you've no

objection, I will settle the captain's business first. He owes me thirty-seven hundred pounds. Are you going to pay me, here and now, or am I to lock up Sir Jasper Goldthorpe's son in Cursitor Street ?"

"I would do all I could to satisfy the claims against him, but I fear that he has other liabilities."

"Others! By that I suppose you mean that there are more Filoes and Co. than one. I dare say twenty thousand wouldn't cover the paper he has out, let alone the nice little nest-egg he's laid for the Derby. There's scarcely a bill-discounter in London who hasn't got his precious autograph. They think he's pretty safe, knowing what his father seems to be, but not knowing what he really is so well as I do. And yet *I* don't know anything, do I, Sir Jasper? But I'll tell you what: our people are getting shy even of the son of such a rich man as Sir Jasper Goldthorpe. He's but a younger son, you know, after all. One off the title; might have been two but for that accident."

Sir Jasper groaned again.

"Yes," the merciful Sims continued, "I dare say you do feel that. Terrible drop it was, to be sure. How are the mighty fallen! and the rest of it. Dreadful blow to Miss Hill too, whom our little lady yonder is so fond of. But, mark my words, Sir J., young Hopeful's creditors will sell him up, and that in two twos. Not but what they'll lend him plenty more money by and by; but they want to see what he's made of, and how far his governor will shell out. As to his betting-book, you'll have to pay that on the nail, if Orcus goes to the bad. That's a case of must. Captain Goldthorpe can't be a defaulter."

"Is there no compromising his imprudent wagers?"

"There's very little compromising down on the south side of St. George's Hospital, Hyde Park Corner. Hungry and sharp's the word, and if there's any meat on him, they'll have it. You'll get much more quarter at the hands of our people. The Jews will take anything so long as it's double the amount they originally advanced. It's only Christians that go in for two hundred and fifty per cent. But even they'll compromise, if you stick out and threaten sale of commission, Insolvent Court, cutting off with a shilling, and so on. Take Filoe and Co. for instance. I'm not unreasonable, any more than the Co., who has ten shillings a week, paid every Saturday at two p.m. We're open to an offer, we're to be squared. The captain owes us thirty-seven hundred pounds. Give us a cheque for three thousand, and we'll cry quits."

"And how much actual money has the wretched boy had at usurious interest ? "

" If by usurious interest at sixty per cent., and the renewals and et ceteras, which, after you've paid the original debt, always leave you more in debt than you were before, you mean ' actual money,' I dare say the captain's had a cool fifteen hundred pounds, and that's liberal. All hard cash, mind. I never give wine or pictures, or any of that sort of trumpery."

" I will give you a cheque for two thousand five hundred pounds to-morrow."

" Won't do," Mr. Sims calmly returned. " When Filoe and Co. make an offer, F. and Company never depart from it. The Co. in the next room wouldn't abate a sixpence for half a week's salary. Say, when will you send us the cheque ? "

" You shall have the money, if it be imperatively necessary. A letter enclosing it shall be left for any messenger you choose to send after ten o'clock to-morrow morning. But there are other liabilities. Money is much in demand, and is very hard to get just now."

" That speech from Sir Jasper Goldthorpe," Mr. Sims exclaimed, in graceful raillery,—" those words from a gentleman who coins golds, who eats, drinks, and sleeps upon money-bags ! Bah ! you are jesting."

" I am not indeed. The operations of our house are tremendous, but they are equalled by the calls made upon us."

" There, that will do. And how about the surplus ? But we won't be hard upon you. Our cheque we must have, because we want it ; but Filoe and Co. will undertake to satisfy all outstanding calls against young Hopeful, and get in all the stamped paper from all the tribes of Israel, lost ones and all, for ten shillings in the pound paid down."

" If I accede to this, will you do me one favour ? "

" What is it ? "

" Not to lend William any more money."

"Yes," replied Mr. Sims, very slowly and drily. "I think I can promise that the captain won't get another shilling from Filoe and Co. until we see our way a great deal more clearly. Do you know, Sir Jasper Goldthorpe, that I'm not quite so well satisfied with the security as I was an hour ago? I begin to be of your opinion, that money is much in demand and very hard to get; and that although the operations of your house are tremendous, they are equalled by the calls made upon it. *Is* there any tangible surplus, Sir J.?" The richest man in London moved uneasily in his chair, and a faint flush overspread his pallid cheek.

"You shall have your cheque," he said with an effort, "and I will give you authority to compound with my son's creditors."

"I ask you 'eye,' and you answer 'elbow,'" Mr. Sims continued. "But let that pass. We have settled the captain's little business, and relieved Filoe and Co. from the painful necessity of issuing twenty-eight Victorias by the grace of, at two pounds fourteen each, commanding William Goldthorpe to put in an appearance before Fred. Pollock at Westminster. Now about your own concerns. May I ask to what I am indebted for the pleasure of et cetera, et cetera, et cetera, and how the deuce you came to stumble across me and Coger's Inn?"

"She sent me here."

"Clever little minx, I dare say she did. And what was I to do?"

"In an interview I had with her only yesterday, I begged, I implored, I almost went on my knees to her to name a sum for which she would consent to resign those fatal papers."

"What fatal papers?"

"Oh, Desborough, Desborough, you know too well."

"Upon my word, Sir Jasper Goldthorpe, I don't; and I can't see what any papers, fatal or otherwise, have to do with your visit to me."

"She said that she could do nothing without your sanction. She implied that you were a participator in the secret which is the curse and agony of my life. She resisted my entreaties, my supplications, my offers, always on the plea of being unable to act without you. And finally, saying that you might prove tractable, she bade me come to you, and told me where to find you."

"I declare that were you to give me fifty thousand pounds, I couldn't help you," Sims replied, with a very disturbed and puzzled expression of countenance. "It seems to me that she has been making fools of both of us. She was always good at lying," muttered Mr. Filoe Sims to himself, "and this is decidedly an elephantine lie. I'm too fond of money," he continued to the baronet, "to refuse a good offer if I've anything to sell; but I don't happen to be in partnership with Mrs. A. in this particular instance."

He was speaking with perfect frankness. Mr. Sims never told untruths when mendacity was unnecessary. Mrs. Armytage lied from predilection. There are some people who will lie about the day of the week and the time of the day. Sims had taken a comprehensive view of the situation. He saw there was nothing to be gained by deceiving Sir Jasper Goldthorpe on this point, and was for that reason quite candid and truthful.

"Then, you know nothing?" the baronet asked, but not in a relieved tone, as though he would rather have been in the power of Mr. Sims, than in that of Mrs. Armytage.

"Nothing beyond a general impression that our lively little friend has a hold over you, by which she manages to extract about two thousand a year from Beryl Court. Do you receive her rents for her, or are you the agent for her late husband's pension?"

Sir Jasper moved towards the door.

"I must try again," he murmured. "The continuance of this thraldom will either kill or drive me mad."

"Nay," said Mr. Sims, "though I know nothing at present, there is no reason why I shouldn't screw all that is to be known out of our captivating acquaintance. If she has a hold over you, I have a hold over her."

"And I one, and no light hold, over you, Desborough," Sir Jasper interposed in a low, sad voice.

"And so we all hold, and may all hang together," gaily responded Mr. Sims, with a short dry laugh, and positively snapping his fingers. "A hold over me, bah! I defy you. Not all the oaths of all the witnesses, true and perjured in the world,

could make me out to be Hugh Desborough. To those I choose
I am Sims, to others Filoe. I may call myself Sardanapalus, or
Tippoo Saib, if I like; but Hugh Desborough I never can and
never will be. He is a dead man, dead and buried, and I have
come into his property."

Sir Jasper Goldthorpe looked at this mean, grey, ill-favoured
little man, with his rogue's face and shabby raiment, and his
thoughts rolled back long years. He was among the twenties,
and saw himself humble and struggling behind a country-shop
counter, his wife in the back parlour nursing a baby boy. He
saw the man, who, in despite of truth and knowledge, he was to
call Filoe, not Desborough, young, natty, spruce, rosy—a jaunty
little man in a white hat, blue coat, yellow waistcoat, stocking-net
pantaloons, and Hessian boots—a merry little man, fond of his
bottle of port, his rubber of whist, and his Anacreontic song,
which he piped in a chirping voice when business-hours were over.
Yes, there was the shop, his little boy playing with the brooms,
and brushes, and fagots of wood at the door; his wife in the
back parlour nursing a baby. He saw, in the lazy summer afternoon, the jaunty little man coming across the high street. His
blue shadow fell across the threshold. Anon he was in the shop,
and spoke him cheeringly but decisively. For the little man was
his superior, and had authority over him. There was a talk
about a lottery-ticket. Six of "thirty thousand pounds," "the
last lottery ever to be drawn." "Bish, contractor," jangled in
his ears like chimes. And the little man changed; ah, how he
changed! and he saw himself change no less. He was on a jury.
The little man in soiled and sordid raiment, stood in a wooden pen
in a hot crowded room; an inverted mirror over his head, a man
with keys behind, rue on the ledge before him. Guilty, Death.
It was a banker's prosecution—a private banker's, a Quaker firm,
luckily. The quiet Friends were always averse to capital punishment. "Guilty, Death;" and he saw a ship slowly working out
of dock, the men at the capstan crooning forth their dull song,
the soldier with his bright bayonet standing over the hatchway
where the exiles lay fettered. Hugh Desborough was dead
indeed. His name was written in the midst of the great Pacific
wave, and a great golden rock rolled across Sir Jasper Gold-

thorpe's field of vision, and left him face to face with Filoe and
Co. composedly grinning.

"There is nothing more," Sir Jasper said, with a deep, deep
sigh.

"But one word." Mr. Sims placed himself in front of Mammon. He had the audacity to take him by the lapels of that
revered frock-coat, to look him full in the eyes, to draw him
towards as much light as would pass through the murky window-
pane.

"See here," said Mr. Sims, very softly, almost kindly. "We
are very old acquaintances, and have each seen our ups and downs,
though business makes a gulf between us as wide as Chelsea
Reach. Is all right with you? Is Beryl Court really built of
gold, or is it only straw and stamped paper? Be frank. You
are the most specious, but yet the duller rascal of the two. You
may deceive yourself. I never do, save when I back the red or
take the box in my hand. Are you going to the bad?"

"The reputation of my house,"—Sir Jasper began in his grave
plodding voice.

"May become so much infamy to-morrow. If you were to lay
me down fifty thousand pounds in gold on that table, you might
be still on the very eve of a Smash. I can understand when a man's
head gets muddled with millions. If you are ruined, of course the
ruin will be of the most splendid description. Come, speak out."

The baronet looked round for his hat, and muttered something
about a cheque awaiting the pleasure of Filoe and Co.

"I suppose I must let you go your own gate," observed Mr.
Sims, releasing his hold on Sir Jasper's lapels, and thrusting his
hand into his pocket again. "We have touched for a moment,
and must now fly asunder farther than ever. Don't come here
any more. It won't do you any good. It may be part of my
subsequent duty to assist in smashing you. Keep your promise
to Filoe and Co., and they'll let you be; if not, they will be
compelled to do you a mischief."

"You will remember old times, Des— Filoe."

"I shall remember nothing," Mr. Sims tartly replied, "but
business. Let us trust that our mutual business transactions
won't bring us into collision. I say again that Desborough is

dead, and that the ghosts of Townsend or Ruthven, the Bow
Street runners, couldn't identify him. Go, and return no more.
If you had spoken to me frankly, I might have forgotten the
wrong you once did me, and helped you. I have no means of
judging, but I can swear you need help."

"I do indeed, in one instance—that of the woman who tortures
me."

"What, of little Florence, little Flo? She is useful to me; but
you have still my full leave to poison her, or have her kidnapped
and locked up in a coal cellar for life. I shall be obliged to do
something of the same sort myself; for, do you know, my good
sir, her Impulse makes her dangerous."

He had his hand on the door, and was about to open it.

"Remember," he said, "you are doing wrong. This is the last
time of asking. As you knew me once, I am now—a common
swindler and cheat. But I have means, aha! I have means. The
mouse might help the lion. Coger's Inn might come to the aid of
Beryl Court with benefit to both parties. Once more, have you
anything to say?"

"Nothing, nothing," Sir Jasper falteringly made answer; and
he was given over to Buffalmacco the Ruthless, and conducted out
of Coger's Castle.

"Go," said Mr. Sims, apostrophising a cupboard in default of
his late visitor. "Go to your clerks, your slaves, and your toadies;
go, till the smash comes. What a smash it will be! I might have
disentangled the web. I should like to be the bosom friend at
Beryl Court. But it's too late, evidently; and he's far too deeply
dipped. This makes the second of my acquaintances who have
Smash written in their way-bills. The little woman must go.
There is no help for it. Her Impulse grows stronger and
stronger."

He became aware of the presence of a fragment of biscuit on
the window-sill, and, pouncing upon it, devoured it with great
gusto.

"She's an artful little hussy, too," he thought, still munching.
"She's moved that heavy, senseless, spooney lubber away from
Hoogendracht. Yes; the Lay Brother went away on the 10th of
May. Next Wednesday is the 24th. She thought to spirit him

away from her Sims; and here's a letter telling me that he's safe and sound at Belleriport. A *garde-chiourme*, aha! a *garde-chiourme*. She doesn't give parties in the Rue Neuve for nothing. Her influence with the maritime Prefect must be enormous. The *chiourme* too. How fond she is of the old locality! Memory will bring back the feeling. *Mon enfant, tu finiras là, où tu as commencée.*"

May I be permitted to observe, that people who have passed many years of their lives in a foreign country, thoroughly isolated from the companionship of their own countrymen, frequently express their thoughts in the language which they have been accustomed to hear spoken.

"Buff," said Mr. Sims, passing into the adjoining room, "here are five sovereigns to pay for the usual postages and advertisements. Twelve more insertions, on alternate days, for Professor Merryscope, if you please. I shall not be here to-morrow. And now," continued Mr. Sims, "I'll go and enjoy myself."

Mr. Sims's curriculum of enjoyment was peculiar. He took a walk up Regent Street, and passed into Piccadilly by the Burlington Arcade, peering into a variety of shops for the display of fashionable wares, and chuckling to think how many bills of sale he held over those gay stocks-in-trade, and how many of the dashing proprietors, male and female, he had under the thumb-screw. Then he took a little walk in Hyde Park, and looked at the distinguished personages on foot, on horseback, and in heraldry-covered carriages, who owed Filoe and Co. money. Then he had a nice little dinner at a sixpenny eating-house; and then, after a quiet tumbler at a tavern, of which the landlord was obsequiously polite to the customer who held his lease, his life-policy, and his dock-warrants, Mr. Sims thought that he would go to the play. He had paid his gold into a bank, and had a pocketful of silver. He came back from the play about three o'clock in the morning, very haggard, with bloodshot eyes, and with very nearly three hundred pounds in gold and notes about him.

"What's the good?" he muttered, turning into a wretched bed at a coffee-shop in Long Acre—he seldom slept twice in the same place. "I lost a thousand the night before last."

CHAPTER XIV.

MRS. ARMYTAGE'S IMPULSE.

DEAR ladies, who are good enough to read this story, don't you think that there is a great deal too much about money and not half enough about love in its pages? There has not been, positively, a scene of downright honest sweethearting in one single chapter. Is it possible for that wicked and most objectionable little person, Mrs. Armytage, to love any one? Besides, who is the *prétendu,* who the *soupirant?* What man has been fortunate or unhappy enough to find a place in that cankered heart, deceitful above all things, and desperately wicked? There is Miss Magdalen Hill, too. She is rich, she is accomplished, she is pious; and she loses one lover by a railway-accident, and has another, a clergyman, too, almost turned out of doors. And that rude hoyden, Miss Letitia Salusbury, is *she* susceptible of the soft passion? When is the real love-making going to begin? you may ask, ladies. Why, even a little servants'-hall *tendresse,* between Sir Jasper Goldthorpe's fifth footman and the scullerymaid in Onyx Square, might alleviate the intolerable dreariness of this history of money-bags, bills for discount, postage-stamps, cheques, bank-notes, and naughty people who live in ugly places and lend money at sixty per cent. Ladies, you must be just. If you want love-making novels, Mr. Mudie will pile up your carriage-cushions with any amount of three-volume sentimentality. If you require theological novels about High Church, Low Church, Broad Church, or no Church at all, the circulating libraries and the railway book-stalls will meet your every wish. How am I to write about Love, of which I know nothing, and never did know aught that would bear the dwelling upon? You seek the placid lake, the green boughs, the birds singing in the calm sky of affection. I have been far out to sea, and can only discourse of

howling waves and inky clouds, of jagged rocks and drifting spars
of wreck, of storm-birds hovering over the foam, and bunches of
tangled seaweed floating Heaven knows whither. This story is
not about the Seven Sons of Venus, could Cupid so multiply himself. It is called the Seven Sons of Mammon. It treats of the
low and squalid, the sordid and the base, of dross-getting and
dross-spending; it tells of the good and evil that by money may
be wrought. I asked in the outset if gold were a chimera, and
denied the postulate. For gold gives us power and scorn, and the
accomplishment of desire, and the working-out of long-nursed
hatreds and revenges; and by gold in Mammon and Mammon in
gold this book must stand or fall.

And you, good gentlemen, have you not a crow to pluck with
me, for that I have but as yet introduced you to three of
Mammon's seven sons? One of them dead and buried, too, at
Kensal Green. Have patience: let the months and years roll on,
There is time enough for the sailor to come home from sea, for
the Eton boy to grow up to man's estate, for his two brothers to
make themselves a place in history. All this may take place in
the twelfth volume or thereabouts of this work. There is time
enough for the very dead to—but enough: I must attend to the
affairs of the living.

Mrs. Armytage, for instance, was as lively as the liveliest of
kittens, when, the cheque of Filoo and Co. in her porte-monnaie,
she trotted down the crazy stairs of Coger's Inn. She was an
ephemeral creature. She hoped and feared, sorrowed and joyed,
but for the moment. She was an April in flounces and crinoline,
and the sunshine far predominated over the showers. When a
storm did come, it was short, but sharp.

In the shameful old courtyard of Coger's Inn her brougham
was waiting. Have you observed how partial the little woman
was to riding about? She seldom walked. People whose life is
one criminal hurry are obliged to ride. Somebody else was in
waiting, too, being no other than Mr. Tigg's man, who—being
well aware of the ins and outs of Coger's Inn, and so well persuaded that, unless Mrs. Armytage threw herself out of a window,
or took up her permanent abode in one of the sets of chambers,
she must necessarily come out by the same door by which she had

entered—was basking in the sun, which made him look very dusty, and lit up his greasy hat and coat-collar with golden flakes. He had been amusing himself by chewing the end of a lucifer-match with great apparent relish. Mr. Tigg's man was youthful, and a highly disagreeable young man he was, both to sight and to smell, to say nothing of hearing. Why his hat was much too large for him, and was worn at the back of his head; why his coat was too long, and his trousers too short, and his boots too big; why he should dangle one hideous Berlin glove, which, in antediluvian times, may have been white, and which had not the remotest reference to a fellow; why he should have strings and pins where buttons should have been; why no vestige of under-linen should have been perceptible about him, save and except only one striped sock, which flapped idly over one unlaced high-low; why his blue cotton pocket-handkerchief should have been deposited in his hat, allowing one small triangle of clouded cerulean to brand his pasty brow; why the mud, seemingly of last summer, should have encrusted his lower extremities; why the grease of the year before last slashed his jerkin and pinked his sleeves, and the patches of perhaps the last century spotted him over, as though he had made his coat from a particoloured counterpane, or had been a harlequin, fallen upon evil days, and into a gutter;—all these were matters between the young man, his tailor, and his conscience. His chewing the ends of lucifer-matches might likewise be looked upon as an idiosyncracy. The continual blinking of his lashless eyelids, and the occasional spasmodic twitch of his limbs, which gave him the appearance of a clumsy pupil in St. Vitus's school, who had failed even to master his Dance to perfection, might be put down to the score of natural infirmities. Nor could he help his large ears, his wide and idiotically simpering mouth, his beardless chin and cheeks, his scant hair, which had been apparently half-singed off, while the other moiety had been cut with a knife and fork, and his many pimples. But he was a slovenly young man, for soap and water are cheap: there was even a pump in Coger's Inn, and washing would have done him no harm, and made his purse none the leaner. And he was an inconsistent young man; for while in the aggregate he looked like a beggar, he quite dissipated any notion of pauperism that may have been formed respecting him, first by wearing in his foul old stock a diamond brooch of great brilliance, and next by allowing a golden chain of massive form and curious workmanship to meander over the breast of his exceedingly ragged waistcoat. This young man might have been about twenty-three years of age. There hung about him a mingled and decidedly unpleasant odour, in which a chandler's shop, a tobacconist's, and a tap-room contended for preëminence; and he had a voice which reminded you at once of a person naturally gruff, and with a cold in his head besides, whispering down a gutta-percha tube. The young man's name was Reuben.

"A pretty cavalier, upon my word, to ride with," quoth Mrs. Armytage, shaking her sunny ringlets. "And that diamond must be worth a hundred and fifty pounds, if its worth a penny. If you please, sir." she continued,—as a pleasant compromise between "wretch" and "fellow,"—"everything is settled, and we will go back to Mr. Tigg's, if you please."

"Ham Hi," asked the young man, "to go hinside, or ham Hi to go hout? Thof a follerer, Hi ham a gent, and 'av moved among the very fust."

The fact is, that the young man had ridden all the way from Stockwell on the box of the brougham, and the driver had in no qualified terms imparted to him his opinion that pumping on first, and rubbing down with a bath-brick afterwards, were about the best remedies for his complaint.

"Hi ham respected," continued the young man, evidently much hurt in his feelings, "him tho 'all an' bin the robin' room. Hi ham well known at jidge's chambers. Ham Hi to go hinside, or ham Hi to go hout?"

If the young man's face had not been of the precise hue of cold boiled veal, it might have been likened to an aitchbone of beef, so full of h's in the wrong place was he.

Mrs. Armytage was in an excellent temper. "You had better get inside, I think," she said. "I'm sure I didn't mean to offend you. Will you drive back to the same place, if you please?" she added to the coachman.

"I'm glad it's inside this time," grumbled the charioteer; "I'll be danged if I drive over Westminster Bridge again with that scarecrow by the side of me." The brougham was only a hired one; and the man thought, it may be presumed, that he had a right to be impertinent.

"If you would be kind enough, sir," suggested Mrs. Army-tage, "to sit as far away on that side"—indicating the one opposite to her—"as you can; and if you'd just pull the window down: and,—yes, thank you, if you wouldn't mind my—it's so very refreshing this warm weather."

On hearing the two magic syllables "refresh," the dull eye of the young man brightened up, and he grinned fawningly. But on the word terminating with "ing" instead of "ment," the eye subsided into fishy gloom, and the young man's mouth relapsed into its normal expression of hopeless vacancy; while Mrs. Armytage proceeded to sprinkle herself with eau de Cologne.

"May I ask," the conversational little lady proceeded, with unabated politeness, "how you employ yourself generally?"

"Hi follers 'em habout," was the reply of the young man.

"Whom did you say you were good enough to follow?"

"Father's customers. Them has 'es down hupon, sich as you; and Hi follers them as 'as to be took."

"Took?"

"Capture. Middlesex and Surrey to wit. Capias," explained the young man, with as many nods as words. "Hi follers; and hif they means boltin', Hi 'angs hon. Hi oughter for to take myself. Hi oughter, but Hi aint lucky. Father says Hi'm a fool."

"I wish your papa would get a new tailor for you, and wouldn't let you smoke such strong tobacco," thought Mrs. Armytage.

"Hi oughter," continued the young man, a deep sense of injury in his tone, "to be 'igh hup in the lor. Hif not a hofficer, han attorney. My brother's one, and lives hin Gray's Hinn. 'E's a swell, and Hi'm holder than 'im, but Hi'm honly Mr. Tigg's little boy."

"Dear me," murmured Mrs. Armytage sympathisingly, and gazing at the victim of parental partiality through her eye-glass.

"Hit's cos Hi haint a scoller," proceeded the aggrieved young man. "Hi wenter school, and Hi couldn't fix the words. The master 'ammered me and Hi 'owled. The more Hi 'owled, the

more 'e 'ammered me. Hit was 'ammerin and 'owlin, 'owlin and
'ammerin all day long; but Hi never could fix them words; and
Hi'm honly good forter serve writs, and swear affidavitches, and
foller parties habout."

He sank into moody silence after this affecting narrative, and
chewed the cud of sweet and bitter fancies—and another lucifer-
match—during the remainder of the journey.

Mrs. Armytage thought of a thousand things;—of some that
made her eyes glisten, of others that darkened her fair face, and
stamped a tiny little horseshoe—but only for a moment—between
her brows. And ever and anon she opened her portemonnaie, and
glanced triumphantly at a little bit of grey paper that lay neatly
folded in a compartment by itself; and if, graceless little body,
she could invoke a blessing upon anything, she must have blessed
her lucky stars at the sight of that same grey paper.

The residence of Mr. Ephraim Tigg was in Badger Lane, a
portion of the charming suburb of Stockwell which has not yet
become susceptible to the influence of metropolitan improvements.
On a mouldy zinc plate, from whose sunken letters the black
annealing had cracked away, Mr. Tigg called himself an auctioneer,
estate-agent, appraiser, and upholder. Those who were familiar
with the business he carried on might have opined that casting
down was much more his province than holding up; but, at any
rate, it would have been more consistent with the announcement
on his door-plate if Mr. Tigg had occupied himself a little with
upholding his own residence, which had the craziest and most
dilapidated appearance. The nucleus of this tenement had, to all
seeming, been originally a showman's van; the wheels being
removed to insure a firm foundation. This *corps de logis* had two
wings, one in the guise of a washhouse, and the other in that of a
parochial cage in a country town. Behind, 'something like a
ruined brick-kiln struggled for architectural ascendancy with a
barn. Before the place stretched by way of lawn a model, on a
diminutive scale, of the great Desert of Sahara, with one oasis in
the shape of a boot, much worn, which had perhaps slipped from
some angry wayfarer, who had shaken the dust off his feet on
leaving Mr. Tigg's premises. The whole was fenced about with
rusty spear-headed rails, pointing in various directions, as though

N

the sheriff of Surrey had buried a posse of javelin-men beneath,. and their imprisoned ghosts were piercing the earth with lethal weapons. There were plenty of flower-pots about, likewise saucers, generally broken; and a plentiful supply of mould, but not any flowers. The place was called Paradise Cottage. This name was displayed on a black board gibbeted between two poles, looking very much like one that had served for conveyance of announce- - ments that rubbish might here be shot. The satirical artists among the neighbouring youth had also made it a medium for the display of cartoons in chalk, representing a personage of monstrous mien, presumedly the proprietor of Paradise Cottage, suspended from a gallows, and smoking a pipe meanwhile. He was likewise shown as selling himself for a bag labelled " 2s. 6d." to a dreadful creature with horns, hoofs, and a tail, and who might reasonably be supposed to be the Enemy of Mankind. These drawings were accompanied by insulting legends, generally assuming an interro-gative form, and inquiring whether Mr. Tigg was the person who skinned the flea for the hide and fat, and who made beef-tea out of paving-stones.

Badger Lane did not seem precisely the locality for carriages; but as Mrs. Armytage's brougham drove towards Paradise Cot-tage, the way was found to be stopped by a very splendid mail-phaeton, with two very splendid and champing grey horses, splendidly harnessed. The fittings of the vehicle—silver-mounted lamps, tiger-skin rugs, morocco cushions—were on an equal scale of splendour; and behind was a solemn groom in a blue-and-silver livery, who sat with his arms folded, mute and contemplative, as though he were twin brother to the Emperor Napoleon, brought by the exigences of fortune down to the service of a livery-stable, instead of St. Helena.

The proprietor of all this splendour was absolutely sumptuous. He stood in the midst of the Desert of Sahara talking to Mr. Tigg. He was a fat gentleman; and with his vast abdomen and pursy cheeks, but sallow complexion, and black beard and ringlets, quite fulfilled the idea of an Oriental Alderman. He glittered very much with chains, rings, and brooches, and he had a very large cigar, at which he drew with such vigour and persistence, that you might have thought it was his slave, and that he was determined to have a good day's work out of it. And the fat gentleman had very yellow gloves, and smelt very strongly of musk.

"You won't, then, you won't come to terms," the fat gentleman said, loud enough for Mrs. Armytage to hear, as, finding the narrow lane blocked, she cheerfully descended from her brougham; "you won't take nineteen and sevenpence in the pound! You're wrong, Mr. Tigg; upon my life and word and honour, now, you're wrong indeed."

"I wouldn't take nineteen and ninepence—I wouldn't take nineteen and elevenpence threefarthings—there!" Mr. Tigg made answer.

"Then you're wrong," pursued the fat gentleman; "you're wrong, my dear friend; bless you, and good-bye. Bless you—." He was forced to make his sentences short, the cigar entailing much expenditure of respiration. "When will you come and dine?"

"I never come and dine," replied Mr. Tigg.

"Come and dine in the Regency Park. Why don't you live in the Regency Park, instead of in this mousetrap?"

"We have all our different ways of enjoying life," Mr. Tigg observed sententiously.

"Truly so, truly so, my dear friend," went on the fat gentleman, still puffing. "I like to enjoy myself. You like to live in a dog-kennel. Good-bye, and bless you. Stop," he said, as though a novel idea had struck him, "perhaps you prefer to lock up in Surrey?"

"Maybe."

"Ah, there's something in that—something in that. By the way, will you go halves in another five hundred at three months for young Goldthorpe?"

"Hush!" cried Mr. Tigg; "don't mention names out of doors. Don't you see there's somebody coming?"

He pointed to Mrs. Armytage and the young man Reuben, who were just then at the hingeless gate which gave entrance to the Great Desert of Sahara.

The fat and splendid gentleman glanced over his shoulder, and took instantaneous stock of the new arrival. Badger Lane was scarcely an appropriate place wherein to discuss the merits of the lyric drama, but he immediately began to talk about the Italian Opera. He mentioned Persiani at once, and took leave of Mr. Tigg with a reference to the *Sonnambula*. He could not shake hands with Mr. Tigg, however; for the sufficient reason that his host leaned habitually on two crutch-sticks; but he blessed him a great many times, and, removing the cigar from his lips to hum an air from *Norma*, mounted into his chariot of state. The brougham had backed out of Badger Lane, and the fat gentleman in his mail-phaeton had it all his own way.

"Where have I met that woman before?" he said reflectively, as he drove into the high-road. "One doesn't see that grin and those curls twice in a life."

Mr. Tigg was delighted to see Mrs. Armytage, and in his joy positively gave his boy Reuben a shilling. It is remarkable that a very few minutes afterwards the pungent odour of the very strongest tobacco pervaded the dwelling of Mr. Tigg. Nature is, after all, but an aggregate of systems of compensation; and while Ephraim Tigg hardened his heart with usury, his son Reuben softened his brain with coarse tobacco and a short pipe.

The fumes of this calumet made Mrs. Armytage cough a little even in the kitchen, where she sat with Mr. Tigg. For it was on the basement floor, and in the apartment ordinarily devoted to culinary purposes, that the Stockwell Rasper elected to dwell. A lean and hungry cat with admirably defined ribs kept him company, while the young man Reuben smoked his pipe above stairs, until required to follow people about. The furniture of Mr. Tigg's kitchen was eccentric. There were plenty of dish-covers, but no dishes, and not a scrap of anything eatable to put in them, if dishes there had been. The place of a larder was supplied by a very large iron safe, and that of a dresser by a nest of drawers and pigeon-holes. The huge hobs of the kitchen-range were covered with a neat assortment of ink-bottles past service, and the open oven and plate-warmer appeared to contain newspapers. A common kitchen-table was littered with files of documents. A hanging shelf contained Mr. Tigg's library: to wit, a Post-Office Directory, a Peerage and Baronetage, an Army List, a Navy List, a Clergy List, a Law List, and a Racing Calendar,—all books essential to the due carrying on of Mr. Tigg's vocation. Remote as was his residence from the abodes of wealth and the haunts of fashion, peers, baronets, members of the House of Commons, officers of the household cavalry and of her Majesty's navy, sages of the law, and dignitaries of the Church, had travelled to Stock-well, and sat in that squalid kitchen, and sometimes trembled before its master, as they vainly pleaded for "time." For when the mountain lends money, and Mahomet wants money, he must needs go to the mountain.

Regarding Mr. Ephraim Tigg himself, it may be a tenable theory to assume that this eminent Rasper chose to live in a kitchen, either through a fellow feeling for the rats which infested it, or else in salutary memory that it was somewhat nearer to that grave to which he seemed destined at no distant date to descend.

Whether he had attained the age of one hundred years, or was a few years short of the century, must remain a moot-point. On the principle of extremes meeting, he was a very Hercules of infir-mities. His head was quite bald; and, more for use than orna-ment, there was perched on the crown thereof a black skull-cap of threadbare cotton velvet. The wags of his craft declared that he had lost all his teeth in gnawing up a certain great bankrupt's estate in the year 1825. He was slightly paralytic on one side of his face, and in one arm, and so lurched at you when he lent you money, or sued you for the triple of that which he had lent. His legs and feet were thickly bandaged up; so were his hands, much afflicted with chalkstones. He walked, or hobbled, or limped, or lurched, as has been before mentioned, by the aid of two crutch-sticks. He wore a filthy, old, grey flannel dressing-gown, closely buttoned up. A yellow string that hung down from his throat, and belonging probably to his night-shirt, and a pair of misshapen slippers that had once been of red leather, marked what remain-ing sacrifices he had made to the Graces.

Mrs. Armytage knew his person and peculiarities by heart, and his appearance was scarcely repulsive to her. Indeed, she once said that he had a *belle tête de mort*. She chose the least rickety of the two wretched chairs the kitchen contained, opened her porte-monnaie, took out the slip of grey paper, unfolded it, and displayed the cheque bearing the signature of Filoe and Co. to the eyes of the Rasper.

He received it very philosophically, seeming neither pleased nor displeased, but carefully scanning the signature and the private mark, and mumbling to himself meanwhile.

"It's righteous, mum," he said, "it's righteous. A many and a many of Filoe's cheques I've seen. Deara, deara me, the little tricks he used to be up to. It was his custom, mum, always to stop the payment of the cheques he drew. You went to the bank and couldn't get 'em cashed, or paid 'em in and they was refused. Then you went back to him in a rage, and he said he was very sorry, and gave you another cheque, which was to be as right as ninepence.—he'd made a little error in his balance, he said then ; and deara, deara me, you used to get the money, and Filoe and Co. used to get sometimes twenty-four hours', and sometimes forty-eight hours' more profit on their little balances. Ah! but he wouldn't serve poor old Ephy such a trick."

Mrs. Armytage listened with amused composure to this anecdote of Messrs. Filoe's ingenuity.

"You wouldn't take my check," she remarked, "although you seem glad enough to accept one from a person who, it appears, was in the habit of cheating those with whom he dealt. You are a strange old man. Will you be good enough to give me back that—that paper, now you have the money ? "

"In a moment, in a moment, mum," answered the Rasper. "It's up-stairs—I'll fetch it directly ; but I'm very lame to-day. and very short of breath. Won't you have a glass of sherry wine and a sweet cake now you are here, mum ? "

Once, in the earlier days of her acquaintance with the Rasper, and feeling exceedingly faint, Mrs. Armytage had been tempted to accept such an invitation. Preserving, however, a lively remembrance of the dreadful dregs, and of the apparently calca-reous fragments powdered with grit, of which she had partaken on that occasion, she declined the hospitable offer with an outward smile and an inward shudder.

"And how did you get along with my little boy ? " the Rasper asked, tottering backwards and forwards, either in quest of some-

thing, or being anxious to obtain delay. "How did young
Reuben behave, mum?"

"Ugh!" exclaimed the little woman, with profound disgust;
"the wretch!"

"I know he isn't popular," his papa, with a leer, went on.
"Reuben's eccentric—he's peculiar. He's a character, mum."

"So it seems," remarked Mrs. Armytage drily.

"I grant he's a fool at his book learning," resumed the fond
parent. "I never could get him to be articled, nor nothing of
that sort; but he's as sharp, mum—he's as sharp as a *ne exeat*.
He's made his little pickings, too, poor fellow, out of his pocket-
money, and what he's got from the gentlefolks he's followed."

"He won't get any pickings out of *me*," was the mental resolve
of Mrs. Armytage.

"You'd scarcely believe it, mum," the Rasper went on, dilating
with the congenial theme, "that my boy, young as he is, has got
houses—houses of his own, mum—in the thickest part of the Old
Kent Road."

"Woe betide his tenants!" was the observation of the little
lady.

"Ah, woe betide 'em, indeed, if they don't pay. Sharp's the
word with my Reuben; and Monday's his selling-up day regular.
That boy will put the brokers in to the most obstroperous tenant
as clean as a whistle, as quick as lightning, and as welcome as the
flowers in May."

Mrs. Armytage bowed her head in mute acknowledgment of
the talents of the younger Rasper, and the force and justice of
his father's similes.

"The way he took an Arabian bedstead worth at least two-ten,
and with a real feather-bed, from under a case of Fever, and had
it smoked in the back yard with sulphur and mahogany-shavings,
that it might go quite sound and healthy to the sheriff's sale, was
grand—grand and noble, mum. Think of the courage of the
thing. It reminded a friend of mine of the conduct of Boney-
partey at the bridge of Waterloo."

The bridge of Arcola or Lodi might possibly have been mentioned by the Rasper's friend in connection with the career of the
late Emperor of the French, but it did not matter:—decidedly

not to Mrs. Armytage, who, yawning and drumming her pretty
little fingers on the table, again requested Mr. Tigg to let her
have what she wanted, and allow her to depart.

"Directly, directly," he answered. "Bless us, what a hurry
we're in! Sometimes we can stop by the hour together with old
Ephy. You won't have no sherry wine; you won't have no cake?
Don't you want a little accommodation; a tiny little bit of something at three months at, oh! so moderate a price. I'll renew,
mum, I'll always renew for you. Don't you want some pretty
article of jewellery to set off that charming little figure with?
Say the word. Old Ephy's always ready to do business with you,
and bears no malice for any mistakes made."

She laughed scornfully,—was it at the compliment or at the
offer?—but she bit her lips and turned her head away. She had
just then plenty of money at the banker's.

"Not to-day," she said; "don't tempt me, you wicked old
man. Go and fetch me the paper, and let me go."

"A little bracelet now, just a fifty-pun' note to buy sweet
scents with," the Rasper persuasively continued, and leering at
her like a worn-out satyr in whom avarice had extinguished
desire. "Say the word, pretty Mrs. Armytage. Say the word.
Look here, and here, mum."

He had been pottering about since the conversation commenced, and, piece by piece, had brought out from his iron safe
a quantity of flat, oval, morocco cases. He opened them with
seeming carelessness, keeping her in conversation meanwhile.
She cast her eyes—she could not help it—on the glittering gems
as they lay in their nests of white satin. There were massive
bracelets and tiny trinkets of gold filagree; there were big drop-
ear-rings of pearl; there were necklaces of emerald and sapphire;
there were *rivières* of diamonds, serpents of diamonds, lockets
studded with diamonds, Lilliputian watches bristling with brilliants; there were pencil-cases with amethyst tops, and even
snuff-boxes and *bonbonnières* of gold and mosaic and enamel; there
were brooches and chatelaines of dull, heavy-looking, red gold,
all chased and bossed and graven; and there were legions of
rings of every shape, of every size, that gleamed and glistened
with a fascinating shimmer from among the dingy old papers on

the kitchen-table, like the eyes of so many wild beasts crouching in their lair and waiting for their prey.

"Look at them," cried Ephraim Tigg, his own old eyes sparkling as he greedily contemplated all this treasure; "look at the pooty things! Ain't they better than all the meat and drink and fine clothes in the world? *They* don't wear out, bless them. Think of the pretty things they'll purchase. These real pearls will buy coronets with sham ones round them. These diamonds will bring the brightest eyes in England down to the poor old beggarman's kitchen. They'll buy houses and lands, and honours and friends. When I die," quoth Ephraim Tigg, "I should like to be buried in di'monds."

Mrs. Armytage gazed but for a minute or so. She resolutely closed her eyes and clenched her hands, and once more entreated Mr. Tigg to do her bidding. With many leers and whinings, and much expatiating on the beauty and costliness of his wares—in truth, they were superb—the Rasper at length consented to totter out of the room. With her eyes still closed, the woman heard him clumping up-stairs with his crutch-sticks; then, a lambent flame in her face, and, presaging evil, she started up.

She, and the jewels, and her Impulse were together. She hung over the table; she touched and fondled the gems; she tried now one bracelet and now another on her arm. Her fingers fluttered among the rings, and had a pretty palsy. She cursed because there was no looking-glass. She clutched at necklaces. She wounded her hands with the pins of brooches. Oh, but to have one of them! "Take one," said Impulse. "Take one, Mrs. Armytage," cried twenty thousand little fiends nestling in her golden curls. She felt sick and dizzy. Her breath came short and hot. Her heart leapt up to the bars of its cage, and her busy fingers still went wandering, and wandering, and wandering among the perilous stuff.

"What can a poor little woman do with a parasol?" she muttered bitterly. "I can't strangle him with a cambric pocket-handkerchief. Upon my word, if I were a man, I'd brain him with one of his own crutches, and force my way out of the house with all these things."

Just at this moment her Impulse whispered, "Look there—

look at that book, Mrs. Armytage; that's safe enough." In her
agitation, rearranging a necklace in its case, she had disturbed and
well-nigh thrown to the ground a portly folio volume. She knew
it well. It was Ephraim Tigg's cheque-book. How many times
had she seen and gloated over it! No longitudinal pamphlet of
single cheques sufficed for the extended banking transactions of
the Rasper. There were at least twenty on each page of the
folio volume. Mrs. Armytage looked upon them, and, in her
mind's eye, filled up the blanks between the graven forms with
sums and with signatures. But the writing she pictured to herself all seemed to be in red ink. Some two or three cheques had
already been cut from the page that lay open before her. The
cheques were on white paper; the cuttings on the page
looked by no means conspicuous. Would the abstraction of one,
one little cheque only, be missed? No longer twenty thousand
minor fiends among her curls, but the very Devil himself cried,
"Take it, woman! be bold, and take it!"

A sharp penknife lay invitingly near, when just the tiniest
creak in the world of the kitchen door alarmed her. It had been
left half open. She looked up, and saw Ephraim Tigg of Stockwell, the Rasper, through the aperture, leaning on his two crutch-
sticks and watching her.

She caught his eye at once, and he hobbled in. "Aha!" he
said cunningly, "we have been travelling on Tom Tiddler's
ground I see. Pretty travelling, pretty travelling, isn't it?"

She was confused, and dropped her veil, and yet in her inmost
heart was as thankful as one so fallen as she was could be, that for
once she had not obeyed the promptings of that Impulse of hers.
Ephraim Tigg swept in a moment the table with his hungry eye.
He saw that nothing was missing:—nor gem nor cheque.

There was one loose draught, however, and that he had
brought with him. It was similar in form to those in his book.
It was much crumpled, as though it had passed through many
hands. Was there not a big black word branded or stamped
across its face—a word that began with F? The draft was for
two hundred pounds, and bore in the usual place of signature his
own name, Ephraim Tigg, or something very like it, appended
thereto. With never a word he handed it to Mrs. Armytage, who,

in equal silence, tore the document into minute fragments, and thrust them into her portemonnaie. She made the usurer a low curtsey, laughed her little silver laugh, and was her own old charming self again.

"*Quitte pour cette fois*," she murmured between her shining teeth ; " but it has cost me a hundred pounds."

The Rasper let her go, and when her skirts had ceased to rustle in his hearing, sate down, and nursed one of his bandaged legs.

" Not this·time, but the next," he said, with a cunning smile. " Not this time, but the next she surely will. The bird must be caught : the pretty little song-bird must be caged and fed on Old Bailey grunsel."

Mrs. Armytage was unusually grave and meditative until the brougham had brought her to the Middlesex side of Westminster Bridge. She leant her cheek on her hand, and through her clustering curls looked wistfully at the passing crowds who sped about their several concernments, pure and honest ones mainly, it is to be hoped, not errands of sin and death. She passed a girls' charity-school, and wondered to see how white the children's caps and pinners and sleeves were; how smooth and rosy their faces. " I could do without diamonds if I were a charity-girl," she thought. At the corner of the New Cut there was, as usual, the great flaunting ragged crowd reeking of fried fish and vitriol. " Is there any one among those wretches wickeder or more miserable than I am ? " Mrs. Armytage asked herself. It was late in the May afternoon, the sun danced on the river, which the cloudless sky made blue against its will, hiding all the mud and the corruption beneath. She saw the myriad panes in the Parliament House all twinkling in golden sparkles; the sharp crocketed pinnacles piercing the clear azure ; the long purple shadow that the great tower cast upon the flood. She brightened up herself now, perhaps in compliment to the House of Lords and Commons, and by the time her brougham had entered Birdcage Walk was quite radiant, and had bowed, smiled, shaken her ringlets, and waved her finger-tips to at least a score of fashionable acquaintances.

She was still a bird of passage, and had no house in London ;

but for the present was staying not in an hotel, but in grand furnished lodgings close to Albert Gate, Knightsbridge. She dismissed the brougham at the door, and bade the driver go to the stables and tell them to send round the horses. In a quarter of an hour or so came a mounted groom, with a cockade in his hat, —had not her late husband military rank?—leading her own saddle-horse, an exquisitely-formed and satin-skinned chesnut. And forth came Mrs. Armytage, in the most graceful of riding-habits and the tightest-fitting of riding trousers, and a little Spanish hat with a white feather swaling in it. The Spanish hat was a novelty in 1851. The great Sombrero and pork-pie revolution had not yet taken place. Reine, her faithful chamber-maid, had dressed her. "She is perfect," Reine exclaimed, as she stood at the door, and in unfeigned admiration saw her mistress assisted into her saddle:—she scarcely seemed to touch the outstretched palm of the groom—and giving her horse a light touch of the whip on the flank, caused him to curvet and paw his way up the street.

"Yes," soliloquised Mademoiselle Reine, "she is perfect. She can do the *haute école* to a marvel. She would be a treasure at Franconi's. *Elle y ira un jour, peut-être.* She is not a bad mistress, and never looks to see what there is between the pear and the cheese. *Mais, quelle drôlesse!*" And Mademoiselle Reine, shrugging her shoulders, shut the door.

Mrs. Armytage passed some hundreds of acquaintances in the park. Amazons and cavaliers in the ride; guardsmen and dandies lounging at the rails. She patronised them all. She puzzled the men; she was the *femme libre*, but allowed no liberties. No one could say anything against her, and yet everybody had an innate conviction that she did not belong to the category of the immaculate. The Southbank, who was in great force in the Park that afternoon, hated Mrs. Armytage even worse than she did Miss Salusbury. "She's neither flesh nor fowl nor good red-herring," was the disparaging remark of the plain-spoken Southbank. The more cynical among the dandies said, that when she had a fixed residence in town, her house was one where you played at being well-behaved, and made believe to be proper.

But everybody liked Mrs. Armytage's little dinners and card-parties, her dry Sillery, her sparkling Burgundy, and her conversation.

As she cantered homewards, she caught sight of Captain William Goldthorpe, leaning over the rails. He was as splendid as the sartor, sutor, shirt-maker, and jeweller's art could make him; but his moustache hung down, his eyelids drooped, and he looked on the whole a very dejected dragoon indeed. She reined in her horse, and looked at him long and earnestly.

"Poor Willy Goldthorpe," she said, "to be so young and good-looking, and to have so rich a papa, and yet to be in such dreadful difficulties."

The dragoon recognised her, and raised his hat.

"Just like his own fair curls," thought the widow. "Yes, Willy is very like Hugh. Poor Hugh!"

And so she rode through Albert Gate.

CHAPTER XV.

QUIS CUSTODIET IPSOS CUSTODES?

THEY had brought him away from Hoogendracht, and made a *garde-chiourme*—a keeper of gaol-birds—of him. He was not master of his own actions. He was in the hands of Fate; and Fate, through the intermediary of the Maritime Prefect of the department of the Bouches-du-Scampre, had brought him to Belleriport-upon-the-Sea, and made a gaoler of him.

The place was not one that was much coveted, although it entailed the wearing of a military uniform, even by people ordinarily so hungry for office, and so fond of wearing uniform as are the French. An old soldier is glad enough to get a place as a game-keeper or a *garde-champêtre*, or to slumber and snarl in the porter's lodge in some public establishment. He will not object to a place in the custom-house, or at the Octroi barriers in Paris. He will accept even at a pinch the appointment of *porte-clefs* or guardian in a Parisian prison, or in a *maison centrale*. But he shuns the *chiourme*. An ineffaceable infamy attaches to all that is connected with the galleys. The *gardes-chiourme* are looked upon as cousins-german to the hangman. Although the convicts have been transferred to dry land, and (ten years since) were lodged in the Belle-riport barracks, instead of being chained to the oar in monstrous bi-remes and tri-remes; the duties of their task-masters were still analogous to those which they fulfilled in the days when the galley-master walked backwards and forwards, from stem to stern, along the plank between the lines of rowers, and, with threats and execrations, let fall his lash on the shoulders of the slaves who faltered at the oar.

The gendarmes are accustomed to handle malefactors; but they shrink from the *chiourme*. They conduct the convicts to its gates, and give them over to the keepers, but there their office ends.

Were they to accept the detestable functions attached to the place itself, their yellow belts would be tarnished, their moustaches would wax limp, and their jack-boots dull; and the glory of their cocked hats would be diminished. For there is no greater error than to suppose that a gendarme occupies a humiliatingly inferior position in the military hierarchy of France. The gendarmerie is a *service d'élite*. No rude boys dare deride the tall man in the cocked hat as they do the humble "Bobby" in England. They fear and respect him, nay, even admire his imposing dress and resplendent accoutrements. He is favoured by the municipal authorities, and frequently deferred to,—not ordered hither and thither like a dog or an English policeman. I have heard a private in this force called "Monsieur le gendarme" by a shopkeeper.

So he had been brought from the peaceful Flemish convent,—from innocent labours, from the calm abode where, if the evil passions of men were not absolutely extinguished, they were latent and subdued—to this Aceldama of Southern France, and put in authority over thieves and murderers. Out of a gang of twenty toiling at their slavish drudgery, the comrade who was to initiate him into his duty could point out fourteen who had taken the life of a man.

His duties were not many, and not difficult to learn. He was to be a common *garde-chiourme*. The commissary of the Bagne—the governor of this Tartarus—read the minister's *placet*, and a sealed letter of recommendation from the office of the Maritime Prefect. He asked him nothing about his antecedents. Any stick is considered good enough to beat a dog with, and at Belle-riport any man whose hand was strong enough to hold the stick was looked upon as qualified to wield it. The commissary asked him if he could read and write. He answered, Yes, and by command read a passage or two from the framed rules and regulations of the place hanging on the wall. He wrote, from dictation, an extract from the penal code of the Bagne, inflicting ten years' imprisonment with hard labour on any *garde-chiourme* convicted of having favoured the escape of a convict. The commissary glanced at his handwriting, and remarked to a subordinate, "He can spell." His name, François Vireloque,—it was so on his passport, and was as good as any other for such a nameless wretch

as he,—his age, his height, were entered in a huge book. He
was told to sign a certain declaration, promising obedience and
fidelity, and he did so.

"There is nothing else that I can do for you," said the commissary, closing the great book. "We ask questions neither from
our sheep nor our shepherds. All those we want to know are
answered in writing. You will be given over to a *planton*, who
will show you your duty, and I should counsel you to attend to
it. After four days' looking about you, it will be time enough
to go to work. *Allez, mon garçon.* You look strong and muscular enough to make a charming *garde-chiourme*, although I suppose you were pretty well tired of the world before you entered
into this dog's life."

The commissary threw himself back into his arm-chair, and
blew his nose in a depreciatory manner. Even he despised his
subordinates. He forgot to despise himself; for, you see, that
is a lack of memory not very uncommon; and, besides, there *is*
something in possessing power, well-nigh as absolute as that of an
Oriental pasha, over two thousand five hundred men, even though
they happen to be the greatest rascals in creation. The Maritime
Prefect was ostensibly the commissary's superior; but he had a
perfect horror of the Bagne, seldom ventured within its precincts,
and was very loth to interfere by word or deed with the scoundrelism
it contained. "There is pitch enough in my ships," observed the
prefect, "without my soiling my hands with those miscreants."
So he kept grand state at the Hotel of the Prefecture, and
approved all the reports and memoranda of the commissary.
This functionary was himself a very good-natured person, with a
profound disgust for the place and the people among whom he
was doomed to pass his life. He had once been a commissary of
police in Paris,—in the brilliant Quartier de l'Opera, in fact—
but breaking down in not discovering one of the innumerable
conspiracies of Louis Philippe's reign, had been very nearly
losing his situation, when a friend, who was *chef de bureau* in the
department of marine, recommended him for the vacant post of
commissary of the Bagne at Belleriport. "'Tis an easy place,
my friend," he said. "'Tis as easy as being a schoolmaster.
Now there are schoolmasters and schoolmasters. If one has to

QUIS CUSTODIET IPSOS CUSTODES ?

progress, the calling has its difficulties and its responsibilities;
but if one has only to teach incorrigible blockheads, whom no
one expects to learn anything, the life becomes easy. You have
nothing to do but punish." The commissary in difficulties
accepted the situation, and held it satisfactorily. He was now in
his tenth year of service. When the pious ecclesiastic who was
almoner of the Bagne talked to him of reclaiming any of the
outcasts under his charge, he made answer, "There is nothing
about reclaiming prisoners in the government instructions; but
there is a great deal touching upon double irons, the 'grande
fatigue,' and the bastinado. Reclaim your penitents as much as
ever you like, my dear abbé, only let them not shirk their work.
It is with me they will have to deal if they do." The commissary
had a pretty faded little wife, who had been an actress at the
Opéra Comique. When she was in a good temper, she made him
nice dishes, and they talked of the dear old days of masked balls,
and dinners at the Café Anglais, and when on the morrow of
the carnival disorderly *débardeurs* and *titis* used to be brought
before him in their masquerade costume. When she was cross
and had the *migraine*, he would come down into the Bagne and
lead the convicts a terrible life. His lady called the two thousand
five hundred prisoners "*ces gueux.*" The commissary allowed
himself two hours' absence every evening, which he spent at the
principal café in the town of Belleriport. The town commissary,
the brigadier of gendarmerie, and some of the inferior *employés* of
the prefecture would smoke, and take their *dimi-tasse*, and play
draughts with him; but the general public avoided the terrible
commissary of the Bagne. *Il sentait la chiourme*—"he smelt of
the hulks," they said. At home, in addition to the conversation
of Madame, he cultivated jonquils, and played dismal overtures on
the violoncello. A weary life this, but the commissary bore it,
for his pay was four times larger than he would have received in
an ordinary capacity elsewhere. He had his tenderness, his weak
point, this stern commissaire. He had a pretty little daughter,
Amanda, fourteen years of age, at school, in the convent of the
Sacred Heart in Paris; and every franc of his savings helped to
swell the fund which was one day to culminate in Amanda's

o

wedding portion. *Elle sera dotée par le Bagne*—"the hulks shall give her a dowry," the commissary was wont gleefully to exclaim. But little Amanda had never been within fifty leagues of that abhorred Belleriport.

François Vireloque, the newly-appointed gaol-guard, was duly handed over to the *planton* or guide. This man's name was a mystery. The commissary knew it of course; but he never mentioned it himself, and seemed profoundly indifferent about having a name at all. His comrades called him "Le Camus," the "Snub," from the conformation of his nose. Even the commissary became accustomed to address him by this not very complimentary epithet. Le Camus seemed to care nothing about his nose, and went about his business tranquilly. He was an old hand at convict keeping, and had been at Belleriport twenty years. Previously, he admitted to have been a *garde* at Toulon, at Rochfort, and at Brest. "I like it," said Le Camus. "I am a philosopher, and there is quite enough to make me contented with my lot in the fact that I have to drive convicts about, instead of being one myself." He was a man of ancient and venerable appearance, with snowy hair, a rosy cheek, and a mild blue eye. These gifts of nature did not, however, prevent the Sieur le Camus from being an unconscionable old villain, with a hard heart and a cruel hand, and with an insatiable penchant for anisette.

"You are welcome, my friend, to Belleriport," he chuckled, as he led the new-comer to the storehouse, where he was to be supplied with his uniform. "We want new blood down here terribly. The commissary is a mere jackass, and the majority of our comrades have their brains in the soles of their boots. You will not enjoy much of the esteem of society at large,"—Le Camus habitually spoke in the inflated style common to the half-educated Frenchmen ;—"there is a prejudice, a most unjust prejudice, against the profession of *garde-chiourme ;* but you will know how to make yourself respected among these gentlemen. There is one of them. You will make him respect you. Tchaoup !" And, with this curious interjection, he raised the thin cane or *badine* which with the rest of his fellows he bore as a symbol of authority, and brought it down with all his strength—which, his age notwithstanding, was by no means contemptible—across the shoulders

of a wretched creature in coarse drab vestments, and with a red
woollen nightcap on his shaven head, who had been gaping and
staring at the stranger ; while his companion, another forlorn
specimen of humanity, in similar attire, and to whom he was
attached by strong leg-shackles, was busily polishing a cannon-
ball with sand.　He sat to this work, like a stone-breaker, with his
legs wide apart, and his work-mate had to stoop a little.　There
was a pile of balls on either side of him, one rusty and the other
polished.

It did not appear that the convict standing up had been guilty
of any offence beyond gaping and staring.　Le Camus merely
struck him with his cane because he was fond of hitting people
who dared not hit him again.　The poor creature took his stripe
as a matter of course, uttering a short, sharp yell, writhing his
shoulders, and looking a curse at his tormentor.　The polisher of
cannon-balls looked up with a grin, as though he thought it an
exceedingly lucky thing to have escaped this stroke of practical
humour on the part of the *garde-chiourme ;* and a sailor-marine
standing sentry—not over the convicts, but over the government
storehouse—close by remarked in gruff approval, " *Il l'a attrappé :
c'est très bien.*"

" The only way to get on with these brute beasts, comrade,"
the Sieur le Camus said, by way of explanation, as they entered
the storehouse.

François Vireloque was speedily provided with his uniform, and
with the kit and accoutrements allotted to a *garde-chiourme.*　The
dress was exceedingly hideous, and the convict element struggled
with the military for predominance in it.　A coarse greatcoat of
blue drab, with red cuffs, collars, and epaulettes, grey trousers
with a red stripe, thick boots, over which came clumsy white
gaiters, a *bonnet de police* with a red worsted tassel, and a pipe-
clayed sword-belt, from which hung a short heavy sabre, and his
equipment was complete.　Then they gave him a dark lantern, a
pair of pocket-pistols, a pair of handcuffs, an iron *bâillon* or gag,
and a *livret* or pamphlet containing the rules and regulations for
the life of a *garde-chiourme.*

He reported himself before the commissary, was inspected,
approved, and dismissed.　The *planton* took him in hand again,

and the remainder of that day, with the whole of the next, was devoted to exploring every nook and cranny of the great Bagne of Belleriport. He saw the convicts' dormitories, their solitary cells, their work-rooms for wet weather, their hospital, and their grave-yard. As the *garde-chiourme* was destined to remain long enough in Belleriport to become acquainted with all the features and peculiarities of his abode, it is not expedient at present to antici-pate matters by describing any of these apartments in detail. By-and-by, you may know all about them, and why the *garde-chiourme* was sent thither, and why he had ceased to be a Lay Brother, and who and what he was, and whether he had ever worn the cassock of a clergyman, or the scarlet and gold-lace of a soldier, instead of the friar's duffle-frock or the convict-keeper's belt and *bonnet de police.*

When every part of the barrack had been visited, they entered a boat, manned by convicts, with a *garde-chiourme* as coxswain, who moved the tiller with one hand, and plied his cane with the other, and crossed a sheet of water to the immense dockyard and arsenal of Belleriport. There the Lay Brother saw the convicts at work in gangs of hundreds together, always linked two and two. They were sawing blocks of stone, piling timber, dragging huge tumbrils full of stone and gravel, hauling weights up, and other-wise performing the duties of beasts of burden. And among them continually circulated the *gardes-chiourme*, calling them abusive names, and bringing down their lithe canes on their backs.

"At Brest," observed Le Camus, "we are not permitted to use our *badines*. At Belleriport a system more sage prevails. Tchaoup!" he cried again, flicking but not absolutely striking with his cane a tall and athletic convict, who with his mate was trundling a wheelbarrow full of sand up a plank, somewhat too lazily as the officer thought.

"Hands off!" cried the convict fiercely, and in the English tongue; but he took care not to return the insult, and kept a firm grip upon the wheelbarrow, as if fearful of giving liberty to his hands.

"It is well," sneered Le Camus, "it is well, Mr. John Bull. I dare say your words were mutinous enough, but you are too artful to get yourself into trouble. After all," he whispered to

François Vireloque, "I was not quite *en règle* in touching him ; the fellow was doing nothing that immediately called for punishment, and might have reported me to the sergeant, and so on to the commissary, for cruelty. To be sure, I might have said that he was skulking: and a *garde-chiourme's* word is always taken before a convict's. Look at the fellow. What a robust scoundrel he is ! Are they all like him, I wonder, those Englishmen? When he came here first he had magnificent auburn hair, moustache, and beard. He is just your build—not to offend you by the comparison ; and,'upon my word, compère Vireloque, you have somewhat of an English look."

"I have been in England," answered the *garde-chiourme* slowly, "many, many years ago. I have seen many Englishmen like him yonder with the wheelbarrow. How sunburnt he is!"

"Yes, one might imagine that he had passed half his life in the Indies. But it is nothing, after all, but our southern sun. It soon tans the fairest convict, and if that doesn't tan him, the bastinado will. Here he is, coming down the plank."

The athletic Englishman, with his chain-fellow, came down with the empty wheelbarrow. The chain-fellow could not have been of much assistance to him in his work. He was a diminutive and almost deformed negro—an old negro, too, who had dreadful white eyebrows seaming his black face, and with his red woollen nightcap wanted only a tricoloured cockade to look like a monstrous caricature of Toussaint L'Ouverture. He also had grinned and shown his teeth when the *garde-chiourme* had wantonly insulted him who shared his misery. The convicts of Belleriport were strictly practical believers in the philosophy of La Rochefoucault, and always found something to rejoice over in the misfortunes of their best friends.

The Englishman gazed with some interest at the new *garde-chiourme*, muttered something to himself in English, and then something to his yoke-fellow in French. Anon he was called away to some fresh task.

"What is he here for?" asked François Vireloque.

"Do you mean the negro?" returned Le Camus. "*Meurtre.* Killing a cattle-dealer of Poissy. He got off the major sentence for *assassinat.* He didn't shoot or stab his man with a knife, but bit his nose off, tore one of his eyes nearly from the socket, and then knelt upon and strangled him. There being no lethal weapon used, the jury found him guilty with 'extenuating circumstances,' and he only had *travaux forcés à vie*. He is a lifer. Don't you see his double irons. If he misconducts himself, he has triple ones; and as he can't walk with them, is obliged to lie on the floor of a cell."

"I don't mean the negro. I mean the other."

"Oh, the Englishman. He's a lifer too. Burglary and attempt to murder too; that's his little affair. It took hard swearing, though, to convict him. He very nearly proved an *alibi*. Was at a railway-station, his counsel protested, when he was said to have been at Chaillot. All the eloquence of M. le Procureur Impérial had to be employed to drum a persuasion of his guilt into the heads of the jury. They are so stupid, those juries."

"At Chaillot, did you say?"

"Yes, at Chaillot. It was necessary to prove that he had been at Chaillot; though of course M. le Procureur Impérial could have proved him to have been anywhere he pleased. A very clever man M. le Procureur Impérial."

"Is he quiet?"

"Yes; *il est assez bon diable*. He has not yet been punished, although he frequently suffers for the sins of his black friend; for when the negro has triple irons for three days or so, our Englishman has to sit or stand by his side: and when the blackamoor gets the bastinado, which is his pleasant fate about once a month, his comrade has to stand by and look on."

"Horrible!"

"Horrible! Ah, you are but young to the business. You'll soon get all that nonsense out of your head, after you've seen a few more horrible things."

"Is he always chained to that black demon?"

"Always! Death alone can unrivet his manacles. You see, our lambs are never uncoupled save when one dies, or is sentenced to death for killing his brother convict."

"They kill each other, then?"

"Occasionally. *C'est une petite distraction;* it relieves the monotony of their existence."

"Do they never kill their jailers?"

"Jailers! Oh, you mean us? Bah, it is not a pretty word, jailer! Well, sometimes they murder a *garde-chiourme* who is fool enough to be looking the wrong way, but that is his own fault. And now, my friend," Le Camus continued, "I think we have seen everything that is to be seen in the dockyard and the Bagne to boot. Two of our little institutions you have not witnessed, the infliction of the bastinado and of the guillotine. But you will have time enough to assist at both these ceremonies. We don't trouble the *exécuteur des hautes œuvres* of the department when we have a capital case. *La chiourme* keeps a guillotine on its own premises."

They took boat again, and went back to the Bagne. That evening Le Camus was on leave, and he took François Vireloque to a wretched *cabaret* just outside the dockyard gates, and frequented exclusively by *gardes-chiourme.* Here le Sieur le Camus submitted to be treated to several glasses of absinthe, and became convivially conversational.

"You had better enjoy yourself to-night," he said, "for to-morrow you will have to study your *livret* of duties, and will be examined upon them by M. le Commissaire. Burn M. le Commissaire! I hate him. Yes; I will have yet another pipe and another absinthe. You are a silent fellow, but you are generous. How like an Englishman you are!"

"I am an Alsatian. I come from Strasbourg," answered François Vireloque.

"Ah, that's half a German, and a German's half an Englishman. By the way, I forgot to tell you that our friend who is chained to the negro always stoutly protests his innocence. M. le Commissaire even says that he has doubts about his case. I remember once, when that wretched black was in trouble, and the Englishman had to keep him company in his cell, that it was my duty to take them their victuals. The negro was sleeping in his triple irons, the lazy old rascal, and I had some talk with the Englishman. He is not generally very communicative, but that evening I got him to loosen his tongue. I remember well the finish of his conversation. '*Garde-chiourme*,' he said, almost solemnly, 'I am the victim of an infernal plot. I am here

through the wickedness and the treachery of a she-demon with
yellow ringlets, who has been my Evil Genius through life.'
What on earth is the matter with you, Brother Vireloque?" he
exclaimed, suddenly stopping in his discourse.

The Lay Brother, the *garde-chiourme*, had buried his face in
his hands, and, his head prono to the *cabaret*-table, was sobbing
violently.

CHAPTER XVI.

MRS. CÆSAR DONKIN.

As a freeborn Englishman, of full age, unconvicted of any offence, and with means amply sufficient to defray any costs of charges, you might be desirous, I assume, to obtain board and lodging in a genteel family where, at a moderate outlay, all the comforts, luxuries, and refinements of life were offered. Turning over the supplement of a great daily journal, a well-worded advertisement informed you as to the place where that board and lodging with its concomitants might be obtained. Mrs. Cæsar Donkin was a lady of much experience in advertising, and was generally fortunate enough to secure a left-hand top-corner. To see herself there on a fine Monday morning in the boarding and lodging season was, next to affixing a receipt to a bill for a month's hospitality, her chief delight. To ladies and gentlemen seeking a truly English home her doors stood widely open. You were to apply, by letter only, post-paid, to Omicron, care of Mr. Tryfell, pastrycook, Bergen-op-Zoom Terrace, Ticonderago Square. The highest references were offered and required; and as regards the first, a letter to Omicron very speedily brought about an interview with Mrs. Cæsar Donkin, who referred you to the pastrycook, to several neighbouring tradesmen, to a beneficed clergyman of the Established Church residing in the immediate neighbourhood of the Giant's Causeway, Ireland, and to herself. To look at Mrs. Cæsar Donkin was generally found sufficient. You made up your mind and boarded, or didn't board, after five minutes' parley. As to your own references, a month's payment in advance was held by Mrs. Cæsar Donkin to be far more conclusive of a candidate's respectability than any number of testimonials from peers of the realm, members of Parliament, or dignitaries of the Church. But there was a proviso, there was a

saving clause,—there was one little requirement which the hostess
of 15, Bergen-op-Zoom Terrace, expected you to fulfil; and if
you were unable to do so, a gentleman might just as well hope to
occupy a front parlour furnished in Buckingham Palace, with
partial board from the royal kitchen, and Phipps the Ineffable to
officiate as a boy in buttons, as to become an inmate of Mrs.
Cæsar Donkin's boarding-house. She received no gentleman
under sixty years of age. Above that age, she gave ample scope
and verge enough,—she would have welcomed Methuselah with
affable gladness,—but sixty was her minimum. Her rule was
inflexible. The laws of the Medes and Persians might have been
summed up in her advertisement. She never departed from its
terms. Read it.

> BOARD AND RESIDENCE.—In the immediate vicinity of Ken-
> sington Gardens, the Marble Arch, Madame Tussaud's Exhibition,
> and within an easy distance of Kensal-Green Cemetery, and other
> fashionable places of amusement, all the comforts of home and the
> luxuries of refined life are offered, by a lady moving in the first circles,
> to ladies and gentlemen of means and position. The highest references
> given and required. Address, by letter only, post-paid, to 'Omicron,'
> care of Mr. Tryfell, pastrycook, Bergen-op-Zoom Terrace, Ticonderago
> Square. N.B. No gentleman under sixty need apply.

The sting of the announcement was in this caudal postscript.
You might be as rich as Crœsus, but unless you were sixty Mrs.
Cæsar Donkin would have nothing to say to you. Once, and
once only, she had relaxed her rule, and had consented to receive
a battered East Indian reputed to be enormously rich, and who
would only own to fifty-nine. Mr. Jaghire stayed many months.
He went away one morning to Malvern to drink the waters. He
didn't come back. After the lapse of about a year, he wrote to
Mrs. Cæsar Donkin, professedly from some unpronounceable place
in Hindostan, whither he had proceeded, he said, in the hope of
repairing his fortune, which had been grievously injured by disastrous speculations in indigo. He intreated her to take the
greatest care of a very old and ragged shawl dressing-gown, and
of a hubblebubble pipe much damaged, which, with a file of the
Bengal Hurkaru, and a slack-baked cat called Ginger, were the
only chattels he had left at Bergen-op-Zoom Terrace. The slack-
baked cat he requested Mrs. Donkin to accept as a present. He

talked of making her speedy remittances,—of sending her draughts
at sight, jars of chutnee, kincobs, uncut gems, all the wealth of
the Indies, for aught that appeared,—but he regretted that at
present, owing to "the infamous conduct of his agents," he was
unable to send anything. Stay: he sent his compliments, and
had the honour to inform Mrs. Cæsar Donkin that he was forty-
five next birthday.

The dismal falling-off of this depraved Anglo-Indian—it was
years before the mutiny, but he *must* have been Nana Sahib in
disguise—was a heavy blow to Mrs. Cæsar Donkin; but the perfidy
of Jaghire taught her wisdom, and thenceforth she took care that
none of the male sex but sexagenarians entered her doors. When
a gentleman called on Mrs. Donkin, she took stock of him narrowly. Five minutes' inspection generally sufficed to enable her
to come to a decision. She could see through paint and padding
and bracing-up and buckling-in. No form of wiggery was unfa-
miliar to her. She asked for no certificate of baptism. She said
to herself, "This gentleman is either over or under sixty," and
accepted or rejected him accordingly. After the Jaghire catastrophe she was never known to err. The loss she sustained was
in some sense salutary to her; and all her sexagenarian guests
declared that, since that "Indian fellow" went away, her monthly
bills always contained items for which she had never thought of
charging before. There was no disputing those bills; they were,
like her laws, unalterable. If an old gentleman grumbled, Mrs.
Cæsar Donkin curtsied, and requested him to provide himself
with another domicile by that day month. In most cases the old
gentleman was senile enough to cry, and beg pardon, and was
re-admitted to the privilege of paying about three guineas a week
for his board and lodging; but he never grumbled again.

Mrs. Cæsar Donkin had an enemy, Mrs. Grabblecheese, of
Great Aboukir Street, a rival lodging-house keeper. Mrs. Grabblecheese used to call the establishment in Bergen-op-Zoom
Terrace "the hospital," "the paralytic asylum," "the refuge for
the destitute," "Crutchstick Castle," and the like opprobrious
names. Mrs. Cæsar Donkin laughed her bitter laugh, and asked
how it was that Mrs. Grabblecheese could only get commercial
clerks, half-pay lieutenants, and decayed old maids as boarders;

why she didn't pay the butcher, baker, candlestick-maker, and so forth ; and what she had done with the money of that *poor deceived* Miss Gumm, whom she had taken into partnership, and with whom she had, after some six months, quarrelled, even to the unseemly extent of public litigation ? In the Paddington County Court the cross actions of Grabblecheese *versus* Gumm (disputed right of property in a Pembroke table and a volume of Blair's Sermons), and Gumm *versus* Grabblecheese (money lent), are yet reckoned among the *causes célèbres* of the district. The quondam partners were very nearly going up to the Common Pleas, each with her several plaint of assault and battery. That Gumm had torn off Grabblecheese's false front the milkman and the newspaper boy could testify ; but, then, were not 'Liza the housemaid, and Stampell the postman, ready to swear that Grabblecheese had knocked out one of Gumm's false teeth with her matronly and by no means feeble fist, in the very passage of the house in Great Aboukir Street? How Mrs. Cæsar Donkin gloated over the feuds of her foewomen ! "*I* never go to law," she said, with a toss of her head. The legal gentlemen who fomented the quarrels between Gumm and Grabblecheese earnestly wished that she would. "*I* pay my bills," Mrs. Donkin proudly declared. It was certain that Mrs. Grabblecheese didn't; and when Miss Gumm's money, which wasn't much, was spent, the firm oscillated for a considerable period between Great Aboukir Street and Portugal Street, Lincoln's Inn Fields. It was, indeed, notoriously insolvent; and Mrs. G.'s only defence was, that if she paid nobody, nobody, on the other hand, paid her. "*My* husband doesn't drink," Mrs. Donkin used to say. Mr. Grabblecheese, it is useless to conceal, *did* drink. He was a dissolute corn-chandler ; that is to say, he professed to have once dealt in cereals on commission, but he had come to a very draffy and husky stage, and imbibed continu-. ously. He was not unfrequently laid up in lavender, or in tobacco and malt-liquor rather, in Whitecross Street; and his periodical appearance before the Commissioner made much mirth among the tipstaves and the attorneys' clerks. "The low wretches," Mrs. Cæsar Donkin used to say, with a supreme curl of her lip, when she alluded to the entire Grabblecheese interest and connection.

The male Donkin, her husband, was a musician. He was pro-

fessional, and played every night during the season in the orchestra
of the Surrey Theatre. In the summer months he went to the
sea-side, or to some suburban music-hall; at all events, he was not
visible from July to September. His instrument was the violin;
he dressed in rusty black; his demeanour was placid, and his nose
was red. If he did not drink, his next neighbour must decidedly
have been an ardent votary of Bacchus, and he, Donkin, have
caught the convivial infection. He never mingled with the
domestic concerns of Bergen-op-Zoom Terrace. He came home
very late, and breakfasted in the kitchen, and departed quietly
and unostentatiously, as he came. The Grabblecheeses declared
that the area-steps were his ordinary channel of ingress and egress.
He was the meekest and mildest of fiddlers, and had a smooth,
shining, old, bald head, which the boys in the Surrey Gallery at
Easter time, and on Boxing-night, used to find an irresistible
target whereat to aim nutshells and orange-peel. He bore all
with equanimity. He would have endured even a ginger-beer
bottle, and smiled under concussion of the brain. "Where's the
use," he would say to his comrade who played the flageolet, when
advised to resent scornful epithets of "catgut," and when insult-
ingly desired to "strike up,"—"where's the use? I'm a disappointed man." The old gentlemen boarders who by chance met
him about Bergen-op-Zoom Terrace merely saw in him a shabby
elderly man with a blue bag. There might be boots in the bag,
or law-papers, anything. Few suspected the fiddle; and only
from the occasional presence of a lump of rosin on the mantelpiece
of Mrs. Cæsar Donkin's sanctum, and a stray strand of horsehair
floating about, could you have inferred anything as to the vocation
of her husband.

The dinner-hour in Bergen-op-Zoom Terrace was seven o'clock,
and at about thirty minutes before that hour, and on a fine evening
in the latter part of May, Mrs. Cæsar Donkin sate in the sanctum
before named busily occupied in arranging the dessert for the
coming banquet. She always gave her guests dessert. It helped
them on with their wine. She liked them to dine late. They
lunched at their clubs or abroad,—not but what she had a midday
refection of the genteelest description,—and a late dinner made
them less hungry than thirsty. She liked the old boys to be

thirsty, and to have plenty of wine, and of the very best, from
their own wine-merchants. Tithe and toll Mrs. Donkin might
indeed have taken on the decanters of the ancient boarders, but
she would have scorned to adulterate or to dilute their potations ;
nay, when their own stores were temporarily exhausted, she was
glad to supply them with wines and liqueurs of the very best
vintages, for which she did not forget to charge a handsome price.
"No Cape sherry, no logwood port, no British brandy for me,"
was Mrs. Cæsar Donkin's maxim. She sent for the finest wines
with which Mr. Harrington Parker, of Pall Mall, could furnish
her, and was quite contented with a profit not exceeding seventy-
five per cent.

"My gentlemen like port," she said ; "it warms the cockles of
their old hearts. Once get 'em over their wine, and they don't
want to go out ; do they, Puffin ? "

Words similar to these rose to Mrs. Cæsar Donkin's lips on the
very afternoon of which I am speaking. The young person
addressed as Puffin meekly acquiesced, as it was her practice to
acquiesce in everything that everybody said. Miss Puffin was an
incarnate affirmative. It would be inappropriate to call her an
animated one, for she was the stillest and quietest of womankind. There had never been any animation about her ; it wasn't
in her.

Mrs. Donkin's sanctum was a kind of polygonal excrescence
which had been partly robbed from the kitchen-stairs, and partly
from the back-parlour, and incommoded the entrance to both.
There had, it is presumable, once been a window to it, which had
been bricked up and papered over in the days of the window-tax ;
but a sunken tracery of its outline was still visible, throwing the
impossible dragons and abnormal flower-baskets in the wall-paper
violently out of perspective. To compensate its disappearance, a
hole had been knocked in the ceiling, and a skylight fitted, through
which slippery vantage-ground the ill-omened cat Ginger frequently looked down with baleful eyes on the confabulations of
Mrs. Donkin and Miss Puffin. The mistress of the house had a
strange leaning to this animal, sole relic of the faithless Jaghire ;
for the shawl dressing-gown, the hubblebubble, and the *Bengal
Hurkaru*, had long since gone the way of all rubbish. Ginger

was repulsive in aspect, profligate and felonious in disposition ; yet still Mrs. Cæsar leaned towards him, sometimes with affection, sometimes with a hearth-broom. He was a cynical cat, and from long acquaintance with every missile that could be propelled against his ribs and head, had grown callous. When he was not on the skylight, he sat habitually among the fragments of bottle-glass in the roughcast on the wall of the back yard. Now and then he caught a sparrow whose senses had become stupefied by the London smoke, and had so become weak upon the wing, and then, having eaten him, Ginger rejoiced over the wing in a manner horrible to behold.

The polygonal sanctum was full of cupboards with locks that would have defied Hobbs, to say nothing of the tampering of any evilly-disposed housemaid. It being May, and warm weather, the meagre little fireplace was garnished with a neatly-crumpled supplement of the *Times*, from which, however, the Bergen-op-Zoom advertisement had been carefully cut. Mrs. Donkin had an almost superstitious reverence for these aids to publicity, look-ing upon them as things that had cost money and brought money, and were not to be lightly cast away. She kept the scissored fragments in an old volume of Elegant Extracts, and designed to make an album of them some day.

On the mantelshelf reposed the male Donkin's lump of rosin, and a couple of pit orders for the theatre, the which, judiciously distributed, were found to be very serviceable in inducing trades-people of a gay turn of mind to send in articles of first-rate quality at reduced prices. The rosin was flanked on either side by two little weasened black profile portraits in the sticking-plaster style of art, one representing Mr. Cæsar Donkin in an enormous coat-collar and an aggressively protuberant shirt-frill, the other, Mrs. Cæsar Donkin in leg-of-mutton sleeves and a hat like a cart wheel placed horizontally. The gum had long since become desiccated, and portions of the heads and busts of the personages represented curled away from the fly-blown Bristol board. Little triangles of glass stuck in the corners of the warped frames. The bronzing with which the high lights had been relieved had become discoloured, and dotted Mr. Donkin's whiskers and Mrs. Donkin's hat-ribbons with a tar-

nished fluff, giving them the appearance of rusted Ethiopians.
A little inscription in pencil beneath each portrait told the
spectator that they were executed on the Chain Pier, Brighton,
in July, 1829. Had there ever been a time, I wonder, when
Mrs. Cæsar Donkin cared less about Mammon than about matrimony? Perhaps. On the wall fronting the fireplace there hung
another little portrait, a worn-out, mangy miniature, the carnations all faded, and one eye smeared out, on a bulging scrap
of ivory. It was the picture of an unhealthy, inane-looking
child in a frock and frills,—a mournful little object, who seemed
to be weakly lisping, "I always had the rickets, and died of water
on the brain, if you please." Such, it may be, was the end of
young Cæsar Donkin, if there ever had been a Cæsar Donkin
who was young, and wore a frock and frills, and had his miniature
taken.

The dessert on the table—it was one of the order called by
upholsterers "occasional," and a French furniture dealer would
decidedly have put it down as a *meuble d'occasion*—was not such a
display as Mr. Duffield or Miss Mutrie would have longed to have
painted. It was mainly of the dry and gritty description. There
were some argillaceous-looking biscuits; several pippins, whose
bruised countenances gave them the appearance of fighting pippins,
and of having been in the Ring, and heavily grassed in a contest
with the Blustering Railer; some apparently petrified plums; a
few dropsical oranges, suggesting boiled or blown-out integuments
and woolly interiors; a plateful of almonds and raisins, very dried
up and shrivelled; and some squabby flattened figs. This, with a
seed-cake, presenting a curious model of different geological strata,
completed the dessert. There was seldom any need to renew it.
The old gentlemen who sat at Mrs. Donkin's table were in general
toothless; and as for the ladies, they had more reasons for pleasing
the landlady than the landlady had for pleasing them, and so Mrs.
Donkin did not study them much. Now and then the old gentlemen were generous, and on birthdays and the like brought home
choice pears and strawberries, nay, grapes and pines even, from
Covent Garden. Mrs. Donkin did not in the least object, and
the improved dessert made a gala-day for herself, the ladies, and
Puffin.

A word may be spared for a glance at the two ladies I have mentioned by name. With Mrs. Donkin's age I have nothing to do; it would be ungallant to make inquiry into it; but taking her appearance for all in all, it is much to be feared that if Mrs. Donkin had lived in the reign of Elizabeth or James I., she would have been summarily sent to the stake, or at least dragged through a series of horseponds as a witch. The very sight of her would have set Mr. Hopkins itching to tie her thumbs together, and her facial *ensemble* would have been irresistible to the Reverend Cotton Mather. We know how many perfectly innocent and virtuous, albeit hideous, old ladies were unjustly burnt alive in the days of witchcraft persecution; and, remembering this, the ill-favouredness of Mrs. Donkin's appearance should not have militated against the presumption that she was in all respects a most estimable personage. Granting that she wore on her head a faded silken mutch, or hood, or calash, or something very much resembling the head-gear of the ladies who met on the blasted heath what time Macbeth was made Thane of Cawdor; granting that from beneath this headdress there hung elf-locks of grizzled and dishevelled hair; granting that Mrs. Cæsar Donkin's countenance was, in the way of wrinkles and crow's-feet, a chart of defiance to Mr. Wyld and all other eminent geographers; granting that on her upper lip and dented chin some sparse and bristly hairs of undefinable hue asserted themselves: granting that two discoloured fangs made an unpleasantly prominent appearance when she opened her withered lips; granting that what little of her neck was visible presented a remarkable series of gnarled corrugations; granting that her shoulders were very high, her back very round, and her hands long, lean, and garnished with orange-tawny nails that approached the form of claws;—granting all these peculiarities, it would be manifestly unjust to attach the stigma of sorcery to a lady who doubtless possessed every quality of head and heart necessary to endear her to her own sex and to the community at large.

That implacable Mrs. Grabblecheese boldly insinuated and resolutely maintained that Mrs. Cæsar Donkin never washed. Well, supposing that she never did? We can be virtuous without soap, I presume. Some of the holiest hermits of antiquity were quite unacquainted with the use of the flesh-brush and the foot-bath. If Mrs. Cæsar Donkin was averse from lavatory exertion, her boarders had never to complain of a deficiency of towels or brown Windsor. Everything in her house, herself always excepted, was as clean as a new pin. The furniture and metal work were as bright as the sun, and she was one of the spots on it.

The captious complained of her attire; surely she had a right to wear what clothes she liked. Her garments were of silk, although they certainly had seen their best, and perhaps their worst, days; for, short of absolute tatters, they had reached the superlative degree of shabbiness. From Mrs. Cæsar Donkin's girdle there hung a bunch of keys, which gave her a pleasant *chatelaine* look, compounded of a cellaress in a nunnery and a female warder in the House of Correction. She wore, too, an apron, conjectured, from its colour and texture, to have belonged to Mr. Cæsar Donkin in his early days of snuff-taking, and to have served him as a pocket-handkerchief. When to this you add very roomy list slippers, and a very remarkable brooch set in silver, and the stone of which was very like a petrified whelk, Mrs. Cæsar Donkin stands, or rather sits, before you in that unadorned beauty which is said to be adorned the most.

Respecting her companion, Miss Puffin, there is no need to enter into such minuteness of detail. Everybody felt and said that Puffin was nobody. Mrs. Cæsar Donkin told her so at least five hundred times a-day, and the worthy body seemed perfectly contented to be regarded as a nullity. She was a very placable little woman, with hair that had seemingly been carefully boiled until all the colour had been expressed from it, and with a complexion that had also undergone an analogous process of stewing down. If Puffin never smiled, it may be for the reason that her teeth were uneven, or that she had nothing to laugh at. If she seldom looked you in the face, it was perhaps because her eyes were very weak, and the lids thereof given to inflammation. If her hands were so very thin and bluely transparent, incessant hard work may have been the cause; and if, to sum up her personality, her poor little *barége* frock was dismally frayed and faded, it may be accounted for by the fact that it was very nearly the only dress which Puffin had to wear.

Being Nobody did not prevent people occasionally asking, in a lazy kind of way, how she came to be nobody and nothing. A few surmises respecting her were hazarded, but they involved no interest, and were seldom carried out to investigation. Some said she had been a partner of Mrs. Cæsar Donkin, and had been cozened out of her share in the business; others that she had been a boarder with a small annuity which had ceased, and being destitute, was now dependent on Mrs. Cæsar Donkin's bounty, and did what household work she could to assist her, for her keep. Then there was a party who said that she was a bankrupt day-school keeper hiding from her creditors. Another risked the conjecture that she was Mrs. Donkin's sister, niece, daughter even; but the most generally received opinion was, that Miss Puffin had been a domestic servant, elevated from the kitchen to the parlour, and admitted to the full confidence of the lady of the house, and intrusted with all her secrets, because "she knew something about her," and could do her an injury if she chose. Don't for one moment imagine that one ten-thousandth part of the charity which exists in London is to be found in the dinner and asylum announcements that appear every day in the newspapers. Puffin was about thirty years of age, and was, it need not be said, "a maiden all forlorn," at whom there is too much reason to fear that "the man all tattered and torn" of the nursery rhyme, albeit excited by the morn-crowing of an early village cock, and an offer from a "priest all shaven and shorn" to perform the marriage service gratuitously, would have turned up his nose.

CHAPTER XVII

THE SEXAGENARIANS.

THE preparation of a dessert is no such very momentous matter, particularly when there are no strawberries to pick, and no grapes to prune with silver scissors or dress with vine-leaves. Mrs. Cæsar Donkin, however, considered the daily occasion as one of great importance, and, with the assistance of Puffin, went through it with a considerable amount of state and ceremony. The half-hour before dinner was her time for descanting on the virtues and the failings of her boarders, for comparing the experience of the past with the occurrences of the present, and for devising those crafty little additions to her monthly bills which redounded so greatly to the credit of her ingenuity, and were by no means unserviceable in swelling her monthly profits.

"But as for General Tibby, Puffin," Mrs. Cæsar remarked, twisting a raisin which was obviously past service from its stalk, "he must go."

Puffin, who was polishing a pippin, did not verbally respond to this observation; but she gave utterance to a plaintive bleat, which may have been either a negative or an affirmative, or nothing at all, as the case stood.

"You mean that you think he ought to go," pursued Mrs. Donkin, quite satisfied as it seemed with the reply. "I can stand him and his carryings-on no longer. The nasty, mean, old hunks! I wish he'd never come here, that I'm sure I do."

This time Miss Puffin spake: "He's very old," she timidly ventured to remark.

"Old!" repeated the boarding-house keeper; "he's as old as the hills. He's one of the screws out of Noah's ark, and as rusty. What's the good of his being old and half-silly, if he's got nothing besides his half-pay and an annuity which dies with him?"

Miss Puffin winced at the mention of an annuity. It recalled, perhaps, unpleasant reminiscences.

"His half-pay," Mrs. Donkin continued, in a true philanthropic spirit, "he can't help. Not that he ever fought for it, I should imagine. He never went further than Wormwood Scrubbs, you may be sure. But it's his annuity that drives me wild with him. A man who would sink his savings in an annuity, and give up some comfortable thousands in a lump for a paltry six hundred a-year, would poison his grandmother."

"Ah, that he would!" acquiesced Miss Puffin, who would have agreed with Mrs. Donkin if she had accused General Tibby of a design to blow up the Houses of Parliament or set the Thames on fire.

"The man pays punctually enough," Mrs. Donkin was just enough to admit. "But where's the use of his money, if he's got nothing to leave? He might make his will on the back of a postage-stamp, and his handsomest legacy would be the silver buckle to his stock, his old wig, or his shower-bath. Stop; he's got a rouge-pot, too, and a hare's-foot. I'm sick and tired of him, Puffin. He gives himself all the airs of a bashaw of three tails. He grumbles at everything. He tastes the milk at breakfast before it goes into his tea, and talks of adulteration. He smells his bread, and says he's sure there are ground bones in it. He finds out my extras and scratches them out. He never offers anybody a glass of wine, though he drinks shamefully: and, worse than all, he takes my gentlemen out at night, and keeps them till two o'clock in the morning at his nasty clubs, smoking and guzzling, I'll be bound. He's half-ruined that poor Mr. Fogo, who was never anything more than a cotton-broker at Liverpool, but always wishes to pass himself off as a military man."

From the tenor of Mrs. Donkin's remarks it may be reasonably inferred that General Tibby was by no means a favourite with that lady. Previous to the discovery of the annuity, indeed, he had held a high place in her estimation. Although convicted of the heinous offence of having sunk his capital, he might have continued on the footing of an ordinary boarder; but his most unpardonable crime was the seduction into dissipated ways of the ex-cotton-

broker, Fogo, who was very wealthy and had *not* invested his property in an annuity.

"Give Tibby warning," was the sententious advice proffered by
Miss Puffin, when her companion had come to the end of her
complaints.

"I must and will," replied Mrs. Cæsar, "though it's a hard
matter to lose something very like two hundred a year. But I
can't stand him, Puffin, and that's the truth. He ought to be
charged a pound a week for his cough, and another pound for the
stupid nonsense he talks, and thirty shillings for the trouble he
gives the servants for his baths, and his I don't-know-what's, and
then he ought to be hung for an old skin-flint."

"He's a wretch," Miss Puffin agreed, pensively musing over
the plate of figs.

"Ah," retorted Mrs. Donkin, with some asperity, "it's all
very well for you to call him a wretch; and yet I've heard you
flattering the old nuisance up to his very eyes. You shan't sit
next to him any more, Puffin."

"I won't," returned Miss P., with perfect equanimity.

"Why don't you try your sheep's eyes upon Mr. Chatwynd,"
Mrs. Donkin resumed, "or upon Mr. Maunder, or on Captain
O'Ballygrumble, or on Mr. Tiddydoll, or on that dear, good, kind
old creature the Governor?"

It may have been intended as a compliment to speak of Miss
Puffin's orbs of vision having any resemblance to sheep's eyes.
It would have been nearer the mark to have likened them
to those of a lamb sorely afflicted with ophthalmia. To the
patient Puffin, however, all epithets were equally indifferent.
She was the kind of woman whom you could have called a
griffin or a hippopotamus without in the least disturbing her
tranquillity.

"Poor old Governor!" she said softly.

"Poor old Governor! Rich old Governor, you mean. At all
events, if he isn't rich, his daughter must be rolling in money. I
believe that if the old gentleman could eat gold, she'd let him
have it. She's always bringing him something. She's always making him presents. She turns the servants' heads with half-crowns
and new caps. She's promised me a gold watch from Benson's

on her papa's next birthday. Such a lady as she is too! such horses and carriages, such diamonds and pearls, and such a dear little duck of a Blenheim spaniel!"

"I don't like her," Miss Puffin remarked quietly.

"That's because you're jealous of her, you mean-spirited thing. You hate her because she's pretty, and has plenty of money, and hasn't a face like a sick rabbit with pink eyes."

Miss Puffin just raised those same ill-spoken-of eyes to about a level with the scraggy neck of the old woman.

"She's very kind to her father," she returned, "and does her best to make the Governor happy; apart from that, I think—I don't know why, but I'm sure of it—that Mrs. Armytage is a very wicked woman. Her very laugh makes one shudder."

This was an exceedingly long speech for the ordinarily taciturn Puffin, and she was quite confused with her loquacity; so, plunging into silence she proceeded to carry the plates, two by two, from the room. At this stage, it wanting but ten minutes to dinner-time, it was Mrs. Cæsar Donkin's invariable custom to remark that she must really go and make herself tidy. The memory of Puffin ran not to the contrary regarding this remark; and Mrs. Donkin used duly to disappear to some mysterious chamber in the upper stories which served as her sleeping apartment. When she reappeared, her hands were invested with a pair of curiously brown and ragged mittens, in which the fissures of age struggled with the original interstices of the network; and those who were permitted to approach Mrs. Donkin could not avoid an impression, palpable to the olfactory sense, that the completion of her toilette had been in some way assisted by the consumption, either by herself or by her twin-sister, of some alcoholic preparation into which the cordial known as peppermint had entered.

Miss Puffin took the dessert to the dining-room by easy stages, and had just landed the figs on the sideboard when a double knock of alarming length and resonance echoed through the house.

For the matter of that, all the boarders knocked loud; some whose hands were stiff or chalkstony plied the knocker somewhat tremulously and in uncertain cadence; but all the sexagenarians did their best to produce sonorous rat-tats. Their strength was in the main but labour and sorrow now; and there was some feeble pleasure to be derived even from the power of knocking a good loud series of reverberations. The ring which passed through the lion's head on the door was good to them, and thundered on its little anvil bravely. Mrs. Cæsar Donkin let them knock as vigorously as they could and chose to do. It was an indulgence for which she forbore to charge in the monthly bills.

The double knock, or rather the personage whose advent it announced, was duly ushered upstairs; and a few moments afterwards a succession of double knocks more or less resounding was heard, as the old gentlemen came from their clubs, their trots in the Park, and the other amusements they devised for killing their old enemy Time. He it was that most of all they had to fear. Like a usurer who begins to have doubts of the solvency of a spendthrift deep in his books, he exacted heavier and heavier interest for every year of life he granted them; yet the poor old moths could not help wasting the brief span that remained to them, and puzzled their wits to get rid of the precious moments that Time in his tolerance permitted them still to enjoy.

Let the venue be changed to the dining-room, an intensely respectable and gloomy apartment of the family-vault order of architecture, the windows of which commanded an extensive view of the premises of a statuary opposite, whose front garden was decorated in a lively manner with cenotaphs, broken columns, monumental tablets, garden vases, the Venus of Milo, the bald-faced stag, the Discobolus, the dog of Alcibiades, the late Mr. Wilberforce, and the late Duke of Wellington. There was the usual sarcophagus wine-cooler under the side-board of the dining-room; a cheerful bust of a Grecian philosopher with his nose broken off; and a water-colour view of a building that might have been either a union workhouse, a baths and washhouses, or a baronial hall, and which seemed to have been borrowed from the fine-arts' gallery of a house-agent.

A bell that was suggestive of mingled reminiscences of a sexton's tolling for the departing and of the proximity of muffins had been tinkling for some five minutes to warn the inmates of Mrs. Cæsar Donkin's establishment that dinner was served; and at a few minutes after seven the old boys came shambling and tottering down the staircase from the drawing-room, each with a lady on his arm.

I have called them for conciseness the Sexagenarians, but it has already been pointed out that while Mrs. Cæsar insisted on a minimum, she totally ignored the maximum in age. Some of the gentlemen present had passed their seventh, some were rapidly approaching their eighth lustre. Old General Tibby, it was clear, would never see seventy-three again. This hero of a hundred field-days was immensely decrepit and fatuous, and as sprightly as his manifold infirmities would allow him to be. He was elaborately got up, and there was nothing true about him but his voice, which, as all the paint and padding in the world will not mend flaws in the vocal organ, was cracked and shrill, as beseemed his advanced age. Mr. Fogo was not so old by half a score of years, and wore much better. Something of the Lancastrian muscle—of the thew and sinew of the strong men who hail from the backbone of England, and bulk large, so to speak, in the forefront of English humanity—yet adhered to him. It has already been hinted that this retired and affluent cotton-broker had a fancy for being mistaken for a military gentleman. It would have been indeed a very great mistake to assume that he was one; for "*bourgeois*" was written in every line of his healthy vacuous countenance; but, as Mr. Fogo was over six feet high, and had sufficiently broad shoulders, and did not stoop much, he took to wearing a black stock, without any perceptible shirt collar, a blue surtout tightly buttoned up to his throat, and a stripe down either leg of his trowsers. He affected high heels to his boots likewise, carried a bamboo-cane in one hand, and dangled a stout buckskin glove in the other. He subscribed to the *Army List*, knew all the military clubs by sight, frequently hovered on their door-steps when there was the slightest shadow of a pretence to ask for one of the members, and would have dearly liked to belong to either of the United Service re-unions, could he have got any one to propose and second him. Before coming to Mrs. Donkin's he had occupied apartments in that great half-pay Patmos St. Alban's Place, Haymarket; but the red-jackets and crossing-sweepers soon found out that he was no soldier. When they called him "captain" it was ironically, and when they touched their ragged caps to him, it was with a sneer. In the end he fled the purlieus of the camp in disgust; but on levee-days he was still to be found haunting the avenues to St. James's and the Horse Guards. He knew all the promotions and appointments in the *Gazette*; he was familiar with the facings, services, and motto of every regiment in the service; he was glib in the use of abstruse terms relative to fortifications and military tactics; and he was an adept at the configuration of a plan of the battle of Waterloo, on the mahogany after dinner:—the positions of the French and allied armies being marked out by means of nut-crackers, bits of orange peel, and thin streaks of port-wine. Beyond this he was perfectly harmless, and paid his way like a gentleman.

There were altogether eight old men who partook of the dignified hospitality of Bergen-op-Zoom Terrace. Tibby and Fogo you have been already introduced to. Captain O'Ballygrumble's energies—he was seventy—were mainly confined to the endeavour to conceal the fact that he was an Irishman. When it is mentioned that his appearance was as Hibernian as his name, and that his speech was of the purest Dublin jackeen just racked through a cask of Cork whisky, it is unnecessary to add that his attempt did not succeed. He was called captain—or called himself so—from having formerly held a commission in a militia regiment. He was a ladies' man, but of the ferocious, not the sentimental order. He bragged much of having blown out the brains of many brothers who objected to the attentions he had paid to their sisters. When a divorce case in high life became a topic of conversation, he was used to wink significantly, and to hint that he could say a great deal more about that "litthle matther" if he chose. He pleaded guilty to the charge of ogling the ladies in Kensington Gardens. The truth is, that he glared at them horribly, brushed past them offensively, and addressed them impertinently, whenever he had an opportunity; and his dyed whiskers and large white teeth were the terror of well-disposed nursery-maids and young ladies' boarding schools. It was whispered that he had been tried in early life for the abduction of an heiress; and it was known that he had made an offer of marriage to Lady Madapolam, widow of the great City alderman Sir Callimauco Madapolam, who had over two hundred thousand pounds to her jointure. His suit was scornfully rejected; but, nothing deterred, O'Ballygrumble followed the lady about from watering-place to watering-place,—from Brighton to Cheltenham, from Nice to Aix-la-Chapelle,—pursuing her with his odious attentions. The lady had been foolish enough to send a few curt replies to the oceans of love-letters with which he inundated her; and his last *coup* was to threaten to publish all the correspondence that had passed between them. After this, it was said that Lady Mada-polam—whose servants, male and female, he had alternately cajoled and caned into his interest—had bought her persecutor off with a handsome annual allowance. The good lady didn't require a second husband. She spent her dividends very comfort-ably in eating and drinking, in pills and potions,—she was known to every *Pharmacien Anglais* from the Seine to the Danube; in forming a library of theological literature; in subscribing to charitable associations for recondite philanthropic purposes, and which generally, after the third annual dinner, ended by the secretary's absconding, and the whole affair turning out to be a gross swindle and imposition. The respected name of Lady Mada-polam headed the subscription to the Infant Hottentot's Gra-tuitous Hockey-Stick and Tip-cat Distribution Society, in con-nection with the Additional Knife and Fork and Digestive Pill Aid to Destitute Cannibals Association. Friendly George Gaf-ferer was in the last-named bubble. George was Sec. *pro tem.*, and laid the foundations of many future dinner-invitations among his private friends by distributing gratuitous tickets among them for the first grand festival at the Freemasons' Tavern. The Gaf-ferer was great while the society lasted. He was wont to boast of his "interest with the Press," and absolutely procured the insertion of a ten-line paragraph in the *Weekly Cad* newspaper, in which the pressing claims of the destitute cannibals, more especially in the Fee-jee and Cruel Islands, to a large supply of knives, forks, and Cockle's pills were dwelt upon. "Shall these embyro Christians," asked the paragraph ("embyro" was a good term, and told immensely), "die of indigestion? Missionaries are well known to be tough. Who would refuse the poor cannibal his knife, his fork, and his pill-box?" O'Howler wrote the above glowing lines, and lived at free quarters on the charity for a month afterwards. Friendly George Gafferer constituted himself into a committee of taste, and delivered some opinions most valuable in an epicurean point of view, when asked into the bar-parlour of the Freemasons', and regaled, free of expense, with turtle-soup for lunch, peculiar Madeira, and choice Regalias. A good soul George Gafferer, and nobody's friend but his own.

But Captain O'Ballygrumble has been left in the lurch while I have been digressing upon George Gafferer. (The Additional Aid Society turned out to be an awful delusion; and it was with difficulty that the Treasurer and Sec. *pro tem.* escaped legal proceedings.) The Captain was *en retraite* now, and lived gaily enough upon his property, whencesoever it may have proceeded. He said that he bore Lady Madapolam no malice; but that he had been "skyandalously threated throughout the affair, and that she would have done much better to marry a Milesian gentleman of ancient descent, than to spend thousands in building churches where they were not wanted." Such was the Captain. He would have been very much like the bragging and fortune-hunting Irishman so familiar to us on the stage, had he not been the very image of the bragging and fortune-hunting Irishman we see off the stage and in real life.

Mr. Chatwynd was very old, thin, silent, gentlemanly, and inoffensive. He was known to be rich, to be a member of the Society of Antiquaries, and of the Travellers' Club. Second-hand booksellers and dealers in mediæval wares were continually sending him catalogues by post. He had chambers in Staple Inn, Holborn, where he was supposed to possess a magnificent collection of pictures, busts, gems, China, and rare editions. Beyond a habit of taking snuff at dinner time, and an abhorrence of fat meat, he had no very remarkable peculiarities.

The rest of the old men, with one exception, claim no special notice. They were nonentities. They wheezed and grumbled, they coughed and cooed, they hemmed and hawed, and occasionally drivelled. They were frightened at the ferocity of Captain O'Ballygrumble, and awed by the quiet contempt of Mr. Chatwynd, who, for all his ripe age, was erect and valid, and was known to be a person of superior attainments. Their conversation was the very baldest chat. Take away their clothes, and chains and rings, their well-spread table, and soft couches, and there was not much to choose between these ancients and the frieze-clad dotards you see warming their wafer-like palms over the stoves in the old man's ward of a workhouse. It was not good to look upon them, either when they were solitary, and doddered about in blank search of their health and their memory, or when meat had warmed them into active munching and slavering, or drink had made them garrulous. Poor old men, where were they all going? There was nothing about them to remind him who considered them of those reverend hermits of old, who dwelt in caves and fed on roots, and prayed continually. They were all self-indulgent, and, most of them, sordidly avaricious. The coarse dirty old woman who ruled over the house rather frightened than persuaded them out of their money. A greedy old man needs often to be terrified with stripes as though he were a greedy schoolboy; and not one of Mrs. Donkin's boarders could stand the lashings of her tongue. For the rest, they were the kind of dilapidated gentlemen you see wandering about Pall Mall and the Opera Colonnade on warm afternoons; who leer into the milliners' shops in the Burlington Arcade, and the pastrycook's at the Regent Circus, and sometimes totter through the Pantheon Bazaar to the conservatory, where the macaws and cockatoos scream at them. And more than one of Mrs. Cæsar Donkin's boarders were, it is to be feared, very wicked old boys indeed. But "the Governor"? Who was he? what was he like? and how came he by the gubernatorial title? you may ask. The Governor was the oldest inmate of the caravanserai in Bergen-op-Zoom Terrace. Indeed, he was an old, old man, and venerable to look upon. His silky, snowy locks flowed down his shoulders; his linen was scrupulously clean and white; and through his great infirmities, he was permitted by Mrs. Donkin to appear at the dinner-table in his dressing gown and slippers. When he spoke, his speech was gentle, courteous, and dignified; but he was, perforce, not very talkative for he was almost entirely deaf; and his reverend head was garnished with a pair of ear-trumpets, secured by elastic bands round his white forehead, and which in their convolutions reminded one of a ram of the highest respectability and the greatest antiquity.

He was so feeble that when his daughter was not present to assist him he had to be wheeled in and out of the dining-room in an arm-chair, and he was propped up by pillows during the repast. He rose very late, breakfasted in his room, and retired to rest very early. He was continually visited by eminent physicians. A most handsome stipend was paid for his lodging and maintenance; Mrs. Cæsar Donkin was devoted to him; and even the undemonstrative Puffin showed how much she was interested in him. Often the Governor would say, in his refined and dignified manner, that, but "for his great age and infirmities, nothing would afford him greater gratification than to offer his hand to a virtuous and well-conducted young woman, who could bring herself to cheer the winter of an old man's days." At this the sensitive Puffin would tremble, and grow pale and red by turns; and then, mustering up courage, she would shout into one of the ear-trumpets, that he had plenty more years before him, and that Dr. Sardonix's good care would speedily restore him to health and strength. At which the Governor would shake his head with an expression of resigned negation.

Yes: Dr. Sardonix attended the Governor. He talked everywhere of his patience under suffering, his amiable disposition, and his distinguished manners. A true gentleman, the doctor declared him to be, and one of the old school. He extolled the filial devotion of the Governor's daughter to the skies. "It is true," the doctor would say, "that the brilliant position which Mrs. Armytage fills in society frequently calls her abroad: but no sooner does she arrive in England, than she flies, literally flies, my dear sir,—to the side of her venerated parent. Ah, what a daughter! what a model for all daughters, high and low!"

"I am glad there is some good in that artful and designing creature," Miss Magdalen Hill once chose to remark when the name of the detested widow was mentioned and her filial piety eulogised.

"Artful and designing!" the doctor echoed, holding up his white hands in well-simulated astonishment. "Come, come, let us not be too hard upon this most charming of butterflies,—this most seductive of gilded moths."

"Say serpents, doctor," poor Lady Goldthorpe chimed in.

"She's a nasty hypocritical rattlesnake. I never could a-bear the creature, with her fly-by-night curls. I wish they were false; but they ain't, I know, and more's the pity. I tell you she's no good. Years ago, when my poor dear dead darling Hugh came back from India on his leave, and stopped in Paris, that woman tried to wind him round her finger. I found one of her yellow curls in his cigar-case once—"

"Mamma!" Magdalen expostulated, with a warning finger, a blush, and a sigh.

"You may call her anything you like, dear ladies," the discreet physician would remark; "but what would you have? She is a woman of the world. She occupies the exceptional and invidious place of a rich and pretty—well, not pretty, but engaging—widow. She belongs to Vanity Fair, dear Lady Goldthorpe. Surely you remember the charming character of Becky Sharpe."

"No," the simple lady replied; "I never read no novels. I had a maid called Becky Sharpe once, and she ran away with three bottles of eau-de-cologne, a true lover's knot brooch, and all the silver stoppers off the bottles in my dressing-case, let alone a pair of laced sleeves and a false character she left behind her. Her name turned out to be—when Sir Jasper transported her,—not Sharpe at all, but Bowdler."

"I," Magdalen said, rising at this stage of the colloquy, "have read the wonderful drama of human life to which Dr. Sardonix refers. Unless I am mistaken, Becky Sharpe was in the end found out. It may be that the same fate will happen, some day or another, to this pattern and paragon of filial piety, whose name I disdain to recall."

It is said that when people are talking about us our ears burn. I wonder which one it is, the right or the left, that tingles and feels hot when people are talking against us. It is well that the little widow had curls; for giving one ear to the men, and appropriating another to the women, what flaming lobes Mrs. Army-tage must have had from morning till night underneath those shining locks of hers!

Had she known, or did she divine half the evil that was spoken against her, she would not have deviated from the path of duty she had traced out for herself regarding her papa. Her behaviour

towards him was more than amiable, more than admirable : it was
incomparable. Mrs. Cæsar Donkin looked upon her as the ancients might have looked upon the Grecian daughter, or the Sans-
culottes of the Reign of Terror upon the young lady who drank
a glass of blood to save her father from the scaffold. Puffin, to
be sure, disparaged her ; but then Puffin had her motives. Perhaps
Magdalen had her motives also, but she was too haughty to own
them. The chest of that young person's thoughts closed with a
spring, the key was lost, and the thoughts mouldered into skeletons
within.

The Governor took the homage and the affection of which he
was the object with his unvarying and dignified serenity. He was
good enough to express to Mrs. Donkin his belief that in the
whole world there was not such another daughter to be found as his
Florence ; beyond that admission he suffered himself to be loved
se laissait aimer, and repaid the almost idolatory which was lavished
on him with beaming smiles, of which he had, to all appearance, an
inexhaustible stock. It was doubtful why he was called "the
Governor," what he had governed, or where had been the seat of
his government. He was too fine a gentleman to be asked impertinent questions, even if he had not been too deaf to answer
them. He had had something to do with the colonies—with the
West India Islands, it was generally understood. A chance
reference to Tobago had once been dropped by his daughter. Was
he the original

> "Old man of Tobago,
> Who lived on rice, sugar, and sago,
>   Till the doctor one day
>   Unto him did say,
> To a roast leg of mutton you may go ?"

No one could give an opinion with certainty as to this important
question. It was, however, generally agreed that he was not only
wealthy himself but the cause of wealth in others ; to wit, in his
daughter, whom he had splendidly dowered, and who was the
widow besides of an Indian officer of large means. Mrs. Donkin
had lost her faith in affluent Orientals. The remembrance of the
perfidy of Jaghire was a wound not yet healed ; but even she did
not refuse to place credence in the many lacs of rupees left to his
relict by Major Armytage.

It must appear to the reader that while these personal matters were under discussion the ancient boarders of Bergen-op-Zoom Terrace have been kept waiting an unconscionably long time for their dinners ; and they were crusty old gentlemen, believe me, who resented even a three minutes' delay in the appearance of the soup. Be not alarmed, however ; while we have been wandering from the Governor to the Goldthorpes, and from Bergen-op-Zoom Terrace to Onyx Square,—there was not a mile distance between the boarding-house and the palace of Mammon,—Mrs. Cæsar Donkin's *pensionnaires* have been proceeding with their repast as well as ever their teeth and their trembling hands would let them. They have had soup ; they have had fish—brill, falsely called turbot, at the top, skate at the bottom ; they have had *entrées*—Pshaw ! why should I give you the entire bill of fare ? It is enough to say that the entire banquet was a capital imitation of a first-rate dinner, but that it was in reality a very bad one. There was plenty of electro-plate about, *épergnes* filled with artificial flowers, chased vases for the champagne—which, out of compliment to the ladies, was provided in turns by the old gentlemen,—filigree bread-baskets, finger-glasses, table-napkins, a battered old waiter full of weak rose-water, passed round after the cheese,—all the paraphernalia, in fact, of an expensive and well-served feast. All that was wanting were good meats and vegetables. Herein lay the profit of Mrs. Cæsar Donkin, and herein was displayed her ingenuity and state-craft. The rose-water didn't cost a farthing a day, the electro-plate wore well, the artificial flowers were in perennial bloom, the table-napkins were washed, like every article of linen in the establishment, by the dozen, and surely finger-glasses are cheap enough ! Altogether, however, these odds-and-ends of good society made a brave show. It was the style that did it, Mrs. Donkin said ; and even those who came away hungry from her symposia admitted that she certainly did give very stylish dinners. With a judicious and discriminating use of style, you may do almost everything in this sublunary world. In letters you may conceal your ignorance and your dullness,—in art you may atone for imperfect drawing and clumsy manipulation,—in the concerns of domestic life you may hide half your meannesses and shabbinesses, by artful recourse to style. For it is an impalpable

Q

powder which, when dexterously thrown in the eyes of mankind, affects them with a happy blindness.

There: the clattering of knives and forks is over. A remarkable cheese, very much like a dilapidated drum, and coming, it is to be suspected, from North Wiltshire, but which Mrs. Cæsar Donkin's stylishness caused to do duty as a Stilton, has been removed. The grand cut-glass stand, with three lamentable forked sprigs of celery drooping from it, and the little pellet of butter, with its elaborate knife of electro ware, have been handed round ; the cloth has been drawn, as the reporters write of public dinners; the famous dessert has been put on the table; the decanters of port or claret belonging to each boarder, and each labelled with his name, have been produced from the recesses of the sideboard ; and the Sexagenarians begin to enjoy themselves. They are but a feeble folk, and scant of that breath from a total want of which they must all, at no very distant period, perish. *Oras nobis*, my hearty companions ;—and the conversation is rather by fits and starts than sustained ; but there is a little squabble now and then, and perhaps a weak morsel of love-making ; and these relieve the monotony of the chatter.

Love-making? Yes, madam ; and that reminds the narrator of a serious error of omission. It is customary, I am aware, at public banquets to make the toast of " the ladies " one of, if not *the* very last of, the evening. There is surely no need in private life to be so ungallant; so with the first glass of wine, if you please, let us look towards the ladies, and evince a due solicitude for their very good health. I bow towards the end of the table where sits Mrs. Cæsar Donkin, looking more like a witch than ever. Beyond the mittens, Mrs. Donkin scorned to make any alteration in her toilette, even on the most festive occasions. The Sexagenarians feared her too much to remonstrate. Miss Puffin, indeed, spruced herself up to the extent of putting on over her faded *barége* a black silk jacket, which in a strong light showed reflections of an orange tawney hue, and which was currently reported to have been made out of a hatband presented to her grandfather on the occasion of his attending the obsequies of the late lamented Marquis of Granby. But Mrs. Cæsar Donkin and Miss Puffin were not the only members of their charming

sex who graced the dinner-table. There were lady boarders in
Bergen-op-Zoom Terrace. For example, on the left of General
Tibby—the post of his right being occupied by Puffin—sat old
Mrs. Vanderpant, widow of a former consul at the port of Bristol
of his majesty the king of the Netherlands. She was very fat,
she was very good-tempered. From whatever part of Holland
she came, it could not have been from the clean village of Brock,
near Amsterdam; for she did not show the slightest distaste to
Mrs. Cæsar Donkin's slatternliness. Mrs. Vanderpant had a
comfortable pension paid to her quarterly by a Dutch house in
the cheese and butter trade in Trinity Square, and in which her
deceased husband had held a share. She walked resolutely every
Sunday morning to the old Dutch church in Austin Friars,
returning in a cab, and always having a terrific dispute with the
driver on the question of sixpence. First she refused to pay him;
then she offered him some of the minor coinage of the Low
Countries, which she kept by her in a wash-leather bag; then
she abused him roundly in Dutch; finally, she paid him, slammed
the door in his face, drank two glasses of cherry-brandy, informed
any one who might be present that all cabmen were "tam tieves,"
and went to bed until dinner-time. There was little variety in
her life; but beyond an ugly word (imperfectly pronounced,
which may have divested it of some of its sinfulness) there was no
harm in Mrs. Vanderpant.

Captain O'Ballygrumble, who was croupier,—Mr. Cæsar Donkin never putting in an appearance at meal-times,—had for right
hand neighbour a countrywoman of his own, Miss MacShandrydan
(of the Shandrydans of Booterstown); while his attentions to the
left were due to Miss Bubb. Alethea MacShandrydan was fifty,
and an invalid. She suffered from chronic sickness. Not love-
sickness; there was but one person in the world for whom Miss
MacShandrydan cared one potato-peeling, and that was herself.
Not bodily sickness; she was as strong as a grenadier, and had as
fine an appetite as the celebrated bold dragoon, "with his long
sword, saddle, bridle, O," of the ballad. She was simply sick, and
nearly sick to death with affectation. She had shone many years
before in a kind of meteoric gleam of the reflex of the reflection
of the Irish viceregal court. The shadow of one of the Lord-

Lieutenant's footmen had once crossed her path, and made her
aristocratic for ever. She was Sackville Street at secondhand,
a washed-out Westmoreland Street, a faded Phantom of the
Phœnix Park. She made you very nearly as sick as she was
herself with her meagre prattle about "the Kyastle" and the
"Juke of Richmond's aid-du-cong's." She called a street cab
"a ;floy," and asked people what the inside of an omnibus was
like. The old hypocrite! She was the bane and torment of
every cad between the Marble Arch and Charing Cross. She
was so affected that she could scarcely speak, and, although she
had a fine native brogue of her own, lisped, and chewed her silly
words, marching as mincingly in her speech as Agag on the earth,
and driving irritable people to meditate the hewing of her in
pieces, even as it befel Agag.

She had just enough money to pay her expenses in Bergen-op-
Zoom Terrace, and to buy portraits of crowned heads and of the
higher nobility at the secondhand-print shops. Her bed-chamber
was hung round with pale effigies of his late H.R.H. the Duke of
Gloucester, George the Fourth in a brown jasey and silk-covered
pianoforte legs, the Earl of Liverpool, and the Hetman Platoff.
She had a large wardrobe, which Mrs. Donkin greedily coveted,
and of which the shawls, dresses, laces, and other woman's frip-
pery, might have made a somewhat handsome appearance at certain Castle levees and theatrical command nights in Dublin early
in the century. She always bought the Red-Book of the year
before last cheap; and, so far as you could understand her for
lisping, was fond of dilating on the claims of her brother Hercules
MacShandrydan, "kinnected with the Governmhent," to the dormant peerage of Derrymacash. Captain O'Ballygrumble hated
her with a fierce and implacable loathing, and declared that she
had never been anything more than a governess in a day-school
at Dunleary, and that Hercules her brother had first been a tithe-
proctor, and next an exciseman, and was now a retired sergeant
in the constabulary.

Miss Bubb was of English extraction. She made no secret of
the fact of her family being connected with that branch of commerce involving a traffic in grocery. Don't you remember Bubb
and Grubb, family tea-dealers, at the Golden Biggin in Oxford

Street? It was Bubb who introduced the "Efflorescent Gunpowder at Two and Eleven," by selling which (in four-pound packages) he realised a fortune. Matilda Bubb had in early life made up many parcels; but the sugar of her career was sanded by the treachery of a shopman, who made violent love to her, and actually proposed, but, finding that old Bubb would give nothing down to his daughter, married Miss Pruin of the Golden Caddy, the opposition grocer's directly opposite; and by dint of puffing advertisements, plate-glass, an electro-plated coffee-mill with a working steam-engine, and a vast display of cartoons representing the cultivation and preparation of the fragrant herb as pursued by the natives in the interior of China, succeeded in depriving Bubb and Grubb of nineteenths of their customers. Old Bubb, however, dying, left his only daughter a corpulent independence; and Matilda was scarcely out of her mourning ere she had the gratification of seeing her faithless swain made condignly bankrupt. He fled to Tasmania, without a certificate, and with incipient delirium tremens, and his wife was compelled to take in needlework for a livelihood. Such is very frequently the end of plate-glass windows, electro-plated coffee-mills, and Chinese cartoons.

Miss Bubb was the only boarder in Bergen-op-Zoom Terrace who kept a carriage—a roomy old fly of the glass-coach order. She was very soft, impressionable, and, in a melancholy manner, good-humoured. She read sentimental novels from morning to night. She nourished a long and pensive curl of an ashen hue by the side of either wan cheek, and her left eye was a glass one. Poor Miss Bubb!

The two Misses Cherrygo would have been exceedingly annoyed if you had not taken notice of them; but really there was little in their persons or character to call, in this place at least, for extended notice. They were middle-aged twins, who dressed alike, and wore their hair alike, and frequently had their arms round one another's waists. They sang duets together at the piano in the drawing-room. They went shopping together. In fact, they were inseparable. Old Cherrygo, their papa, who had formerly been connected in some manner with the Commissariat, and was said to owe the major part of his handsome competence to successful malversations in bullocks and rum,—to him was attributed the celebrated *mot*, that "for a forlorn hope there's nothing like fasting,"—had formerly occupied apartments beneath Mrs. Donkin's roof. He had the egregious folly and baseness to go away and marry a designing creature who kept a fancy repository in Praed Street, Paddington, and who, I am delighted to say, made his married life one continuous series of aggravated assaults on her part. Is not the case of Cherrygo *versus* Cherrygo even now down for trial before Sir Cresswell Cresswell, and is not the wretched old Commissary seeking a judicial separation on the ground of cruelty? When he left Bergen-op-Zoom Terrace, a reprobate and a deceiver, this elderly outcast formally disinherited his daughters. The lady who kept the fancy repository is said, indeed, to have declared to a confidential charwoman, on the very eve of their bridal, that the daughters of that old fool should never darken her doors. Fortunately the Misses Cherrygo were not destitute. An uncle, who had made a nice little fortune during the great war by buying up sailors' claims to prize-money at a discount of about seventy-five per cent., bequeathed his virtuous savings to his nieces, and they had quite enough to live upon. The Misses Cherrygo passed, then, a quiet and tranquil life, alternately executing elaborate chair-covers in Berlin wool, and abusing the abandoned Commissary their papa. To that same Berlin wool must be ascribed, as a first cause, their alienation from a never fond but still convenient parent. Had they never requested the elder Cherrygo to call at the repository in Praed Street, for the purpose of matching two shades of orange and one of purple, he would probably have never seen Miss Brownmake, the designing person who subsequently became his wife.

These were all the lady boarders. Mrs. Donkin made no stipulation as to their age, and even charged them less for their board than she did the gentlemen. The ladies were useful to her. It was part of Mrs. Donkin's policy so to contrive matters that every Sexagenarian should be in love with at least one, if not two, of her female inmates. Most of them fell into Cupid's trap easily enough. Chatwynd, indeed, was shy and reticent; but he was so quiet, and in every way so desirable a lodger, that his want of susceptibility was overlooked. Captain O'Ballygrumble made love to the ladies all round, when he was in a good temper, and always excepting Miss Shandrydan; and as for the poor old Governor, it quite suited Mrs. Cæsar Donkin's purpose that all he had to do with love should be in enjoying the worship of his daughter.

She, the daughter, Mrs. Armytage, was the guest this evening. She often came to dine. She liked to sit next to her darling papa. She complimented Mrs. Donkin. She complimented the ladies. She complimented the gentlemen. There was little individual love-making on the days she came, for all the Sexagenarians were wild after Mrs. Armytage, and their homage was centred in her. Curiously the older ladies were not jealous of her. She seemed to be so dazzling, so accomplished, so distinguished, as to belong quite to another world. She could not, it was argued, be setting her cap at any of these poor worn-out, creeping, chattering, dotards. If her aim was wealthy caducity, she might marry a gouty marquis, or a paralytic duke, if she liked. The Governor was good enough to remark one day that his daughter had refused the Russian Ambassador to a foreign Court, who was the owner of half the Ukraine, and half the peasants living thereupon. "But," continued the Governor, "my beloved Florence will never form a fresh alliance so long as her poor old father lives." So the little lady was highly popular in Bergen-op-Zoom Terrace, and was a queen there, as she was everywhere else, save in a certain dingy chamber in Coger's Inn, Strand, and a certain mouldy back kitchen in Badger-lane, Stockwell. Aha! what king, what queen may there be, I wonder, who in some place or another is not reckoned of any more account than a beggar, and, with a crown on head and sceptre in hand, has not to eat the humblest of humble pie?

The Governor did not stay long over his wine. He drank three glasses of sound old port-wine, of which he always kept an abundant store, and which he or his daughter freely dispensed to the company in general, and to Mrs. Donkin in particular. It was not his custom to join the ladies in the drawing-room. He was too much of an invalid to bear so much fatigue. It was a very beautiful and interesting sight to see his tottering steps directed to the door by his devoted daughter. She always assisted him to his bedchamber; and the parent and child passed an hour or so in the solace of cheerful and innocent conversation, before the good old Governor retired to rest. He was unusually feeble on this present evening, and leant on his daughter's arm with unusual pressure. All the Sexagenarians rose as the pair took their departure; and even the ferocious O'Ballgrumble rushed to the door, and held it obsequiously open.

"What a charming creature!" mumbled General Tibby.

"A model daughter," sighed Mr. Bowdler.

"A doosed fine woman," remarked Mr. Fogo, in his peremptory military voice.

The ladies joined their little twitterings in the chorus of applause, and, when they reached the drawing-room, proceeded to criticise Mrs. Armytage's jewellery, her lace, her flounces, and her ringlets. There was but one voice heard in disparagement, and that was, oddly, from good-natured Mrs. Vanderpant.

"I not like her laugh, he, he!" the good lady remarked, sinking on a sofa; "and, 'pon my word, I tink she paint."

The Governor occupied a large and commodious bedchamber on the second-floor. He had furnished it himself, and, as this involved no diminution of Mrs. Donkin's usual charges, that lady was quite content to allow him to furnish it in what manner he pleased. It was by no means an uncomfortable apartment, and, to judge from the number of books and papers scattered about, the Governor was a gentleman of studious, if not literary pursuits.

Florence led the old man into this chamber, and, until they had passed the very threshold, he continued to totter, and she to guide his footsteps, looking up in his face meanwhile with an expression of the tenderest solicitude. They were no sooner inside the door, however, and that door was no sooner closed upon them, and carefully locked, than a very remarkable change took place in the demeanour both of Mrs. Florence Armytage and of her venerable papa. She was no longer the Grecian daughter, the modern Mademoiselle de Sombreuil, ready to quaff a glass of blood as though it were one of Chateau Lafitte to redeem the head of her papa from the glaive of the guillotine. She became, with electric rapidity, our own familiar Mrs. Armytage, the fascinating widow, the laughing tenant of the first-floor in the Rue Grande-des-

Petites-Maisons—the airy, saucy, *débonnaire* little creature, who was wont to shake her sunny ringlets and play with her lap-dog. Her pathetic veneration for the Governor had all vanished; not an iota was left of her affectionate solicitude. She dropped his arm without the slightest ceremony, and tripping to a large easy-chair, flung herself on to the cushions, and laughed long and heartily in her old, merry, satirical, desperately-wicked fashion.

But if the change that had occurred in this pattern of filial affection was sudden and astonishing, not less speedy and peculiar was that which came over the respected gentleman who was dignified with the name of Governor. The deformed became all at once transformed, and Mr. Hartley Livingstone, who had entered the room a confirmed valetudinarian, to whom the seldom-erring judgment of Mrs. Donkin would have given at least seventy-seven years, sat down in an arm-chair opposite his daughter, a hale, strong, personable man to all appearance short of fifty years of age. For he had plucked off his flowing white locks; he had cast aside his ram-like ear-trumpets; he had discarded his green shade; he had divested his neck of its thick swathings of linen. His halt, his hobble, and his stoop had all disappeared; and he sat grinning with a remarkably fine set of even white teeth, a pair of gleaming hazel eyes, and a closely-cropped bullet-head of crisp black hair. It was the story of Sixtus the Fifth over again; and the perfidy of Jaghire was repeated, with five hundred per cent. in its audacious deception added.

The first act of this metamorphosed patriarch was to produce from a cheffonier a black bottle and a glass, and to mix himself a comfortably stiff glass of brandy-and-water. He next opened a cigar-case, and, producing a fine havannah, lighted and proceeded to smoke it, with an aspect of cheerful deliberation.

"My medical attendants recommend the use of the aromatic herb tobacco for the poor old Governor," he remarked, with a coarse laugh, entirely different from his former calmly-dignified manner. "Nobody but the invalid Governor is allowed to smoke in this house; but he pays so well, that the Witch of Endor would allow him to walk on the ceiling, or have a brass band at the window, if it was agreeable to him. He does what he likes, the interesting old sufferer. Ho, ho!"

The man's laugh was inexpressibly repulsive. He seldom spoke without a hard metallic "Ho, ho!" as a refrain. It was his daughter's laugh in its crude and rugose stage;—his was the vocal bronze to her shining silver. He had a habit, too, of speaking of himself in the third person, of flattering himself grossly, and of slapping his large thigh, which by no means enhanced the geniality of his manner.

"He drinks the best and smokes the best, the poor old Governor does," he went on. "Legs and feet, what a start it is!"

"He smokes very strong tobacco and drinks more than is good for him," his daughter—yes, she was his daughter—replied; "and in private life resembles Gallows Dick the bushranger much more than Mr. Hartley Livingstone, sometime Member of Council at St. Kitts, and said to have been Governor of Nevis."

"It wasn't Nevis," broke in the Governor, "it was Tobago. They all say it was Tobago, down-stairs. Ho! ho! and it was at Demerara, not at St. Kitts, that I exercised legislative functions as a member of the Court of Policy. Won't you have a little drop of something that'll do you good, Flo?"

To a third person—if such a third had been present at this interview—there could not have been from the outset the slightest doubt that Mr. Hartley Livingstone of the West Indies, or Gallows Dick of the bush, or the Governor of Bergen-op-Zoom Terrace, Bayswater, was an undisguised and unmitigated Ruffian. Villain and ruffian, coarse, low, cunning, and unscrupulous, were written in every line of his perfectly healthy face. Withal the man's eyes glistened with an ardent, devouring, almost savage love and admiration for his daughter. Their positions were reversed. He no longer suffered himself to be loved, as at the dinner-table. 'Twas she who endured endearment, and, to do Mrs. Armytage justice, she took all her papa's affection in a philosophical if not a demonstrative spirit.

Just then there came a little knock at the door.

CHAPTER XVIII.

THERE were fortunately two doors to the Governor's bed-chamber, and the place was as secure from intrusion as the sanctum of Mr. Sims in Coger's Inn. Mr. Livingstone being very subject to colds, was necessarily very much afraid of draughts; and he had not only carefully listed and sand-bagged the top and bottom of the outer door, but, at his own expense, had fitted up an inner portal, covered with green baize. Those who knocked had to use their knuckles pretty freely before the sound penetrated to the chamber itself.

Mrs. Armytage rose at the summons, went to the door, and in a few moments returned.

"It was the woman of the house," she said, reseating herself.

"What! the Witch of Endor? What did the old sorceress want?"

"She asked some idle question about gruel, or foot-baths, or something equally trivial. She is always prowling and prying about. Do you think it is mere old woman's curiosity, or do you imagine that she suspects anything?"

"She had better not suspect anything," replied Mr. Hartley Livingstone, with a very grim and significant leer. "I don't think she would have many more opportunities for indulging her suspicions."

"What do you mean?" his daughter asked, quietly raising her pretty eyes.

"He means what he says, this party does," returned the ruffian. "He means this."

He drove one clenched fist against the open palm of his other hand. It made a hard dull sound. Mrs. Armytage smiled bitterly.

"You are still a child, father," she said. "Have you worked and studied so long that you do not know that fists, and knives, and pistols are the weapons of fools? You are a good actor enough, and down-stairs you really look and act like a gentleman. I wish you could divest yourself of your ruffianism when you retire into private life."

"Don't call names, Flo," the Governor responded, with his ugly grin, half-jokingly and half-angrily. "If Dick's a ruffian, my fine ladyship is a ruffian's daughter. He doesn't like to be called a ruffian, he doesn't. It riles him. Come and kiss me, Flo, or by Jove I'll box your ears."

Mr. Hartley Livingstone—I suppress the many maledictions that garnished his conversation—was a man of his word. His hand was large and heavy, and Mrs. Armytage knew that the threat he had just uttered was not by any means a vain one. So she went up and kissed him, not reluctantly, and still not heartily, but with that calm and equable philosophy which was apparent in her private behaviour towards her papa.

"And now," the Governor resumed, a thorough reconciliation having been effected, "to business. How stands the money market, my duck of diamonds?"

"Ready money, ready money, nothing but ready money," answered Mrs. Armytage, in a vexed tone. "The business we are carrying on is too large a one. We have too many irons in the fire, father, and we shall be broken for the want of ready money."

"I don't see how that can be. We've two capital strings to our bow. There's Sir Jasper Goldthorpe as good as the dividends on Plough Monday. If ever we want to kill the goose for its golden eggs, you can drive down to Beryl Court, and give the old gentleman a receipt in full for ten thousand down. Why, he's got millions!"

"I don't know. I'm nervous; I'm anxious about Sir Jasper. His life hangs on a thread, and were he to die, we could prove nothing. Besides, when I saw him last, he seemed géné and embarrassed, and spoke of the scarcity of money."

"Surely he can't be travelling to Queer Street. Where did you see him last?"

"In Paris."

" Has he come back to England yet ? "

" He returns to-day. He is to bring that Magdalen Hill up from Swordsley, and there are to be grand doings again in Onyx Square."

" And the young fellow ? "

" What young fellow ? " and Florence Armytage first flushed crimson, and then turned deadly pale.

" There, I don't want to interfere in your little love-affairs, my dear. They're expensive ; but they give you pleasure, and they don't concern me."

" They give me the pleasure of revenge," Mrs. Armytage said slowly ; " of revenge the most signal, the most crushing, and yet the most secret, over one that I love and one that I hate more than ever man or woman was hated on this side the plains of heaven or the sulphur of the bottomless pit."

" You are poetical, my child. Have your own way. It has cost you a good many hundred pounds since last January twelve-mouths ; but you know your own affairs best. The young fellow I spoke of is the soldier-officer—the dragoon Goldthorpe."

" Poor Willy !" replied Mrs. Armytage, with a look of relief, " he is desperately dipped, I fear. His father is angry with him. Even Sims won't lend him any more money."

" That's bad ; when that old rat deserts a ship, it must be sinking indeed. Are there any manufactured articles, ho, ho ! of ours, my dear, about with the Captain's signature to them ?"

" A few."

" Figure ?"

" Three or four hundred pounds."

" Is he likely to pay ?"

" There is a talk of his compounding with his creditors ; and Sims is to have the management of the affair."

" Then our little manufactured articles can be lumped in with the rest, and Sims must go snacks. I dare say the Captain won't holloa. He's been giving blank acceptances for the last two years, and I dare say he doesn't know his own golden signature from the manufactured article—from the Sheffield plate, my dear. Ho, ho !"

It had grown dark by this time, and Mr. Livingstone, having carefully drawn the curtains, lighted a pair of wax-candles.

"I'm growing deuced weary of this confinement," he said, yawning and stretching his great arms. "For eleven months I've never stirred out of this doghole of a house; for eleven months I've been acting a part like Mr. Farren in the play; for eleven months I've borne all the extortions of that foul old hag down-stairs. But your father's got patience, Florence, and he knows that it'll all come right at last, and that he'll win the big stake."

He began walking to and fro in the room, but cautiously used a stick, and stumped it now and then on the carpet, lest those below should wonder at so firm and ponderous a footstep.

"Irons in the fire!" he continued to himself. "Dick Livingstone's got half a dozen, nearly red-hot by this time. There's the gold, Florence, there's the gold!"

"Do you still think the enterprise will succeed?"

"Think! I'm sure of it. Grindle, and Naylor, and Everest, are all good men and true. They must get it; and if between this and next November we don't have twenty thousand pounds' worth of bright red gold in dust, ingots, Mexican doubloons, and Russian pauls, there isn't such a thing as the Great Eastern Railway in England, and I'm a Dutchman."

"It's weary work."

"It's safer than your little game, my dear. Your father helps you in it, because he writes a neat hand, and you're fond of seeing his little pothooks and hangers. Ho, ho! And it certainly brings in ready money; but it's dangerous, Florence. What was it the little boy confessed when his papa's house had been burnt down? 'Last night I played with Tommy lighting straws.' Wasn't that it? You're always playing with Tommy lighting straws, and if you don't take care, the house will all be in a blaze some of these fine days."

"I know it, I know it;" Mrs. Armytage exclaimed; "Sims has told me so over and over again. I would give it up, but it brings in the ready money of which we stand so much in need."

"Exactly so; and so long as we are so very gay and so very fashionable, and spend such quantities of money on our little fancies, the ready money will be required."

"You can spend some yourself, father, if you please."

" Yes, I can get rid of any amount, although I never stir beyond the walls of this house. Your papa's a scientific inventor, my dear. Hasn't he laid out large sums in the perfection of a little machine the results of which, some of these days, will rather astonish the Governor and Company of the Bank of England? Hasn't he his engravers and his paper-makers at work at half a dozen places, and even beyond sea? Then there's the little letter-of-credit concern. That costs money, my child; but it will bring in thousands before you are two years older. And, last of all, isn't there this? isn't there the laboratory? Where's a greater alchymist to be found than your fond father? Ho, ho! I want to find more than the Philosopher's Stone, more than the Elixir of Life. I want the Elixir of Death, my Florence."

The ruffian turned a key in a lock, and flung open the door of what had originally been intended for a dressing-closet. He took one of the candles from the table, and, holding it over his head, looked exultingly into his laboratory. There were many shelves within it laden with jars and phials, full of variously-coloured liquids. There was a still. There was even a little furnace with a flue that went up the chimney. There were glass rods, and steel pincers, many bunches of herbs and bundles of roots hanging from nails on the walls, and a well-thumbed volume or two.

" It's all here, it's all here," Hartley, alias Dick, Livingstone repeated; " but it wants bringing out; it wants trying by the level and the square."

He took a phial from the shelf, and held it to the light.

" There's death in this," he said, " sure enough; but it's the death I don't want. Its death with agony, with convulsions, with grinding, and foaming, and writhing, and stiffening into the shape of a half moon. There's death in that blue bottle, in that red one; in this black stick of Cavendish, in that gray powder; but they're all no good to me. I don't want any colour in my elixir, I don't want any smell, I don't want any taste, nor any nasty preparations that make people pull ugly faces, and turn them livid and swollen when the job is done. No, no. I want the real elixir, the genuine article, the universal cure-all; and I'll find it out, if I blow the roof of this house off."

"I wonder where it will all end?" Mrs. Armytage murmured half to herself, and tapping one foot on the carpet.

"End!" echoed the ruffian, replacing the phial on its shelf, and setting down the candle. "Where should it all end but in success and in riches? You little peddling rogue, you, with your twopenny-halfpenny rascalities, I go in for thousands! I want men's lives to be of no more account to me than those of sheep with the rot! I'll rot 'em—I'll warm 'em!"

"Is it necessary?"

"Ay; it is. You'd like to kill somebody, wouldn't you. You'd like me to cheat Magdalen Hill out of her fortune, and then have her life, wouldn't you? All shall be done. All we want to do shall be effected. Leave your father alone. He's going to make your fortune. You shall marry a duke; and, by jingo, the money we'll make shall turn me into a Man again; shall give me one real name instead of half a dozen aliases; shall sink and burn the memory of the convict who ran into the bush from Hobart Town, and who, ho, ho! was supposed to have been murdered by the natives. Many a time have I talked with Hugh Desborough about it. He was my mate in the chain-gang, Flo. I wonder what's become of him? I wonder whether your friend Mr. Sims knows anything about him? By your account he seems to know everything. I should like to have a word with that Mr. Sims. We might work together."

"I think you are better apart," his daughter observed. "You are too desperate in your speculations for him, father. Sims is always on the safe side. Heigho!" she added, "I wish I were; but I'm in the labyrinth, and must grope my way about as best I can."

She rose to go, and held up her face to the ruffian to be kissed again.

"Can I do anything more for you, my darling?" he asked.

"Stay!" she exclaimed hastily, "you can. I had forgotten. Here are half a dozen signatures to be written. I must have the money by Tuesday next. It is the eve of the Derby Day."

"What! have you made a book?" asked Livingstone, as he received an oblong packet of papers from her, and began to look over them.

"Never mind. I must have the money, that's enough. I have only given you signatures that are beyond my powers. Tibby and Chatwynd I could never manage. Lord Fortyscore's original you have. I will come for them in the course of to-morrow. Good-night, father."

"Good-night, my chickabiddy," the urbane Governor replied, once more kissing his daughter. "Good-night, and God bless you." Yes, he bade God bless her, he did—this ruffian.

Mrs. Armytage took a cab to her grand furnished apartments at Albert Gate. As she alighted from the vehicle and stood on the doorstep, some large drops of rain began to patter on the pavement.

"It will rain in torrents before morning," she thought. "I've often wished that a Deluge might come to drown all us wicked people in a heap. It would be better, perhaps."

Perhaps. The rain did fall in torrents within an hour's time. Was there indeed a Deluge coming, in which all the wicked people were to be submerged, and only the Just saved?

There are those who will read these sheets, and who, wading through the Slough of villanous Despond which the chronicler has mapped out, may cry "absurd!" "improbable!" "preposterous!" and "impossible!" when they take note of the characters and weigh the incidents in this story. The cry would be, at best, but a parrot one, which I have heard five hundred times. When we have not seen, and when we do not know, things, there is nothing easier than to doubt their probability, or even to deny their existence. Not later than yesterday I heard an ass question whether Richard Burton ever went to Mecca or to the Mormon country; and another, more malevolent, ascribe to M. du Chaillu the exuberant imaginativeness of Baron Münchausen. I dare say that few persons find anything astonishing in the wealth of my Sir Jasper Goldthorpe, in the good-humour and vulgarity of his wife, in the self-possessed reticence of Miss Magdalen Hill, in the politeness of Dr. Sardonix, or in the easy profligacy of the Captain of Dragoons. There are things which we see every day, and with which we are all familiar. To be told what we know flatters our sense of self-esteem, and makes us think what clever fellows we are: it is when we are told that of which we had previously no

R

knowledge that we begin to sneer our " oh, indeeds!" and resent,
as an impertinence, information which, from want of evidence, we
reject at once as untrustworthy.   There is my Miss Salusbury, for
instance.   The majority of my female friends are enraged at the
portraiture given of that young lady.   They declare that a nobleman's daughter who swears, who bets, who reads *Bell's Life*, and
who talks slang, is a monstrous impossibility.   I can only shrug my
shoulders, and say that I have known the Honourable Letitia
Salusbury in the flesh.   So with Mrs. Armytage.   I grant that
she is an uncommon specimen of wickedness; but only last Sunday
I dined with a friend who knew her, her face, her ringlets, her
wiles, her thefts, and her forgeries by heart; only, you see, her
name was not Armytage, but something else.   Are you to stigmatise Mr. Sims, again, as an overdrawn character, because you never
met him ?   For the reason that you never boarded at Mrs. Cæsar
Donkin's, are you to deny the verisemblance of the witch of
Bergen-op-Zoom Terrace ?   Finally, because you were never
cheated or poisoned by a returned convict disguised as an invalid
dotard, are you, with impunity, to asseverate that the picture of
Mr. Hartley Livingstone is grossly overcharged ?   Bah!   I tell
you that I have known these people, and they must play their
several parts round the shrine of Mammon until that Deluge
which threatens them all arrives.

CHAPTER XIX.

"Only to die! It is not, after all, so difficult? Only to die Have I not heard, over and over again, the man in *Hamlet* slowly mouthing out the poet's magnificent reflections on the easiness of death? Yes; who would bear all this wretchedness and misery when the quietus offers itself at once in the shape of a bare bodkin? The Romans used to throw themselves on their swords. Could I throw myself on this half-blunted vilely-forged cutlass? Psha! I might as well attempt to cut my throat with a pedlar's razor. It is bad enough to have one's neck half sawn through with a leathern stock, without hacking and hewing at it with this rusty plough-share. Ah! if I had but one of my Sowars' swords far away—the keen glittering blade in its wooden scabbard, the sword that, like Saladin's, would divide a veil cast upon it, or cleave a down-cushion in twain. How many years is it since I read the *Talisman?* I remember: it was at school. Lowman, the usher, lent it me. I think I lent the poor fellow five shillings in return, for he was desperately poor, and we were always laughing at his torn elbows and great ragged collars. 'Cocky Lowman' we called him, from his one eye that used to look round the corner. I wonder where he is by this time. Happier than I am, Heaven help me! Dead perhaps. Only to die! Number one hundred and three went off last night, quietly and calmly as a lamb, and gently murmuring about his mother in Heaven. It was consumption. *La poitrine,* as the Chirurgeon-Major called it. His mother, ay, his mother! We found her portrait in a locket hung round his neck, when the *infirmier* came to put the *linceul* on him. I am forgetting my own language. And yet the young ruffian was here but last night, and had committed, the commissary said, two murders. His mother: —and mine?

"I am hale and strong, and absolutely relish the abominable victuals they give us, just as I used to do in our old bivouac days. Wretched and forlorn as I am, I find myself counting the minutes to dinner, and then again to my pipe, and the *cabaret*, and the dominoes. Will it end, I wonder, in my becoming a callous ruffian like that villanous old Le Camus? Perhaps. I might cease then to Think.

"But only to die! If I could only die! How does a man set about blowing his brains out? There are pistols enough to be had. But could I kill the Secret as well as myself? Ah, Florence Armytage, Florence Armytage! if I had you here, I would show you that the companionship of these wretches has made me as desperate as they, and either you or I should perish, but there should be an end now and for ever to our infernal compact.

"The woman says she loves me. 'Love me in return,' she never ceases to write; 'give me but one little word of love, and riches, freedom, happiness shall be yours.' Yes, freedom, and riches, and happiness, and a fiend for a helpmate. I cannot even bring myself to lie to her. I detest, I abhor her too much.

"I am hidden from the world, and have no country and no name. Dominique Cosson, Frère laïque of the Marist Fathers of Good Works at Hoogendracht, or François Vircloque, of the Hulks, Belleriport, it is all one. To-morrow it may please her to give me a new alias, and to conceal me under some fresh disguise. What if I broke the oath she extorted from me? What if I defied her to do her worst? Ah! that worst. Father, mother, brethren, honour, position, and fame, would be all sunk in one great gulf of ruin and dishonour. Can my father have been as insane, as guilty, as would appear from those fatal papers? How did she become possessed of them? Would their production have the blasting result she predicted? I dare not hope otherwise. It must be so. The lighted match is in my hand, and one spark would set our house in a blaze.

"For how many years has that woman been the curse of my life? If, when I came home first I had gone straight to England, I might have avoided falling into her toils. But Fate ruled that I was to tarry in Paris, to know her, and become her slave. Am

I wholly guiltless either? Did I never fan the flame of her wretched love? Have I ever been false, even for a moment, even in thought, to the woman who gave me her heart, and who should now be my bride? What is she doing now? Where is she? To her I am dead—dead and buried. Has she forgotten me? Has she ever felt grief at my loss? Is it assuaged now, and is she intent on becoming another man's wife? A strange girl! I dare not doubt the love she professed for me. I admire, I esteem, I revere her; but do I love her as I should? Was there not always something austere and frigid about her that repelled me when I would have grown fond? Her letters were as haughty as she herself was. Lovers talk nonsense. She never did. She never responded to one word of endearment; and when she sub-scribed herself as 'with sincere affection,' it was as though she had stated herself to be my 'obedient servant.'

"Is this to be the end of my miserable life? Are there any more scenes wanting to complete the drama of sorrow? Will despair pass from sullenness to desperation? and shall I have at last the despicable courage to kill myself? I should not be the first guardian of this pest-house who had made an end of his intolerable captivity. Did not Le Camus tell me about Briffard, my predecessor, who, months ago, hanged himself in a saw pit? He had been a *garde-chasse*,—a gamekeeper,—and had shot a poacher dead. Even the sulky and morose comrades he had here, avoided and mistrusted the man upon whose hands there was blood. He had never been punished for his crime, nay, had received reward—such as it was — for an act of 'courageous devotion,' as the Procureur Imperial called it; but he was none the less a pariah and an outcast. The poacher whom he had slain left a wife and children. The woman his widow used to make a journey to Belleriport every Easter and every New Year, —she had to come over a hundred miles on foot, poor woman,— and wait for Briffard at the dockyard-gates, and show him her dead husband's shirt, with the bloody rent in the breast where his slugs had entered, and solemnly curse him. Easter and New Year, New Year and Easter, she never missed. The convicts used to call the doomed man Cain. Like Cain, his punishment was greater than he could bear, and one day he hanged himself. The

shop where he bought the rope is close to the *cabaret*. I pass it
every day. He wanted the halter, he said, for a dog. It was for
himself. The commissary never liked Briffard. He told him one
day that it was only through a lucky accident that he did not
wear a brand on his shoulder and irons on his ankles. The
manner of his death was an excuse for denying military honours
to his funeral. 'Military honours?' Yes; they go through that
mockery even with a dead *garde-chiourme*. We are supposed to
form part of the armed force, and to be under *les drapeaux de l'état*
—the banners of the State; its upas-tree, rather.

"I have not killed a man as Briffard did; yet he could not have
been wretcheder than I am. A phantom continually haunted
him, it was said—the ghost of the poacher he had shot. I too am
haunted, by the phantom of Myself. My own phantom! A
strange one to be pursued by. I see myself rich and prosperous,
and caressed. Coming home to a feast of love and happiness,
Poor men were envious of me even while they flattered. Mothers
intrigued and fawned, and strove to palm off their daughters upon
one who was heir to so many thousands a year! Thousands a
year! How long is it since I had any money? How I hunger for
the paltry copper dole a day which is allotted to me for my hangman's office! Thousands a year! I have not five francs in the
world. I used to buy watches and jewellery, horses, fine clothes,
every imaginable luxury. I betted, I played at cards. I have
scattered handfuls of rupees. Now I am glad enough to have
sufficient pelf to buy an extra half-ounce of tobacco, a dram of
absinthe, or two sous-worth of fried potatoes.

"I should be better off as a convict. The degraded brutes who
shared my punishment might sympathise with, or perhaps admire
me, were my crime great enough. The active principle would be
at work. I should have work to do, punishment to elude by craft;
an escape perhaps to plan, a term to my torture to anticipate. I
have known even those condemned for life indulge in hopes of
some fortuitous deliverance, through the accession of a king,
through a fire, a pestilence, a revolution, a hundred other accidents. For me there is no hope. A *garde-chiourme* has no
friends. We are always grumbling and disputing among ourselves, and seeking to curry favour with the commissary by

denouncing one another for neglect of duty. The townspeople
avoid and abhor us; not the pettiest tradesman or tavern-keeper
will trust a *garde-chiourme.* The soldiers are chary of drinking or
smoking with us; and the sailors of the men-of-war in port make
no secret of their contempt and dislike for men whose duty it is
to keep guard over galley-slaves; and every *garde-chiourme* knows
that he is surrounded by hundreds of bitter foes, all chained as
they are, who hate him, who curse him in their hearts, and would
take his life, if they could, as though it were a dog's.

"There, I will think no more or I shall go mad. Mad! it
would be a luxury, a relief, for one's wits to turn: I should not
dwell upon the past then; I should have a new world—all wild
and unreal as it may be—to dwell in. But my mind seems as
unclouded as my body is strong. I am not to go mad, nor to die
yet awhile. But how long is this horrible While to last?"

Now these words were neither spoken nor written, nor, all
loose and fragmentary as they may seem, were they uttered even
with the coherence that I have given them. They came and went
and crossed each other's path in straggling and capricious order.
They rose up unbidden, and departed unawares. They were the
inner speech—the thoughts that coursed through the brain of the
man known as FRANÇOIS VIRELOQUE, as, in coarse and clumsy
garb and awkward forage cap, he slouched to and fro on his beat
in the dockyard of Belleriport.

It was a glorious summer noon, and the sky one blaze of sunshine. Not till you had blinked and winked and rid yourself of
your first bedazzlement, and shaded your eyes with your hand,
could you discover that the heavens were not all Sun, but that
away from the great orb there stretched a boundless arch of deep
azure. There were no clouds, no mists, no fogs, nor smoke below,
either of marsh or of man's making: nothing but God's sky, and
in the midst of it God's Eye looking down upon the folly and
wickedness and cruelty of His children. What millions, billions,
trillions of francs and centimes had there not been spent here
within two centuries! what giant buildings erected, what cunning
schemes of man's ingenuity perfected, what triumphant monu-
ments of his industry achieved! and all for what? One half the

great work done had been for the carrying out the great trade of
Murder.   Saw-pits and rope-walks, forges and block-cutting
machines, powder magazines and provision stores, great piles of
seasoned timber, great pyramids now of cannon-balls, now of tar-
barrels, armories and warehouses full of clothes and munitions,—
what were they all for?   Not for the comfort or improvement of
mankind, but for the equipment of huge war-ships, that were to
deal forth fire and destruction into other war-ships, merely because
they carried flags of other colours, and were manned by creatures
of another race.   These scores of great guns so admirably adjusted,
so exquisitely mounted, which the foundries and wheelwright's
shop turned out with ceaseless activity, what were they for but to
make murder swifter and easier?   Those stalwart men-o'-war's
men who rowed ashore, with spruce captains and lieutenants, all
cocked-hats and gold-lace, sitting in the stern sheets, were taught
to call their profession a glorious one.   What was its end?
Slaughter.   Those trim surgeons, with their long surtouts and
instrument cases covered with shagreen, trotting to and fro
between ships and hospitals, had only learnt the merciful art of
healing to cure the hideous gashes and maimings inflicted by
those with whom they dined at mess and smoked cigars day after
day.   It was handy-dandy, give and take, the Doctrine of Compensation, forsooth.   The State paid one set of men to smash
their fellow creatures' legs and arms, and then paid another set of
men to mind them, and pays them still, elsewhere than at Belleriport.   It is all right and proper, no doubt; and to call war
murder, and to maintain that the massacre of human beings by
broadsides or by bayonet charges, whole crews and whole batta-
lions at a time, is a hideous and enormous sin, and one that in the
end Heaven will judge and Heaven will punish, is to be sneered
at as a sentimentalist, or scouted as a visionary.   There were no
iron-cased frigates, no Armstrong or Dahlgren guns ten years ago,
but there were plenty of ships with plenty of guns that would kill
well enough when fired off.   The rudest and most uncivilised
nations have from the earliest times found little difficulty in
hacking and hewing their enemies.   It is all right and proper, I
suppose and repeat, and glory is to be glory to the end of the
chapter.   If I hide behind a hedge waiting for my foe, and,

catching him in the nick of time, send a bullet through his head;
if I beat out his brains with a hammer, or drug his posset with
strychnine,—it is murder before the law. The jury put their heads
together; the judge shakes his, and writes *sus. per coll.* against
my name in his calendar; and I belong thenceforth to the ordinary, and the sheriff, and the hangman, who, after I have been
exemplarily strangled, sells my clothes to Madame Tussaud.
Miscreant that I am! hasten to get me a niche in the Chamber
of Horrors between Hocker and Mrs. Manning. But if I hide
behind a hedge, and am dressed in a smart tunic and shako; if I
pick off not one but twenty enemies, against whom I have no
grudge, and never saw them probably in my life before; if I march
across the open, and with drums beating and colours flying allow
other people, equally strangers to me, to have a chance of blowing
my brains out; if I point a cannon towards a town, and load and
fire it, and send so much lead, or so many jagged pieces of iron so
many thousand paces to kill, for aught I know, besides my so-
called "enemies" (whom I don't know from Adam), the patriarch
of eighty, the new-made bride, nay, perhaps the babe that is
unborn; if I dash into a river on horseback, and meeting another
mounted man cleave him to the chine with a sword, or batter in
his skull with the butt-end of a carbine, and having taken from
him a silk rag tied to a pole, ride away rejoicing,—all this is not
Murder: it is Courage, heroism, chivalry, glory; I am rewarded
with titles, stars, crosses, freedoms of the City in golden boxes,
diamond-hilted swords, and so much money for each limb I lose.
They may hang up my portrait as a tavern-sign, and name a street,
a bridge, or a boot, after me; my ultimate bourne on earth—for
all that I may be laid in St. Paul's and Westminster Abbey—will
still be Madame Tussaud's, where, however, no extra sixpence will
be paid to view my effigy. I shall herd among the heroes, and be
admired with Napoleon the Great and the Emperor Alexander's
gigantic drummer. Again, and for the last time, I say that all
this is perfectly right and proper, that war is no doubt a necessary
evil, and that it is mere mawkish puling sentimentalism to decry
glory and stigmatise as murderous the heroic achievements of the
battle-field. Of course; but for my part, I must express the
opinion that society has been rather hard in modern times upon

Cannibals. Why should we so loathe a poor Fiji-Islander or New
Zealander for making a meal of a fallen foe ? If it be justifiable
to slash and maim and carve and gird and thrust and burn and
stab and wrench and grind and tear the life out of a man whom
we never saw before, and who has never done us any manner of
harm, why should it not be equally justifiable to cook and eat
our enemy after we have killed him ?

Meanwhile the sun shone upon the ships of the war of the
French Republic,—upon stately three-deckers, upon frigates
armed *en flûte*, and slim corvettes, and stealthy sable war-steam-
ers sliding in and out of port with an adder's swiftness and
subtlety. The sun shone upon the tall three-deckers laid up in
ordinary, with their sides painted dockyard drab, and their decks
protected by awnings of blinding white ; upon the boats cleaving
the water to and fro ;—some barges or lighters lading or unlading
powder and provisions ;—some wherries, manned by the red-
nightcapped convicts, a seafaring *garde-chiourme* steering ; some
the smart gigs and launches of the war-ships, with crews strong and
well-clad enough, but on whom an English jack-tar at Portsmouth
or Plymouth could not have helped looking with a kind of amused
astonishment. A French man-o'-war's man is in outward appearance a compound between Mr. T. P. Cooke in *Black-eyed Susan*,
and the rider of a " trick act " in a circus. He is a brave fellow
without doubt, and can handle his cutlass and boarding-pike in
the most approved manner : but still he gives the spectator
the impression of being far more accustomed to *eau sucrée* than
salt water. He is *such* a dandy ; he is *so* theatrical. His whiskers have such a boulevard cut ; his shirt and jacket and straw
hat such a *bal-masqué* fashion. He is the descendant of the old
French Sea-kings,—of the Jean Barts and Duguay Trouins,—
who shall gainsay it ? He would have cheered lustily when the
Vengeur didn't go down with the tricolour of the Republic one
and indivisible flaunting at the main ; but what are we to say to a
man-o'-war's man who wears a red stripe down each leg of his
trousers ?

As the sun shone upon Belleriport,—upon its forts and ships
and soldiers and sailors and convicts,—so had it shone long before
Republic and Empire, and far into the days of the Bourbon

monarchy.   Up yonder creek rotted one of the ancient galleys of
Louis the Fourteenth's time—galleys which made their last
appearance in warlike life at the battle of La Hogue—galleys
which, when felons were scarce, had seen chained to their oars
Turks and Arabs taken from the piratical cruisers of Tunis and
Sallee, and forced into slavery, as a retaliation for the captivity of
Christians among the fierce powers of Barbary.   High and dry
in the mud was the dismantled hull of a hundred-and-twenty gun-
ship, which, completely armed and equipped, the town of Belleriport had offered to Louis the Sixteenth on his wedding-day;
while by her side, and sinking daily deeper into the ooze, were
the crazy timbers of a little schooner that had done good service
in the times of the American War; for she had taken—so old
men said—Rochambeau and Lafayette across the Atlantic, and
brought the printer philosopher, Benjamin Franklin, back as
ambassador to the court of the most Christian king.   More than
this, she had once borne the flag of a famous filibuster, and every
old sailor in Belleriport boasted of the days when the *Bonhomme
Richard* went up the Frith of Forth with Paul Jones.

Forts! there were forts everywhere.   Not a cask of pitch, not
a coil of rope, not a heap of rusty anchors, not a crane or pair of
towering sheers for lifting ships' masts, but seemed protected by
a shining granite wall bristling with cannon.   Not to speak of the
great fortresses looming far out to sea, cutting the blue waters at
all kinds of eccentric angles, and surmounted every one of them
by the tricolour lazily flapping in the hot air.   Not to speak of
the huge outer fortifications surrounding dockyard and convict
prison, with a preposterous vandyked collar of moats and earthworks.   Not to speak of the hoary old chateau, built by Francis
the First, which defended the entrance to the mercantile port,—
a tower, venerable and picturesque, which stranger artists often
came to sketch, and were as often warned off, or threatened
with the terrors of the Maritime Prefect by stolid sentinels, who
knew nothing of the fine arts, but whose rigorous *consigne* it was
to prevent any one making plans of the fortifications of Belleriport.

The town, its port, and warehouses, for it still possessed considerable commercial importance, lay to the left of the *garde-*

chiourme as he slouched on his beat. He could look down on the narrow streets, the tall white houses and green blinds, the littered quays that were odorous with tobacco and coffee, and seemed sticky with sugar. Far away in the remote distance were more white houses and green blinds, standing in the midst of orange and fig groves. But no mountain range closed up the distance. For scores of miles on every side behind Belleriport stretched the red, arid, burnt-up country of the South, treeless, houseless, and hedgeless, only relieved here and there by dusky patches of some vegetation, so dry and stunted-looking that travellers stared with amazement when they were told that these patches teemed with olives and with grapes.

Still sweltered François Vireloque, the *garde-chiourme,* in his uniform suit of coarse woollen, and thoughts came over him of the cool linen garb and shady pith-hat he used to wear in the scarcely hotter East far away; of his day-dawn rides, when the breeze came refreshingly when the sun was up; of tiffin and iced drinks and bottled beer, and Manilla cheroots; and then his thoughts went back, and reverted to English summer evenings, and deep pools among the alders, whither he and his school-mates came to bathe. What was that boy's name who came to such grief because he could not swim? What an awful moment was that when he was seized with the agonies of cramp, and was only saved from sinking by his foot clutching with convulsive energy at some tall weeds! What a lucky escape it was! He remembered the pool, the alders, the pollards, the legend of the old water-rat that was said to dwell there, that had fangs long and yellow and hooked, that darted out of his hole sometimes as the boys were undressing and made them shudder, and was said to have such a horrible appetite for the legs of children of tender years. It was a perilous pool indeed; for it was on the ground of a farmer who continually muttered dire threats concerning trespassing, and pursued timid boys with a stock-whip until he had hunted them down, and forced them, trembling, to give their names that he might report them to the Doctor. But he never did so report them, and contented himself with "danging" them; and they bathed in his pool and ate his apples, but gave a wide berth to his great bull that guarded the orchard from the adjoining meadow, as the

dragon guarded the Hesperides, and by a sudden rush and feint
—but was it a feint?—of butting would often force the biggest
and bravest boy to drop a whole capful of ruddy-cheeked pippins.
Dried up for ever, O *garde-chiourme!* is that pool. The hole of
the water-rat, the long-toothed vermin itself, would be welcome
here, where every outlet is guarded, where every chink and
cranny is stopped. That gray old rascal with his cunning eye!
See! there are seven hundred rascals, old and young, and clothed
in gray, toiling on the great *digue,*—the breakwater—which lies,
a giant bar of granite, glistening diamond-like, across the harbour
that mocks nature and makes a false horizon.

The orange and the myrtle groves have sweet odours, they say.
They were plentiful outside this Tartarus, but their scent never
passed beyond the high stone walls. In their lieu came the
sickening smell from the basin in the town where the merchant-
ships lay moored; a smell that was overpowering, and almost dense
enough to be felt and cut asunder.

It was noon, and a clock struck, the great clock of the yard
followed by a score of ill-conditioned horologes, from the churches
and public buildings in the town, and that seemed to whine and
grumble while they proclaimed the hour. And then the great bell
of the *bagne* began to toll. It was for no man's death. It was
only for dinner.

Such a dinner! The felons came trooping from their labours,
scrambling over piles of wood, clumsily clambering from boats
clanking along in their chain-gangs. The guards followed them
up closely, making their canes felt if the wretches straggled or
exchanged any conversation. It was François Vireloque's duty to
be last; and last he slouched into the inner yard of the *bagne,*—
they had to pass through half a dozen ere they reached their
refectory,—and saw each heavy gate locked by the *porte-clefs*
after him.

Such a dinner, and such a dining-room! It must be granted
that the repast was an *al fresco* one; for between the four white
walls of the prison-yard the fierce sun poured down its wrath on
the creatures condemned to dine without shade. The sun made
so many blazing lakes of a series of huge tubs filled with Heaven
knows what sickening hell-broth of herbs and hot water; only I

know that large marigolds floated on the surface, and that here
and there a bone with a scrap of gristle attached to it bobbed up
and down, and that the whole distilled a rank and acrid perfume.
Each convict as he entered the yard took a tin pannikin from a
rack, and a lump of black bread from a basket, over which a *garde-
chiourme* kept guard. Then if he belonged to mess number one,
he went to tub number one, and if to mess number two, to the
corresponding tub, and there fell to like a wild beast. I say like
a wild beast—or rather like some caged hyæna that yells and
crunches over his shin-bone of horse-flesh. The creatures crowded
round the tubs and fought and cursed for places. The weakest
went to the wall; the timid criminal had his lump of bread
wrenched from him by the stronger hands of the athletic scoundrel. Some positively bit at one another, or shuffled their
chained legs against them to gall their sides. They baled canfuls
of abomination from the seething slough that was called soup ;
they splashed and scalded one another, now in horse-play, now in
spite ; they screamed over a chance piece of flesh, and battled for
it till their callous hands were slippery; they licked the precious
drops of grease that had fallen on their sleeves; and when from
time to time some fiercer contest than ordinary over a meaty bone
converted the scramble into a fray, the guards swooped down upon
them, and beat them off with their *badines*.

"Pretty animals, *n'est-ce pas, mon gars ?*" was the observation
of le Sieur le Camus to his comrade Vireloque. "You would not
see a more charming sight in the Jardin des Plantes at feeding
time."

"They are not like human beings," his companion said.

"*Ma foi !* they are like just what they are. A *forçat* is a *forçat*.
In this place, my friend, one grows only to care for the *stricte
nécessaire*, and their soup and bread is all in all to them. After
all, shall we not relish our *gamelle* of harricoes when *ces messieurs*
have dined ? My stomach says yes unmistakeably. See, the
repast is at an end. The lambs are going to drink."

About eight minutes had been allowed for this tub-diet,
and every one of them was by this time empty. The convicts
were called off by the tap of a drum, and came crowding, with
the same pannikins from which they had swallowed their

soup, to a species of stone bar, between which and some upright casks stood several *gardes chiourme*, who had donned blue aprons over their uniforms. Here wine was served out to each felon —wine mingled with thrice its body of water, wine thick and muddy, of a vile livid colour, a viler smell, and vilest, most loath-some, most abhorrent taste of all, but still the residue, in some form or another, of some monstrous degeneration and perversion of the fermented juice of the grape. The wretches drank this hideous mixture as greedily as they had gnawed their bread and gulped their soup ; then they were marched out again, clattering and clanking from yard to yard, into the open. About twenty minutes were allowed them—for " recreation "—that is, they were permitted to stand still, without working, in the sun, or find what sheltering shade they could from pent-house roofs or behind logs of timber. And then they were driven to their toil again. A detachment was left behind in the prison, not to sweep up the fragments,—for not a scrap remained of the wolfish feed,—but to scrub the pannikins, and sluice out the tubs with water. At six o'clock they would have their evening meal ; no more soup, but another lump of bread, and another ration of the mixture of ink and cask-lees which was dignified with the name of wine.

" And now," said Le Camus, " it is time, I think, brother of mine, that we went to our own little *ordinaire*. I smell the haricoes at a distance. The fare of those brutes is coarse enough; and yet putting on one side a morsel of beef, we dine scarcely better than they do. Better, we often dine worse ; for a poor fellow of a *garde-chiourme* has often nothing but his pay to depend upon, and that will only get him his pipe and his *goutte* beyond his rations, whereas those among *ces messieurs* who have money may feed as sumptuously as though they were at the Trois Frères Provençaux, instead of here *en Provence*."

" Feed sumptuously ! " repeated François Vircloque.   " Of what use can money be to them, strictly guarded and narrowly watched as they are ! "

" O scarcely fledged and thoroughly unsophisticated *garde-chiourme !* " Le Camus said with a sneer, " were you born yes-terday, that you do not know that money is of use everywhere ? Shut me up in a rock, and keep me there for three centuries, like a toad, but put a *billet de banque* beside me; lay me in my grave, but put a sackful of five-franc pieces beside me,—and I will find out a way to turn them to good account."

"But what is the use of money to a convict chained to another, who at any moment may betray him?"

"The rich are not betrayed; it is only when one grows poor that treachery steps in to sup us up. Did you observe, among those brawling gangs howling and squabbling over the buckets, certain groups that kept close together, that were very still and quiet, and that seemed by no means anxious to dip their pannikins into the soup?"

"I did. What then?"

"Well, to every one of those groups were scouts and outlying pickets, who were fed by lumps of bread, pinches of tobacco, or a *gros sous* or two to give warning of the coming of some sharp-eyed *garde-chiourme* among us. In every one of those groups there was feasting going on. I tell you we have those among our convicts who dine every day on white bread, on cold roast fowl, and Lyons sausage; who have ripe figs and peaches, and rich *fromage de Brie*, the rascals; and wash all down with choice burgundy or genial cognac."

"Whence do they procure these luxuries?"

"How should I know?" the elder gaoler answered, shrugging his shoulders. "They have money, that is enough. Perhaps the sailors from the ships, perhaps the free shipwrights or labourers in the dockyard, bring them these little delicacies. We *gardes-chiourme* are too closely watched to carry provisions for them, or to take bribes. Is it not so? The sergeant has his eye on us, the commissary has his eye on us; and then not one of us can make sure but that his comrade may be a spy. All I know is, that not a day passes but some convict is placed *au cachot* for being in possession of tobacco; that scarcely a week elapses without another getting the bastinado for being drunk. When we discover them they are punished of course; when they are not discovered, they eat and smoke and drink and enjoy themselves much more than we do. But they must have the five-franc pieces, my brother. Woe be to the convict who has no money."

"Will money help them to escape?"

"Chut! you are venturing upon forbidden ground. *On ne parle pas d'évasion du bagne de Belleriport.* Your English friend tried to escape only last week, you remember, and was retaken in scaling the very last of the walls. A nice dose of the *corde goudronnée* he would have had, but that an imbecile of a sentinel shot him through the back, and sent him to the hospital. I don't think he will ever come out of it."

" Is he worse ? "

"Much worse this morning; but bah! Why waste words upon *cette canaille.* Hark! there is our bell. It is time for us to go and eat our haricoes."

CHAPTER XX.

THE sun was tired out with excess of wrath, and in a red rage had set, and gone to sleep. The slavish toil of the *bagne* was over, and the convicts lay by hundreds, in their dormitories, on the bare boards of shelving barrack-pallets. They were still chained. A slight uprising of the boards made their pillow; there was a scanty coverlet for each four men, and that was all. So they lay until one side was sore and bruised, and then turned over, until the other was as bruised and sore. Mattresses could not be had even for money at Belleriport, though cushions and soft pads had been detected in being smuggled in sometimes for villains of wealth. At either end of these vast dormitories, ventilated by iron louvre casements, like those in the cooling-room of a brew-house, burnt with dim light a lamp of oil. Up and down the long lane between the rows of barrack-beds walked all night, but relieved at intervals, with drawn cutlass and pistols in his belt, a *garde-chiourme.* The convicts were either supposed to sleep soundly enough after the toils of the day not to have their dreams disturbed by the tramping of the watchman, or else authority in its wisdom did not care a centime whether their slumbers were broken or not. But for all the lanterns and watchfulness of the guardians of the night, dark deeds were whispered, plots for escape hatched, dire schemes of revenge planned and matured. The seemingly chance clink of a fetter, as its wearer turned on his couch of distress, veiled a watchword. A tug at a coverlet became a signal. Men spoke in snoring, and shrouded secret intelligence in the incoherent babble of feigned sleep. Freemasons, there is a *camaraderie,* a Rosicrucian code among convicts, defying the acutest surveillance, the most lynx-eyed supervision, which we wot not of. So when the sun was down François

Vireloque repaired to his usual cabaret outside the gates,—he was
not on guard that evening,—and smoked his usual pipe, and drank
his usual tumbler of wine. Drams of spirit were the ordinary
stimulants with which the *gardes-chiourme* regaled themselves:
but they took no inconvenient notice of their comrade's absti-
nence. He was a sulky fellow, and had not come there for
nothing; that was all they said. The disparagement mattered
little; they were all well-nigh as sulky as he; and each man had
doubtless as good reasons as Vireloque for being what he was.

This evening there was a *fête* at the cabaret. It was the
festival of St. Somebody,— perhaps of St. Nicholas, patron of
thieves,—but at any rate the mean little wine-shop of the *Etoile
qui file* was *en goguettes*. Very simple decorations sufficed to give
it a festal appearance. There was some coloured calico about.
There were some tallow candles stuck in sconces. There were
some flowers in tin jugs, and an image of the saint in plaster of
Paris. Double prices were charged for everything. The landlady
had a new cap, and the landlord was drunk. Individually, these
things were not, perhaps, out of the common way. In the aggregate they made a capital *fête*. There were ladies to add to the
enjoyment of the evening—ladies who danced, ladies who sang,
ladies who, if the truth must be told, drank and smoked as vigorously as the male guests, and, when the festivities reached their
apogee, mounted the tables, and bellowed in convivial ecstasy. It
was difficult to say to what class of the community these ladies
belonged. They were perfectly virtuous. There was not the
slightest stain upon their reputation. They were not *lorettes*,
grisettes, *dames de la halle*, or *fleuristes*. They were mostly of
robust and athletic build, did not occasionally disdain a pea-jacket
as an outer garment, knew well how to use their fists, and, better
still, their tongues. It would not perhaps be libellous to hint that
they were in some way connected with fish, and with the docks,
and with carrying burdens, and generally with the commercial
prosperity of Belleriport.

With these ladies the *gardes-chiourme* danced in an ungainly
and bear-like manner. Them too they treated to *cassis* and other
cheap refreshments. With them they joined in ranting choruses,
always ending with a " Tra! la! la! " or a "youp! youp! youp! "

Everything was very merry indeed; and the landlord, after proposing the health of *Messieurs les gardes-chiourme* in a few delirious words, sank exhausted by festivity into the midst of a wreck of broken bottles and battered tin jugs. The gaolers in the prison within could hear the sounds of the gay carols floating on the night air, and growled bitter complaints of their unlucky lot in not being able to join the *fête*.

François Vireloque sat aloof and smoked his pipe, as was his wont, thinking perhaps of some nautch he may have seen in the far East. When one of the Bayaderes of Belleriport twitted him upon his moodiness, he offered her refreshment, but declined to dance; and at last they forbore to tease him. The clock-hand pointed to nine, when he heard his name pronounced beside him.

He turned and saw a little imp named Crapaudin, a shock-headed urchin, who was the orphan of a *garde-chiourme mort sur le champ du devoir*,—in other words, slain by a convict with whom he was struggling in the endeavour of the latter to escape,—and who was growing up the *protégé* and adopted child of the Devil's regiment. He blacked the Commissary's boots; ran errands for Madame; fetched and carried to and fro; and looked forward to becoming one day a *garde-chiourme*, provided always that his incorrigible propensities for lying and thieving did not insure him, at some time or another, gratuitous board and lodging for a term of years within the *chiourme* itself as a convict. "*Il a une figure de cour d'assises*," said the Commissary of Crapudin, meaning that he possessed what we might term a Central-Criminal-Court countenance.

"*Garde-chiourme*," said this engaging youth to Vireloque, "you are wanted instantly inside."

"Wanted! by whom?" exclaimed François, rising. The blood rushed to his heart. The poor captive thought, perhaps, that his deliverance was at hand.

"Wanted by Sister Marie des Douleurs. A rendezvous, oho! Nuns are fond of making appointments with fine young fellows such as you are. *Car tu es bel homme, garde-chiourme*."

"Silence, you little reptile!" cried François, "or I'll wring your neck. How dare you talk in that manner of the good sisters?"

"Oh yes, I dare say. Good in the light. Bad in the light.

I don't like nuns. *Ça n'est pas gai, les sœurs grises.* At all events,
she wants you immediately ; and if you don't go, she'll be sure to
report you to the Commissary."

" Where is the good sister, jackanapes ? "

" Jackanapes yourself. She is in the *parloir* of the infirmary.
She is with the almoner. Perhaps they have been drinking hot wine
together. *Ah, que c'est bon, le vin chaud!* Say, *M. le garde-
chiourme*, will you treat me to a glass of mulled *ordinaire* before
you go ? "

" I will treat you to a sound cuff over the ears, you young
monkey," replied the moody man as he paid his reckoning. "Stay,
here are three sous. Spend them in drink, or in tobacco, or in
gaming, or in anything else you choose. Whatever it is it will
do you some harm, I am sure. I go to obey the sister's order."
And so, buckling on his cutlass, he left the place.

" Three sous!" cried Crapaudin, fingering the coins which had
been flung to him. "That isn't much; but it will buy something
to wash out one's windpipe with, won't it, Mother Cayenne-
pepper?" The landlady of the *Etoile qui file* was, from the fiery
nature of her temper, generally known among her guests by the
nickname of "*La Mère Poivre rouge.*"

"*A-t-on jamais vu pareille vermine?*" she exclaimed, pinching
the boy's ear, but not by any means indignantly. "What will
you have that will make you ill, *pendard?*" she continued. "We
are *en fête*, and you shall be treated." Crapaudin was a favourite
at the *cabaret*, and was indulged accordingly.

Meanwhile the *garde-chiourme* strode with heavy footsteps
towards the prison-gate, gave the pass-word to the sentinel, and
was admitted. He knew his way well enough about the place by
this time ; and, passing range after range of low barrack buildings
with penthouse roofs and heavily-grated windows, came at last to
a square edifice standing alone, and looking very white and
ghastly in the moonlight. The windows, which were larger than
the ordinary ones, were not grated, but protected from sill to lintel
by a strong close wirework.

The *parloir* was a bare whitewashed room, with no other decorations than a framed list of the rules of the infirmary and a plain
wooden crucifix, and no other furniture than two long forms of

unpainted deal. The first among the rules was alarming. "*Sera puni de la bastonnade,*" it ran, " *tout forçat convaincu d'avoir feint une maladie.*" Every convict detected in "malingering," or simulating sickness, was threatened with the bastinado.

A *garde-malade*,—a convict with white apron and canvas sleeves over his prison dress, which gave him somewhat the air of a criminal cook,—was dozing on one of the benches, starting spasmodically now and then, either at the pricks of his evil conscience, or at the hardness of his resting-place.

"Sister Marie wants me, number five hundred," said the *garde-chiourme.* " Where is she ? "

" She is in the dispensary," the nurse replied. " You can go there to her. So she said. *Que Dieu lui soit bonne !*"

It was seldom that a pious aspiration was ever uttered save by the chaplain in that abode of crime and woe, yet the convict-nurse, who was otherwise a most villanous rascal to look at, seemed quite sincere as he bade Heaven bless Sister Marie. He was under a twenty years' sentence for an atrocious crime ; yet it is a fact that, as he spoke, he crossed himself.

François Vireloque stepped as softly as he could to the door of an adjoining apartment on the ground-floor, and discreetly tapped thereat. It was opened by a Sister of Charity in the long, coarse, black robe with heavy sleeves and white-flapped cap and wimple of her order. She made the man a sign to enter, and went on compounding some medicament from the bottles and gallipots before her.

The light from the oil-wick, swung in an ugly cresset from a chain, threw monstrous shadows from her robe and head-dress— shadows that eddied in black waves over the floor. Her busy hands went and came among the bottles and gallipots ; otherwise her form was motionless as that of a statue.

The *garde-chiourme* had doffed his cap, and stood motionless too, but in an attitude of patient respect, waiting to be spoken to.

" What is your name, *mon brave ?*" she asked, in a low sweet voice.

" François Vireloque, good sister."

" So he said when he entreated me to send for you. You speak the English language ? "

"Sufficiently well. I have been in England."

"It is well. You must wait a little. The almoner is with him now in the infirmary. He is not of our creed; but the Abbé's prayers will not be thrown away. He is very penitent. We do not wish to convert him; only to soothe his dying pillow."

She said this more to herself than to the man, and said it almost in a whisper. When she had finished her task, she sat down on a form like those in the *parloir*, and took out a little book, and read by the light of the swinging cresset full ten minutes, moving her lips meanwhile as in prayer. The *garde-chiourme* stole a furtive look at her. He had heard much of her good deeds, but had never seen her before. Her hair, poor thing, had been ruthlessly cut off according to the grim usage, her eyes were cast down, her lips closed, her whole countenance composed in deep and earnest devotion; but François Vireloque could tell at once that the Sister of Charity was young and eminently beautiful.

Of what avail were her soft lineaments and sweet quiet manner in this den? Of much. They made savage men meek and tender. They brought a spark—were it ever so slight—of the better feelings of humanity into minds seared and callous, into hearts harder than the nether millstone. They brought a sunshine into a place that was less shady than black as pitch with unutterable crimes and nameless horrors. They whispered the one divine word, Mercy, in the midst of a Babel of threats and execrations, of the groans of misery, and the shrieks of despair.

Six Sisters of Charity were permitted by the government to exercise their beneficent ministrations in the infirmary of Belleriport. Beyond its precincts, and those of the closely adjoining chapel, they never strayed. Their errand had but one purpose—consolation. Of the labours, the crimes, the punishments of that dire place, they knew nothing; they only knew that when the sick and suffering were brought to the infirmary, it was their blessed function to tend them night and day, and strive their utmost to heal them. Now it was a recaptured slave who had been badly wounded in his mad attempt at evasion, and had been brought to the hospital to die. Now it was some miserable wretch whose frame, from neck to loins, had been mangled by the tarred rope,—the infliction of which still goes under the name of the

"bastinado,"—and was sent to the infirmary to lie on his face, and
groan and screech till lint and unguent had done their work, and his
back was healed. And now it was some puny criminal, some
effeminate villain,—for crime and bodily strength go not always
together, — whose constitution had broken down beneath the
hideous toil of the *Grande Fatigue*, and who was glad to crawl to
the pallet of the infirmary to be rid of his chains and be peaceful
for awhile; and find Pity at last in the arms of a Sister of Charity,
and of Death, the great pardoner of human sentences.

Of the six sisters whose noiseless feet were ever on the move
between the sick wards and the dispensary, four were elderly and
wrinkled, two young and fair as she upon whom the *garde-chiourme*
was looking. But Sister Marie des Douleurs was the youngest
and the fairest, the kindest and the best.

Anon there came down the stone staircase from above the
almoner,—the prison chaplain, a ruddy ecclesiastic, in orthodox
soutane and *rabat*, a worthy soul enough, who did his duty, but
could not help yawning sometimes as he did it. He had been so
long ghostly director to the scum of the earth. He had heard so
many lies, so many false professions of repentance. He had the
more justification in yawning to-night; for was not his penitent a
heretic, for whom, without recantation, the Church could do nothing?

He murmured as much to Sister Marie, and saying that he
must have his supper, went away.

Then the sister gravely beckoned to the *garde-chiourme*, and
they went upstairs together.

The patient whom they were to visit was the convict Englishman. He was dying. He lay on his back, and from that quick,
heavy, ceaseless breathing, which came not from his lungs, but
from his throat rather, there could be little doubt that the sands
were fast running down, and that his earthly career would soon
be over. A convict nurse stood by him with a sponge dipped in
some aromatic liquid, with which he occasionally bathed the
temples of the moribund. An *aide-chirurgien*—for the Surgeon-
in-Chief had given the case over, and had gone to play his evening
game at billiards—was seated at a little table a short distance off.
He too was accustomed to such scenes, and, to tell truth, was
reading a novel.

The sister and the *garde* approached the bed, and the former laid her hand upon the shoulder of the dying man.

"Number five hundred and thirty," she said, in her low soft voice, "I have brought the person to you whom you so much desired to see."

The breathing came quicker and heavier, the dull eyes opened; but there was no response.

"Call him by his name, sister," the *aide-chirurgien* interposed.

"I do not know his name, M. Cantagul," Sister Marie replied.

"Nor I scarcely. Stay, what was it the Commissary called him? Ah! I have it—Hugh."

At the sound of the name the Englishman started up in bed, and gazed about him with wild eyes.

"Who wants me? who called Hugh?" he exclaimed in guttural accents.

But dreadful sight as in his pallor and his death-sweat he was, the *garde-chiourme* looked well-nigh as fearful in the lamp-light. For every line of his face was convulsed by horror and amazement, as he kept muttering,

"Hugh! Hugh! who is this man that calls himself Hugh?"

CHAPTER XXI

WHAT is the proverbial dish known as "Humble Pie" made of? "Sugar and spice, and all that's nice," as is suited to the appetite of little girls? "Snips and snails, and puppy-dogs' tails," as beseems the ruder stomachs of little boys? It is questionable. Many consider Humble Pie to be a mere figure of speech—a rhetorical viand, which might furnish the table of him who dines with Duke Humphrey, having previously breakfasted with a Barmecide, lunched on diagrams, and filled himself with the east wind. Still, there is reason to believe that Humble Pie was a viand actually consumed by our great grandmothers; and taking into account the ingredients in a recipe, which the writer has found in a very old volume of the *Gentleman's Magazine*, the pie need have been by no means so untoothsome as its name would imply: "Take the humbles of a deer," says the recipe,—you see, there is venison for you to begin with,—and then it goes on to enumerate slices of bacon, condiments, buttered crust, and so forth: all things by no means suggestive of humility. He who first decried Humble Pie, and libelled it as a mean and shabby kind of victuals, was very probably some envious one who came late to the feast, and of the succulent pasty found only the pie-dish and some brown flakes of crust remaining.

The Humble Pie which the ex-curate Ruthyn Pendragon was invited to eat soon after his departure from Swordsley was, however, the metaphorical, and not the dainty dish. He looked at it with loathing, but dreaded lest he might have to eat it perforce, as Pistol ate his leek,—fortune cudgelling him the while,—and had he not been a clergyman, he might have said, again with ancient Pistol, "I eat, and eke I swear." Not but that I think swearing to be quite practicable without verbal maledictions. Good manners have banished oaths from the drawing-room and the dinner-table; but pray, did you never see the master of the house *look* a very unmistakable malison at the servants if the side-dishes were not handed round properly, or the wines were corked? Did you never detect your charming neighbour in the ocular utterance of at least a score naughty words, when, by unskilful carving, you have given her the wings of a bird which would *not* enable her to fly away, or when in the dance it has been your misfortune to tread on and tear one of her hundred-and-fifty flounces? We are commanded not to swear at all; but having stifled the *gros mots*, let us carry out the good work by putting a bit between our teeth, lest they too should grind themselves in mute curses; let us put a bearing-rein on our shoulders, lest they should shrug, and a kicking-strap on our fingers, lest they should be clenched in rage, and especially blinkers over our eyes, far too prone as they are, on slight provocation, to dart malignant expletives to the right and to the left.

So Ruthyn Pendragon, being reverend, did not swear—at least out loud; but his brow grew darker, and his eye fiercer, and he bit his lip more closely every day. It is a hard fight, that tussle with the strong, rich, well-backed-up world—and you all untrained, underfed, and friendless; you think you may win the contest by science and finish. Well, if you be wondrous wise, you may do so; but in general the brute force of your opponent carries the day, and one swashing blow from the Hercules you are battling with sends you sprawling. And pray mark the philosophy in the rhyme of the nursery hero, who was "wondrous wise:" He jumped into a quickset hedge, and scratched out both his eyes; that is to say, he got into difficulties; he was broken, ruined, sold up; he went to the dogs; his enemies exulted, and said, "There is an end of our friend. It is all up with him. We always thought so." Indeed: the man's wondrous wisdom came to his aid; for by mere force of marvellous sagacity and strong will, did he not *scratch his eyes in again?*

Ruthyn Pendragon found that of his own motion he had thrown up the means of earning a decent and reputable livelihood. He had got nothing in exchange but a gratuitous seat at an ordinary, at which the staple in the bill of fare was Humble Pie. Where-

soever he turned, he found the detested dish paraded before him.
It was Humble Pie hot and Humble Pie cold; Humble Pie roast
and boiled; *pâté à l'humble serviteur*, and not at all *à la financière*.
He was haunted by the ghost of this grim victual, not knowing
what day his resolution might fail, and he be compelled to devour
it ravenously. He had determined not to be a curate any more.
He had said to the church at Swordsley that henceforth it was to
be a struggle between it and him. But he meant a grander and
more potent Church when he apostrophised the humble little
structure of St. Mary-la-Douce. The most abhorred form that
Humble Pie could assume, was in his being possibly driven to ask
the Reverend Ernest Goldthorpe for testimonials as to his moral
character,—for the Rector of Swordsley would scarcely refuse him
those,—and seek, if he were pressed by want, for another curacy.
Before he would do that, he thought, he would hang himself.
What! abase himself in the sight of the supercilious High
Churchman, at whose little follies and weaknesses he, with his
great, strong, logical mind, had so often laughed! What! humi-
liate himself in the sight of the proud and scornful lady who, for
a mere declaration of love, had treated him as one would treat a
lacquey that had stolen spoons! No; sooner the suicide's halter,
the suicide's opium bottle, than that. All was over between him
and the vocation for which he had so carefully trained himself.
He had torn his cassock and rent his bands, he said to himself,
irrevocably. The arrow was shot; the battle had commenced, and
the strongest should win.

He had very little money, and a fortnight in London brought
him well nigh to the lowest ebb. He found that lodging, even in
a mean hotel in a back-street of Blackfriars, was too expensive for
him. He tried a Temperance Coffee-house, which was very dirty
and very expensive, and that too proved beyond his means. He
sought at very many private houses, but could not hear of a
decent sleeping-room under six or seven shillings a week. He
began to part with his clothes, which were few and of no great
account, and with his books, which were numerous, and in some
sort valuable. He had many college prizes, with the old arms
emblazoned on the covers; many expensive editions of the classics,
to purchase which he had denied himself many a meal; and not a

few choice volumes presented to him by old college friends. Away
went Elzevirs and Aldines. Away went college prizes. Away
went Liddell and Scott, and the Corpus Poetarum. With great
fear and trembling he had first essayed to pawn his library, as he
had been prudent enough to do with his clothes; but he found
that the pawnbrokers would scarcely lend the value of their
weight in paper on them, and that one pair of pantaloons was
worth three lexicons. With secret rage and anguish he began
selling his beloved folios. He certainly got more by their vendi-
tion outright; but the sacrifice was still enormous. The second-
hand booksellers in Holborn and Holywell Street told him that
Greek and Latin books were worth scarcely anything now; and
the prices they allowed certainly gave an *ex parte* confirmation to
their opinion. One candid bookvendor, indeed, who rejoiced
much in the sale of albums and gift-books, told him that he only
bought his volumes for their "jackets," meaning their handsome
bindings; and that so long as he could keep a stock of books
well bound in vellum or tooled morrocco, he could find customers,
who would not care if the book itself was the *Iliad* or the *Keep-
sake* for 1836. "The greatest Hauthor of the Hage, Sir,"
remarked this worthy tradesman, "next to the gent that signs the
fi'pun' notes, is 'Ayday. Hanything with 'Ayday's name to it is
sure to sell." And when Ruthyn Pendragon parted with a book
"bound by Hayday," he dined somewhat more copiously than
was his wont.

He led a perfectly solitary life. To not one of his old friends,
although many were wealthy and influential, did he care to appeal,
either for assistance or advice. If he met them in the street, he
did his best to avoid them, or at most returned a furtive or sullen
response to their greetings. Ruthyn had preserved just this link
of connection with the world, as, when he left Swordsley, to
desire that all letters which arrived for him after his departure
might be forwarded to the Chapter Coffee-house in St. Paul's
Churchyard. That hostelry has been long since pulled down;
but at the date to which this story refers the Chapter was a queer,
rambling place, with a darkling coffee-room and several mouldy
old waiters, who were supposed to remember the Great Fire of
London, and that Cathedral of St. Paul which was Gothic, and

not Corinthian. It was a great house of call for parsons more or less dilapidated, who plied for hire there in a not much less overt manner than did the red-nosed and white-aproned ticket-porters at the entrance to Doctors' Commons, hard by. Yet the Chapter Coffee-house had its *fasti*, literary as well as theological; for did not poor Charlotte Brontë and her sister stay there when they came to London after the wonderful success of that most marvellous book *Jane Eyre?*

Every other day or so Pendragon looked in at the Chapter for his letters. A good many came. There were offers of help, which he deliberately tore up. There was a curt note from the Reverend Ernest, informing him that, although they had parted in anger, their differences had in no way impaired the esteem he entertained for Mr. Pendragon's character, and that if his recommendation could be of any service to Mr. P. at any future stage of his career, it was very heartily at his service. Not for many years afterwards was the ex-curate to know at whose instance this letter was written, or by whose hand it was dropped into the letter-box of the Swordsley post-office. There was another note, too, in a bold, dashing scrawl, with plenty of blots and plenty of capital letters, in which L. S. informed R. P. that she thought H. M. was sorry for having used him so cruelly, and that matters might yet be mended if he "squared" the Rector. And the epistle wound up by reminding him that he had always a friend in need in the person of Lord Chalkstonehengist. But I don't think his Lordship wrote the letter, and I think that Ruthyn Pendragon knew perfectly well who did.

He kept both these letters for a day or two, often re-perusing them, and musing over their contents. But that unlucky flavour of Humble Pie pervaded both. He tore the Reverend Ernest Goldthorpe's note into very symmetrical little bits, and having, for his own solace and satisfaction, trampled them under foot, he collected the fragments, and flung them in a handful to the ducks in the ornamental water in St. James's Park. The ducks ate them, as they will eat anything,—bread crumbs, cigar-ends, or tenpenny nails; and it is to be hoped that their omnivorous stomachs derived benefit from the conciliatory expressions of the Rector of Swordsley.

Letter number two Ruthyn did not treat quite so cavalierly. He returned no answer to it; but he kept it about him, at first in his pocket-book, whence, finding that its corners were getting frayed, he transferred it to his bosom. I think he sewed it up in a glove which did not belong to him, and which he had acquired in a surreptitious and—for a clergyman—somewhat dishonest manner, and then he hung the little packet round his neck by a silken string, and felt that when he was laid in his grave he should wish to have that short blotted letter next his heart.

All this time he was very strenuously striving to earn his livelihood; for his means were very exigent, and he felt that his scanty stock of ready money would hold out but a little time longer. When he first went to the Chapter, he used to take a dish of tea there; but soon he began to grudge the cost of that luxury, and was fain to shamble past the waiter, and ask in a shamefaced manner at the bar for his letters. The waiters contemned him accordingly, and soon began to look upon him as a kind of hedge-parson or hackney-chaplain, who would do any absentee's duty, and preach some one else's sermon for ten shillings and a dinner. "If I am doomed to eat that kind of Humble Pie," thought Ruthyn Pendragon, "I shall have to hire a gown and a surplice, for I have parted with both." He had by this time but one suit of what may be termed clerical undress uniform, and it had grown wofully shabby and white at the seams. He had never acquired that art—in which some young curates are so expert—of tying his cravat in a captivating manner; and now, when he could only afford two clean ones in a week, the ill-knotted kerchief gave him a more slovenly appearance than ever. Walking—prowling down Whitehall, rather—one morning, Ruthyn Pendragon met a Bishop. His Lordship was probably on his way to the Athenæum, from some visit he had paid to the Ecclesiastical Commissioners or the Home Secretary. Perhaps he had been sitting in Convocation. There he was, plump, rosy, trimly-shaven, aproned, shovel-hatted, and silk-stockinged; one of the most prosperous-looking descendants, perhaps, of the Twelve who were bidden to set no store by worldly wealth, that you could light upon in a summer's day. He quickened his pace as the disconsolate curate approached; and his episcopal trot almost became a run as, with averted face, he hastened towards King Charles's statue. Why did his Lordship avoid his needy brother? Pendragon concluded that it was through pride, and that this was some lucky college Don who had just exchanged his trencher-cap for a mitre, and who, having known him in the old days, was ashamed to be recognised by so very shabby (albeit, dearly beloved) a brother. Alas, how little we know of one another's motives! The Right Reverend Timothy Stephen, Lord Bishop of Rougemullet (Portsonkin Palace, Binnsborough, is the epis-copal residence), was one of the most charitable prelates on the bench, and had he known Mr. Pendragon, or had he been properly recommended to him, would have done everything in his power to assist a deserving object, but the plain truth must be told :— the Bishop was being continually made the victim of persons who imposed on his benevolence by fictitious tales of woe, and, being exceedingly short-sighted, had mistaken the shabby curate for one Chowsleton, who affected the clerical garb, but who was a notorious begging-letter impostor, and had bled the good Bishop many a time and oft.

Although he disdained to seek employment in that Church against which he had set his face, Pendragon was not too haughty to try for a situation as usher in a school. He advertised once or twice, although the shillings he had to disburse were as so many drops of his heart's blood, and he received a few answers in return. They were all worthless. One schoolmaster wanted an assistant who was perfectly conversant with Hebrew, Hindostani, and Tamil, could play on the harmonium, and take charge of the boys during school-hours, for twenty pounds per annum. Another required an awakened Christian, who could lecture upon chemistry, had some knowledge of therapeutics, and was willing to serve for a year without any salary. A third suggested that literary accom-plishments were less an object than a thorough acquaintance with calisthenics and gymnastic exercises, and a military character; from which Pendragon inferred that his correspondent wanted a drill-sergeant, and not an usher. While a fourth, writing from Broom-back Scrubs, Ferulum, Yorkshire, plainly informed the advertiser that he wanted an usher who was a "cappital skollar,"—so wrote the Yorkshire preceptor,—and "was akkustumed to hoarses." "I

should not mind being a groom," thought Pendragon; "but if I
became one, I would rather ride after Miss Salusbury in the park
than fill up my leisure by teaching little boys, and rubbing my
master's horse down."

There was nothing to be got out of the scholastic profession.
He called on a firm in a dingy street of the Strand who had an
"Educational Registry," and professed to procure situations for
ushers and tutors; but the firm, represented by a bald-headed
man with a red face, who had something to do with corn and coals,
and companies and matrimonial agencies, as well as with education,
talked so much about the commission he expected, that Ruthyn
fled from him in terror. Then he took to answering advertisements, but with an equal want of success. He applied for clerkships to employers who told him they would be glad to engage him
at a rising salary if he would advance the sum of two hundred and
fifty pounds on undeniable security, and bearing interest at the rate
of fifteen per cent. per annum. He was tempted by announcements
that he could clear a handsome income as canvasser for the sale of
an article in general demand, and found that town-travellers were
wanted for a powder to kill fleas, and a liquid that washed linen
(and burnt holes in it *par dessus le marché*) without soap or water.
He was informed, always through the medium of the newspapers,
that he could be taught) in common with other ladies and gentlemen, and in six lessons) an accomplishment by which from three
to five pounds a week could be realised. He sent, as requested,
half-a-crown's worth of postage-stamps to a given address, and
received, by return of post, an envelope containing a dirty scrap
of paper, on which some absurd recipes for painting on leather
and modelling wax-flowers were written in a schoolboy hand. The
dupes were to send their postage-stamps to a certain number in
Coger's Inn, Strand, W.C., and it is not improbable that a party
by the name of Sims may have had something to do with teaching
those accomplishments by which from three to five pounds a week
might be realised.

He wrote to the secretaries of one or two literary institutions,
offering to deliver lectures. He was politely informed in return
that the services of gentlemen unknown to the public were not
available, but that the lecture-theatre of the institution could be

T

engaged for so many pounds per night. He haunted a few law-stationers' shops about the Temple and Lincoln's Inn, in the hope of obtaining some work in copying legal documents. He wrote a bold, nervous hand, but it was loose and irregular. A friendly law-stationer in Carey Street, having glanced over his best specimens of caligraphy, was good enough to say to him, " Look here ; you see these two folios, don't you? Ain't they beautifully written ? Ain't the upstrokes and downstrokes nice? Ain't they like copper-plate ? You see this indenture ? it's on parchment. Ain't the engrossing first-rate ? Did you ever see black letter done better than that ? Well, all this writing's done by a chap that lives in a garret in Bear Yard, and oftener sleeps on a doorstep than at home. He drinks a pint and a half of spirits every day, and will die in the hospital most likely. He's the beautifullest writer and the biggest vagabond I know. When you've learnt a good law hand—it won't take you more than six months—you may come to me again, and if you want employment you shall have it ; though between you and me, I think you'd better take a broom and sweep a crossing than go to law-writing." And treasuring up this valuable advice in his heart, Mr. Pendragon bade adieu to Carey Street.

"An odd thing, wasn't it, for a clergyman to want a copying job ? " remarked the law-stationer to his wife, shortly afterwards. " He was shocking seedy, but he had the real parson-cut about him. I suppose he's taken to drinking, or gone to smash somehow, or done something bad, and the bishop has taken his gown away. Poor fellow ! "

So nothing was wanting to the humiliation of Ruthyn Pendragon ; not even the compassion of a commander of quill-drivers,—not even the pity of this man of pleas, and pounce, and parchment.

Wandering through Soho one day, as being the locality where he thought the cheapest lodgings might be obtained, but revolving in his mind, meanwhile, whether the displacement of so much water, covering so much of the reeds and ooze of the Thames at Twickenham, by casting himself therein, might not be about the cheapest lodging he could find, Pendragon came upon a caravan-serai which suited his lean purse. It was a kind of model lodging-house,—not one of the imposing structures in red-brick with stone dressings which the Society for Improving the Dwellings of the Labouring Classes have since set up here and there in London, but an old warehouse or factory, which a few well-wishers of their kind had furnished in a rough-and-ready manner for the accommodation of men of scanty means. They had called it a model lodging-house at first; but they found the term distasteful to the tenants,—poverty has its proper, as well as its improper, side,—so the name was changed to that of the Monmouth Chambers, and thenceforth its cabins filled wonderfully. They were in truth cabins; for space was of great value in the house, and its distribution a matter of cunning arrangement; and so every room on every floor had been partitioned off by boards, not reaching within some fourteen inches to the ceiling, into so many numbered nooks, a narrow passage running between. Each cabin, however, had its door and its lock. The furniture was simple, but sufficient. A little iron bedstead, a peg or two for clothes, a locker to hold small personal chattels,—and these were all. To each floor was attached a lavatory; and on the basement was a kitchen where the lodgers could cook their victuals, and clean their boots in the adjoining area. There was a room for them to eat in, and a large reading-room supplied with daily and weekly papers and periodicals, and containing a fair library of books. There the inmates sat and read or wrote, or played at chess or draughts, or brooded over their prospects and their poverty. There was even a smoking-room, from which only the introduction of spirits was prohibited. The taboo was merely for form's sake; for the Monmouthians were no topers, and a roysterer would have died there of dulness in a week. A steward, or "Econome," as the Russians call him, managed the discipline of the place; and all its advantages were to be enjoyed for three-and-sixpence a week, paid in advance.

Ruthyn Pendragon eagerly availed himself of a vacant cabin in the Monmouth Chambers. By disposing of every superfluous article in his possession, he had managed to scrape together about four pounds. This sum, he said to himself, must enable him to hold out for six weeks, and then if no succour came he must do— he knew not what; but he was certain that something must be done. A carpet-bag held now his linen and the few needments for his toilet and studies,—his Bible, his Greek Testament, his favourite Horace (it was too ragged to sell), his Paley's *Evidences*, and his Jeremy Taylor's *Liberty of Prophesying*. How many times had he devoured that eloquent treatise? how many times asked mentally, "Shall not I too have liberty of prophesying—of preaching the Word—the Word that has flesh and blood in it, and is not merely so many shrivelled sinews and dry bones?" The house was full, and, like every other house where many people dwelt, was split up into cliques. There was the kitchen party,—reduced tradesmen, old worn-out clerks and commission-agents,—whose chief amusement and employment were in pottering over messes made from cheap scraps, and in squabbling over the reversions of places for their saucepans and fryingpans. They seldom ventured aboveground, but burrowed, like the farrier in Kenilworth. They seemed to have very little to eat, yet to be always breakfasting, dining, and supping.

There were two foreign parties, socially as well as politically divided, hating each other cordially. One was monarchical, the other republican. In the coffee-room all day long, and as far into the night as the rules of the house would permit (save only on occasions that will afterwards be referred to), toiled at a Dictionary a snuffy little old French gentleman, who had been a marquis. Had been, I say,—for, abating his snuff, and two weak eyes poring over the hard words, and a trembling hand that transcribed them, and a meagre little carcase swathed in a woful dressing-gown of striped flannel, he belonged wholly to the past tense. Feebly, very feebly burnt the last drops of oil in that rusted, battered lamp for which Time, the great marine-store dealer, waited with growing impatience. O Beauty, he is waiting for your diamond-head lustre! O brilliant youth, he is waiting for your flashing gig-lamps! O Mammon, he is waiting for your golden candelabra! O virgins wise and virgins foolish, he is waiting for all your lamps to burn out, that he may add them to his heap of rags, and bones, and old metal:—among which, there is but one thing keen and bright,—his own sharp consuming sickle. But render grace for that a greater magician there is than Time—a magician who gives us new lamps for old ones—lamps that are never to burn low or wax pale, or cast lowering shadows, but shall be firmly stayed upon everlasting tripods.

Very long hours the little old Frenchman slaved at the Dictionary. Now and again he would take a bundle of manuscripts out with him (having previously donned, for walking-costume, a kind of woollen sack of olive green, very ragged, in lieu of the flannel dressing-gown). Sometimes he would come back with a little brightness in the weak eyes. Then his companions knew that he had been receiving money, had been paid for some portion of his labour, or had been permitted to draw half-a-sovereign on account. Then he would feed, poorly enough, Heaven knows! on little scraps of cook-shop meat, and ha'porths of bread, and sugar, and coffee, screwed up in odd little cocked hats of paper,—but still feed and satisfy his meagre appetite. More frequently, he would return quite penniless, and with an additional redness in the eyes. It was conjectured then that the hard bookseller in Holborn, who some day or another was to publish the Dictionary, had taken exception to the manner in which his task had been performed, had bidden him recommence, and had refused him an advance. He never complained, and, valiantly enough, would try to gird himself to his task again, but generally went to bed, and lay there some ten hours, half-starving and crying, until the steward would batter at his door with knuckles of authority, and tell him that it was against the regulations of the chambers to lie a-bed by day,—thus routing the poor old Dictionary-maker from his lair; but only to press some coppers into his hand, or force him to come and share his dinner in the little panelled cabin which he called his lodge. The steward was a big-boned man, full six feet high, who had been a boatswain's mate on board a man-of-war, and had, I doubt not, handled many a rope's end in his time; but he had a heart as soft as toast-and-butter, and was governed by a shrewish little wife not much bigger than a Dutch doll, who, on her part, was governed by a baby diminutive but insubordinate, a baby that, without much difficulty, might have been put into a quart pot.

It was mean and ignoble for a foreign nobleman to live in a model lodging-house, among next door to paupers, and cry when he could not get any money from a bookseller, was it not? But

it was difficult to avoid pitying him. He was so old and so broken.
Two-and-seventy years had passed over his head. It was very
long since he was born,—years before the great Revolution,—heir
to an historic name and to vast estates. Why, he was eleven years
of age when his father, mother, sisters, almost every relative he
had, were guillotined by Robespierre. Why, he was past thirty
when at the downfall of Napoleon the old abbé who had sheltered
him and brought him to England told him that it was time to
return to France, and pay his court to Louis the Restored, and
take possession of his long-sequestered inheritance. But he never
got his broad acres back. They had been swallowed up among
the *Domaines Nationaux*, and the new grantees stuck to them.
He managed to get places, employments, was a captain in the
Gardes du Corps,—this poor little shrivelled old Dictionary-maker;
but at last came 1830, and down he came again, never to rise any
more. His days of prosperity had been few and transient. The
morning of his life was misery; the noontide was capricious and
showery; the night threatened to be as miserable as the commencement. He has been dead, I should surmise, this poor old
barnacle *de la vieille roche*, these many years; and I don't think
that he ever finished the Dictionary.

Ruthyn Pendragon would have made advances to this decayed
old gentleman, but he was almost too weak and nervous for conversation, and, like some animal or neglected child long accustomed
to ill-treatment, winced and drew back, even when you spoke to
him kindly, as though he expected, as a matter of course, that the
word would be accompanied by a blow. There was another old
Frenchman, with a closely cropped head and long moustache—
both as white as snow—who wore a discoloured ribbon at his
button-hole, and was addressed as Colonel. He was a Legitimist,
but for pure love of his country had preferred serving in the grand
army under Napoleon to remaining inactive or to emigrating. He
taught fencing when any one would take lessons of him, and,
when they wouldn't, coloured engravings for a livelihood. He
was of a somewhat boisterous temperament, however, and preferred taking his evening solace at an ill-conditioned little coffee-
shop in the neighbourhood, frequented chiefly by foreign gentlemen in difficulties, where until late at night you could hear the

jingling of dominoes, and the wrangling of politicians who never could agree.

The foreign democratic element had also a shelter at the Chambers, and a very bearded, restless, uncomfortable element it was, with apparently as great a hatred to paying its rent in advance, laving itself with soap and water, refraining from smoking tobacco in its bed-chambers, and otherwise conforming to the rules of the establishment, as to tyranny and military coercion. The foreign democratic element was always squabbling with the steward, and now and then endeavoured (mutually) to bruise and stab itself, accusing itself (mutually) of being a traitor and spy in the employ of tyrants. Ruthyn Pendragon avoided the foreign democratic element, then, as all men in their senses would act wisely in avoiding it now.

Of English lodgers—British, rather, for there were Scotchmen and Welshmen among them—there was a sufficiently curious variety. All kinds of waifs and strays had drifted to this lone shore, and lay here in a tangled heap of shingle and seaweed. It was certain that few of them could see worse, but it was generally understood that many of them had seen better, days. There was a tall and old man who had been at one time the possessor of a large fortune. He talked of the days when he had been in the commission of the peace, and kept a pack of hounds. He always posted, he said, from Warrington to London, and with four horses, in defiance of the London and North-Western Railway, which he considered as a dangerous innovation. He had been an extravagant man, and boasted of some orgie he had had in George the Fourth's days, when he had dammed up a fountain, and made punch in the basin. Nobody believed this: but few refused to place credence in the report that he had been a very wicked old fellow, who had wasted his substance in riotous living, broken his wife's heart, and turned his children out of doors. Of his fortune nothing was left now but two or three Chancery suits. He had lain long in the Fleet and in the Bench for contempt, and for costs, and other offences against the High Court at Lincoln's Inn, until at last Chancery itself had got tired of him, and Lord Brougham, one fine morning in his chancellorship, had inexorably, but mercifully, turned him out. It was an equal mercy when he discovered

the chambers, a quiet place where he could live for next to nothing,
and grumble at his ease, and even find an audience to listen to his
"case," and sympathise with his grievances. How he managed
to live was no small mystery; but he had plenty of bundles of
yellow dog-eared papers left, and there appears to be some power
of living by suction given to Chancery suitors, and which makes
their interminable papers a source of nutriment to them. At
least Clidger, that was the tall suitor's name, managed to rub
along, and to find stationery wherewith perpetually to memorialise,
petition, and otherwise bore almost to desperation the Lord Chancellor who was in, and the Lord Chancellor who was out, and the
rising lawyer who was supposed to have a chance of becoming
Lord Chancellor some day or another,—to say nothing of the
Vice-Chancellors, the daily and weekly newspapers, and the
Houses of Lords and Commons.

There was Tottlepot, too. Tottlepot had been a lieutenant in
the Marines, a coal-merchant, and a schoolmaster, and now
existed on a small annual pension granted him by his brother, a
clergyman in Somersetshire, on the express condition that he
should never come within twenty-five miles of his residence.
Tottlepot's three great misfortunes were, that he had once been a
very handsome man, and still considered himself (he was fifty) to
be so; that he was intolerably conceited; and that he wrote a
very bold, legible, and symmetrical hand. These circumstances
concurred in making the unhappy wretch believe that he was a
poet. He wrote rhyme continually, on every kind of subject,
and in every kind of metre. That which he indited was so
legible, that he found no difficulty in reading it aloud, on all
occasions, in a disgustingly flowing and sonorous voice—couplet
after couplet, and stanza after stanza. Had he stammered or
boggled over it, the man might have entertained some doubt as to
his poetic faculty; but rolling out his verses as he could, and did,
by the hundred dozen, he had not the remotest shadow of uncertainty as to his great and transcendent genius. A man to be
avoided, struck dumb with a sledgehammer, or struck dumb at
any rate, was Tottlepot, late of the Marines, the Coal Exchange,
and the Scholastic Profession. He spoke of himself, now rever-
ently, affectionately, soothingly, as the "poor poet,"—and now

arrogantly and boastfully as one with a divine inheritance, one who had stolen fire from Heaven, Sir, and suffered for it, like Prometheus. If the newspapers were late, he recorded their tardiness in a sonnet. He wrote poems on fine days, on wet days, and on foggy ones. He described a cold in his head, or a corn that he had cut, in the Spenserian stanza, and when he had a disagreement with the steward, which was about twice in every three days, withered that functionary, to his own—Tottlepot's— thinking, in Popeian heroics. Who has not known these insufferably vain and empty men, who, on the strength of much wordiness and a half-clouded intellect, turn down their collars, neglect to comb their hair, or fulfil their responsibilities in this life, and give themselves out as Poets? Did they ever abound more than at present? Will some kind, real satirist be good enough to come forward and fustigate them into a sense of shame, and a knowledge of their own position as average rate-paying Christians? Was there ever a time when they more needed the warning hammered into them half a century since by one who was no poet, but who, unless I greatly err, has since become one of the greatest men of letters, lawyers, and sages that the world has seen? Say, was it Brougham, or was it Jeffrey, who wrote, "We really cannot permit all the shallow coxcombs who languish under the burden of existence to take themselves for spell-bound geniuses. The most powerful stream, indeed, will stagnate the most deeply, and will burst out to more wild devastation when obstructed in its peaceful course; but the weakly current is, upon the whole, more liable to obstruction, and will mantle and rot, at least, as dismally as its betters. The innumerable blockheads, in short, who betake themselves to suicide, dram-drinking, and dozing in dirty nightcaps, will not allow us to suppose that there is any real connection between ennui and talent, or that fellows who are fit for nothing better than mending shoes or cracking stones may not be very miserable if they are unfortunately raised above their proper occupations."*

Tottlepot and Clidger,—the one with his poetry, the other with his grievances,—together with the silent misery of the little old

* Edinburgh Review, 1818.

snufly Marquis de la Vieille Roche, and the beards and bluster of the foreign democratic element, were not very conducive to Ruthyn Pendragon's peace of mind. But for the cheapness of the chambers, he might have been speedily tempted to leave them; but he found companions less demonstrative, and, ultimately, two or three almost congenial to his ways of thought. There was a quiet population of broken-down tradesmen, clerks timeworn and shattered, yet still able to scrape a weekly subsistence by making up the books of butchers and tailors in the evening, and collecting debts. There were a few small commission-agents, who were satisfied with their legitimate gains, and therefore did not prosper much. There was a reduced farmer named Cherfit—one of those sad spectacles, a fat man grown thin, and whose skin was as baggy as the clothes he wore. A great speculation in corn, or hops, or clover, had made him bankrupt; but he had not lost his equanimity. He calmly remembered the days when he used to farm a thousand acres; was perfectly contented with criticising the points of the cab and cart horses he saw passing the window; was almost an infallible judge of the weather; was a staunch Protectionist, and assiduously perused the prices current of those markets whose fluctuations were nothing to him now. Add to these, if you please, a dapper little man, whose name was, aptly enough, Mr. Smart, who had taught writing, arithmetic, and the use of the globes any time these fifty years in ladies' schools, chiefly in the neighbourhood of Camberwell and Kensington; a wan, sunburnt man, who had been agent for a Chinese opium house at Canton for many years, who had *not* made a fortune out of that traffic, and was suspected of habitually chewing the narcotic drug in which he had once dealt; and a superannuated theatrical prompter, whose sight was now too bad to enable him to " hold the book," who was, to his great good luck, " on the Fund," and who was looked upon as an infallible authority as to new pieces and first appearances: he never went to the theatre, but attended the performances through the intermediary of a newspaper, and always with a saving clause, disparaging to the present state of the drama, and laudatory of those glorious days when John Kemble and Jack Bannister, Joey Munden and Jerry Sneak Russell, flourished. In what manner

of gyrations do people flourish, I wonder?—angularly, or in
curves, or in "parabolic envelopes," as that unexpected comet,
the other day, is said to have done.

Ah! let me not forget; there was an artist, too, at the chambers. His name was Clere;—John Clere—nothing more. He
was so desperately poor, and so painfully struggling an artist, that
he should properly have lived in a garret, worn a threadbare black-
velvet coat, continually smoked a short pipe, abused the Hanging
Committee of the Royal Academy, and the extortionate race of
picture-dealers, and lain on his back all day on a flock-bed, waiting
for patronage. He did nothing at all of the kind. Although not
three-and-twenty years of age, he never smoked, and did not even
wear a moustache; nor, although his hair was of an auburn hue,
and abundant in quantity, did he part it down the middle, torture
it into ringlets, or allow it to flow over the collar of his coat
behind. He avowed, with much simplicity, that he was the son
of a butcher at Norwich, that he had been bred at a charity-
school, and, disliking the paternal calling, was on the eve of being
apprenticed to a shoemaker, when he thought that he would come
to London and see if he could earn a crust by the exercise of that
taste for drawing which he had shown, chiefly in chalk and slate-
pencil, from the very earliest days that he had worn a muffin-cap
and leathers. At St. Wackleburga's charity-school he had learned
to read and write imperfectly; all the rest he had taught himself.
He was fortunate enough to arrive in the great town, a raw lad, in
1845, when there was a great railway mania. More iron roads were
projected than there were towns and villages, almost, for them to
connect with one another. Certain standing orders of Parliament
had to be complied with, and certain maps and plans to be deposited at the offices of the Board of Trade, by midnight at a given
date. These maps and plans were lithographed; and lithographic
draughtsmen—nay, any ticket-writer who could make a mark on
stone or tracing-paper—were at a premium. John Clere went in
with the rest to a great lithographer in the City, about a fortnight
before the great day. He had been dropping prospectuses down
areas at a penny a-piece—everybody, the lame, the halt, and the
blind, found employment in connection with railways in the
famous "forty-five:" beggars were directors, and alms-men

members of provisional committees—when a youthful acquaintance, engaged in the same pursuit, told him of the great run on
lithographic draughtsmen. He remembered that he had once
made a chalk drawing or two on stone of a popular churchwarden
and a new pump, for a printer in Norwich, who had paid the
clever charity boy a few shillings for his pains. He went with
specimens of his proficiency, and a neatly-written character from
the master of St. Wackleburga ; who, good pedagogue, always
predicted that John Clere would become either president of the
Royal Academy, or coach-painter in ordinary to her Majesty.
The great lithographer cared nothing at all about his character,
and very little about his specimens. He wanted hands. He gave
everybody a chance who said that he understood map-drawing.
If the neophyte made blots, and showed manifest incapability, he
was forthwith turned out. If he was up to his work, he was paid
five shillings an hour for it, and might go on drawing maps and
plans all day and all night. John Clere had a lithographic pen
put in his hand, a stone before him, and a map to copy from. He
proved neat and expeditious ; and before a week was out his hire
was raised to ten—to fifteen shillings an hour, to say nothing of
refreshments laid on gratis and supplied at discretion. He made
junctions between Stoke Pogis and Walton-on-the-Naze, with a
branch to Stony Stratford, calling at Ashton-under-Lyne. He
drew sections of the great Saddleback tunnel, and the great Lough
Swilly bridge, and the great Ben Nevis viaduct. Ah, if those
halcyon days could have lasted for ever ! They did not. The fixed
day for delivery arrived. Cabs tore up to the Board of Trade, dis-
gorging frantic engineers and foaming agents laden with bolsters,
with bales, with pillows of maps and plans. I suppose that not
one-hundredth of those projected railways were ever completed,
ever commenced indeed. However, John Clere found himself the
better by fifty pounds in hard cash when that memorable midnight
hour struck. He had secured, too, a friend in the lithographer,
who saw his talent and admired his wondrous perseverance ; but
alas! while the lithographer had paid his workmen on the nail, the
projecting companies neglected to pay the lithographer. The
Stoke Pogis and Walton-on-the-Naze people, the Lough Swillyites
and the Saddlebackians, owed him hundreds. He went bankrupt,

and to the colony of Natal, whence he wrote now and then to John
Clere, advising him to save up money enough to emigrate to that
flourishing settlement.

John Clere had no luck for six years afterwards. He lived for
a very long time on the fifty pounds the railway mania had brought
him, and then sank down into a day-to-day fight for bread-and-
cheese. When he could earn enough to buy bread with, he spent
it in a subscription to a night-school in Frith-street, Soho, where
he could draw from the " round," or plaster casts from the antique; and hoped some day to be able to subscribe to another
school, where he could draw from the living model. He felt that
he had everything to learn, and so went on learning, and found
his account in it. I wish that Mr. Samuel Smiles could have
known John Clere. He would have added another chapter then
to his good book on Self Help.

John Clere could not paint much. He dreaded the idleness of
companionship, and the temptations to mooning and day-dreaming
of a studio. The steward was kind to him, and there being an un-
occupied cabin at the top of the house with, fortunately, a window
in it—for the majority of the chambers only enjoyed a dim illumination from a common studio—allowed him to go up there and
try his hand at painting, which he did now and then, in a rough-
and-ready fashion, with a board propped against a locker for an
easel. He had a taste for mediæval art too, and was dexterous at
missal painting; but those were long before the days of illuminating Art Union, and the missals would not bring in bread. He
had a mingled scorn and loathing for the picture-dealers, and so
did not devote himself to the production of the hasty oil-sketches
known as " pot-boilers," or the money-bringing daubs that turn
up in cheap auctions. He cultivated a few of the rougher species
of design, and lived by it, preferring mostly to work in the common reading-room below, where the poor old Dictionary-maker
used sometimes to watch his labours in meek admiration; and
Clidger used to scowl at him because he had no grievances, and
Tottlepot rail at him because he did not cultivate High Art, and
had no sense of the Beautiful. He would have conciliated Tottlepot by listening to any amount of his poetry, which rather amused
him than otherwise, but for a falling-off of which you are speedily

to hear.   So he worked and worked, and sufficient for the day was
the Humble Pie thereof.   He drew cheap valentines; he touched
up portraits for cheap miniatures (great is photography in the land
now, but it was only a weak and suckling art then); he drew
cartoons on wood of landaus, and electro-plate, and artificial
limbs, and gentlemen measuring themselves with a view to being
provided by cheap tailors at their provincial residences with exquisitely fitting habiliments—the destination of most of which
cartoons was the advertising columns of newspapers.   And now
and then he had a romance to illustrate for a cheap publisher,
or a portrait to draw on stone, and was quite happy on about
fifteen shillings a week, reserving any overplus for the develop-
ment of a certain purpose, of which only his strong human will
and the Power who had given it to him knew the purport.

Pendragon had not been many days in the chambers before he
struck up something like a friendship with this simple, quiet,
earnest young man.   But for his dread of eating that Humble
Pie, of which the other partook every day quite contentedly, and
even thankfully, he would have asked him to recommend him to
any employment he knew of; but he refrained; and John Clere,
who had a habit of minding his own business, naturally thought
that the parson had some private means, or that he would not sit
all day long reading books and biting his nails.   Pendragon found
out, little by little, that Clere took an interest in Church matters,
and that he used to go to early service every morning to a certain
celebrated and much-decorated church in Wells Street, Oxford
Street, and on Sundays to a fane even more highly decorated at
Knightsbridge.   He began to hesitate whether it were not incumbent upon him—who had sacrificed so much for conscience' sake—
who had given up his curacy at Swordsley because he differed from
the rector as to red crosses, and surplices, and brass work, and
artificial flowers, and candlesticks—to hate this poor toiling young
artist because he was a Puseyite, and confessed that he read Alban
Butler's *Lives of the Saints*.   But was he a Puseyite?   Somehow
Ruthyn had to own to himself that John Clere did not talk as the
Reverend Ernest Goldthorpe talked; that he showed much more
knowledge and much more liberality than the aristocratic rector,
that he seemed to have made a deep and earnest study of things

which Ernest Goldthorpe—so his ex-curate thought—had only
adopted as a fashion and a whim. "This Puseyism, or whatever
it is," said Pendragon, "has made yonder magnifico at Swordsley
supercilious ; it has made Magdalen Hill proud and disdainful :
but it seems to have instilled into this young man only a profound
humility, and a desire to go on learning good things." It was
easy to see that John Clere was no bigot. If he leant even
Romewards, and on this Pendragon pressed him hard, but un-
availingly, it was with no supine reliance. If he turned away from
cant, and howling Boanergism, and the puling shabby piety which
prompts some people, with no fear of the Mendicity Society before
their eyes, to be perpetually scrawling begging-letters to Heaven :
not honest prayers, but selfish petitions based on good deeds they
affect to have done but never have—it was without intolerance and
without severity. John Clere belonged to a little knot of theologians who lived quietly and contentedly at the chambers, and
who, when Pendragon had been admitted to their intimacy, and
had made up his mind not to hate the artist for his Puseyism, he
discovered could agree excellently well among themselves. There
was one of the hardest of Scotchmen, who had something to do
with a Manchester warehouse, and who held by Crown-Court
prophecy and Doctor Cumming. There was a mild old man in a
large black stock and a larger black wig, and who, in-doors and
out-of-doors, wore a blue cloak with a fur collar ; who sat under a
famous preacher, then wont to hold forth at a chapel in Oxendon
Street, Haymarket. He was slightly afraid, the mild old gentleman in the stock and wig used to remark, that the Doctor had
Socinian tendencies ; but he could not help admiring his eloquence,
and revering his truly practical piety. There was a Unitarian,
who attended a place of worship where Gray's *Elegy* or Camp-
bell's *Last Man* were occasionally sung by way of hymns, and
whom Pendragon at first regarded with the kind of feeling with
which Torquemada might have regarded a lapsed heretic, but who
was nevertheless a very quiet, honest, God-fearing man, of grave
conversation and blameless life. There was a Welsh Baptist, who
had been an usher in a school ; and a Methodist mechanic from
Lancashire. And these five, and John Clere the Puseyite, and
Ruthyn Pendragon, who had sacrificed so much for conscience'

sake, would sit and talk together seriously on new connections
and old connections, and orthodoxy and heterodoxy—arguing
closely and sternly too, but never quarrelling. Only one trifling
squall troubled the tranquil sea of their daily discourse. There
came a Calvinist, a town traveller, I think, for a firework manu-
facturer. He was well read, and a fluent speaker, and at first was
a welcome addition to the little knot of those whom the censorious
Clidger used to stigmatise as "the Hypocrites," and the satirical
Tottlepot deride as "the Saints." But there was no eliminating
the brimstone and saltpetre from the Calvinist. He would persist
in maintaining that only the elect could be saved: that he was one
of the elect, and that his companions were not. This was personal,
and the quiet theologians of the chambers declined to argue further
with him; and the Calvinist went away in dudgeon, to travel for
fireworks among a people who had more grace.

How happily Ruthyn Pendragon thought the days would pass
if he could continue to dwell among these tranquil and charitably
minded men. But, alack, the silver sands of his purse were fast
running out. He had now only a few shillings left, and the
dreadful alternative of Humble Pie or Starvation stared him in
the face.

CHAPTER XXII.

WOMAN'S WORK.

ONYX Square, Tyburnia, was itself again. The auriferous tide
had once more its ebb and flow between Beryl Court and the
mansion of Mammon; and splendour, if not gaiety, resumed its
reign in the domains of Sir Jasper Goldthorpe.

The Baronet had come home for the London season, Lady
Goldthorpe with him; and Miss Magdalen Hill had come up from
The Casements to join her adopted mother. Sir Jasper's health,
said Dr. Sardonix, was entirely restored. It was a mercy—it was
a blessing, quoth Dr. Sardonix. If it were not impertinent to
say, neatly observed the Physician, that one to whom Society
owed so much owed something likewise to Society, he, the Doctor,
could state, that his distinguished patient was perfectly prepared
to discharge that debt. His place had long been vacant, but he
was now ready to fill it again, and would do so, as worthily as
ever.

This was very neat language, and from a courtly doctor who had
numbers of distinguished patients to conciliate, came very appro-
priately; but it was not the less a lie. Perhaps Society could not
get on without such elegant untruths: at any rate, they are told
every day of Society's life, and, in Society, prosper exceedingly.
"There is not the slightest foundation," says the *Morning
Smoother*, "for the absurd statement to which an unscrupulous
contemporary just gave currency, that the pecuniary embarrassments of a certain gallant officer in the Household Brigade have
led to his quitting the country in a precipitate manner." It is
perfectly well known at all Captain De Loos' clubs, that he has
been cheating at cards, that the usurers refuse to renew any more
of the Captain's bills, and, tired of large interests, uproariously
demand their principal in full. The Captain is rusticating at

U

Kissingen, whence he will speedily remove to some northern
clime, where extradition treaties with England are not known;
for, lo, in a scandalous trial in the Common Pleas steps into the
witness-box De Loos' great chum, Viscount Groomporter, and
maketh oath and sweareth that the signatures to half-a-dozen bills
of exchange, which the Captain has been getting discounted as
accepted by his lordship, are none of his handwriting. Not a
word of truth, I can assure you, in the story about the *fracas*
between Lord Raffborough and his wife, Tom Soapley—that
eminent professor of the art of making things comfortable—is
instructed to say to anybody who will believe him. But nobody
will believe him, for the reason that it is perfectly well known
that Lord Raffborough has broken Lady Raffborough's *cache-
peigne*, and very nearly her head into the bargain, with a cham-
pagne-bottle, and that her Ladyship has run away with Signor
Mercandotti, the music-master.

Nobody who heard Dr. Sardonix believed a word that he said
about Sir Jasper Goldthorpe's complete restoration to health.
Everybody could see that Mammon looked exceedingly ill and
exceedingly shaky. Indeed, some went so far as to say that the
Baronet's lengthened tour on the Continent was all a pretence,
and that he had been sojourning in a private lunatic asylum.
Still it was a kind and charitable thing for Dr. Sardonix to trot
about town reporting his entire convalescence; and Society, to
say nothing of Mammon, was very grateful to him for it. When
Madame de Genlis's Palace of Truth is built, the window-blind
makers will all realise rapid fortunes.

However, Dr. Sardonix's amiable fictions notwithstanding,
there was no denying that pomp and luxury had reasserted themselves in Onyx Square. If the dead man, and the awful circumstances of his death, were not, and could never be, forgotten, his
remains, at least, were interred in a pompous catafalque, and he
was mourned for beneath veils of gold-and-silver tissue. His
mother still wore mourning for him; still shed tears when,
routing among the drawers of her dressing-table, or in some of
her woman's hiding-places,—and what woman has not a hiding-
place?—she came upon some boyish memento of him who was
gone, never to return:—now a glove, now the agate-mounted whip

he had with his first pony, now a school theme, beautifully
engrossed over faintly-ruled lines, and elaborately flourished with
swans and cherubims by the writing-master attached to the well-
known classical establishment of Dr. Budds, Broomley Heath,
Birchshire. These and dozens of other things—his epaulette-box,
the cashmere shawl and ivory chessmen he had sent her from
India, a rough pen-and-ink drawing he had made of himself in
cantonments, in white jacket and pith hat, lounging in a rocking
chair, smoking a monstrous Trichinopoly cheroot, with a glass of
brandy pawnee beside him,—all these were so many mute but
eloquent disclaimers of the possibility of his ever quite fading
away from the memory of his parents. We can't get rid of
these awfully silent legacies of the dead, these whispers from
beyond the grave. Poor Lady Goldthorpe did not lose the
memory of her sorrow, but she ceased to dwell upon it: she only
bethought herself of it with a chastened sadness : the image of the
lost son was as that of a country visited long, long ago, of which
only the dim outline is permanent in the mind, but which now
and again, and in a transient manner, starts up distinct and vivid.
Moreover she was a cheerful woman by nature, and her suscepti-
bilities were not of the keenest. Heartily grieve as she might,
sorrow seldom spoilt her appetite : she might cry over her dinner,
but she was rarely so wretched as to go utterly dinnerless. New
cares, new pre-occupations, conspired, however, about this time to
cast a shade over Lady Goldthorpe's generally beaming temperament. The chief care was her husband's infirm state of health,
coupled with an uneasy sensation that he was brooding over some
deep and secret sorrow, to which the loss of his son was comparatively trifling. What it was she did not know ; but that
there was something lying dark in his path—something evil
lowering over his head—her womanly instinct persuaded her.

"My Goldy usen't to take on so," she would remark to the
confidential Cashman. "He's had troubles enough in his time,
poor dear; but he always got over them, and was as merry as a
grig a fortnight afterwards. He's had losses and people to worrit
him ; but he never seemed so down as he is now. Depend upon
it, Cash,"—Lady Goldthorpe had a pleasant liking for abbre-
viation,—"there's more in it than either of us think for. What

vexes me most is, that he never tells me anything. He used to
tell me everything; and now he has scarcely a word to throw at
a dog."

In Mrs. Cashman's mind there was one prime and fundamental
root for all human evil. It was not money which Mrs. Cashman,
who had saved a comfortable little *peculium* of her own, so
staunchly held to be the root of all good. The *fons et origo* of
all misery and disaster had in her philosophy an intimate and
inseparable connection with the human abdomen and the human
liver. She considered the two as identical, and seldom mentioned
one without the other.

"P'raps it's the stommick, my lady," she suggested. "P'raps
it's the boil" (Mrs. Cashman always called the biliary secretion
the "boil") "that's the matter with the poor dear gentleman."

"Cashman," replied her mistress, with decision, but without
acrimony, "you're a fool. Sir Jasper never had anything the
matter with his liver. Bless his heart, he could digest a saddle
and bridle for breakfast, and a copper stewpan for dinner. No,
Cash; there's something else. It's something in the City that
troubles my——"

"The fun's, my Lady, maybe," meekly hinted the rebuked
housekeeper.

"Ay, the Funds, or the National Debt, or the Bank Stocks,
or the what's-his-names," pursued Lady Goldthorpe, snappishly.
"Drat the City; I wish there had never been such a place as the
City, I do declare, though we were as poor as church-mice before
we went there, and got all our money out of it. The City!
bother the City; it's the bane of every woman's life. If your
husband comes home as cross as two sticks, and as surly as a bear
with a sore head, things are sure to have been going contrariwise
in the City. If you wish him to take you to Greenwich or
Richmond, he's got an appointment in the City. If he comes
home at two in the morning, with one collar up and the other
down, and a lighted cigar-end in his waistcoat-pocket, he's been
meeting a friend in the City. If you want the horses, he's going
to take them into the City. It's all City, City, City, though it's
made us as rich as Water Creases" (presumably Crœsus); "and
I wish the City was at Jericho, that I'm sure I do."

I wonder how many ladies of my acquaintance are of the same opinion with Lady Goldthorpe,—albeit they may express their thoughts in language slightly more refined.

These were the cares of the wife of Mammon. Her preoccupations were to find a wife for her son Ernest, and a husband for her adopted child Magdalen Hill.

"I don't see why they shouldn't come together now poor dear Hugh's gone," she reasoned to herself. "Her fortun' would join very nicely with Ernest; they're both clever, and pious, and charitable, and they'd make a very pretty pair. Ah, but would they? Would they agree, I wonder? He's proud, and she's proud. He's got a will of his own, and so has she; and when pride and pride come together, Old Scratch comes and sits bodkin."—You must really excuse Lady Goldthorpe's want of refinement, but you must remember that she was of humble extraction, and had once been the wife of a small shopkeeper.— "No, I'm afraid the match wouldn't do. As for Ernest, I must and will marry him off before he's a year older ; but Magdalen— I don't think she would have anybody, if he was Emperor of Japan, and had a mint of money : 'I wear the weeds of a virgin widow,' she told me yesterday. Stuff and nonsense. Girls ought to be married, particular when they have plenty of money. I hadn't any money when Goldy married me. I had but two frocks,—a brown merino, and a silver-gray lustring for Sundays,— and I was as happy as the day was long. But Maggy loved Hugh too dearly to be false to his memory ; so she said. Ah, Hugh, Hugh! poor dear Hugh! We shall meet in Heaven, where the wicked cease from worritin', and there's no more bother, and the weary are nice and comfortable."

This was the usual burden of the good woman's complaints, and although she misquoted the sacred text, she thoroughly believed in it.

There were more persons in Onyx House besides Lady Goldthorpe and the confidential Cashman who shrugged surmises and whispered misgivings about Sir Jasper's altered manner, his bowed and drooping head, his anxious face. His footmen noticed it ; but as it did not affect their wages, their uniform, or their hair-powder, they did not trouble their ineffabilities about it, much. Argent, Sir Jasper's body-servant, remarked it. Argent was a shrewd man, and ventured to sound Mr. Drossleigh, the financial factotum, who still came backwards and forwards between Onyx Square and Beryl Court, Sir Jasper's ill-health frequently compelling him to absent himself for days together from business. Argent did this with great fear and trembling; but Mr. Drossleigh did not, as he expected, reprove him with any extraordinary sternness.

"It's no business of yours, and none of mine, Argent, for the matter of that," he remarked, "and it would be worth both our situations if Sir Jasper found us out prying into his affairs; but between you and me, his goings-on puzzle me quite as much as they do you. I suppose we both see about as much of him, you in your way, and I in mine. I can't understand what's up, Argent. There's something in the wind, and that's the truth. I do hope that Sir Jasper hasn't got into any trouble about a bit of white muslin."

For, as the peculiar idiosyncrasy of the confidential Cashman was to imagine that there could be no trouble without a derangement of the stomach and liver, so did the confidential Drossleigh attribute every moral and physical ailment to one source—namely, to white muslin; otherwise, the womankind enveloped therein. Mr. Drossleigh was a confirmed misogynist, and those familiar with his personal history affirmed that in early life he had been the victim of a subtle adventuress, habitually wearing white muslin, who, having decoyed him into presenting her with his portrait, and addressing to her some absurd versicles, in which "utter" rhymed with "butter," and "pledge" with "edge," had, on his declining to purchase a special licence, and make a handsome settlement upon her forthwith, brought an action for breach of promise of marriage against him, and recovered damages to the extent of three hundred and fifty pounds. Drossleigh paid the damages and costs, and thenceforth looked with an evil eye on white muslin, constantly traducing the wearers of that textile fabric, and ascribing to their agency all woe that is worked beneath the sun. Nor did Sir Jasper Goldthorpe's condition escape the notice and the comments of two young ladies at that time resident in his mansion. Magdalen Hill saw his sorrow, and

grieved. Letitia Salusbury saw Magdalen's grief in a stronger
light than even she did Sir Jasper's, and sympathised with her to
the full. They were not a very well assorted pair. Magdalen
was as little communicative as ever; and her frank and voluble
companion was compelled to judge mostly by inference of that
which was passing in the mind of her taciturn companion.

I have said that they were ill-assorted. Seldom, perhaps, were
two young ladies brought together who had so few tastes in
common, or who seemed so widely to diverge in their views and
dispositions. Magdalen grew sterner and more ascetic, so to
speak, every day. In a few cold words she told her friend that
she, Magdalen, had long neglected her duties; that she had long
been blind to her responsibilities; but that her eyes were at
length opened, and that she was determined to discharge the task
which she knew devolved upon her, and to which she felt that she
was called.

"What is the task, Meg?"—Miss Salusbury persisted in
addressing Miss Hill in the least refined diminutives.—"What
is the duty? What are the responsibilities? Have you got any
bills to take up, like the young men in the Heavies whom one
knew at Swordsley? Are you obliged to get up early in the
morning for drill, or stable-duty? Do you want to go to matins
at St. Barnabas, or, better still, at the Oratory at Brompton?
Or do you feel it your solemn vocation to wear a horse-hair next
your skin, and whip yourself three times a day, like St. Catha-
rine of Sienna, or the saints and martyrs you are always
painting?"

Ah, those saints and martyrs!—'tis the writer who puts in the
interlocutory. How we have degenerated from the fine old times
of maceration and mortification! The saintesses of old wore horse-
hair chemisettes: our modern devotees only wear them in the form
of crinoline skirts. The primitive pietists scourged themselves
with wire: the saints of Belgravia make the wire into "cases," to
distend their skirts withal.

"I think," Miss Hill calmly answered, "that I have painted
saints and martyrs enough. I hope to look henceforth at those
holy exemplars from quite a different point of view. I have done
with those vanities of gold and vellum and gaudiness."

"Ah, I thought what it was coming to. I guessed what was going to happen. A narrow cell, a hard pallet, a crucifix, a rosary, a skull, a big book, and a pair of shears for your back hair;—all is vanity, that's it. You are going to take the veil."

"I have no such intentions. Although the communion by which I hold recognises, under certain circumstances, the excellence and usefulness of the monastic system; although conventual institutions, properly modified, are not wholly foreign to my views on Church matters,—I look at utter seclusion from the world, and denial of the claims which the world has upon our services, as selfish and hypocritical. When I feel that I can no longer do good, I may think again of becoming a nun."

"I dare say you've thought of it over and over again; as it is, you're a walking Lady Abbess. I'm half afraid that you'll order me to be bricked up for my sins in the wall of Tattersall's yard. Charmingly edifying it would be; just like Constance de Beverley in *Marmion*. Fancy the skeleton of Lord Chalkstonehengist's daughter being discovered fifty years hence standing bolt upright in a niche made in the bricks and mortar: nothing on her but some mouldy grave-clothes, nothing beside her but an empty pitcher."

"You jest upon everything, Letitia."

"I jest upon monks and nuns, because I believe the vast majority of the tales told about them to be silly trash. Do you think I believe all those old women's fables about dungeons, and living sepulchres, and iron rods, and clanking chains, and the like? Constance de Beverley's niche was in all probability a rabbit-hutch. I've no patience with your monks and your nuns, and the stupid girls who allow artful priests to caricature nowadays horrors that never existed. Convents in England are not, and never will be any more than a caricature. Abroad you have the genuine article,—and what is it? Do you think it's all midnight chanting and mortifying of the flesh? I knew a girl at school in Paris who had been brought up at the Sacré Cœur. She said that the young nuns did nothing out of class-hours but talk scandal and abuse the abbess, and that the old ones were always taking snuff and quarrelling as to who made the best preserves and the nicest cherry-brandy. I believe they're all the same, monks, and that

they'd all be much better if they could go across country a bit,
and back a horse now and then for a trifle."

"And the Sisters of Charity?"

"Well, they're bricks; that I'll admit. When we were staying
at Brussels, there were some good girls, called *Petites Sœurs des
Pauvres*, who not only nursed the poor, but went out begging for
them. Only imagine a young lady by birth and education going
out every morning in a donkey-cart full of tin-cans, and begging
broken meat and tea-leaves from hotel to hotel. There's no kissing the pavement, no thrashing oneself, and no midnight chanting
among the Sisters of Charity or the *Petites Sœurs*, you may be
sure; and I don't see why there should be any among the nuns,
or the monks either."

So the Honourable Letitia Salusbury said, thinking herself
exceedingly wise in her generation. She had been to Brussels.
She may have visited Louvain. I wonder whether she had ever
heard of a certain Monastery of the Fathers of Good Works, at
a place called Hoogendracht?

Miss Salusbury, however, outspoken as she was, by no means
regarded Magdalen's expression of opinion as to the laxity with
which her duties had hitherto been performed with anything approaching aversion or contempt. She respected her friend. She
was glad to recognise in her superior qualities of mind, and a
stronger sense of rectitude. It might not be within poor Letitia's
power to understand the purport of Magdalen's mission; but she
could admire her for the inflexible manner in which she began to
carry it out.

If the heiress had consulted her own tastes, and had been selfish
enough to have her own way now that she had come to be the
guest of the Mammon family in Onyx Square, she would have
employed her time in a very different manner to that which made
the programme traced out for Miss Hill. For operas, or balls, or
concerts, Miss Salusbury did not much care; but she was very
fond of the theatre; she was fonder of the park; she delighted in
what she called "jollifications," whether those jollifications took
place at flower-shows, at public breakfasts, or at pic-nics. Mundane entertainments of that description did not enter into the
social scheme of Miss Magdalen Hill. She did not insist upon

Letitia's accompanying her in her daily pilgrimage, but she looked sadder and graver than her wont when the other manifested a disinclination to join her; and so, with a good-humoured protest against the whole thing being immensely slow and a great—I am afraid she said a confounded—bore, she went willingly whithersoever she was led. As to Lady Goldthorpe, she declared point blank that she couldn't be bothered with Magdalen's whims and fancies, and that she would be glad enough to give any money to the little beggars and the destitute crossing-sweepers, but would prefer not to cultivate their personal acquaintance. "Go along with the likes of such ragamuffins." Such was Lady Goldthorpe's more expressive locution.

Magdalen and Letitia did however "go along," and mingle with not only the likes of the classes just alluded to, but among men, women, and children of even lower degrees. Each morning was devoted to the exploration of the wretchedest—often of the most depraved—haunts of London. They entered hovels, and passed through scenes, and conversed with and succoured miserable beings, such as even the clergyman, the city missionary, and the police-officer seldom saw—such as the sunlight seldom glanced upon. Their reception was various. Sometimes the inquiries they made were received with respect: the relief they gave, with gratitude. Sometimes, but not seldom, they were met by sullen denials, by hypocritical lies, by rudeness, and abuse. But Magdalen went on her way, and the more rebuffs she met with seemed the more determined not to swerve from her appointed path.

It was not all black and dismal, however; now and then they visited some place where there was brightness, and cheerfulness, and hope. Now it was a training school, a ragged school, a school of industry, or cookery, or housekeeping; now the workroom of some associated seamstresses; now a new and improved habitation for the poor.

"There is a place," Magdalen Hill said one morning, "which I have never visited, and about which ——" (she mentioned some philanthropic bishop or nobleman's name) "has often talked to me. It is a kind of model lodging-house,—not exactly for the poor, but persons of the male sex very reduced in circumstances, or struggling hard against adversity. Shall we go there, Letitia?"

"Anywhere," answered Miss Salusbury blithely; "anything for a change after the sweeps and the beggars. What's the place called, Maggy?"

"It is called," Miss Hill answered, referring to her list for the day, "the Monmouth Chambers, and is situated somewhere in Soho; we will drive there at once."

CHAPTER XXIII.

WHO but the genial Frenchman? Who but he? Who but jovial, careless, candid, confiding, simple-minded, good-hearted Simon Lefranc?

He wore his heart upon his sleeve. It was not a handsome sleeve. Indeed, it was somewhat white at the seams, greasy at the elbows, and frayed as to the cuffs and button-holes. Nor was the sleeve beneath it distinguished for whiteness of hue or fineness of texture. But upon this sleeve Simon Lefranc wore his heart; and I should like to know whether that fact did not at once convert a well-worn, and, to tell truth, somewhat shabby sleeve into one of purple velvet, embroidered with gold and seed-pearls.

He had no secrets from anybody. He was as open as the day or the Liverpool Free Library. He abhorred disguises. He execrated concealment. He told his simple life-story to all who chose to listen, and expected, although he did not exact, an equal amount of confidence in return. " *Racontez moi votre histoire* " —" Narrate to me the events of your life," he would say to chance companions in railways, in steamboats, on the knife-boards of omnibuses, even. Simon was not precisely a fascinating man, yet there was something irresistibly winning in his speech and manner. His persuasive volubility was marvellous. He would have made a fortune as a quack-doctor, a cheap-jack, a popular preacher, a secretary to a charity, or a travelling lecturer on life-assurance. People did tell him their histories. Old gentlemen, almost entirely strangers to him, had revealed to him the investments in which their wealth was placed. Landlords of hotels where he stopped had consulted him as to the proper mode of carrying on business. He was a man who on first acquaintance would be permitted by women to hold their babies, and to whom, on a second interview,

would be imparted the details of domestic cares and troubles connected with tallymen, evil-speaking neighbours, and husbands who
stopped out late. He knew what Mrs. Timms had said (malevo-
lently and abusively) of Mrs. Pimms. People showed him letters,
and asked his advice. He had been known to knock at the door
of a strange house in quest of lodgings, to take tea the same
evening with the landlady, to be hand and glove with all the neighbours in a week, and to stand godfather to one of their children
within a month.

These people, who hammer out acquaintances as quickly and
dexterously as a smith hammers out horseshoes, are a wonder and
a terror to me. I, the narrator, live at some distance from Baby-
lon the bricky, and travel up and down by rail every day. I have
the same travelling companions—ladies, gentlemen, and children
—day after day for months. We never interchange a word—
scarcely so much as a grunt on the question of a window open or
shut—scarcely so much as a surly bow as acknowledgment of the
courtesy of passing a ticket to the collector. I scowl at them, and
they scowl at me. The other morning there travelled with us, a
lithe, ready-tongued man, wearing of course his heart upon his
sleeve. He was a perfect stranger to us all; but we had not gone
five miles before he had told a particularly surly and speechless
neighbour of mine how many years he had been connected with
the cork-cutting trade, how many shares he owned in the Imperial
Gas Company, and how many acres of potatoes he had lately lost
through blight. As I stepped on to the platform at the London
terminus, my surly and speechless neighbour was explaining to
the heart-upon-his-sleeve-wearing man his views on the Treaty of
Commerce, and I should not have been at all surprised to see them
walk away together arm-in-arm. Once, many years ago, it occurred to me to court a widow. She wouldn't have me,—an error
in taste and judgment very prevalent at that time among the
softer sex. As stupid men will do, I introduced a friend to her,
with a vague idea that he would plead my cause or help my suit
somehow. He was no traitor, and didn't carry off the widow
himself, as Daly, in *Gilbert Gurney*, abducted the heiress; but I
declare that when, a month after his introduction to her, the
preposterous female I courted accepted the hand of some man

who had made a fortune out of melting tallow in Australia—I forgive him now, for she led him, ha! ha! such a deuce of a—but no matter—my friend was one of the trustees under the marriage settlement; and five weeks before she hadn't known him from Adam.

Such an adept at impromptu acquaintances and improvised friendships was Simon Lefranc. By profession he was a commercial traveller; and his line of business was—well, ladies, there is nothing to blush at—Parisian corsets. You may call them *articles de Paris*, if you please; but Simon Lefranc was nevertheless a bagman to a large foreign house in the stay-making branch of commerce. For there is a very large ready-made trade in boddices; and perhaps not a tithe of the ladies who are measured for those adjuncts to female elegance so much decried by doctors really have them made to order.

With his easy, fluent, jovial manner, his perfect knowledge of the world and of business, his equal command of the French and English languages, Simon Lefranc should properly, it might be imagined, have been able to live in luxury, or at least in ease. But he had been overtaken by misfortune. He told you so with charming frankness. His little savings had been swallowed up in a disastrous speculation. A friend for whom he had pledged his credit had used him with the grossest ingratitude. He had sacrificed all to meet the calls of duty and integrity. It was necessary that he should work hard for the benefit of one near and dear to him—his little Adèle, in good sooth—in France, his smiling native land. Meanwhile he must retrench, he must pinch himself, he must practise the strictest economy; and so he became a temporary inmate of the Monmouth Chambers, Soho, and cheerfully nibbled at his self-imposed Humble Pie, in company with Tottlepot the poet, and the starving Marquis de la Vieille Roche, and the all but penniless Ruthyn Pendragon, ex-curate of Swordsley. Did not such abnegation of self do honour to the heart which Simon Lefranc wore upon his sleeve?

There were no other commercial travellers at the Chambers. The convivial gentlemen who draw a guinea a day for their expenses, and always drink a pint of wine at dinner, would have disdained that humble caravanserai. Simon Lefranc did not always sleep at the Chambers. A fellow countryman who had a little villa at Tottenham—he pronounced the word very syllabically—was kind enough, two or three nights a week, to *héberger* him, to give him a bed. Simon Lefranc gave the history of his friend at Tot-ten-ham with pleasing minuteness. John Clere, the painter, could have drawn from the description he gave a portrait of M. Griboulard, retired basket-maker, of the three Angola cats he kept, of the French Protestant pastor, M. Chanoinet, who visited him. For Simon Lefranc was of the Huguenot faith, and owed much of his popularity among his friends and customers to his dissent from the errors of Rome.

Stout, well-built, about fifty years of age, gray hair closely cropped, an excellent set of teeth, a bright eye, a full lip, an active forefinger, with which he was always tapping people's waistcoats, a merry manner of snuff-taking, of kerchief waving, of pirouetting on the points of his toes, of humming little airs from popular vaudevilles, a never-failing willingness to oblige, to do little services: put these together, and you have the outward and visible presentment of Simon Lefranc. Stay; I have omitted to mention his heart, which he wore—not ostentatiously, but plain as a pikestaff in the eyes of most men and all women—on his sleeve.

It was a bright, warm, cheery morning, and Simon Lefranc came into the coffee-room, blithely murmuring one of his little vaudeville couplets. " With a tra la la, with a tra la la,'' the mercurial Frenchman sang. He brought his modest breakfast with him. He had just prepared it, singing all the while, below. A cup of coffee, skilfully prepared in his own percolator, a little loaf purchased from a neighbouring French baker, a tiny pat of butter,—these formed his simple meal. He could not afford luxuries, he said, either in food or in apparel. To tell the truth, Simon was wofully shabby, and his coat was in such evil case as to inspire a surmise that some day or other he would have to pin his heart to one of the flexors or extensors of his arm, for want of a sleeve to wear it upon.

"I could carry the purple and the fine linen," he would say ; " I could eat of the truffle and the ortolan ; I could drink of the *crûs* of the Clos Vougeot; but why should I consume the pro-

perty of others? Why should I eat and drink away the dowry
of my Adèle? *Va! ma petite. Tu n'iras pas sans dot.*" And
a tear would stand in Simon Lefranc's bright eye.

"And my Tottlepot, my poet," the lively traveller exclaimed,
sitting down to his meal; "how is my possessor of the *feu sacré?*
Ah, if I could but write poetry! Ah, if I had the *feu sacré!*
Still at work, my Tottlepot. *Voyons!* a new stanza?"

His hand was cheerily travelling towards a little portfolio
which lay beside the poet. He was the kind of man who,
wearing his heart upon his sleeve, might have taken a letter from
under your nose, and read it from beginning to end without your
being offended with him. Strangely enough, Tottlepot made a
sudden clutch at his portfolio,—he was fond enough, in general,
of showing his fine bold, copperplate-like handwriting,—and red-
dened, and looked alarmed.

"It isn't—it isn't poetry," he stammered. "I'm not in the
vein this morning. I've been hard at work since six, copying
some business manuscripts."

Tottlepot eked out his slender livelihood by his caligraphy.
He had established a species of connection. And if you have
a connection, even in the picking-up-cigar-ends, or spent-lucifer-
match, or broken-egg-shell trade you may live.

"Industrious man! How different from my desultory Bo-
hemian existence! I was always *volage—le vrai Parisien, enfin.*"

It is to be observed that Simon Lefranc spoke English with
perfect fluency, but with a strong foreign accent, which it would
be embarrassing to attempt to imitate orthographically, but which
had more a Provençal than a Parisian tone.

"After all, sir, Poetry——" the vain Tottlepot began.

"Is divine. The poet is a man alone. He should be crowned
with laurels in the Capitol. *Sont-ils rares, ces lauriers; et les
cancres qui en sont couronnés, comme ils abondent!* Fools are
smothered with what is denied to Tottlepot."

The poet blushed again. No flattery was too gross or too
fulsome for him. You could not give him too much of it. He
would bask and writhe himself about when flattered, like a dog
on a sunny door-mat.

"And our charming client," pursued Simon the flatterer; "we

are still doing business for her, eh? We still copy out her
romances. *Diantre*, what a pretty little woman our charming
client is!"

"She is a lady occupying the most exalted of social positions,"
Tottlepot rejoined, with a lofty air. "Nature, Art, and Fortune
have been alike prodigal in the bestowal of their gifts upon
her."

"And she comes all the way to Soho to have her romances
copied into the *belle écriture* of Tottlepot. Does she intend to
publish them, these romances? Will she be another George
Sand, another Madame de Girardin, another Comtesse Dash?
Or does a *tendresse* bring her towards her Tottlepot?"—Simon
pronounced the word Tot-tle-potte. "Ah, lucky rogue, lucky
rogue! You are not wholly an insulary, my friend. You have
some of the old Gaulish blood in you,—the spirit of the Comte
Oury,—the manner of the Frenchman who by nature *a le don de
plaire*."

Tottlepot was certainly a sham poet; but his eyes began,
nevertheless, to roll in a fine frenzy, and his ears to tingle at
these intoxicating words. He could have hugged the Frenchman
in his rapture. As he put his breakfast things together, they
clattered in his nervous hands; and he was going away delighted
to his cabin, which he called "the poet's studio," and where he
was by special favour allowed to have a little table and the fourth
part of a window. He was always squabbling with the steward,
and girding at him, it is true; but still that functionary had the
respect for his genius which simple-minded men persist in enter-
taining towards those who talk largely.

He was on the threshold, when the Frenchman called him
back.

"Fly not from Paradise, my Tottlepot," he cried; "seek not
too suddenly the Parnassus of the *quatrième étage*. Unless I am
much mistaken, I just saw your charming client pass the window.
'Tis a scandal that such a charming creature should be compelled
to walk. Why has she not carriage, horses, powdered lacqueys?"

Simon's observant eye—yes, it was as observant as it was
bright and roving—had not deceived him. The form of a lady
had flitted across the window looking into the street; and anon

x

the steward put his head in at the coffee-room door, and, in a tone half surly and half deferential, announced that Mr. Tottlepot was wanted.

As a rule, ladies were not encouraged at the Monmouth Chambers, and those who were admitted to the precincts thereof were chiefly connected with the profession of washing linen. The purpose of the visit of Tottlepot's client was, however, held by the steward to be sufficiently legitimate to warrant her reception; and the lady herself would even condescend occasionally to enter the steward's lodge, to converse with the steward's wife, who pronounced her a "lady every inch of her,"—and to dandle the diminutive baby. She was the kindest and most urbane of ladies. She made little presents to the steward and his wife. She endowed the baby with a cloth robe, elaborately braided, which, when put on the poor little thing, on high days and holidays, very nearly smothered it. She took an interest, she said, in Tottlepot, and admired his talents. She feared that the world had not used him very well, and, in the kindness of her heart, she made work for him in copying manuscript.

Tottlepot went out into the entry, and found the lady there waiting for him, with some impatience it would seem, for she was tapping a little foot on the mat. He made her a low bow, and inclined his head downwards, for Tottlepot was tall, and the lady was but a slight and fragile little thing.

"Come out into the street," she said.

They went out. Tottlepot moved a little on one side, and stood with his back to the coffee-room window. Had his position been different, he might have seen the jovial face and bright observant eye of Simon Lefranc beaming through the glass. One could have seen his sleeve, too, and the heart he wore upon it.

"It is imprudent," the lady said, hurriedly, "to talk to you here; but time presses, and I have no alternative. Can you write Sir Jasper Goldthorpe's name? It is the only one I cannot manage. There is a tremulous curve to the G that drives me to despair."

"I have tried at least a hundred times, and have mastered it at last. Old Kraussen in Lambeth could not do it better."

"Old Kraussen was a fool to get transported just as I wanted him. He was not such a fool though as you are, with your poetry."

"Madam!"—and the poet, wounded in his tenderest point, drew himself up haughtily.

"There, there, remember we are in the street. Get a little closer to the wall. Inside this roll of manuscript to copy you will find the paper. The name is to be across, as usual. I have used the old 'made payable' stamp—the old red ink. It must be ready in an hour. Will it be ready in an hour?"

"It will."

"You will meet me, then, on the south side of Leicester Square, by the auction-rooms, at noon precisely. How much am I to give you for this?"

"The name is a difficult one—the most difficult I have ever attempted. Twenty pounds."

"I will give you ten."

"Make it fifteen."

"There, poet, you shall have your fifteen, only let it be done within the time."

"I will be in Leicester Square precisely at twelve."

The lady, who was exactly and entirely Mrs. Armytage, did not take the trouble of saying good-by to the poet, but placing a portly roll of manuscript in his hand, nodded her ringlets in token of farewell, and waved her hand in dismissal. Tottlepot hurried into the Chambers and up-stairs to his cabin, where he at once shot the door-bolt and set to work.

The lady, left alone, hesitated for a moment, as if uncertain in which direction to proceed. And yet Mrs. Armytage knew her way perfectly well about Soho. She was lowering her veil, as a preliminary measure, when she caught sight of Simon Lefranc's broad jovial face beaming through the window-pane.

"What an impudent-looking fellow!" she thought. "He looks like a *paillasse*—a merry-andrew to a quack doctor."

And so she raised her flowing drapery a little, and would have crossed the street, when a handsome equipage drove rapidly up and stopped at the door of the Chambers. She started, drew back, and uttered an exclamation of surprise.

"She knows the people in the carriage," said Simon Lefranc to himself, and, for a wonder, without the slightest foreign accent so far as his mental speech was concerned. "From what I hear of her, my Duchess knows everybody; what can be her game with that miserable Tottlepot? Is the fellow a rogue, as well as a fool? However, that is not my affair. I dare say they have been doing a quiet bit of swindling together; but Miss Duchess is far above swindling in the eyes of S. Lefranc. Simon contemplates her from a far more isolated point of view. Ah, my Duchess, my Duchess, what a career you have had on our side of the water, and what a career you seem to be having on this!"

The persons in the carriage had alighted, and Mrs. Armytage was conversing with them.

"She knows the swells," mused Simon Lefranc, with a countenance no longer jovial, no longer beaming, but with a very grave and serious expression overshadowing his features. "I have been so long out of England that I have forgotten the heraldry I used to study from the hatchments and the coach-makers in Long Acre, and can't tell a bit to whom the carriage belongs. I can make out three somethings on a golden shield, and a bloody hand, —the swell must be a Bart.; and, let's see—what's the motto on the thingum-bob? Ah, I see—*Ex sudore, aurum.* I'll have a closer look at it, and at the swells too."

It certainly must have been by the merest chance in the world. Mrs. Armytage, having despatched her business with her client Tottlepot, was tranquilly going away, when this same carriage drove up, and one of the tall footmen assisted four persons to alight. There was Magdalen; there was Letitia; there was a harmless curate belonging to the parish, who took much interest in the Chambers, and was acting as cicerone on the present occasion; and there was a distinguished nobleman, officiating as escort to the ladies,—none other, indeed, than the Earl of Carnation. He was a very pink young peer, with weak eyes, very fair curly hair, and the fluffy phantom of a moustache. I believe that Nature had fully intended him to be a Fool; but his noble mamma, who was in the secret, dying very young, his papa had him brought up, quite by mistake, to be clever, Dear me, how they had crammed the Earl of Carnation! His mind was something like an over-boiled egg. It had been kept so long at an excessive temperature, that the shell had cracked a little, and the yolk shrivelled up slightly. He would have known everything, if he could have remembered anything; but a malicious imp seemed to follow him about with a sponge, and wipe out everything that, with feeble slate pencil, he had inscribed on the tablet of his memory. Philanthropy was thought to be his forte. It was certainly his foible, and he was perpetually being trotted through prisons, hospitals, soup-kitchens, ragged-schools, and baths and wash-houses. At public meetings he could second a resolution moved by an archbishop, or propose a vote of thanks to the chairman. He had at one time been the hope of the Conservative party, and was backed heavily for an attack on the ministry,—it was before he came to the title, and when he was the Honourable Claude Crichton,—but he broke down in the first paragraph of his speech, beginning, "The weiterated wemonstwances of honourable gentlemen opposite confirm me in the wesolve of weviewing their weasons for weceding," and so forth. The head of the party said, after this, that Claude Crichton was no good, and that the sooner he went up to the Lords the better. In due process of time he came to his coronet, and addicted himself to philanthropy. He never spoke in the House; but he was an industrious attendant at the debates, and even at the morning judicial sittings, where his eye-glass and his simper must have been of great assistance to the law lords in determining the appeal of Gottee Humguffi Baloa Raffee Loll v. Chowder Ram Buffee Cowric Jug (from Bombay). His chaplain wrote a little pamphlet for him now and then, about crime, or education, or wash-houses, which Mr. Hatchard published, and which was favourably reviewed in the *John Bull*. He didn't do anybody any harm; but he didn't do much good; for the Earl of Carnation was inconceivably stingy, and, had he not been a peer of the realm, would have made a model bill-discounter. At Eton he used to be called "Skinflint," and at Oxford "Spooney."

Mrs. Armytage and he were very old friends. She was always profoundly obsequious to him, and flattered him enormously; and his lordship was good enough to say he thought her a very superior kind of woman. Florence regretted sometimes that she had not cultivated his acquaintance more; even as Napoleon sighed in the midst of his despotism to be able to nestle *dans les draps d'un roi constitutionnel.* She often thought how nice and comfortable it would be to give up intrigue and excitement and impulse, and settle down quietly in the philanthropic and beneficent line of business. "It can't be so very difficult to do good," she reasoned. "How many envious and malicious and stupid people I know who torment their husbands and persecute their children, and yet out of doors might be photographed as Dorcas or the good Samaritan. But, then, you want so much ready money, and they are so uninteresting these ragged-school and wash-house creatures, and it's such a bore. I can understand the Pope and the Cardinals washing the feet of the pilgrims, and waiting upon them at dinner. It's a ceremony, and grand and stately, and that kind of thing. There's the *guardia nobile* looking on, and the Roman ladies and the *corps diplomatique,* and there are horse-races afterwards, and St. Peter's illuminated in the evening. I wish they would make being good in England a little livelier. Why are they all dull, and obtuse, and bilious, these good people? They physic themselves quite as much as they do the poor, they preach temperance because their digestion is all wrong, and a glass of Madeira half kills them. They insist upon people reading tracts because they can't understand Thackeray and think Dickens's fun wickedness. I wish there was a funny clergyman like the Rowland Hill they talk about. I am sure he would draw. I'm sure I'd go to church." So reasoned this wicked little woman of the world, and from her last remark you may gather that she flourished before the era of the sainted Spurgeon.

A great deal of polite gesticulation, but very little real conversation, took place among the party who met so oddly on the pavement in front of the Monmouth Chambers. There is a kind of discourse, very prevalent in genteel society, which mainly consists in the rustling of silks, the showing of teeth, the liberal dispensation of curtsies and smiles, the repetition of expressions of pleasure and surprise, but into which words that have any tangible meaning enter for but very little. If there be a lapdog close by, or a servant to order about, this art of saying nothing, with much ado about it, becomes easier. Ladies are the great adepts in this art of simulating speech. You shall hear two women who have actually nothing to say to one another go in for half an hour in the interchange of elegant flummeries. Men are not so clever. If they don't know one another, they stare, and look black, and at the first opportunity make a rush. It was for this reason that glees and songs were introduced between the speeches at public dinners. They save men who are strangers to one another from a silence which might at last become intolerable, and lead a tongue-tied man to hurl a bottle at his opposite neighbour by way of relief. For, somehow or another, it is difficult for an *attaché* of the House of Montague to divest himself of the idea that the other fellow yonder, who belongs to the Capulet faction, and is consequently to be hated and avoided, is biting his thumb at him. The greatest enemy I ever had was a man I had never met; and the week after we became acquainted he wanted to lend me a hundred pounds.

Magdalen had never spoken to Mrs. Armytage since that well-remembered evening at the Goldthorpe, late Pogthorpe Road, Station. Miss Salusbury had seen the celebrated little Indian widow, and had heard of her countless times. You may imagine how pleasant the task of introduction was to Miss Hill; how touching were Mrs. Armytage's inquiries after dear Lady Gold-thorpe, and Sir Jasper, and Captain William, and all the living Sons of Mammon. Miss Salusbury gave Florence a good broad look of hearty dislike, and would have instantly commanded Lord Carnation to escort her into the Chambers; but that meek and philanthropic nobleman was in the trammels of the widow. Hercules in a street in Soho, and Omphale in a walking-dress and her bonnet on, and no more than a parasol for a distaff, are not very realisable images; but Florence Omphale Armytage held Hercules, Earl of Carnation, very tightly in the summer sun and on the Soho pavement, and wound him round her finger several times before she permitted him to depart. "A monstrous clever woman," thought the egregious young man, as she fluttered and shook her ringlets at him.

"If I were clear and had a thousand pounds," thought Florence, "I'd be Countess of Carnation in a month, and be as good as gold; but it can't be done for less, and I don't see how it can be done at all. Heigho!"

She thought "Heigho!" but she didn't say "Heigho!"
Nobody does, any more than they say "Tush!" or "Psha!" or,
as Mr. Kinglake once pointed out, "Alas!"

Of course the ladies explained their errand in Soho. They had
come to see a most meritorious institution, admirably conducted—
at which the curate who had not been introduced to anybody, and
was staring uneasily at the steward, who was bowing backwards,
after the manner of theatrical managers when royalty comes to
the theatre, only without the wax-candles, and so nearly tripping
up his wife, who was peeping from under his arms at the gentlefolks who had come in the grand carriage—at which the curate, I
repeat, blushed violently and looked at his watch. Whereupon
Mrs. Armytage looked at a tiny jewelled toy she carried at her
waist likewise ; and there were more curtsies and genuflections,
and showings of teeth and rustlings of dresses, and Florence,
saying, in an airy manner that as a widow she was privileged to
walk alone, and that she had left her carriage in Regent Street,
took an affectionate leave of Lord Carnation, and a gracious one of
Magdalen, and a cool one of Letitia, and a peeress-to-a-puppy one
of the curate, and patronised everybody, including the steward
and his wife, including the lodgers looking from the windows, and
fluttered away. O gorgeous little galley with silken sails and
prow of gold! O gondola of delights, built to float upon the
Idle Lake, and not to be tempest-tost and tempest-lost upon the
great Black Sea of Crime!

"A real lady," the steward remarked deferentially, as he
ushered the distinguished party into the corridor; " very rich, I'm
told; came here first with the Lord Bishop of St. Blaise—a
French Bishop. Most charitable lady. Half keeps one of our
poor gentlemen, who is a beautiful poet, and does a bit of copying.
This way, ladies, if you please."

"A little saucy, impudent, artful-looking thing," Miss Salusbury remarked energetically. "I should like to box her ears. Is
there no by-law in society for turning that woman out of it ? "

"There is nothing against her," Magdalen remarked gently—
she was not wont to speak of her in so tolerant a manner. "She
is rich, and a widow, and has lived much abroad. She is very
eccentric, and knows quantities of strange people, but there has

been nothing in her conduct to justify her exclusion from what we term society."

"I dare say," quoth Miss Salusbury, "that she knows no people who can be stranger or can be better than they should be, or than she is herself. She's after no good. She's on the cross, and not at all upon the square."

"The cross! the square! what do you mean?"

"Never mind; let's go through this wonderful dingy old place. I do hope that the people are washed, and are not in rags, and that I'm not to see the Eighth Commandment hung up everywhere. I often wonder how it is that the people who are always supposed to be stealing seldom have anything to eat, and never have any money, and that the people who never steal roll in riches. I wonder whether my papa would have been quite so well off if my Norman ancestors had learnt the Eighth Commandment by heart and acted upon it!"

By this time the curate had fallen into a cold fit of horror, and looked upon Letitia as a beauteous image of heterodoxy. Miss Hill did not proffer any reply to her companion's remarks; indeed, she was an inveterate illuminator of moral and Scriptural placards, from the precepts against stealing to the warning, "Eat, but pocket nothing," of Sunday-school treats. Lord Carnation was rather amused than otherwise. Miss Salusbury was a relief in his dreary pilgrimage of duty.

CHAPTER XXIV

"Miss Salusbury is not so clever as the little widow," said Lord Carnation to himself; "but she's plucky, and knows a lot. But the widow!—what a committee she might get up for a burnt-out or a famine-relief fund. If the women didn't hate her so, she ought to go in against slavery. I wish she'd cram me about crime and reformation, and that sort of thing. I wonder where she lives! Where *does* she live?" he asked aloud, turning to Magdalen.

"To whom do you allude, my lord?"

"Why, our little friend, Mrs. What'shername—Mrs. Army-tage."

"Behind the scenes, I should think," broke in Letitia petulantly. "Inquire at the stage-door. This way for the riders. You'll soon find her out, Lord Carnation."

The curate—they were inspecting the dormitories by this time—passed from a cold into a hot perspiration of dismay. "Beautiful, but lost creature," he mentally exclaimed, "deprived, no doubt, of maternal care at an early age; undisciplined mind, misapplied talents! Ah, what an Eden choked with weeds and tares!"

The curate wasn't a humbug. He was only an amiable young man, who had been his mother's pet and the joy of a High-Church watering-place in Devonshire, where devotion and pretty things went hand in hand. He had looked at life through the stained-glass oriel of a gimcrack chapel, and had suddenly been trans-planted from the carved-and-gilt and vellum-bound and wax-candled Vale of Rest in the sweet south, to this great brabbling, murky, gas-lit Soho, where he had his corns trodden on and the angles of his fine feelings chipped off every day in the week. He was a curate with an Ideal; but to have turned it to any practical use, he should have been a police-constable, and taken a spell of night duty for a fortnight. To a clergyman who really wishes to do good among the poor and the vicious, a bull's-eye is an admirable companion to a Bible.

"Mrs. Armytage," Magdalen said slowly, in reply to the earl's query, "resides habitually in Paris and in Brighton. Sometimes, I believe, she stays with her aged father, who lives in some boarding-house near Bayswater, I believe, and to whom she is very kind. But she is of course free to go where she lists, and, as I have said, is very eccentric, and, I am told, stays a great deal at hotels, and even in furnished lodgings."

"I have her address, if you please, my lady," the steward said. "Here it is, in Albert Street, Knightsbridge. She gave me the card the first time she employed Mr. Tottlepot,—that's one of our poor gentlemen,—the poet that she gives copying to."

It was noticed afterwards, as strange circumstances in the career of this woman, that she never assumed an alias, and that she never concealed her dwelling-place. What she did was done in the open. You remember the story of the First Napoleon and Cardinal Fesch, when the latter endeavoured to dissuade him from undertaking the invasion of Russia. He led the Cardinal to the window, opened it, and pointed out into the sky. It was night, and a black one. "Do you see that star?" he asked. "No, sire," answered the Cardinal. "But I do," said the Emperor, and shut the window, and invaded Russia, and came to the end you all know. Florence Armytage had her star, invisible to other eyes, and it bade her keep straight on in the broad, smooth, shining road, unto the end that was coming.

The distinguished party saw all that was to be seen in the Monmouth Chambers:—dormitories, kitchens, coffee-room, smoking-room even, and, of course, praised and admired the general air of neatness, cleanliness, and comfort that reigned. I wonder they did not ask to see the refractory-ward or the solitary cell, or the cat-o'-nine tails, sealed with the seal of the visiting justice. For it is a strange, but nevertheless a very true thing, that people who haunt "institutions" grow hardened to them. Whatever the place be,—hospital, school, gaol, asylum, or madhouse,—an indefinable sensation comes over the visitor that he is a superior being, and that the inmates have got into some inexplicable scrape.

I have been myself over some hundreds of these institutions, but have tried in vain to attain the hardened stage which comes so naturally to professed philanthropists. I always feel uneasy, and ask myself what right I have to be there, and how I should like myself to be put into a description of moral cage, and exhibited by a kind of Moral Beef-eater, as though I were a wombat or a giraffe, and inspected, patronised, and approved of. For who knows what to-morrow may bring forth? Who is so sane but he may need the douche-bath and the padded room some day? Who so virtuous but he may have to hold up his hand at the bidding of the clerk of the arraigns and plead? Who so hale and strong but he may find the water-bed a luxury, and the hospital-nurse his best friend? Who so rich but the time may come when his only refuge shall be the old man's ward, and he look out eagerly for meat-days, and remember Christmas chiefly in connection with an allowance of snuff and a pint of strong ale:—the bounty of the guardians? Haughty and insolent salt ones of the earth, take down a book written by one who was the pride of his age, and the favourite of a queen, and lay for years a captive in a hole of the White Tower. Read what Raleigh writes of Darius. How he wore purple and a crown of gold in the morning, and was the master of millions, and how at night he lay naked and bleeding and forlorn on the ground. Velvet and brocade, carving and gilding, may fade away, and leave nothing but the pauper's pallet, or, worse, a whitewashed cell, and the prison task-master instructing you in the art of cobbling shoes, or making cane-bottoms for chairs. And the first shall be last, and the last first; and the High Sheriff take a turn in the dock, and the beggar make out Dive's mittimus for sleeping under a hedge instead of a four-poster with an eider-down quilt; and thank God for it, or the gorge of pride would rise and burst us asunder.

The Earl of Carnation troubled not his noble mind with such reflections. Don't you who read them think them stale and trite, —if, indeed, you have not skipped them altogether? But the mania for patronising and placarding the Eighth Commandment, and showering tracts, and "going over institutions," is one of the great curses of this age, next to the eternal "talkee, talkee" about people's "missions" and "Social Science," and similar lunacies of distempered vanity; and many philanthropists would do well to remember what Richard Oastler said to Sir Robert Peel in the picture-gallery at Tamworth. "Good God, Sir Robert,"—looking at an exquisite child-picture by Landseer,—"your daughter might have been a factory-girl." Yes; and the factory-girl might have been cited as a shining example of all the virtues, regal as well as domestic, had she been born to be Empress of Mofussilistan, with twenty millions a year for a Civil List.

The tour of inspection came to an end at last. It was close upon noon, and the horizon of the Earl of Carnation began to be gilt with the prospect of luncheon. There was but one place more to visit—the reading-room. To the library the harmless curate had been a munificent donor, and had made the shelves creak beneath High-Church chronicles, tales, tracts, and poetry. Just as the steward was opening the door, there glided by, coming from the regions above, the poet Tottlepot. He had his little portfolio under his arm, and seemed in a great hurry. Poets are not always so punctual in keeping their appointments.

"That's the poor gentleman I spoke about to your lordship and ladyships," the steward remarked, as the bard passed down the corridor. "His handwriting's beautiful; but if it wasn't for the kind lady who employs him, I do believe that he'd half starve."

Magdalen made a note on her tablets. The heart of Tottlepot, she thought, should be rejoiced that night. She little knew that the poet had just earned a pocketful of sovereigns.

"He looks very much like an old humbug," remarked Miss Salusbury. "I suppose he'd be offended if one were to give him any money. There was a man who used to write in the poet's corner of our county newspaper, and who wanted to fight a duel with papa because he wasn't asked to dinner. I don't believe in any poets except 'Yates' of the *Morning Advertiser*, and he's more a prophet than a poet. However, your poet looks very poor. Lord Carnation, you'd better leave him a check for five pounds."

The young nobleman looked very uneasy at this recommendation, and murmured something about "the many calls upon him."

It is true that an infinity of calls were made upon the Earl of

Carnation; but one of the most difficult things in the world was to find his lordship at home.

"And it is thus they pass the bard," Tottlepot said with a bitter groan, as he emerged into the street : "pass him with contumely and neglect. But a day will come—a day will come." And away went Tottlepot to keep his appointment in Leicester Square.

Simon Lefranc saw him—Who but he? Simon had been wearing his heart upon his sleeve, and airing it in the sunshine, in front of a little tobacconist's and periodical shop opposite the Chambers. As Tottlepot crossed the road, Simon passed behind him, and smote him in a jovial manner on the shoulder.

The poor poet turned round. His face was very livid, and he trembled all over.

"*Courage, mon garçon;* courage, my Tottlepot," Simon said in his cheery manner. "Bright days are in store for thee, my poet." And having dismissed him somewhat reassured, but still very nervous, Simon took to sporting that heart of his—always on his sleeve, I need not say—round the adjacent street-corners, and in front of the cab-stand, and in the entries of half a dozen little shops. The mid-day beer-boy was delighted with him, and almost felt inclined to give him eleemosynary refreshment from his can. The little children danced round him, and made much of a half-penny which he bestowed on one of their number. A troupe of Ethiopian serenaders sang, it seemed, their most enlivening ditties specially for him. The very sparrows of Soho appeared to peck their morsels round about his feet without diffidence. Ah, it is a fine thing to wear our heart upon our sleeve, and to make a sunshine wherever we go! For all his little trips about, however, I don't think for two consecutive minutes Simon ever lost sight of the doorway of the Monmouth Chambers, or the grand carriage there drawn up.

Ruthyn Pendragon was in the reading-room brooding over a book as the distinguished party entered. The little old marquis was close by, pottering too over his interminable and never-to-be-terminated Dictionary. Ruthyn looked up as the ladies and gentlemen entered. He heard the steward whisper, "French nobleman," and then "Clergyman of the Church of England." He knew himself to be alluded to. He felt his face on fire. He felt first a cataract of molten lead, and then one of ice, flow down his back. He felt the moisture at the roots of his hair, on his eyelids. He felt his heart bound, like a newly-caged wild beast striving to dash itself to death against the bars of its den. He felt that if one mercy could be bestowed upon him, one crowning act of grace and pity, it would be for the floor of this mean room to open and swallow him up from sight and shame. But it was not to be so; and he was to eat his Humble Pie to the very last flake of the crust.

The curate, usually so harmless, and always well-meaning, was enabled, quite unconsciously, to do at this time a very pretty piece of mischief. He came up to where Pendragon sat, his hair almost touching the book before him, and made use of some simperingly good-hearted expressions, setting forth, it may have been, that he was sorry to see a clergyman so reduced in circumstances, but that he was glad to see him engaged in study, and the like.

Ruthyn Pendragon started to his feet with a cry.

" What the devil is that to you ?" he demanded ferociously of the amazed curate.

The steward, quite shocked, stepped forward, for he thought the clergyman was about to hurl the book he had been reading at his brother parson. As for Lord Carnation, he looked more amused than otherwise.

"Wides wusty," he simpered, adjusting his eye-glass; "don't like being asked questions sometimes. Wemember a man in Bedlam wanting to stwangle me because I asked why he cut his wife and thwee childwen's heads off. Only yesterday, burglar in penitentiary twied to stab chaplain, because he asked him to say ' Twinkle, twinkle, little '—what was it ?"—here Lord Carnation's memory played him false—"before self' and the Dean of Dorking."

Letitia and Magdalen had both recognised the ex-curate of Swordsley, the shabby lodger in the shabby Chambers. The generous Amazon would have rushed forward to shake hands with Pendragon ; but a stern grasp withheld, a stern, albeit low, voice forbade her.

" Let us go," said Magdalen Hill, and positively forced her companion from the room.

"This is no place for us," she added, pale and scared, when they were in the corridor.

"It's no place for him," Letitia exclaimed indignantly. "Poor fellow! he looks half-starved. Let us go back, Magdalen. Curb your devilish pride for once. Say but one word. Shall I call him to us?"

She would not curb her pride, all demoniacal as it may have been. She would not move. She would not say the word. Ah, that tug at the bridle! Ah, that step in advance! Ah, that word, which women will not speak! It may be that it was but a little word, after all, that first sowed dissension between Menelaus and Helen, and that had the word been spoken in good season all the woes of Troy might have been spared.

As it was, Magdalen Hill marched resolutely towards her carriage, and Lord Carnation, still amused, and the curate, still amazed, followed. The steward would have lingered for a moment to give the unmannerly lodger a week's notice to quit the Chambers; but Miss Salusbury prevented him.

"You know that gentleman?" she asked.

"I'm sure, madam, I'm very sorry that he should have so misbehaved himself. The committee won't allow him to stay after this, I needn't say."

"I hope they won't. He ought never to have been here at all. I ask you if you know him."

"Surely, madam. He gave his name. He doesn't seem to be ashamed of it. The Reverend Ruthyn Pendragon—that's it."

"Very well, give him this piece of paper. You need not say anything about it to anybody. You seem a very decent sort of fellow; there's a sovereign for you." And Miss Salusbury hurried after her companions, and the carriage drove away.

They dropped the curate at a schoolhouse, where some eighty children howled hymns from morning till night, and could read all the genealogies in Scripture with tolerable fluency, but were utterly unable to spell through an ordinary paragraph in the newspaper. They dropped Lord Carnation at his club in Pall Mall, where he lunched,—at the expense of the club. And then Letitia Salusbury turned to Magdalen Hill and said,

"Magdalen,"—she would not condescend to use a diminutive,—"you have treated that man shamefully."

"I am not well. Let us go home," was all that Magdalen would reply, hiding her face in her handkerchief—but not to weep, I am afraid.

When the carriage had been bowed away from the Chambers by the steward and his wife, the former imparted to his helpmate the strange incident that had occurred in the reading-room, and showed her the paper that he was to deliver to Pendragon. It was not sealed, and I fear that Mrs. Steward, incited by the natural curiosity of her sex,—and has *our* sex no "natural curiosity," I should like to know?—would have had little hesitation in gleaning some knowledge of its contents, but for the salutary rigid ideas of discipline entertained by her husband.

"No, no," he said; "no pollprying. I'll go and take it to the parson at once, for fear of accidents."

He met Ruthyn Pendragon coming hurriedly from the reading-room.

"I am going away," Ruthyn said, in a thick strange voice. "I owe nothing, and am free to depart."

"That you may please yourself about," retorted the steward; "but one of the ladies left this for you, and you may as well read it before you go."

Pendragon took the paper from the other's hand. It had been hastily folded, or rather crumpled, together. He read it, and turned his head away, for his eyes were full of tears.

CHAPTER XXV.

NEMESIS IN PLAIN CLOTHES.

THE greatest men have their weaknesses: their little *penchants* and propensities. Thus the weakness of Inspector Millament was for reading cheap periodicals, and that of Sergeant South for studying playbills.

Our old acquaintance, Mr. Sims, who has been very busy all this time, although you have not heard so much about him, used to be very partial to theatrical performances, and went to the play, in more senses than one, two or three times a week; but the dramatic fancy of Sergeant South took more of a theoretical than of a practical turn. If *veluti in speculum* were his motto, it was more to look in the window where the playbill hung than to gaze into the mirror of the proscenium. Now and then the Sergeant entered the doors of a theatre; but he went habitually behind the scenes, and eschewed the audience part of the house. It was said that Sergeant South had once passed three months of his existence as a supernumerary at one of our principal places of Thespian amusement, and that he went on the stage regularly every night, either accoutred in a plumed bonnet and red tights, and carrying a banner, or else arrayed in a tunic and buff boots, and bearing a tin javelin as one of the retainers of a ruthless baron. Humble as was his standing in that Theatre Royal, it did not prevent his holding frequent and secret conference with the manager; and at the end of the three months it so happened that Sergeant South disappeared without warning, and without troubling the "super-master" for his outstanding salary; and that two or three days afterwards he was constrained, through a keen sense of duty towards his country in general, and the ends of justice in particular, to give evidence at the Marlborough Street Police Court against one Mouchy, a felonious *employé* of the theatre, who had pilfered many articles of rich costume from the dressing-rooms. The Sergeant was highly complimented by the presiding magistrate on the astuteness and sagacity he had displayed in tracing the perpetrator of so many robberies.

But it was, after all, towards the playbills that Sergeant South displayed the most ardent and disinterested affection. He was always pondering over these black and red letter documents, and spelling over their contents with a solicitude that was more than affectionate : it was paternal. His hands in his pockets and his head on one side, Sergeant South would go through the entire contents, from the name of the theatre and the address of the manager and lessee to the *Vivant Regina et Princeps* and " No Money returned," at the bottom. He would bestow the same amount of attention on the bill of some transpontine saloon, with three monstrous and murderous melodramas per night, as upon the lordly proclamations of the Italian Opera, with their announcements of *Don Giovanni* " by command," or a grand ballet " by desire." Nothing in playbill literature came amiss to him. He did not disdain the placards of music-halls, of suburban gardens, of raree-shows, or dwarf and giant exhibitions, or nigger-singers, or "drawing-room entertainments"—which last I take to be the very lowest kind of popular amusement that this, our present era of civilisation, has seen. Sergeant South had an eye for all these waifs and strays of recreation. He liked to linger at stationers' and tobacconists' shops and see his beloved playbill-boards reposing on the area-railings. He knew all the bill-stickers, and watched them at their work assiduously. There was a large theatrical public-house which he specially affected, and of which not only the coffee-room, but the very walls of the bar were thickly covered with playbills. The inexpressibly dilapidated men and women—where do they all come from, and whither are they all going?—who sell programmes, " books of the Hopera," and " bills of the play " in the purlieus of our dramatic and lyric fanes were all known to Sergeant South. He was known, likewise, to all those gentry, and, to tell truth, a little feared by them.

Sergeant South, in age, was wavering between the thirties and the forties : but seemed unable to make up his mind towards the

latter. He was the youngest looking of middle-aged men, with
a fresh blue eye, and chestnut hair, and a little pink spot on each
cheek, and an almost downy whisker. But for thick-serried
ranges of crow's-feet under his eyes, and some ominous lines
about his mouth, he would have looked a mere boy; as it was, he
had somewhat the appearance of a youth who had been stopping
up rather late on the night-side of life. Sergeant South dressed
with exquisite neatness, and not without a certain kind of
elegance. His turn-down collar was irreproachably white; his
scarf beautifully tied; his horse-shoe pin quiet, but handsome.
His hair was always well brushed. He wore a natty watch-guard
and a neat signet-ring. If there was one particular in which he
did not display taste, or elegance, or, indeed, neatness, it was in
that of boots. Those leathern casings were very thick and clumsy,
and had hobnails, and were but indifferently well polished. It is a
curious fact, but you may in general recognize gentlemen of the
profession of Sergeant South, and under what would otherwise be
the most impenetrable of disguises, by their boots.

Sergeant South's staunch friend, confidential comrade, and
superior, indeed, in the hierarchy to which both belonged, was
Inspector Millament. He should have been mentioned first
perhaps; but there is yet time to make him full amends.
Besides, he was a tranquil, peace-loving man, who never cared to
thrust himself foremost. Give him but the "Parlour Magazine,"
the "Family Miscellany," the "Backstairs Herald," all highly
popular penny journals at that day, and he was satisfied. He
waded through the endless romances published in his beloved
serials with a calm and never-failing delight. "To be continued
in our next" were words of hope and joy to him. It is true that
he habitually mixed up the plots of the novels he read into an
inextricable jumble of perplexity; that the marquis in one story
became dovetailed on to the gipsy-chief in the other, and the
abducted heiress's adventures were frequently intertwined with
those of the much-wronged ballet-dancer. Inspector Millament
vexed himself very little about such trifling incongruities. He
read and read on, and wandered in a world of dormant peerages,
of murderous baronets, and ladies of title addicted to the study
of toxicology, of gipsies and brigand-chiefs, men with masks and

women with daggers, of stolen children, withered hags, heartless
gamesters, nefarious roués, foreign princesses, Jesuit fathers,
grave-diggers, resurrection-men, lunatics, and ghosts. This was
his ideal world. Just deducting the ghosts, I don't think that
the world he really lived and played a very powerful and occult
part in, was a world much less strange or much less terrible; but
who regards the marvels that surround him? who takes account
of the things that lie at his feet? who will believe that the events
enacting under his eyes are History? We have all of us a
horizon at the end of our noses; but we disdain to look so closely,
and must strain our eyes far, far afield. Not many weeks since,
a good friend was kind enough to remonstrate with me on the
utter and glaring improbability, nay impossibility of some of the
characters I have drawn in this story. In vain I strove to
assure him that I had taken the world as I found it, and painted
(with a free brush, it might be) but from the very life. With
great difficulty he granted Mrs. Armytage. I had something to
show him which disarmed even his scepticism as to the verisemblance of that lady; but as for Mr. Sims, or for Ephraim Tigg
the Rasper, he would not hear of them for a moment. And yet
I think I know where to put my hand on people ten times stranger
in their ways of life than Sims or Tigg, poor, common rogues as
they are; and but a very few days after our controversy, my
friend came well nigh raving to me about the details of the
"Northumberland Street Tragedy!" Tragedy! a wretched Co-
burg melodrama it was, at best; there are real five-act tragedies
going on about us, every day,—far more fearful, far more horrify-
ing than that slaughter-house fray. The ladies are even more
difficult to convince than the gentlemen. They *won't* have Mrs.
Armytage. There was never anybody like her, they say. Miss
Salusbury also is to them simply an impossible character. These
complaints, these protests, constantly reach me. I am bidden to
write a story all about purity and honesty, and truth, and the
home-affections, and the rest of it. Well, I will try to do so; but
you must not be surprised to find my narrative so many blank
pages. It would be writing so many lines in white chalk on so
many planes of virgin snow. If you want *lait d'ânesse* fresh from
the animal, you must go elsewhere. I have none to sell. Which

is best, I wonder: to write namby-pamby *historiettes* of Jemmy
and Jenny Jessamy's love passages; to describe monsters of
innocence and loveliness; to paint a twopenny Garden of Eden,
with no serpent in it more dangerous than a Jesuit priest,—the
poor Jesuits! they have never done half the harm that the people
who go into frenzies of bigotry about them have done,—or to
describe the world as it wags, not only in its good, but in its evil
fashion? Do all the good books that are written about good
people save their readers from being covetous, and lying, and
slanderous, and sensual? Are the gentlefolks who come up to
the Divorce Court quite ignorant of the nature of cold-boiled-
veal-without-salt novels (in three vols.)? And, finally, how
would you like a newspaper in which there were no police-reports,
no law or assize intelligence, no leading articles on any other sub-
jects save missionary societies, governess institutions, the art of
pickling onions, and the best means of obliterating freckles?
While I live, and while I write, I shall just tell the stories of the
people I have met, and of the lives they have led,—so far as I
have known them,—in my own fashion; and when I begin to paint
the Graces from imagination, and the Virtues from hearsay, it will
be time for me to retire to the Asylum for Idiots at Earlswood,
and gibber.

There is another kind of story-telling in which, perhaps, with
some moderate faculty of humour and observation, and with a
liver very much out of order, one might succeed. Shall I map out
a world for you bounded on one side by Belgravia, and on the
other by Russell Square: assume that all my acquaintances are in
the habit of dining at seven o'clock, going to court, and keeping
carriages and pair, and sneer at the unhappy wretches who have
" plated side-dishes " at their feasts, call their eighteenpenny claret
Laflitte, hire greengrocers to wait upon them on state occasions, and
proceed to the Drawing-Room at St. James's in a hired cab? or shall
I be in a perpetual fume because people " go about saying things
about me," because Jones accuses me of opium-eating, and Tompkins of having poisoned my grandmother, and Robinson of being
a returned convict? Goodness gracious! what does it all matter?
what harm is there in the greengrocer so long as he is an honest
man, and has clean hands, and doesn't spill the lobster-sauce

over our pantaloons? I would rather help myself from the table; but am I to quarrel with my neighbour for preferring the green-grocer and the grim ceremony of handing things round? And the eighteenpenny claret. Who does not tell fibs about his wine? Cambacérès, Talleyrand, were not always to be depended upon in their stories about their vintages. I have heard even teetotallers grow Münchausenesque about the virtues of strange pumps. There is a certain stage of good-fellowship when all men—to the most truthful—have a tendency towards glorifying themselves and telling lies. And the people who "go about saying things," —a *fico* for them all!—have they got ninety-eight thousand pounds snugly lying in consols? Are they the only living descendants of Timour the Tartar, and Marino Faliero? Can they squeeze a pewter-pot flat between their fingers, or swallow a red-hot poker, or play the overture to *Der Freischütz* on their chins? I may have these powers and possessions, or I may not. Do you think that you can say more against me than I can against you? How about that eight-day clock? How about that little affair at Torquay? I knew the scale in a contested election turned once by this simple placard, "Ask Mr. A. (one of the candidates) about the widow of poor Mr. Smith." There had never been a widow of poor Mr. Smith, there had never been a poor Mr. Smith at all; but the placard took amazingly; it was copied and repeated everywhere : the candidate was pursued by howling mobs demanding what he had done with poor Mr. Smith's widow ; and in the end he was beaten by a humiliating majority. There is nothing like the "poor Mr. Smith" system of attack. Aha! traducer! *Tu quoque:* you're another! and the traitor Benedict Arnold used to confess that the accusation, perfectly unfounded, of having once "killed a man in a claret-coloured coat," sometimes lay heavier on his mind than the curses of his country and the blood of André.

It is so seldom, nowadays, that I allow myself a good hearty digression, that having once begun, I thought it as well to proceed until you were exasperated, and I was satiated. This agreeable state of things being, I conclude, attained, I will return to Inspector Millament and Sergeant South, promising not to digress again for a great many chapters.

A word as to the personal appearance of the Inspector. He

was tall, like his attendant Sergeant, but he had long since given
up all youthful vanities in attire. Inspector Millament assumed
the imposing, the paternal, the venerable. He was stately in
mien, of a grave countenance, rubicund, but abundant in white
hair and whiskers, almost approaching the full beard. He wore a
broad-brimmed hat and gold-rimmed spectacles. His manly chest
was covered by a black-velvet waistcoat of comfortable, but austere
cut. He wore gaiters. He was never seen without an umbrella
with a crutched handle. From one of his side-pockets usually
bulged a packet of his adored periodicals. There was about him
an indefinable combination of the "heavy father" in a comedy
and a retired military officer in real life.

Both Inspector Millament and Sergeant South were married.
They had pretty little cottages at Camberwell, and were as close
neighbours as they were close friends. At home they smoked
their pipes and drank their social glass; and read—the Inspector
his continuous romances, and the Sergeant the theatrical advertisements, in default of playbills—in peace and comfort. Both
had large families; and it may be mentioned as a somewhat
curious feature in their respective domesticities, that neither Mrs.
Inspector Millament nor Mrs. Sergeant South ever made the
slightest disturbance if the liege lord of one or the other stopped
out until the unholiest hours in the night-morning, or, leaving
home for a quiet stroll, didn't come back again for a fortnight.
They were quite accustomed to such vagaries.

Millament without South, or South without Millament, would
have been trustworthy and efficient officers, I have no doubt; but
they were seldom seen asunder. They hunted much better together. The newspapers always associated their names; nay,
police-magistrates experienced a kind of pleasure when they were
told that such or such an important case was under the management of Inspector Millament and Sergeant South.

It was about half-after one p.m. on the day when the distinguished party visited the Monmouth Chambers that the Inspector and his colleague were sauntering by the northern
approach to Waterloo Bridge. There were plenty of announcements relative to entertainments, *poses plastiques*, and theatrical
novelties for the Sergeant to peruse; and there was apparently

plenty of leisure for the Inspector to finish the last chapter of "Amy Montmorenci, or the Odd-Fellow's Niece." The day was delightful; everything wore a cheerful and sunshiny aspect, and the people who passed to and fro glanced approvingly at the two friends, doubtless thinking them a very nice pair of gentlemen indeed. As, indeed, they were.

"It don't finish well, South, and that's a fact," the Inspector remarked, shutting up "Amy Montmorenci," and replacing the periodical in his pocket. "She ought to have come into the fortune in her own right, instead of marrying that lily-livered son of a gun who was made out to be an earl."

"That way of finishing it would never have done for the 'Vic.,'" mused the Sergeant, intent on a playbill. "The women ought always to have the best of it. Virtue rewarded, and that sort of thing. Halloa! here's the French Plays a-coming."

There was no bill of Mr. Mitchell's (then) charming little theatre near; but Inspector Millament seemed perfectly well to understand what was meant by the "French Plays."

"On to the bridge," he said quickly to his subordinate, and passed through the turnstile.

The collector who took his halfpenny and that of Sergeant South gave a respectful grin as they went through, and remarked subsequently to a youth, with a face like a muffin and a cap like a crumpet, who assisted him in his fiscal duties, that "there was something up." Many a time had the toll-collector seen Inspector Millament and Sergeant South pass through his wicket, until at last he seemed to have almost an intuitive knowledge of when they were going quietly to their own homes, and when "there was something up."

The two sauntered along the bridge; the Inspector taking a smiling survey of Somerset House, the Sergeant gazing with rapt attention, first at the shot-tower, and then at the lion on the summit of the brewery on the Surrey side. Then both faced about and stood still.

There came towards them from Middlesex a gentleman of gay and jaunty carriage, and attired in the first style of fashion. I say in the first style of fashion; for his raiment was splendid and well cut; his hat was shiny, and his boots were bright.

His linen was of the finest and whitest. He had many chains and many rings, and curious to relate, he wore his heart upon his sleeve.

"What swells they do come out to be sure, sometimes," Sergeant South remarked, half in admiration, half in disparagement. "I've seen that chap as seedy as a scarecrow."

"A theatrical lot, South, a theatrical lot," returned his superior; "no offence to you, though," he added, as though he feared the Sergeant might take the remark as a reflection on his liking for playbill literature. "There's no man admires the drama more than I do, South. But they're always acting a part, those Frenchmen; and there's no denying it. Look at that French count in *Love and Madness*. Makes use of his whiskers and braiding to betray a poor trusting widow-woman. They're all alike."

"The last part I saw him acting," the Sergeant said with a grin, "was one where clean linen wasn't wanted."

"They *are* slovenly," acquiesced the Inspector. "They've no notion of the neat and quiet in apparel: the real Old English Gentleman cut," and he glanced approvingly at his black-velvet waistcoat and gaiters. "But they're a knowing lot, South— a shrewd, a very shrewd and artful lot I can assure you."

The bravely-attired gentleman who wore his heart upon his sleeve rapidly neared them. He was, to all seeming, in the best of spirits, and sang a little song, of which the refrain was,

"Eh, vive le Roi, et Simon Lefranc,
Son favori, son favori!"

"There's a deal in that way he has of singing," the Sergeant whispered, enticingly but approvingly.

"It does carry things off; but it's too stagy for me," was the Inspector's verdict. "But here he is. Ah, Monsieur Lefranc, good morning to you."

M. Simon Lefranc, no longer a commercial traveller in difficulties, but a dandy of the very first water, was enchanted, ravished, to behold his dear friends. He pressed both their hands warmly. He longed for the day when he could enjoy, more at his ease, the pleasure of their society. But business must be attended to. "At all events," he added, "we shall have a charming day to-morrow at the races."

"Yes; it's likely enough to be fine, Monsieur," said the Inspector, "and there'll be plenty of enjoyment on the road and on the course. But we'll all get our hands full of business, I think, to-morrow; eh, South?" he concluded, turning to his companion.

"Chock-full," replied the Sergeant; "so has Monsieur Lefranc there."

"Bah! a trifle! a mere bagatelle! My little affair might have been over an hour ago. I could have caged my bird before noon, but we had agreed to wait, and for certain reasons to strike all our *coups* together. She is certain to be at the races, you say?"

"As sure as eggs is eggs," the Sergeant conclusively responded. "She won't miss, nor any of *our* birds either. Besides, they'll all be well watched during the night. You've got all the papers?"

"Everything. Warrant of extradition. All complete."

"Is there anything else, Monsieur Lefranc? unless, indeed, you'd like to take a pint of wine," asked Inspector Millament.

"There is nothing else; and a million thanks for your hospitable offer; but I am engaged to lunch at Long's Hotel at two."

"Then we won't detain you. My mate and I have a little business down the Cut, and shall be at it all the afternoon: you'll be down the Yard, I suppose, to-night? The Commissioner may wish to see you."

"I shall be there at ten o'clock precisely. I have a little document to get signed."

"Perhaps," continued the hospitable Inspector, "you'll be able to spare an hour; and we'll go and hear a song, and take a quiet tumbler and a cigar. If not, our appointment stands for to-morrow; three o'clock in front of the Grand Stand. South and I are coming down by the rail early. You're going to do the road, I presume?"

"Precisely; I am about to intrust my person to a barouche and four."

"Ah, nobody knows you," the Inspector said, with something like a sigh; "I daren't be seen even on the roof of a four-horse

omnibus. Everybody would say, 'There goes Inspector Millament. I wonder what he's after.' South and I are obliged to
slink down by rail and prowl about as though we had something
to be ashamed of."

"*Qui fit Mæcenas, ut nemo—*" Well, who *is* contented with
his lot? Inspector Millament was the most famous thief-catcher
in England, feared and deferred to, and trembled at. And yet
even *he* could find something to grumble about.

"One word," Sergeant South said, as the Frenchman, lifting
his hat, was about to retrace his steps northward. "We've been
wanting this woman for months. Have wanted her for a dozen
little transportable matters; but she's always had the art to talk
the prosecutors over before an information was sworn. She's
slipped through our fingers twenty times. Do you really think
that she will be nailed on your little matter?"

"I am sure of it. In France we do not let our little birds
escape so easily. I have a treble-barrelled gun for her. Do you
know what kind of bullets they carry?"

"I can just guess," answered Sergeant South.

"Number one, *faux en écritures privées*,—Forgery. Number
two, complicity in a *vol avec effraction*,—Burglary. Number
three, *assassinat*,—MURDER."

"By Jove!" exclaimed the ordinarily equable Inspector Millament, whilst Sergeant South uttered a prolonged whistle.

"Yes, I think that pretty little mouth may *cracher dans le
son*, grin in sawdust yet. We have her, hard and fast. Do you
know a man named Sims?" he added rapidly.

"Known him for years; very clever, but a bad lot," replied
the Inspector.

"Is he an accomplice?" asked the Sergeant, eagerly.

"An accomplice!" echoed the Frenchman, with a look of
surprise; "he's been one of us for years; but *dans la politique:*
in the State department. This will be a sad blow to my old
colleague; for he was very fond of our little friend, and tried to
prevent her compromising herself so deeply as she has done.
Bonjour, mes enfants. A demain."

And so each of these hunters of human kind went on his
way.

CHAPTER XXVI

THE RACE.

Up, Florence Armytage! up and away! for the hunters are after thee for thy destruction.

Why does she tarry? why does she linger? Rash and desperate little woman, the hounds have slipped their leash; you may almost hear their baying. They will be upon thee presently, and pull thee down, and tear thy throat, and rend thee asunder. The game is up. The last stake has been played. The decree has gone forth. Fly, miserable little woman! There is yet time. Fly!

But there was no one by to say this to Florence, and she stayed. What cause had she to fly? Everything had been going well with her lately. Her last little adventure had succeeded marvellously. The offspring of Tottlepot's caligraphy, planted in a safe quarter, had filled her pocket with hundreds, as it had filled his wth golden units. Fly, indeed! Do we go on wings to the Races?

She came home to her Knightsbridge lodgings about five, very, very tired, but radiant. She was too fatigued to ride on horseback, and had a pretty little dinner sent in to her from a neighbouring confectioner's. The salmon-cutlet was delicious. There was an exquisite little duck and a truffle, and a morsel of iced pudding. The wicked little woman drank a whole pint of Moselle. It did her good, she said. There were times—they were only times of recent date, however—when at the conclusion of a day's hard campaigning she had been obliged to take a little cognac; sometimes with water, sometimes without. She did not want cognac to-day, no, nor the laudanum in her dressing-case.

"Poison," she said gaily to herself, "poison, indeed. I could get enough of it from papa without ever troubling the chemist for it. Poor dear papa, I ought to have gone to see him to-day. I'm afraid he's not so comfortable as he ought to be with that Mrs. Donkin.

"Papa's is a desperate game," she pursued. "If he succeeds, what a fortune! if he fails,—ah, I shudder to think of it." And she did shudder.

She sat toying with the remains of her repast,—it had been followed, of course, by a choice dessert,—until past eight o'clock. There was yet time for her to fly. She might have caught the mail-train for Dover, and have been at Ostend by morning. She might have caught the great night-mail for the North at Euston Square, and have been at Carlisle by dawn. There were scores of outlets open to her, and there was no one to tell her that the hunters were up, and that the hounds had slipped their leash. She lighted her little cigarette, and sent tiny wreaths of blue smoke circling towards the ceiling. To her they did not look like halters.

The French maid came in due time, and dressed her in elaborate magnificence. She was covered in jewels. Some that she had on were owed for, and some had been gotten from usurers, and some had been stolen. But no matter. A little carriage waited for her, and she drove to the French plays at the St. James's Theatre.

What were the performances that evening? *L'Auberge des Adrets, Vingt Ans de la Vie d'un Joueur?* I forget. Ah, now I remember; it was *La Dame de St. Tropez*. She had a little closely-curtained stage-box. She shivered a little at the death-scene, but was soon herself again, and, returning, stopped the carriage at Verrey's, and had an ice and a glass of Curaçoa brought out to her.

She did not go to bed after the play. She went home and had a bath, and the maid dressed her again more elaborately and magnificently than before. But there were certain of her diamonds,—the most gorgeous among them perhaps,—which she did not put on. She was driven this time but a very short distance. Whereabouts on the confines of Belgravia or Pimlico it was situated is a matter of no present concern. It was a very grand house, lighted up from top to bottom with wax-candles. The

Baroness despised gas. Yes; it was a Baroness who officiated as hostess: a foreign lady of title, whose husband, M. le Baron, was grave in appearance, portly in build, and was decorated with the ribbons of many orders. There were many ladies,—none of them so pretty as Florence Armytage, but many young and comely, and many more who could not lay pretensions to extreme youth, but were nevertheless stately and superb. All the toilettes were ravishing; and the diamonds glistened so that you might have imagined the ladies so many walking chandeliers, with the gauze-coverings which careful housewives put about them floating by way of drapery. There were a great many gentlemen, some of them the greatest dandies in London. There was a duke. There were Russian and Turkish *diplomates.* The conversation was brilliant, but strictly decorous. Not even the tiny pinches of Attic salt sometimes permitted by the Lady on the First Floor at her charming *réunions* in the Rue Grande-des-Petites-Maisons, Paris, were tolerated here. There was singing and playing, and of the very best description, in one room. There was dancing in another. There was play, and of the very deepest, in another. None of your sixpenny-pointed whist or eighteenpenny vingt-un, but good, sound, ruinous roulette. The Baroness was kind enough to keep the bank; her stately husband did not disdain to officiate as croupier. How the gold gave out its red glow, and the crisp bank-notes crackled on the green-baize table! How merrily the ball spun round in its parti-coloured wheel! With what dulcet tones the Baroness proclaimed the chances of the game! Florence Armytage was in luck that night. She won two hundred pounds. She sang and danced afterwards, and enchanted everybody. She was taken in to supper by the Duke, and drank more Moselle; but it was iced, and had a seductive bouquet about it, and it did her good, she said. She reached home at three in the morning, fatigued, but unconquered; and bade her discreet Abigail wake her at eleven, at which time her own snug little brougham, but with four post-horses attached, was to call and take her to the Downs. And who do you think was to be her cavalier on the occasion? I dare not tell you yet; but you shall hear speedily.

Yes; the parties given by the Baroness de la Haute Gueuse

were undeniably splendid, although their locality was certainly in
the Debateable Land. They were not like Mrs. Armytage's
Parisian *soirées*. They did not in the least resemble the dull and
vulgar, yet pretentious, shams of well-conducted parties, common
among the "upper five hundred" of a class I disdain to parti-
cularise. The Southbank might have sighed as often and as
vainly as Queen Dido in the ballad before she could have obtained
a card for the Baroness's parties. The oddest thing about them
was that nobody seemed to know exactly where she lived. The
great dandies, the gorgeous guardsmen, the foreign *diplomates*,
used to be taken there late at night by other dandies, guardsmen,
and *diplomates*, who, in their turn, had been taken there by others.
You used to wake late the next morning with a headache, and a
misty consciousness of having had a very good supper over-
night, and had rather too much champagne. You had seen a
multitude of wax-candles and many jewels. You had been
permitted at one stage of the entertainment to smoke. Perhaps
you found a white camellia or a lady's glove in your pocket. It
was as though you had been to see the Adelantado of the Seven
Cities whom Washington Irving discourses of so sweetly : the
only drawbacks to the pleasurable reminiscences of the evening
were that champagne-headache and the discovery that you had
lost all the money you had about you. Generally you found a
cabman's ticket in lieu of your *port-monnaie*. The cabman would
call for his fare about noon, demanding seven-and-sixpence; and
in answer to your inquiries would politely inform you that you
and another gentleman had hailed him at Hyde-Park Corner,
whence you were driven, at your own request, to Paddington
Green, where the other gentleman alighted, and so you had been
driven eventually home. You paid the cabman, but you never
saw that other gentleman again.

It would have been well for Florence Armytage if she, too, had
been driven to Paddington, and to the terminus of the Great
Western Railway, and had so taken train anywhere away from
the hunters. Of what close and narrow chances is Life made up !
But for the merest chance in the world Mr. Sims might have
dropped in at the Baroness's—where he was very well known—
and there met not only Mrs. Armytage, but a gentleman of

cheerful guise and jocund conversation, who, as a strange adjunct to full evening-costume, wore his heart upon his sleeve. Oh! Simon Lefranc was there; and Florence was introduced to him. He was Count Somebody, and wore a full moustache and whisker and a curly black wig; and the little woman thought him very droll, and did not in the least recognise him as the impudent-looking person with a face like that of a *paillasse*, who had stared at her that morning through the coffee-room window of the Soho Chambers.

The Race on the Downs that May-day was the most brilliant that had ever been seen for years. The sun shone glaring hot, and the dust was somewhat choking; but summer toilettes and parasols will defy the sun, and lobster-salads and iced drinks will allay the dust. There were more things which took place at this particular Race than had been known to occur for many years. "Teddy the Tyler" was the horse that won the great stake; but the events that accompanied his progress to the judge's chair are of too much importance to be dismissed at the fag-end of a chapter. If you please, we will let "Teddy the Tyler," and the champagne, and the lobsters wait a little. Very shortly you shall have a correct card of the entire proceedings.

Three gentlemen had to meet by appointment at the Grand Stand at three p.m. The police were rapidly clearing the course, in their admired broom-like fashion, about that time; for "Teddy the Tyler," with his three-and-twenty competitors, were all saddled and bridled, and Teddy the Tyler's jockey, with *his* three-and-twenty competitors, had all received their last instructions from their trainers and owners. The superintendent of police, who was directing the clearing of the course, gave a friendly nod as he passed the three gentlemen, who, too discreet to interfere with the discipline of the day, were retiring from the course.

"Pleasure or business?" asked the Superintendent, leaning over his saddle-bow.

"A little of both," answered Inspector Millament; "more of the former, perhaps."

"Lots of tip-top swells here," remarked Sergeant South.

"Everybody. Sir Jasper Goldthorpe and party just driven on to the Hill. His son the captain's betting away in the ring like

z

mad.   Friend of yours ? " and the Superintendent indicated with
a wave of his whip Simon Lefranc, who, with his heart pinned to
the sleeve of a gauzy coat, constructed expressly " for the races,"
was standing a little apart.

    " French—just come across," the Inspector returned in a hasty
whisper. " Deuce of a heavy job. Murder. One of their best
men.   Good bye."

    So the course was cleared, and, after many false starts, the race
was run, " Teddy the Tyler " winning by a neck.

    " My horse ! my horse ! " cried little Mrs. Armytage, in great
glee, from her carriage-window. She was not the owner of the
animal ; but she had backed him heavily, and stood to win a good
deal of money.

    How lucky Florence Armytage had been that week, to be
sure !

CHAPTER XXVII.

AFTER THE RACE.

AND the Tower of Babel, Messieurs Essayists and Reviewers. Is that au Allegory? is that to be taken "ideologically?" Granted that it is to be so accepted, let us allegorise and idealise it, here, upon the Downs.

Yonder is the Tower of Babel, there, the Grand Stand. But for the infirm and impotent purpose of Man it would have mounted higher, higher, and higher, until it had soared miles beyond the altitude ever attained by the carrier-pigeons liberated each race-day from the summit, with the news of the great Event tied under their wings. But a term was to be put to Babel, and the Builder stayed his hand, and then all around arose the confusion of tongues.

The myriad-langued brabble had ceased at the starting; and respiration paused in a hundred thousand pair of lungs as the horses came round the Corner. He who stood at the end of the Stand nearest the Judge's chair, and looked at the hive of heads upon it, saw but a mass of black; when by came the horses, and forthwith the black ant-hill turned pallid white, as the mass of faces, blanched with anxiety, were turned towards the goal. Then Teddy the Tyler came out of a squad of three that had long since abandoned the rest, and leaving Shandrydan to admire his tail, and beating Brother to Desdichado by a neck cleverly, came in triumphantly, and won the Race.

I often wonder what the last jockey on the last horse thinks about as the turf gives out sullen echoes to the hoofs of his lagging steed. Do hopes of "better luck next time" encourage him under defeat, or did he never mean to win the race at all? Somebody must be last, of course; somebody must be beaten. What

did the last cuirassier escorting Napoleon from the lost field of
Waterloo towards Genappe think about? "Here is a pretty
piece of business. It is all over with the Chief—*fini* with the
Little Corporal. Shall we ever get to Genappe? Shall I be
sabred by the Prussians, or taken prisoner by the Rosbifs? Shall
I ever see Fanchon again, or the Champs Elysées, or drink *petit
bleu* at the Barrier, or get admitted to the Invalides if I lose my
leg?" Thus may run the thoughts coursing through such a
trooper's mind! and yet just as probably he may be like "the
jolly young waterman," not rowing but riding along, "thinking
of nothing at all." A great power, that temporary but complete
suspension of thought! Perhaps the last jockey in the race can
so give himself a mental holiday. I have often noticed a vacuous
and abstracted expression beneath the velvet or parti-coloured
cap. What does it matter, after all? He has lost the blue
ribbon of the turf, but he may win some gaudy little bit of tape
at Northampton or Goodwood. He is young yet. There are
plenty of gentlemen who will give him a mount; meanwhile he
rides and thinks not, unless indeed he has sold the race, and
"pulled" his steed at some knave's bidding; and then he may be
half-chuckling in his silken sleeve to think that it is lined with
bank-notes, and half-apprehensive of the Vehmgericht of the
Jockey Club, with their "cord-and-dagger" decrees of suspension
or expulsion from the ring and turf; or else he may be a mere
child, as many jockeys are, who has ridden carelessly or clumsily,
and dreads fierce reprehension, or fiercer double-thonging, when
he returns to the training-stable. The confusion of tongues,
stilled at the starting, surging again as the horses swept away,
hushed again at the critical turn of the Corner, breaking into a
delirious dropping-fire of "It is!" "It isn't!" "Red wins!"
"Yellow wins!" "Hurrah for Blue-cap!" "Lord Punter's horse
wins!" "I'll bet against the Tyler!"—now, when the event was
decided, burst into a huge frenzy of howling, yelling, cheering,
bawling, screaming, cursing, laughing, screeching, hooting, yelp-
ing, and general mad gabbling and turmoil. And the Ring, all
whose thoughts a moment before had been centered on this race,
forthwith began to speculate on the race for the ensuing year,
and back Teddy the Tyler for the Leger.

Inspector Millament, his Sergeant, and his French friend, seemed in no kind of hurry to get through their little business.

"There's plenty of time," the Inspector remarked, quietly.

"Let 'em have their lunch," said the Sergeant, with a grin.

"With all my heart," acquiesced the genial Simon Lefranc. "We too will lunch, and eat of the *salade du homard*, and *sabler* the *petit vin mousseux.*"

They kept their eyes open, however. From ten minutes to ten minutes people passed them who had a sign of intelligence to give, a word of intelligence to whisper. Now it was a hot hostler hurrying by, with a wisp of straw and a pail of water. Now a little ragamuffin, bawling forth the correctness of race-cards of the year before last. Now a monstrously attired Ethiopian serenader, with his Welsh wig all awry, and the blackening streaming off his pockmarked face with heat. Now came a trampish woman with a tambourine, but also with a nod and a wink for Sergeant South. Now a remarkably dingy foreign gentleman, seemingly of the interpreting persuasion from Leicester Square, who carelessly flung a half-burnt cigar on the turf,—no sooner flung than picked up by Simon Lefranc.

"You do not manage your agents well in England," the volatile Simon remarked; "I observe that you let them speak to you. *I* never let mine say a word. *Tenez*, this bit of cigar is a whole phrase to me."

"We're not so clever at the deaf-and-dumb language, maybe, as you are," retorted Sergeant South, somewhat nettled.

"That isn't it," interposed the pacific Inspector Millament; "our men are so confoundedly free and independent. We're obliged to pick 'em up where we can, and they will have their own way. You have 'em all under your control. We haven't. Our Government's dreadfully shabby to the Force, and it's as much as we can do to make both ends meet."

"There may be something in that," remarked Simon Lefranc, reflectively. "That's one of your constitutional weaknesses. *Chez nous on a carte blanche.*"

"And then, you see," continued the Inspector, "whenever one of these gentry has got rather clever in picking up information, and has done us a good turn in a pretty stiffish case or two, what does he do but set up in business for himself, and start a 'private inquiry' office, to set genteel families by the ears, and rip up all the secrets of the first nobility of the land. I've no patience with 'em."

"Nor I," the accommodating M. Lefranc agreed. "Nor would I, nor would M. le Prefet. *Peste!* we suffer no amateurs in our vocation. *Il faut être à nous corps et ame, sinon on va là d'où l'on vient.* By which I mean, my friends," he continued, "that we know a little too much about our assistants; and that if they play us any little tricks, we send them back to where we took them from. You understand, eh?"

"I wonder where *he* came from, at the first going off," whispered Sergeant South to his superior. "He can't be under fifty. He must have seen a lot, and have been in a lot of queer places; ay, and done a lot of queer things in his time. I should like to know where he learnt to speak English so well."

"Hush," the inspector returned, just with a movement of an eyelid, sufficient to indicate the near neighbourhood of Simon Lefranc, who, wearing his heart upon his sleeve, according to custom, seemed likewise to have eyes in his coat-back and in his boot-heels, and to see laterally, and dorsally, and obliquely, and everywhere.

None of the three gentlemen had tickets for the Grand Stand; but they all passed unquestioned in and out of the enclosure, and up and down the staircase of that Tower of Babel. Their business was at present in the midst of the confusion of tongues in the Ring.

A strange and edifying sight that enclosure and its occupants were to see. A more marvellous one was that Ring,—not to be equalled in any country but our own,—without a parallel in any age of civilisation but the present one. Simon Lefranc looked upon all he saw with a calmly critical eye, and in contemptuous disparagement thought on what comparatively lean and barren sights Chantilly and other Continental race-courses presented. An Englishman, even, familiar with the thousand and one "events" with which our racing calendar teems, must have been fain to acknowledge that these Downs, this Enclosure, this Ring, were unequalled in his experience, and in the world.

The great tournament was over—gone and done with, to be remembered only gleefully or ruefully on settling day; to find only its record as the "Teddy the Tyler year" among the *fasti* of the turf; to be perpetuated only in garish mezzotint engravings, that are framed and hung up in tavern parlours. Well, and is that not fame enough? Do the great enjoy a much brighter, a much more durable renown when they have passed away to the cold dark house, where you and I, and all the world,—athletes and paralytics, Adonis and Quasimodo, the Prime Minister and Blondin the tight-rope dancer,—must one day find a home and peace? Here is a veteran who has filled Europe with his fame, stormed redoubts, planted banners on earthworks, done all the deeds of a Paladin. He has won crosses and orders, titles and a pension. Years before he dies, the world, which was wont to applaud him so loudly, has quite forgotten him. His laurels are as withered as the orange-flowers in the chaplet of last year's bride. Nobody cares to inquire who that feeble old gentleman in the blue frock and buff waistcoat may be, who hobbles from his lodgings in St. Alban's place to the United Service Club, and scolds the waiters, and is voted a nuisance in the library because he wheezes and coughs so. One day he does not come down stairs to breakfast: the undertakers go up stairs to him, instead. His man-servant improves the occasion, and his own particular wardrobe. Somebody puts a *distringas* upon his balance at the banker's; sometimes it happens that he has lived so long as not even to leave nephews and nieces to squabble over his heritage. He dies, and they bury him: but for one brief day one paragraph of the military intelligence in the newspapers is illuminated by a flash of his old fame; the laurels bloom once more; again is the trumpet sounded, as we are told that the poor old gentleman deceased was the gallant Sir Hercules Lyon Choker, the hero of—where was it?—Walcheren, Orthes, Nivelle, Ticonderoga?—it might have been the Battle of Blenheim for aught the public care about it twenty-four hours afterwards;—the intrepid General, whose first commission bore date January 1st, 1787; who was all through the Peninsular War; who was at Washington, and only missed Waterloo through his services being required on the other side of the Atlantic. He was a K.C.B., he was a

General, he was a Colonel of the Fifth Toughs; and so he ends: and this is Fame.

The three police-officers, too, this race-day, were elbowing their way through a compact mass of fame. Even they, thief-catchers as they were, had a kind of celebrity, and felt proud of it. Now and then Inspector Millament and Sergeant South were recognised by some wary turfite, by some experienced man about town, who would thrust his tongue in his cheek, and chuckle, and say, unconsciously echoing the toll-taker on the bridge in London, "There they go—on the hunt, as usual; I wonder what's up."

Round and about they elbowed their way. Deeper and deeper they plunged into the great cauldron wherein seethed the children of Mammon; South and Millament proceeding with a calm and practised motion of the arms, and even M. Lefranc insinuating his way along in a manner which seemed to argue that he thoroughly understood the ins and outs of an English crowd.

"There's his Lordship," muttered the inspector to his companions; "he looks first-rate to-day."

His Lordship was apparent but for a moment. Anon he was surrounded by other lordships, and disappeared. He was a nobleman full fifty years of age, and wrinkled and grey, and plainly dressed; and yet, gazing upon him for the first time in your life, you might at once have made an affidavit that this was one of the proudest patricians in England. He looked his Lordship all over. There was an indescribable distance, reserve, and *morgue*, an almost sneering, almost spiteful expression of pride in his Lordship's face, which gave him a very unlovely, but a very aristocratic expression. A plain frock, a black satin stock of the fashion worn five-and-twenty years ago, and pepper-and-salt trousers very quaintly cut about the boot, are not, surely, very sumptuous articles of attire; yet had his Lordship worn an embroidered surcoat on his noble breast, and a damascened morion with a plume of feathers, and gauntlets of silver, and greaves of gold, and a tremendous coat-of-arms blazoned on his shining shield, he could not have looked one whit more or less the true patrician than in the simple garb I have described. This was his

Lordship, eloquent in debate, sage in council, generous, albeit imperious, among his vassals, learned and witty, and pungent and ill-tempered, and very fond of horseflesh.

"He's not a bad sort," Sergeant South opined; "but he can't win the blue ribbon of the turf for all his trying."

His Lordship! why, half the peerage found representatives in or about the Grand Stand that memorable day when Teddy the Tyler won. There were plump old lords very tightly braced and girthed up, very stiff about the neckerchief, very shiny about the hat, very rosy, and sometimes slightly purple about their pendulous cheeks:—jolly old patricians! how many races had they seen, long before railways were dreamt of, and when the course was kept clear by smock-frocked rustics, temporarily sworn in as special constables, and armed with cartwhips, instead of being swept by that long irresistible blue broom of the Metropolitan Police; when there was open and undisturbed gambling in all the booths, instead of here and there a little furtive, cowering, timorous thimblerigging and cardsharping, and half a dozen stand-up fights, if not more, between every race! Then there were middle-aged noblemen, inclined, in general, to look somewhat seriously and disparagingly at mundane amusements, especially at those in which the lower classes of society were permitted to mingle, but who had somehow found themselves in the Grand Stand inclosure early in the afternoon,—as they had similarly found themselves any time these twenty years past,—with the carriages containing their families, their retainers, and their Fortnum-and-Mason hampers on the Hill opposite. The old lords and the middle-aged lords, and the tall, severe-looking baronets with the white hats and the pendent whiskers, and the stalwart gentlemen in body-coats and drab cords, who bore the appearance of being members for the county, or chairmen of Quarter-sessions, and who, very probably, were entitled to such high styles and dignities, had nothing whatever to do with the rude, hectoring, betting fraternity—oh dear, no! If ever they were seen down Tattersall's Yard, say on a Sunday afternoon towards the close of the merry month of May, it was merely for a saunter before dinner. *They* wouldn't bet on a week-day even, to say nothing of the Sabbath they were so fond, in Parliament and elsewhere, of making laws about:—always for the better preservation of that holy day, and the coercion (for their soul's health) of the wicked worldlings of the lower classes. They only attended the leading races through an unfeigned love for national sports, and a laudably patriotic desire to improve the breed of the British racer. Most meritorious gentlemen, had they not their desire! Had they not so improved horse-racing that the animal itself has come to be a kind of four-legged acrobat, a tight-rope dancer with a mane and tail,—a quadruped so precious as to be sometimes the joint-stock property of a company of speculators, —so precious, that a cold in the head or a pebble in the hoof is a ten thousand pound matter,—so precious, that police-guards and detectives have to be kept in his stable to prevent his being "nobbled," or poisoned, or maimed by other ardently patriotic improvers of the breed of British racers, only a little too anxious that some other horse, and not the particular racer in question, should win the day?' Had they not improved it until a thousand and one ruses, stratagems, intrigues, frauds, and bedevilments have come to environ one of the simplest operations in equine nature,—that of a horse going as fast as his legs will carry or his rider can compel him? Had they not improved it till jockeys have dwindled and dwindled from strong men into little weazened brats of children, riding "feather-weight," forsooth, till the wind almost blows them from their saddles to dash them against the posts on the course? Had they not improved it till the whole Turf has become one huge arena of knavery and villany and common cheating, the vantage-ground of shameless rascals who no longer sleeve cards or cog dice, because the law has left no common gaming-houses for them to play the Greek in?

These worthy gentlemen, I say, never betted. They left the odds to the professedly sporting aristocracy and gentry, who made no secret of their propensity, and carried their betting-books in their hands as openly as Simon Lefranc wore his heart upon his sleeve; but they heard something from time to time about large bets that were made, about thousands that were won and lost by persons very intimately known to them,—their own mothers' sons indeed. "Commission" did it all. Stealthy Mr. Wriggles, trust-worthy Mr. Wraggles, confidential Mr. Baggles, the great com-mission agents of the Ring, knew how much to put on Cantharides

for Lord Lofty, how much to lay against Bloodsucker for Lord
Whitechokerly, how much Sir John stood to win on the Ascot
Cup. Wriggles, Wraggles, and Baggles never knew their patrons
in public. They called very early in the morning, and were supposed to have something to do with the estates, or the tenantry,
or the drains down in the country. They were to be seen at
private houses of call. Had you met them in public, and not been
one of the thoroughly initiated, you would not have been able to
recognise them as having anything to do with the Ring. Wriggles
affected the clerical in his appearance; Wraggles' aspect partook
half of the schoolmaster and half of the well-to-do tradesman;
and Baggles positively dressed and looked like a gentleman, and
was more than ninety-five per cent. of one. Commission is a great
power in the state: hidden, undemonstrative, but not the less
potent. The Archbishop of Canterbury might bet on commission;
and in the ordinary course of his affairs, no human being would
be the wiser for his Grace's transactions. Occasionally, it must
be admitted, the occult arcana of commission are opened up, and
a great exposure takes place. Then, when Sir John has blown his
brains out, it is whispered that the trigger of his gun did *not* catch
in a button-hole while he was out shooting, but that he killed
himself because he could not pay his losses on the Derby. Thus,
when my Lord levants and the bailiffs go down as unbidden guests
to his country-seat, it is rumoured that he has lost many thousands
on the St. Leger:—he was never seen to book a bet in his life.

Leave we these devotees of dark and crooked ways, to whom
the sport of horse-racing has lost its zest and savour, these ten
years past, and to whom the turf is only another board of green
cloth, on which the hoofs of horses, in lieu of ivory dice, are
rattled. There is plenty more matter for observation as we
wander about. Here, in brilliant, noisy knots, are the young
fledglings of turf gambling, the wild young lords, the "noble
captains,"—so called by runners and touts and doorkeepers,—the
sporting Guardsmen, the smooth-faced young subalterns in infantry
regiments, sometimes, who are wasting their patrimony, or ruining
the clergymen, their papas—ruining them in the military clubs
and worse places, and whose lives, when they can scamper up from
Aldershott, are made up of betting, soda-and-brandy guzzling, bill-

discounters, chamber-haunting, lobsters, oysters, late hours and loose company, and who wake up some morning to be arrested on parade, to become the cynosure of the Insolvent Court and the theme of the newspapers, and who, having begun as fools, often end as rogues, fade away into Continental billiard-rooms and *table d'hôtes,* and seduce other fools in their turn. Given a subaltern's pay in a marching regiment, to find the means of living at the rate of two thousand a year. This is the problem many gallant, and at first well-meaning youths have to solve :—with what ruinous, despairful results, let clergymen with sequestered livings, let sisters robbed of their portions, let defrauded tailors, and usurers frantic at being " done,"—" by such a good man, too, as everybody thought him," wheezes Ephraim Tigg the Rasper,—let swindled hotel-keepers and billiard-markers with tremendous scores unpaid, essay to tell.

Shall not a place be found, too, for the sporting Government clerks, and stockbrokers, and rich young tradesmen, just a step lower in the hierarchy of " swelldom," who are at all the races, and bet, and drink, and " carry on," as the phrase is, but who seldom come to such desperate grief as their more aristocratic competitors, for the simple reason that they have not so far to fall, and have a way of letting the mud into which they have fallen dry, and then rubbing it off with a will? Many more young sparks of the sporting world might I descant upon ; but they are cheaper swells : they don't patronise the Grand Stand ; they come down by the rail, and not in four-in-hands, or even Hansom cabs ; and their losses and winnings are on a scale not at all pretentious.

But there must not be passed over a variety of the genuine " swell " tribe,—noble in birth often, generally affluent, at least, in means,—the only remnant we possess, in this hard-working age,—when almost every man, high or low, prince or peasant, does *something,* whether it be for good or evil,—of the " dandies " of bygone times. They are growing rarer every day, like that intolerable old (and young) nuisance, — the " gent," who has been all but absorbed by the Volunteer Movement ; but you may still see the perfectly listless, do-nothing, care-for-nothing—I trust not good-for-nothing : and yet what *is* he good for ?—

dandy in the Grand Stand on a great race day. He is always exquisitely dressed; his hair and appendages are marvels of True-fitism. His jewellery is resplendent; his linen irreproachable. He carries, wet or dry, a slim umbrella. Mr. John Leech has drawn him in *Punch* five hundred times. I wish that he could fix him to a wood-block, so that he pervaded society no longer. He smokes as he talks, in a languid, drawling kind of way, and wastes half of his weeds, as he wastes half of his words. He never knows what to do with his legs. He *does* know what to do with his hands, and thrusts them, nearly up to the elbows, into his pockets. He comes to the "races" in the most elaborate equi-page and costume attainable, simply because it is "the thing." He does not bet. It is a bore to bet. The men in his set don't bet. He is quite unsusceptible to the excitement of the race, and has just completed the leisurely adjustment of his eye-glass by the time the winning horse has passed the post. He does not even take much interest in the brilliant ladies in the carriages outside,—save to remark to a friend and duplicate that he has seen Baby Molyneux, or Ada Tressilian (*née* Runt), and that "she looks older." He does not in the least understand the rude witticisms of the road homewards; and at a handful of salt more or less attic being flung at him, returns a look of such calm bewilderment as to disarm the most practised "chaffer." He has been known to take more champagne than was good for him, and to have gone to the length of assuming a false nose at the "Cock" at Sutton; but he goes to sleep when tipsy: there are always, at least, seven dandies as solemn as he to take care of him, and he comes to no harm. He never comes to any good. The age of this silent, languid dandy is from twenty-five to thirty. I want to know what becomes of him when he reaches middle age, or approaches fogeyism. Does he emigrate? Does he enlist? Does he expire from pure inanition? Does he take heart of grace and hit somebody, or do something, and approve himself a Man? Even girls who are worth anything don't seem to care much about him, save as a butt to laugh at; and although I have occasionally seen the languid and listless dandy feebly struggling between billows of crinoline, and carrying a gorgeous church service to and from Belgravian places of worship on Sundays, it is not with great frequency, I opine, that his Common Prayer is opened at the Order for the Solemnisation of Matrimony. I fancy that when the dandy does marry, it is to one of those strong-minded British females who are in the habit of trotting their tall, gaunt, melancholy-looking, uncomplaining husbands from one Continental watering-place to another. You know the unhappy being I mean. He is a patient and uxorious drudge, an amiable and contented packhorse. He is always in trouble about the luggage. He is the "Monsieur" with whom hotel-keepers are threatened when the bills are exorbitant, and who would pay the bills out of his own private funds for peace and quietness' sake if he had any private funds; but he hasn't. He gave up all those, years ago, for splendid board and lodging. He takes his wife's children— she has generally been a widow—out a-walking very meekly. He fetches their physic from the *pharmacien Anglais,*—"*Trois graines de pilule bleue, et une dose noire, s'il vous plait;*" and he is as harmless and, perhaps, slightly more useful than of yore.

Add to the people I have endeavoured to sketch the foreigners who always muster in great force in the Grand Stand and its precincts, and think they are up to their eyes in *Le Sport* when they are elbowed and pushed about by the contending crowd. Almost every foreign legation in London has its minister or secretary or *attaché* here, generally got up in the most approved racing style, with white hats and green veils, and diaphanous coats, and white jean boots with varnished tips and spurs,— whether they ride or not,—and white trousers. How is it that we, of all people in the world, should have almost entirely abandoned the use of those candid nether garments? Foreigners adhere to them with pleasing persistence; but, save on board a man-o'-war, who ever sees an Englishman with a pair of white ducks on nowadays? Easter Sunday used to be the great day for inaugurating their wear; but, of late years, we have had a succession of rainy Easters. That may have something to do with it. Or is it because the great Duke of Wellington, who wore white ducks winter and summer, is no more, and that the fashion has gone out with him?

There are the diplomatic foreigners, who have seen races in every town in Europe almost; and there are the simple sight-

seeing foreigners, who are lost in their amazement at the Babel
sight and the Babel sounds; there are the country gentlemen of
the neighbourhood, who really enjoy the race, and take a genuine
interest in the " improvement of the racer." There would be a
good many more members of the swell-mob on the look-out for
gold watches, dropped pencil-cases, bank-notes, and similar trifles,
than are actually present, but that each member of the pocket-
picking fraternity is perfectly aware of the Argus-eyed attributes
of Inspector Millament, Sergeant South, and sundry other officers
of the police force then and there present in plain clothes; and so
the thieves prudently make themselves scarce at the earliest convenient opportunity. There are the reporters of the sporting
newspapers, flitting in and out, rushing from pillar to post, and
from post to paddock, and from paddock to Ring, back again,—
seeing everything: the weighing, saddling, starting, racing, winning, losing, buying, selling, judging, and betting,—passing to
and fro unquestioned, quite as well recognised by the officials as
the police, and by some almost as much feared, working like
galley-slaves in pursuit of their vocation, and delighting in it,
moreover. The great owners of race-horses, the solid, serious
turfites, the substantial, grave-eyed trainers, are seldom seen,
and then but for an instant. They have other and weightier
business further afield, where the grass is greener, and the throng
is not so dense.

Aï! Aï!—which is an ejaculation I hope will be pardoned to
me by the critics,—the hullaballoo, the hue and cry, the frenzied
exclamation of the book-makers. They will bet against everything: who will lay against the field? who will back anything?
They will do everything. Bar one; bar two; bar three. What
will anybody do on the event? His Lordship wins; the Captain wins in a canter. Didn't they say so? Green wins; Black
wins; Red wins. The very Fiend himself would seem to be
winning to listen to the unearthly screeching of those men.

Such hot, dusty, streaming, common, knavish, or brutal faces,
too! Now the wolf-type, hungry and savage; now the fox-type,
cunning and cynical, and, the day being warm, of not too sweet a
savour; now the terrier-type, honest enough, but exceeding
ravenous after rats. Men—old betting-men—with faces like

owls, like magpies, like ravens; not many of the eagle-type, I
fancy, save in so far as aquiline noses reach. Of these, with the
accompaniment of greasy ringlets, pulpy lips, and much glittering
jewellery, there is sufficiency, and a little to spare, it may be.
And there are weasel faces, ferret faces, grinning-otter faces,
hawk faces, bull-dog faces, and *bull faces;* but on every human
face, among the book-making crew, there is always and ever the
unmistakeable stamp and brand of the Gambler,—the nervous
tick of the head from side to side, the teeth busy with the lips,
the fingers busy with the chin, the unrest in the eye. In a lesser
degree, you may see these signs among bargainers in coal and
corn marts, among chafferers upon exchanges, among punters at
rouge-et-noir tables, among bidders at auctions; but for the
gambler's look,—*l'allure de celui qui joue gros jeu,*—commend me
to the book-makers in the Ring.

They are of every variety of build and stature, and of all ages;
but they have all gotten their symbol, and have taken Mammon's
arles, and are soldiers in his great black-and-yellow regiment.
Whence came they? From Manchester, Preston, Blackpool,
Rochdale, Stockport, Blackburn,—from the great black, striving,
working, gaming, spinning, heaving, savage north of England:—
many of them, I think, from the dialect in which they yell. The
harder, but not harsher, Yorkshire makes itself heard, too, with a
vengeance. The unadulterated cockney, showering its "h's"
about as from a pepper-castor, is not behindhand; every province
in England seems to have sent a contingent. It is Babel; but
Babel with a universal tongue, concurrent with the confusion
thereof, for every one of these money-mongers understands the
one primeval language taught by Professor Mammon.

What were they ere they took to "making books?" Did they
write them, or keep them, or sell them? This is a mystery which
I, for one, do not pretend to solve; but I have heard that a man
is fit to go into the Ring after he has been a beershop-keeper, a
miner in a coal-pit, a railway-porter, a journeyman carpenter, the
setter-up in a skittle-alley, the steward of a steamer, a helper in
a stable, a prize-fighter, an omnibus-driver, and a gentleman's
servant. I have heard that some of these men, the coarsest,
commonest of their kind, unable to read or write, scarcely able to

speak their native tongue, have yet been gifted with powers, or have acquired habits, of mental calculation which would, if tested, somewhat astonish Mr. Bidder, ex-calculating boy, and Mr. Babbage, present constructor of figure-grinding machines, and hater of music-grinding ditto. I have heard that the word of many of these men may be taken for tens of thousands of pounds, and that, amidst an amount of trickery and roguery—not always among these coarse and common fellows from Lancashire and Whitechapel—which has brought scandal and discredit on the English turf, there are some who are strictly honest and scrupulously honourable : therein setting an example to many refined and many aristocratic frequenters of Tattersall's.

"They're a queer lot, and that's a fact," Inspector Millament remarked to Sergeant South. "How they do get along without breaking oftener than they do is a wonder to me."

"They do break sometimes, though," the Sergeant said. "There's too many of 'em, Inspector. My belief is, in horse-racing, that there's more cats than mice for 'm to catch."

"And when they do break,—when they cannot pay?" asked Simon Lefranc.

"Why, then they have to go over yonder," explained the Sergeant, pointing to an outer Babel beyond the barrier of the Stand, and where multitudes of betting-men, shabbier in attire, but with the same types of face,—oh, the very same types of face,—were exchanging yells of intelligence, and receiving yells back again, and occasionally leaping high in air to catch the eyes of those within the Ring.

"They have to go over yonder," said the Sergeant, "and make their bets as they can. It's about our time. Suppose we go out and look at 'em ; and then, if you're agreeable, Inspector and Monsieur, we'll have a little lunch. One of my men has just given me the office, and four o'clock will do very well for our little business. Unless your little party ties herself to the wing of a carrier pigeon, or telegraphs herself to London, she can't very well get away from the eyes that are watching her. This way, Monsieur."

And so the three went out among the outsiders ; each man with the fate of a human being—it may be—in his breast-pocket.

A A

CHAPTER XXVIII.

CAUGHT.

"My horse! my horse!" had cried little Mrs. Armytage from her brougham window, as "Teddy the Tyler" won by a neck. Yes; he was her horse—her favourite—the colt she would win so much money by. She could have kissed the jockey, so delighted was she. Miserable little woman! she did not see Black Care mounted behind that skilful rider as he was paraded along the course amidst the shouting crowds!

It was too late to fly. She was encompassed. The swarthy gipsy-woman who came to beg her to cross her hand with silver, and, as she laughingly held out her palm, mumbled to her about a fair young man who had gone a long journey, but who would see her again shortly, had her eye upon her. The post-boy who was regaling on the dinner drawn from her own hamper, who was devouring her own viands, and fuddling himself with her own wines, had been bribed to watch her, and did watch her, mingled liquids notwithstanding. There was an Ethiopian serenader with a straw hat and a monstrous shirt-collar, and who came and serenaded her with a broken banjo, who was appointed to spy over her. Her horses were in safe keeping, and would be harnessed only by superior order. For Florence Armytage was wanted very badly indeed, and no expense was spared for the accomplishment of the purpose certain parties held in view.

And who do you think was to have been Mrs. Armytage's cavalier on this occasion? The cavalier had not come yet. *Il se faisait attendre.* He was coming. Ah, Florence, he was coming; and he was to take her home.

There was a prodigious gathering of carriages on the Hill. Threading the maze at Hampton Court was a light and easy task compared with the labour of following the ins and outs of the close-clustered carriages. There they were, axle to axle, and pole to panel, in anything but comfortable proximity : so the gentlemen thought who had to perform acrobatic feats on the tires of wheels, and clamber over splinterbars, and, judging from landmarks or flags or tents or stands opposite, kept continually finding themselves five hundred yards away from the carriages they wished to get. The ladies were better off, for they seldom stirred from the chariots in which they throned it in dazzling state. However, everybody found his carriage at last, and then everybody went to lunch.

The first meal after a shipwreck, or the relief of a beleaguered city, is said to afford a very fair sample of the ravenous faculties of humanity. The poor Turks whom the Russian General put down to the first good dinner they had eaten for months after he had starved them out of Kars, were not reckoned bad trencher-men ; and the onslaught on the eatables at a subscription ball in the country is a sufficiently ferocious spectacle to witness. I have witnessed, too, some edifying little specimens of knife-and-fork practice at picnics. But great as is said to be the delight experienced at finding that the salt has been forgotten, and that the salad-dressing has spread itself all over the table-cloth, and has not left a drop of lubrication for the salad, a picnic is, after all, a very tame and colourless affair. The provender wants the relish, the excitement. If you can get up something like a good quarrel among the guests *en route*, it is an advantge, and makes those who haven't quarrelled fall to more heartily. But then unanimity of temper will sometimes prevail even at picnics. A thunderstorm isn't bad, or a big dog that suddenly rushes from a thicket and carries off a lobster or a leg of lamb; but these additional zests to good cheer cannot always be counted on with certainty. For real, staunch, predatory, rapacious feeding, commend me to the lunch after a great race. There is every variety of excitement to sharpen and heighten the appetite. You are out for a holiday, to begin with, and are partaking of fare to which you are not accustomed; for few people are so Apician or Luculline in their ways as to cram themselves all the year round with the good things they consume on a Derby or Ascot Cup Day. If you have won, you eat and drink tremendously, of course. If you have lost, you eat for spite and drink for despair, likewise tremendously, and equally of course. If the weather be fine, what can there be more pleasant than to see the sun making the sparkling Moselle more sparkling, and tipping the crisp lettuce-leaves with diamond sparks? If it be wet, there is some consolation in cowering under a phaeton hood to crunch chicken-bones, or gorging pigeon-pie in the *huis clos* of a drag. Then you are continually under a nervous apprehension—by no means devoid of pleasurable sensations,—that the gipsies and tramps will run away with half the things out of the hamper; that the evilly-disposed will steal the great double-handled silver tankard or champagne cup; that all the glasses will be broken, and the knives, forks, and napkins mislaid; that the post-boys—who are in a fair way already—will get hopelessly inebriated; and that everything you have eaten or drunk will disagree with you to-morrow morning. There is but one drawback to the varied excitements of a race-course lunch, and that is, to find when feeding time has arrived that your hamper has been cut away from the back of your carriage, and that, unless you choose to jostle your way to a horrible booth, into which a lady cannot enter, and where you pay half-a-crown for a bone and some beer-slops, there is no lunch and no dinner for you at all.

It may be contended that this out-of-door feeding does not develope the finer feelings of humanity. To me it seems that it developes something quite as good,—the fine old English custom of carrying your victuals with you, sitting down to eat them when you are a hungered, and letting the beggar who looks wistfully on have his share in the fragments. The merest churl will not deny a portion from his venison-pasty to a beggar-woman on Derby Day. How the ragged rogues riot in dainty flesh, and wheaten bread, and choice liquors! I say that this is an English custom. It is the good old institution of the bread-and-cheese which Hudibras carried in his sword-scabbard. It is the institution of the "parcel,"—the rich meaty packet of good things which stage-coach travellers used to carry with them, which third-class and sensible-class passengers by railway carry with them now, and which, were the fashion only followed by the first-class journeyers, would very speedily shame the proprietors

of railway refreshment-rooms into providing something better
for wayfarers than the mouldy rubbish which, at extortionate
rates, they sell now. Yes; the practice of "parcel" carrying
is purely Anglo-Saxon. Sancho Panza, I admit, had onions,
cheese, and other things in his wallet; but Sancho Panza was
wise enough to be an Englishman, and I never knew a modern
Spaniard who had anything in *his* wallet beyond a stick of chocolate and some paper and tobacco for his *cigaritos*. I have
heard of a Scottish army who, marching to the wars, was provided
each and every man with a little bag of oatmeal, and an iron plate
whereon to knead and bake it. *It was that Scottish army that won
the Battle of Bannockburn.* They may have burnt their bannocks:
but for once they beat us. Had they trusted to a commissariat,
they would have been beaten. The Highlanders who defeated
Johnny Cope at Preston Pans *had had their breakfasts*, not
"cauld kail in Aberdeen," but a hearty meal. I was reading,
the other day, Mr. Thomas Francis Meagher's vindication of the
"stampedo" of his corps at the battle of Bull's Run. "It is not
in the nature of an Irishman," pleaded Mr. Meagher, "to fight
with four or five pounds of salt pork and biscuit hanging to his
hip;" and so the Irish at Manassas threw away their rations,
and ultimately stampeded. O Thomas Francis, this was a grievous
error! I believe that it is in the nature of an Irishman to fight,
had he a whole fat pig and a barrel of biscuit on his head; but
he would fight much better with his belly full, or with the
materials for his dinner in his pouch. It was when the commons
were short that our troops came to grief in the Crimea. Directly
beef became abundant, and the porter-casks began to flow steadily,
Gortschakoff began to tremble; and to me, next to Florence
Nightingale's heroism, and Raglan's death, and the deed of that
good French General who caught up the wounded English
soldier to his saddle-bow, landed him safely, kissed his hand,
left him, and never told his name, there is nothing so simply
touching in the whole story of the Crimean War as that of the
English matrons heaping up mighty plum-puddings, and huge
pasties, and great mince-pies, and sending them far, far away
to the black Taurida, where our gallant hearts were keeping
Christmas in the teeth of the Muscovite.

Florence had quite a little court about her, although there were dozens of carriages around that were far more splendid than her own equipage. Those who saw her that day, for the last time, declared that never had she looked prettier, or been more fascinating. She was once more *La Dame au Premier*—the gay, impetuous, triumphant Lady on the First Floor, dominating all, dismayed by none; not the careworn, excited, ever-seeking, never-finding Florence Armytage that we have sometimes known in London. They were five hundred miles away from her, all those carking cares and troubles, those fears and dark suspicions of impending discovery and ruin. Bills! what did she care about bills? Forgery! who had committed forgery? She would win Lord Carnation, she thought. She would quit the life, and be good. "I'll retire on my laurels," she said to herself, with a malicious little laugh.

Retire on her laurels! Win Lord Carnation! Was there not a place in the north called Hoogendracht? was there not a place in the south called Belleriport?

"I'll win *him* too," she muttered, and she looked at her locket, as she had done in the room at Paris, and clenched her little fist; and the smile went away, but came again in an instant.

Retire on her laurels! Win the hearts of men! What had she done with Tottlepot's handwriting only the day before? The thought caused her scarcely any uneasiness. It was sure to come right, she thought. She had a strange fancy that Tottlepot would die, that Sir Jasper Goldthorpe would have a fit of apoplexy, that something would occur to secure immunity for what she had done. At other times, she would have started and shivered when the question arose stark and hideous, like a nightmare: "Florence Armytage, what is to be done?" Now she laughed, and made light of the nightmare. There was a perpetual panorama of people she knew passing, or rather dodging, along the narrow passage of which her carriage made one of the innumerable angles. Now it was courtly Doctor Sardonix, complimenting her upon her good looks, and upon her thorough restoration to health. It was a way the Doctor had of assuming that everybody had been ill, but was now looking better than ever, and that he, Dr. Sardonix, had been somehow instrumental in effecting the cure.

"But I haven't been ill at all, Doctor," Mrs. Armytage insisted.

"Tut, tut, we know, we know," the physician returned, with polite denial. "Bronchial affection at Brighton. Our little prescriptions were, I hear, remembered at Kemp and Glaisher's. The best chemists,—*the* very best chemists in the town. I shall be always happy to do anything for you that my poor skill will afford." And the Doctor was picking his way gingerly between the wheels and the servants who were regaling on the grass, when Florence, who did not care to argue the point of her fabulous illness with him any longer, called him back.

"Well, I *am* better," she admitted, "and I'm very much obliged to you, dear Doctor Sardonix. Are any of the Goldthorpes here—I mean, besides Willy? He passed me at Ewell, in a drag full of Guardsmen."

The doctor elevated his eyebrows a little at the word "drag;" but he answered with unabated urbanity.

"Sir Jasper is here; indeed it was solicitude lest my illustrious patient should in any way over exert himself that has brought me, a grave physician, little accustomed to these giddy scenes, here to-day."

This was the neatest of little fibs that was ever told by a Fellow of the College of Physicians. The Doctor had come down in a snug barouche-and-four with old Sir Jernigan Jernigan, —"Garter Jernigan" he used to be called,—who had once been valet to King George the Fourth, and had risen, nobody knew how, to be his apothecary, and his Privy Purse, and other things besides,—so the chronicle of the time said. Sir Jernigan never missed a great race. "My royal master was a patron of the turf," he said, "and I'll be one too, till old Jernigan Jernigan" —his real Christian name was John, but he had doubled the surname on promotion—"is laid with his fathers." I think it would have puzzled the heralds, to say nothing of the authorities of Lambeth parish, to discover who John Jernigan's father was.

"Sir Jasper, ah, Sir Jasper," mused Mrs. Armytage. "Any one else, Dr. Sardonix?"

"Lady Goldthorpe is here, dear madam, more in obedience to

my illustrious patient's wishes than for any pleasure she takes in this revelry. Miss Hill, I need scarcely say, is *not* here. Miss Salusbury is here, with the Earl of Carnation, and a gentleman, who, I believe ordinarily attends his Lordship in a clerical capacity, but is to-day in a lay habit."

The Doctor was right. The Earl's chaplain (who wrote his pamphlets for him) was of a decidedly sporting turn, and not altogether free from the suspicion of having gone down to Millington to see the fight between Boss Belper (the Mauleyton Pet) and Puggy Wiggins's Black for a hundred pounds a side, laying rather heavily on the darkey's colours. He generally managed to get down to the Downs without compromising himself, and on this occasion, in a shooting-coat and a wide-awake, passed all but unrecognised in the rumble of the Goldthorpe,—I mean of one of the Goldthorpe carriages. His noble patron had an indistinct idea that this wasn't quite correct in the Reverend James Feldspar, and that it wasn't philanthropic, and that kind of thing; but he was afraid of the chaplain, who was more than any one else in the secret of his Lordship's having been "over-educated for his intellect," and who might, were he driven to it, write a pamphlet against *him*. So he let him have his way.

Florence started when she heard the name of Lord Carnation. "He is sure to be this way soon," she thought. "The thing shall be done this very afternoon. He shall come back with me, for all those Goldthorpes. Yes, he shall. Am I not a widow? Ha, ha, cannot I do as I like? One moment, dear Doctor," she continued. "Have you heard what Willy Goldthorpe has done on this race? You know he bets dreadfully."

The Doctor had not heard one word about the upshot of the Captain's transactions, and he was very anxious to get back to Sir Jernigan Jernigan, who was waiting lunch for him, and was a man not to be trifled with. So he shot a good bouncing fib at what the old artillery man used to call "full random."

"As usual, the favourite of Fortune,—carrying all before him; but I *must* leave you, my dear madam. Good bye, goodbye."

And away went the Doctor, not only anxious about his lunch, but somewhat nervous of compromising himself with some of the more fastidious of his acquaintance by further parley with that delightful but inexplicable Mrs. Armytage.

"I don't believe a word that man says," she thought on her part. "How he fawns and lies, to be sure! What need is there for him to do so? They say he is both rich and clever. Edmund, you may unpack the hamper. I shall have half a dozen guests to lunch before I have eaten a mouthful. Stay, there is that man Gafferer prowling about as usual. If he sees a sign of lunch, he'll want me to give him some. Well, yes, Edmund," she continued aloud, "you may go on unpacking. Mr. Gafferer, here!"

Her little silver voice was never raised to discordant accents, but it always reached far enough. It struck at once on the tympanum of friendly George Gafferer, who was—well, not exactly prowling about, or wandering about, or sneaking about, but, we will say walking about, in the hope of being asked to lunch by somebody. George had come down alone, very early, by the rail. He had not taken a return-ticket. Somebody, he opined, would be sure to give him a cast home. And the sanguine man was right. Somebody always did.

George was always getting things for nothing. If people didn't leave him much in their wills, they at least took care that his friendly heart should be bedewed with a refreshing shower of little legacies during their lives. These came more pleasantly, as he had to pay no duty upon them. Now it was Jack Lindo, who went away to Australia and left George half the furniture in his chambers, his tiger-skin rug, and his great Turkish pipe. Now Plantagenet Rosencrantz, who had at one time been crazy after private theatricals, grew disgusted therewith, and bestowed his Hamlet and his Macbeth dresses, his stage jewelry and his broad-swords, upon friendly George Gafferer. Somebody once gave him a valuable diamond-ring—at least Mr. Attenborough's mortgage-note for the same, which would have been well nigh as valuable as the article itself, only the liberal soul who had mortgaged it forgot that it ran only for six months in lieu of a year; and so George got nothing by it, after all.

George knew Mrs. Armytage, and trembled before her. To him she was a duchess, a queen, and an empress. He had written some little words to a song she had composed. She had once asked him to an evening party. George's boon companions—he had many boon companions—used to rally him about the "pretty little widow," and tell him that he was a "lucky fellow." Then George would blush—he could blush—and chuckle. In Mrs. Armytage's presence he blushed, but did not chuckle.

"Mr. Gafferer, will you have some lunch?" the little lady asked, with a patronising nod, and without offering him her hand.

George was delighted, enchanted. He was not asked into the carriage. He sat contentedly upon a wheel, and ate and drank his fill; and then the widow said to him,

"I want to hear about Captain Goldthorpe. What has he done on the race? Tell me the truth."

Friendly George Gafferer could not certainly be accused of telling less than the truth. He always told more than the truth, an extreme which may sometimes be as dangerously inconvenient as its opposite.

"Dear, dear me," George began, shaking his friendly head. "Sad news, sad news, madam."

"What is the matter?"

"Ruin, my dear lady, ruin! Utter and irremediable ruin, unless Sir Jasper pays all. Seven-and-thirty thousand, my dear madam. Fifteen thousand three hundred to a biscuit-baker in Orchard-street, Portman-square. They say the Captain laid ten-pound notes to fourpenny-pieces on Jumping Jemmy."

"What is Jumping Jemmy? A man or a horse?"

"A horse, my dear madam; a dreadful bright bay creature, with long legs, and a star on the forehead. They say that good was never known to come out of a horse with a star on the forehead. This 'Jumping Jemmy' has been the ruin of half the young men about town."

"And William Goldthorpe is ruined, then?"

"As ruined as a young man with his magnificent prospects can be."

"What do you know about his prospects, and whether they are magnificent or not?"

"I only know what I hear, and what everybody talks about. Extravagant as he has been, Sir Jasper will hardly allow his son's

name to be compromised. But it's not only in horse-flesh that
the poor captain's dipped."

" What, can there be anything else ?" exclaimed Mrs. Armytage,
who knew perhaps about five hundred times more than George
Gafferer what William Goldthorpe's embarrassments really were,
and what means he had of getting rid of them. " For goodness'
sake, dear Mr. Gafferer, tell me all about it."

" Ah, dear me, madam, it would take hours ; but, at all events,
I can tell you this much, that——"

Just as George was commencing a fresh lamentable revelation,
William Goldthorpe himself, with Lord Groomporter and one
or two kindred spirits, came up, certainly looking very disconsolate.

" Thank you," said Mrs. Armytage to George. It was impossible for her to say in plainer terms, " Go away." The friendly
man took the hint. He was only too glad to have been in her
society even for a few minutes, and to have refreshed himself with
her hospitality. So he went away rejoicing, hoping that somebody
had seen him, and would rally and envy him for having been seen
sitting on the pretty little widow's carriage-wheel. A contented
spirit was friendly George Gafferer, and his pleasures were very
cheap.

Florence was very eager to know the extent of the Captain's
losses ; but she could not elicit any very definite information from
him. The young man was sulky, and said that he had had a
" doose of a bad time of it," and that there would be " a doose of
a blow-up with the governor." He did not respect Mrs. Armytage
quite enough to speak to her as ladies are accustomed to be spoken
to. Then Groomporter was with him, and his lordship, who was
the best-dressed and the most habitually tipsy young peer in
England, was already very far gone in iced wines ; and on being
asked what might be offered to him, replied in a voice somewhat
thick and husky that he should like some " braiorsoawarr," by
which it is to be presumed that Viscount Groomporter meant
brandy and soda-water. Very wealthy, very young, exceedingly
good-natured, was Viscount Groomporter. He was always a good
friend to the people who were his greatest enemies : forgave
Captain de Loos three months after the trial at which it was

proved that the disreputable captain had forged his name, and
positively sent him money to Kissingen to enable him to go
salmon-fishing in Norway. Viscount Groomporter was, I have
observed, one of the best-dressed noblemen in the peerage. His
blue surtout with the velvet collar, his scarf, his pin, his white hat,
were perfection. Dandies sighed in vain to know the address of
his trousers-maker, or of the artist who modelled those boots so
carefully to his feet. When people saw him, superlatively attired,
gloved, handkerchiefed, say about three in the afternoon, going up
the steps of Pall Mall, their first impulse was one of admiration
to see such a well-looking, well-dressed young gentleman; their
next was one of astonishment that his eyes should be so bloodshot,
and his gait so unsteady. For Viscount Groomporter was precisely that which Oliver Cromwell declared Charles the Second to
be, and what the reticence of the nineteenth century forbids me
to repeat. In truth, his lordship was incorrigible, and his thirty
thousand a year seemed to have a fair chance of being submerged
in "braiorsoawarr."

There was not much, as you see, to be gleaned by Florence from
the conversation of these young patricians. They were, besides,
anxious to be after their own devices,—throwing at sticks, conversing with the occupants of broughams far more equivocal than
that of the Indian widow, wandering among the booths, and so
forth,—and she let them go. She shook hands, however, with
William Goldthorpe; and when the young man found his hand
released, there was a bank-note in it crumpled up.

"Don't look at it," whispered Mrs. Armytage hurriedly;
"never mind what it is. Keep it till you get away from here, and
then spend it. It'll pay for something."

"But I can't, Mrs. Armytage," the Captain murmured hesi-
tatingly, blushing up to the tips of his ears.

"Yes, you can. Am I not a soldier's widow? Mayn't I do
what I like with my own? There, get along with you after your
friends. *Bon jour.*" And so dismissed him.

Her own! She had assuredly never come honestly by that
money; but she had nevertheless given him a bank-note for fifty
pounds, and she had given it him in pure good nature and sympathy for his misfortunes. As he retreated she put her head out

of the carriage-window, and, not for the first time, whispered softly to herself,

"Poor fellow, how like Hugh he is!"

As she drew her head back, she found the door on the other side open. As she turned her face in surprise towards it, she found the figure of a man standing in the aperture. He was stout and of good stature; he was about fifty years of age. She had met him the night before; but she did not recognise him as Count somebody, with a full moustache and whisker and a curly black wig, who was the affable guest of the Baroness de la Haute Gueuse. She recognised in him instead the man with a face impudent as that of a jack-pudding, a *paillasse*, who had leered at her so audaciously from the coffee-room window of the Chambers in Soho. But both the Jack-pudding and the Paillasse wore their heart upon their sleeve, and both were Simon Lefranc.

"The saucy fellow!" she cried in easy indignation, and extended her hand to close the door and shut the intruder out. But another hand came forth,—the hand of which the sleeve had the heart upon it; and Florence Armytage's wrist was suddenly caught in a grip like that of steel.

She knew the worst had come. Her disengaged hand sought, quick as lightning, her side. There should have been nestling there, in an embroidered pouch, the tiny revolver, without which she never travelled. It was her custom to assure herself of its presence at least twice in an hour. This verification had become a habit. The pistol had been safe twenty minutes since; but I think the swarthy gipsey who had told her about the fair young man who was gone on a journey knew something of the embroidered pouch and its pretty, murderous contents.

"The little dog that barks is gone away," whispered Simon Lefranc. "Florence Armytage, you are my prisoner. *Veuve Armytage, se servant de plusieurs noms et prénoms faux. De par la République, une et indivisible, et par mandat d'amener sous seing officiel, je vous arrête.*"

"I took her," said Simon subsequently to his chief, "with all the formalities. It was charming."

She saw that all was over. She did not faint, but her face was the colour of bleached wax; and had any been privileged to place

their hands between her shoulder-blades, they would have found
a cold dew there. Her knees knocked together; her hand
quivered like a bird in the thief-catcher's grip; but she did not
faint. Not she.

"What is it?" she asked? "what is it for?"

"Murder, burglary, and forgery. You know as well as I do.
Ah, *ma mie, je t'accroche à la longue.*"

Florence's postboy's duty was quite over, and he was asleep
comfortably under the carriage-pole, with his head in a salad-bowl.
Three intelligent foreigners stood before the window opposite to
Simon. They had drawn the blinds down. Nothing could have
been better managed—it was charming.

The policeman got into the carriage, and sat down close to
Mrs. Armytage's side. She shrank away from him shuddering,
but made no effort to scream or to resist.

"We will have the other blind down, so; that is nice and comfortable," Simon remarked, suiting the action to the word. "You
are not afraid of being alone with Papa Lallouet in this *crépuscule,*
eh, *ma petite?*"

Simon Lefranc had many names; Florence knew him by this
one. She had often heard of, but never seen, the dreaded personage whom for years she had started at in her sleep. Papa
Lallouet was called the *Parrain de la Guillotine,* but I prefer still
to call him Simon Lefranc, the man who wore his heart upon his
sleeve.

"Which will you do?" he asked. "Will you make a fuss,—a
tintamarre,—and oblige me to have you carried away by the
English police, and before an English magistrate, to have your
warrant of extradition read, and be publicly consigned to my cus-
tody? or will you go away quietly with Papa Lallouet, like a good
little girl, as you ought to be? If you accompany me of your
own free will, it will save all the *esclandre* of an examination in a
police-court; and we can be as happy as two turtle-doves till we
get home."

She had reason indeed to be afraid of the publicity of her arrest
in England. Five hundred creditors—five hundred people whom
she had defrauded, robbed, forged upon—would read the story of
her crimes, and rush forward to be confronted with and to identify

her. It was better, she thought, now the worst had come to the worst, to go with this man. She knew that in France she had a certain Influence, and with the hand that was not a captive she felt her soft neck, and thought, "At least this is safe."

"Don't be too sure," said Simon, who even in the gloom had marked her movement, and seemed to divine her thought. "Remember, it is *assassinat*—what the English law calls wilful murder —that I arrest you for. You go with me without promise or condition on my part. Make up your mind, or the English police will come to my help."

"Do they know of my fate?" she asked.

"They know everything; but the thing is arranged. They could get a dozen warrants for your arrest on charges for all you have done here in England by ten o'clock to-morrow morning."

"And, pray, what have I done here, Monsieur Lallouet?" the wretched little creature, with a touch of her old disdain and her old impertinence, interposed.

"Ta, ta, ta!" the police agent replied. "Don't try to put me off my guard, you little crocodile. I am too old *pour conter sornettes*. What have you done in England? What have you not done? Do you think that we, of the Rue de Jerusalem, have not kept the history of your life and adventures by double entry, *en partie double*, these five years past? We know all about you, *ma petite bonne femme*:—how you have lied and cheated and swindled; how you have stolen and forged; how you have perhaps done worse things,—for which you will have to sit on the benches of the *cour d'assises*."

"I will go with you," Mrs. Armytage murmured, and with a gesture of despair.

"Very well; but, remember, it is murder. *On n'y ricane pas en France, ma belle*."

"I am innocent," she answered. "Besides—" She halted; but her hand sought her neck again, and, with a smile,—a ghastly smile, almost the last that ever visited those now livid lips,—she thought, "Ah! I have still one Influence left. They will never guillotine poor little Me."

"In that case," pursued Simon Lefranc, "we will wait quietly and comfortably with the blinds down until such time as we can got away. In this throng nobody, without some distinguishing mark, will be able to recognise your carriage. Are you content ? "

She shrugged her shoulders.

"Silence gives consent. Permit me, then, to trouble you ;" and Simon Lefranc slipped the neatest little handcuff in the world over Florence's wrist, on which he had not for one moment loosened his hold. The handcuff was attached by a ring to another of larger size, and this Simon slipped over his own wrist, cheerfully humming a little tune the while. " *Là, nous voilà dans les menottes*," he said. " Not quite so comfortable perhaps as your diamond-bracelets ; but still I hope this little ornament does not hurt you."

She never answered.

" Go to sleep, *ma petite*," Simon paternally advised, " or think about your defence for the day of trial. If I were you, I would retain Maître Paillet, or at least Chaix d'Estange. There, you shall be treated like a lady, and have the best to eat and drink till we are safe at home. I can't take you across the Channel handcuffed like this; but you shall be carried on board the steamer at Dover as a lady very sick. You *are* very sick. We will have you nicely wrapped up in shawls and blankets, so that nobody will see the bright little bracelets which we will take the liberty of placing round your wrists and round your ancles."

She heard, but she let the man have his say, and answered him naught. She was thinking. She was in the toils. What mattered it if the net round her were tight or loose ? They had got her, and might lead her along as they chose.

She closed her eyes, and, strange as it may seem, experienced something like a relaxation of anxiety, something that approached comparative relief and ease. Naturalists have surmised that a feeling somewhat analogous may be experienced by the hunted hare, the hopelessly beset deer, when there is not one chance more left, when the hounds are close at hand, and there is nothing more left but to lie down and die. She had been hunted and harried so long ; so many years had elapsed since she first began to sleep with her eyes open—to start at every shadow, to fancy every bush an officer, to be continually and perpetually in dread

of discovery and seizure—that the mere reaction now soothed her.
There was nothing more to fly from, no more lies to tell, no more
stratagems to devise, no more gulfs to bridge over. So, at least,
she thought. So it might be, if she chose. Should she plead
guilty to all that was brought against her, and let them use her
as they pleased? She experienced an indefinable reluctance to
concoct any story for her defence, to employ any means for ex-
tricating herself from her deadly peril. To-morrow, next week,
next month, next year—would do for all that, she seemed to think.
It was a matter that concerned her lawyers. She would have to
employ lawyers, she supposed. There was plenty of time for
that—plenty of time for all. She was drowsy with doing evil.
She was tired with crime. She wanted rest. The thing was bad
enough, certainly; but it could not be much worse, and it was a
relief to know that the storm which had so long blackened the
sky had burst.

And while her mind refused to dwell with any intensity on her
present situation, or the circumstances which had led to it, it
returned over and over again to her early youth—to the days
when she was young and happy and—God help her!—innocent.
She was saying the old lessons, playing at the same childish games,
romping about the same playground, dancing at her first party,
reading her first love-letter, starting on her first voyage to
India.

She had been in captivity about half an hour—it seemed to
have been ten years—when a discreet tap came against the glass
of the window nearest to Simon Lefranc. The police-agent drew
it down, and inclined his bullet-head to hear what was spoken to
him from without; but, at the same time, he contrived to throw
a cloak between him and his prisoner so dexterously and in folds
so thick as to muffle any sound that might pass between that
window and her ear.

It was Inspector Millament who had tapped at the window.
The roar of the Babel outside first wafted through the aperture,
and let Florence know of its vicinage; but the Inspector was an
adept at whispering, and not a word that he uttered could reach
her through the heavy mass of drapery.

"Have you got your bird?" he asked.

" *Oui, mon vieux.* I have, my dear friend," responded Simon. "She fluttered her wings a little at first; but she is quiet and peaceable as a dove, now."

"There is no necessity for our services, then?"

"Not the least. All will be managed without publicity and scandal, which can only defeat the ends of justice. In fifteen hours she will be safe in Paris."

"She is wanted very badly here, more by person than by name; and when she is tried, she will be sure to be recognised by some one who knew her in England, and it will all come out."

"Let it. We have our instructions, and act by them. If you like, I kidnapped her, and got her across the Channel without your knowing anything about it. *On n'y regardera pas de si près, à Paris.* His chiefs will bear Papa Lallouet out, and say to Simon Lefranc, ' My son, thou hast done well.' "

"Well, you know best. I wish you joy of your capture. She's worth having. You Frenchmen have certainly a very neat way of doing business. If it had been our duty to take her, there would have been a row, and lots of screaming, and a mob. The whole thing would have been known in five minutes, and half-a-dozen 'gentlemen of the press,' as they call themselves, would have been pestering me with questions, and rushing off to the station to telegraph the news to London."

"Yes," Simon observed with a quiet grin, " she is indeed worth having. She is a pearl beyond price. She will be worth my *retraite,* my retiring pension to me, monsieur, all the more surely as I have taken her quietly. For we want to pluck a few little feathers off our pigeon before she is ready to be trussed and roasted, and served up at the table of Madame la Justice. A dainty morsel, *ma foi;* ha, ha!"

He laughed quietly enough, but still in a tone loud enough to make his victim start uneasily. He gave her handcuffed wrist a warning shake, and in a savage undertone muttered "Be quiet!" and she was still as she was mute.

"And you," Simon continued, turning again to the Inspector, "Have you done your business? Have you caged *your* birds?"

"Most extraordinary thing, we haven't," returned Inspector

Millament, in a tone of disappointment. "Journey down for nothing; and I'd such a sweet little bit of business cut out for me in Bergen-op-Zoom Terrace, Bayswater! However, we've had the pleasure of your company, and seen your way of doing business."

"Truly, you flatter me. The pleasure is, believe me, mutual. But how have you missed your game? It was well watched enough. Has Sir Jasper Goldthorpe got away?"

"No; his carriage and party are within fifty yards of us; but within a minute of your leaving comes down a telegraphic message to us to hold over all our warrants against him, leave off watching him even, and come back to town."

"He is still very rich, perhaps, and very powerful, and has influential friends."

"There's no man in England," retorted the vexed Inspector, "powerful enough to step between a criminal and his prosecutors when informations have once been sworn, and a warrant has once been granted. We don't do things in a corner or in the dark here, monsieur. 'Fair and above board' is our motto. I was to have taken him here, and I ought to have taken him here, and it's deuced provoking."

The true Englishman spoke in Inspector Millament. All detective policeman as he was, and accustomed to track his prey very much in the manner of a sleuth hound, he would have been shocked to learn that any of his prisoners—"customers," as he called them—had been arrested without all due legal formalities being observed; or that, after capture, they had been deprived of any legal means of defence. And, moreover, Inspector Millament was mortal. Though he railed at the "gentlemen of the press," he was not insensible to the flattering notices frequently bestowed on his sagacity and acumen by the newspaper reporters, and ranked in the highest class of literary composition those wondrously-spun paragraphs in which the "skilful recapture of an escaped convict," or the "extraordinary detection of a bank-robbery," or the "clever discovery of a fugitive bankrupt," was ascribed to the pluck and energy of Sergeant South, or the zeal tempered with discretion of Mr.—they always gave him the Mister—Mr. Inspector Millament.

The baffled Inspector was preparing to take leave of Simon, when there came pressing through the throng Sergeant South, beckoning hastily to his superior. The Inspector closed the window; Simon drew the blind down, and they were once more in the gloom again.

But not for long. Florence heard the clanking of a chain, the lumbering of the carriage-pole, the shouts and curses of drivers and post-boys who were being made to move their vehicles on one side by the police. She strained her ears to catch some words; but the din of minstrels and niggers with their music, and the roaring of the stick-throwing, and the brawlers and the chaffers and the roysterers, made up only one harsh humming noise, and she could distinguish nothing.

Let us pass for the moment from the interior of that silken prison to the outside. It has always been to me a marvel of marvels how ever people manage to get a carriage off the Hill on a great race-day without smashing five hundred coach-panels, and crushing five thousand toes. It is done somehow. There are always people who want to leave early, and they manage to leave and get clear of the labyrinth of wheels, and drive away through the grinning, scampering crowd; but the operation is nevertheless astounding. So, in youth, were these four puzzling and bewildering things to me: first, to know how a ship got into a dock, and how she got out of dock, without being stove in at some stage or another; next, to know how ever the great Duke of Wellington, in extreme old age, managed to get on his horse, and, finally, how he contrived to get off it.

The four posters brought down by Mrs. Armytage were in due time, that is to say, after a good long lapse of it, harnessed to the carriage. The post-boy, who was tipsy, had disappeared; so had his comrade, not much superior to him, it must be admitted, in sobriety. Their places were supplied by two new postillions of great gravity of countenance, and who were thoroughly impervious to the witticisms of the road. As the carriage, with the blinds still down, was painfully manœuvred out of the ruck of its surroundings, at least half a dozen mounted policemen showed themselves exceedingly active in directing its movements and clearing the way; conspicuous among them was the Superintendent who had spoken to Millament and his companions on the course.

The throng had of course their jest at the fact of the blinds of the carriage being so closely drawn down, and various opinions were hazarded as to the occupants having taken a little more than was good for them. Derisive cries were heard of "Didn't it agree with you?" "Never mind if your head aches!" "Come out and have some fresh air!" Then soda-water corks and farthing dolls were playfully thrown against the windows; then the post-boys were recommended to "go gently over the stones;" then it was surmised that there was a lady inside with a "wicked old marquis," who was adjured to "come out and show hisself." But there is an end to everything, even to getting off the Hill at Epsom. Away the carriage and its occupants went at last. Away from the booths and the gipsy-tents, the hucksters' stalls, the temporary stables. Away from the mad medley of lords and ladies, gamblers, *roués*, thieves, fools, grooms, hostlers, gipsies, beggars, policemen, mountebanks, and vagrant children.

There was an open barouche to which the horses were being put, and which was full of the Daughters of Folly, all blazing in paint and jewellery, and rich silks and laces. The poor creatures within were half uproarious and half fractious with champagne. A knot of dissipated young men were lounging over this carriage, perched on wheels and box and rumble, and bandying about loose talk and silver tankards. Among them, I am sorry to say, were Captain Goldthorpe, already half consoled for his losses, and Viscount Groomporter, who was growing more and more flushed as to his countenance, and less and less steady as to his legs.

The carriage came thudding by on the soft turf, and the young nobleman seeing it cried,

"Why, Goldie, isn't that your friend Mrs. A.'s trap?"

The dragoon looked and saw that it was.

"What's she going away so early for?"

"Because she chooses, I suppose, Groomporter."

"Yes,"—I am afraid his Lordship pronounced the affirmative "yesh;"—"but what has she got the blinds down for?"

"She may be tired; she may have some one with her that she doesn't care about being seen with."

"Goldie," pursued Viscount Groomporter, with much tipsy gravity, "my opinion is, that the little widow's very spoons upon you."

The Captain, remembering the fifty-pound note, which, by the way, had been nearly doubled since he received it by a lucky draw in a sweepstakes on one of the minor races, blushed, and was silent.

The curtained carriage drove away, and all association between Florence Armytage and the British aristocracy faded away forever. She was thoroughly worn out, and fell into a sleep. Simon Lefranc was not at all surprised to see her slumber. Had he not, in his time, watched murderers sleeping in the condemned cell the very night before their execution, galley-slaves reposing on their hard deal boards? "Why shouldn't she sleep, if she's tired? and tired enough I dare say she is," quoth Simon Lefranc to himself.

The carriage was driven along the most sequestered roads that the postillions could hit upon, in order to avoid as much as possible the noise and confusion inseparable, as it would seem, from coming home after a great race; yet with the minutest precautions, and following bye-lane after bye-lane, they could not help coming from time to time upon some carriage filled with choice spirits, who roared, and laughed, and "chaffed," and gave many other unmistakable signs of the wine being in and the wit being out. Comparatively early as they had started, they took so many *détours* that it was ten o'clock at night before they came to Clapham Common.

When Florence Armytage woke for the first time, which was after about an hour's rest, she found that the carriage had halted, and that the door was half open, with a man—not Simon, he had not yet stirred from her side—standing thereat. A cup of tea was handed to her, which she drank greedily—as she would have drunk anything, from prussic acid to curaçoa. It must have been very good tea, and very strong tea; for she went to sleep again five minutes after she had emptied the cup, and did not wake for full three hours afterwards.

Then she woke thoroughly, and found, to her amazement, that Simon Lefranc was no longer with her, and that her wrist was manacled to that of a woman. A little swinging lamp had been lit; and she could see that she had yet another travelling companion, a woman who sat opposite to her.

She started, and would have screamed. The looks of these two women terrified her ten thousand times more than the policeman had done. Her terror was increased when the woman to whom she was handcuffed bade her to "give them none of her nonsense, for if she did she should be gagged." She bowed her head, and spake no more till London was reached, and her new life commenced.

CHAPTER XXIX.

In the first place, people said in the City, and knew it for a fact, that the Bank of England had raised its rate of discount. The tightening of that financial screw, of course, had immediately produced a corresponding tightness in the money market. Money was no longer to be had on easy terms "in the street;" —I wish that I knew when it was to be had on easy terms in the houses;—holders were firm, and wouldn't look even at the best of paper. Merchants reputed wealthy came with gloomy countenances out of the parlours of the great discount houses in Lombard and Throgmorton Streets, their still unnegotiated securities in their pockets. Things, to be brief, did not look at all well in the City.

Things looked up the next day a little; then they looked straightforward; then sideways; then down again, and worse than ever. There could not be a panic, there could not be a crash, people said, because, you see, there had never been so much money in the country, or so many visitors in London Trade was flourishing; gold was coming in from California; mechanics and labourers were in full work; many of the great houses which had begun to falter and tremble a little gradually recovered themselves. The Bank screw was relaxed; the merchants reputed wealthy went into Lombard Street parlours with hopeful, and came out with joyful, countenances; the Stock Exchange resumed its wonted joviality; there were no shadows but one—a great black Shadow it was—where money-mongers most do congregate. Peace and prosperity in the world, commercial and financial, seemed to be returning, and yet,—things did not look at all well in the City.

Things had their worst aspect; the **great Shadow** had its

blackest hue, and hung like an imminent pall in and over a place called Beryl Court. People—that is, the people who were supposed to know a thing or two—talked all day long about Beryl Court, and about Mammon, the proprietor and potentate thereof. And, while they talked, it was curious to mark that they did not seem to know on what particular peg to hang their conversation. They fastened, of course, as a preliminary peg upon Sir Jasper Gold-thorpe: but the baronet was convalescent; he had been to the Derby; he was at business the next day, and in the evening was to give a grand dinner-party to certain illustrious foreigners, then sojourning in the British metropolis. The banquet was to be followed by a grand ball. It was during the day of which this was to be the triumphant conclusion that people in the City talked most about Sir Jasper Goldthorpe.

Who were those people? I cannot with certainty determine, any more than I can fix with exactitude upon him who first states authoritatively that Consols shall be ninety-seven and an eighth ; that French Three per Cents. shall be sixty-five and a quarter. Some-body must say so in the first instance, of course, in deference, per-haps, to somebody else. Somebody else agrees with him; a third assentient adds his voice, and the quotation of the Funds is stricken.

But it may have been in Cornhill or in Capel Court, in Lombard or Old Broad Street, that a White Waistcoat (corpu-lent) brushes against a Blue Frock-coat (sparely built). To them enter a Drab Felt Hat; and a Brown Silk Umbrella with an ivory handle makes up a fourth.

Says White Waistcoat, " I hear for a certainty that it's all over with him."

"You don't say so," ejaculates Blue Frock-coat. "It's true I did hear some very queer rumours at the club this morning."

"He can't last twenty-four hours. He *must* go ; I know it for a fact," Brown Silk Umbrella adds, giving himself a thwack on the pavement.

"That's bad," joins in Drab Hat; "and, to tell the truth, I've heard a good deal about it myself since yesterday afternoon. They say it's been a long time coming. He was always a close custo-mer, and kept things pretty snugly to himself; but the truth will ooze out somehow."

"Ah," remarks White Waistcoat, "he'd better have taken partners."

"He never would, though," Drab Hat continues, shaking a shrewd head inside it. "They might have known a great deal too much about the affairs of the House to be quite convenient."

"How much will he go for?"

"A couple of millions at least."

"Say a million and a half."

"I'll bet it's over two, and that there won't be half-a-crown in the pound assets. There never is in these great paper-crashes. Money will make money of itself, just by turning itself over; but when paper goes to the bad, it doesn't leave enough revenue to light a rushlight with."

"What's the secret? What has he been doing? He's been in no great speculations in our market lately."

"You don't know how many hundred he's been at the bottom of, and behind the scenes of. He was always such an old Slyboots. They say he bolstered up the Luffbury Bank for years."

"Ah! I've heard that. He had something to do, too, with Jubson's patents for raising wrecks with spun-glass cables."

"That big mill that was burnt down at Rochdale in May, and wasn't insured, was his property, so I've heard."

"Hadn't he something to do with the Inland Heliogabalus Docks in Paris?"

"Don't know; but I'm sure he had the concession of the Montevidean Railway. I saw it in *Galignani*. You know, the one that was to join the General South and Central American Trunk Line;—tunnel under Chimborazo, and run a branch to Tehucantepec."

"Ah! that was a nice little spec; to say nothing of the Ulululu copper-mines."

"And the Pitcairn's Island Packet-service."

"And the loan to the Republic of Prigas."

"And the quicksilver affair in Barataria."

"And the Grand Lama of Tibet's Lottery."

"And the Polar Circle Tallow-melting and Ice-preserving Company."

"Pshaw! any one of these things might have turned up trumps,"—it was Silk Umbrella who spoke;—"it's all touch and go. It isn't that rock he's split upon. It's paper! Giving good money for bad bills, and lending huge sums to Houses that never existed."

"And borrowing bigger sums to pay the interest," opines White Waistcoat.

"It isn't that," breaks in Drab Hat, shaking the shrewd head inside again. "I'll tell you what it is. *It's Austria.*"

"Austria!"

"Yes, Austria. Who lent the ready cash for the Austrians to get Lombardy back again, taking a million Cremona fiddles as security, which turned out to be Lowther Arcade ones? Goldthorpe's House. Who kept up the war in Hungary, and was promised a lien on the crown of St. Stephen, till Kossuth ran away with it? Goldthorpe's House. Who filled the military chest for the Austrians who garrisoned Leghorn? Who contracted for the new fortifications at Venice and Mantua? Who kept the Tyrol in order, and took the Archduchess Sophia's jewels out of pawn? Who, if he hadn't been sniffing after an English peerage, which he'll never get, and if he hadn't been—more's the shame—an Englishman, would have liked to go to Vienna, and be made a German baron of? I say, Goldthorpe's House, and Jasper Goldthorpe; and if he smashes to-day, it's his own fault for a fool, and the Austrian government's for a pack of rogues."

"But they may cash up," interposes Silk Umbrella.

"Cash up! They'll never cash up a farthing-piece; I know them of old, sir. They're on the verge of bankruptcy. To my certain knowledge Austria—"

But I will not be so cruel to the reader as to repeat in detail all that the Drab Hat (who is in the Russia Trade, by-the-bye) has to say about Austria. He is the greatest authority extant as to the ways and means of that chronically embarrassed empire. It is edifying, but terrific, to hear him on Austrian finance. He is the only English politician who reads the *Œsterreichische Zeitung* in the original. He is great upon the by-gone horrors of the Spielburg; upon the wrongs of Silvio Pellico; upon the whipping of Madame de Maderspach; upon the execution of Ciceroacchio and Ugo Bassi. Austria is his bugbear, his nightmare. He is Prometheus with a double-headed eagle gnawing at his vitals. They say at his Club that it is for his sole use and benefit that the daily press entertain long-winded correspondents at Vienna; and, at all events, this is beyond doubt, that in all places save City marts and exchanges, where, being immensely wealthy, he is an oracle, and listened to with reverence, he is generally known as "the Austrian bore." In club reading-room, at social dinner-table, in gay saloon, people shudder and gather themselves up, and if possible fly from the face of this insatiate Austromane. Hence he likes the City much better than the West End, and thinks of becoming a member of a Club in Old Broad Street, and taking his name off the books in Pall Mall. "Would you believe it," he says to Silk Umbrella, "that only yesterday, as I was trying to explain the history of the Aulic Council to Dr. Scoggles at the Bonassus, that impudent fellow, Scanderbeg, who's only a literary man, and hasn't got a penny in the world, told me that he wished the Aulic Council was at Jericho!"

White Waistcoat, Silk Umbrella, Blue Frock-coat, Drab Hat, all of them go their several ways, and by-and-by form into other groups with other articles of raiment with human beings within them; and the rumour swells and swells, and is a rolling stone that gathers moss, and a snowball that grows bigger, and an avalanche that comes tumbling, and a cataract that comes splashing, and a thunder-cloud that bursts, and a volcano that vomits forth its lava and sends up its scoriæ, and a tempest that tears up the golden trees by the roots and scathes the silver plains, and an earthquake that yawns sudden and tremendous, and engulfs Mammon and his millions for ever.

"Have you heard the news," friendly George Gafferer asks Tom Soapley,—with whom he is most intimate and friendly, and whom he cordially hates,—"have you heard the news, my dearest chick?"

It is half-past two o'clock in the afternoon, and George, who has always some "business" in the City, although neither he nor anybody else can tell what it is, has looked in at the Bay-

Tree in quest of a chop and a glass of sherry, and finds Soapley there on the same errand.

" What news ? "

"The great house of Goldthorpe has stopped payment,—stopped payment ! gone to utter, hopeless smash ! Sir Jasper Goldthorpe's cut his throat—his own throat, my chick ; Lady Goldthorpe poisoned herself with naphtha—no, camphine—out of a lamp. Sir Jasper's ward—you know—Miss Hill,—all her savings are swallowed up ; and they say that the head clerk in Beryl Court has bolted with ninety thousand, and that before Sir Jasper committed suicide he tried to set fire to the house in Onyx Square, only the flames were extinguished by Dr. Sardonix and the under-butler. And he was at the race only yesterday, looking better than ever, and was to have given a grand dinner and ball this evening, to which I was invited. I've got the card, as big as a pancake, at home, my dear chick."

" I don't believe it," Soapley returns.

" Sir ! " George exclaims, drawing himself up.

" I don't mean about the invitation,—I was invited myself " (both are lying),—" but the smash. I *can't* believe it, my dear Mr. Gatherer ;" Soapley never condescended to familiarity with his rival, and was always profoundly obsequious to him. " Sir Jasper Goldthorpe's position is too high in the City of London, his fortune is too ample, his means are too vast, for such a disaster to overtake him,—that is, taking human probabilities into consideration. Let us not, therefore, on the faith of an idle rumour rashly assume—"

" Idle rumour ! rashly assume ! " cries George in amazement. " Why, it's as well known as the Royal Exchange. It's in the second edition of the *Times*."

Soapley knows well enough that the intelligence of the catastrophe is to be found in the second issue of the morning journal. He has seen it perhaps before George ; but it is Soapley's policy to deny all the rumours he has heard, and half the news. They may be contradicted, he reckons. There are such things as blunders, false statements, and hoaxes. The very opposite to what has been written or rumoured may be published to-morrow ; and then the parties interested may say, " Such and such a report was flying about town, and the only man who wouldn't believe it was Tom Soapley. Shrewd dog!" By which means Thomas hopes, some day, to get made something by somebody.

There was a considerable admixture of the fabulous in Gafferer's budget of intelligence, and not a tithe of what his idle tongue gave currency to had appeared in the paper; but in two particulars he was correct. The great house of Goldthorpe was bankrupt, and Magdalen Hill was a beggar.

CHAPTER XXX

THE walls of Beryl Court, like those of Balclutha, were desolate. That *feu d'enfer* at Sebastopol, of which Menschikoff wrote
such rueful accounts to his Emperor, was a mere popgun cannon-
ade compared with the devastating bombardment of Bankruptcy.
A fiat from Basinghall Street is like a trumpet, blowing down
the walls of Jericho, commercial and financial, in an instant.
No pantomimic change that Farley or Bradwell ever dreamt of
is half so rapid as that which takes place when a great merchant's
house is turned out of windows. 'Tis the old story of Aladdin's
palace over again. The inestimable old, albeit rusty, lamp has
been incautiously exchanged—beware of people who cry things
in the street—for a bran-new, tawdry, utterly worthless affair ;
and, presto, away goes palace, and down comes Aladdin, like
Humpty Dumpty from the top of his wall.

It was speedily manifest that not all the king's horses nor all
the king's men could ever set Sir Jasper Goldthorpe up again.
His fall had been too violent; the Smash was too great. A wise
man has said, that the success of the wicked resembles only the
progress of some wretch urged towards the summit of the Tar-
peian rock to be ruinously flung therefrom. I leave for the
moment the question of Mammon's wickedness or virtue in abey-
ance. I only look at him as he lies, bleeding, mangled, crushed
out of all solvent semblance, at the bottom of the precipice, to
the brink of which he clomb so arrogantly.

Where Mammon had been only yesterday absolute,—supreme,
well-nigh, in his earthly way, and among his earthly vassals
omnipotent,—a Messenger in Bankruptcy now held undisputed
sway. The Emperor was nowhere. He had been beaten; he
had abdicated ; his throne was vacant. The Messenger was the

Provisional Government. He appointed a provisional ministry, and took provisional command of the remaining finances. *Le Roi était mort;* but the kingly line was extinct, and there was no new sovereign to shout *" Vive le roi !"* for. The Messenger in Bankruptcy was a pleasant man in a Marseilles waistcoat, and with a bald pate so polished, that when he took off his hat the birds might have used his shining occiput for a mirror, and plumed themselves by its reflection. The Messenger netted a comfortable salary of two or three thousand a year by getting other people to execute his messages. He was a high Tory, and spent a portion of his earnings in the maintenance of a moribund, but highly orthodox, Church and State newspaper, of which the last proprietor had been a Unitarian, and the last but one a converted Jew. The *Morning Mitre*—thus was the Messenger's journal called—has since been sold, the True-Blue Club refusing to advance any more money for its support. It is now edited by a gentleman of Mormon tendencies, and is said to be the sub-sidised organ of the Turkish government,—since the black ambassador from Hayti wouldn't have anything to do with it,—but it is as orthodox and as Conservative as ever.

So the Messenger put his merry men into Beryl Court, and accountants began to range through the extensive library of ledgers, cash-books, journals, and so forth, in which the prodigious transactions of Goldthorpe and Co. were recorded. I am advancing matters if I speak of meetings for the choice of assignees, certificate discussions, and similar preliminaries to the great five-act drama of fivepence in the pound. I am now but at the morrow of the disaster; but was it fivepence, or was it nothing at all in the pound, that Goldthorpe's estate, after seven years' delay, rendered to the creditors?

Goldthorpe's estate! That now became the misty, hazy semi-entity into which the countless treasures of Mammon had resolved themselves. Everything now belonged to the "estate," and seemed to wither and grow blighted under the baneful influence of Basinghall Street. The marble fronted palace in Beryl Court seemed suddenly afflicted with the same leprosy that is said to have attacked the stonework of the New Houses of Parliament. Of course the people whose business it was left off cleaning the

windows, sweeping the door-step, and polishing the brass-plate.
The muddy highlows of the Messenger's merry men made tesse-
lations for themselves on the pavement of the entrance-hall. Bits
of straw,—however is it that bits of straw seem indissolubly connected with every case in bankruptcy?—began to be noticed
about the Court, and even in offices and ante-chambers. The
merry men belonging to the Messenger chewed bits of straw continually. The trim servitors, who were wont to glide about so
noiselessly and so obediently on the behests of Mammon and the
heads of his departments, suddenly disappeared, and were replaced,
no one knew how or why, by an inconceivable female of great but
uncertain age, who had a face like an exaggerated Norfolk biffin,
and the arrangement of whose costume was after the engraved
portrait of Mother Bunch, and whose pattens were perpetual,
and who wore a bonnet that may be said to have resembled the
design of a Turkey carpet, for it was like nothing in the sky, or
upon the earth, or in the waters under them. This phenomenon
announced herself to be Mrs. Runt, laundress, and invariably
soiled every article with which she came in contact. She was
always sipping half-pints of porter, and always talking with indecorous glibness about the "estate" and the assignees. In all the
catastrophes of life,—in childbirth, in bankruptcy, in captivity, in
sickness, and in death,—these appalling women start up unbidden,
and have dominion almost as great as that claimed by commissioners, by turnkeys, by doctors, and by undertakers. When they
are not prattling about the "assignees," their theme is the "trustees," or the "executors." They are all sisters. Mrs. Runt
pervades Beryl Court, and Mrs. Bunt, when you are sick in chambers, administers to you, internally, the liniment instead of the
draught. Mrs. Grunt comes to the lying-in, and Mrs. Hunt
lays you out. Were they ever young, these standing protests
against the laws on witchcraft? Had they ever good looks?
Did they ever know what it was to be pretty, and cheerful,
and honest, and sober? What were their husbands, if they
ever had any,—mutes or dissecting-room porters, or resurrec-
tion men, or watchmen? I think, myself, that they were all
born old, that they had the rheumatism in their cradles, and
were suckled on beer and weaned on gin, and that their fathers

c c

were all Chelsea pensioners, and their mothers all workhouse nurses.

The clerks and other *employés* of the great House did not take the ruin of Mammon much to heart. There was something in having belonged to a firm that had smashed for so tremendous an amount. The sage heads of other City firms looked on a man out of Goldthorpe's as one whose experiences had been vast, whose knowledge of monetary ramifications must be prodigious, and who must necessarily be up, not to a thing or two, but to a thing or twenty. So, when the brief notice accorded to them had expired, they readily found other engagements. The heads of departments were as undismayed. One gentleman positively married on the strength of Goldthorpe's bankruptcy. Another, as precautionary measures, immediately increased his tailor's bill, ordered some peculiar port from his wine-merchant, and took a house on a long lease. A third published a book on the History of Great Speculations, which had a rapid sale, and obtained for its gifted author the appointment of Secretary of the Imperial Clerical and General Purchase of Pawnbrokers' Duplicates Association (offices in Cannon Street and Pall Mall); and one gentleman, more aspiring than the rest, added another horse to his brougham, took a house in Tyburnia, went into business for himself, and was blithely bankrupt at the end of twelve months. He had so closely imitated the system of operations pursued by his great chief, that his Smash was the very image of Mammon's seen through the small end of an opera-glass.

The fountain in the Court ceased playing of course; and then it came out how much money was owing to the Water Company, in which Sir Jasper was a shareholder. The scrip, it is needless to say, had been mortgaged for twice its value. Money had been raised upon everything on which it was possible to raise a stiver,—upon title-deeds and dock-warrants, upon bills and cheques, upon bills-of-sale of phantom furniture, upon shares, and bonds, and bills of lading, and policies of insurance, and reversions, and the contents of Mammon's waste-paper basket generally. The assets, if they could only have been realized, ought to have been enormous. Hundreds of thousands of pounds sterling were owed to Sir Jasper Goldthorpe; only Brumm Brothers of Finsbury Circus, and Poulgar

and Tyke of Manchester, and J. C. Whittlestool of New York,
and Solomon Bennosey and Co. of Vienna and Trieste, and Jacob
van Scholdup and Nephews of the Hague, and Caïkjee, Ferikjee,
and Bostandji-Bashi of Constantinople,—those great Greek bankers and farmers of the Moldavio-Wallachian tribute,—all happened to smash up simultaneously with Sir Jasper Goldthorpe, or
as early, at least, as the return of post would permit them. None
of these reputedly-wealthy houses had any assets worth speaking
of; and people did say that Brumm Brothers never had any more
tangible representatives than a very large mahogany desk, and an
office-boy at fifteen shillings a week; that Poulgar and Tyke of
Manchester were simply myths; that J. C. Whittlestool of New
York was a gentleman of the "loafing" persuasion, who, after an
unsuccessful speculation in dry goods, had taken to school-teaching,
and to lecturing on the Od Force, and to writing epic poems and
five-act tragedies, purporting to be the composition of Edmund
Spenser and William Shakespeare respectively, for a spirit-rapping
circle at Fantombrowski City, Mass. Ugly rumours also got
abroad that Solomon Bennosey and Jacob van Scholdup, Company, Nephews, and all, were personages equally fabulous with
the foregoing; and that Caïkjee, Ferikjee, and Bostandji-Bashi
were only petty money-changers in the Grand Rue de Péra. Be
it as it may, nothing came out of the stoppage or the "liquida-
tion" of these shadowy firms; in fact, they liquidated themselves so completely that their names might have been written in
water.

Sir Jasper Goldthorpe was seen no more on his accustomed
walk in the Royal Exchange. He took his name off the books of
the Callipash Club in Old Broad Street. He was one of the
Wardens of the Worshipful Company of Battle-axe Makers; but
he did not join that ancient Society at their June feast in Battle-
axe Makers' Hall, or drink prosperity to the Company "root and
branch." He was to have taken the chair at the annual dinner of
the Hospital for Elephantiasis; but declining the honour, for
obvious reasons, the indefatigable Secretary, W. R. Y. Noccros,
Esq. (subsequently public prosecutor to the Royal Society for the
Prevention of Cruelty to Fleas,—the post which friendly George
Gafferer tried so hard to obtain), succeeded in persuading His

Grace the Duke of Clubfoot to officiate as chairman, who, had he
not been stone-deaf, and had he not in his speech in advocacy of
the claims of the Institution confounded it with the Royal Queen-
Charlotte Institution for supplying Wet-nurses with Snuff, would
have afforded the highest satisfaction to the numerous and distinguished company present.

It was about this time that Sir Jasper's former chums and
associates—if a man so mighty can be said to have ever had chums
or associates—were found to turn their heads the other way, or to
cross discreetly to the other side of the road, when the ruined
man crept by on his way to his lawyers. The cabmen, too, whom
he had once held in such awe, now openly scorned him, and would
have over-charged him because he was poor, and braved his ire
had he remonstrated. The red-nosed and white-aproned ticket-
porters, the ward-beadles and turncocks, the hangers-on at City
taverns and coffee-houses, even the man who sold dog-collars,
pocket-books, and toy copper coal-scuttles and coffee-pots, under
the lee of Bow Church and the Poultry Chapel, quite forgot to
touch their hats now when the Baronet passed. With that
idiosyncrasy peculiar to ruined men, he persisted in hanging about
the scenes of his former glories;—a poor broken-down old Marius,
wandering amidst the ruins of a golden Carthage. There was no
great need for him to be seen on the eastern side of Temple Bar.
He was not often wanted at his lawyers' or at Basinghall Street;
in fact, they could have got on quite as well there without as with
him. But he would hanker after the old scenes; he would prowl
about Beryl Court, and the marts and exchanges where he had
been so well known, and where he had achieved in bygone times
such triumphant successes. Some of his former companions took
it quite ill that he did not absent himself for good and all. He
was smashed; he was done for; he belonged henceforth to the
Court and the Commissioners. What did he want "humbugging"
—I use their terms, not mine—about Cheapside and Cornhill?

"There's a want of decency in it," quoth one. "He ought to
know better," said another. "Hain't proper," was the opinion
of a third. Joddles, of Joddles and Toddles, Turkey brokers, had
a dreadful dream about Sir Jasper Goldthorpe, and told it the
next morning, coldly perspiring as he spoke, to a friend. "By

Jove, sir!" he said, "I dreamt last night of that fellow Goldthorpe coming to my place, and wanting to borrow half-a-sufferin
of me. And of course I wouldn't lend it to him. And then he
seized me by the throat; and then he changed into the Rotunda
of the Bank of England; and then I fell into a tureenful of
scalding hot turtle; and then I woke. Sir, if that man had any
sense of decency in him, he'd emigrate."

The Church had something to say, too, about the luckless
wretch. The Reverend Hugh Mango Hollowpenny, who, through
Sir Jasper's influence, had been presented to the comfortable
living of St.-Pogis-under-Pump (resident population thirteen
hundred and thirteen, average congregation nine and a half,—the
half being a hunch-backed charity-boy), took the ruined Goldthorpe as the text for a very neat sermon preached in the ancient
church of St. Pogis, the first Sunday after the decline of Mammon.
He showed how, even when the ex-millionnaire was a rich man, he
had doubtless scorned the beggar in his gate, and sent him disdainfully the crumbs that fell from his children's table; whereas now
the beggar was an infinitely better man than he, and would go to
glory;—whereas he—but I desist.

The minor organs of the public press would have been wanting
to their high attributes and functions, had they not made a trifling
moral capital out of the great catastrophe which had convulsed
the City of London. The money-articles in all the dailies were
full of Goldthorpiana for at least a fortnight. Then came two or
three stinging leaders, in which it was irrefragably proved that
such a system of business as that pursued by Jasper Goldthorpe
must inevitably find its culmination in ruin and disgrace, and in
which he was likened to John Law, to Rowland Stephenson, and,
by implication, to the late Mr. Fauntleroy. The weekly journals
teemed with tiny paragraphs, contributed by industrious penny-a-
liners, not quite certain on Friday as to where their Sunday's
dinner was to come from, and alluding to the Sardanapalian extra-
vagance of Sir Jasper, to the wasteful prodigality of the Sons of
Mammon, to the Persian splendour of Beryl Court, the Versailles-
like magnificence of Onyx Square, and the Arcadian beauty of
Goldthorpe Manor. There were little anecdotes, too, about Sir
Jasper having been in the habit of purchasing early green peas at

a guinea a quart, feeding his horses on Jamaica arrowroot, and cane-bottoming the chairs in his servants' hall with gold wire. Fortunately Magdalen Hill was only ruined, and was not a gazetted bankrupt, else the minor organs of the press might have had something to say against her as well.

All these anecdotes and calumnies, all these lies and scandals, Ernest Goldthorpe read in his rectory at Swordsley;—for he had plenty of kind friends to send him the papers, however trashy they were, which contained them;—all these he perused with a secret rage and burning shame. There are few things more terrible in the eventualities of life than when misfortune creates a grief between parents and their children,—than when inevitable fate abases the sire, and leaves the son honoured and prosperous. Ask my lady yonder who has married a peer, whether she is comfortable in the knowledge that her poor old mother once kept a grocer's shop, and is still partial to snuff and to ardent spirits. Ask the gallant officer, who has won rank and fame and the Cross of the Bath in far distant lands, how he likes coming home from the East, and finding that his father has failed as a stock-broker, and has taken to the corn-and-coal-commission business for a livelihood. Of course Ernest Goldthorpe, as a son and as a clergyman, meant to do everything that was proper and generous for his family, when this dreadful crisis was over, and these sad affairs were arranged; but, meanwhile, he could not help thinking in his heart of hearts that it would be an exceedingly comfortable thing and an infinite relief if, for some brief period, say six months, his papa and mamma could be relegated to the antipodes, or sunk (without any peril to their lives) at the bottom of the sea.

CHAPTER XXXI.

AT THE WEST-END.

IT would be difficult to describe with precision the immediate effect which the failure of Sir Jasper Goldthorpe had upon that polite world of which he had been for so long the envy and the ornament. A thunderbolt, an earthquake, a tornado, the explosion of a powder-magazine,—all these are, if not vulgar, at least hackneyed images, and will scarcely bear re-quoting when this most gigantic Smash is taken into consideration. The news of Goldthorpe's stoppage was wafted, of course, on a thousand wings through Temple Bar,—another edition came round Newgate Street and Holborn way,—rushed with lightning swiftness up Fleet Street, and so to Charing Cross, where, bifurcating, it was transmitted, in duplicate, westward to Tyburnia and southward to Belgravia. Consternation, amazement, rage, mortification,—all these feelings were certainly experienced by the polite world on the receipt of the disastrous intelligence ; but with regard to any sentiment of pity, sorrow, condolence, or compassion, my information is by no means so exact. The polite world felt, in the first place, naturally vexed and humiliated at the collapse of a sumptuous Entity to whom they had so long bowed the knee, whom, together with its belongings, they had courted, flattered, not to say beslavered with adulation ; to whose feasts they had rejoiced to be bidden ; in whose sunshine they had basked ; and in whose temporal Eternity—for many persons, gross as seems the paradox, do positively believe that Riches will last for ever—they had reposed so strong a faith ; and Sir Jasper Goldthorpe, they argued, had no right to set himself up as a rich man, since the foundations of his formidably gigantic fortune were, after all, built upon a quicksand. For the polite world, as a rule, profess to be entirely ignorant of the fluctuations of financial and commercial speculations. The polite world screeches in agony when their banker breaks, or their stock-broker runs away, and want to hang all Lombard Street, and all Capel Court immediately. They say they can't understand panics and hard times, and so forth. Their only notion of a firm tangible fortune is one that consists of snug dividends upon Bank or India Stock, on bonds and rent-charges, and especially on national pensions; and so long as the Bank of England doesn't break, and the British Government still holds its own, they imagine that their fortunes must necessarily be secure.

Thus, while in the City Sir Jasper Goldthorpe was looked upon as a simply unfortunate man who had gone a little too fast, over-traded, and had found at last things turn out badly, he was regarded at the West End, and by the impulsive polite world, as little short of a swindler. They had no patience with him. This, forsooth, was the financier worth millions, the man made of money, the auriferous oligarch who could buy and sell half the Peerage, who had been made a baronet because he was so rich, and was to be made a peer because he was growing richer. This was the Idol to whom all had bowed down; whose feasts were like those of Marly in the reign of the Grand Monarque; whose daughters, had he possessed any, might have wedded with princes; who was, in fact, MAMMON, and in consequence to be worshipped, and made much of, so long as he would shower gold about him. Now he was down. Now his fortune turned out to be a myth, and his riches not worth a peck of cowries. Of course the polite world were shocked, irritated, and mortified that they had been deceived; and, equally of course, their just suspicions, which they had entertained for a very long period,—only twenty-four hours since they had been caressing Mammon's shoe-strings!—were only verified. They had always thought how it would end. There was always something suspicious, *louche*, about this man. He never looked you in the face. He was evidently, and had been for a long time, tormented by the stings of conscience. And finally, drawing a neat and genteel moral from the downfall of this rich man, who had so wickedly proved to be poorer than Job, the polite world bade its admirers, dependents, toadies, and hangers-on take warning by the fate of the Goldthorpes, beware in future of these City sharpers and adventurers, and mark the

results which followed the encouragement and the admission into
society of mere plebeians; for although Sir Jasper Goldthorpe's
name was in Burke and in Debrett, and he had a handle to his
name, and a bloody hand in his escutcheon, he had not been two
days bankrupt ere the polite world found out that he was of the
meanest possible extraction, and, not many years ago, had kept a
shop in a little country town.

This is the way of the world, and has been these thousand
years; and there is small use, perhaps, in moralising upon it. To
hit a man when he is down, and find out that the wretch who
stands convicted of murder has committed half-a-dozen desperate
assassinations in addition to the one for which he is to be hanged
next Monday: to throw a stone at the drowning man, and trip up
the lame dog that is trying to get over the style; to declare that
"the woman who has made one false step has tumbled down a
whole flight of stairs" (as a great wit once said); to swear,
because a man wears a wig, that his teeth are false and his moustaches dyed; to give unto him who has plenty, and to take away
from him who has nothing;—we say that we don't do these things,
and brand as cynics and man-haters those who declare that we
do. But we do them, nevertheless, and, in ourselves, glory in
them, every day.

Courtly Doctor Sardonix was inexpressibly shocked by the
catastrophe which had laid desolate Beryl Court and Onyx
Square. It was a terrible blow to him, almost as severe as
though he had been put down in consultation before a third party
who was an enemy, or as though some beautiful duchess whom he
had been attending for the tooth-ache had died. The worst
of the matter was, that there was no denying it. You cannot
quite ignore the sun at noonday. The courteous Doctor did his
best for a few hours to shuffle, and evade, and stall off the awful
truth with discreet shrugs and simpers; but when the Messenger
(how sorry I am to learn on the authority of Mr. Commissioner
Goulbourn, that the salary of that ill-used functionary has been
reduced to the paltry stipend of five hundred a year—a mere
catchpole's wage)—when the Messenger, travelling westward, as
well as the evil news, put in an appearance in Onyx Square, and
laid his hand on all that the House of Mammon contained, it

was time for Doctor Sardonix to speak out, and to express himself
on a concern about which the whole polite world were talking as
a Man and a physician. He comported himself, as usual, with
exquisite discretion. *He* had nothing to say against the fallen
man.

"The soul of liberality, my dear sir!" he repeated everywhere.
"Just and upright in all his dealings, so far as your humble
servant is concerned. Let us have some Christian charity. Let
us not break the bruised reed. He erred, it may be,—erred from
excess of energy and enterprise; but who is not liable to error?
Humanum est errare."

This was the pleasing refrain of the physician's song. There is
something to be got even out of toadying the unfortunate. The
Doctor's present reward was to be called a good kind soul; and
to hear on every side rumours that, contrary to the usual exigent
etiquette of the profession, he had allowed the Goldthorpe family
to run in his debt for hundreds of fees. His hope of future
guerdon lay, perhaps, in the bare possibility that, some day or
another, some member of the Goldthorpe family might hold his
head up again, and, by his bounty, recall the gladsome days when
he scarcely ever met a Goldthorpe without having his smooth
palm crossed with gold.

I am bound to admit that Doctor Sardonix refrained (purely
through motives of delicacy) from leaving his card at the house of
the ruined family, and that Zenobia his spouse "improved the
occasion," as the diplomatists say, to make the Goldthorpe bankruptcy a frequent text for exhortations to her family and friends
on the pomps and vanities of earthly things, and the sinfulness of
a mere reliance on perishable dross. A good many of the neighbouring clergy, orthodox and heterodox, also, "improved the
occasion," as that other reverend gentleman had done at the
East-End, even as they improved all other occasions,—wars,
tumults, pestilences, famines, and railway-accidents, to suit the
stops on their own particular barrel-organs. Bolsover, M.P., was
neutral. He remarked that Goldthorpe might have played his
cards better. This was in the lobby of the House. In the Park,
hearing further details of the Smash, he opined that Sir Jasper
had brought his pigs to a fine market; and after dinner, at the

Club, between his rubbers, he observed that he didn't see how G.
was to get out of the mess. But Bolsover was always a man of
strong common sense, dealing in platitudes which everybody
could understand. He is sure to be a Lord of the Treasury some
day.

The great West-End lawyers looked at the tragedy philosophically, and only regretted that they were not for the nonce East-
End lawyers, and that they might have something to do with the
case and the assigness. "There'll be pretty pickings on that
estate, sir," Deedes (Deedes, Ferret, and Wax, Old Cavendish
Street) remarked to Probate, of Bedford Row: in which the
latter acquiesced, adding that if the case were in his hands, he
would put half-a-dozen extra clerks on his establishment on the
mere strength of it; and, quoth wicked old Mr. Jehoshophat, of
St. James's Place,—that terrible, terrible limb of the law, who
was reputed to have made a hundred and ten thousand pounds
out of four bankruptcies, and to have patented a machine for the
legal grinding of widows' and orphans' faces,—said this most
redoubtable of solicitors,—a man who seemed to labour under a
natural incapacity for being *for* you in a cause, and was always,
and, as a matter of course, against you, suing you horribly, and
selling you up at all hours of the day and night, in term and out
of term,—"Since Bulgrummer's affair (the East Swindlesbury
Bank and Universal Wind-winnowing Company), there hasn't
been, within my recollection (and I'm sixty-nine, sir), a bankruptcy with more meat upon it."

Mr. Plumer Ravenbury—who may certainly be said to have
belonged to the polite world, inasmuch as it was his function to
conduct so many polite worldlings out of it—received the news
with a soft sigh. He consulted his books, and found that the
funeral of Hugh Jasper Goldthorpe had been paid for at the
expiration of the customary year of grace, and that not one of the
costly items had been disputed by the family. So *he* had nothing
to say against Mammon. Besides, Plumer was a disciple of the
school of Dr. Sardonix; and the two played into each other's
hands much oftener than was imagined, although quite unconsciously, perhaps. Undertakers are hereditary retainers of the
poor as well as the rich; and if you, or any of your ancestors,

have ever paid them a good long bill without questioning any of the charges, they will go on burying you and your descendants until the crack of doom. But once let a tray of feathers be quibbled at, or a silken scarf objected to, and your undertaker repudiates you, and is of opinion that you or your representatives —yourself being out of court—had better go to some cheap Funeral Company or advertising person. Every man, to the meanest, has his Boswell, I have been told, and—it is a very dreadful thing to think of—his undertaker, also a sable little cherub who sits down below, and looks out for the death of poor Jack Pudding.

The Bosuns (Admiral Bosun), neighbours of Mammon in Onyx Square, had never known the Goldthorpes. They were glad and *thankful* now, yes, thankful, Admiral Bosun, that they had been spared the disgrace and contamination of contact with those unworthy people. And Miss Magdalen Hill was ruined too, was she ? No good ever came out of such wicked, wicked pride as hers. The Bosuns were not to be appeased by what they termed the shameful backsliding of their neighbours. You will generally find that the people whom you have never offended will never forgive you. Old Mrs. Twizzle, from Maida Hill, was furious against the whole Goldthorpe race. She was a wealthy but not well-educated woman, and spoke of them, with more force than elegance, as "a pack of trumpery rubbage." That gloomy spinster, Miss Ashtaroth, from the Harrow Road, moaned much over the abasement of pride, and the trampling under foot of the disdainful man. She made reference to Dives; she quoted Job; and if that patriarch had been afflicted with any female friends, Miss Ashtaroth, for a surety, would have been one of them. She too " improved the occasion," according to her lights ; and being the authoress of that suggestive volume of poetry (privately printed) entitled " The Hatchment,"—there are some powerful verses, too, in "The Pall with the Patched Lining," although that last-named work is still in MS.,—she sat down to write some album-verses on the misfortunes of the people she had never met. I think she commenced one powerful apostrophe with "How are the mighty fallen ! " but being reminded by "too partial friends " that somebody had given utterance to the same sentiments on a

previous occasion, she began anew, "Mammon, Mammon! thou
art not as thou hast been!" when, finding that she had unconsciously paraphrased a certain Felicia Hemans, and that, moreover, her first line wouldn't scan with her second, she abandoned
poesy for the nonce, made a pilgrimage to Kensal Green, meditated some occasional lines on Hugh Jasper Goldthorpe's tomb,
and, on her return, gave warning to her maid Vaunter, and
severely chastised her poodle for eating black sealing-wax—a
refreshment to which that pampered animal was much addicted.

Hawksley, R.N., albeit devoted to the Bosuns,—he has been
engaged to all the girls in succession, and it is hoped may still
make a good end of it when Mrs. Admiral becomes a widow,—
behaved very well under the circumstances. He said that Goldthorpe didn't owe him any money, and that he used to give very
capital dinners and very jolly parties; that the old woman,
meaning Lady Goldthorpe, was a trump; and that if he wasn't
a poor devil of a sea-captain on half-pay, he would lend him some
money, he would. Chewke, late of Riga, instructed Chipp, his
body-servant, to purchase the *Times* for him every morning until
the proceedings in Goldthorpe's bankruptcy were terminated.
He could not wait for the City article and the Basinghall
Street record until it was time for him to take his noontide walk
to the Union Club. He read all about the choice of assignees.
and the proof-of-debts meetings, over hot pigeon-pie, on which
he had lately taken to breakfasting in bed. Gryggor, the joker,
was taciturn and morose on the whole subject. It is probable
that he was nursing a store of facetiæ and conundrums against
the unhappy Baronet's hanging himself or Lady Goldthorpe's
dying of a broken heart. Lord Groomporter drowned his grief
in "braiorsoawarr," and, in the excess of exhilaration caused by
that stimulant, made up his mind to offer marriage to Magdalen
Hill. On taking plain soda-water the next morning he thought
better of his resolve, and instructed his man-servant to procure
him devilled kidneys, with plenty of cayenne, for his breakfast
at 2·30. Lord Carnation—the truth must be told—ran away.
At least, he found it convenient to pass over for a season to a
cheap German Spa, where his chaplain wrote pamphlets in the
morning, and played at *trente et quarante* in the evening, Lord

Carnation cramming himself meanwhile from the German news-papers. In the Teutonic language his lordship was, I need not say, a proficient. He knew almost every word, and didn't under-stand half-a-dozen, in it. Why did Lord Carnation run away? The truth must again be told; and I am afraid that the Noble Childe departed this country in sore dismay, and extreme terror lest the Goldthorpes and their connections might want to borrow money, or seek some favour at his hands. "One can never tell what may happen, you know," he said candidly to his chaplain. "Old man may want to get into the Charterhouse, or old woman may turn begging-letter-writer. There's that girl too. Fool she was to trust old man with her money! I wonder whether that little Mrs. Armytage lost anything by him. Rather too knowing, I should think." From which it may be inferred that the Earl of Carnation, although intellectually a ninny, was not deficient in worldly wisdom.

And those ruined cast-out men and women,—where were they? In Onyx Square? No; the Messenger and his merry men were fast in possession there. At Goldthorpe Manor—that marvel of a place? No; there also the Messenger and his merry men were chiefs and suzerains over park and terrace, over woods and forests, over rosery and drapery, over vert and venison, over chamber and hall, wherein beards by no means merrily wagged, but rather men of brokerlike aspect confabulated over their inevitable pewter measures of porter. We have all heard of the noble bard who awoke one morning to find himself famous. Edmond Malone, the critic, used to say that he went to bed in one street and woke the next day in another—the name of the thoroughfare in which he resided having been changed from Queen-Anne Street East to Foley Place. It is not agreeable to go to bed hale and hearty and to wake in a raging fever, or with your limbs shackled by sciatica. There may be pleasanter things than to find your morning pillow guarded by alguazils; or to read in the damp news-sheet that your last night's farce, which you were too nervous to witness in person, was signally damned; or to learn, through the same medium, that the Trans-Caucasian Railways, in which you have invested a few thousands, and which have been so long at a glowing premium, are down to three and an eighth discount; or that—a mere *on dit* this—a marriage is on the *tapis* between some wretch in the Guards and the peerless beauty with whom you were waltzing and flirting on the previous evening. These are the kicks which Fortune gives us as she passes; but the sorest, cruellest buffet that she can have in store for us is surely to retire to rest honoured and rich, and to rise up in the morning disgraced and a beggar.

So had it been with each and every one of the pampered children of Mammon. The Brazen Idol himself must have long foreseen the blow—must have felt his clay feet tottering and crumbling beneath him;—but They! It was all over in a moment. Onyx Square, Goldthorpe Manor, treasures, honours, dignities, alliances, friendships, luxuries, whims and caprices,— all faded away "like the breath from off the mirror," and "like the foam from off the sea," and like the shadow of the shadow of smoke.

Persian splendour and Assyrian magnificence speedily resolved themselves into a mean lodging in Praed Street, Paddington. They were still of Tyburnia, you see, even as the dwellers of Pimlico purlieus are close upon Belgravia; but what a gulf between Praed Street and the proud Square! The rent was, I think, five-and-twenty shillings a week: parlours, of course,— poor people always choose parlours to live in,—with a landlady who had seen better days, and grumbled because there was nothing to steal. She had found out all about her guests before they had been six hours in her house ; and looked sharply after her rent on the ensuing Saturday, you may be sure. In this narrow crib, with a lady professor of the pianoforte—terms one-and-sixpence an hour—over head; with a tailor, not too rarely inebriated, above that, and a pack of howling children perpetually executing gymnastic feats on the staircase, and settling their little differences in the passage,—were content to abide Sir Jasper and Lady Goldthorpe and Magdalen Hill. For the first time in her life that young lady became acquainted with the price of potatoes, and learned what the tongue of a coarse, violent, ignorant, envious, and gossiping lodging-house keeper was like. For Captain William Goldthorpe, and on the very morrow of his father's bankruptcy, apartments of a more expensive, but of a less agreeable, nature had been found. That unhappy officer of cavalry was arrested at early morn at a friend's chambers, where he thought himself perfectly free from pursuit, and conveyed by Mr. Morris Hyams, officer to the Sheriff of Middlesex, assisted by Mr. Melphibosheth Hashbaz, his retainer and follower, to the lock-up of Mr. Nebuchadnezzar Barney-winkle, in Cursitor Street, Chancery Lane, where, at the trifling outlay of a guinea a day, he was indulged in the luxury of a private room, well-nigh as dirty as a dog-kennel, and not much bigger than a bird-cage. The Captain was only " took," to use Mr. Hyam's locution, on four executions,—three bill-discounters' and a military tailor's ; but ere he had been an hour in hold the detainers against him came pouring in like applications for the office of common hangman, when that post happens to be vacant (there were seventy-seven last time) ; and by two in the afternoon the Captain was "to the bad for two-and-twenty thou," as Mr. Barneywinkle cheerfully observed to Mr. Hyams, thereby mean-ing twenty-two thousand pounds. William Goldthorpe had plenty of squander-cash friends, who were only too happy to supply him with the necessary guineas for his rent, which, with admirable promptitude and punctuality, was always exacted in advance. He could have set up a cigar-shop with the stock of choice Regalias, and packets of Milo's honey-dew tobacco, which were daily forwarded to him by sympathising friends in the Household Brigade, the Line, and the Artillery. Hampers of wine were continually sent to the captive, much to the disgust of Mr. Nebuchadnezzar Barneywinkle, whose pleasure and profit it was to supply vinous and alchoholic beverages from his own cellars to the lambs in his fold ; but who found consolation in taking toll on the Captain's wine, at so much per cork, as it passed through his grated wicket. Also, there were plenty of young men, with the longest of legs and of moustaches, and the largest of whiskers, who were glad to come and sit with Willy Goldthorpe during the permitted hours,—to abuse his creditors, to cheer him up, to recount to him the latest sporting intelligence fresh from *Bell's Life*, to smoke and drink, and occasionally take a friendly hand at loo or vingt'un with him. All this certainly made a sunshine in the very shady place of Cursitor Street ; but wine and cigars and cards, and the odds on the Leger, won't pay two-and-twenty thousand pounds' worth of debt. Jack Butts told Willy so plainly. Jack Butts was always saying cruel things, and doing kind actions. He owed more money than any man of his means (which were *nil*) in London. His creditors despaired of, but were fond of him. "What's the good of suing Captain Jack?" such a one would urge; "he's stood godfather to all the sheriff's officers' children, and they always turn the blind side to him when he passes." When Jack Butts went to a bill-discounter with a piece of stamped paper for negotiation, the usurer would say, "No, Jack; we've had quite enough of your blessed signature at three months; but if you want a ten-pun' note in a friendly way, here it is, and welcome." "He owes me a cool hundred, the capting does," observed Mr. Chevron, tailor, of New Burlington Street; "but if he'd only promise to drop in sometimes of a Sunday, and take a bit of dinner on the quiet at my little place at Forest Hill, I'd write his name off my ledger to-morrow. That man's conversation over a bottle of the right sort is worth forty shillings in the pound alone." Jack Butts was a man of the world, and could give good advice to anybody but himself.

"It's a bad job, Willy," he remarked in Cursitor Street, "and no mistake, and it can't be squared. The Philistines have made you sing comic songs at three months' date quite long enough, my boy; and it's time to pull Stamp Castle down upon their heads. You've gone to smash, and your governor's gone to smash, and except that Basinghall Street lies to the east of Temple Bar, and Portugal Street to the west, I don't see much difference between the two. You must go over to the Bench, old fellow, and order a pail of whitewash. As you owe such a precious lot, I don't think it will go very hard with you. If you were a poor devil owing a couple of hundred or so, you'd be sure to be remanded for six months. You'd have to stand the Commissioner's bullying. I've stood it. It didn't turn *my* hair gray. It isn't so bad as a wigging from the Chief on a field day. And then you'll come out as clean as a new pin; and we must set you up as a 'vet.,' or a commission-agent, or a riding-master at Brighton, or a billiard-marker, or something genteel and easy in that line; and if you

D D

want a fiver towards helping you to file your schedule, you've only to say the word to Jack Butts, and if he can't beg it, he'll borrow it; and if he can't borrow it, he'll steal it."

These were not, perhaps, the words of strict morality, but they were decidedly the words of worldly wisdom, and William Goldthorpe did not fail to lay them well to heart. It would have been well, perhaps, for the forlorn circle in Praed Street, Paddington, if they had found comforters as practical. But they had none. Sir Jasper had ever been a shy and reticent man, and those whom he had shunned in his prosperity shunned him now in his adversity. With the polite world the family had clearly nothing more to do. The polite portals were closed against them, even if they had chosen to knock thereat, and they were ostracised in perpetuity from the sacred precincts. This was truly hard, but perhaps necessary, and certainly salutary. Not that they were entirely destitute of friends. Some old clients to whom Mammon had been generous from his abundant store, some old servants who remembered what good living, and what comfortable quarters they had enjoyed in the old time, were anxious to do their former master and mistress such services as lay in their power. Gratitude is not quite dead in the world; if it were, it would be as well for us to go and live in a pit full of devils.

Lady Goldthorpe "bore up"—she used the expression herself —far better than had been expected. Perhaps it was that the good woman found herself once more in an element familiar, and, to a certain extent, comfortable to her. She fretted little; she repined not at all. She was cheerful. She called her husband "Goldie," as in the old days, and strove to cheer him up. She cooked him nice little dishes, and tried to persuade him to take suppers, and something warm after it.

"There's nothing like supper," said simple Lady Goldthorpe, "for a wounded heart. Don't you remember what nice little suppers we used to have, years and years ago, when we were in those little difficulties about Mr. D.? Poor Mr. D., I wonder what became of him! Do have a rump-steak and kidney pudding at ten, Goldie."

The Baronet shuddered at the word "difficulties." "They exist still, Maria," he remarked gloomily.

"Oh, nonsense!" Lady Goldthorpe continued, "that botheration of a bankruptcy can't last for ever. Why, wasn't Pybus, in our town, bankrupt over and over again, and didn't he always get over it? He always seemed to be better off after he had failed for a good lot. You can pay something in the pound, can't you, Goldie?"

"I don't know: perhaps I may; perhaps not a penny."

"Well, if you can't, you can't—that's positive. Blood can't be got out of a stone. They can't hang you, Goldie, for being unfortunate."

"No; but they can——"

"What?"

"Never mind what," Sir Jasper cried, in an agonising voice. "They can do that to me which would bring ruin—utter ruin—on me, and disgrace on all our children."

"Ruin and disgrace!"

"Yes, Maria. There is one dreadful secret I have never confided to you,—to you, my own true wife, the companion of my early poverty, and in whose bosom I have reposed all my cares and troubles,—all but this terrible one, which now hangs over me and threatens to crush me."

"Jasper Goldthorpe," his wife said, with something like dignity in her homely way, "to me you have always been a good and faithful husband; to me you have always acted as an honest man. Why should I think that you would do the thing that isn't right to others? When one's a rogue at home, one's generally a rogue abroad. Come now, Goldie dear, tell me what it's all about."

"I cannot, I dare not, Maria. I should blush to do so. I tremble to speak about the awful thing, for fear that the very walls might have ears."

"Walls *have* ears, Sir Jasper," a voice close behind the baronet said; "and so have people behind parlour-doors; and pretty sharp ones, too."

The voice belonged to Filoe and Co., of Coger's Inn; the voice belonged to Mr. Sims, of London, Paris, and the world generally. And Mr. Sims had knocked a soft rat-tat at the street-door, while the bankrupt baronet and his wife were in conversation,—Magdalen was away—gone in quest of work, she had said, in her proud way,—and after a brief parley on the door-mat, ending with his slipping a five-shilling piece into the landlady's hand,—a great outlay for the usually economical Mr. Sims,—he had been permitted to remain in ambush for a few minutes in the narrow little passage; had doubtless—thanks to a flimsy lodging-house parlour-door and his sharp ears—heard the concluding part of the colloquy between Sir Jasper and Lady Goldthorpe, and now entered the room, cool, confident, and suggestive of no science being to him a mystery.

But when Lady Goldthorpe turned round at the entrance of the unexpected visitor, it was not as Mr. Sims or as Mr. Filoe that she addressed him. She stared at him in blank amazement; she suppressed a rising shriek, and lifting up her hands, and sinking into her chair, the good woman murmured, "Hugh Desborough, my husband's old partner, by all that's wonderful!"

CHAPTER XXXII

A BRIGHT day in Paris is, perhaps, the brightest that can be
seen anywhere in the world; and it was the brightest, the sun-
niest, and the cheeriest that Lutetia had known for many months
—this June morning. It was so bright that the sun turned the
crooks of the rag-pickers into gold, and tipped with silver the
strips of iron, and fragments of saucepan-lids, and nails, and boot-
heels twinkling in their baskets. It was so bright that the
Morgue, that gruesome dead-house, looked quite classical and
picturesque,—a little temple of antiquity, with the ashes of dead
heroes inside, instead of a dank and dismal charnel-place, where
the livid corpses lie on the stone slabs, a wonder and a horror to
the sight-seers. It was so bright that the bayonets of a regiment
of infantry marching down the Rue de Rivoli flashed and glittered
in the sunlight like a *chevaux-de-frise* of diamonds. Of course the
nursemaids in the Palais Royal, and the plump Normandy nurses
outside the Café de Paris, took advantage of the occasion to hire
chairs at two sous an hour, and sun themselves, with their young
charges, to the admiration of all passers-by, especially the red-
legged warriors attached to the garrison at Paris. Of course the
little girls in the great quadrangle of the Palace aforesaid, and in
the Tuileries Gardens,—those wonderful little Parisian children
with scragged-up hair, vandyked trousers, black-silk pinafores,
who are coquettes in their cradles, and flirts in their leading-
strings,—availed themselves of the sunshine to indulge in more
than ordinarily graceful and elaborate gymnastic exercises as connected with the skipping-rope. Of course while they skipped
they looked round for the customary murmur of applause never
denied, and quite as gratifying to their little eyes and ears,
whether it proceeded from the toothless old gentlemen sipping

their morning coffee, and reading their tiny rags of newspapers outside the Café de la Rotonde, or from the ingenuous provincials in blouses, sabots, and red-tasselled nightcaps, who were loitering about to see the Guard paraded, and the sun-dial cannon fired by Phœbus' rays at high noon. It was so bright and sunny, that the five hundred thousand ladies and gentlemen who have nothing to do in Paris all the year round began to do it with all their minds and with all their strength,—that the rattling of dominoes, the clinking of glasses, the clattering of billiard-cues, the shuffling of cards, began to be heard an hour earlier than usual,—and that the fumes of prematurely matutinal cigars curled blue in the morning sunshine from at least two hundred and fifty thousand pairs of happy idle lips. It was so bright and sunny, that you forgot the beggars, with their rags and their sores, on the Pavis Notre-Dame, and the steps of St. Roche (ye beggars, ye have been swept away under the Imperial dispensation!),—that you forgot the gutters, and the discordant cries of the old-clothes men, and the dust and ashes which the house-porters persisted in sweeping over your clean boots,—that you forgot there was a great deal of want, and a great deal of misery, and a great deal of vice, a great deal of crime, in this teeming city of Paris. *Sol lucet omnibus.* The sun made amends for all. The sun made the beggar rich, and bade the cripple forget his hurts, and the paralytic that he was bed-ridden, and the debtor that he was in Clichy, and the pickpocket that the spies were on his track, and the *gamin* that his dinner was problematical, and the sempstress that she was making shirts for forty sous a dozen. The sun was meat to the famished, and drink to those who were athirst, and lodging to the houseless. So it must have been in all times, I fancy, in this wonderful city, whose dark shadows only looked the blacker by the dazzling sunshine which contrasts with them. There must have been sunny mornings during the Reign of Terror, when Robespierre enjoyed his breakfast and Fouquier-Tinville smiled, when the procession of the tumbrils down the Rue St.-Honoré must have looked quite a glittering pageant; and the sun must have shone so on the red guillotine, on the Place of the Revolution, that you could scarcely distinguish it from a *galante* show in the neighbouring Elysian fields.

Sol lucet omnibus. Everywhere the sun shone, and for all;—
for the Ministers of the Republic in their cabinets; for the
students in the taverns and coffee-houses of the Latin Quarter;
for the *grisettes* in their garrets, the soldiers in their barracks,
the mountebanks in their booths, the great *dames* of the Faubourg
St.-Germain in their boudoirs, the artisans in their workrooms,
the cobblers and umbrella-menders in their underground cabins.
The sun brought many innocent youths, between the ages of six
and twelve, in the divers schools and colleges at Paris, to grief,
prompting them as it did to catch its rays in burning-glasses, and
so perforate copybooks supplied to them by their pastors and
masters. Yes, the sun shone in all places and for all, save in the
tomb and for its inmates. There all was dark enough, as usual.
In two notable places it shone this morning in the month of June.
First it streamed gallantly and defiantly into a splendid suite of
rooms in the Rue Grande-des-Petites-Maisons, and through a
stained casement into a sumptuous little boudoir, and upon a man
lolling on a luxurious ottoman, and who was dressed to all substantial seeming in plain burgess's apparel, but who figuratively,
and curiously enough, wore his heart upon his sleeve.

Our old friend Simon Lefranc! the genial, airy, volatile child
of Gaul (was he a child of Gaul?); the ex-commercial traveller
in the corset-trade; the ex-denizen of the Monmouth Chambers,
Soho; the *ex-paillasse* who had looked through the coffee-room
window; the ex-dandy who had met with Inspector Millament
and Sergeant South on the Bridge of Waterloo; the ex-Count
Somebody, in curly black wig, who had been so welcome a guest
at the entertainment of the Baroness de la Haute Gueuse; the
present Papa Lallouet;—Simon Lefranc, call him what you
will.

Simon was quite at home, a man of the world; and in it he
could accommodate himself to any circumstances in life; but the
present were, to tell truth, somewhat snug, somewhat cozy, not
to say luxurious circumstances. Simon never exceeded, he was
too wary for that, but he certainly enjoyed himself thoroughly.
A nice succulent little breakfast was laid out before him. The
remains of some truffled turkey, the crust of a slice of Strasbourg
pie, the bones of some cutlets, some oyster-shells warranted

Ostend, a champagne-cork, and the lees of a right good bottle of Chambertin, showed that he had known during the last half-hour how to appreciate the good things of this life. And now Simon's *demi tasse*, and Simon's *petit verre*, had been brought him by an obsequious *bonne ;* and Simon himself, producing from a cigar-case a lengthy and fragrant Trabuco, did not look, as he sipped and he puffed the goods with which the gods had provided him, in the least like the same Simon who was a traveller to a stay-maker, and associated with the half-starved inhabitants of a model lodging-house, who had lost his all in disastrous speculations, and was obliged to pinch himself now for the sake of his little Adèle.

And while Simon so sipped and puffed he meditated; but whether his thoughts ran in the French or the English language, it concerns me not to tell. Who can? For aught you know, your seemingly English neighbour may be thinking in Swedish, or Sclavoniac, or Mauri, or the one primeval language known only to himself; as poor Hartley Coleridge used to declare that he thought in the language of the Eujaxrians, his self-created tongue. When I am excited, I think in Teloogoo ; and does not Rabelais tell us of the nation who saw with their ears and understood with their elbows ? So I will use the romancer's privilege, and translate Simon Lefranc's meditations into indifferent English.

" There never was," he thought, " such an artificial baffling little minx; she is almost too clever, even for me. Where are those papers ? What has she done with them ? She has defied that most sagacious Mrs. Skinner, whose fingers are like cork-screws, and whose eyes like probes—a searcher at Scotland Yard. She has defied even our paragon La Mère Camuse at the Prefecture, that dauntless woman who would take the skin off a blacka-moor, if there was anything to be found underneath; who would take all the teeth out of your head, if there was anything worth finding in the cavities. But Mrs. Skinner and La Mère Camuse can do nothing with her ; they have turned her, so to speak, in-side out. I myself, and Riflard my man,—bah ! half-a-dozen men, —have ransacked every table, every drawer, every chair-covering, every feather-bed, every curtain-lining in these fine show-rooms ; —we have looked behind the mirrors, and under the carpet, and up the chimney : we have found enough, goodness knows, but

THE AGONY OF FLORENCE ARMYTAGE.

THE AGONY OF FLORENCE ARMYTAGE. 409

have yet failed to discover the one thing needful. Now I, Simon Lefranc, flatter myself that I could find out the secret of the Man in the Iron Mask, if that secret remained to be discovered; and yet so far as this one tiny particular secret is concerned, Florence Armytage masters and defies me, as she has mastered and defied Mrs. Skinner and La Mère Camuse." He rang a little silver bell,—no luxury was deficient in Simon's housekeeping,—which anon was answered by the obsequious *bonne*. This *bonne* had never formed part of the household of the lady on the first-floor. She was, like Simon Lefranc, her master, in the pay and the service of the grand master of all of them—the Prefecture. "Send Riflard here."

The *bonne* curtsied and withdrew.

Soon appeared on the scene Monsieur Riflard, by profession *garde de commerce*, a catchpole to the civil tribunals; by predilection scamp and spy. Monsieur Riflard wore a long bottle-green surtout, and his countenance was of a bilio-greenish hue, and the nap of his hat had a tinge of green in it; and it was with great difficulty that he could ever be persuaded to release his hold of a green cotton umbrella; and altogether Monsieur Riflard, had he had anything to be jealous of, would have made a very admirable representation of the green-eyed monster.

"Any new discoveries, Riflard?"

"None, master."

"Has the porter's lodge below been searched?"

"Everything has been searched, master; nothing found but what you have."

"It is well. I am going to the Palace; there is an examination on this morning. We must get the papers from her by fair or by foul means. Meanwhile go on searching. You may play a game of cards, if you are tired; but I should prefer your not getting tipsy, as you did yesterday. Remember, there are those about who will report to me all that has been done. Good bye, and keep your eyes open."

Monsieur Riflard, whose only weakness was absinthe, made a shambling bow of great deference, for Simon was an emperor among his subordinates. Then the Chief of the Spies took his hat and his cane and his gloves, and proceeded majestically, as beseemed a gentleman of his degree, from the first-floor to the basement, where he found waiting for him a snug little *coupé* to convey him to the Palace. What Palace? You are shortly to learn.

Simon and his retainers had been in judicial possession of that memorable first-floor for fourteen days, routing amongst its gorgeous furniture, turning up and prying into its cupboards and shelves, and cabinets of price, scattering the books in the library, ripping up the draperies, gauging the key-holes almost, for the one absorbing object of their *search*. They were still seeking, and had not yet found. They lived on the very best, for Simon had command of abundant funds. They drank of the very choicest, for the cellar of the lady on the first-floor was abundantly furnished with rare vintages and curious seals. Oddly enough, 'twas found on inquiry that she who owed money almost everywhere, and had defrauded almost every soul with whom she came in contact, had paid the rent of this place with undeviating punctuality. "She was the best of lodgers," quoth the *concierge*, "the best and most generous at Easter and the New Year." *Pauvre petite dame!* the *concierge* pitied her, and it was something to be pitied even by a porter. He and his wife, and the keeper of the *café* over the way, and the proprietor of the wine-shop at the corner, knew very well that Simon and his men were on the first-floor, and what they were there for. Beyond that, nobody in or out of the house, in that neighbourhood at least, knew anything about the matter. You may live a hundred years in a house at Paris without being aware in the slightest degree of whom your next neighbour may be. Our famous first-floor, our once gay and brilliant abode of mirth, and wit, and feasting, and splendour, our bygone haunt of fair women and brave men, our fairy court of beauty and intellect, of which the little sovereign with her golden hair throned it in so queenly a manner, our first-floor of the Rue Grande-des-Petites-Maisons,—what are you now, and where is your lady?

"What a career!" muttered Simon, stepping into his *coupé*; "what a career, how long continued, how triumphantly carried on, and what a sorry end! *Cocher, au Palais!*" The coachman knew well enough what Palace was meant, and blithely drove on to the

Boulevards, and down the crowded Rue Montmartre, and so down towards the Quay, and over the bridge; and the idlers and the dandies recked little that the Chief of the Spies was passing in their midst.

Sol lucet omnibus. And the sun shone that morning in and all about that great Palace. Shone on the emblazoned clock on the Quay. Shone on the peaked turrets of the grim Conciergerie. Shone on the bars of the dungeon whence Marie-Antoinette once looked out. Shone on the golden spire of the Sainte-Chapelle. Shone in great courtyard and on heavy bronze railing. Shone in the huge Hall of the Lost Footsteps, where the suitors paced up and down nibbling oyster-shells, while their black-capped and black-robed advocates regaled themselves with fat oysters, taken now from the Plaintiff, and now from the Defendant. Into tribunals of correctional police; into courts of assize decorated with inscriptions about Liberty, Equality, and Fraternity; into judges' chambers and *greffiers'* offices and *huissiers'* cabinets,—the same sun shone.

Sol lucet omnibus. One ray—a pitying ray, a ray of grief, not of mercy,—came through a barred window, and fell on the trucklebed where Florence Armytage was sitting. They had put her *au secret*, not in solitary confinement; that paragon of the Prefecture, La Mère Camuse, who very much resembled a grenadier of the Old Guard, moustaches and all, in a chintz bed-gown, was with her day and night. She was in secret confinement, being sequestered from all communication with visitors from without. The precaution seemed almost needless; for since her imprisonment not one human being had sought admission to the presence of Florence Armytage, who knew everybody that was noble, or rich, or witty, or wicked enough to be worth knowing in London and Paris.

Another precaution, not quite so needless, had also been adopted. They had put on the wretched little woman the *camisole de force*— the strait-waistcoat, a horrible arrangement of canvas, of straps and tags and laces, with the sleeves knotted together. The *camisole de force*, the prison authorities maintain, was a far more humane and delicate instrument of coercion, where a lady was concerned, than handcuffs; and so she who had worn so many silks and velvets, and mantles of sable, and bracelets of diamond, and necklaces of pearl, sat huddled together in the coarse prison *peignoir*, with her golden hair thrust underneath the coarse black prison coif; and in these hideous swaddling bands of canvas and leather she could just clench her hands, and raise them to her fevered forehead, when La Mère Camuse fed her with a spoon like a child. They had not forced her to wear this dress of torture and ignominy owing to any attempt she had made to commit suicide, or any fear that she would so attempt it; but Florence had been, to tell the truth, somewhat of a refractory prisoner. She had scratched, she had fought, she had bitten, she had kicked, she had wrestled with the two horrible beldames who had brought her from England, and who had subjected her to what she considered unspeakable indignities. But they had found nothing,—not that, at least, for which they were in search,—and Florence Armytage, even in the *camisole de force*, was in one respect triumphant.

Stay, they had found something. Her locket. However, no questions had been asked about that; not even Simon Lefranc could know whose portrait that locket contained.

In the early days of her imprisonment, she had begged passionately for writing materials, but in vain. She wanted to exert her Influence. She wanted to tell her Influence where she was, and how he might help her. The gaolers only grinned at her, and refused her the much-coveted pens, ink, and paper. What was she to do? How was she to assist herself? She gnashed her teeth when she remembered that she was in a country where she might be detained for an indefinite period without trial, without even examination. "Oh, for an English station-house!" she muttered to herself. "At least, they would bring me up before a magistrate within twenty-four hours, and I could not be remanded for more than a week at a time." You see that Florence knew something of English law.

Although access to pens, ink, and paper was denied her, and although, when she asked for legal advice, she was told with a grin that by-and-by would be quite soon enough for her to retain an advocate, examination came soon and frequently enough. An intolerable personage, in a suit of black and a white neckcloth, accompanied by a snake-like secretary, also in black turned up with white, but both rusty and dingy in hue, came to her day by day, and asked her interminable questions. They sat by her for hours, pestering, almost maddening, her with bland interrogations. It was strange to her that they said very little about the crimes which she was accused of having committed in France, and for which she had been arrested at the races by Simon Lefranc. They appeared to be far more anxious concerning her antecedents in England and in India. They asked her the minutest, and apparently the most trivial, questions about events in her early life;— about her education, her juvenile peccadilloes, her school-friends, her courtship, her marriage, her parents, her connections; who her husband was, what he was, when he died; how she came to return to Europe, whereabouts in London and Brighton she had had her many residences, what brought her first to think of living in Paris, and taking that first-floor in the Rue Grande-des-Petites-Maisons. But they tarried very little in Paris, and went back again to England and India, travelling over the same ground again and again, for no earthly or available purpose save barren curiosity and prying impertinence; so Florence Armytage thought. She little knew, with all her astuteness, the slow and cautious steps, the painful and elaborate minuteness, necessary to the composition of that remarkable document, at once denunciatory and biographical, known as an *Acte d'Accusation.*

At first she answered these perpetual questions in a confused and rambling, flighty, almost jaunty manner. She could scarcely take the sable inquisitor and his snake-like secretary *au sérieux.* She tried her old blandishments, her old cat-like purrings and gambols, on them. She thought that if she was indeed to die, she would go to her death like Agag, mincingly. But she found that though the functionaries were urbane enough,—the chief was the very soul of politeness,—the polished surface of their countenances only concealed visors of thrice-tempered steel. They administered the torture in white kid gloves; and the cords to the pulleys of their rack were made of silk; and their ordeal by water was one of rose-water; but all these were not the less tortures, and frightful to endure. There is a story told, in *Knickerbocker's History of New York,* how a shrewd, down-east

Yankee once questioned a simple Dutchman out of his well-fed
steed, and left him instead a vile calico-mare in exchange. In a
similar spirit, the polite inquisitors almost questioned Florence
Armytage out of her five senses, out of her skin, out of her life,
and left her a poor, trembling, bewildered thread-paper of a
woman, rocking herself on her pallet-bed; and wishing that she
had never been born to undergo such cross-questioning. Then
she grew testy, and wayward, and irritable. She did not know,
she was sure; it was so long ago, she could not remember; how
was she to tell? what did they mean by asking such things?—
and similar evasions. Then she pleaded her inability to converse
any longer in French; and then the chief inquisitor resumed his
queries in the most grammatical English, dashed by the slightest
foreign accent. She lost all patience at last, and flatly refused to
answer any more questions. Her tormentors did not lose their
temper, but left her for a while, and then came back to resume
the verbal infliction. All this was necessary, perhaps, for Justice
and for expiation. It formed the first stage of the agony of
Florence Armytage. It was the preface to a voluminous and
terrific Act of Accusation.

She had been in another prison—where, she knew not, but it
seemed to be in the centre of Paris—for at least a week before
she was brought within the precincts of the Palace of Justice,
and immured *au secret* in a cell belonging to the Conciergerie.
Before she came hither, they gave her nothing but bread and
water morning and evening, with some thin soup at noonday.
They told her at the Conciergerie that she was now *à la pistole*,—
that is, she could order any sustenance she liked, which would be
paid for from the funds found upon her. She might have pens,
ink, and paper, and write as many letters as she chose. She
might have any books to read,—novels and *vaudevilles* even, if
she pleased. She might smoke her cigarette, if it were agreeable
to her, and take her glass of curaçoa after dinner: she would be
treated in all respects like a lady. Nay, Justice itself might not
feel indisposed to look benignantly on her manifold offences,
if she would but consent to answer certain questions, and
to deliver up a certain packet of papers, of which she
was either the possessor, or of which she knew the place

of concealment. It was but a trifling favour they asked from her; it might add some years of liberty to a life already doomed to incarceration; it might save that life itself. They sent the almoner of the prison to her,—a worthy ecclesiastic, with an oily smile and a sugared tongue. He called her his dear erring child, his strayed lamb, his stricken dove; he spoke of that Mercy which is Infinite; he touched, now on the chastisements of this world, whose severity, by prudence, might be mitigated,—now on the punishments of the next, which no human art, no human cunning could evade. Was it not better, after all, to *transiger avec la Justice?* Was it not worth while to try and mollify the furies, who were already plaiting their scorpion-whips for her? She was deaf to persuasions and deaf to entreaty. The old fiend came up within her, and made her incurably stubborn and rebellious. It was thus when she was a child, and could have avoided punishment by saying one little word, and would not say it, and suffered stripes and hunger and solitary durance. No, she would not say the word now; no, she would not give up the thing they wanted. No, she would NOT. Let them send her to the *travaux forcés* for life; let them shave her head, and dress her in the infamous grey flannel of the convict; let them drag her to the Place de la Roquette, and subject her to the same awful fate as that which Madame Laffarge so narrowly escaped; let them cut her to pieces, let them roast her over a slow fire; she was in their power, and they could do with her as it seemed best to them; but she would *not* say the word, and she would *not* deliver up the secret.

The tactics of her gaolers changed; the pious almoner, with oily smile and sugared tongue, kept away. He would return no more, they told her, in threatening tones, until the morrow of her condemnation to death, until the dawn of her execution-day. In lieu of the priest came a harsh prison-director, came the substitute of the Procurator of the Republic, with bitter reproach and stern menace. She must be subdued, they said. Her writing materials, her books, were taken away from her. The bread and water diet was resumed. She had been searched in London at the police-office, where Simon Lefranc had first taken her. She had been searched again at the Prefecture on her first arrival in Paris. She was again delivered over to the horrible crooked fingers of La Mère Camuse. It was then she began to bite and scratch, and kick and struggle; it was then they put the degrading *camisole de force* upon her.

And so God's sun, that shines for all, cast his radiance upon this wretched, forlorn, hopeless sinner, for she had no hope left. She had ceased even to trust in her Influence. She was in a rage at her capture, as a tigress might be in a rage when caught in the toils. She hated herself; and could see, in her soul's mirror, how black and stained with loathsome crimes she was; but she did not repent. They would kill her now, she supposed; let them. The guillotine was the last infliction she could suffer in this life—and beyond that? She saw the Place de la Roquette, two tall posts, the board on rollers, the impending knife, the long red basket filled with saw-dust. She felt in imagination the cold steel of the executioner's scissors, as he sheared her shining tresses from the back of her neck to give the axe's edge full play. And she felt the last awful stroke; heard the heavy thud of the axe as it fell: that was death of a surety; but beyond that was nothing but a huge, black, boundless, and eternal voyage. Was ever woman in worse case than this?

On the morning when the sun was shining, there came a tap at the wicket of her cell; and the Judas-hole was opened, and an impudent face peered through the grating.

"Open, Mère Camuse," said the voice of Simon Lefranc; "open, and let us look at our little caged bird."

The searcher gave admission to the Chief of the Spies, who had ingress everywhere.

"You can wait outside for a few minutes," Simon said, sauntering into the dungeon with his hands in his pockets, his hat on one side, and his heart on his sleeve as usual.

The old woman began to grumble a little, and plead her orders not to leave her prisoner alone even for a moment; but Simon put her aside with a confident shrug and a confident grin, telling her that she knew the prisoner was perfectly safe with him, and that if he could not manage her, the whole body of the French police, *gendarmerie*, spies, and political agents to boot, would be unequal to the task. So the Mère Camuse, still grumbling, but quite subservient, surrendered her key of office to the spy, and submitted to be locked out. Simon took the additional precaution of shutting the trap of the Judas-hole, which could be pulled inwards if a certain spring was touched. Then he advanced to where the prisoner sat on her truckle-bed, haggard and wan, in the sunshine; then he pulled a stool towards her, and sat down facing his caged bird; then he produced his never-failing cigar-case, took out a Trabuco, bit off the tip, moistened the stump, kindled a fusee on the sole of his boot, lighted his cigar, crossed one leg over the other, rested one hand on his hip, one elbow on his knee, and, tranquilly emitting little skeins of smoke, contemplated the prisoner with quite a paternal air.

"And how is our little bird?" he asked, in a tone that was meant to be soothing, and might have been so had it not been inconceivably insolent.

The little bird made, as well as her muffled hands would allow, a gesture of disdain, and uttered an inarticulate murmur of repugnance towards her visitor.

"Come, come; we must not be angry with our Simon; we must not grieve the heart of our good Papa."

At the word Papa the thoughts of Florence Armytage darted, straight as an arrow from the Tartar's bow, three hundred miles away from that dreary Conciergerie cell to an up-stair room in a boarding-house at Bayswater, where a man with the face of a ruffian was working in a little laboratory,—she lounging in a great easy-chair, he laughing and joking as he poured one liquid from one phial to another, and calling her his Florence and his darling, and saying that he would find out the great secret yet, and make all their fortunes.

"Papa!" Mrs. Armytage almost mechanically repeated, but with an accent of bitter scorn.

"Yes, Papa," resumed Simon, "Grandpapa, Uncle, Cousin, Guardian—everything now except Judge and Jury. We must be obedient to our Papa; we must listen to what he says for his own satisfaction and our own good. Else things will go hardly with us. They have gone a little hardly with us lately. Eh, *ma mie?*"

She groaned bitterly. "They have indeed, Heaven knows," she muttered.

E E

"That is because we have been naughty. Naughty children must be punished; when they are good, they are kissed, and have *bon-bons* given them : we have been punished with the *camisole de force*, and bread and water, and the attentions of the Mère Camuse. Would we not like to be good, and have our books and papers back again? have a nice little roast chicken and a bottle of Moselle for dinner ? and wear a nice morning wrapper instead of that ugly *camisole*, and take a walk in the courtyard and see the sky, and a green tree or two, and the faces of our fellow-creatures ? "

"I should like to be out of this place," said Mrs. Armytage. "I would be sooner torn to pieces by wild horses than remain in it two days longer. Why don't they try me, and send me to the galleys at once ? "

"They don't send ladies to the galleys in this polite country, *ma petite maman*," replied Simon; "they send them to a nice little *maison centrale*, where they shave their heads, and put them to nice hard work. Besides, do you know, *mon ange*, that you have done some funny little things that M. le Procureur de la République knows all about, and which may lead him to demand, not that you be sent to the galleys, but that your pretty little head be cut off ? "

"I am not guilty," said Mrs. Armytage.

"Bah!" cried the spy, rising, knocking the ash off his cigar, changing his tone as he did so from banter to harshness. "*A d'autres, ces contes jaunes.* Listen to me, Widow Armytage; listen to me, woman with half-a-dozen names and half-a-thousand crimes; listen to me, forger, murderess, swindler, thief! You will not be tried before you have been found guilty between the four walls of this cell, or those of the cabinet of the examining judge. Little by little the Act of Accusation has been building up ; it will not take the jury ten minutes to decide your fate ; it will not take the Advocate-General twenty minutes to plead your head off your white shoulders. Justice has got hold of you, my pet; that Justice which never loosens its grip till the bird is dead, or the mouse is torn to pieces. You are in the claws of the cat of the Palace of Justice. *La chatte que ne perd jamais son rat.* Do you want to live or die? "

"I want to have this strait-waistcoat taken off, and to be allowed to comb my hair." Her poor golden ringlets! they were indeed wofully dishevelled.

"The only way to have your wish, the only way to save your life, is to reply to that which has been asked of you,—is to render up those papers which you have, or of which you know the hiding-place."

"Indeed!"

"Will you consent?"

"No! a thousand times no!"

"Under those circumstances," said Simon Lefranc, again returning to his tone of bantering politeness, "I have the honour to wish you, Madame Armytage, a very good morning. A few more questions will shortly be put to you by some one who has even more authority than I have to ask them, and who will perhaps be more successful in his interrogations."

He moved towards the door, unlocked it, and went out into the corridor; then gave some whispered orders in a low tone to the Mère Camuse, and so departed. Five minutes after he was lounging, with his hat on one side, and his hands in his pockets, and his heart upon his sleeve, through the great Hall of the Lost Footsteps; and as he paced those well-worn flags he said mentally, "We have but one more resource left,—the locket,—and that, I think, will not fail us."

The female turnkey did not inflict her abhorred presence upon the prisoner for a full half-hour after the departure of Simon Lefranc; then she entered the cell accompanied by another assistant, almost as tall, and quite as forbidding in appearance, as herself. Florence Armytage turned to see what new tortures were in store for her. To her surprise, the two women approached her with something like gentleness in their manner, and addressed her in language which was almost kind. They took from her the hated *camisole de force;* they had brought with them a bundle containing a suit of her own apparel, rich and dainty as she was wont to wear; not, however, the toilet in which she had been taken prisoner, but another. In this they would with their own hands have attired her; but, with an invincible feeling of repulsion, she declined the services of these

E E 2

ghastly chamber-maids, and when bidden to dress herself, did so
with much meekness.   They let her comb her pretty hair, holding
a mirror for her as she arranged it in the old fascinating clusters
of ringlets.   They gave her a bonnet, a glistening toy of ribbons
and beads and feathers ; they gave her a pair of her old Houbi-
gant six-and-a-quarter gloves ; they gave her a cambric handkerchief, artfully scented; they even, with a sardonic smile, offered
her some *rouge*.   She allowed them to lace her little *bottines*,
those wonderful little *bottines* the heels of which had been so
often tapped in petty petulance on the soft carpets, those *bottines*
which had covered the little feet that had trodden so often the
paths of vanity, and vice, and crime.   They then gave her her
parasol, and bade her put her Brussels lace veil down ; and, but
that she had no jewels, no chains of gold, but that she had no
little dog to follow her, but that her face was deadly pale and
that there were livid lines under her eyes and at the corners of
her mouth, she was the old Florence Armytage of the golden
ringlets and the rustling drapery.

They asked her if she would have some refreshment; and all
proud and rebellious as the little woman had been, she valued
her creature-comforts too highly not to accept an improvement
in her bill-of-fare, when it could be accepted without damaging
concessions.   So with sufficient appetite, yet in somewhat of a
mechanical manner likewise, she ate a little meat and drank a
little wine, and felt a little stronger for that which was to come
next: what that was to be, she did not know.   She waited after
this repast another full half-hour, then another tap came to the
wicket, and one of the *huissiers* of the Palace, a grave man in
black, with a silver chain round his neck, entered the cell,
accompanied by two *gendarmes*.

"The Widow Armytage," said the *huissier*, in as sonorous a
tone as though he had been addressing a crowded audience
instead of a wretched prisoner, to the gaolers, "is summoned to
appear before *M. le Juge d'Instruction* in his cabinet.   Widow
Armytage, you will accompany me."

The Widow Armytage rose submissively from the truckle-bed,
where she had been sitting ready dressed.   A *gendarme* placed
himself on either side of her, and the *huissier* preceding, the

little procession passed through the door, and began to move
through the corridors of the prison.

The two she-gaolers were left together.

"Her affair will soon be settled," said the Mère Camuse,
beginning to arrange the prisoner's bed.

"Not so soon, perhaps, as you imagine," replied the second
harridan. She will give *M. le Juge d'Instruction*, and the whole
Palace of Justice into the bargain, more trouble than half-a-dozen
brigands and assassins. *Une fameuse! Allez.*"

"What is she accused of?" said the Mère Camuse. "I know
she nearly kicked me to pieces, and bit my hand through, when
I was making my little perquisitions."

"How do I know?" replied the other; "it is none of our
business to inquire. We shall know soon enough when the Court
of Assizes opens."

You see that they manage these things so much better in
France.

The corridors and the passages through which the *gendarmes*,
the *huissier*, and Florence Armytage passed, the staircases they
ascended and descended, seemed interminable. Once they
emerged into a narrow iron gallery, running along the wall, but
close to the roof of the great Hall of the Lost Footsteps. The
gendarmes kept closer to Florence as they traversed this gallery.
She could look down, however, and see far below on the pavement the straggling groups of weary suitors nibbling oyster-
shells; the little knots of black-capped, black-robed advocates
swallowing fat oysters. She did not see, but was clearly seen by,
our friend with his hands in his pockets and his heart on his
sleeve, who, as he craned his neck to watch her pass with her
escort, gave a low whistle, and said "*Bon!* Our little affair is
about to be decided. Let us see what *M. le Juge* will make of
our obstinate little friend."

And Simon Lefranc was seen no more that day in the Hall of
the Lost Footsteps.

The *gendarmes* and their charge passed through a little swing
door covered with baize, descended a wide and somewhat handsome staircase, and entered a long, lofty, vaulted corridor, into
which opened many doors, each bearing a name inscribed upon

its centre panel; each door had beside a number. These were
the cabinets of *MM. les Juges d'Instruction*; and into cabinet
No. 5, Florence Armytage was ushered, the *huissier* preceding her,
but the *gendarmes* remaining outside.

The door was immediately locked behind her, a chair was
pointed out to her, and she was bidden to sit down. After the
gloomy sternness of the cell she had just left, after the cold and
naked want and misery in which she had passed the days of her
captivity—she who had passed her wicked life in tremor and
anxiety certainly, but still in silken luxury and wanton plenty
and soft repose,—it was a relief to Florence to find herself in an
apartment which offered no signs of being in contiguity to the
sternest and most repellent of French prisons. Cabinet No. 5,
was an apartment of considerable size, comfortably, and even
handsomely furnished, thickly carpeted, with heavy curtains to
the windows, a number of easy-chairs about, and with a handsome
clock ticking on the marble mantel-piece beneath the insignia of
the Republic one and indivisible. There were two large book-
cases, and in the centre of the room was a huge official table
covered with leather, and strewed with filed and docketed papers.
Before it was a vacant arm-chair; and directly in a line with this,
facing the table, Florence Armytage and *her chair* were planted
by the silent and dexterous *huissier*.

The clock on the mantel-piece had marked the passage of ten
minutes, when a side door, not the one by which Florence had
entered, opened, and there entered, smirking and smiling, and
clad in the invariable black with a white neckcloth, but with the
ribbon of the Legion of Honour at his button-hole, a charming
gentleman of middle age, a bald head and a blue eye, a fair whisker
and a rosy cheek, and a gleaming set of teeth, and a white soft
hand decorated with a snowy wristband, and a diamond brooch in
his frill, and a signet-ring on his right fore-finger, and a heavy
chain and seals, and polished boots and a large yellow China silk
pocket-handkerchief, of which he made frequent and sounding use.
This was the *Juge d'Instruction*. He looked much less like a
judge attached to a court of criminal judicature than like a prosperous linen-draper's assistant, or an English ladies' physician, or
a fashionable undertaker—say Plumer Ravenbury for instance—

who did not wish to look too professional, but liked to combine the
mortuary with the mundane. Yet M. Plon was the *Juge d'Instruction* all over, the sharp astute criminal inquisitor, who had
had to do with many scores of assassins, robbers, and vagabonds,
male and female, in his time, and who, though shorn of his quondam powers of rack and thumb-screw, was in spirit the lineal
descendant of those old counsellors of the Parliament, in the
ancien régime, who, when they went home at night, used to be
asked by their pretty wives whether they had applied the torture
to any one that day. And M. Plon, making a sidelong bow as he
entered, to Justice in general, and the prisoner in particular,
seated himself in his great arm-chair, first threw himself back in a
critical manner, and, shading his blue eyes with one of the white
hands, looked long and keenly at Florence. Then he leant forward on his table, folded his white hands about six inches in
advance, so that his signet-ring might be displayed to the best
advantage, flashed his white teeth on the captive widow, and took
another keen glance at her with the blue eyes. This was what
M. Plon called " fixing his subject."

He fixed her so well that she flinched under his gaze, as
birds are said to do beneath the fascination of the basilisk.
There was nothing terrifying either in M. Plon or in his speech.
He was simply fascinating, and murdered while he fascinated.

" And your state of health, madame?" he asked, with polite
suddenness.

" I am as well as I can expect to be," Florence answered.

" You have been subject to some severities. Justice regrets
them ; but you have left us no other alternative. Even as it is,
you have been treated with certain *égards* and certain *ménage-
ments* which, to one in your position, might justifiably have been
withheld."

" I know that I have been stripped and searched over and over
again, and treated with the most revolting indignity, by two horrible old women. I know that I have been thrust into a strait-
waistcoat, as though I were a raving maniac. I know that I have
been half-starved, and debarred, not only from writing to my
friends and to my professional advisers, but from even reading
a book."

"The exigencies of the case, my dear madame,—only consider the exigencies of the case. The provocation,—you must bear the provocation in mind. We acted towards you with the tenderest solicitude until we were compelled, through your contumacy, to have recourse to harsh measures. Your arrest in England was surrounded by elements of the most chivalrous courtesy"—*M. le Juge* was speaking in French—"on the part of the agents of authority. Only judge of what a scandal, what an exposure, what an *esclandre*, from your capture in so public a place in a public manner!"

"Yes," Florence said, "I was captured, that is to say, kidnapped, in the most private manner. I was brought over here like a bale of contraband goods. I have been smuggled from prison to prison, and tormented in every imaginable way. Are these your notions of Law and Justice, *M. le Juge?*"

"My dear madame, we manage things differently on this side of the water. You have probably heard that sentiment before. All that has been done could be justified to you by rule and precedent, if justification were needed; but it is not. We have here, my dear madame, within the walls of the Palais de Justice, and the adjacent Conciergerie, what is called *le pouvoir matériel*, the material power; and, within the limits of reason, we act as we please, and how we please. However, I am not about to bandy words with you. I have one or two little questions to ask you, and we will at once proceed to business."

He unclasped the white hands, and taking a little silver bell which stood on the table beside him, softly tinkled it. In a minute or two a *huissier*—not Florence's *huissier*, he had been motionless all this while behind her chair—made his appearance at the side door.

"Beg *M. le Greffier* to step hither."

The *huissier* retired, and almost immediately afterwards the snake-like personage in the rusty black and the dingy white, who had accompanied the first inquisitor to Florence's dungeon, made his appearance.

"Will you be good enough, monsieur, to take a seat and transcribe while I proceed with the examination of this lady?"

"I cannot bear it! I cannot bear it!" cried Florence, covering her face with her hands. "Do anything to me; but spare me the infliction of that frightful ordeal. Send these men away, and I will answer any questions you like to put to me."

"*M. le Greffier*," said M. Plon, his white teeth blandly beaming, "will you have the goodness to retire? *Huissiers*," he added, "you may withdraw. If there be any further necessity for your services, I will ring."

When they were left alone, the *Juge d'Instruction* once more threw himself back in his great arm-chair, and took a survey of his prisoner in the critical manner, shading his blue eyes with his hand meanwhile. Then he bent forward, clasped his hands before him, and said, as blandly as ever:

"Now, madame, do you know anything of the original of the portrait contained in this locket?"

And, so saying, he held aloft a little golden locket attached to a slender chain. It was open, and framed within it was the portrait of a fair young man, clad in English military uniform, and with very full auburn moustaches.

CHAPTER XXXIII

"*L'affaire de la Rue des Oursins?*" The particulars of that affair at Finchley? The mystery of the Man with the Iron Mask? The Gowrie conspiracy? The Spanish marriages? Don Pacifico's wrongs? The Crimean war? Fauntleroy's bankruptcy? Mrs. Potiphar's divorce case? Mrs. Faggot's diamonds? The gold-dust robbery? Mr. Toadycram's Peerage? The great literary quarrel between Mr. Sphoon and Doctor Bunglecrumpus? Why Miss Cygnet left the stage, and how Jack Elbowsout manages to give dinner parties? Signor Cobra di Capello's hold on my Lord Fitzgypesland; and Signora Mercandotti's relationship to the Bishop of Bosfursus—she is said to be his niece; friendly George Gafferer's daily dinner, and clean shirt even? Does everybody know all about those enigmas? Have those mysteries been quite solved? Has the *dernier mot* been spoken? and does nothing more remain to be told in connection with those histories?

The noble prayer of the historian Niebuhr was to live until he could bring his Roman record down to the period where Gibbon began. He was not spared to accomplish a tithe of his task; and there is a dark yawning gulf between the end of exploded Roman fable, and the beginning of Roman fact. Was Mr. Gibbon quite certain about his facts either? Truly, he quotes Ammianus, and Zosimus, and the Abbé de la Bléterie, and a thousand others; but might not Ammianus, and Zosimus, and the Abbé de la Bléterie, with their thousand brethren, have lied sometimes? My great-grandson may be fortunate enough to receive a somewhat better education than his ancestor. He may turn historian and write the chronicle of the last Tuscan revolution, taking the Marquis of Normanby, and Sir George Bowyer, as guides for his facts. *Your* great-grandson may condescend to undertake a similar task, adopting the state papers of Baron Ricasoli as his authorities. I don't think the two historians will agree very closely. How, too, is M. Thiers' biography of Napoleon I., in the *Consulate and the Empire*, to be reconciled with our old friend, the Père Loriquet's statement that Louis XVIII. returned to his dominions in 1815, on the "resignation" of the "Marquis de Bonaparte," who during fifteen years had governed France for him? And the panegyrics of MM. Méry and Belmontet upon the present order of things? How will they tally with M. Hugo's opuscule "Napoleon the Little?" And the *Penny Trumpet's* eulogy on my last epic, as compared with the *Sixpenny Slaughter-house's* demolition of the same? Will the truth, the whole truth, and nothing but the truth, ever come out, I wonder? Did Sir Hector Haynau really beat his wife, or did Lady Haynau (she was a Miss Brownrigg) beat him? There are people who are ready to take an affidavit that they have seen the letters which passed between Mrs. Aholibah and Captain Lawless, containing, they say, a clear confession of her guilt; there are others who maintain that she was the most injured of women, and that all her troubles were due to the machinations of that wicked Miss Blackadder. I read the other day in a paper called the *Spiritual Magazine*, that I had been *incognito* to a spirit-rapping medium, and expressed myself much surprised and edified by what I saw and heard. The whole narrative—beyond the fact of my having once paid half-a-crown to a very clumsy Witch of Endor in Red Lion Street, Holborn, who was about as successful in raising the ghost of Samuel as though she had tried to evoke the spirit of Samuel Hall—was from beginning to end a tissue of abominable lies; and yet, I dare say, there are people who believe in the *Spiritual Magazine*, and that my conversion to rappology has been quoted by many devout rapparees. If I am ever unlucky enough to be hanged, I doubt not but that the Seven Dials Plutarch, who compiles my biography, will add a belief in spirit-rapping to the catalogue of my crimes.

It is all very well to put together a neat collection of state-ments, and weave an ingenious theory round them, and found a variety of more or less sage comments upon them; but is this,

after all, history? I am afraid not, and that my account of the
transactions entered into by Mammon, and his several sons, their
friends and acquaintances, may be proved in the main to be as
unreliable, say as Herodotus, or as Guicciardini, or as Roger of
Wendover. You see that I have an implicit belief in the reality
of my story, and of my characters. There is not an incident or a
personage in these pages that is wholly imaginary, any more than
in a dream; there is not a single thing, however wild and improbable it may appear, but has formed part, at some time or another,
of the action of our lives; only, in this tale, as in a vision of the
night, coherence may be to some extent absent, and time and
place slightly confused, and the unities violated, and the round
people put, sometimes, into the square holes, or *vice versâ*. But
my chief difficulty lies in the uncertainty as to whether the events
I am about to narrate came about precisely in the order and in
the manner I have followed. Somebody may know the history of
Sir Jasper's misfortunes, of Mrs. Armytage's agony, better than
I do, and may be enabled to give a version of the affair differing
very widely from mine. What says the governor of Lewes Gaol?
What sayest thou, T. R., attorney-at-law? *You* knew Florence,
well enough. How much have I left unsaid? How much have I
added? How much altered? And the catastrophe—the wind-
ing-up—which is imminent? Is *that*, strictly in accordance with
what actually took place? We shall never know, probably, any
more than we shall ever be enabled to tell, with exactitude,
whether Troy was ever besieged for the sake of a quarrel about
Mrs. Menelaus; whether Dick Whittington was ever indebted to
a cat for his fortune and his fame; and whether there was ever a
British king called Arthur, who had a queen (not over prudent)
named Guinevere. The false is ever mixed with the true; there
is always the golden as well as the silver side to the shield; there
are always people ready to come into court and make oath that
they saw the chameleon of a bright sky-blue colour, and others
who persist in swearing that he was pink; and the balance will
not be struck, and the needle will not be eliminated from the
bottle of hay, and the pearl picked from the dunghill, until human
lying and human blundering are of no more account than tobacco
ashes,—until the fools who wrote "Essays and Reviews" are con-

founded at their own impudent ignorance, and the mud in the
wine-glass becomes clearer than the crystal, and a towering tree
springs from the grain of mustard seed, and all our tiny cock-
boats of fancied learning, and fancied reason, and fancied logic,
are swallowed up in the great dazzling ocean of God's Truth.

A year, so I assume, had passed. The greensward once more
showed itself in Hyde Park on the site of the Exhibition building,
and the ingenious persons who had speculated on finding thousands
of pounds in bracelets, sleeve buttons, and porte-monnaies, dropped
by careless visitors between the interstices of the flooring, had
reaped an abundant crop of disappointment. The world had gone
on pretty much as usual. There had been, to be sure, a *coup d'état,*
and a change of government in a neighbouring country, but the
fact of the Empire being Peace had not caused larks to fall ready-
roasted from the skies ; while a certain ruler's change of residence
from the Elysée to the Tuileries had not materially affected the
receipts of the Pompes Funèbres. When you and I die, the sun
will not necessarily put on a mourning hatband ; and I am afraid
that the undertaker's men will be as merry and as thirsty as ever,
as they swing their legs over the black roof coming homewards. I
have heard of a whole nation being "plunged in grief" at the death
of a king or a great man. I want to know whether this immersion
in sorrow ever caused an appreciable diminution in the consumption of butcher's meat. When the great Mirabeau died, Mr.
Carlyle tells us that the populace, in the exuberance of their grief,
would not permit the playgoers to enter the theatres, so the baffled
amusement hunters thronged all the cafés instead, and wept over
the departed patriot and their *petits verres* until two o'clock in the
morning. Do you remember the eve and the day of the great
Duke of Wellington's funeral ? The nights belonging to them
were two of the most drunken ever known in the metropolis of
Britain. I think John Evelyn has something to the same effect
to say concerning the interment of Oliver Cromwell, and Horace
Walpole of the obsequies of George the Second. It is curious to
mark how impulsively a nation "plunged in grief" betakes itself
to drinking.

Well, a year had passed, and friendly George Gafferer dined
and wore clean linen as usual. The years passed lightly over the

amicable creature's head. He was discreet, and, like Fontenelle, took care not to remind the ruling powers too often of how old he was and how undeserving. So they, having matters of more moment in hand, seemed to let him be. It chanced one mellow evening, in the summer of 1852, that George was bidden to the annual feast of the Hospital for Hare Lip, held at the Freemasons'. Doctor Tooth, the honorary physician, had sent him a card, under a vague impression that George was connected with the press. He had about as much connexion with it as an ex-fifer in the German Legion has with the British army. George was in high feather on the Hare Lip night; worthy Mr. Splitmug, the secretary to the institution, had received him most courteously in the ante-chamber, and bidden the head waiter to take special care of him, as of the other gentlemen of the press, in the way of choice wines with curious seals, grapes of rarity, and peaches of price. Mr. Widemouth, treasurer, had come down and tapped him on the back, and whispered to him that his last paragraph on the claims of the Hospital for public support in *The Tinkling Cymbal* was capital. The friendly man had no more written it than he had climbed up Mont Blanc that morning before breakfast. Nay, more than this, to crown his cornucopia of pleasure, the Royal Duke who was to take the chair had, in squeezing past him, positively accosted him and vouchsafed to say, "How do—how do—hope you are quite well—quite well, hay?" George was in ecstasies; these condescending words were spoken in the hearing of at least six waiters, and of all the gentlemen of the press. Cabinet Steinwein was immediately brought for him to drink with his turbot. Old Mopps, of *The Vulture*, the man who always takes three times salmon, and curses the waiters, and hates and envies everybody, looked up with a wolfish glare as the Gafferer was thus honoured. The truth is, that His Royal Highness did not know George from Adam, but he had seen his friendly phiz so often at reviews, dinners, fancy-fairs, and other meetings of a public nature, that he fancied he must know him, although whether George was a lord of the bedchamber or a half-pay quartermaster with a grievance, or a member of Parliament, or a rural dean, was quite a matter of uncertainty to the royal mind. But what he said was uttered in his blue riband and his star, and amidst the strains of "See the Conquering Hero comes," and George well-nigh boarded and lodged on the strength of the royal notice for the next three months.

Little Topinamboo, of *The Mosquito*, was George's right-hand neighbour. O'Crawl, of *The Gutter Lane Chronicle*, was on his left. Mopps, of *The Vulture*, and Thuggy, of *The Hempen Record*, one of the oldest of the London reporters, the man who saw Thistlewood's head cut off, *and knows who cut it off*, ha, ha! he darkly boasts over his second bottle, were opposite. The gentlemen of the press were very merry, and the eloquent orators who made speeches half-an-hour long, and expected a verbatim report of their orations, were somewhat mortified to find the next morning that the whole narrative of the dinner in aid of the funds for the Hospital for Hare Lip was comprised in a twenty-line paragraph. *Sic itur ad astra ;* only we don't always go starward the same way, and it is a long time in the estimation of the gentlemen of the press before we ourselves become "stars" enough to be reported verbatim.

Said George to Mopps (who was leading the waiter a terrible life about ice-pudding), " Do you recollect Sir Jasper Goldthorpe's being in the chair here for the Hare Lips in '47 ? "

"It was not for the Hare Lips," grumbled Mopps, who had secured two slices of pudding from two different waiters, and who was not even then quite satisfied. "It was the Institution for supplying Wellington boots to people with wooden legs. And it wasn't at the Freemasons', it was at the London Tavern; and you were there, and ate up all the olives, as usual."

"Mopps is right," quoth little Topinamboo; "what a memory you have, Mopps. I remember Sir Jasper's being in the chair well, and how we had to give a column and a half of his speech, for he was such a great gun, and was going to be made a lord, so everybody said."

"That Gafferer is always making blunders," muttered O'Crawl, who loathed our friend, and would willingly have drowned him in water-souché. "H'what does he want here, saying that he belongs to the press, when he never had anything more to do with a newspaper than to collect advertisements for *The Pawnbrokers' Gazette*."

"Well," continued George, somewhat abashed, "Hare lip or wooden legs, it does not much matter, you need not be so hard upon a fellow. I only wanted to say that I saw Sir Jasper Gold-thorpe to-day."

"I thought he had hanged himself," growled Mopps, who was putting a composite finish to his dinner, with a plate full of pestachio ice, blanc mange, plovers' eggs, macaroons, and Stilton cheese, and was draining his vast array of wine-glasses lest the waiters carrying them off should find any "ullages" in them for surreptitious tippling on staircases.

"I heard he had gone into the Charterhouse or the workhouse," Mr. Topinamboo observed.

"I had heard he had emigrated, and got into trouble about stealing a horse," charitably observed Mr. Thuggy.

"Sure I heard he was dead," tranquilly observed O'Crawl, slicing a pine-apple.

"Not the least in the world," resumed George. "I saw him to-day in Regent Street, quite old and broken, and with his hair as white as snow."

"Seedy?" asked Mopps.

"Dreadfully!"

"I am glad of it," the Samaritan opposite observed, with a savage grin; "then there is no new swindle up for him to fatten on."

"He was always a poor mean-spirited creature," chimed in little Topinamboo, who had not courage enough to say bo to a goose, to say nothing of Goldthorpe.

"And of the very lowest origin," Mr. O'Crawl remarked, dis-dainfully. Mr. O'Crawl was a member of the Fawn-coloured Kid Glove Club, and was the son, people said, of a tinker somewhere in Tipperary.

"I thought," honest Mr. Thuggy, who was a man of slow and deliberate utterance, said, "that the affair would have ended criminally. It always struck me that Goldthorpe had a hanging face; he was just like the portrait of the elder Perreau, and walked precisely like Dr. Dodd."

"Did you see Dr. Dodd hanged, Thuggy?" asked George, desperately diving, in the attempt to say something smart.

"I did not, sir," replied, with great solemnity, the attaché of
The Hempen Record, and finishing his last glass of Madeira; "but
I shall have the very greatest pleasure in seeing you hung, George,
and have no doubt that I shall, and that the time is not far
distant. You smell of rue, sir, and have a gallows look; and if
you live anywhere, you ought to take lodgings in a rope-walk."

George was not very comfortable after this, and felt rather
relieved than otherwise when the cloth was drawn, and the port
came on, and the speechifying began, and he could make a show
of taking short-hand notes, which, for any useful purpose they
served, might just as well have been a catalogue in stenography
of the kings of England from the Conquest.

But we must leave these jovial members of the Fourth Estate,
good fellows with all their failings, and liking each other very
well, notwithstanding their occasional squabblings. George
Gafferer was right, for a wonder, in what he had said concerning
Sir Jasper Goldthorpe. *He had* seen the Baronet that day in
Regent Street, and more than this, the former magnate of the
City was to be seen every day in the great fashionable West End
thoroughfare between four and five in the afternoon.

One can scarcely tell why, it may be, knowing that an impassable gulf lay between him and the City, where once he had reigned
supreme, he had some feeble idea that the bloody hand which still
glowered in his shield gave him a kind of grasp on the polite world.
He was, as George described him, wofully "seedy;" but his seedi-
ness had now a more woful tinge of faded dandyism in it. The
poor old thread-bare coat had a velvet collar, the boots down at
heel were of varnished leather, the trousers, frayed at the bottoms,
had a stripe down the sides, the gloves were dingy, but they had
been of white buckskin. Thus accoutred, with a cheap cane in
his shaking hand, he was an object ten times more pitiable than
had he been more tattered and torn than the man in the nursery
rhyme. He was very changed. He was very old. He was
scarcely fifty-two, but he looked seventy. He halted in his
speech, and forgot people's names. He was a long time in finding
his glasses, and when he had found them, had much trouble in
reading manuscript even by their aid. His hand-writing, once
so bold and firm, was now scarcely legible; he, the great financier,

F F

blundered over the slightest arithmetical calculation. A year had
done all this.   Have you never known instances as terrible of the
utter wholesale shipwreck made of men and women by disaster?
They are not the same people, they walk and talk, and eat and
drink in a different manner.   I knew once a hale, rollicking,
lusty, speculative kind of a man, full of talk of dogs and horses,
and loose company, and living riotously on the best, who had a
year's imprisonment and hard labour, for some fraudulent dealings
of his with a Company.   I saw him the day after he came forth
from his captivity,—he was another man.   It was not only that
the full beard and moustachios were shaved off, that the eyes
were sunken and the cheeks hollow, that he no more drove mail-
phaetons or gave dinners at Greenwich, that he was humbled and
contrite, but he had somebody else's manner—somebody who
skulked rather than walked,—somebody else's voice—and somebody's who for the last twelve months had been apparently residing in the catacombs—somebody else's ways, and tastes, and
thoughts.   He who, before his incarceration, had been a practical
and matter-of-fact sybarite, had turned poet in his captivity, and
showed me sentimental stanzas "On being put on the treadmill
for scratching my nose," " On having forty-eight hours of solitary
confinement for being found in possession of a lead pencil."
These changes are horrible.   To find, after a year, the woman
whom you have known beautiful, haughty, and fascinating, to·find
her dowdy and slipshod, with a flushed face, a moist lip, a bloodshot eye, and a lock of hair hanging over her forehead, and to be
told by a good-natured friend, with a significant conveyance of
the finger and thumb to the mouth, and a throwing back of the
head, that she has taken to—never mind what.   To hear the man
whose strong, vigorous, brilliant intellect awed and astonished you
twelve months ago, bubble forth maudlin inanities ; to be accosted
in a sheepish manner and asked for half-a-crown by the old schoolmaster who used to cane you,—these seem revulsions improbable,
nay, almost impossible, yet they occur around us every day.

Fate had been good to Sir Jasper Goldthorpe in one sense,
but had dealt hardly with him in another.   Fate had at least
decreed that he should emerge from his ruin personally unharmed.
The enemies who predicted that he must necessarily be convicted

of swindling, robbery, and fraud, were disappointed. He went through the long and tedious ordeal of bankruptcy, not, indeed, without difficulty nor without discredit, but he came out of Basinghall Street safe and sound, and in dread of no penal clauses. It is true that, some of his transactions appearing to the Commissioner as somewhat dubious, his certificate, when granted, was of the third class, was suspended for awhile, and without protection. He had the consolation of being informed by one of the messenger's merry men, that in the then temper of the Chief Commissioner he wouldn't grant a first-class certificate to an angel, even if he could pay fifty shillings in the pound, and that, as things went, a third class was as good as a second class, and infinitely better than no certificate at all. The withholding of protection was a more serious matter; and, indeed, Sir Jasper was taken in execution ten minutes after he had left the tribunal of fiats and dockets, by the trustees of an infuriated widow at Muswell Hill, of whose jointure he had made ducks and drakes. He sojourned for a season, I am ashamed to say, in Whitecross Street; for his allowance from the creditors while the bankruptcy was pending had stopped, and he was temporarily without even the necessary funds to purchase a habeas corpus for conveyance to the Queen's Bench. For although that famous writ is one of right, and is granted as a matter of course to every suffering Englishman, it has become, like every other thing in England, purchaseable; and if you want the palladium of English liberty you must pay for it a matter of some two pounds ten shillings. So, to the Middlesex side of Whitecross Street Prison the baronet was duly taken, after a brief enjoyment of the cordial but costly hospitality of Mr. Nebuchadnezzar Barneywinkle, in Cursitor Street. Mr. Morris Hyams was good enough to officiate as cicerone towards the vile slum where the gaol is situated, and informed Sir Jasper that he had lately had an opportunity of "doing the polite" to his son, "the Capting," who, in Mr. Hyams' opinion was "a real swell, and no mistake." Father and son were spared the humiliation of meeting within the prison walls; Captain William had gone straight from Cursitor Street to the more aristocratic place of confinement in Southwark; but that brave woman, Lady Goldthorpe, came over to the regions of

Barbican so soon as she heard that her Goldie was in trouble,
walked with him in the narrow yard, and sat by him in the
reeking coffee-room, where the smell of beer, tobacco, steaks that
were broiling, and onions that were frying, and the sounds of
swearing, quarrelling, and singing, were mingled in one stifling
Babel of brawl and greasy vapour. The change had begun to
set in with Sir Jasper Goldthorpe. It was a very sad and curious
thing to watch him purchasing his petty groceries at the chandler's
shop in the yard; to see him wait anxiously at the grate for the
beer-boy; to see him at the huge roaring fire in the coffee-room,
with the inscription " *Dum spiro, spero* " flourished on the mantel
above, meekly waiting his turn to cook his half-pound of beef-
skirt. He dined at the stewards' table at first, but found that
too expensive. He, the erst richest man in the City of London,
was now to be seen peeling potatoes. He blacked his own boots.
He conciliated the turnkeys. He held a haggard baby while a
haggard husband dictated to a haggard wife some letter of vain
entreaty to a creditor with a heart as hard as the nether millstone.

Thank God that Pity is not dead! and if you would behold it
in its most beautiful and cheering form, go visit the wards of a
debtor's prison. You will see the very poor helping the very
poorest. You will see Pride, all tumbled down from its golden
throne, glad to consort with and to assist the very humblest and
meanest of mankind. You will see athletic men gladly performing menial offices, yet with a thoughtfulness and delicacy that
make quite a bright sunshine in the gloom and dolour of the
House of Sorrow. It is pity—mutual pity and succour and
compassion that lead captivity captive, that pad the fetters and
smooth the straw pallet—that make the spikes on the wall look
like a jasmine hedge, and change the bars at the casement into
a garden-trellis. I remember hearing once of an insolvent pig-
jobber in Horsemonger Lane Goal, who had struck up a friendship with a knavish attorney, likewise confined for debt, who had
a very pretty pale-faced wife. The little woman used to come to
see her husband—an arrant scamp who would have stolen the
gold setting from his grandmother's false teeth after she was
dead—every day. It was bitter wintry weather, and the poor

thing's feet were on the ground. Literally so, in a double sense, for she wore the shamefullest pair of lavender jean boots that ever you saw, and of which the dilapidated soles were sopped in mud one day, and frozen to her toes the next. This pig-jobber had a pair of clumping anklejacks, with soles as thick as the head of an Essayist and Reviewer—perfectly hideous to the view, but quite weatherworthy. He had no money, and his last pig had been jobbed at a loss, but he followed the pale-faced woman from the yard one day, and by the humane connivance of a turnkey— and there are many humane creatures among turnkeys—decoyed her into the inner lodge, and then and there half persuaded, half forced her to take off the lavender jean rags and to put on the anklejacks. She would have resisted, but he told her, in very bad grammar, that he had children of his own in Essex, and that he knew what it was. "They ain't handsome," quoth the pig-jobber—meaning his *chaussure*, not his offspring—when he had insisted on officiating as *valet de chambre*, and had laced on the boots—very tightly, for they were a world too large, and the laces had to be wound a dozen times round the little woman's ankles— "they ain't handsome, and they'd be better, p'r'aps, for a trifle of cotton stuffed into the toes; but I'll warrant 'em to stand all the mud in Smiffel on a market morning in Janiwerry." The pig-jobber went about for a fortnight afterwards in a pair of slippers of curious fashion, manufactured by himself, and made, apparently, from a scrap of matting and a fragment of engine hose; but I think that had he gone just then before the Great Commissioner of Insolvent Audit, he would not have been asked many questions as to why he was so shod, and what he had done with his stout serviceable anklejacks.

Of course the Reverend Ernest Goldthorpe could not permit his father to remain for any length of time in Whitecross Street. He was communicated with, and Sir Jasper was transferred by habeas to the Bench. There he had a room to himself, neatly furnished, and was attended by Mrs. Punt, laundress, own sister to Mesdames Grunt, Runt, Bunt, and Hunt, who "did for him," to use the classical term; made his bed, washed up his tea-things, stole his tea and sugar, and strongly adjured him, morning and night, to "go up like a man and ha' done with it." For Mrs.

Punt wisely considered, though to offer the counsel was somewhat against her own interest, that it was the bounden duty of every *detenu* in the Bench to proceed forthwith to the Insolvent Court and be purged from their debts. "When they stops here for a little," reasoned Mrs. Punt, "they've got money, and pays liberal. Then they goes up like men and has done with it, and gives me a crownd for luck when they gets their discharge. But when they won't file their sheddles, and turns aggerwating, and stops here for years, they've got no money left, or saves it all to bring hactions against the Governor, and they does for theirselves, and they ain't worth tuppence farden. A short life and a merry one for me." From which it may be gathered that Mrs. Punt was, after her fashion, a philosopher, and indeed was imbued with principles not very dissimilar to those subsequently embodied in the Bethell Bankruptcy Bill. She was an uncleanly female, neither too honest or too sober, but she had the heart that could feel for another, and was continually getting into trouble with the prison authorities for smuggling ardent spirits into its precincts in a bladder, worn by way of bustle. Within a month a few of Sir Jasper's old friends, the Reverend Ernest lending his assistance of course, made up a purse among them; the trustees of the infuriated widow at Muswell Hill were appeased, and Sir Jasper Goldthorpe came out into Belvidere Place, Southwark, quite a free man. We said he had friends who still clung to him, but they were mostly of those who in earlier days had been reckoned very low down indeed in the scale of his vassals and retainers. The polite world had done with him of course; the plutocracy of the City had formally repudiated him; but Argent, his former body-servant, who had set up a lodging-house in St. James's with the savings acquired in his service to Mammon, insisted on giving his old master a bank-note for fifty pounds, while the confidential Mr. Drossleigh informed Sir Jasper that he was instructed by a client to pay him ten pounds per quarter until further notice; and I have every reason to believe that the confidential Mr. Drossleigh's client was in this instance no other than the confidential Mr. Drossleigh himself. Misfortune had not, however, done with the bankrupt baronet. Within a month after his release, he began to mix himself up

with all kinds of petty cracked tea-kettle speculations. A few
bubble companies were glad of his name in the direction list; one
or two feeble and ephemeral schemes floated languidly for a time
in the stagnant atmosphere of Bartholomew Lane, with such
wind-bag assistance as he could give them. He even went into
the City and bought some ginger on speculation, and failed to
realise in time, and sold at a grievous loss. He drew bills which
Ernest Goldthorpe declined to accept. He began to scatter his
own signature about at three months, although it was now scarcely
worth the paper on which it was written. He muddled himself
with corn and coals. He had one or two agencies which did not
turn out prosperously. A fat and splendid gentleman driving a
very splendid mail phæton, with two very splendid and champing
grey horses splendidly harnessed—the same splendid gentleman,
in fact, whom Mrs. Armytage had seen at Paradise Cottage,
Badger Lane, Stockwell, the residence of Ephraim Tigg, Esq., the
Rasper—and who was indeed Mr. Montmorenci Sheenysson, the
fashionable bill-discounter of St. James's Place, entertained some
thoughts of employing Sir Jasper, on the strength of his baronetcy, as a runner, touter, or decoy-duck for young men about
town who wanted money, but he found the poor wretched ex-
millionaire quite unsuitable for his purpose. "He is aged," Mr.
Sheenysson, who was a sporting character, said conclusively; "he
is gone at the knees, and spavined. There is no pace and no
action in him; he is only fit for a night cab, and I am afraid it
won't be long before poor old G. goes to the knackers."

He was going thither, or to the dogs, or to the deuce, or on
some equally dreary pilgrimage, to his own bewilderment and the
despair of his wife, when Mr. Sims from Coger's Inn once more
appeared upon the stage. Months had passed since Mr. Sims had
made a momentous appearance in the lodging-house parlour in
Praed Street, Paddington. It was then that, in a few words, he
had relieved Sir Jasper's mind from a great burden, that he had
extricated him from an awful peril, that he had taken away the
sword of Damocles so long impending over him, that he had
rolled away for ever the stone like unto that which overhung the
sultan's bed, and for years had threatened to topple over and
crush him. It was done in a moment—done in that lodging-

house parlour. Lady Goldthorpe was horror-struck, but inevitably grateful. "Goldthorpe," he said, "Hugh Desborough is
come to save his old partner from wearing fetters on his ankles,
and working on the roads at Sydney. You have been a fool, and
worse than a fool, but it is very long ago, and let bygones be
bygones. Do you know these bills?"

He took out an oblong packet of papers, yellow and crumpled,
and fly-blown, with signatures crossing the body of the manuscripts at right angles.

"Good God!" cried the baronet; "they are the papers which
were held by that woman."

"They are; they are all forgeries, as you know. There is no
statute of limitation for felony. There are twenty years' trans-
portation in every one of those scraps of worthless paper; they
have been got from our little friend, never mind how. I got
them. I want to get something else from her, and will if I can.
And now, my friend, we will burn all these little acceptances."

He took the oblong packet—it was summer—and thrust it
between the bars of the bright little grate, with its trumpery
garniture of paper and tinsel shavings. He kindled a match, and
thrust it into the heap, and away up the chimney, with a thin
flame, and a thick cloud of white smoke, and a few bright sparks,
went garniture of paper and tinsel shavings, Judge, Jury, Counsel
for the Prosecution, sentence, hulks, chain gang, disgrace, and
ruin. Sir Jasper Goldthorpe was free, and to the world as innocent as the babe unborn.

He drew a long breath, and put his hand to his heart.

"You have nothing more of the same kind out," asked Mr.
Sims; "nothing more at three months, five-and-twenty-years old,
with a little mistake in the handwriting, have you?"

"Nothing, so help me Heaven!"

"Then, oh be joyful," observed Mr. Sims, scattering the
blackened embers of the paper with the poker. "I should just
like to know, however, how much Mrs. A. has had out of you on
the strength of those valuable securities."

"Thousands, thousands," murmured the baronet, rocking himself to and fro.

"How many thousands,—ten?"

" More, much more! "

" Whew! " and Mr. Sims indulged in a prolonged whistle.
" Of all the artful little parties I ever heard of, our friend was
certainly the artfullest. What a pity it is she could not resist
her Impulse."

" Where is she now ? " asked Sir Jasper.

" Abroad; she will never come home ; she is quite safe, but
scarcely sound. She is very ill, but I have not quite done with her
yet."

And it was thus Sir Jasper escaped dreadful consequences.

Think it not strange for me to have dismissed his deliverance
so rapidly. In life such eventualities are quite as instantaneous.
'Tis the merest chance, the turn of a hair, the weight of a grain
of sand, whether black or red turns up, whether escape or catastrophe come. I knew a prosperous merchant once, who told me
that in early youth he was dismissed from the great counting-
house, where he was an office-boy, dismissed through no fault of
his own, and left friendless and almost destitute in the Great
Desert of London. He knew not what to do, or where to go to
seek employment. He had been in the habit of paying in money
and drawing money out at his employer's bank ; he had been in
the habit of obtaining fresh cheque-books for the firm when
needed. A mad, desperate thought came over him one morning,
when he felt most hungry and most forlorn. Should he go to the
bank, ask for a cheque-book—the clerks might not know of his
dismissal—forge a draft for money, get it cashed, and fly to
America with the proceeds. He paced the great hall of the
General Post Office, revolving this wicked project in his mind.
He was on the point of yielding to the devil that was within him,
when, as it seemed to him, the expression of a human countenance came over the dial of the Post Office great clock. It
seemed to warn, to conjure, to implore him to turn back from
his black design. By God's mercy he did so ; and, although he
had no bed and no supper that night, he obtained employment
the very next day, and when he told me the story he was a rich
man. But his honesty had trembled in the balance, and a hair's
breadth, or the weight of a sand-grain, might have turned the

scale. " To be or not to be," translated into " Do or not to do,"
is one of the swiftest but one of the fiercest conflicts that has ever
waged in the human heart. And the decision is made in a moment. I will marry Miss Jones, I won't marry Miss Jones,
either the one or the other, and you vault into Paradise or are
plunged into Tophet for life. The most sensible determination to
come to is, perhaps, not to marry Miss Jones; tell her that you
will regard her as a sister, and you have no idea how fond she will
be of her dear brother.

This was Mr. Sims' first active deliverance of Sir Jasper from
his self-created Philistines. " You must get out of this, Goldthorpe," he said, when the Baronet sheepishly confided to him his
wretched embarrassments caused by corn and coal and bubble
schemes. " You are not fit for business, and business is not fit
for you; you'll get yourself into some mess, and write your own
name or somebody else's once too often. You must do the quiet
gentleman, and live upon your means. I'll find the means, and
speak to Lady G. about it."

Mr. Sims found the means and spoke to Lady G. A ten-
roomed house was taken at Kentish Town. Mr. Sims had it
neatly but not expensively furnished from a cheap upholsterer's
in Tottenham Court Road; and Lady Goldthorpe—there is no
use in disguising the fact—took to letting lodgings. But so far
as the house at Kentish Town was concerned, the hereditary
dignity was dropped. It was Mr. and Mrs. Mordaunt, who were
happy to let apartments furnished to single gentlemen, with
partial board if required,—not Sir Jasper and Lady Goldthorpe.
The single gentlemen came, and had decent accommodation for
their ten or twelve shillings a week. One gentleman from the
Custom House insisted on practising on the trombone early in
the morning and late at night, and had speedy warning in consequence. Another was troubled with fits, and fell down stairs
regularly every Sunday morning. A third was an entomologist,
and formed a collection of live cockroaches, which crawled about
the house generally in an embarrassing manner. Then there was
one gentleman who turned out to be a swindler, and brought a
trunk, neatly packed with bricks; and when he went away, with-

out paying his rent, took with him a few books, chimney ornaments, and other articles of trifling value. But, on the whole,
Mr. and Mrs. Mordaunt got on very satisfactorily with their
single-gentlemen lodgers, sat rent free, and were enabled to lay
by some little surplus. To see Mrs. Mordaunt, once Lady Goldthorpe, bustling about the house with its cheap furniture, painted
washhand-stands, and printed druggets; making out the little bills
of her single-gentlemen lodgers, wrangling in the little kitchen with
an Irish servant, with a face like a kidney potato, who had an incorrigible propensity for black-leading her face as well as the
stoves, and with her successor, a stolid young person from the
workhouse, aged fourteen, who was sulky and lazy, and obstinate
and vicious, and who was once detected in eating raw beefsteak;
to watch her parleying on the door-step with a gentleman in highlows, corduroys, and a seal-skin cap, who came with a donkey and
sold cauliflowers : you would have had much difficulty in recog-
nising the magnificent Lady Goldthorpe in her palace at Onyx
Square, throning it on silken couches and sumptuous carpets,
scattering her gold about her in boundless profusion, waited upon
by giants in plush and powder and gold lace. The world sees
changes just as curious. One thinks of Napoleon at St. Helena,
squabbling over the quantity and quality of his rations, grumbling
because his cocked hat had lost its nap, and his uniform coat was
growing white at the seams. And yet I think that Lady Goldthorpe was happier now than when she lived in Onyx Square—
almost as happy, indeed, as when she was the tenant of a back
parlour of a little shop in a petty country town.

The Reverend Ernest Goldthorpe allowed his parents a hundred and fifty pounds a year; the pittance was paid to them
weekly; for Ernest had an uneasy sensation that his father would
begin to speculate so soon as he had any considerable amount of
money in his hands. The young gentleman in the Foreign Office
was reduced to the dire necessity of living upon his salary, which
to a young gentleman in the Foreign Office is a very dire necessity indeed. I am constrained to say that he thought himself
very much ill-used by his father, that he imagined himself to have
been in some degree defrauded of a share in a splendid inheritance, and that he bore some malice to the author of his days in

consequence. He could no longer be called Bullion Goldthorpe by his fellow-clerks. Livery-stable keepers, tailors, cigar-dealers, did not compete for his custom. He was no longer a young man of expectations. He alluded to his degenerate papa as seldom as possible, and devoted himself with much ardour to the cultivation of his opportunities at evening parties, in the hope of marrying a young lady with money. As nature had endowed him with a smooth pretty face and a pleasing tenor voice, and as he had acquired the difficult art of parting his hair up and down the middle, even from the nape of his neck to within an inch of his eyebrows, so neatly and so accurately as to make you think that his head was in halves, and was about to fall asunder, he became very popular at Brompton and Kensington. The under-graduate, who was of a studious turn, sensibly left the University and took a tutorship in a private family; he wrote dutifully but rarely to Kentish Town: he must bear his hard lot, he said. A hard lot indeed, to be bred up in the hope of your father leaving you fifty thousand pounds some day, and to find out suddenly that he is not worth sixpence. The Eton boy was kept at Eton by his stern, conscientious brother, who destined him for the Church; but I am afraid that Dr. Hawtrey did not spare him so frequently as he might have done when he was a son of Mammon, and that his tutor was not very much inclined to condone his offences when he remembered that the quarterly bills for his board and instruction must be kept within very narrow limits. It sometimes occurred to his youthful companions to call him a beggar, whereupon he fought them, and thrashed them or was thrashed, as capricious Fortune chose to decide. It was all for the best. Alfred had very little pocket-money now, but if he had had more he might have injured his constitution by excesses in sweetstuff and shrub. The wind is tempered even to the shorn schoolboy, and the Etonian made up for less luxury by more football and more paper chases.

The sailor abroad had his profession to depend upon. He was a lieutenant now, and could live on his pay. Just previous to the Smash he had been, according to custom, drawing bills with some prodigality upon his papa. Matters looked somewhat serious when those documents were returned protested; but his Captain,

who was rich and liked the young man, compounded with his
creditors, and lent him money to liquidate the composition. So
all that Lieutenant Goldthorpe, R.N., had to wish for was a good
sharp war, which would bring him a little fame and a little prize-
money.

Captain William Goldthorpe, late of the Dragoons, for he prudently managed to sell his commission just before it lapsed through
his having overstayed his leave, made his appearance in due course
at the Insolvent Debtors' Court. His debts, I need scarcely say,
were prodigious; his assets might have been put into one of those
walnut shells which hold Limerick gloves, silver thimbles, and
miniature scissors. Where the price of the Captain's commission
went to was never correctly known. He was asked so many
questions at the Insolvent Court, and bullied on so many sides by
enraged creditors, that this one was somehow passed by. Jack
Butts charitably spread about the story that he owed all the
money and more to the regimental agents; but friendly George
Gafferer darkly insinuated that the quondam Captain had made a
private purse for himself. His case was a very flagrant one, and
would have fully justified a remand for eighteen months; but fortunately for Willy Goldthorpe, the Commissioner before whom
he was examined happened to be himself in a chronically insolvent
condition, and had recently passed through his own Court, and
beautified the sepulchre of his debts with his own whitewash.
His Honour held bill discounters of every degree in utter abomination; so when the Captain's schedule came to be discussed, he
mainly confined himself to blowing up the gentlemen who lent
money at sixty per cent.; and, in discharging William Goldthorpe,
told him that he left that Court without a stain on his character,
with the esteem and commiseration of all who knew him, and
with the earnest expression of a hope on his, the Commissioner's,
part, that he would be able to retrieve his fallen fortune and employ his brilliant talents for the benefit of that society of which
he bade fair to be a conspicuous ornament. It is thus that some
of us do *not* get our deserts, and that a great many of us *do*
'scape the whipping. As to the other poor rogues, let them be
triced up to the halberds, and, drummer, see that you warm their
shoulders thoroughly—the rascals!—with wholesome whipcord.

Captain Goldthorpe—once a Captain, always a Captain—drove down to his club in the rapidest of Hansoms, gave the driver half-a-crown instead of a shilling for his fare, had a very nice little dinner, drank a bottle of very sound Pomard, and afterwards, over his 'Seltzer-water and Cognac and the most fragrant of Havan-nahs, put the smoking-room in a roar with an account of his recent ordeal, of the humours of the Commissioner, and specially of the examination of an insolvent umbrella-maker, with a club-foot and an impediment in his speech, who, after undergoing a stern and terrifying lecture, had been remanded for six months by the indignant judicial functionary, who had recently gone through his own Court, for the heinous offence of contracting a debt of nine pounds seven shillings without reasonable expectations of payment. A hardened wretch, this umbrella-maker, clearly; and you see there are some people who *do* get their deserts, and are soundly swinged by outraged Justice.

Captain Goldthorpe consoled himself very well under his mis-fortunes. He had a handsome figure, a good constitution, very long moustachios, and a cheerful disposition. He could ride and drive, and fence, and shoot, and box, and by a large circle of acquaintances was deemed pre-eminently a good fellow. He was not compelled, so far as his adventures in this chronicle are set down, to turn riding-master or veterinary surgeon or commission agent. The Captain went abroad. In the gay circles of Paris, in the cheerful Passages of Brussels, but chiefly at those delightful places on the Rhine where a medical regimen is combined with the pursuit of *roulette* and *rouge et noir*, Captain Goldthorpe found diversion after his many troubles. He ate of the best, and drank of the best, and rode blood horses, and was highly popular amongst scores of good fellows and dashing and adventurous spirits like himself. Time works wonders, and a great many changes take place in twelve months. In eighteen hundred and fifty-two Captain Goldthorpe, principally of the Rhine, was in a transition state. I think the state he had left was that of the pigeon, and I am afraid that the state into which he was entering was that of the hawk. He was as good-natured as ever, and would have written to his parents and assisted them, only he was such a bird of passage, and he had not time, and it was a bore, you see, and he could not do much now for the poor old governor, and he had lost the address in Kentish Town; and so he did not write, and at the end of the year for aught he cared for the father that begat, or the mother that bore him, he might have been a foundling.

These are the separations that money, or the loss of money, makes between parents and children, between kinsmen and kins-women, and schoolfellows and old friends. These are the things that make life terrible, and change flesh and blood into stone and warm blood into brine, and turn our hair grey before the time.

CHAPTER XXXIV.

"There is a sore evil which I have seen under the sun, namely, riches kept for the owners thereof to their hurt. But those riches perish by evil travail, and he begetteth a son and there is nothing in his hand." The Preacher is secular as well as sacred, and he may surely be quoted without irreverence in a work about worldlings. For who knew so much of the world and its way as King Solomon, the Jewish merchant, as Mr. Ruskin called him, the Sir Charles Coldstream, the used-up, blasé sovereign, rather, he may be called, of antiquity. He who found that all was vanity, and turned to behold Wisdom in Madness and Folly, and held that there should be no remembrance of the Wise any more than of the Fool for ever, and that there was nothing better than that a man should rejoice in his own works, and that money answereth all things, must have been acquainted with Mammon, and known the power and the importance of silver and golden dross.

Sir Jasper Goldthorpe had kept riches to his hurt, and had lost it through evil travail, and had begotten sons, and there was nothing in their hands. And yet Sir Jasper Goldthorpe walked Regent Street, and was a Baronet there. At home, in Milliken Street, Kentish Town, he was Mrs. Mordaunt's the lodging-house keeper's husband, at whom the Irish servant girl, with a face like a kidney potato, and the young person from the workhouse who ate raw beef, jeered. The single-gentlemen lodgers called him the man of the house, and were under the general impression that he cleaned the knives and blacked the boots. He had been seen fetching in the beer from the Bag o' Nails hostelry round the corner. Chype, the landlord, was of opinion that he had been unfortunate in the retail shoe trade. He was held in no estimation by the butcher. The greengrocer disdained him and called him "a party." The baker hesitated to execute his orders without instructions from Mrs. Mordaunt. The tax-collector did not lift his hat to him. The gas was rude to him. The water rates said in an imperious voice that he could not call again when the ex-millionaire meekly opened the door to that official. He had taken to snuffing, but he had no credit at the tobacco shop. The omnibus conductors at the Eyre Arms, when he purposed travelling east-ward, called him "Guv'n'r," and enjoined him to look alive. He was thoroughly despised, for he was in the scrape, as Mr. King-lake has it, of being alive and old and poor. Not one of the paltry and shabby beings with whom he had commerce dreamt that this had been a King of Men, a captain of fifties and of thousands; a potentate who could write *Io el rey*—who could compel friendship and adulation, and flattery and lip-service by the lifting of his little finger; who could raise men to riches or fling them into beggary by a stroke of his pen. Mr. Mordaunt, of Milliken Street, was the shabbiest of old broken-down hacks dis-carded from the chariot of Fortune. He was not richer in Regent Street, but he enjoyed more consideration. The milliners' girls, gossiping in their workrooms as he tottered past, called him a fine old gentleman. He ventured sometimes so far as the Burlington Arcade, and would be looked upon by its idle frequenters as a nobleman whose eccentricities led him to dress so shabbily. Now and then some old patrician acquaintance coming from the clubs or alighting from his carriage would recognise and hold him in chat for a minute or so, and returning home say, "I met poor old Goldthorpe to-day; he is quite worn out." He was known at some half-dozen shops in the purlieus of Regent Street, and the shop people bowed to him and called him Sir Jasper. He belonged to a little club held at a tavern in Beak Street, whose members were chiefly poor artists, struggling newspaper men, briefless barristers, patientless surgeons, with one or two rich Regent Street tradesfolk, and these jolly dogs were kind to him and made much of him, partly for fun, partly through pity, and partly through that odd esteem for a man with a handle to his name which lingers in the British breast. There is something in knowing a live Baronet, even if he be not worth twopence-halfpenny in the world.

G G

Sir Jasper would meet his club acquaintances in Regent Street, and they would take his arm and show him off, and introduce him to their acquaintances as a kind of lion. He was wont to brag in a feeble manner of his past riches, and to point with tremulous cane to such and such a haughty one rolling by in his chariot, who affected not to know him now, but whom he had lifted from the mud, and whose fortune he had made. He throve on these miserable little vanities, grew quite gay and jaunty towards five o'clock, and would lift his napless hat in defiance to the rolling chariots for all that their occupants turned their heads the other way. "The obtrusiveness of that man is disgusting," quoth Tom Tadpole on his hired hack, when the Baronet persisted in saluting him; "he still thinks he is one of us." "The bankrupt old beggar," muttered the envious Mopps, who always took a walk in Regent Street on fine afternoons, in order to glower at and to curse the people who seemed richer than he. "He had the impudence to bow to *me* the other day while I was talking to Mr. Secretary Calipash, on the strength, forsooth, of having met me at dinner; he was always a cad and made long speeches. I hate long speeches and cads." Thus Mopps.

It would have been twenty times better for this wretched old man had his name really been Mordaunt, and had he and his wife really been born to the condition of letting lodgings, and had his baronetcy faded away like Alnaschar's vision of riches. But it was not to be so. He clung to his baronetcy with a feeble fierceness. He grudged that it should descend to his son—his cruel, cold-hearted, upstart son, he called him now. Towards five o'clock he would slink into a little pastrycook's shop in Cranbourne Steect, and in whose back parlour he had a chop, potatoes, and a cup of coffee for ninepence; or he would lurk into a cheap French ordinary behind the Quadrant, where he would feed on leather and prunella, or stale fish dressed up with cunning sauces. The waiter at Bagaboshe's restaurant called him "Milor," and when trade was dull he would discourse with that servitor, who was a Swiss by an Italian mother and a Polish father, on his bygone prosperity and the ingratitude of the world. Then, unless it happened to be club night, he would fade away into a tavern in Warwick Street, and drink his cold gin-and-water, and prattle about the city articles in the newspapers, and be looked up to as a sort of second-hand oracle by the small tradesmen in the neighbourhood. There was a barmaid who was compassionate to him, and gave him snuff from a large Scotch mull for nothing. He would reach home by omnibus by ten o'clock, and be put to bed by Lady Goldthorpe; and sometimes, when he had taken a little too much gin-and-water, he would cry, and take the stumps of his many cheque-books from their drawer, and maunder over them in a pitiable manner. We will drop the curtain, if you please, upon this not too cheerful spectacle.

And Magdalen Hill, where was she? Why, was she not by the side of her old friend, her old guardian? Magdalen had gone away. And, as usual, pride had done it all. In the very earliest days of Sir Jasper's bankruptcy, Letitia Salusbury had sought her out with offers of assistance. Lord Chalkstonchengist's daughter was as generous as she was good : she would have given her ears away ; she would have pawned her earrings to help any one in distress. "What can I do for you?" was her first question to Magdalen. "Your fortune, I know, is gone, but mine remains. You know that papa is very rich, and that he will do anything I ask him. Only say what we are to do when this dreadful botheration of a bankruptcy is over." So far all promised well ; but the two girls had not been a quarter of an hour together before they had a fierce, hot, deadly quarrel. It was about Ruthyn Pendragon. That exceedingly vulgar person once more came on the *tapis*, and with his clumsy feet was once more the means of tearing the carpet to pieces. I believe that Letitia pressed Magdalen to marry him. I fear that Miss Hill spoke with even fiercer scorn and disdain of the ex-curate than had hitherto been her wont. She accused him of living on Letitia's bounty. "You gave him money in the lodging-house, you know you did," she said, in passionate tones. The two women wrangled as only proud and passionate women with no listeners by can wrangle. They parted not to meet again. Letitia flung away in a rage, telling Magdalen that she might starve for a proud and obstinate wretch. Miss Hill, with drawn-up form, white face, and quivering lip, said things not so violent, but that were more pointed and left deeper marks behind them. And could ladies

who had moved in the best society so wrangle? I thought
it was only the common people who quarrelled. "Tush!"
answers Señor Asmodeus, "if you will wait while I unroof this
house in Belgravia, you shall see my Lady fling the silver tea-pot
at my Lord's head, and the Honourable Mrs. Lamb box her
grown-up daughter's ears; and hear what a fine clatter of
crockeryware is made when the breakfast table is overturned;
and what an edifying war of words is waged in that very low life
which is sometimes carried on above stairs." Be quiet, lame
Devil, you are but a deformed cynic, invented by a grinning
Frenchman; and it must be only the common people who quarrel
and throw things at one another. The breach between Letitia
and Magdalen was not to be healed, and the whole Goldthorpe
family suffered through that deadly feud. Sir Jasper was inclined to be querulous, and to murmur at the injury which
Magdalen's stupid pride, as he called it, had inflicted on his
prospects of assistance from the wealthy Lord Chalkstonehengist
and his open-handed daughter. His wife, as wives will, took her
husband's part; and there was sullen animosity in the wretched
little household even before they left Paddington. So Magdalen
went away, stern, proud, and unforgiving. She sold her trinkets,
she sold almost all her clothes, save the black garb she continued
to wear in remembrance of the dead Hugh. She advertised, with
a grim persistency, day after day in the *Times* for a situation as
governess. She got one at last in a school at Clapham, where
she was to teach everything, and have thirty pounds a year and
her washing. The place was the wretchedest of wretched ones.
The schoolmistress was the daughter of a cheesemonger, and had
in early life been a lady's maid. She could not spell; the
writing-master made out her quarterly bills; but she was scrupulously particular as to references, and in taking only the
daughters of gentlemen as pupils. She had a parlour-boarder
at a hundred guineas a year, who was forty years old, and mad,
and used to cut her dress into snippets with a pair of scissors,
and wolf her food with her fingers, and wander about the house
with her hair down like a Banshee, nearly frightening the scholars
into fits. There was a French governess who almost set the
house on fire about once a week with reading novels in bed; and

an English teacher, who maintained an amatory correspondence with a dancing-master, and subsequently with one of the big boys at Dr. Wackerbath's establishment close by. The governesses all hated one another; and the schoolmistress bullied everybody, from the servants to the parlour-boarders; and in this educational Inferno Miss Magdalen Hill passed eight months. It was good for her pride. Perhaps it is good for pomp to take physic sometimes and repent. Did she? I am afraid not. She was as cold and self-possessed as ever, and went about her duties in a strict, unbending way. She bore the abuse of the coarse, avaricious hag who ruled the school, and the envy and malice of the shrewish women who were her fellow-governesses, and the ceaseless teasing of half a hundred tiresome girls. She was very cool and calm without; but I think, nevertheless, there was still a raging fever within her. The Spanish Inquisition is abolished, as you know: the thumb-screws and the scavenger's daughter in the Tower lie idle; the Smithfield fires are quenched; the pillory is headless; the stocks are legless: but believe me, there are many thousand genteel stucco-covered houses in this fair metropolis and its suburbs, where the amenities of the Inquisition are practised all the year round, and the torture-chamber has its tenants, every day.

CHAPTER XXXV.

THE AGONY OF FLORENCE ARMYTAGE: STAGE THE LAST.

YES, she had been a great traveller. Amiens, St. Lazare, Lewes, Kirkdale, Kilmainham, La Bourbe, Mannheim, Milan, Preston, Nice; from Lancashire to Lombardy, from the Maritime Alps to the Sussex Downs, the little feet, sometimes against their will, had wandered. She had been in twenty gaols, and had undergone twenty sentences. She, the gay and luxurious, had been accustomed from her youth upwards to stone floors and iron doors, to prison gaolers and prison fare. To be arrested and tried, and kept in captivity for robbing and swindling, were no novelties to her. They were the little reverses incidental to a career such as hers had been. It is not surprising she did not talk about them in polite society. We are all of us acquainted with some little topics which we don't mention in the drawing-room. We don't feel it essential to enlighten every chance acquaintance about our wig and our cancer, about our false teeth and our pawn tickets; about our brother in Colney Hatch, and our uncle who was hanged. We are very apt to prate about the skeleton in our neighbour's cupboard, but do not feel inclined to make a show of the very neat specimen of osteology that our own private cabinet may contain. We remember what Napoleon said about domestic laundry-work, and hold our tongues, and are wise. I never yet heard a gentleman volunteer a full, true, and particular account of how he was kicked in Pall Mall, or a lady disclose the precise circumstances which led to her wearing false fronts.

If I were to give you a detailed account of the career of Florence Armytage, it would swell this work to thrice its destined size. If I were to enumerate, even in the driest catalogue-maker's fashion, her escapades, her misdeeds, her triumphs, and her humiliations, the catalogue would fill a volume. When the man, Agar, was under cross-examination at a famous trial, the advocate, thinking to pose him, asked him how he earned his livelihood during the past twenty years. He answered, confidently, "By crime." It was the naked simple truth. Precisely the same may be said of Florence. By crime, and crime alone, she had lived for years. Reticence and evasion are of no use now; it was *tempus abire* for her. The truth must be told about the woman. This poor little popinjay must be stripped of its silken rags and golden gewgaws, and exposed as a poor trembling forked radish of a criminal as she was. These are hard words to say, but they must be said. She had been a liar and a thief from her cradle. She had been expelled from innumerable schools for misconduct. She robbed the aunt who brought her up. But in all the anguish of all the punishments her sins brought upon her, she was always obstinate and defiant. She had a fatal gift for caligraphy, and forged her school-fellows' names in her earliest copy-books. How, when she went to India, the passengers in the ship lost rings and money; how winners at play suddenly found their stakes disappear; how at the up-country station where she lived with her husband, wretched native servants were discharged for robberies which she had committed; how, when she came back to Europe, she plundered and cheated right and left; how many ladies' maids were discharged for the sake of trinkets which she had purloined; how many tradespeople in England and on the Continent, bankers, hotel-keepers, money-changers were fleeced: but it is useless to pursue the sickening chronicle. The edifice that she had built up, glistening white as snow without, black as hell within, had toppled down upon her miserable head and crushed her. There had come an end to the lying, and cogging, and fawning, and deceiving. Under one of her innumerable false names she had been tried at the Court of Assizes of the Seine for forgery and jewel robbery, and had been sentenced to twenty years' hard labour.

It would have been easy for the authorities to have tried her under her own name, which they knew perfectly well, and for far graver crimes. They could have had her head off her shoulders in a trice: her guilt was patent to at least a dozen shrewd lawyers and police spies. Simon Lefranc, the examining Judge, the Procurator-General, the President of the Criminal Court, knew well that she was a murderess, and had killed a man. But she had listened in time to judicial argument and judicial persuasion, and compromised with justice, and saved her head. At the nick of time her Influence bestirred himself. Her Influence was powerful, but the scandal created by her crimes would have been so horrible had all that had been known about her been published, that her Influence, potent as he was, was forced to be cautious. Her Influence could do almost, but not quite, everything in France. A week since her last examination by Monsieur Plon had passed, when her Influence was admitted in the dead of night into her cell. A close carriage had brought him from a side door in the Rue de Rivoli to the Quai de l'Horloge. Her Influence said little, and made no noise. He was wrapped in a cloak, and no one saw his face. It was the last time that Florence and her Influence were to meet on earth.

"*Tenez, madame, il faut en finir*," was said to her in a voice accustomed to command.

"You used to call me Florence," she remarked bitterly.

"It was long ago, the end has come, ask what you want."

"Set me free."

"It is impossible; you must be imprisoned for twenty years."

"You are very different from what you used to be. Do you forget the old days?"

"I remember them too well. What I tell you is for the best. You must be sentenced for twenty years, *et puis on verra*." He went away, and she saw him no more; but orders were given that night that not a day of her sentence was to be remitted, that no prayer or petition from her was to be received, and that her name was never to be mentioned in high places.

"It was time to put a stop to her," her Influence said, as he sat that night smoking his cigar, with his feet on the fender. "She has played the *diable à quatre* long enough. If we could have another Troy to-morrow, that woman would burn it down."

Florence's compromise with Justice was not without some sacrifice on her part. The authorities wanted an oblong packet of papers from her. After a last sharp struggle she gave them up. There were certain little revelations too concerning a portrait in a golden locket. These revelations she made,—they were probably no secrets to her Influence. The secret of her last and greatest crime was now buried in her own breast. It was safe from the lawyers and police spies. It was safe with her Influence ; it was safe with her accomplice. A young English desperado, who had been tried for burglary and murder at Chaillot more than two years before, who narrowly escaped the capital penalty, and died from a wound he received in an attempt to escape from the galleys at Belleriport, whither he had been sent to hard labour for life. How clever she had been to avoid being arraigned with him !—and what had all her cleverness come to now ?

Her disappearance from England was but a nine days' wonder. In the polite world she had always been but a bird of passage, and, for aught they knew, she might be enjoying herself in Paris or Italy, or in the East even. Only Lord Carnation happening to be in Paris in the autumn of '51, and strolling into the Court of Assizes of the Seine one morning, to see if he could get up a little useful cramming as to the French judicial system, saw sitting on the bench of the accused, between two *gendarmes*, a woman with yellow hair, and in the coarse prison dress, the sight of whose face made him turn white as a sheet, and tremble all over. The yellow-haired woman's eye met his as he stood among the auditory, and a livid spot came to each of her cheeks, and she grinned a ghastly grin. But the woman was arraigned as *Femme* Maillard, of Belle-ville. She was interrogated, and she answered in the purest French. She was tried, and sentenced to twenty years' hard labour in the usual way, and Lord Carnation, rubbing his eyes, murmured that it was very odd, very odd indeed, but that he must have made a mistake. He had *not* made a mistake. He *had* seen Florence Armytage ; but I have been told that a day or two after the trial his lordship received an anonymous letter, in which he was particularly advised to hold his tongue about what he had seen at the Palais de Justice, and was moreover informed in the politest of terms, that whatever he said would be sure to come to the writer's ears, and that if ever he hazarded any indiscreet comments tending to establish an identity between the *Femme* Maillard and any other living creature, he, the writer, would be under the painful necessity of blowing out his lordship's brains on the first convenient opportunity. The letter was signed, " One who keeps his word," and Lord Carnation, whose moral courage was not of the very highest calibre, took the advice volunteered to him in good part, and carefully refrained from any reference to Mrs. Armytage in his future conversations. Only once, when Lord Groomporter, whose notions of things were generally of the most confused order, declared he had seen her at Baden Baden with a Russian Prince to whom she was married, the Earl of Carnation said he had heard that she was on the Continent, but he did not think she would be back for twenty years.

There were persons in England, however, even more interested in her exodus. The commercial and financial world—that is to say, a vast number of shopkeepers and bill-discounters, both in town and country—had been swindled and forged upon by her to an almost inconceivable amount. They began to have a dim perception that the fashionable Mrs. Armytage was also the notorious Miss Armlet, was also the Countess Prigolski from Popoff in Poland, that she was the twin-sister of Lady Arabella Tothill Fielding, if not that distinguished, though spurious and felonious, member of the aristocracy herself. Then it was discovered that she and Mrs. Hicks Hall were one and the same person:—in fact, there was no end to Florence's aliases and Florence's felonies. Saddington and Dedwards, Wittle and Gumtickler, innumerable hosiers, haberdashers, milliners, jewellers, and mantuamakers, had been honoured by her custom, and had suffered by her. Ephraim Tigg, of Stockwell, was in a fury. She had robbed him of thousands, he said; he wanted to send Daniel Forrester to the World's End after her. He wanted to go before the grand jury and prefer a bill against her. He would have her hanged, he would have her burnt alive, he piped out. But a person named Sims went discreetly about and threw oil upon the troubled waters. Filoe and Co. of Coger's Inn took up a great many of her bills. Five shillings in the pound satisfied many of her creditors. More than one West End bill-discounter had good reasons for not mentioning her name with harshness, nay, even for remembering her with a certain kind of gratitude for the good things she had put in their way.

" By Jove, sir ! " Mr. Domitian Doo, of Argyle Street, would remark to his familiars, " that woman was the best tout in London ! She would bring the Horse Guards down in a body, jackboots and all, to do a bit of stiff at three months. She would gammon the whole bar of England into taking half wine, and the 'ouse of Peers into taking one-third cash and the rest in ivory frigates and camels' bits. If she had not bust up so sudden, she would have brought the Bench of Bishops and the Board of Admiralty down to my shop for a trifle in the way of accommodation."

Was she chaste ? I declare that I do not know. No one ever knew. There might have been one pure spot on that blackened heart, one unsullied moment in that wicked life. Liar, swindler, forger, thief, she was known to be. Murderess, the French lawyers and police spies declared she was ; but of Florence Armytage as a chaste or unchaste woman none could speak with certainty. Her Influence perhaps knew, but he was silent.

She was the yellow-haired woman Lord Carnation had seen in Paris, but no Lord Groomporter had ever seen her in Baden Baden. She was taken away, three days after her sentence, in a cellular van,—a horrible dungeon upon wheels, which almost jolted and rattled her to death, and within whose narrow confines she passed three days and nights of agony, in darkness and stifling heat,—to a great prison in the centre of France. She was to have undergone twenty years' hard labour, but she never performed one hour of that penance. The day after her arrival at her prison house, she broke with her fist the glass window of her cell,— it was secured by brass without,—powdered some pieces into minute fragments, and actually swallowed a handful of splintered glass. That was to kill herself. Her throat was frightfully lacerated ; her hands and lips and tongue were almost cut to pieces ; but she did not die. She had a long, long illness, but recovered. She had a horrible fever, and her hair fell off, and she became ugly. She knew that herself ; for she clawed off a pewter button from a gaoler's coat, and polished it till she could see her face in the tiny mirror, and so found that she was hideous. Her hair fell off, as I have said ; but her vanity was not quite gone, for she was found skimming the grease off her broth with a scrap of woollen rag, to

use it as pomatum. When she recovered, she tried to hang herself over and over again. She assayed to dash her head against
the wall of her cell ; she once bit a piece out of her right arm in
the attempt to open a vein ; she had heard that Negro slaves,
under punishment, had contrived to wedge their tongues into the
œsophagus, and so suffocate themselves ;—but there was no use in
it, and she could not die. She was reserved for expiation in this
world ; who dares predicate about the next ? She went through,
time after time, all the old tortures of dark dungeons, strait-waist-
coats, fetters, even watchers by day and by night, hunger, and pri-
vation. But they could not tame her. Priests tried to mollify her,
but in vain. She was placed, for many weeks, in a ward set apart
for lunatic prisoners. There was a talk about sending her to the
madhouse at Bicêtre ; but she kept her senses, and was only in a
rage with herself and with the world.

At length, by Heaven's mercy, which is never denied but
only withheld for a season for Heaven's wise purpose, this most
miserable of His creatures fell ill. It was a decline. It proved
one of the very rapidest nature. " *Elle dépérissait à vue d'œil*,"
the prison surgeons said. She wasted away day by day, and the
two livid spots which showed themselves on her cheeks when
from her bench she had seen the English nobleman at her trial
became permanent there. Her lips were all scarred with those
old marks made by the broken glass, dark-brown rings encircled
her eyes ; if they had put curtain-rings upon her now instead of
handcuffs, they would have slid off her poor shrunken wrists ; her
bones asserted themselves sharply beneath her skin. She was a
terrible sight to see.

The summer sun shone very pleasantly into her prison-room
one June evening in 1852. *Sol lucet omnibus*. Ah, bah ! how
trite it is to repeat the saw ; but still the sun that shines for all
shone mercifully upon her now. She was dying, and knew it.
But upright by her bed sat a Sister of Charity ; not young and
well-favoured, like that Sister Marie des Douleurs you wot of, but
old and harsh-featured. Sister Marie-Catherine this was. She
was sixty ; but she had nursed her patient with angelic care and
tenderness. She had another watcher by her bed too—only her
man Sims. He had permission to be with her. Mr. Sims was a

great traveller in his way, but a more prudent one than that lost creature in the bed. He came and went as he listed; and since his arrival she had been denied no care and no delicacy, and had been removed from the prison infirmary to a cell by herself.

Sims was a man of the world and worldly, and is so still, and thrives. Never mind as to whether he had a heart or not. Who are we that we shall glibly declare our neighbour's bosom to be empty, or filled only with flints? How about our own vacuum? How about that paving-stone beneath our own fifth rib? He tended the dying woman with unceasing solicitude. He may have had about as much religious conviction as Tom Paine; but I know that he brought her an English Bible. He gave it to her just as though it had been an orange or a spoonful of jelly. "Perhaps you'd like something in that way," he said quietly, and walked to the window.

The Romish nun knew what he had done, but, although she was of another faith, interposed no word of inhibition. Only, when Florence turned her eyes towards her, as though in quest of some permission,—for she was very meek and humble now,—the Sister of Charity bowed her head in encouragement, and said, "*Lisez, ma fille. La miséricorde de Dieu est infinie.*"

And whenever Florence Armytage turned inquiring eyes towards Sister Marie-Catherine, the nun wearied not to tell her that God's mercy was infinite.

She lay on her back many hours, day after day, and read the book. She lay hours more, not reading; her eyes closed, but not asleep; her lips softly moving.

"*Elle prie!*" murmured the nun, and took her rosary, and began to pray too in her fashion.

She was so quietly lying on the evening when Mr. Sims came to her for the last time. He sate by her motionless, revolving in his mind who knows how many schemes, combinations, worldly intrigues, and knaveries. But he never took his eyes off hers.

She opened them, and murmured something inarticulately.

"Drink?" inquired Sims, his hand moving towards a jug of cooling beverage.

She shook her head.

"Fan?" he asked, pointing to a screen of paper.

" No," she said with an effort, and suddenly sitting up in bed. " Sims, let me see a clergyman."

" There is but the almoner of the gaol."

" It's no use! Where's the use of confessing my sins to him. I've no religion ; I'm neither Catholic nor Protestant."

The nun seemed to understand what she said, albeit, good woman, she spake not a word of English. She rose and took the English Bible, and gave it to the dying woman, saying softly,

" *Priez, ma fille. Cela vous fera du bien.*"

" You are a good woman," said Florence to her ; " kiss me ! "

She held up her face and spoke in French ; and the nun bent over her, and put her lips to her scarred mouth.

She was silent for half an hour, and then, as suddenly as before, said,

"Sims, I am sorry. I should like to do some good. I should like to save my father. Sims, he is as wicked as I am."

"He will do no more harm. He is dead."

"Dead ! "

" It was for the best. He might have died in a different manner. He flew at very high game."

She gave a long shudder.

" How was it ? " she asked.

" As I predicted all along. He carried his little chemical experiments too far. He died of apoplexy, at Mrs. Donkin's—of apoplexy, you understand. But there were some little things found in his laboratory that led me to a very different conclusion. There was no fuss made about it. He died just after—so far as I can judge—he had discovered the Grand Secret,—a poison which has neither taste nor smell, and which leaves no vestige of its presence in the human body ; but which, I am afraid, is rather apt to kill those who inhale its vapour without putting a glass mask over their faces."

She did not seem to hear him. It was certain that she was not paying attention to him. She was evidently sinking, and near her end.

All at once, and with a sharp spasmodic cry, she asked:

"Where is Hugh ? Is he dead too ? "

" Hugh the convict ? "

"No; Hugh Goldthorpe. Hugh that was to have married Magdalen Hill. Hugh that I killed."

"Why, you know you have seen him half-a-dozen times within these three days."

"I want to see him again. I want him to forgive me."

"You silly little creature, has he not told you over and over again that he forgives you—that he bears you no malice for having buried him alive in that convent in Belgium—in that prison of Belleriport. He is Hugh Goldthorpe once more, no longer a lay brother or a convicts' gaoler. He is going home to England to his father and mother."

"Sims, I must see him again—for one moment, dear Sims. There is something I have not yet asked him, and which he must do:—be quick, Sims, I am dying."

Her old confederate motioned to the Sister of Charity to keep a watchful eye on the moribund, and left the cell. He returned anon, and brought with him the dead alive. "Resurgam" had been written on his coffin-plate, and he had risen from the tomb. He was pale and worn, and the shadow of his former self; but he was alive.

Sims beckoned to the Sister of Charity: she understood, and followed him. He left Florence and Hugh together for twenty minutes, when the young man, with a scared face, opened the door, and bade them enter, for God's sake.

It was the crisis of her agony. She had risen up to die, and was erect on the bed, but anon began to sway and totter. They laid her down with gentle force, and bathed her forehead, and put wine and jelly to her lips.

Once more she sat up in bed and spake.

"He has promised, he has promised," she gasped, the sobs of death choking her utterance. "He has promised that he will marry Magdalen. Forgive me, Hugh; forgive me, Magdalen; oh, God, forgive me!"

These were the last words she uttered. It was now seven o'clock; but she lay till nearly nine quite still, and giving forth only those quick, husky, regular respirations that betokened the end.

The nun felt her feet, and they were cold; her legs were dead.

The husky breathings grew more rapid—rapider—confused—and stopped. A film was drawn over her eyes, and all at once her flesh changed to marble, and she was dead.

Instinctively, it may be, Sims muttered that it was very hot and close, and threw the cell-door open. The window was open already. And so her soul had elbow-room; and the Something—we know not what—came from between the parted lips of this worn sinner, and passed into the Open; going God knows whither, and to be judged God alone knows how. Truly her sins were scarlet; but there is snow that is white—and who can tell?

The nun drew out a silver watch, and marked the hour.

"*La miséricorde de Dieu est infinie*," she murmured. "She died at nine; at ten they will come to put her in her shroud."

There is little more to be said. Mrs. Armytage made no will; but she had nevertheless an executor—a faithful one too—whose name was Sims. On the day of his marriage with Magdalen Hill, he put into the bridegroom's hands a pocket-book containing bank-notes to the value of three thousand pounds.

"Don't scruple to take it," said Mr. Sims to the astonished recipient; "it is all your own. You see I know a thing or two; and Filoe and Co. were enabled to rescue a trifle out of the fire after our poor little friend's blow-up. A prodigious woman that, sir. She might have gone anywhere, and done anything, like the Peninsular war—was it not the Peninsular war?—if it had not been for her Impulse. Good-bye, my dear Hugh. Good-bye, Mrs. H. I am Hugh's godfather, you know, and knew him when he was a baby in long clothes. I'll take care that the old people don't want for anything. Filoe and Co. are not broken yet. Good-bye; I am going to the play."

And thus dramatically intent, although it was barely one o'clock in the day, Mr. Sims took his departure.

Were Hugh and Magdalen happy, I wonder? I hope so. I know they went to Van Diemen's Land, and that Hugh was very successful as a sheep-farmer.

One word in conclusion. When last I heard of him, Ruthyn Pendragon, all ex-curate of the Church of England as he was, had not quite abandoned the clerical profession. He was still the

Reverend Ruthyn Pendragon; he was the most popular and the most prosperous preacher in London. He had founded a new sect,—that of the Peculiar Christians, indeed—of which he was a shining light and Professor. His wit, his humour, his learning, his eloquence, were admired by hundreds of thousands of weekly worshippers. Bishops and prime ministers came incognito to hear him. The chapel in which he held forth proved a world too small for his enthusiastic admirers, and they built him a monstrous tabernacle on the site of a horse-bazaar. But he was still, and incorrigibly so, an exceedingly vulgar person. He has lately taken to lecturing on Apes and Vermin, and his lectures are listened to as eagerly and applauded as vehemently as his sermons. I should not omit to state that he has taken to himself a wife, and that the lady in question has a right to call herself, if she so chooses, the Honourable Mrs. Pendragon.

"Where are you going?" asked the tract at the Goldthorpe Station. I think the deformed Slave was in the right when, questioned as to his destination, he answered that he knew nothing about it. Where *are* we all going, I wonder?

THE END.

www.ingramcontent.com/pod-product-compliance
Lightning Source LLC
Chambersburg PA
CBHW052346110726
47901CB00005B/1384